AMERICAN EDEN

Also by Marilyn Harris

AMERICAN EDEN

MARILYN HARRIS

Doubleday & Company, Inc., Garden City, New York
1987

FOR JUDGE

Library of Congress Cataloging-in-Publication Data

Harris, Marilyn, 1931–
  American Eden.

  I. Title.
PS3558.A648A8 1987   813'.54   86-16599
ISBN 0-385-18816-1

"What then is the American, this new being?"
Crèvecoeur
1780

Stanhope Hall
Outside Mobile, Alabama
August 3, 1889

By dawn, Mary could feel the heat close in around her. It was too hot to sleep. Memories awakened by the letter from Eden Castle were growing stronger, more painful.

Quietly she left the bed and Burke sleeping and slipped out onto the front gallery of Stanhope Hall. At the door, she lightly touched the white lace curtains which hung unmoving in the absence of an early morning breeze. Her eyes followed the sweep of lawn, canopied by flanking rows of giant live oaks, to where birds sat silent in August heat.

At the gallery railing she stopped and closed her eyes, struggling for control over the memories. The letter from Eden Castle had arrived over a month ago, announcing the imminent arrival of Stephen Eden at Stanhope Hall. John Murrey Eden's son—

The name alone was capable of obliterating the hot Southern morning and replacing it with that cold London autumn evening, the secluded corner of Hyde Park where Mary had gone to meet Burke Stanhope, against the wishes of her guardian, John Murrey Eden, everything against the wishes of John Murrey Eden, who, in an attempt to destroy her love for the American Stanhope, had hired assailants who were waiting for her that day, concealed in bushes. Their orders from John had been merely to cut her long hair, to frighten her. But they had had wills of their own.

Out of the turmoil of heat and old terror, Mary tried to resist the sensations still so vivid after twenty years, and remembered as though it were happening now how she felt herself overpowered, her arms wrenched behind her, a monster with many hands twisting her head to one side, binding her eyes with a foul-smelling cloth.

Then they were upon her, loosening her hair, one hand lifting her head to an upright position with a painful jerk of her head. She had heard a new sound then, metal teeth biting together, her head jerked first one way, then the other, growing lighter.

They had seemed to retreat and she heard their voices in muttering dispute.

"No marks, John Murrey Eden said."

"No marks'll show."

"She's fair—"

"Better than a whore."

"Then be quick."

"And we all get a turn."

As hands had commenced pulling back the layers of her garments, as she had felt the coolness of dirt beneath her bare legs, as the double pressure on her body crushed her arms bound beneath her, she had calmly gathered the few remaining fragments of her soul and taken them to a deeper level. In the last moments of consciousness, she had been aware only of the rhythmic rocking motions of her body.

Shuddering, Mary bent low over the gallery railing and waited for the pain of memory to pass. She thought angrily of that part of her that had been permanently destroyed by John Murrey Eden. Now his son was coming—

"Mama?"

She looked toward the end of the gallery and saw Eve just emerging from her bedchamber. There was concern on her face. "I heard you cry out. Are you ill?"

"No, my darling," Mary replied.

"Are you sure? It's so hot—"

"Only a bad dream, that's all. Come to me, please."

As Eve started toward her, Mary looked at what surely was the most beautiful face God had ever created, a work of art, this daughter, and Mary suffered no immodesty in thinking so. Eve was a true love child with the voice of an angel, conceived on that rough passage from England seventeen years ago when she and Burke had scarcely left each other's arms, hungry for closeness after the hate John Murrey Eden had hurled down upon them.

"Don't ever get sick, Mama." Eve smiled and lightly kissed Mary's cheek. "I don't know what any of us would do without you. I sometimes wonder—"

She walked past Mary toward the end of the gallery, and Mary watched her. On the surface, Eve seemed to possess a serene personality that never faltered. Only when she hesitated could Mary glimpse behind the serene beauty. Her face, now bathed in a breathtaking patina of early morning light, was like pale marble, fine featured, pink lipped; ample loveliness showed silhouetted through her white nightshirt, below her slim white throat. She possessed a contemplative manner that concealed something Mary had never quite been able to identify.

Elizabeth Victoria Eden Stanhope, known simply by her monogram, Eve, liked to do surprising things. She wore her long golden hair in unconventional styles, and Mary knew for a fact that Eve preferred to ride astride a horse, scorning the sidesaddle. And she wrote poems that, according to Burke, ranged from good to excellent.

But her most stunning gift was her voice, with its perfect pitch and a lovely tone the most beautiful that Mary had ever heard. Now she watched this fresh beauty, this rare daughter, as she gazed out over the grounds of Stanhope Hall. For several moments, neither spoke, as though they both were catching their breaths from a difficult night.

Mary felt as tired as though she had never slept. The night had been a restless one, though now the memories were gone and good riddance. Burke had come to bed after midnight, having spent the evening in the library with Mr. Washington, a strange man, sober, humorless, fully aware of his destiny. She had watched them earlier in the evening, these two compatible though mismatched idealists: Booker T. Washington, a black man trying to lead his people to a higher plateau, aided by Burke, a Southern aristocrat who preferred Mr. Washington's company to that of his fellow white Southerners.

Mary drew her dressing gown about her and saw Eve still at the far end of the hall. She seemed to be staring off toward the smoke coming from the slave cabins, though they were no longer occupied by slaves. Now they were refurbished cottages filled with free men, both black and white, who worked for Stanhope Cotton by choice, because the equipment at Stanhope was the newest, the methods the most efficient, the exchange the most humane.

Mary drew even with Eve and stood behind her and lovingly pulled back the long silky blond hair and saw the nape of that white slender neck already dampened with early morning perspiration.

At her touch, Eve turned about, and Mary, shocked, saw tears. "My dearest, what's the matter?" She tried to embrace the girl, who shook free and quickly wiped her eyes and characteristically laughed at her own distress.

"I don't know, I—it's just—I love it here, Mama, I really do, but I can't stay here for the rest of my life. I think I'd go crazy and you'd have another Sis Liz on your hands, and I don't want that, but sometimes I feel as if this house is a prison."

Mary watched and felt a dangerous surge of emotion, part sympathy for Eve, part angry resentment at Burke, whose radical activities and philosophies had left them all isolated and cut off in this already truncated South she was growing to dislike, particularly when it threatened the happiness and well-being of her children.

Eve's tears were well under control. Mary saw the lovely face again, composed, but she knew there still was a great deal to comfort if only she knew how. What could she promise her—that the prison doors would miraculously spring open, that all the hostility and estrangement and resentment would end, that invitations would come flooding down between those silent live oaks, that Eve would have beaux coming from as far away as New Orleans?

Mary couldn't promise that though she would have given anything in her possession to be able to do so. Now she came up beside Eve where she stood at the railing. She had to say something to comfort the girl. Time was limited, the difficult night soon to be followed by what would perhaps prove to be the most difficult day in the history of Stanhope Hall, the younger children awakening, Mr. Washington leaving at noon, then the arrival later today of Mr. Stephen Eden from North Devon, England.

Then Mary had an idea, at best a stopgap measure to occupy her daughter and keep her mind off her painful isolation. "I'm going to put you in charge of Stephen Eden."

Eve commenced to shake her head, and Mary went right on talking.

"There's nothing to be afraid of, Eve. He arrives this afternoon, as you know. Your father is occupied with Paris Boley, seeing that he's settled into his new job, and I have—oh, just everything to do. Eve, you are to be his hostess and see that he is made comfortable."

"Mama, I couldn't."

"Why?"

"I wouldn't know what to say to him."

"Say anything. You have no trouble talking to me, or your father, or David or Christine or any of the servants."

"No. I couldn't."

Her fear and timidity were painful to watch. Quickly she withdrew to the far end of the gallery as though to escape the threat of the very society for which she recently had hungered. And Mary recognized it for what it was—not timidity so much as insecurity. Eve had grown up in limited company at best—her younger brother David, and sister Christine, and her most constant companion, the mad Sis Liz. This was not exactly the ideal training school for a smooth passage into superficial and dangerous Southern society.

Yet the more Mary pondered the spur-of-the-moment idea, the greater the appeal. Why not? She had received the letter a month ago from her brother, Lord Richard, requesting that they extend their hospitality to this young nephew. The mere name of Eden had fanned destructive flames of memory. Burke had been outraged, recalling John Murrey Eden's criminal conduct.

No son of John Murrey Eden will set foot on Stanhope Plantation.

This had been Burke's final reaction, but Mary had successfully tempered that anger while at the same time trying to deal with her own inability to forgive, and pleaded for both their souls that perhaps the son should not be held accountable for the sins of the father, and anyway it was only to be for a limited time. According to her brother, Lord Richard, he was sending his nephew, Stephen, on a business trip to check on a cattle investment in Montana, and if Burke and Mary could help him arrange for this important passage westward, Lord Richard would be forever grateful.

"Eve."

Mary sent her most persuasive voice ahead to where Eve had taken refuge at the end of the gallery, where the good smells of breakfast coffee and sausage were already wafting up from Mrs. Winegar's kitchen annex.

"No, I can't, Mama, don't ask me to. I wouldn't know what to—"

"I need your help, Eve."

"Papa doesn't want him here."

"But he's coming anyway. Today."

"Why does Papa hate him so?"

"He doesn't hate young Stephen. It's his father, John Murrey Eden."

"Why?"

Mary drew a deep breath. She looked toward the end of the avenue of live oaks, thinking she'd seen something. Morning shadows only. The sun was rising. Did she have either the time or the inclination to discuss the complex nature of Burke's hatred for John Murrey Eden?

The answer was simple. No.

"Eve, please, I need your help. I really do—"

Mary broke off, seeing a new expression on Eve's face, curiosity taking the place of apprehension as she stared beyond Mary's shoulder out across the Stanhope lawn to the end of the road.

"Someone's coming, Mama. Look!"

Mary's first thought as she turned about and saw a distant lone horseman on the road was that Stephen Eden had arrived early from Mobile. What in the name of God would she do now? Receive him in her dressing gown?

She heard a noise on the porch directly beneath her and looked down on Ben, an old black man born in slavery at Stanhope Hall who lived here now as a freed man, leading one of the mules toward the grazing pasture. Suddenly he jerked the mule about and headed back toward the barnyard in the direction from which he'd come.

"Ben, wait, who is—"

But he was gone, and she saw that Eve had moved to the center of the gallery the better to see, and Mary saw further that it was no longer a lone rider, saw now that there were eight, no, twelve horsemen, all turning into Stanhope Hall, all riding at a sedate pace, single file, several carrying torches that flamed palely against the rising morning sun, suggesting that this curious parade had commenced in predawn darkness somewhere.

"Mama, who—"

"I don't know. Come on, we should perhaps—"

Go inside, Mary was about to say, but at that moment the horsemen drew near enough for her to see that their faces were obscured by gray hoods, and now she knew why Ben had run.

Dear God no.

This prayer was short-lived and unanswered as the horsemen drew yet nearer. Where was Burke? What did they want?

As the unanswered questions assaulted her mind, she saw Eve standing at the gallery railing, transfixed, nothing of fear in her expression, rather profound curiosity, as though to say, what a unique way to start a day that normally starts like the day before and the day before.

"Mama, look, that's Mr. Higgins's horse." Eve pointed toward the lead rider, whose coal black horse with a white star on his forehead was well known the county over as belonging to Jarmay Higgins.

Still clearly fascinated and without looking back, Eve whispered, "Shouldn't we call Papa?"

Quickly Mary shook her head and tried to draw Eve back, away from the gallery railing, though her own attention was still fixed on the approaching horsemen, specifically the lead rider, whom she suspected was Jarmay Higgins himself.

The Higgins plantation was Stanhope Hall's nearest neighbor to the east, boasting vast timberlands as well as cotton fields. Mr. Higgins owned Mobile's largest lumberyard and had become extremely wealthy during the halcyon days of Reconstruction, when it seemed everyone needed lumber to rebuild after the Yankee fires. A true son of the South, Jarmay Higgins had long ago written off Burke Stanhope as a scalawag, guilty of unforgivable behavior in Southern eyes, one who cooperated with and assisted Republican rule and, worse, made friends with the Yankees, who were second only to niggers as objects of hate.

Now what was Jarmay Higgins doing, hooded, at Stanhope Hall so early on this hot August morning? And why were Eve and Mary the only ones awake to view this macabre parade? The riders were drawing still closer, their gait measured, almost ritualistic and therefore terrifying.

The horsemen had now formed a solid line facing Stanhope Hall, as though waiting for someone to come out and acknowledge them. Mary saw the lead rider slowly dismount, an unhurried movement containing no visible threat, yet Mary knew better, knew that quite probably beneath each gray hood was a recognizable and respected face, many of them neighbors, for these were the scare tactics of the Knights of the White Camellia.

"He's taking something out of his pocket, Mama," Eve murmured, and Mary knew why they had come on this morning. A black man had slept under the roof of Stanhope Hall last night and now it was time for this vigilante group of Southern aristocrats to move into action. Formed after the war, though shortly thereafter outlawed by the federal government, they still were the most active organization in the South. It was difficult to obtain hard, fast evidence on them, primarily because the most prominent lawyers and judges and ministers rode with the Knights of the White Camellia and thus protected them, or so it was rumored.

Their deeds were legend, and they took perverse pride in their sense of fair play. If the "Southern Code" was broken, the offender suffered only property loss at first—the burning of a barn or an outbuilding. If attention was not paid immediately and ways mended, then the knights played a different game and people disappeared, their bodies to be found horribly mutilated.

"Come away, Eve," Mary ordered, certain that by now the men had seen them in their nightclothes standing on the upper gallery.

"It's a flower, Mama, look, a white camellia."

The excitement in Eve's voice drew her back to the gallery railing, where she saw the lead rider just rising from placing a white camellia at the exact center of the red brick steps. As the hooded face was upward bound from his kneeling position, his head lifted to the second floor gallery, his eyes visible through small slits in the gray hood. Mary saw two cold black eyes watching them closely. No one else was moving, the horses as still as a painting, all held fast by those two black eyes frozen in their white ovals.

Mary felt her heart accelerate. She placed an arm protectively around Eve's shoulders. Still the eyes held, and Mary discovered that she couldn't turn away, as if unwittingly she'd become a pawn in this bizarre tableau.

Eve was more than holding her own. She was predominant on the gallery nearest the railing and perhaps even the cause of all those fixed male eyes who were finding sustenance in young female beauty. Mary was certain that the girl was enjoying this unexpected theater.

Then, slowly, the lead rider bowed his head, as though paying homage to the women. At the same time he lifted his hand to his forehead and touched the gray hood in salute. Then he resumed his mount and led the other horsemen in a single-file procession back down the avenue of live oaks. Mary found herself stupidly counting them as they passed in review, and suddenly she remembered that she always counted objects in moments of stress. Then she saw the last rider disappear into swirls of morning ground fog and closed her eyes and heard her heart beating.

"They're gone, Mama. Who were they? Do you know them? Why were their faces hidden? And why did they leave a camellia on the—"

Mary made no attempt to answer any of Eve's persistent questions. For one thing, they were coming too fast and they were unanswerable anyway. There *was* information to be shared, perhaps a lecture on the meaning of this early-morning visitation and, more important, how it would affect all their lives from now on, but first Mary must calm her down.

"Papa, did you see them?" Eve called over the gallery railing to her father, who had just appeared on the front porch below.

Mary hurried back to the edge of the gallery and looked over and down and saw Burke, his hair tousled, his burgundy dressing gown knotted loosely around his waist, slippered, no stockings. Without replying to Eve, he bent and retrieved the white camellia.

"Papa, did you—"

As Eve's excited voice drifted down, Burke looked up from his kneeling position. Mary saw his focus fix on Eve, then move slowly past as it came to rest on her. In that expression she knew so well, she saw love and worry and something else, the fuel that fed Burke's idealism and his sense of justice. Anger. She saw anger that they had dared to violate the peace and sanctity of Stanhope Hall with their scare tactics and stupid rituals.

Still kneeling, he held the white camellia for a moment in the palm of his hand, one finger carefully examining each velvet petal as though searching for clues.

Eve called to him once more, apparently alarmed by his silent kneeling, and Mary was on the verge of joining her, wanting some acknowledgment of what they all had seen, some reassurance. But as she moved closer to the gallery railing, she heard additional footsteps below and leaned out and looked down on a familiar head with white curly hair—the long-boned figure and alertly handsome head of Mr.

Booker T. Washington. He was fully dressed in his black coat and black trousers, and Mary wondered if he had ever been to bed.

Neither man spoke, though at last Mary saw Burke turn and acknowledge Mr. Washington's presence. Then slowly he rose, still holding the white camellia, and for several minutes he stood eyeing the blossom. Suddenly he crushed it in the palm of his hand and hurled it down the steps, where it came to rest in fragments. Then he smiled at Mr. Washington and took his arm and said, "Come, my friend. It is not the season for camellias," and led the way back into Stanhope Hall and left Mary staring down at the crushed camellia, knowing all too well that it could not and would not be dismissed or forgotten that easily.

Belatedly she was aware of Eve at her side, offering comfort despite her own confusion.

"Mama, don't worry, it will be all right. I'll greet Mr. Eden if you want me to. I'm sure I won't do it well, but I'll try, I really will."

Again Mary heard that sweetness of tone blended with loneliness and knew if she started talking right now and talked until the day of her death she could never fully explain to Eve the ways of this world, the evil disguised as goodness, the meaning of a group such as the Knights of the White Camellia, the effects of human deprivation and loneliness, so many lessons the girl must learn and learn soon and Mary was the only one who could teach her.

But for now, most of these lessons would have to wait. For now, there was time for just one, the most important one. "Eve, listen. You must listen and you must promise me. For the next few days, you will not leave Stanhope Hall alone. Is that clear?"

"Mama!"

The reaction was immediate and the anguish sincere. Lacking human companions, Eve had established a warm relationship with her horse, a lovely little sorrel Burke had given her several years ago and whom she had named Clarissa, after Mr. Richardson's novel of the same name. Then there were her other animals, a variety of dogs and cats and birds and two squirrels, to say nothing of her daily pilgrimage to Fan Cottage to visit Sis Liz and White Doll.

"Eve, please," Mary begged in quick response to the rebuttal she saw gathering in those dark blue eyes, "just for a while until I can—"

"Clarissa needs exercise. I can't just—"

"I'll get one of the boys to—"

"She's accustomed to me. She doesn't want the boys."

"It isn't safe."

"Why isn't it safe?"

"You saw those men."

"They did nothing."

"Not yet, but—"

Mary heard footsteps behind her on the gallery and knew they were no longer alone and knew as well that the subject was far from over and that Eve had not yet given her word. "Eve, please, just for a while, for your own—"

Behind her, she heard movement. "Mama, I had a bad dream." It was Christine, her youngest, age eight, but smaller than eight and pale, having spent most of the humid Southern summer in bed with lung congestion, having spent most of her young, fragile life in bed, for that matter.

Mary turned and opened her arms to Christine and gathered in the frail child, who apparently had brought half her bedclothes with her. "Bad dreams are terrible things," Mary said soothingly and kissed the shell pink ear already damp with perspiration. "I had one too. After breakfast I'll tell you mine if you'll tell me yours."

Christine nodded, though Mary felt her thin arms around her neck in a viselike grip. Lacking the heart to dislodge her, she felt torn as she watched Eve stare moodily out over the railing, still not quite able to digest this last restriction.

"Eve, may we talk about this later?" Mary requested gently.

No response, just the graceful image of the young girl bathed in the rose of morning light, resting her forehead as though suffering the weight of the world against one of the powerful doric columns that thrust upward from the porch below.

"Eve—"

"I'm all right, Mama. See to Christine. She needs you more than I do."

"Will you come down to tell Mr. Washington good-bye?"

"Of course."

"And may we talk later? I'll try to help you understand. For now, dress as quickly as possible and find Mrs. Winegar and see if there is anything at all that you can do to help her, and I'll be down immediately."

As Mary talked, she walked back through Eve's bedroom. At the door she stopped and looked back, surprised to see that Eve hadn't left her position on the far gallery. From where she stood, spotlighted by delicate morning sun, her nightshirt falling in graceful folds around her rapidly developing figure, her long blond hair spinning gold out of the sun rays, Mary at last accepted the hard fact that her daughter could not stay confined forever within the safe boundaries of Stanhope Hall, any more than she, Mary, could have stayed an unwilling prisoner within the confines of John Murrey Eden's Lon-

don house. The cord would have to be cut. Under the duress of the
moment and the climbing heat of the morning, Mary breathed a quiet
prayer. *"Dear God, make her passage less painful than mine."*

"Do hurry, Eve," she called back, and quickly closed her daughter's
bedroom door.

Footsteps were coming fast up the hall. Then, "There you are, you
scamp. I'm sorry, Mrs. Stanhope. She gave me a start."

At the sound of the familiar voice, Mary looked up to see Katie, a
young black woman who adored Christine and helped care for her,
hurrying down the shadowed corridor. The expression on Katie's
strong face was one of worry. But as she saw the bundled child in
Mary's arms, the fear dissolved into sudden relief. "You should have
told me you had her, Mrs. Stanhope. I was—"

"She came into Eve's room. I'm sorry."

"Where do you want her?" Katie asked after she had kissed Christine's forehead.

"Let her go back to sleep."

"Are you all right, Mrs. Stanhope?"

Mary nodded, enjoying an easy familiarity with Katie as she did
with all the servants. She was teaching Katie and several others to
read and write, holding classes in the front parlor after the noon meal
and the morning chores were done. The number of her students were
growing to include children of white tenant farmers as well. The
only social division in the class was between those who could read
and those who couldn't, a division that could be conquered by anyone
who had the wit, the time and the patience to learn.

"Did you see—"

Mary nodded quickly. "I saw."

"What do you think?"

"I don't know. You run along now, Katie. Stay close to Christine,
please."

A pointed look passed between the two women as Katie bundled
Christine closer and hurried off down the corridor.

Alone, Mary felt suddenly worn out. The house noises she'd heard
in abundance a few moments earlier had suddenly grown silent. Now
she heard nothing. It was as if she were in the house alone.

She must hurry, must dress, must find Burke and determine how
he was going to respond to this early morning threat. And it was a
threat. She was certain of that.

Suddenly anger, raw and specific, surfaced within her. How dare
they? What right had they to terrorize her entire household, to dis-
rupt so many innocent lives?

Her anger increasing, she considered searching out Burke in her dressing gown and demanding an answer. But good sense intervened. Someplace in those downstairs rooms was Mr. Washington, fully attired, probably giving Paris Boley last-minute instructions. Paris, a young black man born in slavery on the plantation, was now a graduate of the Tuskegee Institute and ready to assume full general manager responsibility for the Stanhope Plantation, a giant step for Mr. Washington and his school and for the South as well. To the best of Mary's knowledge, there were no black general managers in all of Alabama.

No, first she must dress. Decorum and civilized behavior would prevail, despite the hooded bullies. And with this conviction, Mary turned about and started toward her bedchamber and hoped she would find Burke there, but knew better; knew that though he still loved her, his passions were elsewhere. A one-man Reconstruction was what his good friend Thomas Nast had called him as he struggled valiantly, trying to make Southerners see and understand that an inquiring mind need not be considered treasonous in the South that had bred Thomas Jefferson.

Contemplation tempered her anger as she moved slowly down the corridor, feeling herself fall in love all over again with Burke Stanhope, and somehow that awareness of love brought a sense of healing and a greater sense of faith. It would all work out. It always had. The Knights of the White Camellia would come to their senses and see that Burke was not the enemy. Stephen Eden would arrive from England and would be the antithesis of his father, John Murrey Eden. He would be sensitive and polite to a fault and would be at Stanhope Hall only long enough to arrange for his journey westward. And Paris Boley would be accepted by all for the superior young man that he was and the color of his skin wouldn't matter at all, and Eve would suddenly be besieged by invitations and have more suitors than she could ever handle and . . .

Before her bedroom door Mary stopped, overwhelmed by her ability to spin daydreams. Her hope was boundless as was her faith. Nothing had ever destroyed it in the past and nothing was going to destroy it in the future. It was her greatest and most treasured possession.

Dress, a small but wise voice suggested, *and go and put the world to rights.*

"I will," Mary replied to the inner voice and tried not to hear the spurs of doubt that swirled inside her head on this bright, hot, splintered August morning.

* * *

Eve had discovered sometime early last year that she could arouse delightful sensations in her body by gently caressing her left breast. The pleasant feelings never lasted long but were so good that she had grown quite adept at creating them even though when once she'd described them to Sis Liz, the old woman had grown mute. White Doll had merely laughed prettily, and then both old women had exchanged a resigned smile and had served Eve their delicious peppermint tea and had quietly suggested that she tell no one else of her secret pleasures.

Now with her rooms still bearing the muddled scent of her mother's toilet water and Christine's camphor pack, Eve sat slowly in the old rocker and gazed out at the beauty of early morning at Stanhope Hall, though through the balcony looking down she still could see the crushed camellia her father had hurled into the dust.

Slowly her right hand slipped beneath her nightshirt and cupped around her breast, and even at first touch she found the sensation so pleasing. She relaxed further into the chair.

The good feelings were beginning. She closed her eyes the better to enjoy them. Though what these feelings were she had no idea. On occasion they would become quite overwhelming, a kind of pleasant paralysis and therefore frightening and even more mysterious. And still they came, building, accelerating, leaving her ultimately in a state of frozen pleasure, afraid to move for fear the feelings would leave her.

Recovering, she stood rapidly and rebuttoned her nightshirt and looked around the now sun-drenched gallery and felt the promise of more heat and knew that within the hour she would disobey her mother and leave Stanhope Hall, and run to the lower garden and escape through the azalea hedge and into the woods that led to Fan Cottage. She had so much to tell Sis Liz and White Doll this morning and more to ask them. Someone had to talk to her, to tell her the truth, in clear terms—why the world was as it was, largely puzzling and harsh and nonsensical, and why by merely touching her breasts she could set off explosions within her own body that left her gasping with pleasure, and why hooded men came calling in predawn hours and said nothing but left a white camellia on the steps, and why her father had crushed it and hurled it into the dust.

Down below on the side lawn she saw movement, saw her brother David, twelve, bare-chested, running around the corner of the house, heading toward the ice pond. Up until a few years ago she had been permitted to join him, bare-chested as well. And suddenly one day her mother had pronounced it "no longer proper."

Why?

The questions screamed in her head along with hundreds of others, and in an attempt to escape those screams and the rising heat of the morning and the awful day that would bring a stranger to Stanhope Hall in the form of a distant cousin she didn't know and had little desire to meet, Eve abandoned the now steamy gallery, drew the nightshirt over her head without bothering to unbutton the buttons —a habit that annoyed her mother—and continued to stride barefoot and naked across her bedroom toward the bowl and pitcher and mirror on the far wall.

Abruptly she stopped, or rather the reflection in the mirror stopped her. In stunned surprise, she stared back at what appeared to be a madwoman, her long hair hanging limp in places, sticking out and irregular in others, her cheeks aflame, mouth open. But it was her eyes that caused the greatest alarm, wide and distended. She resembled one of those impassioned, tragic and hysterical women in Greek tragedies, the ones who murder their own children.

Newly sobered, she covered her mouth with her hands and focused solely on her eyes, so wild-appearing, eyes not suitable for front parlors and family chapels and welcoming strange cousins.

Softly she moaned, mildly undone by her own face and by the burgeoning heat. She was envious of David. She could hear him splashing in the ice pond with Cleo and Casey. She dreaded putting on long skirts and tight bodices.

Still she must and she lifted the heavy white porcelain pitcher and filled the bowl with tepid water and reached into the shell dish for the rose soap and commenced rubbing vigorously. And she continued to rub until her breasts and arms and stomach were covered with suds and when she again made eye contact with the girl in the mirror, that was all she saw: a girl, not terribly pretty, not ugly, just two plain eyes, a plain nose, a plain mouth, plain, plain, plain.

As she wrapped herself in a large white towel, she pondered her mother's recent command. Her mother had no right, and even if she did, Fan Cottage was within the broad confines of Stanhope Hall, less than a quarter of a mile. Through secluded woods, miles from the main road where no one ever went, though sometimes it could be a spooky place, for she had found rusty old muskets there, and tin plates and empty bottles and worm-eaten pieces of fabric, both blue and gray. Her father had told her once that the Stanhope woods had been sanctified by human blood and that while he lived, no one would ever chop down a tree, for trees were nature's tombstones honoring and marking the graves of the soldiers who had died there.

The thought of her father always sobered her and gave her cause for thought. She adored him, though he seemed so distant of late, so alone and so serious.

Fan Cottage. There was her escape now, as it had been every day of her life for as long as she could remember, that risky though necessary escape to the small paint-peeling exterior of the old slave cabin, Sis Liz and White Doll waiting for her, the tea service gleaming, tea steaming, White Doll's sugared pecans in an Irish belleek bowl, double-chocolate tea cakes, incense, candles, velvet robes, laughter and music, lilacs, paradise.

Hurry.

In order to escape detection, she'd go up into the attic and through the trap door that led down steep and secret steps the length of the house. Sis Liz and White Doll had told her about the passage years ago. They'd used it nightly to "haunt" the Yankee troops who once had occupied Stanhope Hall during the war.

She'd only stay for an hour. Her mother was so busy she'd never miss her. Now as she dressed she reminded herself to tell both Sis Liz and White Doll about the hooded men and the white camellia.

Quickly she secured the high neck buttons of her shirtwaist and kicked aside her petticoats—it would be easier to run without petticoats. Hastily she gathered her long hair into a braid and secured it with a pin and was about to turn away from the mirror when she heard a familiar voice on the porch below the second-floor gallery.

Carefully, wanting to see but not be seen, she crept out and peered over without going directly to the edge of the railing.

It was Papa and old Ben.

Ben was wielding a large shovel and broom, picking up the droppings from the twelve horses who recently had paid them a visit, and Papa was watching, still in his dressing gown, hands shoved into his pockets.

He was thinking, Eve was certain of it. When she was a little girl she had sometimes believed that he thought so hard his brain made a noise.

Suddenly she saw him stoop and scoop up the crushed white camellia that, earlier, he had hurled to the bottom step. Now he lifted it as though it were akin to what old Ben was sweeping up. He carried it toward the gunny sack that Ben was filling with horse droppings. Old Ben stopped sweeping and watched as Papa drew back the edges of the sack and dropped the crushed flower inside.

Ben grinned. Papa brushed off his hands and said something to Ben so low that Eve couldn't hear, and then he walked a few yards away until he was standing at the exact center of the avenue of live oaks.

He simply stood there for a long time, looking out.

Eve felt torn, wanting to speak to him, to go to him, anything to let
him know that he was not alone. But time was passing and breakfast
would be called soon and after that there would be no escape for the
rest of the day.

She took a final look at her father standing statuelike, looking out
over the land that bore his name. Then she ran to her bedroom door,
peered furtively out into the corridor, saw no one, lifted her skirts
and broke into a run toward the attic staircase at the top of the third-
floor landing, her destination, a place where the world was not
flawed, where no one thought until his brain made a noise, in fact,
where no one thought very much at all . . .

* * *

Burke knew that there were at least three people awaiting his company and his immediate attention: Mary, in their bedroom, undoubtedly upset and worried by the early-morning melodrama of hooded
horsemen; Mr. Washington in the library waiting to confer with
Burke on available dates this month when he could return to Stanhope Hall and meet with Mr. Samuel Clemens—at Mr. Clemens's
personal request; and perhaps the most urgent of all, Paris Boley, the
young black man waiting in Burke's office for final instructions before he assumed the responsibility and authority of being general
manager of Stanhope Plantation.

In a minute. They all could wait. For now, Burke needed time
alone to consider for himself all the ramifications of that cowardly
dawn act. My God, didn't they know? Vigilante groups had been
outlawed by the federal government years ago.

How long will it take to make one citizen respect another?

You begin at the bottom and work up.

As this recent discussion with Mr. Washington ran through his
mind, Burke walked slowly down the grassy avenue between the live
oaks, planted a century ago by an early French explorer who stayed
long enough only to plant these huge symmetrical guardians of Stanhope Hall. In full leaf they formed a shaded canopy all the way to the
road about two hundred yards in the distance, and they were in full
leaf now. The shade on soft green grass and the dappled effect of ever-
changing sun and shadow lured Burke down the avenue although he
knew it was inappropriate for the master of Stanhope Hall to be seen
strolling in the early-morning hours in his dressing gown.

Inappropriate!

The true inappropriateness had occurred earlier that morning, and
now what was to be done about it. Jarmay Higgins was in on it.
Burke was certain of that. He had recognized Higgins's horse as who

in the county wouldn't and had recognized Higgins's physique as well and wondered again briefly if all the men had lost their wits.

What had they hoped to accomplish? Fear? There was nothing to fear from faceless men. Change? Reformation? If they were angry because a black man had slept under the roof of Stanhope Hall, they'd better learn to swallow their anger, for surely they'd choke to death when word reached them of the skin pigmentation of Stanhope Plantation's new general manager.

Burke smiled and dug the toe of his slipper into a mound of clover. Foolishness. That was the only crime of these infamous Knights of the White Camellia. Change was no longer coming. Change was here, and the animosities that had extracted so high a price a quarter century ago must at last be put to rest. The Southern soul would survive. The Southern economy and, worse, the Southern future might not.

Lovingly he looked up and scanned this piece of earth that bore his name. Nearby Natchez was English and loved the reel and cotillion. New Orleans was French and loved the chanson. Stanhope Plantation represented the best of both these worlds. Since the beginning, at least for as far back as he could trace or have traced, there had always been a Stanhope on these rich acres.

Indians had come this way once. Spaniards once, the French once, the English once, and after they all had come and gone there forever remained a Stanhope—strong, stubborn, determined men who felt a kinship with this wide flat land and knew well how to fill it with those soft lightly packed cotton bolls that made every new Stanhope richer than the one before.

Slowly Burke walked in a limited circle, surveying the fields for as far as the eye could see, privately thanking those wise progenitors who had spotted and claimed these eight thousand acres ten miles north of Mobile, on the Mobile River.

At the end of the avenue of live oaks he turned about abruptly and saw Stanhope Hall from a distance, crowning the slope, the eye drawn back up the line of live oaks in the clear shining light of morning.

Probably no house in all the South was put up more sturdily, one reason why blue and gray alike had spared it during the war, as though they knew that a more elegant shelter they would find no place.

Thick red brick walls, three-storied, ended in outer cornice working of massive size and elaboration. The portico, a mass of brick and stucco, almost as broad as the building itself, had two pairs of powerful doric columns upholding the pediment. Ironwork bordered the galleries above and below; a balustraded captain's walk on the roof seemed to extend over half the elevation.

Stanhope Hall had had a sophistication and a worldly look about it even in the middle of the 1840s. Now in 1889 it resembled a maturing beautiful woman, her beauty enhanced and ever increasing with the years.

Burke started back toward Stanhope Hall, reveling in what he saw, the best of the South about to take a giant step forward in human reformation and justice.

Now in these last few moments, before the myriad of responsibilities called to him, he found himself eager for the beauty and classical symmetry of the interior of Stanhope Hall and took a final look backward as old Ben swept up the last remnants of their early-morning visitation. Cheap theatrics, that's all it had been, performed by disgruntled and struggling neighbors who perhaps had never forgiven Burke's father for making Stanhope Hall's present prosperity possible by arranging to ship baled Stanhope cotton to Mobile for transport to Northern mills in exchange for a generous reconstruction loan.

On the third step Burke stopped, aware anew of the precise cost of that loan; his father found dead in a Mobile hotel room, a suicide by hanging, his Southern conscience unable to bear the weight of his bargain with the "Yankees."

Saddened, Burke stared down on the veined white marble step. He saw a slight indentation caused by wear over the years and saw his father worn down in the same way. If Burke had been here beside him instead of remaining in England in pursuit of Mary—

No. Quickly he scolded himself and dismissed the damaging thoughts for the ancient postmortems they were.

Suddenly, from behind, he heard laughter and looked over his shoulder to see David, dripping wet, his cotton long johns clinging to his skinny boyish legs, his chest bare and glistening with water from the ice pond, his dark hair hurling a spray of water beads as he shook it in wild pursuit of Cleo and Casey, Ben's grandsons, who lived here at Stanhope Hall while their father tried to earn a living in the Birmingham mills.

Feeling like a truant himself, Burke stood on the steps and watched the boys rolling in the cool shade on soft clover like pups, simply deliriously happy to be alive.

A single thought presented itself to Burke. The world was good. Despite the ugliness of the morning, the world was good.

"Papa."

The call came from David, who apparently had looked up from his impromptu wrestling match.

"Papa, wait."

Burke took immense pleasure in the sight of his son running, a sturdy lad, bright humored, with rare charm and a spontaneous sparkle. Mary often said that everything came too easily for him, that they had not spoiled him so much as nature had.

"Papa, did you see the horses this morning?" David called out.

"I saw," Burke nodded, smiling down on all three boys.

"Well?" David pressed impatiently. "Who were they? What did they want?"

Burke played dumb and shook his head. "Did you see them?" he asked.

As all three heads shook no, fresh water halos spread out like brief jewels.

"Then how did you know?"

David looked mildly defensive. "I heard them, a hundred horses at least and Casey saw them as they were leaving and old Ben saw it all."

Stymied, Burke considered his next move, aware that he must tread carefully. These three young lions were hungry for a war, as all young lions had been since the beginning of time, a flaw in the otherwise near perfect design, perhaps. But let them go elsewhere and find their own battles, away from Stanhope Hall. Burke was weary of this one and only wanted to end it.

"Papa?"

"What did Ben tell you?" Burke asked.

Cleo ventured a step forward. "That they were bad men and meant us no good."

"Well, that's not exactly true, Cleo."

"Then who were they and what did they want?" David persisted, keeping everyone on track.

"I don't know," Burke replied honestly.

"Didn't they say anything?"

Burke shook his head.

Apparently Casey felt compelled to contribute and drew even with the other two. "Mrs. Winegar said they don't talk, they never talk, they just leave a white flower, then someone gets hurt bad."

"Is that true, Papa?"

Burke eased up a step or two and evaded the question. "No one will get hurt at Stanhope Hall, I promise. Hurry and dress, David, and you two as well. I want all of you in the library to bid Mr. Washington farewell. Hurry now."

"But Papa—"

"Later, David, I said later." For the first time Burke employed his "father voice," and all three boys moved obediently backward, though he could see anger in David's face that the central mystery of the morning had been so thoroughly evaded and that in essence his father had pulled rank.

Burke watched them as they disappeared around the side of the house and thought that he probably could get away with that stance for another year, and then it would be too late.

Well, he'd worry about that when the time came. Now he must dress, must speak briefly with Mary and must reassure Eve and rejoin Mr. Washington in the library and escort him to the dining room for breakfast.

Who were they? What did they want?

As David's two questions echoed in his head, Burke realized that he too would like specific answers. But later. For now Stanhope Hall was too busy enjoying the present and anticipating the glorious future to pay serious attention to the melodrama of the past . . .

* * *

It was the dark passage across the top of Stanhope Hall that always frightened Eve most, going down through the trap door into utter black, on down the narrow steps that led to the earth tunnel and eventually led up to the moss-covered grate and the fresh air at the extreme north end of the garden, a treacherous route which, when she was a little girl, she had run with her breath held and one eye closed.

Now it wasn't quite that bad, though she still flinched and jumped when cobwebs caught on her face, and of late the earth tunnel had begun to collect water that seeped in from the ice pond, so that she had to lift her skirts and endure wet shoes until they dried. The route *was* hazardous but it led to freedom and thus was worth it.

Now grateful that once again she had made an effective escape, she bent to restore the grate and observed her wet shoes and was sorry that she was disobeying her mother, but not so sorry that she wanted to turn back. For as long as she could remember, she had needed Sis Liz and White Doll to explain to her the ways of the world, and while their explanations had not made a great deal of sense, at least the questions of the moment seemed less urgent when filtered through their joy and gaiety and continuous celebration of life.

Now as she raised up from sliding the grate back, she paused to brush away the fine-powdered dust that caught on her dark skirts. Sis Liz always took careful note of her appearance and if it was too offensive would waste part of their precious time together scolding and cleaning.

Look at the child, White Doll, not a Stanhope surely, a waif, abandoned—

Prematurely despairing, Eve looked around for a diversion and found it in the gardens themselves. Nothing pleased Sis Liz and White Doll more than to be presented with flowers, and stretching before her was what was rumored to be the prettiest gardens along the Mobile River, though there wasn't much left now in the August heat.

Ah, there was color. Crepe myrtle in abundance, big showy plumes of lavender and coral and purple. Sis Liz would be ecstatic. Eve hurried to the flowery shrubs, snapping the brittle stems one after another until her arms were filled.

Now she retraced her steps back down the central aisle of the garden, sidestepping loose flagstones, hurrying past the grate through which she'd just emerged and on down until she confronted the solid-appearing azalea hedge that marked the end of Stanhope gardens and the beginning of Stanhope woods.

She stole one quick look back over her shoulder to make certain no one was watching, then lifted the greenery and slipped through to the other side, carefully protecting the flowers in her arms. Standing upright, she looked out at the towering forest of pine that kept this part of Stanhope Plantation in constant shadow. The earth was covered with fallen pine needles that, when it rained, made for slippery footing. More than once Eve had started off at a run and found herself flat on her back. Worse was a wind. Then there was a ghostly high-pitched wail that sounded like all the sorrow in the world.

You must learn one lesson, Eve, my child—what you wish to think, think. What you choose to ignore no longer exists.

She smiled at the echo in her head and heard the musical voice of Sis Liz and hungered for her presence, for her magic, and again she renewed her grasp on the large bouquet and found her route, a small path worn clean by the tread of her own footsteps, and she started off at a deliberate pace, tentatively checking each footing, not wanting to slip and do further damage to her already mussed garments.

While her father and mother did not particularly care for her daily visits to Fan Cottage, they both had agreed that Sis Liz had a special quality. Eve loved to hear her father tell stories of Sis Liz as a young woman, beautiful in lace, the belle of Alabama, carriages lined up the length of the Stanhope live oaks, all suitors for Sis Liz.

Then why had she never married?

She had never told Eve, though she had promised her she would tell all when the time was right.

Listen—

Eve held her position. She'd heard something behind her. Now? Nothing. The pine woods were known for their deceptive sounds; even the birds preferred the sunny gardens to these damp shadows.

Moving with greater care, Eve kept to her path and followed it down into a ravine and up the other side. Sometimes in early autumn Sis Liz and White Doll would come here to gather succulent mushrooms that they would cook for Eve in a tangy butter sauce with garlic and red peppers. Not long now until mushroom season.

There it was again, that sound, a movement nearby that did not belong in these woods.

Please don't leave Stanhope Hall alone, Eve, I beg you—

Hurry, pay no attention, though she did pay close attention as she pulled up out of the ravine and heard movement, like horse's hooves sliding on pine needles.

Panic for just a moment, then anger that someone should try to intimidate her, and in a surge of defiance she turned and confronted —nothing but empty shadowy woods and the flickering patterns of ever-changing sun.

Now Eve maintained a sedate pace, head erect, her eyes trained on the shadows ahead, eager for a glimpse of the roof of Fan Cottage and safety. A magical place, Fan Cottage. Years ago it had been occupied by a black woman named Mammy Fan, who had been Sis Liz's nanny. Mammy Fan had died during the yellow fever and cholera epidemic of 1852, an awful time, according to Sis Liz, with frightened Negroes fleeing to these woods only to die here. Mammy Fan died that year and was buried behind Fan Cottage, and poor Sis Liz, desolate, stole off so often to cry alone at the grave that ultimately she decided with Southern practicality to move into Fan Cottage and care for Mammy Fan's only child, a daughter named White Doll because of her diminutive size and mulatto coloring. Rumor had it that Sis Liz's brother, Burke Stanhope's father, had sired the child, thus making her Sis Liz's niece and a blood relation.

Since then the two women had lived together in blissful harmony, in mutual love and adoration.

Over the years the two women had transformed the interior of the plain brown cabin into a small but luxurious parlor. Gradually they had spirited prized pieces out of the big house, and their small rooms were filled with trinkets, ornaments, pictures, strings of paper flowers, whatever the two women remembered with sentimental interest. Sis Liz, older, was the more dominant. She had acquired an almost regal quality with the years, and now, though she was approaching eighty, Eve found her beautiful, tall and irresistible.

In a curious way White Doll was the child Sis Liz had never had. And sometimes Eve suspected that White Doll played the child role just to please Sis Liz.

Restriction and sadness and a failed world in one direction; freedom, joy and an enchanted world in the other. No question which one Eve preferred, and again she increased her step, relieved to find herself drawing nearer to the curve in the path beyond which she would catch her first glimpse of Fan Cottage.

But as she approached this curve, she heard another disturbance behind her, closer this time, and saw a man's face staring at her from a distance of about twenty feet.

Eve turned, unmindful of the treacherous footing, and lifted her skirts and started off at top speed despite her rapidly beating heart and took the curve, too afraid to look back, too afraid to do anything but increase her speed. At the first glimpse of Fan Cottage she cried out, "Sis Liz, please—" her voice echoing through the still pine woods. "Sis Liz, Sis Liz—"

Above her cries she tried to determine if the flat, unmoving eyes were following her.

"Sis Liz, are you—"

She kept her eyes fixed on the front door of Fan Cottage, and at last she saw it open and saw White Doll peering out, a doll-size woman in her mid-fifties, still wearing her white dressing gown. A moment later Eve saw Sis Liz appear behind White Doll, push gently past her and appear full length in the door, wearing a matching white silk dressing gown, their "costumes" for their morning ritual.

Relieved, Eve dared to break speed and looked behind her where she saw the path empty, though she maintained a good speed until she was safely through the white picket gate and gazing up into the regal face of Sis Liz, who stared down at her with a mixed expression of curiosity, love and concern.

Breathless, Eve struggled to speak. "Something in the woods—a horse—a man—I saw him."

She saw Sis Liz step forward and stare back down the dim, shadowy path.

"I see no one," she pronounced, a mild tone of accusation in her voice.

"He was there, I swear it, Sis Liz. He was looking at me."

"Were you running? Only persons of lesser rank run."

"Oh, Sis Liz, for heaven's sake, she's frightened," scolded White Doll, who came around and put her arm about Eve and led her to the stairs.

Ultimately Sis Liz softened and took up a position on Eve's other arm and hugged her. "Well, if anyone was there, obviously you frightened him off with your wild banshee yell. A woman must train her speaking voice to mimic a harp, not a—"

At last she caught sight of what was left of the bouquet of crepe myrtle. "Oh, dearest Eve, how gorgeous. Look, White Doll. In the jade vase. Perfect."

As she took the flowers from Eve's arms, she kissed her on the cheek.

"Come, my dearest child," she soothed. "You do look undone, and I'm sorry for your fright. We need another Buck, don't we, White Doll? Did we ever tell you about our lovely black dog with straw-colored eyes and a red nose who patrolled these woods vigilantly until the day of his death?"

A hundred times at least, Eve thought, beginning to relax and feel safe again.

White Doll led the way through the door and held it open for Eve and Sis Liz, who, Eve observed, was the last one in and who stole a final look at the woods as though she might have believed Eve's story.

But nothing more was said, as though with the closing of the door, they were capable of shutting out "that other world" with all its imperfections.

"Hurry now, White Doll, put the blossoms in the vase and we'll include Eve in our daybreak ceremony. The beauty will help to cleanse her system of all fear."

As the two women scurried about the small interior, Eve straightened a lock of her hair that had fallen loose in her run, and she held her position by the door, feeding as she always did on the unexpected beauty that lay concealed behind plain paint-peeling frame walls. Before her was a comfortable salon, two royal blue velvet settees, and a courting bench, and a lovely muted oriental runner and mahogany what-not shelves and an arrangement of royal blue peacock feather fans and a glass dome filled with shiny wax flowers. And there on the sideboard was a gleaming silver tea service arranged for the daily morning ritual and two rosewood bookcases filled with leather-bound volumes of the classics, predominant among them Sis Liz's "God," the only one who mattered, Sir Walter Scott, and Eve's favorite piece of all, a prize of Stanhopes for generations—a small circular table inlaid with a pattern of birds in mosaics, with small diamonds and emeralds and rubies to represent the eyes.

"Oh, how perfect," Sis Liz exclaimed now as White Doll placed the towering plumes of lilac crepe myrtle in a dark green jade vase, a stunning contrast on the small round white marble tea table.

"Burke had a hand in growing these, I just know he did," Sis Liz announced. The old woman adored her nephew, Eve's father, and always kept her mild resentment of Eve's mother thinly veiled, fearful that Burke had married beneath his station in marrying "that English woman."

"No, Sis Liz," Eve murmured, "the gardens are Mama's. She tends them and you know that."

"Too bad," the old woman mourned. "No fertilizer like the master's footsteps." For a moment she caressed the flowers with an air of faint mourning. Then in an abrupt change of mood she motioned Eve forward. "Come. The day that starts splintered must quickly be made whole again. White Doll, fetch her a hot mint towel so that she can cleanse that exquisite beauty and become whole again."

Eve wished that Sis Liz knew just exactly how splintered this day had begun. Well, in time. She smiled as she realized that Fan Cottage had already started to work its magic, the mystery and fear and apprehension of the morning becoming slowly obliterated by the color and beauty and love to be found in this small cottage and with these two unique women.

"Here. This will put you to right soon enough." Eve looked up at White Doll's black eyes and childlike face and saw her holding a steaming white linen towel between the pair of silver tongs, the perfumed odor of mint blending with hot steam.

Without hesitation, Eve took it and simultaneously recalled the numbers of hot mint towels that had assisted her through childhood, one for every scrape, bump, bruise, cut and splinter. As she covered her face with the towel, she breathed deeply of the fumes and was in the process of washing her forehead when White Doll bent low.

"Here, let me do that, just like when you were a little girl," and those gentle hands took over in a gentle massage of Eve's temples and the sides of her neck and she let her head hang limp and felt White Doll move closer behind her.

"Oh, White Doll," she murmured in pleasure and leaned back against the woman and gave in entirely to the strong fingers and the pleasant combination of warmth and mint.

"Now you know why I shall live forever," Sis Liz called out playfully from across the room, where she was busying herself with the tea service. "And be as beautiful as I was on my eighteenth birthday, far more beautiful even than you, Eve, although I'm sure you won't believe me."

"And as immodest," whispered White Doll. Only Eve saw the caring smile that accompanied the words.

"Did I ever tell you, Eve, about my most important beau?"

"No, Sis Liz, you never did, although you've promised. Tell me about him now, please."

"A doctor, he was," Sis Liz announced, "highly respected, related to the Natchez Stantons, six foot if he was an inch with a soul to match, the most sensitive man I've ever had the privilege of knowing, a beautiful ruddy face and thick auburn sideburns that curled in the breeze. He played the violin, you know, and his features, though slightly irregular, had a dark strength. He could laugh when others fretted and remain at ease when most men shouted out their rage. He was the most superior man I have ever met in my entire life, and I loved him to the point of absolute desperation."

Her voice broke.

With eyes closed, Eve waited, as did White Doll, standing behind her. So powerful was Sis Liz's description of the remarkable Dr. Stanton that Eve was half-certain that if she opened her eyes, she'd find him standing in the room with them.

But there was only silence now, a painful one, Sis Liz frozen over the tea table as though she'd gone too far back in memory and was having trouble finding her way home.

"Sis Liz, what happened?" Eve asked gently in the spirit of throwing the old woman a lifeline.

When still there was no answer, White Doll placed the mint towel in Eve's hand, straightened her dressing gown, which had become twisted during Eve's impromptu massage, and walked slowly toward the woman who was still standing unmoving with her head bowed by the tea table.

"My darling Sis Liz," White Doll began slowly, "Eve has asked you a question. What happened to the remarkable and beautiful Dr. Stanton?"

For a moment, from where Eve sat, she still could see no movement. Then, imperceptibly, one parchmentlike white hand with distended blue veins started up, like a wounded bird, half-fluttering. The old woman herself stood straighter, with renewed regality, and at last the white hand stopped at the side of her cheek, giving her a perplexed air as though she really had to concentrate in order to remember what had happened to Dr. Stanton.

"Nothing," she said airily and followed it with a short laugh. "Absolutely nothing. Now, isn't that just like life?" And she laughed again and White Doll appeared to study her for just a moment; then she too laughed. And at some point the two women felt the need to embrace, and around their laughter they kissed each other's cheek and paused for an exchange of loving glances, and Eve felt herself smiling, a little envious of the rare relationship between these two mismatched friends—one dark and small, the other fair and tall, separated in age by a quarter of a century, in breeding by an ice age, yet so alike, so compassionate, so caring.

"You know, Eve, in my day," Sis Liz went on, adjusting the strands of pearls about her throat, "all that was required of a young lady was that she develop the ability to say nothing with good manners. I never could do that, could I, White Doll?"

White Doll shook her head and took over the arrangement of the tea table.

Now Sis Liz, with head held high, a great peacock fan in her hand for stirring the hot August air, advanced out of her bleak mood. "I always arrived early in order to get it over with, said far too much while I was there, retired to my room and spent the evening in great appreciation of myself."

Eve laughed, as did White Doll. Only Sis Liz's face remained earnest and sober.

"You must learn, my dear child," she said to Eve, "to fill your own world in your own way. Then if you find disappointment in the so-called reality around you, you will be able to carry off your disappointment with a certain aplomb and grace."

The remarkable face of Sis Liz was very close now and so earnest in her delivery of these early-morning lessons Eve did not fully understand but wished she could. Perhaps now was the time to tell Sis Liz of the early morning visitation of hooded riders to Stanhope Hall.

But when White Doll announced from the tea table, "All's ready," Sis Liz rose in a graceful movement and said, "How beautiful," and turned away.

"Come, come." She motioned to Eve, who was in the process of pushing up out of the plush deep settee, so glad now that she'd disobeyed her mother and left Stanhope Hall. "The morning ritual" was a concept invented and refined by Sis Liz and White Doll in which they pledged anew for the day their love and trust and patience and understanding one for the other. They had been doing it for as long as Eve could remember, the brief ceremony always concluded by the exchange of something personal to be worn by the other for the duration of the day as a reminder of their bond to each other.

"Come, child, we've set you a place," Sis Liz urged, "and your gift of flowers is at the exact center. See?"

As Eve took her chair on one side of the tea table, she was doubly glad she'd taken the time to pick the bouquet. White Doll's arrangement in the jade vase was pure artistry and enhanced the already beautiful tea table itself, silver candlesticks and tall white tapers flanking the crepe myrtle, a small silver dish of sugared pecans—Sis

Liz's favorite—at the center. Sis Liz liked to drop them into her hot coffee and always urged everyone else at the table to do the same.

And there were other delicacies on the tea table, leading Eve to believe that the morning ritual had been expanded to include breakfast. There was a pink fluted porcelain platter of White Doll's "mice candy"—sweet meats complete with tails and tiny whiskers. And there was an arrangement of cinnamon buns, and molasses bread and butter, and burnt sugar cakes and Eve's favorite, double toffee cookies, and of course the steaming urn filled with strong black coffee and flanking pitchers of heavy cream.

As the three settled around the tea table, Eve noticed square pale pink linen napkins with a single tiny rose embroidered in each corner. She watched Sis Liz place hers daintily in her lap, then followed suit and waited, hands in lap, for the ritual to commence.

For a moment Sis Liz and White Doll looked at each other over the crepe myrtle plumes. Then slowly Sis Liz reached into the folds of her robe and withdrew a small blue velvet box and placed it on the table. White Doll did the same, except her exchange was larger, flatter and came wrapped in white paper.

After both personal items had been placed on the table, Sis Liz reached across and grasped White Doll's hand, and looking straight into the eyes of her dear friend, she began to speak intimately.

"I want this day, this dawn to hear and know of my proclamation of love for this woman named White Doll, who graces every second of my life and brings warmth to my heart, and eases every step, and soothes every doubt, and fills my days with joy beyond imagination and description, and my first task when I leave this world and arrive in another will be to thank the God there for His gracious gifts to me here, the most gracious of all, my life companion, my sustenance, my hope, my warmth, my one and only love. . . ."

After Sis Liz's pledge, White Doll's was brief, simple and even more moving.

"To the one who makes my life a paradise. To my beloved Sis Liz."

Eve heard the words and wondered bleakly if she would ever know such a person, someone who could make her life a paradise.

Then the exchange of gifts, for Sis Liz from White Doll a rare treasure, a starched lace fan made in the violet pattern by White Doll's mother, Mammy Fan.

Eve watched as Sis Liz took it with obvious tenderness and affection both for what it was and who had made it, her beloved Mammy Fan whose grave was visible through the back window, a grave that Sis Liz still visited and decorated every day as she had since 1852, over thirty-five years ago.

Mammy Fan had earned her nickname because of her artistry with fans such as this one, crocheted pieces she'd then heavily starch and mount on a bone frame. This one that Sis Liz was now admiring was exquisite, done with colored thread, each long bone a green violet stem culminating in a dark lavender violet, all attached to a carved mother-of-pearl handle.

Eve saw Sis Liz bring it closer as though to admire it better. "She's been very close to me of late, you know," she said over the fan to White Doll. "I wish you could have known her, Eve, my Mammy Fan." As she talked she fingered each starched lace violet as though trying to make actual contact with the woman who had created them.

"So strong, the strongest woman I have ever known and the wisest. Do you know, when she died, all the camellia bushes dropped their blossoms upon the soft earth. Only when God is in a very generous and giving mood does He create a soul the caliber of my Mammy Fan, and if He loves you very much, He will put you in close proximity to such a soul."

Her voice trailed off and her memory with it, and there was no sound in the room as Sis Liz communicated in her own way with the dead woman who had raised her and loved her without qualification.

Suddenly Sis Liz laughed and gave a luxurious sigh. "Do you know how truly lucky we are, White Doll? We two old women? On one side we have the rare treasures of the past, our Mammy Fan, and on this side we have the rarest treasure of the future, our own beautiful Eve."

Eve blushed under the sudden close scrutiny of both women and wished they would focus their attention once again on old Mammy Fan, wherever she was.

"Well, coffee's getting cold," Sis Liz said at last and opened the small blue velvet box at her elbow and commanded White Doll to "give me your magical hand."

As White Doll did so, Sis Liz slid a pearl ring on her index finger, a perfect pearl with pale pink tints that sat elevated in a heavy gold mounting and surrounded by diamonds, a beautiful ring made even more beautiful by the contrast of White Doll's dark skin.

"It's beautiful." White Doll smiled in what appeared to be genuine surprise, though Eve was certain that each had exchanged these precise treasures before. It was simply a feature of their affection for each other that they played these roles with surprise and pleasure.

White Doll examined the ring up close and extended it to Eve for her inspection and Eve recognized the sense of celebration, a Christmas morning, only these two had managed to create it every day of the year.

As Sis Liz extended to her a steaming cup of coffee and an invitation to help herself, Eve sat closer to the tea table and willingly did as she was told.

"Now," Sis Liz said as she settled back in her chair, taking her china cup with her and with great elaboration dropping in two sugared pecans, then fixing Eve with a pointed stare. "You must tell us the cause of your unhappiness, and don't deny it, because it hovers over you even now like a cloud, doesn't it, White Doll? I noticed it the moment I saw you, didn't you, White Doll, and we must have no concealment from each other here. Otherwise the magic is rendered impotent."

As she talked, she stirred the sugared pecans into her hot coffee and looked sternly at Eve, who was a little chagrined to find out that her unhappiness showed.

When Sis Liz continued to fix her with that waiting gaze, Eve opened her mouth to speak and the strangest question came out.

"Sis Liz, where is your Dr. Stanton now?"

For a moment all movement on both sides of the tea table ceased. Slowly Sis Liz fished a naked pecan from her coffee, popped it into her mouth and chewed contentedly, all the while gazing down at Eve. Gradually a sweet, knowing smile cracked the pale white face.

"She's curious about love." Sis Liz beamed at White Doll. "Our Eve, our precious baby, all grown up and in exquisite need of that terminal and deadly illness known as love."

She sipped slowly at her hot coffee, all the while shaking her head. "Oh, my dearest, when I contemplate the pain that is in store for you, it breaks my heart. But there's nothing I can do to change you or the ways of the world."

"Inevitable," White Doll agreed.

"Dr. Stanton," Sis Liz announced in a loud voice. "I saw him only once in later years, after nothing happened. His eyes were faded, worldly, embittered, his face had heavy lines, his mouth a look of disillusionment, almost of contempt of everything he saw."

She paused. "But that doesn't mean that your young man will turn out that way."

"I don't have a young man," Eve murmured, embarrassed by their focus and embarrassed even more by the subject.

"Oh, but you do." Sis Liz beamed and stood with regal dignity. "Someplace in this world at this very moment is your twin half, made so by destiny, shaped by nature to a perfection that will cause your breath to catch in your throat, a more pleasing arrangement of flesh and blood and bone you will not find in this world, and he is out there now, perhaps even wondering about his twin half and when he will find you and how he will recognize you and painfully worried about whether the two of you can fight your way through all the hazardous traps of true love. Do you believe me?"

Eve did well to nod, so fascinated was she by the promise of a twin male half somewhere in this world. "I believe you, Sis Liz. But how will I know him or he me?"

All at once Sis Liz laughed, a sound like tinkling crystal, and White Doll joined in on the other side of the tea table, though a portion of her attention was still being channeled toward the pearl ring on the index finger of her right hand.

"How young you are," Sis Liz said sweetly at the end of the laugh. "You may not know him, but your heart will," and she clasped the area of her chest in the vicinity of her heart and looked upward, and Eve, delighted, settled back, hoping the performance would never end.

"One day your heart will become most insistent and nagging and start to hurt. Quite a literal pain, my dearest, so prepare yourself for it, and you will assess your world for something, someone to ease the hurt, and there will be only one, one face, one set of eyes, one pair of lips, one hand, one laugh, one mouth, one fragrance, one essence, one voice, one—man."

Sis Liz paused, still looking heavenward. "And he will take your hand and lead you away with him and then your true life will begin. All this muddled routine, believe me, is merely prelude—"

"But not for you, Sis Liz," Eve questioned, sitting up on the edge of her chair, still fascinated by the mysterious Dr. Stanton.

Sis Liz shook her head sadly. "No, not for me. And not for White Doll. Not that kind of love, not for either one of us."

"Why?"

Sis Liz shrugged, and smiled. "I went visiting the Stanton home in Natchez once, a dreadful journey of unbelievable peril and discomfort. And when I arrived, Dr. Stanton showed me his golden drawing room. The whole chamber had a golden sheen, Aubusson carpet embellished with floral patterns, lines of gold flowers against the gold French hand-blocked paper, satin damask curtains, French mirrors framed in gold leaf, gold leaf cornices, tiebacks at the windows in the shape of gilt bronze leaves holding grapes of solid gold."

She paused as though seeing the splendid scene anew.

"Well, Dr. Stanton's face was flushed with pride, I can tell you, and rightly so. But you know, standing amidst all that gold, he looked for all the world like old King Midas, and when I realized he was looking at me in the exact same way he was looking at his gold carpets and gold cornices, well, I suddenly missed Stanhope Hall and Fan Cottage

and White Doll so much that my heart started hurting and I knew
then precisely where I belonged."

Silence, though Eve was aware of the special glance the two women
exchanged, White Doll starting halfway up out of her chair as though
she wanted in the worst way to be close enough to Sis Liz to touch
her.

But Sis Liz stopped her with a wave of the violet fan as though to
say she needed another minute to make her point.

"You must pay attention, my dear Eve," she said. "There are two
important considerations to make when approaching the difficult subject of love. One—finding the heart's other half, which really isn't all
that difficult. But number two frequently presents major and fatal
problems."

"Sis Liz, what—" Eve asked eagerly, wanting to be as prepared as
possible for an event that probably would never happen.

Sis Liz looked pleased by Eve's interest and drew her chair close
and sat until their knees were touching. "Well, next, my dear, after
the heart has rejoiced, then it's the soul's job to determine as quickly,
as accurately as possible, precisely what it is that the beloved wor-
ships."

Eve didn't understand and allowed the bewilderment to show in
her face.

"Not God," Sis Liz said sternly. "I'm not speaking of God or Sun-
day-school picnics or the empty blather that most people chant in
church like parrots. No, I'm talking about something much deeper,
more significant and crucial to the survival of the two lovers, because
down deep, you see, we all worship something other than ourselves
and other than God, a much greater God, if you will. Dr. Stanton
worshipped that gold drawing room and all it stood for, and as much
as my heart loved him, which I assure you was considerable, my soul
wept when it identified his personal God, and it was a sad bundle that
returned to Stanhope Hall. For a while this sad bundle whom they
called Sis Liz moped and grieved and pulled petals off magnolias and
contemplated the green depths of the Mobile River and crushed
chicken eggs and generally cursed the gods who had spawned her."

Eve held on to her chair, ever fascinated by the drama that was Sis
Liz, better than any traveling theatrical in Mobile, her father had
always said.

"Until one day that dear soul seated there," and she pointed to
White Doll, "met me along the path as we both were deep in mourning for Mammy Fan and she informed me that there was an empty
space in her cottage, and in her heart, and invited me in to fill it. That
same day, on that same path, I saw that she worshipped the same God

that I worshipped—life, duty, love, spirit—and we've been together ever since."

Then apparently White Doll would not be deprived a moment longer and left her side of the tea table in a rush of love and reached Sis Liz's arms just in time and for several long moments the women embraced each other in the rarest love Eve had ever witnessed.

"Well, enough," Sis Liz pronounced at the end of the embrace, and wiped quickly at her eyes, as did White Doll, who kissed Sis Liz before they separated, and still Eve watched closely, and felt no embarrassment, felt privileged to be in the presence of such rare affection, though there was a doubt and Sis Liz apparently saw it on her face.

"What, my dearest? Have we fed you too much too soon? The meal can be too rich if you're not careful."

Eve shook her head. "No, it's just that . . ."

"What?"

"I'll never meet anyone, not here. No one ever comes here except Papa's friends. Even if the other half of my heart is out there, I'll never meet him."

She was hoping for immediate and reassuring refutation. Instead the small interior of the cottage was silent, as though neither woman could refute her sad claim.

Finally, the best Sis Liz could do was to softly promise, "Something will happen, I promise. It always does in life when we least expect it. All that is expected of us is to remain whole while waiting, and that's what I intend to see that you do. Now I must ask, can you spend the entire day with us? White Doll is going to treat us to her special chicken and dumplings, a private recipe given to her by an angel. Can you stay?"

Eve knew she couldn't and said as much. "I must get back." She smiled sadly. "Mama ordered me not to leave Stanhope Hall this morning."

"And you disobeyed?"

Eve nodded. She didn't think Sis Liz would scold. And she didn't.

"I'll hurry," White Doll promised sweetly from the door, her egg basket in hand. "At least let me fix you an omelet before you leave."

As White Doll closed the door behind herself, Sis Liz turned back to the tea table and commenced returning the various delicacies to their tins, safe from the Southern heat and humidity.

Eve stood and wondered if she should leave now, sneak back into Stanhope Hall before anyone noticed she was missing. But she dreaded the walk back through shadowy woods. Besides, she wanted to tell Sis Liz about the hooded riders.

"Sis Liz, may I help?" she asked, turning back only to find Sis Liz in the small kitchen area, a room scarcely large enough to accommodate two.

"No, just make yourself comfortable, my dear. I'll be right out. There's something on your mind, I know, and together we must solve it."

Eve smiled at the wise voice that sailed out over the top of the beaded partition. They would chat briefly until White Doll returned, then maybe the three of them could walk back to Stanhope Hall, at least as far as the gardens.

"Now then, dishes done, a rising sun, the battle won, and time for fun," chanted Sis Liz, smiling as she reappeared, a fresh dot of color on each cheek. "Where shall we sit for each other?" she asked. Then, "Here on the velvet settee where our hands can reach out, and our knees touch, and our words don't have very far to go."

She sat first and arranged her robe, then, using the fan as a pointer, indicated the precise spot where Eve was to sit.

"Sis Liz, I have a question."

"How lucky you are only to have one."

"Well, there's more, but . . ."

"What? Speak up. I'm fairly certain I can answer anything."

Eve looked up to see that the violet fan had grown still, concealing all of Sis Liz's face except her eyes, which peered over the top with piercing intensity.

"Early this morning," Eve began, "I couldn't sleep and apparently neither could Mama. Papa had sat up late talking with Mr. Washington and—"

"Mr. Booker T. Washington, the Negro?"

Eve nodded and wished that Sis Liz wouldn't just peer at her over the top of the fan.

"And Mama went out on the gallery to look for air and she asked for my help, which I gave because she's so busy, and her nephew is coming soon from England, and neither she nor Papa wants him here, but there's nothing they can do about it and then the men came."

"What men?" Sis Liz asked.

Eve tried to be as articulate as possible. "They were on horseback—"

"How many?"

"A dozen. Some carried torches, and we couldn't see their faces."

"Why not?"

"They were covered with gray hoods, all of them—"

Abruptly Sis Liz dropped the fan and stood and glared down on Eve with a fearful expression.

"Sis Liz, what—"

"What else? Tell me, child, everything, quickly, please."

Eve had never seen Sis Liz so alarmed, and within moments that alarm began to spread and Eve wished she'd kept her mouth shut now and said nothing about the hooded men.

"What did they do?" Sis Liz demanded.

"They did nothing," Eve stammered, trying to remember. Everything was getting all mixed up in her head. Did she see the men's faces then or had that been later, in the woods? "No, one of the riders," she went on, remembering, "dismounted and walked to the steps and placed a single white camellia on the—"

"Oh my dear God," whispered Sis Liz, and the prayer caused the hair to stand up on Eve's arms and at the back of her neck.

For several moments Sis Liz took her despair back to the kitchen partition and bowed her head.

"What did Burke say?" Sis Liz demanded, turning back to Eve.

"Nothing," Eve replied, "not to me, at least. He came out on the porch after the men had left."

"And?"

"He threw the flower into the dirt and went back into the house with Mr. Washington."

Suddenly Sis Liz fixed her with an intense stare. "This Mr. Washington, did he pass the night at Stanhope Hall? Did he sleep there?"

It seemed an innocent question. "Of course," Eve nodded.

Sis Liz closed her eyes and lifted her face to the ceiling, and there was such an expression of defeat on her face that her entire appearance seemed changed.

Her behavior alarmed Eve, and she considered fetching White Doll, who would know how to calm her. But she changed her mind. Surely Sis Liz would calm down soon and explain to Eve what had happened, who the men were and the nature of their curious early morning visit.

Then the old woman turned at last and Eve was shocked to see tears, silent ones, cutting small paths across the fields of rouge. "I am constantly amazed and outraged at God's willingness to let evil have its way in His world," she said. "Those men are evil, Eve, hiding behind their hoods, leaving a trail of terror, poisoning everything in their path, and all the while God sits idly by and lets it happen."

She paused, anger replacing fear. "The Knights of the White Camellia," Sis Liz pronounced. Her voice attacked the words and turned each syllable into an unspeakable obscenity. "Cowards," she added further. "And bullies. Burke is right to fight them, as my brother, Burke's father, should have done. But Grant lacked the courage and so hanged himself in a cheap Mobile hotel room."

After a moment's pause Sis Liz looked back with another question. "When is Mr. Washington leaving Stanhope Hall?"

"This morning. Paris is staying."

New suspicion crept over Sis Liz's face. "And who is Paris?"

"You remember Paris Boley," Eve lightly scolded. "You loaned him some of your books once. Mama taught him to read. Remember?"

For a moment Eve could tell from the old woman's expression that she was trying to clear the fog of memory. Apparently it couldn't be done, and ultimately she dismissed the news concerning Paris Boley and returned to the more recognizable and immediate threat. "And your father said nothing?" she asked.

"No, not that I heard."

"Did he confront them?"

"No, he didn't come out of the house until after they had gone."

"And you saw them?"

"Yes. And Mama too."

"Did *she* speak to them?"

Eve smiled. "She was in her nightclothes. On the second-floor gallery. They didn't even know we were there."

"Oh, you're very wrong there, my child," Sis Liz scolded and now commenced to move in sharp movements about the small interior. "They knew everything that was going on this morning at Stanhope Hall. They knew who occupied each room, knew the precise nature of the activities, and knew full well of the two women peering down on them from the upper gallery. Make no mistake of that."

"One did look up. He was riding Jarmay Higgins's horse."

At this information Sis Liz looked back. "Higgins?" she repeated. "The Higginses always were inferior men, for as long as I can remember. Quite baffling, because they have every advantage, adequate education, and yet still each generation manages to produce only inferior men. We just don't understand enough yet, about anything, do we? And I can't help wondering whether it will be better or worse when we do understand it all."

For several moments Eve heard nothing but distant morning sounds outside the window. Time was passing. She should be getting back. She didn't want to further upset her mother, and her father would expect her to bid Mr. Washington farewell.

She looked toward the front door, thinking she'd heard a step, and hoped that White Doll was returning. Apparently Sis Liz was going to brood at the cookstove for a while, and when she got that way, only White Doll could handle her.

But when the door refused to swing open, Eve stood and straightened the waistband of her skirt, already dreading the long dark tunnel that led back into Stanhope Hall.

"Sis Liz, I really should be getting—"

"Stay for a moment," the old woman said, almost plaintively. "Please stay. White Doll will be back soon and tell us of the wonders she has encountered this morning. And you must sing for us. How desperately we need your song this morning. Time, all time is so short . . ."

It was a tone Eve had never heard before from Sis Liz, revealing need and loneliness and perhaps fear.

"I'll stay," Eve promised softly.

Now coming from the kitchen she heard the delicate clink of crystal. Then Sis Liz appeared from behind the kitchen partition bearing a silver tray and three crystal wineglasses and a pitcher. "A small collation," she murmured, "to help us through the bad news until we can reach the shores of the good."

As Sis Liz placed the tray on the table, she caught Eve's eye and winked. "And a special surprise for you this morning. Your first glass of Sis Liz's infamous plum-dumb punch, though just one small glass, you hear, or your father will come after me. Still I firmly believe that if you're old enough to ask questions about the meaning of love, you're old enough to have a sip of plum-dumb punch."

Pleased, Eve smiled. For as long as she could remember she'd watched Sis Liz serve her famous plum-dumb punch to everybody who visited Fan Cottage. Yet every time that Eve would ask for a glass or a sip, she would be told, "Too young. Must grow up first."

Apparently she'd accomplished sufficient years to qualify for the magic elixir that was talked about far and wide, the length and breadth of Alabama.

What the precise ingredients were, Eve had no idea. It resembled pale lemonade. But the strong predominant odor was not that of lemon; it smelled more like the cough medicine that Dr. Melrose gave to Christine for her lung congestion.

"No, we shan't wait," Sis Liz announced, and Eve belatedly realized that she should have waited for White Doll before sniffing the glass.

"She's taking extra long this morning, isn't she?" Eve asked and watched carefully as Sis Liz poured a glass of plum-dumb for herself.

"Oh, sometimes she's quick, sometimes she tarries forever. She was born curious, you know. Mammy Fan used to say her first breath was a question. She'll be along. Don't worry. Obviously she's deep in conversation with her chickens. For now—"

Carefully she lifted her glass and fixed Eve with an intense and sad stare. "I had hoped that the world would behave itself so that you might have an enchanted life from start to finish. But apparently it is not to be. Still, I hope it treats you gently and respects your beautiful face and voice and understands your unique power, for the world's sake." She lifted the glass higher. "To my beloved Eve."

Blushing, Eve followed suit, not understanding all the sentiments but grateful that Sis Liz appeared to be recovered from her earlier state of alarm.

As Sis Liz drank heartily of her plum-dumb, Eve sipped more tentatively. With the first touch of her tongue, her taste buds screamed as though they had touched fire. From this close proximity even the vapors seemed pungent and burned the lining of Eve's nose.

Sis Liz saw her discomfort and explained politely. "Don't sip. That's the worst thing you could do. Like life, hurl yourself into it, welcome the pain, meet it more than halfway, challenge it, then triumph over it."

As Sis Liz gave her instructions, Eve drew a deep breath, tilted her head back and poured several ounces of lemon-flavored liquid fire directly down her throat and objected only to the sensation that she might never again draw a deep breath in this life.

Coughing, sputtering, she placed the glass on the table and accepted a napkin from Sis Liz, who seemed not at all concerned, who in fact advised her to pat her eyes dry so that now she might see more clearly.

The discomfort, though harsh, was short-lived and left a delightful warmth that commenced at the back of Eve's throat and culminated in the tips of her toes. "It's warm," she gasped.

"It's a secret, you know. The original recipe belonged to Mammy Fan. I for one have developed a tolerance for it." And as though by way of demonstration she drained her glass, briefly drew her upper lip across her teeth, took a breath and suddenly looked toward the door.

Eve followed her line of vision, again thinking that at last White Doll had returned. But the door remained closed and there was no sound beyond, not even bird calls, like the silence that precedes a summer storm.

"Are you—too warm, my darling Eve?" Sis Liz asked, though not once did she take her eyes off the door, as though she'd sensed something that warranted her complete attention.

"I'm fine," Eve lied, her eyes still watering from the punch, new alarm creeping up from small insignificant things; the manner in which Sis Liz spoke to Eve but continued to fix her eye on the door, the silence coming from beyond the door, though in the distance Eve thought now she heard the whinnying of a horse.

"White Doll is taking far too long today," Sis Liz whispered with special emphasis. "She can be a disobedient child, did you know that? Oh yes, she drove Mammy Fan to distraction, complete distraction."

As she spoke, she reached, without looking, in the general vicinity of the table where she'd left the violet lace fan. Her gnarled fingers found it and lifted it and she pressed it against the side of her face.

"Did you answer my question, Eve?" she repeated. "Are you too warm? We can open the door for a breeze if you wish."

"No."

Eve surprised even herself with her quick reply. She had no idea why she wanted that door to remain closed. She *was* warm, her hair stuck in perspiration to her forehead.

"Sis Liz," Eve whispered. The alarm had spread for the contagion that it was, both women now staring fixedly at the door.

"We must open it, you know," Sis Liz murmured. "If White Doll has gone and dirtied her robes, I'll—"

Eve saw new anxiety on her face. "Do you want me to go and look for her?"

At last Sis Liz looked at her. "No need. We're both becoming hysterical old hens. We'll go together and find White Doll, and we can take turns scolding her, me first, though, then you."

Eve searched the suspicious facade of strength for weak spots. And found none. On a surge of bravery that she did not wholly feel, she started toward the door and was halfway through the clutter of furnishings when she realized that Sis Liz had yet to leave her chair.

Eve looked back and saw all color drained from the old woman's face. "I—can't, my darling. I'm sorry. I claim few privileges at eighty, but now I claim one. Go and find White Doll for me and bring the disobedient child back to me and I will be eternally grateful."

The ghost voice matched the ghost face, and Eve knew only that she'd never seen Sis Liz so distraught.

Now in answer to Sis Liz's request, Eve continued on toward the door, listening as closely as possible, ready to identify any and all hazards that might be lurking on the other side.

But she heard nothing and tried to keep a tight hold on her imagination, still feeling the warmth from the plum-dumb, feeling that for the first time in her life she must be strong for Sis Liz, who had certainly eased her through enough nonexistent terrors.

"Be right back," she announced cheerily.

Eve twisted the doorknob and heard distant locusts objecting to the heat of the day and drew the door back a few feet and looked out. She saw nothing but the sandy clearing in front of Fan Cottage, two intersecting paths, one leading out of the thick pine woods, the other leading into the woods, and beyond the woods the vast Stanhope cotton fields in the distance.

"Do you see her? That naughty girl?"

As Sis Liz's voice cut through the silent heat, Eve shook her head and felt relief.

One step out of the door and she stopped. There was something—

"Eve, answer me, please."

Something, from where she stood, looking down at a distance about ten feet away to the edge of the porch, the top step—

"Eve, are you—"

The sun struck at a peculiar angle, blinding her.

"Eve—"

A flower, she saw it now, a white flower, or so it appeared, resting on something, a small dark something she couldn't see.

"Eve, do you hear me calling to you?"

This lost voice was so close, directly behind her at the door now. Eve took a single step to the right and suddenly saw too clearly, saw that the cupped curled dark something beneath the white camellia was a human hand, with human fingers, the white camellia resting in the palm, sharp severed tendons protruding from a dark cavity that spilled red over the porch and down the steps.

Eve felt the strong punch she'd recently consumed rise in her throat. She swallowed hard and saw Sis Liz as her eyes fell on the same hideous spectacle, and with what little composure and strength she had left, Eve tried to turn Sis Liz back into the safety of Fan Cottage.

But the old woman with matching strength pulled free and started in a slow and torturous journey toward the newly severed hand holding its bloodstained white camellia.

"Sis Liz, please," Eve begged and felt her knees on the verge of collapse.

But still the old woman moved in a direct path to the atrocity that rested so silently in the hot morning sun, and as Eve stepped backward for the support of the cabin wall, Sis Liz seemed to draw on some deep reserve of strength and proceeded on to the very edge of the step and at last came to a halt and stood motionless over the severed hand and stared down at it without moving or speaking.

"Sis Liz, please come away," Eve whispered and felt the beginning of tears, as the old woman did the unthinkable, reached down and touched the flower, lifted it gently to one side as though it were worthy of tenderness.

"No, Sis Liz." Eve wept and looked straight up to heaven for a moment's rest from the horror that was taking place before her. Despite this new vista, her tears increased and she heard a gasp, followed by a moan, then heard nothing and vowed secretly not to look down.

But no sooner had she made that vow than she broke it and looked down and saw Sis Liz in the act of lifting the small dark severed hand, the fingers cupped at an angle where she caught a clear view of a large pearl ring.

White Doll—

As Sis Liz studied the hand, Eve tried within the limited boundaries of her experience to understand what had happened and failed.

"Come, my child, we have much to do."

This newly weakened voice belonged to Sis Liz, who was standing before her now, cradling the severed hand in her own hand, fragments of bone hanging loose, blood spreading in ever-widening coins down the front of Sis Liz's white dressing gown.

Quickly Eve shook her head and tried to pull away, but Sis Liz reached out and restrained her. "No, my dearest, this, too, is part of life, the senseless, random hard part, and it must be faced with courage and determination and it must not defeat us. We will shed our tears and confront our emptiness soon, but not now. Now you must give me your support and walk with me back to Stanhope Hall, where we must inform Burke of the nature and caliber of his enemies."

"White Doll," Eve said, wanting only to put distance between herself and the horror.

"White Doll, yes," Sis Liz confirmed and immediately her voice broke and Eve looked back to see her head bent over the severed hand.

Then all at once Eve perceived a fleeting hope. "Could she still be alive?"

"She could be, but she isn't. And what rejoicing there must be in heaven now."

Eve tried to control her weeping and tried not to see the object in Sis Liz's hand and tried to concentrate on the beautiful scene she was creating in heaven, though she didn't believe it for a minute.

"White Doll is gone," Sis Liz said at last, "and the emptiness is our problem, not hers. We are left, and despite everything, we must behave within the mold of proper Stanhope behavior. It was that way in Mama and Papa's day and, it must be that way for us."

Sis Liz extended her hand to Eve. "Come, my child. We have sad news to spread and sadder evidence to share. There is still on this earth the matter of justice, and for that we need Burke's help. Now, will you walk with me and give me support?"

It seemed the only sensible thing to do, to walk together back through the woods for help, bearing the grotesque evidence.

"We must take that, too," Sis Liz whispered as she led Eve to the top of the steps, both women gazing down on the white camellia whose velvet petals were tipped with blood like a new hybrid.

Everything in Eve resisted.

We must behave within the mold of proper Stanhope behavior.

How many times Eve had heard that before, from Papa, from Mama, a clear statement that to be a Stanhope was to be special with special privileges, but more important, with greater responsibilities. Generally in the past Eve had always viewed such a claim as empty and old-fashioned. Now for the first time it occurred to her that such a concept protected and endowed as much as it restricted, for there was the proof, in the manner in which Sis Liz bent over with only a moment's hesitation and took painful note of the bloodstained white flower, then carefully lifted it and did not look back again but led the way down the steps.

Eve followed, still feeling ill, though after a few steps she drew her strength from Sis Liz's and took the lead. It seemed so far, the path so long. Shouldn't she be able to see the gallery of Stanhope Hall by now? Were they even on the right path? These thick woods were cunning with criss-crossed paths from slave days when the occupants of the slave cabins each had a different route, heading to a different destination, some to the house, some to the fields, some to the farm.

Then a few minutes later she saw it, that uppermost ridge of Stanhope Hall, like an amen at the end of a long and painful prayer.

"There it is, Sis Liz. I was afraid we were lost," Eve called back.

She now veered toward the back garden gate and tried to peer through the thick lilac hedge to see who was at work in the smithy shed and who was weeding the vegetable gardens.

But she saw no one and in anger she was tempted to call out. Someone must share this with them, must help them, must relieve Sis Liz of her grim cargo.

She was aware then of Sis Liz coming up alongside her, her old eyes searching as Eve's were for a sign of life, someone who would raise the alarm.

But there was no one in sight, the yard empty as though the entire world had gone off and left them alone to deal with their grief and fear and horror.

"Sis Liz?"

"Hush. Someone will come."

"Where are they? All the servants—"

"They see us. They are afraid."

Her voice was low, scarcely a whisper, and slowly Eve sensed eyes all about, behind barn walls, peering out through cracks in the hayloft, all-knowing eyes that had been through this before with their own kind and knew there was no possible defense against it.

Now Eve stood erect beside Sis Liz and felt the sun climb higher in the sky, sweat coursing down the small of her back, and knew she must stand still and not waver and not give in to either the heat of the morning or the silent terror surrounding them.

* * *

"Mr. Stanhope, with your kind permission, I would like a moment alone with Paris before I leave."

Burke acceded readily to Mr. Washington's request. He hadn't had a chance to speak with Mary since the beginning of this splintered day. A moment to Mr. Booker T. Washington could mean anything from fifteen minutes to a half-hour, and he was understandably sad about leaving his prize student at Stanhope Hall and undoubtedly wanted to give him last-minute advice.

Now Burke withdrew to the door of the library and to his surprise and pleasure found Mary waiting on the other side. Together they looked back at the remarkable Mr. Washington, his long-boned figure and alertly handsome head even more distinguished in the direct rays of bright morning sun.

"I'll see to your valises," Burke called back.

"No, please. I'll do it myself," Mr. Washington replied.

Burke could have predicted that. In his school at Tuskegee Mr. Washington preached self-reliance and habits of self-discipline and cleanliness along with academic disciplines and both in companionship with certain skills such as blacksmithing, harness making, brick making and metal work. His philosophy was that there would be room and, more important, acceptance in the new South for such well-trained and self-reliant Negroes.

Burke agreed with all his heart and soul and had devoted a large portion of his energy and money to Mr. Washington and his Tuskegee school. He held the man in the highest esteem and respect and acquiesced now to Mr. Washington's insistence that he could and would carry his own valises out to the waiting carriage.

"Please take your time, gentlemen," Mary called out to Washington and Paris Boley, and brushed lightly against Burke as she passed by him and with only one brief look and no words informed him that she now wanted to speak with him.

Burke took a final glance into the library and saw Mr. Washington standing before the dead fireplace in his customary stance, hands behind his back. Paris Boley stood erect before him, Stanhope Plantation's new general manager, an important position for a white man, a miracle of accomplishment for a black man.

Quietly Burke closed the heavy wood-paneled door behind him, struck with the historical nature of this moment, two black gentlemen conversing quietly in the library of Stanhope Hall, not as servants, not as inferior men in any way, in fact, far superior to the white rabble who had paid a visit to Stanhope Hall earlier, their faces hidden beneath gray hoods.

"Is everything all right?" It was Mary, looking beautiful as ever despite the awful heat, her manner, her bearing, her smile after twenty years still capable of converting Burke's knees to summer aspic.

Now he placed a finger to his lips, indicating a pause, and drew her beneath his arm and sniffed her summer fragrance of spice and lemon and thought, God help him if she preceded him in death, for surely his grief and loneliness would drive him insane.

Now in the manner of a man checking to see if his house was in order, he glanced out through the broad open front doors, the polished floor gleaming like a mirror from the reflected light of morning. Quite a gathering of house and field help had congregated to say good-bye to Mr. Washington. They all were aware, white and black alike, of the remarkable man's presence, and of this historic moment when one of theirs would shortly assume important reins of leadership.

Let them stay. Such a farewell would be helpful in healing the wounds caused by the early-morning visitors, the Knights of the White Camellia.

Merely thinking the name renewed Burke's distress and he looked back to see Mary patiently waiting.

"Come along," he invited and took her hand and led her hurriedly down the long central corridor of the house. At the rear of Stanhope Hall, beyond the dining room, was a small solarium, a present for Mary several years ago, a place to nurture her budding plants and most fragile blossoms.

Now it would provide them with a private place to talk until Mr. Washington was ready to leave. As Burke pushed open the door and ushered Mary into the tropical green lushness, he spied Paul, a young house boy, standing protectively beside Mr. Washington's valise.

Burke motioned him forward. "Paul, will you do something for me?"

The boy nodded brightly.

"Stand here and keep your eye on the library door. The minute you see Mr. Washington emerge, let me know immediately. Do you understand?"

Again the boy nodded. He was sixteen, possibly seventeen, bright. It was Burke's intention to send him to Tuskegee next spring.

Now he closed the door behind him and all at once felt the humidity of the place.

"We don't have long," Burke began. "Are you all right?"

"I wasn't certain if you saw them," she said, "The men, I mean, this morning."

"I saw them. Where's Eve? She wasn't at breakfast."

"In her room, I would imagine," Mary said. "I asked her to come down for breakfast but she was—upset."

"I'll speak with her."

"Yes. I wish you would. Who were they, Burke?"

The question took him by surprise. He knew the organization, if not the individuals. "Knights of the—"

"I know that," she interrupted. "But who were the men?"

"I'm not sure. I can guess."

"It was Jarmay Higgins's horse."

"One of them, yes. And undoubtedly Higgins himself was in there someplace."

"Are we—should we take them seriously? I had no idea what to tell Eve. She's so very unhappy anyway—"

"Why unhappy?"

"Oh, Burke . . ."

In mild exasperation Mary started down one of the aisles, past fall plantings of chrysanthemums. At the far end she stopped and looked back.

"May I ask your plans for the remainder of the day?" she inquired with sad formality. Did she have to adopt that tone? Was he really that inaccessible as a husband, as a father?

Unhappily Burke knew the answer to both questions. Still, "Why do you ask?"

"Have you forgotten?" she accused. "We have a house guest arriving this afternoon."

Burke gaped at her over the new plantings, his mind a sincere and safe blank. Then he remembered and suddenly the humid air of the solarium seemed to close about him in renewed suffocation. *"Your* house guest, not mine," he snapped and glanced back toward the door and wished that Paul would knock.

There was silence between them now, and not a good one, for it gave Burke too much time to think, to remember. Stephen Eden. From North Devon, England. Twenty-two or thereabouts. Son of John Murrey Eden, the only man Burke had ever met whom he despised totally. Oh, he'd known other bastards, to be sure, had come into unhappy contact with a dozen of them only this morning. But none, despite their disjointed and out-of-date philosophies, wore the cloak of villainy with as much arrogance and natural ease as John Murrey Eden. It was Mary's one flaw, one unhappy state of fate and circumstance, that she was half-sister to this male aberration called John Murrey Eden. Burke had had a chance once to kill him, in a no-holds-barred fistfight in the courtyard of Eden castle in North Devon. He'd had him down, seriously injured, bleeding heavily. A simple snap of the neck would have been an easy act to accomplish, and even as he had contemplated it, his Christian conscience had kept strangely silent and nonjudgmental.

But some other impulse, higher hopefully than mere Christian reflex, had intervened and he'd allowed servants to carry off John Murrey Eden or what was left of him and even then had not felt particularly good about the quality of his mercy and now felt even worse. If he'd only had the moral courage to snuff out the man's life then, he would not be faced with the possibility of receiving his son now.

He stared down at a potting shelf, on tender chrysanthemum buds waiting for the gentler sun of autumn planting. Mary's silence informed him of two miseries. Undoubtedly she knew what he was thinking and regretted it while at the same time agreeing with it, for she, even more than Burke, had reason to prefer a world without the presence of John Murrey Eden.

"Mary, I'm sorry," Burke stammered and knew that he really wasn't and if indeed the young man was arriving today, then it would serve the entire household if Burke left immediately for Mobile and perhaps went on to New Orleans and filled his next few days with urgent business matters far from Stanhope Hall. Mary could send word when the boy had departed.

Again he looked up, having momentarily lost her among the plantings. He glanced toward the door, wishing Paul would summon him with news of Mr. Washington's departure. He felt that he and Mary had had enough of this subject, having argued, discussed, debated it endlessly since Lord Richard's letter had first arrived a month ago.

In the hot silence of the solarium, Burke spied an upturned barrel and sat, suffering an unspeakable weariness. As long as silence seemed the order of this day, he'd obey it gladly.

He caught Mary's eye through the foliage. She looked equally as unhappy as he felt.

"My darling," he began and wiped at his brow and began slowly to make his way to her. "Please, let's not discuss it now."

"We must," she insisted. "He's due before the end of this day."

"He might be late," Burke suggested hopefully. "The trains from the East are notoriously slow and irregular."

"Burke, please," she pleaded and looked up at him with an expression of such sweetness.

As long as his handkerchief was out, he refolded it and with great tenderness applied it to her forehead. "The last thing in the world that I want to do is cause you additional grief," he began.

"Then don't—"

"Couldn't he stay in Mobile? You could visit him there."

"Richard asked that we receive him."

"I have business in Mobile and New Orleans—"

"Burke, please, don't do this to me."

Abruptly she stepped away from his ministrations, her back to him. For a moment neither spoke. Then she turned slowly toward him.

"It's wrong of us, you know, to hold the son accountable for the sins of the father."

"Guilty then."

"For years Richard has been speaking of John's reformation."

"John Murrey Eden will be reformed when Satan sits on the right hand of St. Peter."

"Then you won't help me?"

Faced with such an ugly accusation, Burke faltered and again fought to clear his mind of the persistent image of John Murrey Eden's face, which seemed to be hanging suspended in his memory.

"I have much to do."

"Will you help?"

"In what way?"

"Simple ways, really. Civility, kindness, hospitality." Mary paused as though aware that she was asking a great deal. "It's only for a short time, Burke. I dread it as much as you, if not more. I have only one remaining and prevailing nightmare now from those days in England and John Murrey Eden is responsible for it."

She moved closer, one hand reaching up to his shoulder. "He won't be here long, I promise."

"How long?"

"Well, I should imagine we could control that. If we can assist him, with dispatch, to arrange for his trip west, then he'll be gone from Stanhope Hall as quickly as possible."

She was so close to him now, so lovely, so unchanged, really, despite the years and three children and social deprivation and an enormous amount of private pain. All this she had suffered over the years by simply being Mrs. Burke Stanhope. For a moment, looking down on her in the brilliant light of the solarium, Burke saw that same vision of loveliness that had invaded and conquered his heart years ago in Sim's Song and Supper Club in London.

So beautiful she was then, and even more beautiful now. For during their marriage Burke had on more than one occasion glimpsed beneath the surface beauty to a rare heart and rarer soul who now fittingly was pleading for him to love his enemy.

Momentarily overcome not with Christian concerns but with carnal passion, wishing that he had her alone, stripped of her corsets in their big four-poster upstairs, he settled for bowing his head and brushing his lips gently across her breasts, and following the route upward to her lips, which were open and ready to receive him.

Sometimes it worried him, this passion of theirs that refused to abate or diminish but grew and became more intense with each passing year.

At the end of the kiss she stayed in his arms. "I love you so much," she whispered close to his ear.

"When is he due? Stephen Eden, I mean."

"His last letter was from New York," Mary said softly, not looking at him. "He was leaving immediately, approximate arrival August third."

The spoken date echoed sadly through the dense humidity, again punishing Burke with a clear vision of John Murrey Eden.

Although Burke now nodded to Mary, indicating at least unspoken cooperation, he knew in the privacy of his heart that for the next few days he'd find as many responsibilities as he could manage that would take him away from Stanhope Hall. Oh, he would make perfunctory appearances, but as soon as possible he would locate an agent in Mobile to arrange for the boy's overland passage from Dodge City west. The Texas-Pacific Railroad could get him that far. Then, as far as Burke was concerned, the West could swallow him up for good.

"We must get back," Burke said, glancing toward the door, hoping that Paul hadn't fallen asleep on the job.

"Burke, one thing more," Mary added, trailing behind, holding his hand. "When time permits, please speak with Eve."

He looked back.

"I think she's frightened." Mary nodded quickly. "I know she's lonely. And very, restless."

"She has her studies."

"When I was her age, I had you."

The simple declaration was most effective, reminding Burke that Eve was no longer a little girl, that the social isolation he'd imposed upon his entire family because of his Reconstruction philosophies were now proving painfully difficult for a seventeen-year-old girl on the brink of womanhood.

In mute despair he moved to the door, ready to leave whether Mr. Washington was or not. Behind him he was aware of Mary's silence, as though she knew full well the size and nature of the various battles raging within him.

"Burke, are you—"

He turned about, shaking his head. "When did it happen?"

"When did what happen?"

He shrugged and gestured with both hands. "This was a paradise once. When did I convert it into a hell?"

"No," she protested softly and placed a finger upon his lips. "No such thing has happened. We can manage—anything. We always have. Perhaps in a way we should be grateful to John Murrey Eden. He was the one who first put us to severe tests and we passed them then, and we shall pass them now."

"Remind me to thank his son," Burke commented wryly, buoyed as always by Mary's indomitable optimism.

"Then you will receive him?"

"Do I have a choice?"

She paused. "No. But then choices are never as character building as challenges."

In a surge of gratitude and need, he gathered her to him and held her close and briefly felt whole, knowing that all a man could do was work his way slowly, steadily toward the creation of a more perfect world.

Suddenly he felt her stiffen in his arms. "Did you hear that?" she asked.

Then Burke heard something, a distant confusion of voices, running footsteps. What in the— Had Paul fallen asleep on the job, and now was Mr. Washington departing unattended?

"Damn," Burke said and hurried toward the door when suddenly a sharp knock sounded on the other side.

"Mr. Stanhope, quick—hurry."

As Burke opened the door all the way, Paul started moving back, his face fearful. One hand, trembling, gestured toward the kitchen annex and the yard beyond.

"Come quick, please," Paul begged.

"Mr. Washington?" Burke asked hesitantly.

"No sir, not him, he's still in there. Oh sir, please hurry. They're out back. By the kitchen—"

They formed a ragtag procession down the central corridor, Paul in the lead, Burke a few steps behind him and Mary a few steps behind Burke. As they turned into the portico, Burke saw a huddle of house servants directly ahead and was aware of more just coming around the corner of the house.

Burke looked out over the railing and saw a larger congregation clustered around something near the yard gate, though from this distance and because of the obstacle of people, he couldn't see.

"Burke, what is it?"

He was aware of Mary close beside him now. For some reason he commanded her to wait. "You stay here. Let me see first."

Just as he started down the steps, he saw several young girls coming back up the gravel path that led to the yard gate. Their heads were down, their aprons pressed against their mouths. To the right, standing on the porch of the kitchen annex, he saw Mrs. Winegar, broad-based, arms folded over her stained and spotted apron, the lines of her strong face set into harsh, condemnatory angles.

Suddenly, without moving from her broad stance, Mrs. Winegar called out, "Not you, Mrs. Stanhope. I'd stay put if I were you."

Surprised, Burke looked over his shoulder and saw Mary a step behind him. "I told you to wait."

But even as he spoke, she brushed past him and lifted her skirts and broke into a brief run and began to make her way through the crowd.

Exasperated, he hurried after her. Then suddenly all noise ceased, and the silence drew his attention back to the crowds who were no longer filling the air with disjointed voices. Now they appeared to be moving back, clearing a path for someone.

Sis Liz? What was Sis Liz doing here? She seldom ventured up to Stanhope Hall until late afternoon.

Closer now, Burke was near enough to see stains on the front of Sis Liz's white robe, uncharacteristically messy for the normally fastidious old woman. Then all at once she stepped forward in a curious faltering movement, as though she was ill or on the verge of collapse. Both hands were cradling something in the folds of the white robe.

"Burke, my darling. Something—has happened."

She looked so frail that he hurried the last few steps to her side. As he reached out for her arm, something dropped to the ground, a dead leaf, he thought at first, though at the same time it struck the earth, there were several nearby screams, and Burke looked down as Sis Liz knelt to retrieve the something fallen. And Burke saw that it was not a leaf, was of greater substance, with gently curled fingers fixed forever in one position. Blood coated the wrist and had formed coagulated colonies around severed tendons. On the fourth finger, swollen, was a large pearl ring. All at once Burke knew.

White Doll. He knew that Sis Liz would not leave Fan Cottage without White Doll, knew what they would find on the search that would take place within the hour, the remains of the mulatto woman who had been Sis Liz's constant companion for over thirty years, even knew what it was that had fallen with the severed hand, the profane calling card of the men who in a single morning had changed the rules of this world.

Eve—

As he turned, he saw his daughter reach down for the white camellia and hand it to him.

The exchange took place in front of Mary. "I'm sorry," Burke whispered and wanted to gather all three women in his arms, but knew such a gesture was out of the question, knew that the sooner this frightened congregation was dispersed, the better.

To that end he whispered to Mary, "Take Eve back to the house. I'll get—"

But as he turned, he saw Sis Liz step toward him, the grizzly memento swaddled lovingly in the folds of her robe, her head erect, a puzzled expression on her face, "Burke, will you help me find White Doll?" she asked, and the silence deepened.

"Of course," Burke answered. "Let's go inside first. We must—"

But Sis Liz held her ground. "Our problem cannot be solved inside Stanhope Hall. We must find White Doll quickly. She may need us."

Now he looked back at Mary in an unspoken plea for assistance.

Instead, "She's right Burke," Mary agreed readily. "I don't think it would be advisable to waste too much time. A search party, we need to—"

Only at the end, when the words faltered, did he glimpse behind that stern mask to the frightened woman inside. But perhaps they were right. Burke knew he could easily assemble a search party out of the present gathering.

As though their thoughts were running on the same track, Sis Liz stepped toward the yard gate and announced full-voiced, "I'm returning to Fan Cottage now. Anyone who wishes to assist me, follow after."

Burke watched the old woman take charge and marveled at her

strength and knew that she would grieve for White Doll every day for the rest of her life, but no one would ever see her do it.

"All right," he called out over the shifting crowd. At the same time he saw Booker T. Washington standing on the gallery. Paris was close beside him. Did they know? Had someone informed them that the stupidity had commenced again? In the rigid and senseless confines of that insanity known as the Southern Code, black men did not sleep under the roof of a white man, and Burke had an even bigger shock in store for the Knights of the White Camellia. A black man, Paris Boley, at age twenty-six was about to assume the prestigious position of general manager of Stanhope Plantation, which meant, among other things, that he would be handing out pay to all Stanhope workers, white and black alike.

In the apprehension of this thought, he was aware of the increasing confusion around him, Sis Liz already en route back to the yard gate, the crowd falling in behind her, including Mary and Eve, who walked with their arms about each other.

"Wait!" Burke called out, torn between the hastily planned search party and the two men who watched from a safe distance on the gallery.

At his command all stopped and looked back. Now that he had their attention, he floundered, not certain what to do with it.

Then he saw Paris Boley hurrying toward him, coming from the porch of the kitchen annex, where he'd conferred hurriedly with Mrs. Winegar, who obviously had told him the nature of the horror, for Burke was certain from the expression on Paris's face that he knew everything.

The young man paused only briefly. "Mr. Washington is waiting to bid you farewell. I'll tend to this." And with that he hurried past.

Burke held his position long enough to see Paris draw Mary and Eve to one side, where, apparently as surprised as Burke by the young man's leadership, they stayed put. Then Paris hurried to the front of the crowd, and the last Burke saw, he had assigned Dorie, a young housemaid, to see to Sis Liz. Then he started to separate the crowd, singling out a few men, sending the others back to their duties. No one seemed to question his leadership or his judgment. For a moment the tragedy of the moment took second place to the triumph of the moment when a young man born in slavery should now rise up like fresh hope in a time of dire need.

Then Burke hurried back to the gallery where Mr. Washington waited. "I'm sorry, there's been—"

"I know. I think I knew earlier this morning. And so did you."

The men met midway on the gallery and stood for a moment, heads bowed as though mutually mourning the loss of reason and humanity and decency in the world.

"Your aunt, will she be all right?" The inquiry came from Mr. Washington. Burke nodded and knew his time here was limited. He must get back and assist Paris with the search party.

"The knights, of course," Mr. Washington said gently.

Together the two men started walking back toward the door. "I'll see you off," Burke said with dispatch. "Hopefully we can have this matter resolved when you come again."

"I doubt it seriously," Mr. Washington said matter-of-factly. "My experience with the knights has taught me that once stirred, they buzz like hornets until someone has the courage to slap them down."

Now he gazed out over the sun-drenched lawn, his eyes focused on the crowd who still were following Paris Boley's every command. "Did you know her, the woman who—"

Burke nodded. "She was my aunt's lifelong companion. A warm heart, a good heart. Her name was White Doll. Damn them," he said beneath his breath and started away from Mr. Washington, eager to rejoin the search party being formed beside the yard gate.

"Remember, be careful," Mr. Washington called after him. "For your soul's sake, I mean. I used to think that hating the white man did me no harm at all. And one day I saw that it was narrowing my soul and making me a good bit less of a human being. Then I quit hating him. It wasn't worth it."

In this instance Burke didn't give a damn about the narrowing of his soul. He started to say as much but changed his mind. No time for words, a need for action. Let his soul survive, if it could.

"Can you see yourself out?" he called out to Mr. Washington.

"Perhaps I should stay. Perhaps—"

"Nonsense," Burke cut in rapidly. "Your meeting with the bankers in Baltimore is of vast importance. The funding for the new wing—"

Abruptly Washington lifted both hands in a staying gesture, as though he didn't need Burke to remind him of his duties. "Please convey my sympathies to Mrs. Stanhope and all your family. I shall be thinking of you during the next few days."

Burke watched him as he reentered the central corridor, stooping to lift his valise. For several moments his footsteps were heard in echo as he marched off the polished hardwood floor.

Burke held his position until he heard the distant whinnying of a horse. Then he looked back out over the yard at a very different sight.

In place of the milling crowd stood two dozen strapping young men. To one side he saw the three women waiting in the shade of the big oak. From this distance Eve and Sis Liz appeared to be standing together. Mary seemed to be speaking earnestly to both of them.

Then Burke saw Paris start briskly toward him.

"I've tried to get your aunt to give me the—" Paris broke off and wiped his hand across his forehead. "She won't relinquish—"

Burke understood.

"Come," Burke said and hurried down the gallery and joined him on the gravel path.

Ahead now was Mary, her face filled with grief and horror. As Burke grew near, she bowed her head and whispered, "She won't give it up."

"Then let her keep it," he murmured, sickened by the nature of their exchange. He approached Eve and tried to keep his line of vision elevated away from the bloody smeared hand Sis Liz continued to cradle in the folds of her robe.

"Eve, I want you to go back to the house."

"No."

"Yes." The command came out stronger than he might have wished.

Apparently Mary saw the need for intervention. "Please, Eve, we both ask that you return to the house and look after things there for us."

"Mama, I was there when—it happened. Let me—"

"Obey your parents!"

This voice topped all others and came from Sis Liz. "Go back, little Eve," she called over her shoulder. "The woods are full of horrors that will do lasting damage to young eyes."

Burke stirred himself and tried to comfort his daughter. "Eve, please, we're only trying to—"

"I saw them. In the woods this morning."

"Who?"

"The men who hurt White Doll."

"Did you recognize them?"

She shook her head. Her face looked pale and her hands were trembling. "I heard them. They were following me."

"Oh, my dearest," he said and drew her close and tried to comfort her, all the while aware that he must hurry and catch up with the others.

"Will she be all right?" Eve asked at the end of the embrace.

"Sis Liz? I think so. You go on back to the house. And stay there. I mean it, Eve."

She held her ground as he backed away, and he marveled with paternal pride at her youth and loveliness and wished he could keep her safe all her life and now even more resented the ugliness to which she'd been exposed early this morning.

Hating the white man was narrowing my soul.

He took a last look at Eve and wished that she would start moving toward the house and safety. Then, aware that he was being left, he turned about and ran through the yard gate and saw the tag end of the men just being devoured by the shadowed woods and did not look back at Eve and knew that before this day was over there would be a body to be buried, and wished that he could bring to it a Christian charity and strength equal to that of Mr. Washington and knew that he could not.

As he ran to catch up, all he knew for certain was that he was right in his faith in equality and justice, and that such conviction had served him well all his days and would not desert him now. He was certain of it. It had to be so.

* * *

Jarmay Higgins sat uneasily upon his horse, well concealed in the heavy brush at the crossroad that led into Mobile. He knew only one thing: that he was right, that the code had been broken, that justice had to be meted out if Southern civilization was to survive.

Nervously he fingered the gray hood that lay stretched across his lap. Best to have it at the ready in the event he had to slip it back on.

Next to him was Reverend Winthrop Pounders, a good man to have along on such a morning, his figure tall, distinguished, his black coat and backward collar impressive, his beautifully manicured nails concealed inside gray kid riding gloves.

Now Jarmay stole a sideward glance at the distinguished profile belonging to the curate of Mobile's only high Episcopal church.

"What's keeping them?" Jarmay asked, growing more nervous, wishing he could sit coolly and distant upon his mount as Reverend Pounders was doing.

"They will be along," the reverend said. "Relax, Mr. Higgins. I assure you, God is on our side."

Jarmay tried to calm his nerves and remembered who he was— owner of Higgins farm plus the largest lumberyard in Mobile; not as wealthy, of course, as Burke Stanhope, but then neither were his hands stained with the corruption of Yankee money.

"Are you doing well, Mr. Higgins?"

The starched, polite inquiry came from Reverend Pounders, who seemed to eye him somewhat critically from atop his handsome white mare.

"I'm well, thank you, Reverend. Warm, of course, and a bit worried. It does seem they should have been along by now."

Reverend Pounders shook his head only once and sniffed at the air. "A different caliber of man, Higgins. They operate on their own time and in their own way. Still, they are God's hirelings as well as ours."

"Do you—suppose it went well?" Jarmay asked and peered out of the heavy brush at the intersecting dusty roads.

In answer to his questions Reverend Pounders leaned to one side in his saddle and withdrew a delicate white lace handkerchief. "Oh, I'm sure it did. Orlando Dow is reliable and believes in the work as we do and knows precisely what men to hire who will do his bidding cleanly and without question."

Jarmay listened and tried to ignore the clinging fabric of his shirt. "What do you think Stanhope will do now?" he asked and watched a lone black man slumped on a mule who was plodding down the center of the heavily rutted road. The rider looked neither to the right nor to the left, thus reassuring Higgins that their hiding place was secure.

"What will Stanhope do?" Reverend Pounders repeated. "Repent, one would hope. I knew his father, you know, when I first came to Mobile. An honorable son of the South, I assure you, until the war tested him and he failed."

Jarmay recalled all too well that the first Northern money to arrive in Mobile's cotton country had gone straight to Stanhope Hall. The knights had had to remind the senior Stanhope of certain moral obligations. And once he had understood, the old man, with honor, had hanged himself, an effective apology as well as a repentance, both of which the knights had graciously accepted.

But the Stanhope son was a different matter. He'd arrived back on American shores after the bloody conflict had ended, bearing a suspect English bride on one arm and a head full of treasonous notions under his hat. He'd not only failed to cancel the Northern loans, he'd borrowed more, plus he'd entertained every liberal scalawag from here to Natchez and welcomed Yankees to Stanhope Hall as though they were decent men, and worse, this latest offense, which they could not let pass, he had actually permitted a Negro to sleep as a guest under the roof of Stanhope Hall.

The outrage stung Jarmay Higgins anew as though he'd just heard of it from his secret source within the walls of Stanhope Hall.

No, Burke Stanhope had committed a crime against every decent citizen of the South. Punishment was due, and the Knights had hired a circuit riding evangelist named Orlando Dow to act as executioner.

Still Jarmay Higgins waited, perched uncomfortably on his horse in the midst of suffocating brush, waiting for the rascals to come and collect their considerable purse.

"Listen!"

This hissed warning came from Reverend Pounders. Jarmay obeyed. What if something had gone wrong?

Then Jarmay saw them, first Dow's horse, a coal-black beauty the circuit preacher kept brushed and shining like a piece of prized satin.

"It's him." Jarmay smiled in relief, for at that moment he caught sight of Orlando Dow himself, at the head of the procession. Dow was a racy, remarkably powerful fellow with deep-set eyes, a well-chiseled nose and glistening blue-black hair. He always dressed with a style that put river gamblers to shame, never stinted on diamond studs, and his waistcoats were the colors of the rainbow. The ladies loved him, and as Mobile's most famous circuit riding preacher, he featured female salvation.

He heard Reverend Pounders murmur, "Let's get this business concluded as quickly as possible," and turned his horse about and led the way deeper into the underbrush and the meeting with Orlando Dow.

Jarmay always thought it curious that the circuit riding evangelist and the respected Anglican priest should hate each other so, both being men of God. And yet there you were. The two men loathed each other, even though it was Reverend Pounders himself who had suggested hiring Preacher Dow for the "difficult task ahead."

"Is that you, Dow?" the Reverend Pounders called ahead, and Preacher Dow emerged from the thick brush, grinning atop his black horse and followed by his two assistants who'd helped him in this difficult task for the Knights of the White Camellia.

Instead of meeting them where they stood, Reverend Pounders passed them by with a word. "Not here. Follow me." Jarmay Higgins watched as Preacher Dow followed Reverend Pounders deeper into the brush, the two "associates" following suit. A more unappetizing twosome Jarmay had never seen, with flat broad brows and low-slung eyes that stared out from under bushy brows at everything and everyone.

Jarmay brought up the rear, a position that suited him, and wondered where Pounders was leading them and wanted only to get this over with as soon as possible—purse exchanged, accounts given and good-byes said. Amen.

Then he saw a cool shaded glen about thirty yards ahead, well concealed from the road, where this brief meeting could take place in relative comfort and safety.

"This will do," Reverend Pounders pronounced from beneath the dappled shade of an oak. With a wave of his hands he indicated that the others were to stop as well.

"Tell all," Reverend Pounders commanded, and at the same time reached beneath his black coat and withdrew a small leather pouch, drawstring pulled tight.

Preacher Dow smiled and lifted one leg and tucked it inside the saddle horn and rubbed the small of his back as though weary after a morning's work. "What's to say?" He smiled. "The nigger lover has one less nigger to love."

From the far corner the two slack-jawed gentlemen snickered.

Reverend Pounders nodded. "Any difficulties?"

Preacher Dow shook his head and ran the palm of his hand almost sadly over his raised knee. "Almost too easy. We like a challenge, don't we, boys? She didn't scream or nothing. She did offer us some eggs, but we told her we'd had our breakfast. She cried a little and prayed to God while we was getting our knives ready, but she knew we had her, and had her we did."

He threw back his head and laughed, and Jarmay Higgins saw the sun catch on his features and between the sun and the shadows he saw evil lurking about the man.

"We cut off her hand first," Preacher Dow went on. "She never whimpered, just sat down and wrapped the bloody stump in her dressing gown. Then one of the boys played with her for a while, but she weren't no good, no fight, you know. And we had to be careful because of the other two in the cottage and—"

"What other two?" Reverend Pounders asked.

"Stanhope's daughter and that crazy aunt of his."

"Did they see you?"

"Of course not, though we followed the girl all the way from Stanhope Hall through the woods and thought once about taking her. She's a good looker."

"No!"

This command was delivered with such force that all looked up. Reverend Pounders glared out at his audience. "We must play fair," he added. "Only a warning at first. Stanhope must understand we play by the rules. He'll never miss the nigger woman, but his daughter, that's another matter."

He withdrew his pocket watch, conferred with the hands, then returned it to his pocket. "It's time to go." He tossed the purse to Orlando Dow, who caught it with remarkable facility. "Are you certain you can trust your men to keep quiet?" Pounders asked.

"They are Christian men." Dow grinned. "I should know; I baptized them myself."

For a moment a look of censure crossed Reverend Pounders's face. "And you?" he asked pointedly of Orlando Dow. "You will say nothing."

Orlando Dow smiled. He would smile on Judgment Day. "Reverend Pounders, my word is my bond. We did nothing here this morning that God would not approve of."

"Nonetheless," Pounders added, as he turned his horse about, "we must remember that ours is a secret society. Unfortunately we must perform our good deeds under the cloak of anonymity."

Orlando Dow smiled and held up the filled purse.

Reverend Pounders rode to the edge of the clearing and looked back. Quickly Jarmay Higgins caught up, certainly not wanting to be left alone with this company of men.

"One thing more, Dow," Reverend Pounders said with just barely concealed contempt. "Where did you—leave the body?"

Dow looked up from fingering the purse. "Which part of it?" he smiled.

"Which—"

Reverend Pounders tried to question him further but couldn't. Something had drained his face of all color. For the first time Jarmay Higgins saw Reverend Pounders's dignified demeanor falter. Abruptly he brought his horse about and headed out through the brush that led to the road.

Jarmay followed after him, wondering if Reverend Pounders would wait for him or head on into Mobile. Not that they had further business together. The Knights of the White Camellia had perceived a problem and had effected a solution. The next move was up to Burke Stanhope.

Jarmay shuddered at the thought and derived strength from it and knew within his heart that the actions of the morning, no matter how grim and savage, had in the long run been necessary.

"Reverend Pounders?" he called out. But as he approached the road, he saw a dust cloud moving at a high rate of speed and knew it was Reverend Pounders, knew that he too had had enough of this morning that had started earlier than usual, in predawn darkness in Jarmay's large barn when twelve of the knights had met prior to their early-morning visitation to Stanhope Hall. The others had long since returned to their respective plantations and offices and undoubtedly now were awaiting word on the success of this last mission.

For a moment Jarmay slumped atop his horse, overcome by the heat and fatigue. He closed his eyes and tried to imagine the terror and hysteria that undoubtedly was being felt by all the inhabitants of

Stanhope Hall, Stanhope himself, less arrogant, wondering what to do, which way to turn for help, and worst of all, who would be next.

Home. Hurry home. It was imperative that he stop thinking about what had been done. Besides, the Knights of the White Camellia had a friend inside Stanhope Hall. Word would come soon concerning the reaction of Burke Stanhope. Until then there was nothing to do but wait, and not to think.

* * *

Mary felt foolish, her customary emotional stance where Sis Liz was concerned. She'd come along on this grizzly search to assist the old woman. But the old woman was doing very well without her. Mary was the one who felt faint as one of the men called out.

"Something over here."

Although she was standing twenty feet away, she saw too clearly a bloodied piece of a human body lifted from among the dead leaves of the woods, and she slipped heavily down onto a near stump.

"Please let me get one of the men to take you home, Mrs. Stanhope." The thoughtful offer came from Paris Boley.

She shook her head to the offer and withdrew her handkerchief from the sleeve of her dress and tried to stir a slight breeze. "I'll be all right, Paris. I just thought I could be of help with—"

She broke off and looked at Sis Liz about thirty feet ahead, in earnest conference with Burke and three of the men. Twice Sis Liz gestured broadly in opposite directions, as though she were in charge of the search. Mary took a moment to study the remarkable woman, convinced that it was Sis Liz's madness that had kept her safe.

"Are you sure, Mrs. Stanhope? I really think—"

Again she shook her head to Paris's thoughtfulness, although she knew she probably should return to Stanhope Hall. So much was waiting for her there. Eve to tend to, for one thing. The girl had appeared to be intact; stunned, yes, but functioning. Sometimes Mary feared there was too much of Sis Liz in her daughter, that convenient though potentially dangerous way of seeing only what one wanted to see and somehow filtering out the rest. Then there was Christine, poor little Christine who'd been totally ignored during the events of this morning. Then there was the house to be made ready for Stephen Eden's arrival—dear God, he couldn't be coming at a worse time.

"I'll return shortly, Paris. For now let me stay. Surely I can be of help to—someone."

She looked about, embarrassed by her weakness, and remembered that day seventeen years ago when she'd first seen Stanhope Hall, riding in the carriage with Burke, fatigued and exhilarated by the

long voyage from England. How beautiful the hall had appeared at
the end of its avenues of live oaks. There had been a welcoming
committee of one awaiting them on the broad front steps, a diminutive mulatto woman who had helped her down from the carriage, had
greeted Burke warmly and had presented her with a single pink
spring rose and the promise of a cup of tea awaiting them inside.

White Doll.

White Doll had attended her when Eve was born, had moved effortlessly, gracefully between white and black worlds, leaving a wake of
love and kindness and compassion for all.

"Over here."

The male cry shattered Mary's memories. As dozens of boots ran
toward the new macabre discovery, Mary pushed herself slowly up
from the stump, wavered a moment and started in the opposite direction, away from the cry.

"Mary, wait!"

At the sound of Burke's voice, she stopped.

"You shouldn't have come. I told you so, didn't I? This is no place
for—"

"I'm—going back to the house," she whispered.

"Yes," he agreed. "It's for the best."

"Who would do this?" she asked and knew the question sounded
childlike and simple.

He shook his head.

"Why White Doll?"

"It's the way they operate," Burke replied, keeping his voice down.
"The first strike hits as close to the family as possible without—"

"Then they'll come again?"

"It depends."

"On what?"

"On our response."

"And what will that be?"

Burke appeared to study the palms of his hands. "I won't be intimidated by them."

A man called out. "Mr. Stanhope, we need your help. Over here."

Though Mary was in desperate need of his response, it was denied
her. Gradually every member of the search party was drawn to that
spot, all gazing down on something that apparently had rendered
them speechless.

Still using the tree for support, Mary started to turn about. But Sis
Liz caught her eye as she turned, that tall slim column of a woman
whose white robe bore the bloodstains of her beloved friend. She
appeared to be looking up, searching the tops of the trees, commenc-

ing to turn in a slow deliberate circle, one hand lifting to shield her eyes. She seemed impervious to the group of men standing only a short distance away. Mary watched, curious, and saw, incongruously, the woman waving now at the tops of the trees, a broad, joyous smile on her wrinkled and overrouged face.

For a moment Mary debated the wisdom of approaching the woman. Was there really anything Mary could do for her? Unlike White Doll, who had been the first to welcome her to Stanhope Hall, Sis Liz had never accepted her. She'd not been rude, just very formal over the years. For a while Mary had thought it was just her way. But after her first year at Stanhope Hall, she had observed that with everyone else, Sis Liz was warm and theatrical and enchanting. Her Southern formality was reserved only for Mary.

For a while Mary had allowed it to hurt her. And she had to confess, there had been occasions in the last few years when witnessing Eve's deep affection for the old mad woman had caused her great pain, the agony of watching the two of them, age and youth, in such flawless and beautiful communication. Oh, she was certain that Eve loved *her* in a deeper and more profound way. But there was no denying that the girl had found something in Fan Cottage that she could not find in Stanhope Hall.

Mary's tumbling thoughts accomplished one feat at least. She felt stronger. "Sis Liz?"

The old woman looked sharply across the shadows at her, the radiant expression fading from her face as though she were viewing a total stranger. "Who's there?" she challenged, her eyes squinting as though she couldn't see.

"It's me. Mary, Sis Liz. I didn't mean to—"

"I see it's you," Sis Liz pronounced without inflection.

Mary felt the coldness like an open door in January. She started to retreat, her customary habit when confronted with such a chill. But now she changed her mind. In the past White Doll had always stepped between them with the warming thaw of love. Now White Doll was gone, and as a kind of private memorial to the remarkable woman, Mary vowed not to retreat again but to try to the best of her ability to return Sis Liz's hostility with love.

"Why don't you come back to Stanhope Hall with me, Sis Liz?" Mary invited quietly. "We can sit on the gallery and have—"

"I am not a sitting woman," came the measured and toneless reply.

"I—know. I didn't mean—what I meant, Eve would—"

"Eve is fine and will continue to be so. She is the strongest woman I know, next to me."

Mary tried to meet the woman's piercing gaze and heard men's voices in the distance and thought for the first time about funeral services and burial arrangements.

"Sis Liz," she began, changing the subject. "I was wondering if you had thought about funeral services for White Doll."

"I beg your pardon?"

The question was arch, the face more so. Mary paused. "Funeral services for White Doll," she repeated. "They must be—"

"Have you taken complete leave of your senses?" the old woman sternly demanded.

Mary started to defend her inquiry but was not given that opportunity.

"White Doll will require no funeral services."

Mary spoke gently. "Sis Liz, she's dead. You must accept it."

"Not five minutes ago with my own eyes I saw White Doll step through the gates of heaven. Right up there, yes, I did, saw St. Peter as well, greet her and assist her through to the other side."

Mary bowed her head and continued to hear the men searching for remains, heard Sis Liz describing the gates of heaven.

"And first thing, because we pledged it one to the other, she will kindly request of St. Peter to be returned to this earth because we promised each other we would leave together at the same time, and she won't break her promise, not White Doll, now would she?"

Only at the end had the old voice become plaintive. She needed a reply, and Mary gave her one despite her better judgment. "No, White Doll would not go back on her word."

"There, you see. She will return, probably in time for tea, leaving it all to me to prepare. She can be a very lazy girl when she wants to be, did you know that?"

The new intimate tone had nothing to do with Mary and everything to do with White Doll. And Mary saw now how it was to be, a new track of madness laid down carefully, lovingly across that already mad mind, White Doll not dead, Sis Liz addressing questions to the empty corners of Fan Cottage that did not require direct answers.

"Why don't you stay with us tonight in Stanhope Hall?" Mary invited and heard the men's voices fall silent and knew what it meant. "Come, Sis Liz, take my arm."

"I have no need of your arm," the old woman announced and drew herself up. "And there is absolutely nothing for me to do at Stanhope Hall and everything for me to do at Fan Cottage. We left the place in quite a mess, you know, and I must do some baking before White Doll returns. So much to do, so very very much to do."

As she spoke she turned slowly about in a circle, looked up once more toward the top of the pines, then drew a deep breath and started down the path through the fallen pine needles that led to Fan Cottage.

She turned back with only one request. "If Eve is free, tell her she is invited to our tea party this afternoon. I know she'll be thrilled to see White Doll. Will you please convey that invitation to her from me?"

Slowly Mary watched, helpless, as the old woman picked her way carefully across the pine needles.

"Where's she going?"

The question was Burke's, who'd come up behind Mary and now stood with her, both watching Sis Liz as she gained the path and increased her speed.

"Home. To Fan Cottage."

"What about—"

"White Doll isn't dead. White Doll just stepped through the gates of heaven and will immediately request permission of St. Peter to return to earth because she promised Sis Liz she would not go ahead without her."

As Mary spoke, she never took her eyes off Sis Liz, growing smaller with distance. After a few moments, when Burke had not as yet responded, she looked over her shoulder to see a sad yet accepting expression, as though he had known this would be Sis Liz's attitude.

"Is it safe?" Mary asked.

"What?"

"For her to return to Fan Cottage?"

When again he didn't answer, Mary looked back and saw new worry on his face. "I don't know," he confessed. "I don't know anything," he repeated, and Mary could sense the heavy toll the morning had taken on all of them, everyone making whatever adjustments were necessary to deal with violent and savage death.

"I tried to get her to return to Stanhope Hall," Mary commented.

"No, she doesn't care for life there. Never has."

"Why? It's her home."

Burke shook his head. "I heard her tell my father once that she never wanted to live under any roof where she wasn't the sole mistress."

Mary smiled sadly. "No wonder she doesn't like me."

Burke's protest was weak but gallant. "She likes you as much as she's capable."

Mary was grateful for his kindness. She saw Paris Boley approaching.

"Mr. Stanhope?" he called ahead. "The men are waiting. Shall I send them back to work?"

"Poor Paris," Mary murmured. "Not a very pleasant way to start your new job."

The young man shook his head and looked back at the search party, all of the men standing a distance removed from a small mound of unevenly stacked gunnysacks.

"Sir," he began and motioned over his shoulder in the general direction of the men and gunnysacks.

Mary saw the distress on Burke's face. He knew what was being asked of him but had not one answer in his head.

Relieved that there *was* something she could do after all, Mary made a quick decision and delivered it to Paris. "Ask the men to take White Doll to the family cemetery. We will bury her there."

It had occurred to Mary that the most appropriate burial site for White Doll would be next to her mother, Mammy Fan, behind Fan Cottage, but she doubted seriously if Sis Liz would permit such activity. And the most important thing now was to see it done.

She waited to see if Burke had any objection. Apparently he didn't.

"See to it, Paris, please."

The young man hesitated. "I was afraid something like this might happen."

Burke nodded. "We all knew the risks involved. I will see to it that it does not happen again."

Paris's next question was painfully blunt. "How?"

"The crime of murder has been committed. Someone must answer for it. I'll send word to Taylor Quitman immediately. He'll know what to do."

Mary wondered what Burke's lawyer could do with such a crime. Taylor Quitman worked well with land purchases, cost analysis and property settlements. His world consisted of the family mansion on Government Street and his law office in downtown Mobile, and he kept a strict watch on both worlds to make absolutely certain nothing unpleasant entered either of them. Now the thought of Taylor traipsing through these woods in search of clues for a murdered mulatto was ludicrous.

Mary started to say as much but changed her mind. Somehow she was not ready to move on to solutions. There still was the loss to deal with. "Come, Burke," she murmured and took his arm and turned him about from his empty and futile exchange with Paris. And at the same time Paris started off toward the waiting men, still standing guard over the small collection of gunnysacks.

Suddenly and without warning, Mary felt tears. How she would miss White Doll. The velvet of her Southern voice, her smile, her endless capacity to love and forgive and understand.

"Are you—"

She heard Burke's concerned inquiry and felt his arm around her shoulder and was grateful for his support.

"I'm fine," she reassured him and made her way slowly through the thick woods and tried to avoid glancing in the direction of the men who now were carrying the sorrowful burden toward the Stanhope cemetery.

"Lean on me," Burke invited. He kissed her forehead and whispered, "I am sorry."

"Don't."

"All I ever wanted was to create a paradise for you."

"You have."

"More a hell now."

"Will you send word to Taylor Quitman?"

"Of course. Right away."

At that moment she heard Paris calling to Burke from the side yard. Beyond in the distance she saw the high black gates of the cemetery.

"I'd better go and help," Burke said.

She watched as he strode across the distance, joining the others, then pointing the way ahead to the cemetery. She drew a deep breath and saw him turn back and look directly at her. She kept her eyes fixed on his face, using it like a beacon, and thought as long as he loved her, she could accomplish, survive and triumph over literally everything.

 Irma Kingsley's Lodging House
Mobile, Alabama
August 3, 1889

Irma Kingsley ran a third-rate lodging house and knew it, and thus knew that the young gentleman eating the hearty breakfast at the table near the window was foreign born. A native-born Southern gentleman wouldn't dare be seen in this establishment. After getting off the train in the station across the way, a Southern gentleman would travel by carriage a few blocks uptown to the Magnolia Inn on Excelsior Street.

But that one at the window was different, had been different from the beginning. Irma snuffed out the snub end of her morning cigar and continued to watch him, as she'd enjoyed watching him for the past week and a half, literally feeding on his youth and beauty as though he were her breakfast.

Although he'd arrived alone, with one portmanteau and one steamer trunk, he'd seldom been alone since. He made friends easily of both sexes. Look at him single-handedly playing hell with her two serving girls.

"Hey, over there, you got other customers. See to them. Now."

At the sound of her best screech owl voice, Irma saw Millie and Dora look up, smooth their aprons and head in a reluctant path toward the other two "gentlemen" in the small dining room: one the ever-drunk Captain Willing in his tattered and faded gray Confederate officer's coat, the sleeves patched and not a button in sight. The other "gentleman" was a regular, too, Housy Dunbar and his monkey, Abraham Lincoln, who slept with him, ate with him, drank with him and probably did a lot of other things with him as well.

Irma smiled from her position behind the high scarred desk. Goal accomplished. The handsome young foreigner who spoke so prettily was alone at last. And fair game.

Irma stood up from her stool, tried to smooth back her straggled gray hair, readjusted her ample breasts inside their bindings and made an effort to suck in her bulging midsection so that the buttons on her shirtwaist wouldn't yawn open. She stole a quick glance into the jagged piece of a mirror she kept propped atop the unused ledger books. Hopeless. She was what she saw, sixty-three years of hard living, through some damned tight times and a few—precious few— good ones.

"Good morning, Mr. Eden," she called out.

At the sound of her voice, he looked up from his eggs and toast and gave her a smile that thirty years ago would have been her undoing and that even now caused her to go momentarily speechless, a rare condition for Irma Kingsley.

"Good morning to you, Mrs. Kingsley," the young man replied, rising immediately to hold a chair for her, like she was the Queen of Sheba. For a moment and without shame, she focused all of her attention on the dark-haired, dark-eyed young man of impressive physique. There was an ease to him that suggested that despite his youth he'd already learned many of the most important lessons of this hard world.

"Oh, I shouldn't sit, Mr. Eden." Irma smiled, sitting.

"No, please. I want to talk with you."

"Nothing wrong, I trust?"

"Oh, no. Of course not."

"Are you enjoying Mobile?"

"Yes, very much, thank you."

She waited patiently, enjoying herself as he took a final bite of toast.

She loved to hear him speak, a voice like autumn smoke, soft, yet so precise, words sliding out like they were pearls on a string.

Behind, she heard Housy Dunbar's monkey chattering shrilly, as though the little varmint was eager to get out onto the streets of Mobile and earn some coin. And Housy didn't do badly for himself, sometimes earning up to a dollar a day. Lots of Southerners liked to laugh at the monkey named Abraham Lincoln, and Housy had trained him in a good set of tricks that were always good for a penny or two, like scratching his private parts, then licking them.

"Tell Abe to keep his voice down," Irma called over her shoulder as the monkey's shrill chatter climbed even higher. As she looked back, she caught a glimpse of Captain Willing, a sad figure of a man with no past except the one he wore visibly, gray thinning hair, emaciated, a stump for a left leg, that tattered gray officer's coat, and eyes that had seen too much for any one man. Irma had no idea where he'd come from. He'd been at her lodging house for almost a year now, sometimes paying on time, sometimes not.

Now as she turned back from scolding Abraham Lincoln, she gave a passing glance at Captain Willing's face as he hovered over his mug of coffee. It was an expression she'd never seen before. Generally he sat slumped, eyes down, head bowed. Now he was glaring up at the monkey.

Where in the hell were those two useless girls? "Millie?"

Well, no matter. The blasted little monkey was settling down on Housy's shoulder at last, Housy grinning at her like a jack-o'-lantern, most of his teeth missing, as were three of the fingers on his left hand. Lost them in the Battle of Mobile, according to Housy, who claimed that he'd been pressed into service in the closing days of the war and had fallen from a horse and then the horse had stepped on his arm and crushed his hand.

So many fragments of men drifting about after the war, Irma mourned. The miracle was to find a whole one and then you'd probably only find a coward.

"More coffee, sir?" Irma asked, more than willing to shift her vision from the decaying old to the beautiful new.

He smiled. Lord, what a smile. "No, quite enough, Mrs. Kingsley. Thank you."

"I'm just trying to take good care of you, like your mom would want."

He looked up as he placed his coffee mug on the table. He seemed surprised.

She laughed. "Well, you have a mother, don't you? Somewhere?"

He folded his napkin and pushed back in his chair. "She's dead," he said, and the sweet simplicity and loneliness in his voice caused Irma's heart to ache.

"I am sorry," she murmured. "Your father, then?" she asked, knowing that she was prying, but she felt that after a week and a half she was entitled to something.

The young gentleman nodded, as though pleased by the memories evoked by the name. "Oh, very much alive, I assure you."

"Is he nearby?" Irma asked.

"No," the young gentleman said, and glanced out of the window, a curious fascination on his face, as though in addition to his other lavish gifts, he was capable of finding beauty where none existed. Irma was certain that there was nothing outside her windows that could even remotely be defined as beautiful. This main thoroughfare had been labeled by some as the toughest two blocks in Alabama. In doorways leading down to the water's edge were agents for every shipping company looking for prospects to shanghai. Few establishments were ever closed. There was a constant discord of tinny pianos, the shrill laughter of women and clatter of dice. Parrots squawked, half-naked girls leaned out of low windows, revealing their breasts and other wares. That kind were never permitted near Irma's lodging house. The only baggage that men could bring in here was the kind they carried in their hands.

Through the crowded, narrow street raced carts and drays. Over there a line of cattle stumbled under the driver's whip, heading toward the livestock wharf for shipment out. A similar line passed this way every morning, and woe be to the man who'd not finished breakfast before they'd gone by. From where Irma sat, all outside the window was hot and sweaty and congested and stinking. From the hot dirt road itself rose an odor of squalor and decay and death.

Suddenly her curiosity could no longer be contained. "May I ask you a question, sir?"

Almost reluctantly he tore his eyes from the teeming scene outside the window. "Of course, Mrs. Kingsley, anything."

"You're—not from these parts," she began.

"No." He laughed. "I'm from England," he said, leaning close, his arms folded upon the table. "From a place called North Devon. Do you know it?"

Oh, how she would love to have been able to say yes. Sadly she was forced to shake her head.

"It's very far away," he said. "There's not a great deal to see there. Just cows and sheep and lots of rain."

This did not sound like a criticism of his home, merely a sadness at its apparent limitations. "Oh, there's London, of course. But even London is not quite like that."

There was such a tone of admiration in his voice as he gazed out at the scene of dust and heat and filth that Irma was forced to follow his gaze to see if by mistake a piece of paradise had fallen down when she wasn't looking.

"Mrs. Kingsley, I need to ask a favor of you."

"Anything."

He swallowed the last of the coffee from his mug. "I must make a short journey this morning," he explained, "to a place not too far from here. Perhaps you've heard of it—Stanhope Hall?"

Irma tried to keep her mind on his words and off his dark good looks. "Stanhope?" she repeated. "Everyone knows where Stanhope Hall is."

He seemed pleased.

"And everyone knows the bastard who lives there now," she went on before she could catch herself. She saw his look of pleasure fade.

Well, she was sorry for that, but since he was a young innocent, she felt it was her duty to inform him that if he wanted to get on in Mobile, he'd best choose another direction.

"Oh, don't get me wrong." She smiled sweetly. "Rich they are, the Stanhope clan. But traitors all."

He seemed shocked.

"Starting with the old man during the war," she began, enjoying his close interest. "Hanged himself in a hotel room not two blocks from where we're sitting at this very moment," she concluded and with the hem of her apron wiped the gathering sweat from her upper lip and brow.

The young Eden sat back slowly in his chair, never taking his eyes off her face. "Go on."

"Then the son comes home from wherever it was he was hiding out with a foreign-born whore for a wife, and as if that weren't bad enough, he makes deals with niggers and Yankees." Irma shook her head. "What kind of business would you be having with Stanhope Hall?"

"They are my kin. Mrs. Stanhope is my aunt, my father's half-sister."

Now it was Irma's turn to suffer shock and embarrassment. "Well, why in the hell didn't—"

"It's all right, Mrs. Kingsley," he soothed. "I wanted to ask if I could leave my steamer trunk in your safekeeping. You see, I'm due at Stanhope Hall today and I really don't know how long I'll be staying there."

"Of course." She nodded, already looking forward to sliding the handsome leather trunk into her private room and going through the contents at her leisure.

"I am grateful." He smiled, then added, "I'm very sorry to hear of their—misfortunes. It will be an awkward reunion, I'm sure."

"If I were you, I might reconsider going at all."

"I couldn't do that."

"Then don't tell too many others where you're going."

Abe Lincoln's screeching suddenly became deafening. Irma whirled about to see the little monkey leaping as though having a fit, Housy Dunbar on his feet in wild pursuit. She saw those two worthless girls, Millie and Dora, huddled together in the kitchen doorway, both their faces pinched up like they were trying hard not to laugh, while the most sobering sight of all was poor Captain Willing, standing uneasily on his one good leg, supporting himself on his crutch with one hand, and holding an unsheathed knife in his free hand, his cadaverous face and sunken eyes following the antics of the monkey, the knife held in a throwing position, Captain Willing ready to let fly the moment the monkey came to a halt.

Irma started forward, mad as hell. "Hey, you," she shouted to Captain Willing, figuring the knife to be the most immediate threat. "This here is a dining room, not a—"

"Stay where you are, Mrs. Kingsley," the man warned and suddenly turned in her direction, the knife still suspended. He was an expert with a knife. She'd seen him play for sport, halving an apple at fifty paces for a whiskey.

Now at his command she froze. Asleep or drunk, Captain Willing was merely pathetic. Awake and angry, he was a different man, filled with rage. In view of this Irma changed her tone of voice and approached more slowly. "Captain Willing, if you can tell me what has upset you, I—"

"Him," the man snapped and brought the knife forward with such speed that for an instant Irma thought he was going to hurl it. Instead he used it as a pointer, indicating Housy Dunbar and his monkey, Abe Lincoln.

"Look," Captain Willing said with great melodrama. Still using the knife as a pointer, he indicated the floor and a small pile of animal waste. Apparently Abe Lincoln in his chatter had been trying to tell Housy Dunbar something.

Irma ducked her head to hide a grin. "Captain Willing, I'll have it put to rights," Irma said and was just getting ready to wave the two girls forward when Captain Willing issued a new command.

"I want that creature dead," Captain Willing said, his voice low and menacing. "And I'll be doing the killing myself right here and now. I'm tired of seeing it every morning and smelling it every night, and I'm tired of hearing that name that belongs to Satan while I'm drinking my morning coffee."

"Captain Willing, I'm sure you don't mean what you say. The monkey is just a pet, our Abe Lincoln is—"

But Captain Willing raised the knife until it was at eye level. Everything about his stance suggested that the talk was over; it was time for action, and the knife was aimed right at the monkey, which Housy Dunbar was clasping directly to the center of his chest.

"Wait!"

The strong male voice cut through the silent tension and caused everyone to look up. It was him of the dark good looks and the dubious connection to the Stanhope family. Unfortunately Captain Willing looked as well and turned as quickly as his missing leg would allow, but he did nothing to lower the knife, which meant that now it was aimed directly at young Mr. Eden, who either was very brave or very foolish.

"I said please wait, sir," Eden repeated, and there was nothing about his manner that even suggested he knew there was a poised knife aimed at the center of his heart.

For a moment the element of surprise worked wonders on Captain Willing. Irma felt certain the poor old soldier hadn't even known there was anyone else in the dining room with him except Housy Dunbar and the despicable monkey. Now he appeared to be studying young Eden's face closely, as though convinced that he should recognize him and yet was unable to do so.

Finally, "My quarrel is not with you, sir," Captain Willing said with admirable politeness, though he appeared to renew his grip on the knife.

"Oh, it's not a quarrel I want." Young Eden smiled and ventured ever so slowly out from around the table.

"Then mind your own business," Captain Willing snapped, the politeness gone. But as he was about to turn back to his original target, Eden increased his speed until he stood less than five feet from Captain Willing, who now was struggling mightily to keep his eye on everyone at once.

"I said keep your distance," he shouted, and reflexively Irma moved back and was on the verge of advising the foolhardy young Eden to do the same.

But instead he moved slowly forward, displaying no fear, his manner as relaxed and amiable as it had been moments earlier when he had been discussing his home.

"Your hand, sir," Eden smiled and extended his. "Please give me the honor of allowing me to shake hands with a true and noble soldier. I admire the military mind and spirit and discipline, though I'm afraid that fate set me down in a world resting between conflicts. So all I can be is a student of battle. But I assure you I have been a diligent and earnest student and am well acquainted with logistics and strategies of leaders from Julius Caesar to Napoleon at Borodino to the exploits of Alexander the Great, to Genghis Khan, to your George Washington and my Nelson. But still how rare an honor it is to stand in the presence of a man who has experienced firsthand the sights and sounds and smells of battle. So please sir, your hand and a few moments of your time, if you will, to speak to me of your exploits —only briefly, for I'm certain you have much to do, but I would be grateful."

Her eyes glazed, Irma felt mesmerized by the solid stream of lovely words. And she wasn't the only one who'd fallen into a trance. Poor Captain Willing himself now squinted forward at young Eden as though if he could only see clearly, he might stand a better chance of understanding what had just been said to him. Even Housy Dunbar and Abe Lincoln sat silent and at attention.

"Please, sir," Eden prompted again, stepping closer, his hand still extended, his straight young back and broad shoulders such a sad contrast to Captain Willing's slumped and emaciated frame.

Silence. And waiting. Captain Willing had a choice. He could either ignore that hand extended to him and that winning manner and irresistible invitation, or he could place the knife on the table and deliver himself of a proper gentleman's handshake.

Irma smiled, suddenly understanding the young man's ploy. Damn clever. But would Captain Willing fall for it?

"Your hand, sir," Eden murmured, "and then if you'd be so kind as to join me at my table for a coffee."

Finally the knife was lowered, placed upon the table without so much as a clatter, and as soon as the captain's hand was free, Eden grasped it.

"Allow me to introduce myself, sir," he said. "My name is Stephen Eden and I consider this a rare privilege."

Captain Willing blinked and allowed his hand to be shaken and was on the verge of sinking back into his chair, exhausted by his anger, when young Eden drew him forward. "Not there, sir, please. My table, if you will. It's very pleasant, allows one a view of the street beyond."

With great care the young man assisted the older one away from the offensive animal waste on the floor, the true cause of this conflict, and as they passed Irma, she saw the young man's right hand, low at his side, waggling furiously toward Housy Dunbar and the monkey, a gesture that clearly said, *Get them out of here.*

Irma understood and hesitated only a moment to watch the young man assisting Captain Willing into a chair at the window table.

"I'm a stranger here, sir, so you'll have to tell me everything. Leave nothing out from the moment of your conscription to the end. We only received scattered reports on the War Between the States. Civil wars are the most complex, aren't they? Take our Cromwell—oh, Mrs. Kingsley, two coffees if you'd be so kind. And our deepest thanks."

Quickly Irma turned toward Housy Dunbar and flapped her apron at him. She followed after him all the way to the back door of the lodging house, where amid swarming flies and garbage she scolded, "From now on that fleabag monkey stays out here, do you hear?"

As the door slammed behind her, Irma saw the backsides of those two good-for-nothing girls, Millie and Dora, peering out of the kitchen door and into the dining room.

"Git, both of you," she hissed and picked up a broom to make her point.

As Irma slipped quietly across the threshold, she saw a curious sight: young Eden on his feet, standing over Captain Willing, who appeared to be slumped forward, his head resting on the table. Ill? Injured? What in the—

Irma ventured a step closer. "Is he—"

"Exhausted," the young man replied.

For several moments he continued to stare down at the old soldier. From where Irma stood she saw yet another expression on that remarkable face, something soft this time and sad. "Does he live around here?"

"He sleeps here most nights, if he can make it back after his day of drinking."

"Let him be. He'll wake up soon enough. About the steamer trunk, Mrs. Kingsley. May I—"

She nodded, though she was searching for some reason to keep the young man with her for a while longer. "Stanhope Hall, you say? Is that where you're going?"

He lifted his jacket from the back of the chair.

"For how long?" Irma pressed, following him to the door.

"I don't know. I wish I did. To be honest, I have no idea what my reception there will be."

"Then best to stay away, perhaps."

"I can't. I promised my uncle that I would go."

Behind her, she heard the two girls from the kitchen and looked back to see Dora leaving two steaming mugs of coffee on the table. "Won't be needing those, girl. Get back to work."

When she looked back from scolding the girl, she saw that Mr. Eden had hurried on down the long front hall and was now standing at the front door of the lodging house, his jacket in one hand, a small bag in the other.

"Wait, sir, if you will," Irma called out. "I wanted to thank you."

He looked puzzled.

"The ruckus back there, I mean," she explained. "If it hadn't been for you, being a student of war and loving it and all that, well, Captain Willing would have—"

"I hate war, Mrs. Kingsley."

"But you said—"

"I've studied it, yes, enough to know there is no moral, ethical or spiritual defense of it. I find it difficult to believe that our Creator put us here to blow each other to bits."

"B-but you—"

"Thank you for all your kindnesses, Mrs. Kingsley. I'll either send for my trunk or come for it myself within the week. If that's all right."

"That's fine."

She could tell that he was about to take advantage of a lull in the pedestrian traffic and fall into the rhythm of the crowded road when suddenly a large flatbed wagon appeared from around the corner, coming from the direction of the dock. It was gaily decorated with multicolor streamers and was being drawn by six white horses.

But it wasn't the horses or the streamers that caught everyone's attention, including Mr. Eden, who slowly put down his portmanteau and held his position on Irma Kingsley's doorstep.

The women was what caught everyone's attention; the four beautiful women, one standing on each corner of the flatbed wagon, clad only in pastel gossamer silk that, under the slight August breeze, pressed softly into a bold outline of each female body. These four beauties, garbed to represent the four seasons, tossed advertisements out to the ever-growing and largely male crowd. At the exact center of the colorful wagon sat a fifth woman, expertly playing the accordion and accompanied by a sixth, who piped a sweet flute to form an ear-pleasing melody.

Irma knew who they were and leaned back against the doorframe and enjoyed watching the male reaction, specifically young Mr. Eden, who stared as the wagon moved slowly closer, bringing the unique beauties with it.

"Mrs. Kingsley, what—" As he turned back, Irma saw a blush on his face the color of early summer tomatoes.

Irma smiled. "It's an all-female theatrical troupe, sir, that's what it is," she spoke up over the din of the crowd, of men running alongside the wagon, laughing, shouting, trying to touch the pastel hems of the silken gowns. "Adamless Edens, they are called," Irma explained, delighted by this postponement of his departure. "They put on quite a show, I can tell you. You'd better change your mind and stay for a while. They'll be playing at the Rialto tonight, and the lines probably are forming over there right now."

She was certain he was listening, but he'd turned about the better to see the wagon, which now was exactly even with Irma's lodging house. She looked close, seeing if she could recognize any of the girls, and didn't. Six or seven years ago Yorrick Harp had boarded some of his girls with Irma. But they'd gotten so fancy and popular these last few years that now they stayed at the Majestic or the Magnolia Inn.

Irma didn't recognize them anymore, a whole new set of painted female faces, willing to do just about anything a man wanted them to do—for a price.

As the large wagon passed in front of them, the foot traffic of the street was forced back up onto the board sidewalk, which was becoming more congested than ever. But no one seemed to mind, and all the men were scrambling for one of the advertisements the women were tossing from the wagon. Advertisements meant five cents off the price of admission at the door.

"You sure you won't stay?" Irma prodded.

He shook his head. "I'm afraid they're expecting me."

"How are you traveling?"

"I hired a horse from the stable up the street."

The street was clearing, most of the men running after the wagon of women.

"Again, I thank you, Mrs. Kingsley for all your hospitality." And there he was, extending his hand to Irma as though she were the finest lady in all of Mobile.

"You take care," she called after him as he moved down the steps. "Be on your guard at Stanhope Hall. Some think it to be a very dangerous place."

He touched his hand to his forehead, then slipped into the flow of traffic, only the top of his head visible to the end of the street, then that too was gone, leaving Irma seeing nothing but the ugly crowded street, an ugly world except when the Almighty took pity on His creatures and sent down a rare treat, gentle of manner, beautiful of face, like young Mr. Eden.

The first thing she saw as she reentered her lodging house was the smelly and narrow hall that led to the kitchen. Now it stretched before her like her entire life, enclosed, dingy and going nowhere.

To hell with it. She'd sneak into her room and have another cigar and think on Mr. Eden, who had treated her like a lady.

 On the Road to Stanhope Hall

In his wildest imagination Stephen had never envisioned it like this. Though he'd been on American soil for almost two weeks, only now, on this quiet morning ride beyond the noise and smoke and heat of Mobile, before he reached the mystery of Stanhope Hall, was he able for the first time to sit back and marvel at this vast, energetic, undisciplined, alive place called America.

He shifted in the saddle and patted Cicero's mane, not the fastest horse in the world, but he wasn't interested in speed this morning. There had been far too much of that within the last six months, since his uncle Richard had asked him to make this journey, apologizing for disrupting his life in the process. Apologizing! Stephen grinned.

He settled back and lifted his face to the hot August sun and smiled at everything, mainly at Uncle Richard's mistaken concept of Stephen's devotion to the rural life in North Devon. It had been slowly driving him mad, and he lifted his face higher to the sun, that warm yellow globe that seemed designed to chase away twenty-two years of cold English rain.

He heard a noise and saw a tall, gaunt man in a black frock coat approaching at a rapid gait. Stephen pulled to one side of the narrow, dusty road. Obviously the church was in a hurry this morning. As the man passed, Stephen smiled and received nothing in return.

He waited for the dust to clear and took a backward look at the somber man in black. Why did churchmen everywhere seem so unhappy, as though belief were an intolerable burden. Then slowly he started forward again, looping the reins about the saddle horn and allowing Cicero to move forward at whatever speed pleased him while Stephen settled back, rolled up his sleeves and marveled at the several miracles that had brought him to this long-dreamed-of land at this exact time.

His father, for one, John Murrey Eden, a man Stephen loved, but . . .

He stared at Cicero's ears twitching away flies and wondered if every son's relationship with every father contained at least one "but," one fiercely significant qualifier.

Someplace nearby in the still morning heat crickets sang, and that, combined with Cicero's rhythmic shuffle, was the only sound in this world, a pleasant lull from the cacophony that had commenced on the docks of Southampton, his strained good-bye with his father, then the huffing and puffing of the steam engines of *The City of Paris* across the Atlantic, the fierce storm on the third day out during which Stephen had wondered if he would ever see America. Then there had been the din of New York City, the scream and squeal of the train from New York to Mobile, the countless stops, the faces, the cries at stations, shouts, yells, all in that curious flat, indolent American manner of speaking. To be sure, on occasion his ears had hurt from all the differences, but oh, his brain and heart! Never before had they felt more alive, more stimulated, more responsive.

Moved anew by the stroke of good fortune that had delivered his dream to him, he looked down the seemingly endless road that, according to the man at the stables, would eventually bring him to an intersection called Hangman's Folly, where he would take the turn to the right and, fifty yards beyond, according to the same man, he would see the first white fence of Stanhope land. Stanhope Hall itself would not appear for three miles, and even then he wouldn't find the house on the road but at the end of a long avenue of live oaks, "sitting there with all the arrogance of its present owner."

Stephen blinked, hearing the hate in those words again and mystified by it.

He shifted in the saddle and gazed into the distance and saw nothing but the road narrowing and small explosions of dust picked up by the scant breeze and wondered how much farther to Hangman's Folly.

—sitting there with all the arrogance of its present owner

A single bead of sweat raced down the side of his face and into his eyes, where the salty brine momentarily blinded him. Quickly he reached into his waistcoat pocket and withdrew a handkerchief and made a broad swipe at his eyes. The angry gesture only reflected his feelings of the moment, the manner in which everyone at home in North Devon had sidestepped his questions concerning the bad feelings between this branch of the family and the one he'd left behind in England.

His father had come the closest to revealing all in Southampton, in their rooms at the Imperial Hotel. His uncle Richard had gone to check in his steamer trunk—only the three of them had come to Southampton. And with Richard gone, his father had invited Stephen to sit down, and in that halting, bowed-head posture that Stephen had come to recognize as his contrite pose, he told him simply that he'd not told him everything but that he would now, and Stephen had waited patiently through a long sermon on human forgiveness and a man's capacity to change and on the need to try to make amends to those whom one had wronged.

At some point Stephen had urged him to be specific, and all his father had said was that he had wronged his half-sister Mary and her husband, Burke Stanhope. When Stephen had pressed for details, his father had grown strangely silent.

Then his uncle Richard had returned, limping on his cane, claiming that Southampton air was bad for his rheumatism, and the hotel room had sunk into the uncomfortable silence of the aged, with his father brooding out the window, and Uncle Richard, his leg raised on the footstool, rubbing his knee joint and groaning.

Dear lord, how many evenings Stephen had spent in the Great Hall of Eden Castle, imprisoned in that same tableau, his aunt Eleanor constantly scolding the children and tugging at her too tight corset and Susan nodding off before the fire, her snores punctuating Uncle Richard's groans and Aunt Eleanor's complaints and his father's grunts.

Suddenly Stephen shook his head as though to shake free of that past. For a blessed period of time he was out of it, though he did miss his brother Frederick, only two years younger and angry as hell that he'd not been asked to accompany Stephen. He was needed at home, according to all those snoring, groaning, grunting adults, and besides, if all "went well" at Stanhope Hall, perhaps Aunt Mary would extend a broader invitation at some future date to all the inhabitants of Eden Castle.

Thus the matter had ended, with Stephen embarking on the journey of his dreams, though somehow feeling he was lacking all the puzzle pieces. True, the main purpose of the journey did not rest at Stanhope Hall but rather in a place called Montana, thousands of miles away, where two years ago his uncle Richard had invested several thousand pounds sterling in a cattle syndicate that suddenly had gone silent.

Abruptly Stephen shifted in the saddle. The past was exhausting him, not his past but that of others, and for a moment he resented the heavy responsibility that had been dropped on his shoulders, entering into a household that quite possibly did not want him. His father had even denied him knowledge of the offense, and thus he had no concept of the degree of hostility that might greet him.

He breathed a sigh and felt his earlier excitement blunted by the impending confrontation. He considered for a moment turning his horse about, heading back into Mobile and checking with the Texas-Pacific office on Rosemont Street for the schedule of trains out to New Orleans and points west. He was perfectly capable of making his own arrangements.

The sound of a horse intersected his thoughts, and he saw a cadaverously thin black man in faded overalls riding rapidly toward him.

"Lookin' for Doc Melrose," he called out.

Perplexed, Stephen shook his head. "I'm afraid I—"

"Gots to hurry," the old man gasped and renewed his grip on the reins.

"Wait—"

"Can't wait."

"Stanhope Hall. Can you tell me—"

All of a sudden the horse spun about. "Stanhope Hall?" the old man repeated and pointed a gnarled finger in a northeasterly direction. "Over dere, but it ain't a happy place dis mornin'."

Stephen felt as though he should say something else but there was no time, for despite his age the old man handled the horse very well and in only a few moments had urged him to new speed and disappeared in his own dust cloud, leaving Stephen to wave away the billowing clouds and consider these new and ominous half-pieces of information.

Enough! He had made promises to certain people and those promises must be kept. He would make an appearance at Stanhope Hall, be as congenial, as courteous as possible, make inquiry into the nature of this new unhappiness and perhaps even offer his services. Then after a civil interval, perhaps this very afternoon, with his duty discharged, he'd be on this road back to Mobile, where he'd retrieve his luggage from Irma Kingsley's lodging house. Tomorrow morning at the latest he would be on the train for New Orleans, where he would make connection for points west.

The thoughts tumbling after one another revived him and he brought Cicero about, straightened himself in the saddle and aimed for the end of the road, for Hangman's Folly and the right turn that would lead him ultimately to Stanhope Hall.

Only a brief appearance, that was all that was required of him. An hour. Maybe less. Then he could put Stanhope Hall and its inhabitants out of his life and his mind forever.

Stanhope Hall

Noon.

Hot high sun. No breeze. No one in his or her right mind ever came out onto the second-floor gallery at noon, which was why Eve was there now.

She leaned against the railing and looked down the avenue of live oaks, where earlier that morning the strange horsemen had materialized out of the ground fog. She closed her eyes, then quickly opened them, seeing that small dark severed hand resting on Sis Liz's porch.

Again she suffered a rising in her throat, her head throbbing, and for a moment even her thin white chemise seemed too heavy on her bare shoulders. With one hand she gathered up her long hair, which felt like a fur mantle plastered against her neck and shoulders.

White Doll—

Eve let her hair fall back in a hot weight against her neck and sank slowly to the gallery floor and leaned against the railing and found the varnished floor cool and stretched out full-length, certain no one would bother her.

Flat on her back, she gazed up at the white ceiling and saw knots and gnarls in the wood that resembled elf faces and whiskered dwarfs.

White Doll—

No! Quickly she covered her eyes with her hands, as though that simple gesture could blot out the thoughts. But it didn't, and for several moments her mind became a theater and the central character upon the stage was White Doll, that considerate woman with skin like satin and the kindest smile and the softest voice and the most patient and generous heart—

Early violets for you, my pet.

No more bad dreams. White Doll is here.

The world is filled with voices, Eve. The only one that matters is the voice of your heart.

When the tears had started, Eve couldn't quite say, but she was aware of them running down into her hair, the moisture collecting in her ears, muffling the silence of the hot summer day. The bearded dwarf and elf images overhead blurred into a watery white snowscape, and Eve lay still during her grief and felt pain she'd never felt before. The tears came harder and she rolled to her left and clung to the white slats of the balcony railing and saw the world beyond at a distorted angle, and blinked at a distant figure. He had just entered the distortion of her vision at the far end of the live oaks.

A horseman.

Were they returning?

Please God, no.

She rose halfway up from her prone position and saw him again, one lone rider poised at the exact center of the avenue of live oaks, not moving forward or backward, like the game of statues she sometimes played with David and Christine when, hurled into a certain position, the player would have to hold that position as long as possible, despite heat or sweat or buzzing mosquitoes.

Eve renewed her grasp on the slats, which now served as white bars in her gallery prison. What should she do? Should she go and fetch someone? Who? Everyone, she was certain, was still in the woods.

But as yet it wasn't a real emergency. Far from it, for she began to sense something more than hesitancy coming from the end of the avenue. The riders this morning had approached steadily, had ridden directly up to Stanhope Hall in two ordered columns, never once hesitating.

But this rider—

Perplexed, she slid down a couple of slats to get a better view and looked down on him now in a straight line and wished that the distance were not so great so that she could see the specifics of his face.

Maybe she should go fetch someone. He could be merely the advance guard. More men might materialize at any moment, a second visitation, wreaking greater havoc unless she warned someone.

But still she held her position, fascinated by the new movement coming from the end of the avenue, the rider shifting in his saddle, bending to brush something off his trousers, an impromptu grooming.

Slowly she felt her apprehension shift to sympathetic amusement. Someone wanted to make a good impression. But the question remained. Who?

For a moment, baffled by the mystery, Eve bowed her head, then looked up quickly. The rider had apparently found the courage to move and now flicked the reins. The horse responded and started in a slow pace up the avenue of live oaks.

Eve held her position, grasping the turned slats. He was approaching the halfway mark, still guiding his horse at that apprehensive pace, and not once as far as Eve could tell had he taken his eyes off the front door of Stanhope Hall.

Now she saw new specifics. His hair was dark, his shoulders broad. The fabric of his dark jacket was pulled taut across his chest. His boots were black and polished, and the trouser legs that pressed against the flanks of the horse were muscular and straining.

With new fascination she drew up to her knees, still keeping to the concealment of the gallery railing, and watched as the rider made it all the way to the edge of the last live oak. Nothing separated him now from the front steps of Stanhope Hall but about forty feet of green lawn, then the rounded seashell driveway.

Abruptly he dismounted and led his horse to the left side of the avenue and stood close to the trees directly beneath the spreading boughs, as though a storm were imminent and he'd taken premature shelter.

Eve found his hesitancy moving. All of the adults in her world moved with such harmony and vigor and purpose. It was fun to peer down on someone who seemed to suffer from feelings of uncertainty at least as great as her own.

Then should she speak? What would she say? How would she—

Suddenly there was movement coming from beneath the tree. He started forward, and had managed all of about a half-dozen steps when something intervened. He turned immediately back and instantly retraced his steps and almost comically assumed his same identical position, once again directly beneath the protective bough of the tree, again keeping watch on the front door.

Eve had never seen such painful uncertainty, short of her own behavior on occasion. It couldn't go on. It hurt too much to watch.

"Hello."

At that instant the focus of those dark eyes lifted from the front doors of Stanhope Hall and traveled upward rapidly, wildly for a moment until he could locate her, and only then did she realize what she had done, standing there in her white summer chemise, barefoot, her hair loose about her shoulders, smiling down on a perfect stranger, who returned her gaze yet held his position, which was a good thing because she was having trouble enough dealing with the beauty of his face.

Never before had she seen such a face—young, not one of her father's business associates, not fleshy or flabby or lined. This male face was different, so different.

As the tense silence stretched on to embarrassing lengths, the need for movement and speech became acute.

"I'll—be right down," Eve stammered and stepped back out of his range of vision and remembered to breathe at the last moment and felt her heart beating too fast beneath her chemise and experienced the curious sensation that she'd really just imagined him, that if she tiptoed back to the edge of the gallery right now, he'd be gone, having never really been there in the first place.

With held breath, she tiptoed back to the edge of the gallery, looked down and—

He was there, exactly as she had left him. Quickly she withdrew a second time. A distinct possibility occurred. But it couldn't be. They were expecting him late this afternoon. Or so her mother had said. No, it couldn't be. Anyway she'd envisioned someone older, more businesslike, more—

He *was* there, and possibly, just possibly he was her English cousin Stephen Eden, the one her mother had asked her to look after, see to, make welcome.

Well, it was a possibility. Yet somehow in her mind it still did not mesh. How could that hesitant, uncertain young man be the son of John Murrey Eden, one of the few names capable of bringing her father to an absolute rage and causing her mother to go pale and quiet and sad.

No one had ever bothered to tell Eve precisely what had happened in that distant English world to cause such pain to so many people.

She held the thought suspended and looked back through the gallery railing in the still greenness beyond.

Was he Stephen Eden? Or was it someone else? She couldn't very well find out here. And as everyone else at Stanhope Hall was occupied, then it was her job to hurry and make herself presentable and to greet the young man properly at the front door and to find out everything about him, if possible.

* * *

At first Stephen was certain it had been an apparition, a divine apparition, complete with hair of spun gold that caught the light and reflected it and hurled it back into his eyes, momentarily blinding him.

As Cicero tugged at him, Stephen stole a glimpse backward, thinking he'd heard someone at the front door. But the carved white columns shimmered under the intensity of heat. When no one appeared, the same enticing thought entered his mind for the second time that day.

Leave! Now!

After all, he'd put in an appearance, had kept his promise to his uncle and had been most inhospitably received, had not been received at all. No one would want him to intrude into a household where clearly he was not wanted. The offense had been his father's. Then his father would have to make restitution.

Again Cicero tugged him in the opposite direction, as though urging him to follow his good instincts.

But he wanted to survey Stanhope Hall one last time, starting with that singular spot on the second-floor gallery where he'd seen the vision. From there his eyes traveled down each column, scanning windows as they passed and always finding nothing of life or movement or hospitality.

Then leave . . .

He swung Cicero about, and heard a distant, though clear, "Wait, please wait—"

He looked back. He saw a young woman at the top of the steps. She was wearing a dark blue dress and her hair was loose, gold, a long cascading mane that lifted as she started down the steps.

Fascinated, he turned about in his saddle and watched as she ran toward him and saw bare feet beneath the folds of the blue muslin dress. As she drew nearer, he noticed that her bodice was incorrectly buttoned, causing the prim white collar to poke up at an awkward angle above her neck.

But for all the disarray of her apparel, never had Nature been more in perfect harmony than in the specifics of her face, the face of the apparition he'd seen on the gallery, an inquiring, alert, beautiful face that alternately blushed with daring and grew calm and serene with self-confidence.

She came to an abrupt halt about fifteen feet away, two fever spots burning on either side of her smooth white face.

"You're not leaving, are you?" she asked and revealed a breathlessness as though for the last several minutes she'd been engaged in hectic activity.

"I thought there was no one at home," he began and broke off, much preferring simply to look at her. He was quite certain he'd never seen anyone like her in his entire life. She was tall, for one thing, and slim as a reed. The women at home, both Aunt Eleanor and Susan, were short and plump. And there was something about her eyes, dark blue violet, and something about her gaze and something about her stance and something about—

"Were you looking for someone?"

"I was. The Stanhopes. I understood that this was Stanhope Hall."

"It is."

"Mr. and Mrs. Burke Stanhope?"

"They're here. Well, not here. Busy at the moment." She paused. A look of sadness covered her face. "We've had a difficult morning. One of our good friends was—hurt this morning—no, I mean, found dead, killed."

At first Stephen couldn't believe what she had said. "I'm sorry," he said and slid from his horse and allowed the reins to slip from his hand and was concerned only with the deep sorrow he sensed in the young woman.

For a moment he stood silent before her, not knowing how to offer comfort or even if it was his place to do so. Strange, she seemed less tall standing before him, though the curves and angles beneath the incorrectly buttoned bodice were clear and provocative. He moved back a step to give her room to recover from the grief.

She withdrew from her sleeve a lace handkerchief, dabbed once at her eyes and now stood before him, studying the intricate lace design on her handkerchief. Into this vacuum he took a step. "I am—"

"Stephen Eden. I know. We were expecting you, but later today."

"I'm sorry if I arrived too early."

"No need. It has been an awful day, however—"

"I'm sorry about your—friend."

"My name is Eve."

"Eve," he repeated.

"It's my nickname. My whole name is Elizabeth Victoria Eden Stanhope."

"Was it you I saw on the balcony earlier?"

"I was sent home. They wanted to get me out of the way."

"The way of what?"

She looked up and he saw new grief on her face. "I—found it—you know—" she whispered, and he saw the lace handkerchief trembling.

"Found it?" he repeated, sensing she needed assistance but at a loss momentarily to offer it.

She did not look up. "I'd gone to Fan Cottage to see Sis Liz after the men had left. She and White Doll were preparing morning tea. Those men, you know, the horsemen came early this morning and left the flower on the steps right over there"—and she turned and pointed toward the front steps and suddenly her back went rigid.

"Eve, come, let's sit."

He spoke the invitation softly, and took her arm and led her toward the steps and was pleased to find her compliant, though less pleased to see the pain and fear still clearly visible on her face.

About three feet from the steps, she moved away from his support and sat and wiped her brow with a handkerchief and pushed the handkerchief back into her sleeve, simple gestures that held him fascinated. Never had he seen such beauty, such grace. What few women had crossed his path in North Devon had been the plump, jolly daughters of neighboring dairy farmers, or the scheming and small-mouthed daughters of the gentry, or, worse, the snobbish and arrogant daughters of his uncle Richard's titled friends. Thus he had more or less resigned himself to bachelorhood.

But the oceanic distance between those females and this one—

The comparison stunned him into a greater silence, and he found himself recording her every move as though someday he would be called upon to describe her in full to someone who had not had the good fortune to see her.

"I'm sorry," she murmured.

"No need."

"I'm afraid you chose a sad day on which to arrive."

"Would you like me to leave?"

"No."

Was it his imagination, or had she spoken with significant speed? "I'm only sorry my parents are not here to make you feel welcome."

"Are you in the house alone?"

"Oh, no. The servants are here, some of them. They all loved White Doll as much as I did. The house is full of weeping."

Then there was fresh grief, so close to the surface. Although he couldn't begin to piece together an accurate picture of what had happened, he knew a tragedy had occurred of major proportion and wondered if she would tell him about it in specific detail. Obviously it would be to his advantage to know. If her parents were as distraught as she was, then it might be best to return to Mobile. He could come back when the tragedy had been assimilated, perhaps later.

"Eve," he began gently, stepping back to the place where she was sitting on the steps, aware of the impropriety of it all, speaking intimately with a young woman whom he'd only just met and even then not formally. "Would you tell me what happened? If you don't want to, I'll understand."

"It was dawn . . . ."

Still she hadn't looked up and Stephen wasn't certain of her tale or her intent. But when that low musical voice continued in a bizarre narrative about twelve hooded horsemen riding up, materializing out of morning mist, he felt a double excitement at the tale itself and more important that she trusted him to the extent that she could speak frankly, honestly.

"The Knights of—what?" he asked, sitting a step beneath her, turned sideways, watching her.

"The Knights of the White Camellia," she repeated. "A vigilante group of citizens devoted to preserving the Southern way of life."

As she talked, Stephen tried to understand all the subtleties and nuances of life as it was presently being lived in the southern part of the United States, though it was difficult. Slavery was wrong and thus had been brought to an end, but naturally there would be feelings of resentment after any civil war.

As Eve spoke she seemed to slip into and out of a variety of moods, reminiscing about the dead woman named White Doll. She laughed, a magical sound, and then her mood was respectful when she spoke the name Sis Liz, whom she assured Stephen he would meet.

But presiding over the tale of horror was an all-encompassing sadness that Stephen suspected with regret would accompany her for the rest of her life.

"And that's all I know," Eve concluded, and he saw her shoulders go limp, as though the recitation had drained her.

"Death comes so quickly," came the soft voice behind the strands of hair. "I don't think White Doll intended to die today."

He heard something new in that sweet voice, an angry tone, as though at last she'd moved beyond grief.

She was speaking now of her father. "And he'll change nothing. My father says to give in to their demands is to give them a victory."

"And you don't agree?"

For the first time in several long minutes she looked up. "Not where life is concerned. Unless, of course, God sees nothing wrong with the murder of an innocent woman in order to prove a moral point. Do you agree?"

Stephen gaped, speechless. He couldn't answer that question or even begin to address himself to the pain behind it.

"There is so much I don't understand," she said, a plaintive tone in her voice that he recognized instantly.

Now at last he could agree and did. "I know."

She looked up, surprised.

"Oh, I don't mean here," he hurriedly added. "I don't know this place at all except for what my uncle and my father have told me, and my uncle has obtained all his information from your mother's letters."

"Richard," she mused. "My mother's brother. She has a writing time, you know, a special hour every Sunday afternoon at four o'clock."

Stephen listened, amazed. He'd had no idea the correspondence was so regular. "Does she receive a letter every month from North Devon?"

"Yes, though sometimes they're late. But it's a sad month that a dark brown envelope from Eden Castle isn't delivered to Stanhope Hall."

"Does she miss England?" Stephen asked, wanting very much to keep this conversation going.

"No," Eve replied without a moment's hesitation. "At least she's never said so." She rested her chin on her propped up elbows and looked sideways out across the green lawn. "Not that she has much of a life here," she added.

"Why?"

"She never goes calling. And no one ever comes to visit her."

"Why?" he asked, aware of his rudeness, but hoping that she was not.

"My father," she said simply. "I told you. He has Northern friends and he has black friends, but no Southern friends to be trusted."

"I don't understand."

"They have a name for him, you know," she said with sudden lightness. "They call him a scalawag."

"What does it mean?"

"It means a Southerner who likes Yankees."

"The war was over long ago."

"Not here. Here it's still going on."

"Does your father mind? What they call him, I mean?"

She laughed. "Mind?" she repeated. "He takes pride in it, I think. He writes about it."

"He's a writer?"

She nodded. He saw pride on her face. "I write poetry," she said shyly, "but it's not very good."

"I'm sure it is."

"No, nothing like my father writes. He has won awards—not here, but in the North."

"Does he write books?"

"He's working on one. But mostly he does pieces for magazines—*The Century, Harpers, The Atlantic.*"

Stephen hadn't heard of any of them. If Eve thought that life in southern America was isolated, she should try life in North Devon.

"He's just finished a series of articles called 'Battles and Leaders of the Civil War,' " she added.

Stephen smiled. "That should redeem him in the eyes of Southern society."

Slowly she shook her head. "I'm afraid not. He gave equal time and equal praise to blue and gray alike."

In the brief silence that followed Stephen began to perceive the outline of her unhappiness and found it remarkably similar to his own. Presiding over both their heavens and their hells was a father, strong-willed, gifted, contradictory and unreliable.

"Well," she said, and the gloom was dispersed. "As Mama says, we have everything here at Stanhope Hall, and most important, we have each other. But it does make it awkward when company arrives because no one knows how to act. Here we leave you to wander about in the heat of the day—"

"I wasn't wandering," Stephen smiled.

"I saw you. Your poor horse is searching for food and water even now."

"He hasn't had to search very far."

Stephen looked over his shoulder to see Cicero placidly grazing on the opposite side of the avenue, reins hanging free.

"Is he yours?" she asked and came up alongside him. At first it was difficult to answer, he was so acutely aware of her presence beside him. His eyes skimming the top of her head, standing so close, he could see several strands of hair caught in her eyelashes, which instantly she dislodged and drew back into company with the others.

"No. I borrowed him from a stable in Mobile. For a price, of course. He's agreeable enough, though lacking even the smallest bone of a thoroughbred."

"Do you have horses at home, back in England?"

He nodded. "My aunt Eleanor, Richard's wife, adores horses. She has Arabians which she lets me ride now and then. And I have my own. I've had him for ages. A black stallion."

"What's his name?"

"Prodigal."

"Mine's Clarissa. A sorrel. I'll let you ride her if you wish."

As they talked, they walked at an easy pace down the avenue to where Cicero was munching grass.

"How long will you be here?" she asked, head down, the toes of her bare feet visible beneath the dark blue muslin dress.

"I'm not sure. My destination is—"

"West someplace, wasn't it?"

"Montana, yes."

"How will you travel?"

"I'm not certain. My father said I was to ask your father—"

Abruptly she stopped. There appeared to be new worry on her face. "Such a terrible day for you to arrive."

"As I said, I can leave and come back."

"Oh, no, you mustn't."

"It would be no problem."

"No. Come on, let's get your horse and take him to the barn. Then I'll show you to the house." She confronted him directly, standing less than three feet away, leaving him to deal as best he could with her breathtaking beauty. "It's the least I can do to cover for everyone else's rudeness."

"It's not rudeness. I do understand—"

"If I wandered into your Eden Castle in North Devon, would I be treated thus?"

"No, you would not have been kept waiting in the courtyard of Eden Castle," he said. "But then it's a large castle, the household staff quite large as well. Besides, the lookouts would have seen you at least a quarter of an hour before your arrival, riding across the moors."

"It sounds lovely," she said. "Will you tell me more about England and your life there?"

"Of course, if you're interested."

"My mother has spoken of England all my life. From what she has read to me from Richard's letters, I feel as if I know everyone there."

"Including me?"

She blushed. "I knew your name, but you existed only in your uncle's letters. I didn't expect to see you come riding up to Stanhope Hall."

Their eyes met over Cicero's broad back, and he was pleased to see in hers not a trace of fear or anger. Grief was still there, but even that had been tempered and softened.

She glanced away in the opposite direction, across the lawn, which danced with the mirages of summer heat. "Hear that?" she asked, turning back.

Puzzled, Stephen listened, hearing nothing at first. Then, "Water?"

"My brother, David. You'll meet him. The ice pond is over there behind the willows. He goes bathing every day."

"It sounds cool and refreshing."

"Would you like to—I mean—I could call David. He could—"

Quickly Stephen shook his head. "Not now; perhaps later."

In her face, in the unexpected and deepening lights in her eyes, in her shy half-smile, in the manner in which she clung to Cicero's reins, in the way in which she stole glances across the top of Cicero's back, as though fearful that Stephen might disappear, in these and a hundred other small observations, he sensed loneliness—more than sensed it, recognized it, as though he were gazing into a mirror.

They were walking slowly back up the avenue toward Stanhope Hall, Cicero between them. Stephen was finding it increasingly difficult to take his eyes off her. She was walking head down, though he could see a becoming smile on her lips.

Just as he was on the verge of asking the source of her amusement, she looked directly at him. "Promise you'll stay as long as possible. Will you promise me that?"

"If I'm welcome to stay, of course I'll do so."

His answer seemed to please her, for she rewarded him with a dazzling smile. "You'll stay then," she murmured.

"Eve!"

Suddenly, cutting into their soft conversation, there came a voice, masculine, filled with authority.

Abruptly she looked up toward the front porch. "Papa," she whispered and for just a moment Stephen saw a painful contradiction of emotion and fear blended with hope.

Stephen followed her gaze to the porch of Stanhope Hall and saw a man, tall, broad-shouldered, in his shirtsleeves. He stood on a base of absolute authority, his high-top black boots glistening in the noon sun. He was not alone. Behind him was a young black man, also in white shirtsleeves, a coat swung loosely over his shoulder, his stance not so much one of authority but of support, and behind both men, partially emerging from the house, still holding the door as though for protection, he saw a woman, her face partially obscured by the door, though what he could see of her expression was one of alarm.

Just when Stephen thought no one would ever move or speak again, he heard Eve whisper, "Come on, let's get it over with."

As an invitation, it left a little to be desired. But he moved with her as she tugged Cicero forward. As they approached the bottom step, Stephen thought she would relinquish Cicero's reins and spare the horse this human confrontation, but she didn't.

It was Stephen who lagged behind, partly out of courtesy. He would step forward when called.

"Papa, we have a guest," and with this sweet declaration, Eve broke the silence and Stephen wondered how anyone could resist the music of her voice.

But resist it he did. This man whom she had called Papa now answered her in tones even more harsh than the ones before. "You were told to stay in your rooms."

"I did, Papa."

"You are not there now."

"I told you we have a guest."

What the man said next was clearly a command. "Go to your rooms now."

Eve did not respond, nor did she comply. Burke Stanhope had taken one step toward the top of the stairs when the woman who had held back the door moved with admirable resolve, the grace of a smile at last altering her features, which were very attractive.

"You are surely Stephen Eden," were the first words she spoke to him, and up close he found her beauty even more unique, her voice an irresistible combination of pure English speech softened over the years by the Southern cadence.

"Of course, you're Stephen Eden. Either that or you're my half-brother, John Murrey Eden, thirty years younger and soul intact."

He took her hand, and it felt small and cold in his hand and he tried to understand "soul intact."

"Yes," he said in reply to all her charges. "I'm Stephen Eden, and I'm told I bear a resemblance to my father."

"Resemblance!" The woman smiled and seemed to be studying him with closer scrutiny. "It's the same pattern. Don't you agree, Burke?"

Without turning, she tried to involve the man on the step in her discovery. But the man did not respond in any way to her entreaty; nor did he alter his position at the top of the stairs, surveying everyone with the intensity of a watchdog.

The young black man had retired to the side of the porch, leaning against the railing. Apparently Eve had been right on more than one point. Stephen couldn't have come at a worse time. If only he'd known.

"My deepest apologies," the woman was saying now, still holding his hand, or rather allowing him to hold hers. "Normally we are not this remiss at Stanhope Hall. My name is Mary, as I'm sure you know. Your father's half-sister and thus your aunt."

She was irresistible, exhibiting a glow of warmth despite the awkward moment. "I think I knew." He smiled down on her. "And I'm the one who owes all of you an apology for arriving at such an unfortunate time. As I have told Eve, I could very well leave and return—"

Eve, who had been silent, now objected. "No."

That was all she said, and in an attempt to cover the short protest, Stephen added, "And I assure you, I was most warmly received by your daughter, who has made me feel welcome from the beginning."

Mary looked approvingly at Eve. "For that I'm grateful. Come, you must meet everybody." She glanced over her shoulder. "Burke, please come and greet our guest."

"I know who he is. I see the resemblance as well. If you'll excuse me, there is much to do. Come, Paris, we have work."

With that he disappeared through the door, leaving the young black man gaping after him. Then he, too, disappeared and the porch was empty, a vacuum of vast proportions that threatened briefly to pull them all into it.

"You must forgive my husband, Mr. Eden."

"I understand."

"I don't believe you do."

"Eve told me."

Mary looked up, surprised. "Everything?"

Eve continued to smooth Cicero's silky mane. Now she turned to where Mary was standing. "Did they find—"

"Yes."

"Where have you been?"

"In the cemetery."

"I would like to have been there."

"Mr. Eden, we're being rude again."

Abruptly Mary turned back, as if only then aware they had excluded him. "Come, let's go inside. I'll send someone back to take your horse to the stable. I'll show you to your rooms, and in honor of your arrival we'll have tea at four o'clock—an English tea. How I would enjoy that. Then please promise me that you'll stay for dinner."

All the time she talked she gathered Stephen on one arm and Eve on the other, and together the three of them climbed the stairs and crossed the broad front porch of Stanhope Hall. For the first time Stephen felt a surge of relief, as though they were leaving all tragedies, all mysteries, all unanswered questions from the past out in the heat of the day.

Inside he found it difficult at first to see anything at all, so great was the contrast between sun and shadow. Then gradually he brought the two women into focus and saw as well an elegant interior of highly polished floors, oriental runners, two handsome brass chandeliers lighting the long central corridor, which led off into rooms on either side, a simple architectural design.

"Come, Mr. Eden. Here is someone you must meet, the true keeper of Stanhope Hall."

He saw a distinguished-looking black woman with white hair, leaning heavily on a walking stick. She eyed him with suspicion over the top of her spectacles, as though she was certain there was something about him to distrust.

"This is Florence," Mary said.

"I knew your father," Florence said, in level tones with only a trace of a Southern accent.

To Stephen's puzzled expression, she explained, "I've traveled, yes, I have. I served Mr. Stanhope's mother in London, and when she died, God rest her soul, I served Mr. Stanhope. And when these two wed, I served Lady Mary here, and now I've got my sharp eye on that one."

Florence glanced toward Eve, who had taken refuge on the lower steps of the staircase. There she sat, elbows on her knees, her chin propped in the palms of her hands, the scandalous bare feet visible now for all to see, her toes keeping time to a private rhythm.

Apparently Florence was shocked by the bare feet. "Get on up there," she scolded, and Eve was on her feet. As she started up the stairs, she stole a last look down at Stephen.

"I'm glad you're here," she said and smiled.

Though he knew better than to say anything, he returned her smile and realized that every time he looked at her, he saw some new fascination. He wished that she were staying and everyone else were leaving.

As Eve disappeared at the top of the steps, Stephen concentrated all his attention on his aunt, who, up close, seemed newly undone.

"Could we sit for a moment?" he suggested quietly. Through the double doors on his left he saw what appeared to be a handsome parlor, now cast in sepia tones, the heavy drapes drawn against the afternoon sun.

Mary led the way into the parlor, comfortably filled with massive overstuffed leather furniture, four potted palms gracefully filling each corner and handsome arrangements of mahogany chairs and tables pleasantly and intimately grouped about a large fireplace, which now in summer had been blocked from view by an enormous pale blue and green oriental fire screen.

"Sit where it pleases you," she invited and handed him a delicate paper fan, which he took but did not use. He held his position halfway across the room until he saw her settle in the corner of one of the large settees, then sat opposite her. A low table separated them, a large clear bowl filled with multicolor glass balls resting in the center of the table, a copy of *Century* magazine on one end and a silver epergne of potpourri on the other.

"I'm afraid it's necessary," she said, indicating the fan, and by way of demonstration began to sway it back and forth in a rhythmic movement before her face. "It took me forever to get used to it—the heat, I mean." She smiled sadly. "After North Devon I thought I'd fallen into Hades."

He watched for any clue that might aid him in understanding Stanhope Hall and its inhabitants. This woman, this aunt seemed to be making such a monumental effort to receive him well and kindly, and yet the moment was not easy.

He tried to imitate her movement with the fan, but felt foolish and at last placed it on the table. "I'm really not that warm," he apologized.

Suddenly, to his distress, he saw her leave the settee and take refuge in one of the corners of the parlor. Between the heavy brocade drapes and the foliage of the large palm, she almost disappeared, though he heard sniffling and gave her all the time she needed, confident that she would return as soon as she was able.

"My apologies again, Mr. Eden."

She was back, almost restored, only small red rims about her eyes and a mussed handkerchief in her hand to betray her.

"I'm the one who should apologize," he said, standing. "Eve told me of your—sadness this morning. It was wrong of me to press for an audience so soon."

"No, please sit down. I want to talk with you, to hear all your news."

He waited a moment to see if she meant it. And when for the second time she urged him to sit down, he did so and watched as she retrieved her fan and did not use it, but seemed content merely to caress it lovingly.

"Sometimes this is a dangerous place, Mr. Eden, this America. When you least expect it, it can become a dangerous place."

Though her voice was low, her intensity and meaning were clear. Obviously this native-born Englishwoman had gone through a difficult period of adjustment, was perhaps still going through it. Again Stephen felt a strange surge of affection for her and wondered how his father could have wronged her.

"Now," she said as though on fresh breath and fresh energy. "Please tell me that you accept all my apologies for our behavior this morning, Mr. Eden."

"I'll accept all your apologies if you'll stop calling me Mr. Eden and call me Stephen."

"Stephen, then, and I consider it a fair exchange for our rudeness and neglect."

"You did receive Uncle Richard's letter that I was to arrive on this day?"

"Yes. But later. The New York train generally arrives some time after six in the evening."

"I've been in Mobile for several days."

"You what?"

"Yes, I arrived on Tuesday last."

"Well, my goodness, where have you been? What have you—?"

In an attempt to ease her shock, he laughed. "I've been sightseeing, mainly."

"Where have you been staying?"

"I found a lodging house."

"Where?"

"Near the waterfront."

"Oh, my dear. Richard will never forgive me. You should have come to us immediately."

"But I was early."

"It would have made no difference."

"It did today."

"Today was . . ."

The sentence died. These few harmless revelations seemed to have added to her fatigue.

"Shall I call you Mary or Aunt Mary?" He laughed. "We seem to be having difficulty in deciding what to call each other."

"Mary, please. The 'aunt' part makes me sound old and gray-haired. Now, I want to hear all. Tell me, please. I had no idea how much I've missed Eden until this moment, when I have someone before me who can tell me everything about it."

The fatigue seemed to have disappeared, to be replaced by a charming enthusiasm that propelled her back to the edge of the settee, her eyes fixed on him with flattering intensity.

Being thrust into the spotlight so unexpectedly caused him to falter. "Where shall I start?"

"With Richard. Is he well?"

For the first time since they'd entered the parlor, Stephen was aware of the heat, his shirtwaist damp against his back. "Richard is—well," he began, trying to recreate in his mind a valid though flattering picture of his uncle.

"He suffers terribly from gout now and then," Stephen went on. "But generally he enjoys fair health."

"And the children? What are their ages now? Please tell me of the children."

For a moment Stephen was uncertain which children she meant. At times Eden Point seemed like a public school. "Which children?" he asked. "There are several."

She looked up, puzzled.

"My father's family. Susan—"

"Oh, yes."

Her voice turned suddenly winter. She started up from the settee as though the conversation was over, then sat back down, though she looked nervously about as though searching for a legitimate escape route. "There were three, I believe Richard wrote, at last count."

"Four. Alice is thirteen, Albert is ten and Harriet is six. And of course there's my brother Frederick."

"I remember Frederick—a darling child."

"He's at Oxford now. We think he may end up in the church. He's a gentle man in every sense, with a great capacity to love."

"All gifts from your poor dead mother."

"Did you know her?"

"Very well. The most beautiful woman I've ever seen, I believe, and the most tragic. Your father—"

Abruptly she stopped speaking. She bowed her head. Stephen waited out the awkward silence, uncertain whether to press for her to go on or politely excuse himself. Obviously the subject was still as painful to Mary as it was to his father. In fact, for the first time he sensed wounds so deep as to perhaps be beyond healing.

"If you'll excuse me now, Mr. Eden. We will continue our talk later if you wish."

The voice was formal again and took Stephen by surprise. By the time he was on his feet to offer assistance, she was gone, having moved with rapid familiarity through the cluttered room, saying nothing else by way of explanation, her head still bowed, grasping her long skirts, dust smudged from the tragic morning.

For several minutes he stared at the vacuum of the open doors. Now what to do? He had no idea where his rooms were, no idea even where to start looking. What did her hurried exit signify? That she couldn't talk now? That she had no desire to talk—ever?

No answers, only the persistent and deepening silence of the house and the growing sense that he was in a place where he was not wanted, where he was being held responsible for another man's ancient offenses.

Somewhere between his regret and his frustration, he heard his uncle Richard's voice.

Be patient with them. Your father's offenses were great, and as yet there has been no healing forgiveness. You can be a bridge.

A bridge! At the moment he felt most unbridgelike, felt more like a criminal, a trespasser and an interloper.

He turned aimlessly, and for one of the few times in his life felt bereft of reason and incapable of movement. Suddenly it occurred to him that within the unhappy confines of Stanhope Hall, the exciting term "the New World" did not exist. Here in this gloomy sepia-colored heat-ridden place, the Old World still held sway, still manipulated and controlled and influenced everyone in it, like a cold wind that ceaselessly changes direction and against which there is no defense.

There was one clear perception in his tense waiting. No wonder Eve was so lonely. And this thought moved him and heightened his paralysis of will and rendered him fair game for any ghost from the past who might be passing and want to attack.

* * *

Burke felt anger rising, as it had been rising since early morning, when the hooded bastards had first violated the sanctity of Stanhope Hall, to the unspeakable barbarism of their subsequent act—

Someone would pay.

—to the unscheduled arrival of the arrogant young Eden with his insolent Eden face, to this moment in his study, confronting Paris Boley, wondering when old Ben would return with Dr. Melrose, wondering if Sis Liz's collapse had to do with grief or age or both. Now all these events added up to a cruel disintegration of his world order. As he had not yet found a suitable target for his unspent rage, he ordered Paris to scout the Mobile road and see if he could find Ben, while he sought out his wife to tell her that Stephen Eden would have to go now.

"Hurry," he called after Paris, worried about Sis Liz, aware that she had lived far too long as it was but treasuring this link with his youth and reluctant to see it die. A few of the house women were with her now, but one had reported that her heart palpitations were worse than usual, so Burke had sent for old Dr. Melrose.

"He should be on the main road," he called out over the rear gallery as Paris swung up onto his horse. Then he was gone, leaving a cloud of dust to settle over the kitchen garden and Mrs. Winegar's face, which appeared in the small round window of the kitchen gallery.

Slowly he turned back toward the shadowy central corridor. So much needed his attention. Where to start?

Suddenly at the far end of the corridor he saw Mary running from the parlor, head bowed. He started to call out to her, but she was moving too fast, apparently bent on putting as much distance as possible between herself and the parlor.

Something had happened. Burke moved rapidly forward, the echo of his boots on hardwood floors sounding like thunder in the quiet house. And why was it so quiet? Generally the children were playing and laughing on the upstairs gallery, the servants calling back and forth to each other, old Florence trying to keep everything under control. Now where were they all? Where were the voices, the shouts, the laughter?

No need to look very hard for an answer. Death had come this morning to Stanhope Hall. Burke strode on and realized he had yet to grieve for White Doll, who perhaps had shared his blood though no one had ever pressed for the truth and his father had never come forward to claim her. But he'd cared for her, and Sis Liz had adopted her, and she had walked with complete comfort and ease that most difficult line between the white world and the black one.

Suddenly the full weight of what they all had lost pressed down upon him and he reached out for the near support of the open parlor door and longed for an interval of privacy.

Quickly he stepped inside the parlor and closed the door behind him and leaned his forehead against the door and tried to rid himself of the images of the morning that were causing the painful mix of anger and grief.

To his right, on the small mosaic table, he saw a bottle of Madeira. He lifted the bottle and drank and welcomed the pleasant burning and drank again, long deep swallows, before returning it to the table.

He thought he heard movement in the parlor behind him. "Who's there?" he demanded. His first thought as he frantically searched the ever-changing shadows was that they had returned, the Knights of the White Camellia, that they had dared to enter Stanhope Hall and now were prepared to deliver another threat.

"I demand to—"

"Sir, I'm sorry. I don't mean to intrude."

Suddenly his vision cleared, and for one moment he believed that the bastard himself, John Murrey Eden, had slipped unannounced into Stanhope Hall.

"My name is Stephen Eden. I arrived earlier this morning. You were there—"

"What are you doing in this room?"

"Mrs. Stanhope, your—she invited me in."

"For what purpose?"

"To—"

Then Burke could abide his presence no longer. So certain was he that this face before him now was that same face who'd caused him such sorrow years ago, who'd almost cost him Mary's love, that within the instant, and without thinking, Burke was upon him, one hand grasping the front of his shirtwaist in a rigid grip. The all-too-familiar face appeared stunned, clearly taken by surprise. There was no struggle at first. Then suddenly, without warning, arms of incredible strength shot up, dislodging Burke's grip with a single effort. Freed, the young man stepped back, only a pace, his right arm rigid and holding Burke at bay.

"I beg you, sir, it is not my wish to—"

Something about the insolence of the face before him, the certainty of power, the arrogance of youth, all this combined with the fierce resemblance of that other bastard, and all the unspent anger at the tragedy and injustice of the morning caused Burke to push back but once at the arm that held him at bay, and the next step was even simpler, to push again and yet again until at last he sensed defense and loved the feel of it and before the enemy could strike first, Burke drew back his left arm and delivered a stunning blow to the side of that arrogant Eden face.

The boy reeled backward and collided painfully with the marble fireplace. He righted himself with admirable speed and shook his head as though to clear the effects of the blow. His left hand moved up to the corner of his mouth, where a thin trickle of blood was visible. All this Burke recorded, poised a short distance away, amazed at how good it had felt, one lunge of violent action, the sight of the young man injured.

Now Burke saw him quickly withdraw a handkerchief from his waistcoat pocket and dab at the blood. In the same mood of puzzlement, he looked up. "Sir, I beg you, how have I offended you?"

Burke smiled. How easy this pup would be to defeat. He might well bear his father's resemblance and his name, but in no way did he possess the stubborn nature of John Murrey Eden.

"If you wish me to leave, sir—"

What Burke wished for was fewer words and another chance to deliver a blow. There was an aching need in him on this day to pummel something senseless. He'd hoped the boy would be a worthy opponent. Now in answer to his question, he posed another. "Why did you come here in the first place? You were not invited."

The bewilderment on his face increased. "I—had understood that my uncle, Lord Richard, had written to you."

"Not to me. To my wife."

"Then she did not inform you—"

Burke shook his head. It was a lie, but perhaps it would anger the boy enough to strike back.

But it didn't. Instead the boy slowly pocketed his handkerchief, all the time shaking his head. "Then I do owe you an apology, sir," he began, starting away from the fireplace.

Damn! No reconciliation, not now. There still was something painful and sharp lodged sideways in Burke's soul. "How did you offend my wife?" he demanded, refusing to move from the spot where he stood, thus blocking the boy's exit.

"Offend, sir? I wasn't aware that I had offended her."

"I saw her only a few moments ago run from this room in tears."

"Not in tears, sir. She wasn't weeping."

"Then what was the cause of her distress?"

"I said nothing. We were speaking—"

"Of what?"

"Of simple matters."

"Name them."

Burke now heard his own voice in sharp, echoing retort and loathed it. What in the name of God was he doing?

"Sir, I resent your implication."

"You said something offensive to her."

"No, sir, I did not."

"Your father was skilled at this sort of thing."

"I am not my father."

"You bear his name and his resemblance."

"I am my own man."

Despite the nature of what they were saying, they were drawing closer with each exchange, as though the need for battle was a contagion that had spread from one to the other at last.

"Sir, if you'll let me pass, I'll leave Stanhope Hall immediately."

"You owe this household—my wife—an apology."

"For what? What is my offense?"

"You can answer that better than I."

The boy stepped to one side and gave him a look of such insolence that Burke found renewed contact irresistible and reached angrily out for that passive shoulder, only to feel the passivity fall away under his touch, a lightning-fast movement that took Burke completely by surprise, first shaking off his hand, then a surprisingly strong and steadying hand grasping the front of his shirt and at last the blow that Burke had been waiting for, a reeling, spinning blow that sent Burke hurtling backward into the low table containing the large glass bowl filled with colored marbles. The bowl slid, fell and broke under the impact of Burke's fall, the marbles rolling everywhere in a clattering escape, and for several seconds that was the only sound save for Burke's groan as he felt the flesh around his left eye explode in pain. His vision blurred, seeing the young man standing over him now.

"My apologies, sir, for my actions, which I assure you were provoked by yours. I promise you I did nothing to offend your wife or your household. We were talking quite calmly of—"

Burke rose slowly to his knees, waiting out the pain on his left cheek, and from his position saw the boy's highly polished black leather boots and felt new fury at his presence.

Even as the boy was offering him a hand up, Burke lunged forward, catching him by the knees, and the two of them fell like one crashing column, the boy half under the settee, Burke on top, at least for the moment, each struggling to establish supremacy.

The time for speech was over. Burke at last was satisfied, though the boy was stronger than he had at first imagined. The two of them

inflicted as much pain as was possible within the limited confines of
the parlor, fists delivering blow after blow, the furnishings suffering
the most as fringed shawls were pulled to the floor, taking all their
carefully arranged cargo with them, crystal bowls, silver trays, arrangements of dried flowers under glass domes causing a resounding
and echoing cacophony that served as a strident counterpoint to the
soft thud of reciprocal blows.

At one point Burke thought he heard a woman's outcry, but as
Eden had just delivered a series of ringing blows to his right ear,
there was no time to look, for the boy who had appeared weak and
passive had suddenly turned into a dynamo of strength.

The two had just exchanged a painful volley of blows when he
heard a man's voice, indignant, coming from the parlor door.

Suddenly he felt strong arms grab him from behind and hold him
fast. At the same time he saw young Eden jerked back, arms pinned
in similar fashion. Eden struggled and cursed once, but it did no
good. When Burke saw Eden's captors, two strapping young field
hands, he could only guess at his own, and he looked up toward the
door to see a full gallery of frightened faces. Paris was there. Apparently he'd encountered Ben and Dr. Melrose on the road beyond
Stanhope Hall and had just returned. And Mary was there, a handkerchief pressed against her lips as though to prevent another outcry.
And there was Eve, just arriving, her long hair still loosed, a thin
dressing gown wrapped about her shoulders, and old Florence in hot
and irate pursuit.

Burke's neck ached. His head throbbed. He tasted blood and his
ribs hurt every time he breathed. He looked across at Eden, who in
turn glared back, his face looking even worse than Burke's felt.

Now for the first time he noticed the shambles that once had been
the parlor: furniture shattered, glass broken, fabrics torn; and Mary's
pride, a silk oriental fire screen with a table leg punched through the
center. He and the boy would mend. The fire screen would not.

"Have you lost your mind?"

The simple question had been posed by Dr. Melrose, a short, squat,
heavy-set balding man who at one time or another had taken care of
everyone who inhabited Stanhope Plantation.

"My God, look at you," the wheezing voice went on. "And who's
this one?"

There was a pause before Mary answered. "My nephew. Our house
guest. From England."

The information seemed to work a strange effect on Dr. Melrose.
"Is it a family tradition," he asked of Burke, "to beat each other senseless upon greeting?"

Burke pulled free from the two black men. Paris came forward, looking worried and puzzled. "Thank you and that's all," Paris said to the four workers who'd been pressed into service.

Everyone waited quietly until the four men had left the room, as though by consensus not wanting them to witness any further lunacy on the part of the master of Stanhope Hall.

As soon as they were gone, Dr. Melrose took charge again. "The rest of you go on back to your duties as well, all of you, I mean it," he said to the small knot of people who'd gathered at the parlor door. "Eve, you too. Florence, take her."

From where Burke stood he sensed his daughter's protest, but Florence and Mary combined were too much for her. When he glanced back a few moments later the doorway was empty of all save Mary and Paris.

Burke endured their silent condemnation for several moments, hoping someone would speak. "Paris, take him to his room," he commanded, indicating Eden opposite him, who, while bloodied, looked no less insolent.

"No, thank you, Mr. Stanhope. I will be returning to Mobile immediately. If you will tell me where I can find my horse, I'll—"

A perfect suggestion. Nothing could have pleased Burke more. Therefore he was at a loss to understand Mary's protest.

"No," she said, coming forward. "No, Mr. Eden, please," she implored, taking his hand. "I have no idea what transpired here, who was at fault, who to blame. Probably neither, perhaps both, but I'm certain that if we all just persist a bit longer, we'll find a proper and hospitable and perhaps even loving way in which to welcome you as you should be welcomed."

"I don't think I should stay."

"Of course you should. Where else would you go?"

As Mary's soft voice filled the parlor, Burke began to feel his own injuries in the form of a throbbing lip and eye, and as he turned away to wait out his physical discomforts, he felt shame and wondered what had come over him and whether he could ever explain it to Mary.

At the thought of her he looked back and saw her assisting young Eden to the door, where Paris was waiting to receive him.

"Now, you—"

At the sound of the voice Burke turned to find Mary at his side, smiling up at him as though nothing had happened.

"Come," she urged and took his arm and gave the destroyed room only a passing glance and walked with him to the door where he saw Dr. Melrose, his old lined face tight with repressed anger.

"The other one will live. Let's see you."

As his pudgy fingers started toward Burke's face in examination, Burke pulled away. "I'm afraid we'll both live," he muttered.

"That eye will swell."

"No doubt."

"Get some ice on it right away. You made a fool of yourself, you know."

Burke stopped in his slow progress to the staircase. Unfortunately what Melrose had said was true; therefore, rebuttal was difficult.

In the tense moment Mary retreated to the side of the corridor. Beyond Dr. Melrose's shoulder, Burke saw Katie and Dorie slip into the parlor with brooms and dust pans. Apparently restoration had already started.

"I was—sorry to learn of your difficulties this morning," Melrose went on, rolling down his shirtsleeves as he spoke.

Difficulties. It seemed such a polite word to cover such a tragic and senseless death.

Then Burke remembered. "Would you look in on Fan Cottage, Dr. Melrose? Sis Liz might need—"

"Of course."

"And when did you hear about it?" Burke asked.

The old doctor looked up, still fussing with his shirt cuff. "It's all over the county."

"So soon?"

"It was a dreadful thing."

"Yes."

Burke continued to watch the old man. He seemed ill at ease. How could news of White Doll's death be "all over"? It was scarcely past noon, and no one except Ben had left Stanhope Hall since early morning.

"Well, if you'll excuse me. If you're certain you need no—"

"I need nothing."

"Then—I'll—"

The old man *was* unduly nervous.

"I'll go out the back way."

"Yes, of course."

Shirtsleeves restored, Dr. Melrose swung into his ill-fitting black coat and grasped his worn black leather bag and started off at a good pace toward the back gallery and the blazing sun beyond.

How had he known? The only ones who would know what had transpired today at Stanhope Hall would be the men who had planned the crime and those who had executed it.

For several moments Burke stood rigid, staring at the empty rectangle of sun at the end of the corridor.

"Burke?"

At the sound of Mary's voice a new weariness swept over him. It
was one of the tragic by-products of this sad day that from now on he
would punish himself with doubt at every turn.

"Come, Burke, you need rest."

Why didn't she scold, as she had every right to do?

"Oh, Mary. Sometimes I'm—"

"I know. Come on; let's go upstairs."

"The Eden boy—"

"Will stay for dinner. Then I suspect he will leave."

At the bottom of the step she slipped her arm about his waist and
invited, "Lean on me," and the invitation was so sweetly spoken and
the events of the morning so saturated with death, not just White
Doll's death, but the death of trust and faith, that Burke felt suddenly
moved by her closeness.

Without warning and despite his various bruises, he bent over and
picked her up in his arms and waited out her surprised protest, which
slowly faded.

A brief healing interim, that's all he needed, the joy of giving and
receiving love. Apparently her needs matched his, for at the top of
the steps, in the privacy of the corridor that led to their suite, she
kissed him, kissed his bruises, his swollen eye and cheek, while at the
same time her fingers were already moving down the front of his
shirtwaist.

How many times in the past they'd taken refuge in their great four-
poster bed against the assaults and offenses of life beyond Stanhope
Hall. Then they'd do it again, though this time he doubted if they
would achieve anything more than a temporary relief. The enemy
was too large, too faceless, too lacking in conscience or decency or
morality or any of the characteristics upon which a civilized world
ought to be built.

* * *

Paris still was unable to determine the cause of the fight or how
serious were the man's wounds. He seemed more angry than hurt,
though there was considerable blood on his face, down his neck,
staining his shirt.

"In here, I believe. At least this is the one Mrs. Stanhope said." He
stood before the appointed door and tried to recall her hastily whispered instructions.

Take Mr. Eden up to the guest room at the south end of the second-floor corridor on the right.

Stanhope Hall was larger than his entire dormitory at Tuskegee. But he was certain this was it, though now Mr. Eden seemed loathe to enter. Paris opened the door further and stood back and watched what appeared to be fresh anger move across his face and felt a mild resentment of his own. One of the last pieces of advice Mr. Washington had given him only this morning was that he should not allow himself to be pressed into any service save that for which he had been trained.

Be vigilant. Don't let them misuse you. You are your own responsibility.

At first Paris hadn't taken the admonition seriously. Now he'd been in residence at Stanhope Hall for less than a day and already he'd been sent on errands, helped to break up a fight, and now he was a porter, showing woebegone guests to their rooms.

Still, despite Mr. Washington's advice, something deep inside him counseled patience. The day was at odds with harmony, and perhaps he, Paris Boley, was the cause.

"Are you well? Would you like—"

"What's your name?"

The direct question, spoken with such vigor, surprised Paris. "My name is Paris Boley."

"What is your relationship to this house?"

Another curious question, and what a strange pattern of speech. Paris had never heard anything like it before, clipped, harsh, arrogant-sounding, like a too-starched shirt.

"I—work for Mr. Stanhope," he said by way of reply.

Mr. Eden stood at the exact center of the room and winced slightly as he massaged his chest in the vicinity of his ribs.

"Would you like me to fetch Dr. Melrose again?"

"I've seen him."

"He examined your face, not your ribs."

"I'm fine."

But as he made this claim, he appeared to be searching for a place to sit and found it in a gingham flounced chair near the dead fireplace. Paris watched as he made his way across the room and sat with even greater deliberation, a grimace covering his face, head back, at last staring straight up at the ceiling.

"The man is insane. Did you know that?"

Paris blinked at the quiet statement. "I—beg your pardon?"

"I said the man is insane. Mr. Stanhope is insane."

Paris saw the man in profile only, slumped as he was in the chair. But something about the voice, the accusation, the remembered destruction in the downstairs parlor—all these things informed Paris that it was time to leave. "If you'll excuse me . . ."

"Wait." A new grimace covered his face as he turned too rapidly in his chair. "I'm sorry. I didn't mean to offend you as well."

"You didn't."

"I just don't understand what happened down there."

"You obviously offended Mr. Stanhope."

"*I* offended him?" the man repeated incredulously, and painfully drew himself up on the edge of the chair, an effort that left him with head bowed. From this muffled position he asked, "How long have you known the Stanhope family?"

"All my life. I was born here. Mr. Stanhope sent me to school. I'm now general manager of Stanhope Plantation."

"For how long?" the man asked, still holding his side.

Paris hesitated. "Since—this morning."

Silence. Then:

"Come in, close the door. Sit, please."

The invitation was polite and seemed sincere. Should he? How would it hurt for just a moment?

Slowly he closed the door behind him and walked to the chair where the man sat, keeping his eyes on the battered face opposite him, feeling somehow more and more, based on absolutely nothing of substance, that it was a face he could trust.

"I'm Stephen Eden," the man said and extended his hand.

Paris took it and felt a firm grip. Handshake over, Eden leaned back. "Clearly they weren't expecting me," he said and gingerly rubbed the side of his head.

Paris felt a quick smile break the tension. "What *did* happen?"

Eden shrugged. "I was talking to my aunt, Mrs. Stanhope, and suddenly she left the room and that madman charged in."

His bewilderment was sincere. Now Paris began to share it. Mr. Stanhope was noted for his reason, his patience and his understanding. "What did you say?"

"Nothing. I swear it."

"It's been a difficult day."

"I can imagine."

"I arrived only last evening from Tuskegee."

"Clearly we've entered a hostile world, both of us."

Paris smiled. "I was warned."

"Who warned you?"

"Mr. Washington."

"And who is that?"

"He's—my teacher, my guide, my adviser, my—"

Eden smiled and interrupted. "Your God?"

"*He* would not approve of the description."

The brief conversation died, and Paris felt new tension.

"So much for gods on earth," Eden said finally. "Why would Mr. Stanhope attack me?"

"Are you sure you said nothing?"

"I swear it."

"Could you remind him of someone?"

Paris started to say more, but he was stopped by the expression on Eden's face.

"That's it," he exclaimed.

"What's it?"

"I remind him of someone."

"Who?"

"My father, who else?"

Paris saw a kind of bewildered pleasure on his face now, saw him lean back in his chair again, an expression of concentration on his face as though he were trying to work out all the small details of memory.

Then suddenly, "Enough," Eden pronounced. "Tell me of yourself and how you came to be in this present dangerous position?"

Not only the proposition but the question itself caught Paris off guard.

"Come on, I suspect we both could use a friend. I know I could. I'm not going anyplace, at least for a while, and unless you have other—"

"No."

"Then come. Tell me of yourself. I stand in complete admiration of your bravery. How much courage it must take to pay no attention to the color of one's skin when everyone else is paying sharp and singular attention to nothing else."

His manner of speaking still fascinated Paris, and he was beginning to discover that he didn't have to listen quite so closely. The words, though starched, were beginning to be more easily understood. What truly fascinated Paris was Eden's sincere invitation to speak of personal matters. He tried hard to remember if anyone had ever, in his entire life, invited him to speak freely and at length on only one subject: himself. No one had.

Feeling self-conscious, Paris laughed, one short sharp relief of tension. "I'm very much aware of the color of my skin, Mr. Eden."

"But you don't seem to let it make any difference."

"Do you?"

"Of course not. Does this Mr. Washington know of this group of rampaging white men?"

"He was here when they came earlier this morning. Mr. Stanhope is a loyal supporter of Tuskegee, a college for black students. The two had spent the night in talk, planning new fund-raising ventures."

"What did he do—Mr. Washington, I mean?"

"He did nothing. Of course he did not know then of White Doll's death."

For the first time since Paris had assisted with the lowering of the pine coffin into the hastily dug grave, his mind betrayed him and presented him with a painful recollection of White Doll, alive and laughing.

"Look, I'm sorry—"

A moment later Eden asked, "Will you be staying here at Stanhope Hall?"

"Of course. If Mr. Stanhope permits me to stay."

"What if the men return?"

"Oh, they undoubtedly will. Most of them don't even know of my appointment as general manager."

"Then what was this morning all about?"

"They were serving notice on Mr. Stanhope for past offenses."

"Which are?"

"He does business with the North."

"Is that bad?"

"If you're from the South, it is."

"The war is over. Has anyone told them?"

"Not here it isn't."

They stared at each other across the length of the room.

"Then you're in danger," Eden said quietly.

Paris returned his gaze, amazed at how easy it was talking to him. "Perhaps. It was my hope, my intention, to go about my work quietly."

"That might be difficult for a manager."

Paris started to respond and changed his mind and paced now in front of the broad windows. His view was limited. The west side of Stanhope Hall had no vista, only the beginning of the woods that surrounded Fan Cottage. New memory, new defeat.

"I'm sorry." Again Eden apparently had observed the alteration on Paris's face.

"I'm all right. How long will you be at Stanhope Hall?"

Eden answered with a directness that startled. "I promised my aunt I'd stay for dinner. Then it's back to Mobile."

"Then where?"

"West."

"West where?"

"The western part of America—Montana, specifically."

Paris fought envy. All his life he'd dreamed of journeying to the Pacific Ocean, across the entire width of this country. It was only a dream, nothing more, and would never come true. Still geography and social history had been his favorite disciplines in school, and names such as El Paso and Dodge City and San Francisco were capable of making his head spin.

"West," he repeated, the word alone capable of working magic in his system.

Eden nodded. "Business, primarily for my uncle, Mr. Stanhope's brother-in-law. He invested in Montana cattle two years ago and has received one semiannual report and nothing more."

"What happened?"

Eden smiled. "That's what I'm supposed to find out."

He reached into his pocket and withdrew a small white card. "I'm to locate a man by the name of G.H. Teats." He looked up at Paris. "Do you know what the *G.H.* stands for?"

Paris shook his head.

"Grasshopper; Grasshopper Teats."

Paris grinned. "Shouldn't be too hard to find once you get there. How are you traveling?"

"Mr. Stanhope was going to assist me with travel plans. Now . . ."

"He will. If he promised. He is an honorable man. Mr. Washington claims that Tuskegee wouldn't have been built without him."

Eden seemed on the verge of asking further questions but apparently changed his mind and walked to the windows, which gave a view of the woods.

"Look!"

The whispered command came from Stephen Eden, who apparently had seen something that attracted his attention.

Paris arrived at the window in time to see the hem of a flowing white robe disappear into the woods.

"Wait. It'll come again," Eden promised, his voice low, though filled with a sense of excitement.

As they waited, both focused on the woods, Paris's mind kept going back to Eden's earlier revelation that he was soon to be traveling westward. "Will you be going as far as San Francisco?"

Stephen looked up. "Probably. Well, I don't actually know. Montana is the main destination. What happens after that, I—"

As he spoke he kept his eyes on the woods and now gave Paris a nudge. "Look, there."

"Sis Liz," Paris said calmly, having suspected as much from the beginning. She didn't generally wander this far from Fan Cottage, but this day was not ordinary.

Now in further response to the perplexed look on Eden's face, Paris explained, "Mr. Stanhope's aunt, his father's sister. She lives in Fan Cottage. White Doll was her companion."

"The murdered woman."

Paris nodded and looked down, only to find the woods empty again. Sis Liz *was* wandering far afield. Someone should go and take her home. Besides, Paris had thought Dr. Melrose was with her.

"I'd better go and see to her," Paris said and started toward the door.

"May I come?"

The request startled him. He looked back. "I believe Mrs. Stanhope thought you might need a period of rest."

"I'm fine. Eve told me of an ice pond not far from here. If you could direct me there, or better still join me, a cool dip would soothe all wounds."

Paris smiled. The thought had occurred to him as well. He would see if he could find Sis Liz and return her to Fan Cottage. Then they'd take a cooling dip, help clear both their heads, and perhaps Eden would tell him more of his forthcoming journey.

At the door Paris stopped. "Anything wrong?" Eden asked.

"Did you mean it?" Paris asked.

"Mean what?"

"The invitation to join you in the ice pond?"

Eden appeared baffled. "It's not my pond. I don't even know how to get there. If we go, you'll have to show me the way."

The two men held a steady gaze for a moment. Despite his strange manner of speaking, Paris liked this Englishman.

"*Do* you know where it is?" Eden asked.

Paris laughed. "I've spent half my life in it. It's the coolest water in all of Alabama—in all the world—fed by an underground spring."

"Then what are we waiting for?"

The grin was as natural and sincere as the invitation had been, as was everything about Eden. It was as if his only failing was his eyesight, lacking that built-in Southern reaction to any dark face.

But then he wasn't a Southerner, was he, thus confirming Paris's long-time suspicion and dream: that beyond the borders of this South there was a different world, a different breed of men who did not view the Negro as a problem to be solved or done away with.

"I should try to find Sis Liz first," Paris said.

"I'll help."

Paris looked at him and led the way from the guest room, feeling his heart lift and lighten for the first time in this bleak day.

* * *

While daytime intimacy was not Mary's favorite—there were too many possibilities for interruption—the day and Burke's needs had seemed acute, so she'd allowed him to carry her to their bedchamber, had tended to his facial wounds, which were minor, except for the swelling left eye. Then she had disrobed, had kicked off the heavy dress, still dust smudged from the morning, had splashed cool lavender water over her body, had released her hair from atop her head and had at last looked up to see Burke stretched out atop the coverlet, looking exhausted and lost.

The act of love had been quick and silent, as though both had needed the intimacy simply to confirm their own aliveness.

As he rolled, newly exhausted, to one side, she drew up her knees and thought of the thousand and one jobs that needed doing in Stanhope Hall, starting with the damaged parlor downstairs, and wondered whether to ask him about the fight with Stephen Eden. She decided that not to ask right now might be more considerate.

As she started up from the bed, he reached for her arm. "Please. Don't go."

"There's so much to do."

"I'm sorry for what happened."

She was aware of his fingers on her back, playing with her hair in a gentle loving caress. She started away, and again he grasped her arm, a gentle restraint filled with need of a different sort.

"I didn't mean to strike him, I swear it."

"Did he say something to provoke you?"

Burke shoved a pillow beneath his head and grimaced as though the rapid movement had caused new discomfort. "Something?" he repeated. "Everything he said provoked me."

Mary sat on the edge of the high feather bed, her feet dangling, and reached for her dressing gown. "I understand," she murmured. "He disturbed me as well."

"There, you see? I thought so. What did he say?"

She heard relief in his voice, clearly pleased that his assault had been justified after all.

"He said nothing," she replied, looking directly at him. "There was no need. The shock is in the remarkable physical likeness. He could be John Murrey Eden thirty years ago."

Burke sat up, nodding agreement, and supported himself carefully on one hand.

"But I'm convinced the resemblance is only physical," she said. "He seems to be a most gentle and unassuming young man. Obviously John's wife had a hand in raising him."

She was aware of the look of confusion on his face as slowly he lowered himself back down to the pillow. "I saw nothing of gentleness," he muttered and drew the coverlet over himself as though her words had just helped create a new barrier between them. When he spoke again his voice was measured. "I want nothing more to do with him, do you understand? It's what happened this morning before he came that we must not pass over lightly. We must take steps to protect ourselves. The problem is not Stephen Eden. He is merely an annoyance. The problem came riding in on us at dawn this morning."

She looked down on him. "Talk to me. I'm not sure I fully understand."

"I know you don't, and I want you to listen. It's important that you help me warn the others."

He sat up again and confronted her across the mussed bed. His left eye was swelling, and even before he spoke, Mary suddenly understood the physical violence that had occurred in the downstairs parlor. Stephen Eden had been a readily available target, while the true culprits had hidden under hoods of cowardice and anonymity.

"I told you earlier, they will return," Burke said. "I don't know when and I have no idea what they'll do next. But you must warn the children as well as the house servants."

"Against what? What do they look for?"

"Strangers. Men who approach them, perhaps in friendship, seeking their help."

"Why aren't you informing the authorities?"

"Because it's my guess that the authorities already know."

Slowly she felt the effects of new terror. She returned Burke's gaze. "What shall we do?" she whispered.

"Be vigilant," he said. "I must speak with Taylor Quitman."

"Can he be trusted?"

Burke shrugged.

"What if they return?"

"We'll try to be ready. I would like you to convince Sis Liz that she must move out of Fan Cottage and back into Stanhope Hall. She presents a ready target."

"She won't do that."

"If she and White Doll hadn't been alone out there this morning— if they had had the protection of this house—"

Mary understood. But she also understood Sis Liz and her love of

Fan Cottage, which would become even more important to her now after White Doll's death.

"Burke—"

"It will be all right," he soothed. "I must be up now. You too. I'm going into Mobile to see if I can find Taylor Quitman."

She watched as he moved away from the bed and into his dressing room. She thought of Taylor Quitman, his attorney, a trusted friend for years, a regular visitor to Stanhope Hall, Eve's godfather. Surely Taylor Quitman could be trusted.

"Bring him back for dinner," she called out. "He might be of service to Stephen."

There was no sound coming from the small dressing room on the left side of the room. "Burke? Did you hear?"

He appeared in the doorway, towel in hand. "I won't be back in time for dinner."

"Burke, please. He is not John. How would it hurt to help him? He'll only be here a short time."

"Any length of time is too long where he is concerned."

Mary gaped at her husband. As Burke retreated back into the dressing room, she stood and drew the knot on her dressing gown cord tight.

"I'll ask Taylor Quitman to put him on the first train heading west. Then we'll see the end of him and good riddance."

Burke reappeared and spoke with effort, all the while drawing on his hose, then his boots, stopping along the way, to Mary's annoyance, to polish the tips of his black boots with the silken hem of the bedspread.

"I won't send him away, Burke, and you have no right to ask me to do so."

She started to say more and realized their voices were rising and realized it would serve no purpose to continue this discussion, though it angered her that he would not accommodate her on this one matter.

"Please, Burke," she whispered, standing only a few feet before him, employing such a different tone of voice that he looked up.

"Please what?"

"Return in time for dinner. I'll set the hour late. Nine o'clock if you wish. Bring Taylor—bring anyone—everyone—only please be here. It will mean a great deal to me."

For a moment their gaze held. He shook his head. "I can't believe it. The number of threats that have been leveled at this house this day, the tragedy, the sorrow, and we argue about a dinner for an Englishman neither of us has ever met before."

As he piled absurdity upon absurdity, he continued to shake his head. When he ceased talking, without ever giving her his word that he would return for the evening, she watched him draw on his linen riding jacket, pocket his riding gloves and start toward the door.

"Burke—"

Her entreaty stopped him. "For just this once," she began, holding her position near the bed. "Help me emerge triumphant over the past. And the only way I can do that—the only way any of us can do that—is to forgive whatever sins have been committed against us."

"I did nothing to John Murrey Eden."

"It is not John Murrey Eden who is now beneath our roof."

"The same—"

"Not the same."

Now she sensed his growing impatience at the door and suspected that nothing could alter his attitude or change his mind. On this note of resignation she turned away, feeling indescribably weary, and sat on the edge of the bed on which they had only moments before made love.

She knew he had not yet departed. She could sense his presence.

"Remember what I told you," he said. "Keep the children close by. Don't let them wander. I'll tell Paris to place men at the end of the lane. I don't think they'll come back today."

She interrupted for two reasons. One, she didn't want to hear, and two, he had yet to give her an answer. "Burke, will you please promise to—"

"I promise nothing," he replied, too sharply. Then he was gone, closing the door behind him. The echo of his words left her drained.

She lay slowly back across the bed and stared up at the high canopy. It was the day, a nightmare of a day. Why had Burke denied her and denied himself as well the healing power of forgiveness?

But the question died unanswered as a loud knock sounded at the door and the unmistakable voice of Mrs. Winegar cut through the silence.

"Madame, I need your wishes for this evening."

There was a slight trace of a German accent in the voice, which was fading in the years since she'd served as cook for Stanhope Hall. *I need your wishes* was Mrs. Winegar's euphemism for "tell me what to prepare for the evening meal."

"Just a moment, please," Mary called out and sat up quickly and drew her dressing gown more securely about herself.

Burke was gone, but she was here, left to pull this large household together as best she could.

Sometimes, like now, standing alone in the middle of her bedchamber, she wondered how she had come to be here, in this place, with this man and these children, in this country. It was a bewildering sense of lostness, as though she were merely playing another woman's role and would shortly return to the real place where she belonged.

* * *

At first Eve had been angry when Florence dragged her away from downstairs and asked her to stay with her sister Christine, who was upset by the household.

But Eve had peeked out of her door long enough to know the fight had ended, that Paris had escorted the beautiful Mr. Eden to an upstairs guest chamber. Now as she stretched out across her bed—she'd brought Christine into her own bedchamber, which afforded a perfect view of the road and front lane—Eve began to relax and listen to her sister's sweet, high, piping voice speaking of the most incredible things.

"And in the dream I saw hundreds of men, Eve, I really did, burly, unwashed men, not men like Papa, and they all were standing up and shouting and the night was alive with stars."

Propped on her elbow, Eve listened. An enchantress, that's what Sis Liz and White Doll called Christine. She was eight now, but she had been born sickly, fluid on her lungs, and according to Sis Liz, she would not live a full life. But for the brief period of time she would spend on this earth, she would be granted powers the rest of the world would never possess.

Eve adored her, had from the moment of her birth, when Florence had placed her in Eve's arms, a small, red-splotched infant, so weak, though one tiny fist had reached up to Eve's face and their bond of love had been sealed.

"And then what happened?" Eve asked.

Christine turned sideways and looked at her. "I—don't remember," she said flatly. "But you were in it. I remember very clearly seeing you, though not like you are now. You were so beautiful, and all the men were smiling at you and you were singing for them."

Eve lay back beside Christine. "It sounds awful," she said. She rubbed her bare leg and relaxed even more, though she still was curious about the grim scene she'd only briefly witnessed downstairs, her father and Stephen Eden in physical combat. What the cause was she had no idea, and at first, after Florence had sent her up to stay with Christine, she had been terrified that her father would order Stephen Eden out of Stanhope Hall and she would never see him again.

But he was still here, she knew it; and feeling confident that she would see him again, Eve laced her hands behind her head and invited Christine to "go on, what happened next?"

She felt Christine push lightly against her as though cuddling for security. "I told you, I don't remember. But it was a place I had never seen before, not even in books. There were no trees, no houses, no buildings, no water, no flowers, no—"

As the list of negatives grew, Eve laughed. "What *was* there?"

"Nothing, Eve, I told you. Didn't you listen? You were there, and hundreds of shouting, laughing men and lots of stars in a black night and that was all."

Quickly Christine rolled onto her stomach and peered down on Eve over propped elbows. "You weren't unhappy in the dream," she went on thoughtfully. "Sometimes I dream about people and all I can remember from the dream is their unhappiness."

"I just wish you could remember it all so I would know what to look forward to. What happened? You usually remember all your dreams down to the smallest detail."

Christine looked equally perplexed. "Halfway through the dream, something else happened."

So noticeable was the alteration in her voice and manner that Eve looked directly at her. "What do you mean, something happened?"

"I was in another world, not your world of men and black stars."

"I don't understand."

"Neither did I, and I didn't like the new world, although it was very familiar. I knew everything, I could even sniff familiar fragrances, and I wasn't lost at all. I knew where I was, but—"

Suddenly she broke off. Her head fell forward until it was resting on Eve's breast. "I was so scared, Eve. I was alone in the woods—"

"Which woods?"

"Our woods. I was on the way to Fan Cottage and I shouldn't have been there, not alone. Mama had just told me not to go alone."

Eve listened closely, newly alert. "What happened?" she prompted, sensing that it was important for Christine to speak of this dream.

"White Doll—"

"What about White Doll?"

"She was there, in the woods with me. But—"

During this pause Eve wondered if anyone had informed Christine of the events of the morning. She doubted it. Christine generally slept late, then took her morning porridge with Madame Germaine, who launched into morning studies while Christine's energies were at their peak. She tired so easily. So how could she know?

"Eve, will you go with me to Fan Cottage? I want to see White Doll."

Her face lifted, so frightened. Eve returned her gaze. "Now? No, I don't—"

"Please, Eve, you must. White Doll is in trouble. She's hurt. I feel it so acutely, and it's growing stronger. She needs me."

Stunned, Eve could only gape. "What—else did you see in your dream?"

"I couldn't see," Christine whispered and wiped away the beginning of tears. "It was so dark. Sis Liz told me once that the darkest place in this world was our woods on a moonless night."

"Was Sis Liz in the dream?"

"No, at least I didn't see her. I was there alone."

"Except for White Doll."

"White Doll wasn't there. She was—"

Christine broke off, apparently bewildered by her own contradictions. "Oh, I don't know. Eve, come with me, please. White Doll needs us. I can hear her calling."

"Can you still see her?"

"I—think so. No, yes, oh, I wish—"

Suddenly it was as though a new wave of fatigue had swept over Christine. She pushed back from Eve's side and fell flat on her back, arms limp, her forehead dotted with perspiration, breathing too hard.

"I can't remember any more," she whispered. "I—don't want to."

As Eve stared down at her sister, she found herself resentful of the prison of Christine's existence. If Eve had been denied some aspects of the world, Christine had been denied all aspects of it. She seemed to creep further back into her loneliness and sit quietly, and not mind what had been taken from her.

Suddenly Christine's head turned, her eyes opened. "Listen, there's something on our front lawn." As she spoke, she struggled up.

"What are you talking about?" Eve gently protested, trying to calm her down.

"No, come," Christine insisted. "Something good, something beautiful. Oh, hurry, Eve, help me."

She'd already struggled to the edge of the bed. Eve stood in order to get out of her way. But the bed was high, and the small, thin legs were weak. As she stepped down, she would have fallen had Eve not stepped quickly forward and grabbed her.

Christine continued to drag herself and Eve to the open doors, not stopping until she reached the balcony. Both stared down at the front lawns of Stanhope Hall, where nothing was moving except the play of sun and shadow and the ever-present din of the cicadas and bluejays.

Then, softly, she heard voices coming around the left wing of Stanhope Hall, male voices, talking low, steady.

"Look!" Christine whispered, her face alive with pleasurable excitement.

Eve followed the direction of her hand. Two men had just emerged in clear view. One, Paris Boley, looked at ease minus his jacket, his blousy white shirtwaist pulled free, carrying something white draped over his shoulder. Next to him—

"Oh, Eve, look! I told you we would see something beautiful."

Now Eve saw clearly the broad shoulders and remarkable gait of Stephen Eden, who, like Paris, had left his jacket somewhere and now held a large white towel loosely over his shoulder.

"Who is he, Eve? Do you know? Is he a friend of Papa's?"

Eve tried to answer Christine's questions, never taking her eyes off the two men, who were heading toward the ice pond and a refreshing summer afternoon dip.

"I know him." Eve nodded with a degree of pride. "He's our cousin. His name is Stephen Eden and he is—"

"Mama's?"

"Yes. From England."

"Does Papa know?"

"He knows." Apparently Christine had overheard an earlier heated discussion.

"Eve, may I meet him? Please?"

"Of course you'll meet him."

"Now?"

"No, not know. They're going bathing. They—"

"Look."

Christine pointed down at David now, coming from the direction of the ice pond, Cleo and Casey behind him. As the boys saw the two men approaching, they stopped and stood self-consciously to one side of the path.

Paris greeted them first. Cleo and Casey ducked their heads. Then Stephen Eden moved forward with ease and immediately shook each boy's hand after Paris's introduction.

"Look at David," Eve whispered, amazed at how grown up her little brother appeared. When had he grown so tall? And when had he started bearing such a remarkable resemblance to Papa?

Suddenly the sound of male laughter punctuated the hot, still August afternoon. Eve saw them all laughing at something Stephen Eden had said. Then, though the three boys had obviously just completed their bathing, they reversed their direction and joined the two on the path heading for the ice pond a short distance away.

All three boys seemed to be jockeying for the position nearest to

Stephen Eden, who continued to talk, gesturing on both sides, every comment leaving his audience weak with laughter.

"I wish we could be down there with them," Christine whispered.

Then a revolutionary thought occurred. Why not? It might do Christine a world of good. Oh, not literally to go bathing with them, but to watch, from some safe place of concealment close by. Why not? They'd all keep their knickers on, of that Eve was certain.

"Eve, what's the matter?"

"Nothing," she soothed and drew Christine close. "Do you feel up to an adventure?"

The instantaneous light in Christine's eyes provided her with a ready answer.

"Then come on. Let's raid my wardrobe. I have the very thing for you."

Slowly Christine's eyes widened, as did the irrepressible grin on her face. For a moment Eve saw nothing that resembled a chronically ill child. Instead this "invalid" dashed to Eve's large wardrobe, already begging, "Let me wear your new straw, Eve. I tried it on last week. It fits, it really does."

Eve wasn't certain which pleased her more, Christine's enthusiastic response or the awareness that she was going to see Stephen Eden again close at hand. As she joined Christine at the wardrobe, her excitement briefly faltered and from someplace within her surfaced a responsible adult thought. They must not be seen by anyone and could only stay for a few moments. There was a thick hedge of lilac bushes that bordered the ice pond on one side. The foliage would afford them complete protection.

"This one, Eve, this is the one I meant," and Christine held up a broad-brimmed straw hat with a red plaid ribbon that Eve's mother had purchased for her last year in Mobile. Now Christine put it on her head. Though ill-fitting, it did shade her face completely.

"What shall I wear?" Christine asked, her enthusiasm still mounting.

"Your night dress will do, because I'm going to carry you."

"You can't carry me, Eve."

"I can and I will. Now be patient while I dress, and we'll be off."

Carefully she directed Christine to a chair beside the wardrobe and allowed her to hold on to the broad-brimmed straw hat and was amazed at the color newly risen in her cheeks.

Through the crack in the wardrobe door, she saw Christine preening comically in the straw hat, wearing it at a cocked angle, her small face arched into the haughty contours of a lady, her voluminous white nightshirt adding to the silly spectacle.

Eve grinned and was grateful for at least one thing. Again Stephen Eden had somehow managed to temper the fear and sorrow of this day.

"Come on, let's go," Eve whispered and scooped up the giggling Christine and started out at a good pace toward the door, amazed at how eager she was to see Stephen Eden again.

 ## Mobile

From his second-floor law office over the Mobile Security and Exchange Bank, Taylor Quitman looked down on the dusty commerce of Peeler Street and caught sight of Burke Stanhope while he was still a block away. There was an arrogance to the gentleman as he rode his white stallion named Cotton Man, a handsome horse that stood out from the other horses of the crowded street. But it was more than that. It was how Stanhope rode him, as though he were a medieval knight, man and horse erect with the conviction of their rightness in this world.

Taylor Quitman smiled. He knew Burke would be in his office today, knew that something had offended that impractical Stanhope sense of rightness and knew that at last all the years of trust he had carefully built would now pay off.

To the three men waiting in his office with him he said simply, "He's coming," and all men stood with identical speed, Reverend Pounders knocking his chair noisily into the bookcase, Zach Hennessey and Joel Peterson meeting, then colliding at the narrow door.

"Gentlemen," Taylor Quitman scolded. "No need for haste. He's a full block away, and as is his custom, he will stable his horse at Twains and then will take a few minutes to wash the dirt of the road from his hands and his face."

"Still," Reverend Pounders protested, "we should take our concealment. I want the matter done. It's been a long and very difficult day."

The two at the door nodded in agreement. Zach Hennessey reached for the notebook that he'd left on the corner of Taylor's desk, a code ledger belonging to the Knights of the White Camellia. "Are you certain we'll be able to hear everything?" he asked, nervously peering around the corner and into Taylor's small law library. "It seems a distance."

"Would you care to test it, gentlemen?"

Joel Peterson said nervously, "There's no time."

"Of course there is time. Fifteen minutes at most is my guess.

Come, let me show you a lawyer's trick. We call it the solicitor's confessional. Come, all of you."

Aware that he was the only one exhibiting any enthusiasm for the impending meeting, Taylor Quitman led the way around the corner of his office and into the musty stacks of his law library. Just inside the door he found the candle box and matches and lit a candle and lifted the limited illumination high for the benefit of those behind him.

"Here," Taylor Quitman said and led the way down the long narrow room, brushing aside the cobwebs, realizing he'd not used either his library or his "solicitor's confessional" in some time. It required a special case with special needs, like this one.

"Damn hot," Zach Hennessey complained.

"No windows," Joel Peterson observed.

"I doubt if it will be a long meeting," Taylor Quitman promised. "Here 'tis." And carefully he placed the candle to one side and withdrew a half-dozen heavy law books and in the process revealed a patch of wall approximately two feet by two feet in which the wall section itself had been removed and neatly replaced with thin wire mesh.

"Behold, gentlemen," Taylor Quitman said as he gestured toward the opening. "On the other side of this wire mesh is a faded print of Mr. Rembrandt's *Prodigal Son*, of no real value, I assure you, and beyond Mr. Rembrandt's print is my office."

The three men pushed close, Reverend Pounders in the lead.

"But can we hear?"

"Everything. Including the dropping of a pin."

"Will he know?"

"Nothing. But I warn you, you must remain absolutely silent."

As all three men continued their close inspection of the unique room, Taylor could see the questions forming on their faces and tried to answer them before their moral indignation escalated to a dangerous level.

"I don't use it often," he reassured them. "My father swore by it, however, and found it most helpful in difficult cases."

"How? I don't understand." The question was Zach Hennessey's. The bewilderment was everyone's.

"Oh, it's ever so useful in any number of ways," Taylor Quitman hurriedly explained. "A client reluctant to speak directly to a lawyer will speak volumes to a companion when the lawyer vacates the room. Or my father's favorite use of it was to invite the prosecuting attorneys in for a conciliatory chat, then conveniently be called out of the room, thus freeing the enemy to discuss future tactics and strategies. How many times he defeated his opponents with their own battle plans."

The memory was pleasant. Taylor had worshiped his father, a true son of the South who, in all matters, had performed with dignity.

"Not quite ethical, if you ask me," Joel Peterson muttered. "Doubt if I'll ever trust a lawyer again. Not that I ever trusted them before."

Taylor started to answer the criticism but decided against it. Time was of the essence. "Now hold steady," he warned, "and say nothing. I'll let Stanhope talk, and then together we'll judge his repentance."

"He will repent nothing," Reverend Pounders predicted sternly.

Joel Peterson reminded them all of Stanhope's offense. "The nigger Washington slept under the roof of Stanhope Hall."

At the door Taylor looked sternly back at the three men who were chattering full voice as though seated comfortably in a smoker. "You must keep quiet," he warned. "Otherwise we're all found out."

"Well, hurry, damn it. It's hot."

Reverend Pounders was out of sorts, and Taylor Quitman understood why. It had been a long and difficult day for all of them. It was always difficult when disciplining a friend.

Still Taylor was willing to be patient and give Burke another chance. After all, their fathers had been close friends until Stanhope Sr. had become involved with corrupt Northern money. Violent acts such as the one they had hired criminals to commit this morning were repugnant to them all, but the threat of losing what precious little they had left of the Southern Code was even more repugnant.

It had had to be done. On this note of moral certitude, Taylor Quitman quietly closed the door to the library behind him and peered down the long corridor that led to the street. He found it empty and was puzzled that Burke Stanhope was taking longer than usual when, suddenly, coming from the door of his law office, he heard a familiar voice.

"Taylor, here I am. I wondered where you were."

He wheeled on hearing the voice as though under attack and saw Burke Stanhope, still dusty from the road.

"Burke, I—"

"Where were you? I thought I heard voices."

"Well, come," Taylor said too eagerly, wishing his heart would stop pounding, wondering if the terror he felt showed on his face.

"Come," he repeated and led Burke into his office and vowed not to glance at Rembrandt's *Prodigal Son* but glanced anyway, all the time offering, "Take off your jacket. You look miserably hot. Can I get you something cold?"

To all his offers, Burke shook his head and maintained his silence and walked slowly around the office, wiping at his brow and neck with a handkerchief. Then he stopped before the Rembrandt print. "Where were you, Taylor?" he asked again, but of the Rembrandt this time, his back to Taylor.

Did he know? "I—had some filing to do in the stacks," Taylor said hurriedly and sat down behind his mussed desk and counseled himself to be cautious. He'd closed the door to the library stacks. There was no way Burke could know anything.

"We had a tragedy this morning at Stanhope Hall," Burke began, turning away from his inspection of the print and allowing Taylor to see the fatigue and worry and grief on his face.

"I'm sorry," Taylor murmured and sat up in his chair. "What—"

"A murder."

Taylor blinked. "I don't believe you."

"White Doll."

Taylor closed his eyes and shook his head, feigning shock, though in reality it was easier not to see the trust and faith and grief in Burke's face. They'd known each other since boyhood, a spotty friendship to be sure, but a loyal one until two years ago, when Taylor Quitman had joined the Knights of the White Camellia.

"What happened?" he asked, indicating with a gesture that Burke was to take the large leather easy chair opposite the desk.

When Burke did not speak right away, Taylor asked further, "How do you know she was murdered?" and instantly regretted it, for Burke launched forth into a description.

"Her hand had been severed and left on the porch of Fan Cottage. Eve was visiting Sis Liz. Eve, Taylor, for God's sake. She's only a child, and she found it."

The man's anger mixed with grief lifted him out of the chair, where he strode back to the door. For a moment Taylor thought he might leave.

But at the door he stopped. From this position Taylor heard him continue.

"We found her body in the woods—what was left of it to find."

Taylor waited a moment. "Whom do you suspect?" he asked, confident that he was doing a good job of feigning everything, though in truth hearing of the account had not been easy or pleasant. He had known the little mulatto woman, White Doll; had encountered her several times in younger better days on the road to Mobile, in the carriage with Sis Liz. White Doll had discovered in one of those early chance meetings that Taylor enjoyed plum jelly, and thereafter every year in season he had found a small straw basket of plum jelly waiting outside his office door.

The memory did fearful damage and left him gaping forward, unaware that Burke had been speaking for several moments.

"—and so I suspect no one. There is no need for suspicion."

"Oh?"

"I know who did it."

"What do you—"

"Earlier we had an uninvited delegation of men at Stanhope Hall. Twelve of them, to be precise," he said, looking at Taylor as he continued to pace.

"Twelve true Sons of the South, all brazenly riding their own mounts, hiding beneath hoods, though I'd recognize their stench again anyplace. All villains, parading as respectable citizens. Small-minded, narrow-thinking bigots who cannot dream or even perceive of a world going forward in mutual and healing unity, bullies who insist that we march backward to the Dark Ages, where a man could not comfortably exist unless he had a dozen of his own breed beneath the heel of his boot. What is there, Taylor, in the Southern soul that requires that barbaric state?"

The best that Taylor Quitman could do was blink at the eloquent anger that came crashing over him. Suddenly Burke pushed away from the door and seemed to head for the desk at top speed, as though he intended to leap over it and move straight to Taylor himself.

"I need an answer," Burke demanded, "because without one, the senseless emotional cost to my family is too great. Besides, I think they will come again unless I understand precisely what it is they want. So I do need your help, Taylor, or else I shall be forced to arm my entire plantation and convert this corner of Alabama into a blood bath, because I will not remain defenseless against such stupidity."

By the time he'd finished speaking, he was seated in the chair opposite Taylor, looking newly exhausted.

Slowly Taylor drew himself up on the edge of his chair, grateful that the desk was between them. "I *am* sorry about White Doll."

"We all are."

"If you are right in your—suspicions—"

"I am right."

"Then it sounds like the Knights of the White Camellia. But you know as well as I that they were outlawed along with the klan years ago."

"You must tell that to them. Apparently word has not yet reached them."

"All right," Taylor soothed, lifting both hands, biding his time. "Assuming there was a delegation from the knights, why are you so certain that they are responsible for what happened to White Doll? God rest her soul."

"Because," Burke said, "in the severed hand Eve found on the front porch of Fan Cottage was a white camellia."

His eyes were leveled on Taylor Quitman, and the expression in those eyes gave Taylor a chill. The committee listening behind the Rembrandt print was hearing everything *but* repentance and apology.

"All right, Burke, I'll try to help," Taylor said with new energy. No need to prolong it. The men in the library stacks would be growing uncomfortable soon. "May I ask if there is anything you might have done recently to—offend?"

"Offend whom?"

"The Southern conscience, the Southern Code?"

Burke looked genuinely puzzled. "What exactly is the Southern conscience? Does it vary noticeably from the Northern conscience, or, better still, the human conscience?"

There it was again, that arrogance, that willingness to flaunt his offenses and pretend he was doing nothing wrong.

"Have you recently housed niggers beneath the roof of Stanhope Hall?" Taylor asked with a directness that startled.

That got his attention. Slowly Burke looked up out of his fatigue. "Have I—what?" he asked.

"I said, have you recently housed niggers beneath the roof of Stanhope Hall?"

"Of course I have. My entire staff is black."

"I'm not speaking of your staff."

"Then what?"

"A man, a nigger, a guest in Stanhope Hall, treated as an equal in all respects."

The bewilderment on Burke's face appeared genuine. Then, "Oh, I understand," he said. "You're speaking of Mr. Booker T. Washington? Is that the nigger you are referring to? Because if so, you are wrong. He is not my equal in all respects. He is not my equal in any respect."

Taylor sat up, pleased. Perhaps there was hope.

"No, he is by far my superior," Burke added quietly, "in all respects, and I might add he is your superior as well, Taylor."

Taylor looked away from the insult, strangely saddened. It was as he had suspected. Burke had learned nothing, was perhaps capable of learning nothing.

"May I ask you a question, Burke?" Taylor began with all the poise he could muster. "Why did you return to the South?"

"Because it's my home."

"You didn't marry a Southerner, you moved away from the South during its crucible, safe in England. In essence you deserted the South. Why did you return?"

"You know why I went to England during the war, Taylor. Have you forgotten? The Southern Cotton Syndicate sent me, with your blessing and the blessing of every other Southerner, to plead with the mills of northern England not to boycott Southern cotton."

Burke paused, and during the pause Taylor painfully remembered what he had conveniently forgotten; that perhaps, after all, Burke *had* performed as a true Son of the South.

"Your efforts were unsuccessful," Taylor muttered.

"But I tried. I did not abandon the South, as you put it." He paused again. "Am I not welcome here, Taylor?" he asked. "Is that what you're saying?"

The question was quiet and full of pain and made Taylor wish he was a complete villain instead of only a partial one.

"I mean, you might have been happier elsewhere."

"Why?"

"Because you seem out of step."

"In what way out of step?"

"You think differently."

"From what? Who?"

"The South."

"The South is not a region of this country, then, it's a state of mind?"

"In a way, yes."

"A state of mind that encourages prejudice and injustice, that asks of its citizens that they not grow or change, that demands slavish loyalty to a set of principles notable in their lack of dignity and compassion, a society that pays lip service to the social amenities of aristocratic breeding but down deep harbors the smallest minds, the narrowest visions, the most unkempt imaginations ever to stain and disgrace this earth."

Taylor waited out this second barrage of verbal abuse, seated well back in his chair, thinking quite calmly that the man was literally hanging himself, for certainly these heresies were being recorded by the committee behind the Rembrandt print, and these same heresies before nightfall would be reported in full to the entire body of the Knights of the White Camellia.

When at last Burke reached the end of his speech and his rage, Taylor stood, weary of this meeting, doubly weary of the abuse that was being heaped on him and every true Son of the South.

"Then I take it that you will not bar the nigger from entering Stanhope Hall again."

"Bar him?" Burke repeated. "He will continue to be my most honored guest, next arriving at the end of the month along, with the writer Samuel Clemens, who has expressed a desire to meet him. I had planned a small reception for these worthy gentlemen, thinking that there would be many in Mobile who would treasure making their acquaintance. Now, however, due to present unhappy circumstances, I shall simply tell them that the South has not yet fully entered this most progressive last quarter of the nineteenth century where civilized men find themselves capable of grasping all hands, not just those of the same color."

Taylor sat well back in his chair, grateful to his father, who first saw fit to cut the panel out of the wall and conceal it with the Rembrandt in order to eavesdrop on clients and competitors. It was that sort of thinking that had led to this triumphant moment when Burke Stanhope had just provided the Knights of the White Camellia with enough evidence, enough ammunition, to wage a just war against Stanhope Hall and all its inhabitants, until one by one they began to see the error of their ways and either came around or else vacated the South and took their treason with them.

"But I don't think it would make any difference, do you, Taylor?"

Again Taylor Quitman had to jar himself back to the present and the man across the desk, who had earnestly posed the question.

"Make—any—I don't—"

Patiently Burke repeated himself. "I said it probably wouldn't make any difference to launch an investigation, would it?"

Still off track, Taylor continued to flounder. "An investigation of—"

"Of the murder. White Doll's."

Taylor shook his head. "Not if your suspicions are true—that it was not random, that a group was behind it."

"What are you saying?"

The direct question caught him off guard. He heard a noise, the men confined in the narrow stacks growing restless. "What I'm saying—" he began distractedly and was never given a chance to finish.

"What you're saying is that a single criminal can sometimes be caught and brought to justice. But crime by committee is permissible, indeed, safe from prosecution."

"I'm not saying that at all."

"Then what?"

"I'm saying nothing more or less than you already know."

"Which is . . ."

"It would be—difficult at best."

"Why?"

"Because if the Knights of the White Camellia have become orga-
nized again, well, as you know, it is a secret organization."

"What if I could positively identify one of them?"

Taylor looked up, worried. "You told me they were hooded."

"Answer my question. If I could provide proof of my charges, then
what?"

Taylor tried accurately to read the expression on Burke's bruised
face. Did he have such proof, or was he bluffing?

He was bluffing. Taylor smiled. "Then of course we'd press for an
investigation without hesitation."

For the first time in this disjointed meeting, Taylor Quitman began
to feel as though he had the upper hand. As for Stanhope, he looked
even more confused than when he had arrived. He stared at the sleeve
of his jacket, as though seeing for the first time how dusty it was. He
made a faint, distracted, brushing motion as though to restore it, all
the while walking slowly toward the door.

But at the door Burke appeared to lose interest in the sleeve of his
jacket. He looked back. "What would they want me to do?"

Taylor leaned forward. "I don't understand."

"The honorable Knights of the White Camellia. You said I had
offended them. How would they want me to mend my ways, so to
speak?"

Taylor stood cautiously, trying to grasp the true meaning of the
question and all its ramifications. Was Burke accusing *him* of belonging to the knights?

But when Burke refused to withdraw his question, Taylor was
forced to answer it. In a last homage to that dead boyhood friendship,
he framed an answer he felt certain would be in Burke's best interests.

"What would they want you to do?" he repeated, coming out from
behind his desk, then perching on its edge in the position of a fatherly
adviser. "First, I believe they would want some kind of reassurance
from you that at last you understand the social structure of the
South."

"Which is?"

"Which is simple—the white race is superior to the black race. In
all ways. This is not to say that it is not our Christian obligation and
responsibility to treat them with fairness and kindness and compassion, but neither should we do them the cruel injustice of draping
over their genetically weak shoulders mantles that they are, by design
of God and nature, ill equipped to support."

Burke said nothing.

"Next," Taylor went on, warming to his subject, "I think they would need some sort of reassurance that all your Northern alliances have been abandoned now and forever."

"Why? Are Northerners inferior to Southerners as well?"

"No, just different."

"And differences in human beings, if I understand it correctly, are not to be tolerated?"

"Tolerated, yes. Encouraged by acceptance, no. Don't forget it was a Northern mind that conceived of the war that robbed us of all possessions, all property, the lives of our young men."

"A few of theirs died as well."

"Not enough; not nearly enough."

"Anything else?" Burke asked, and when he received no answer, he apparently drew his own conclusions. "Then they would leave us alone?" he asked, one hand on the doorknob.

Taylor looked up suspicious. "But you would have to be demonstrably sincere."

"Of course."

Taylor tried to read the man's new mood. Was he sincere? Was the death of one mulatto woman sufficient to bring about a significant transformation for his own good and certainly for the good of his family? It was impossible to tell. Now Stanhope's expression was one of sorrow more than anything else, as though a new grief had just entered his mind.

"I'm sorry for taking up your time, Taylor," he apologized, still at the door.

Taylor dismissed the apology and only wished now that Burke Stanhope would leave. Their continuing association was an impossibility. They thought differently, reacted differently, their values were vastly different. Those two small boys who had splashed in Stanhope Hall's ice pond while their daddies talked cotton prices were gone, if indeed they had ever existed at all.

When Taylor looked up from his unhappy memories, he found the doorway empty.

For a moment Taylor stood rigidly still, continuing to listen. Then he walked toward the Rembrandt print and whispered, "Are you all well?"

"Is it safe?"

"Yes. He's gone."

Joel Peterson led the way back into the room, brushing dust from the stacks off his jacket. "Damn hot in there," he muttered.

"Sorry I couldn't provide you with a fan," Taylor snapped, suddenly annoyed with the complaining men.

Zach Hennessey followed, wiping his brow with a handkerchief. "Do you think he knew we were in there?"

Taylor moved back to his desk. "I'm not sure."

"He spoke treason." This sepulchral voice belonged to Reverend Pounders, who was the last man to come into the office.

Taylor, sitting behind his desk, closed his eyes, feeling mildly ill from the heat and the circumstances of the day.

"You heard him," Pounders repeated, holding a fixed position in front of the closed door. "You heard his treasonous obscenities on the superiority of the black man."

"Only one particular black man," Taylor corrected, "in all fairness."

"Makes no difference," Reverend Pounders said. "It's dangerous, such thinking. It could lead to hell on earth, to a society that sees no cause for differences in the color of a man's skin, whereas the Bible clearly states that dark pigmentation is a punishment for past sins."

Taylor really wasn't in the mood for a sermon and was fairly certain the others felt the same way. Zach Hennessey had a bank to run. Joel Peterson had a plantation almost as large as Stanhope Hall, though not as rich. Pounders had a church to run, though who would know it.

"Gentlemen, I have a law office to run," Taylor said, standing to give his words impetus. "We'll meet as always this Friday evening at Jarmay Higgins's lumberyard. There we can discuss the matter endlessly if any find it necessary."

"You don't, Mr. Quitman?" This arch question came from Reverend Pounders, who clearly did not like being dismissed in this fashion.

"This matter? No," Taylor said. "I know Burke Stanhope. He's been sorely hurt by the events of this day. He'll do nothing for a while; then he will take action."

"What will he do?" Zach asked, still mopping at his plump face with his handkerchief.

The question seemed to be on everyone's mind, for all the men looked in Taylor's direction.

But for now Taylor lacked an answer. He knew Burke Stanhope well enough to know that the last thing he'd change would be his philosophy and his conviction of the rightness of that philosophy. He would continue to entertain the nigger beneath the roof of Stanhope Hall, he'd continue to see his Yankee friends and write for the Yankee magazines and do any and everything he pleased, because that was the way Burke Stanhope was and always had been and always would be.

But Taylor decided against breaking this bleak news to the gentlemen now. Time later. For now the meeting was over, as was the sad day. Hopefully the memory of the little mulatto woman who made the best plum jelly in these parts would fade soon, along with everything else.

"Gentlemen," Taylor repeated, still trying to herd them toward the door. "Until Friday, when we can discuss the matter at length under better conditions." His mind caught on the words. He doubted if the dusty loft of Jarmay Higgins's lumberyard was a better condition, but certainly it was a safer one.

Reluctantly Reverend Pounders vacated his guardlike position before the door. "I'm not certain we have solved anything on this day."

"A woman is dead," Taylor said, remembering the fact with increasing sorrow.

"An evil woman." Pounders nodded. "A sinful woman with mixed blood in her veins."

"Good-bye," Taylor repeated.

At last only Reverend Pounders stood in the doorway. "Which is stronger, Taylor?" the old Episcopal priest asked. "Your affection for the cause or your affection for Burke Stanhope?"

"I have no affection for Burke Stanhope."

"You did once."

"Years ago, yes, when we were boys."

"Your fathers—"

"I am not my father; neither is Burke his. Now if you will excuse me, Reverend, there really is a tremendous amount of work to be done here."

As he spoke, he moved with admirable speed to the door and the man who stood blocking it. By the time he arrived, Reverend Pounders had stepped back just enough to permit the door to be closed.

It had been a long day, commencing with the predawn meeting at Higgins's loft for the finalization of the day's plans, to hear the strategies of that slime Orlando Dow, who apparently had carried out his bloody scheme to perfection. Then the silent waiting in this room, knowing what was going on—such knowledge took a heavy toll— then the word that it had been accomplished and that curious rush of gossip that had struck the city's saloons and coffeehouses, that the Knights of the White Camellia were back on vigilant duty.

Then Quitman knew beyond the shadow of a doubt that he was on the side of right. It was just that sometimes being right was so difficult, required steady nerves and an unwavering spirit. It was those boyhood memories that had weakened him.

Careful. Get all the weakness out of your system now. Come Friday the Knights of the White Camellia must not be able to glimpse so much as a hint of it.

They didn't approve of weakness in their membership. The South had been weak once before. It must never be allowed to happen again.

 Stanhope Hall

Looking around the dining room of Stanhope Hall, Eve found herself fascinated by the bruised and handsome face of Stephen Eden directly opposite her, which she had first glimpsed through the three-tiered silver epergne of summer fruit.

"I apologize for my husband's absence," Eve heard her mother murmur, and all eyes lifted in that direction toward the end of the table, where Eve saw her mother looking ill at ease.

"I understand," Stephen smiled.

Next to Stephen sat a slavish, adoring David, who mimicked Stephen's every movement. Apparently a bond had taken hold during the afternoon's swim in the ice pond. On Stephen's left sat Christine, who had insisted that she be allowed to join the family for dinner in honor of her English cousin. Eve had helped her dress, had selected her gown, a light green cotton with pale pink roses.

On Eve's right sat her tutor, Madame Germaine, tall, gaunt, her salt-and-pepper hair pulled tightly back into a French knot, the "conscience of the world," or so Papa called her, generally with affection.

Eve's relationship with her was at best tenuous. Though they'd had fierce rows in the past over just about everything, the older Eve got, the easier was her relationship with Madame Germaine. While there was no real affection between them, Eve respected the old Frenchwoman and was grateful for her patience and doubly grateful for the love and care she showered on Christine.

On Eve's left was Paris Boley, looking quite important in his best black suit and white shirtwaist. They'd grown up together, Eve and Paris, had survived Madame Germaine, knew all the twists and turns, both geographically and emotionally, of life at Stanhope Hall. She'd missed him sorely when he left to attend Tuskegee for the last three years, and now she was so pleased to have him home, like the return of a triumphant older brother.

So this was the company, seven in all, not counting her father's empty place at the head of the table that seemed to be proclaiming its emptiness in silence. Earlier Mary had asked old Ben to post a man with a lantern at the end of the road, and as soon as Mr. Stanhope rode into view, the lantern was to signal the house. Thus far the lantern had not moved.

Katie and Dorie and Mrs. Winegar were serving dinner this evening, only the household staff, nothing compared to the larger staff that was pressed into service when Papa entertained his sizable gatherings of Northern friends.

Eve liked it this way—Mrs. Winegar openly scolding Katie for tilting the soup tureen too far to the right. It was more like a family dinner, except no one was laughing and joking like when Papa was here. In fact, no one was even talking at the moment, everyone seeming to concentrate on Katie's manipulation of the heavy white soup tureen as Mrs. Winegar filled each bowl with her velvety cream of celery soup.

As the serving continued around the table, so did the silence, until at last Eve felt compelled to break it.

"Did you enjoy your swim, Mr. Eden?"

The direct question seemed to catch everyone off guard, particularly Mr. Eden.

"I did, yes. How did you—"

"I just asked, that's all."

David sat up in defense of his new hero. "Well, what's the matter with going swimming? Cleo and Casey and I go swimming every afternoon."

"Nothing's wrong with it, David," Eve soothed. "It's just that Christine and I followed—"

"You what?" David's eyes widened. His mouth fell open. Next to him Stephen Eden's expression was approximately the same.

"You didn't. I don't believe you," David scoffed.

"Ask Christine." Eve smiled, delighted at the recall of their afternoon escapade, which really had lasted only a few minutes. Christine had suddenly grown heavy in Eve's arms, and the afternoon had become hot. Eve had become worried that if something happened to Christine, she would be held accountable. So they'd only lingered behind the lilac bushes for a few moments—long enough to see the boys strip off their shirts and shoes and stockings, then plunge half-naked into the cool spring waters of the ice pond.

"We wished we could have joined you," Eve concluded, pleased with the shocked expressions on the faces around her.

"Eve, don't tease," her mother murmured and waved Katie away after only one ladle of soup.

"I'm not teasing, Mama." Eve smiled. "Just ask Christine."

She glanced across the table and saw Christine return her grin.

Would she admit to the prank or not? Sometimes Christine impressed her with her daring, and at other times she seemed little more than a baby and a fraidy cat.

But now she was not given a chance to answer, for Mr. Eden spoke up, between spoonfuls of soup. "You *should* have joined us," he said. "Both of you. The water was perfect, wasn't it, David?"

David nodded all too eagerly and in the manner of an older and wiser counsel whispered to Stephen, "And you don't have to worry. They really weren't there."

"Oh, but they were, David," Stephen Eden assured him, smiling. "I saw them. Paris did too. Didn't you, Paris?"

Eve quickly covered her mouth with her napkin in an attempt to conceal her grin. Such a harmless joke, and yet the shock waves were continuing to vibrate around the table. Madame Germaine and Mary were both apparently speechless.

"I saw—nothing," Paris said and suddenly got very busy over his soup. At the same time Eve lost her appetite for the harmless prank.

"Never mind," Eve said and met Stephen's eyes over the top of her napkin and was grateful for his lighthearted cooperation, but she hoped he understood how difficult it was to laugh or joke on this day.

For several moments all ate in silence. There was no sound except for the click-click of silver on china. When the awkward silence stretched on, Eve tried to conceive of a safe subject for conversation, one that would involve the entire table and be offensive to no one.

It was a large undertaking and one she was still working on when she heard her mother's soft voice pose a simple question.

"Stephen, tell us of your life in England. Tell us of Eden Castle. Though I grew up there, it's been so long. I'm sure it's changed."

"Not really." Stephen smiled and placed his soup spoon alongside the bowl. "My father always says that the only changes that Eden Castle will allow are superficial ones. Its essence remains intact, precisely as it was in the year 1080."

"Imagine, 1080, children," Madame Germaine said. "All right. A quick history lesson. What happened only a few years prior to that? One of the most significant dates in the English-speaking world."

Eve groaned inwardly. David ducked behind his napkin. Christine responded. "William the Conqueror invaded England. The invasion was successful and William early on made it clear that Normandy had the force and the spirit to absorb all of Saxon England."

As the sweet piping voice ceased in its lecture on eleventh-century England, soup spoons around the table hung suspended. Even Madame Germaine seemed stirred by the impressive display of knowledge. Eve saw her mother smile.

"Well done, Christine," she said.

"Indeed," Stephen agreed and turned sideways in his chair, as though wanting a better look at this young font of knowledge. "In your opinion, Christine, was William a good conqueror?"

"Oh, no, not at first. In fact, he was very bloodthirsty. He practiced a form of terrorism known as frightfulness, which meant that he went from village to village committing horrible murders for no apparent reason, other than to try to intimidate and frighten the people, like—"

The lilting voice fell abruptly. Eve saw something cross her sister's face, some lesson of history learned too late, if at all, a parallel racing pell-mell across the centuries.

"Like—"

Again Christine tried to verbalize this new and painful perception, the awareness that William's practice of frightfulness was alive and flourishing in *their* world.

Stephen was the closest to Christine, and he offered both comfort and assistance. "I know, Christine; I understand. We all do."

Eve lost a full awareness of what he was saying and found herself instead concentrating on that most miraculous face, the way the light caught in the contours of the jawline, the way his hair curled about the shell of his ear, the way—

"Eve, don't you agree?"

Good Lord, it was Madame Germaine again, nudging her beneath the table, a rude gesture that was not at all consistent with that civil smiling face leering at her from the right.

Nothing to do but confess. "I'm sorry, Madame Germaine, I'm afraid I didn't hear—"

"Weren't paying attention." The old hag sighed heavily. "The story, I'm afraid, Mr. Eden, of this young lady's life. She wool-gathers endlessly."

"My father accuses me of the same crime, Madame Germaine," Stephen confessed.

Eve sat up and vowed to pay closer attention, grateful again. "What do you wool-gather about, Mr. Eden?" she asked, secretly pleased to shut out Madame Germaine from this conversation, doubly pleased not to have to answer her question.

"Everything," Mr. Eden replied, "Eden Point invites day-dreaming."

Eve saw her mother nod readily. "Oh, it does, it does indeed. You should see it, my children. It is the most beautiful—" Abruptly she broke off, as though self-conscious. "Not beauty in the way we see it here at Stanhope Hall."

"No," Stephen agreed.

"Then how does it differ?" David urged. "Is it bigger? Nothing is bigger than Stanhope Hall."

Mary laughed, a good sound. "Oh, indeed it is, David. It is an entire world."

"Built out of cliffs," Stephen contributed.

"Rising to the sky," Mary added.

"Gray stone."

"Tiled roof."

"The inner courtyard alone would swallow up all of Stanhope Hall."

Their voices were coming in counterpoint. Eve glanced rapidly back and forth, savoring the clear expression and enjoyment of each.

For several moments no one spoke. Mrs. Winegar and Katie and Dorie had reentered the room, each pushing laden serving carts. Beyond David's shoulder Eve caught a glimpse of the puff pastry dome of Mrs. Winegar's company chicken pie.

Suddenly Eve dropped her napkin. Paris bent over to retrieve it. Eve followed suit. "What are you doing after dinner?" she whispered fiercely.

Paris looked puzzled, sideways in her vision.

"Hurry, tell me, where are you going?"

"Noplace."

"Mr. Eden?"

"He's returning to Mobile."

"No, he can't."

"That's what he said."

Mary's voice interrupted. "Is something wrong, Eve?"

"I dropped my napkin. Paris was helping—"

She held the napkin up for display. As Dorie placed a laden platter before Mr. Eden, Eve decided to see if Paris's claim was right.

"I hope you found your rooms comfortable, Mr. Eden."

"Oh, they were, most agreeable. I'm grateful to you all."

"Was the bed to your liking?"

"I did not try the bed. I only—"

"Oh, but you must. The mattress in the guest suite is quite hard. Mr. Gilder, Papa's editor, sleeps there when he visits us. He likes it that way, but you might prefer—"

"I won't be spending the night, Miss Stanhope. I must return to Mobile this evening."

The disappointment around the table was instantaneous. Mary spoke first. "No, Stephen, please stay. I still feel badly."

"No need," he reassured her. "My arrival was poorly timed."

David made a plea. "Don't go, Stephen. You said you might stay. Paris, make him, you can make him."

As the attention shifted, Eve saw Mr. Eden look directly at her, an expression of such intensity in his eyes that she felt a blush creep up her neck.

Next to her, Paris was making lame denials. "Mr. Eden does not need nor has he sought my counsel. He keeps his own, as he should."

Christine now joined in with a charming plea. "Please stay with us for a while, Mr. Eden. We so seldom meet someone from the outside." This entreaty was heartfelt and held appeal for everyone except Mary.

"Christine, you make Stanhope Hall sound like a prison."

"It's true, Mama, and you know it. No one ever visits us except Papa's friends."

Then Mary spoke again with that slight tone of apology. "What are your plans when you leave here, Stephen?"

He shook his head. "My plans. I'm afraid they are as vague as my arrival here."

"I don't understand."

"Uncle Richard gave me only a destination, not an itinerary. Eventually I must make my way to the state of Montana and locate a man named G. H. Teats."

"Why did Richard invest in American cattle?" Mary asked.

"He was invited to participate in a British syndicate, and I suppose at the time it seemed a good investment."

"Of course." Mary nodded and looked upward toward the ceiling and appeared to be thinking. "I recall a severe winter several years ago that affected western cattle. Burke could tell us—"

She seemed to catch herself. Her eyes skimmed over the empty chair at the head of the table.

Obviously Paris sensed her worry and offered quietly, "Mrs. Stanhope, would you like for me to—"

"No, no, finish your supper. Everything will be all right."

"You'll have to fight red Indians, you know," David chirped, his mouth full of Mrs. Winegar's chicken pie.

Mary scolded. "That's not true, David, and please empty your mouth before you speak."

"It is so true," David protested. "There are red Indians, all over out there."

"Who told you that?"

"Sis Liz. She said she was on a stagecoach once, going to Kansas City, and red Indians rode right up alongside the stagecoach and one jumped aboard and took all their money and all their jewelry and they kidnapped a little white girl and that's the last anyone ever saw of her."

Eve along with everyone else at the table listened, doubly fascinated, not only by the tale itself but fascinated by its source, Sis Liz, who stored in her brain beneath her white hair the best stories the world would ever hear.

Stephen ate heartily and between bites promised David, "I'll keep a sharp eye out, I promise. It's not my intention to antagonize any man, my present bruised face notwithstanding."

Smiling, he touched his temple.

"I am sorry, Stephen," Mary whispered. "You must forgive my husband. I don't know what happened between the two of you, but I assure you that normally he is a most placid and agreeable and reasonable man."

"Mary!"

The voice was sudden and angry and drew their attention to the serving door. All gaped at this new apparition, dust covered, his face lined with fatigue and anger as he stared at the back of Mary's head.

"I am capable of speaking for myself," Papa said. "I need no one to apologize for me."

"Burke, I—"

"Paris, I must see you immediately."

Paris dropped his napkin onto the table and murmured a brief "Excuse me" and joined Papa at the door. Then they were gone, leaving the dinner party in ruins.

Eve dared not look up. Something had happened here tonight for the first time in Eve's memory, a sad something. Her father had spoken to her mother without a trace of love in his voice. And if Eve had recognized it, surely her mother had, and now how could they ever end this awful moment.

"Mama." The soft voice came from Christine, who always seemed to feel everything more acutely. Eve looked up and saw her mother hurry to Christine's side and assist her out of her chair and walk with her from the dining room, one arm protectively about her.

Then Madame Germaine felt compelled to show everyone her mantle of authority. "Come, David, you have studies. You, too, Eve."

Madame Germaine held the door for David and followed him out and closed it behind her.

Silence.

At last Eve found the courage to look up, and to her amazement found Stephen staring straight at her.

"I was told," he began quietly, "by everyone at home that it would not be easy."

"It is not your fault, any of it. You must realize that."

"I've caused trouble."

"Trouble was here when you arrived."

"Still—"

He shook his head and broke off speaking and looked about at the empty table with new awareness. "I think it best if I return immediately to Mobile."

"No, please."

He smiled at her quick protest and reminded her, "Others might not agree."

Fascinated by the curious sense of panic that swept over her at the prospect of his departure, Eve pushed back in her chair and made a heartfelt plea, which she hoped made sense.

"It would be wrong for you to leave under these circumstances. You must believe me when I say that both Mama and Papa would want you to stay at least for a while."

Her voice sounded appropriate in echo, and he seemed to be listening.

"Just one night," she proposed. "Give all of us a chance to make amends."

"It's not necessary."

"But it *is*."

Abruptly he stood. Not until he reached the door did he turn back. "Are you permitted to walk with me? Only for a few moments?"

His cautious formality amused her. His invitation pleased her. She joined him at the door with a simple yes and led the way into the corridor, praying that they would not encounter anyone.

The corridor was blessedly empty. At the double front doors she looked back as though to confirm her good fortune.

He was still there behind her. She pushed open the doors and stepped out into the evening shadows, taking refuge in the darkness, at least until her rapid pulse settled down, until she could adjust to the fact that she was alone in the company of this man, this miraculous man who stirred her in ways she had never been stirred before.

* * *

Still smarting from the embarrassment in the dining room, Stephen followed Eve out onto the cool gallery, grateful for the darkness, which obliterated everything except his memory of the unhappy scene, Mr. Stanhope glaring at him over his wife's head, the man's manner as deranged as it had been earlier in the day.

"Would you rather sit or walk?"

The soft inquiry came from Eve, and again Stephen felt himself to be in her debt. Twice on this unhappy day she'd come to his rescue and soothed the awkward moments with her own peculiar grace and kindness.

"Let's sit," he said, indicating the front steps. Ahead the avenue of live oaks appeared as large gnarled sentinels under the patina of pale moonlight.

For several long moments they both seemed content to sit and stare out at the evening. Here and there he saw the faint flicker of a firefly. At the far end of the avenue he saw a lantern and recalled that one had been placed there to mark the return of Mr. Stanhope, who apparently had circumvented the lantern and entered Stanhope Hall through the back courtyard. There were so many questions he wanted to ask Eve yet dared not for fear of appearing to pry.

So he settled for the silence and a private sorrow, that events had gone so against him here.

"Are you comfortable? Would you—"

"We can walk if you wish. It makes no—"

As they both spoke simultaneously, both broke off and gave into a newly embarrassed silence.

Finally, "I'm fine," she murmured, "but we can walk if you wish." There was something so sweet, so gentle in her manner.

"Were you really watching us?" he asked. "In the ice pond?"

"Of course." She smiled. "Though it was Christine's idea. Or was it mine? I don't remember."

"Why did you hide? Why didn't you just come out?"

"It was more fun," she said with blunt honesty. "And besides, Mama would have—"

She broke off and appeared to be staring out at the night alive with fireflies.

He sensed her embarrassment and realized there was no safe ground of conversation. Everything led back to the muddle of the day, the tragic death of the mulatto woman and Mr. Stanhope's antagonism.

"I should be on my way back to Mobile. It's late."

"No, please. You promised. One night. Come morning everything will be different, better—you'll see."

She was most persuasive. But he knew better than to trust her word alone. She was not the one who wanted him gone. She might speak for herself, but not for her father.

"I can't, Eve," he repeated and stood up despite the protestations in her face.

"It's too late now," she said, rising with him. "The road to Mobile is hazardous after dark. Papa would not want you to . . ."

Stephen laughed. "I doubt if anything would please your father more than my having a chance encounter with local villains."

"That's not true, Stephen. My father is a good man. He would wish no man ill."

"I know. I'm sorry."

"Then you must give him another chance."

"He has much on his mind."

"And Mama—"

"Your mother has been kind to a fault. Uncle Richard most specifically wanted word of his sister."

"Well, there you are. You've hardly had a chance to speak with her. How can you possibly relay information to your uncle that you do not have?"

Clever. And again most persuasive. Still he didn't want to linger here overnight and run the risk of another encounter with Burke Stanhope.

"I'll write to you, Eve," he promised, joining her on the step below, seeing her features clearly in the moonlight, feeling certain that there were hidden riches in her personality that would reward any man who took the time and effort to uncover them.

"Please," she begged again. "Stay just one—"

Suddenly there was a noise at the door. Both turned about.

"There you are." Paris smiled from the doorway. "I looked for you in the dining room, which I'm afraid now resembles a battlefield. Have you always possessed this talent, Eden, to convert a harmonious family into two armed camps?"

There was clear good nature in Paris's voice, accompanied by a wide grin. "I have a message," Paris announced now from the top of the porch steps. "From Mr. Stanhope. A reminder and a promise that tomorrow is another day, and he urges you to make yourself at home at Stanhope Hall and to feel free to stay as long as you find it necessary."

Stephen stared at both the message and the messenger.

"He is sincere," Paris added, coming slowly down the steps, hands in pockets. "He is a good man," he said, his voice echoing Eve's earlier claim.

"He has just come back from Mobile," Paris added, keeping his voice down, "where he learned the sad lesson that he has no friend whom he can trust."

Stephen listened, wanting very much to believe that he personally had little or nothing to do with Stanhope's erratic behavior.

"There, you see." Eve smiled, a hint of triumph in her voice. "And if you don't choose to believe me, you must believe Paris, who, according to Papa, has never told an untruth in his life."

Stephen started to challenge the claim in good humor. He looked back at the serious and studious young black man, who obviously had come very far very fast and was now a trusted adviser to Mr. Stanhope and a linchpin in the operation of Stanhope Plantation. He started to say more but saw a shadowy figure now inside the door— old Ben, a lamp in hand—while behind him was yet another figure, looking as mussed and unhappy in shadow as he had earlier in the dining room.

Apparently the other two, Eve and Paris, had seen the flickering light and sensed new presences as well.

"Papa, are you there?"

"Come inside, Eve. Paris will see to all of Mr. Eden's needs."

With reluctance Eve gathered her skirts and started up the steps. As she passed Stephen, she whispered, "Until tomorrow morning. Please sleep well. I want to show you everything."

He gaped at the whispered message and found it an appealing invitation and watched as Ben held the door open for her.

Stephen held his position mid-step. Then he heard that voice again, emerging from the shadows, the same one that had leveled baseless accusations at him that morning, the same one that had brought the dinner party to an abrupt halt.

"You are quite welcome to stay here at Stanhope Hall, Mr. Eden," this voice said. "I apologize for my actions."

Stephen stared after the voice. As the flickering lamp disappeared at the top of the staircase, Stephen thought how similar this man was to his own father, John Murrey Eden.

"So you'll stay, of course." Paris nodded, and he, too, seemed to relax visibly as the staircase inside the front door grew dark and silent and safe again.

"I'd not intended . . ."

"But you will."

"Yes."

"Good. Then come along. Mrs. Winegar said we could finish our dinner in the kitchen annex. Then I want you to tell me all about your trip west, destinations, mode of travel, everything. Well, come on, we now have all of Mrs. Winegar's chicken pie to ourselves."

The pleasure in Paris's voice pleased Stephen, more like the cordial reception he'd hoped for earlier that day. Yes, he would stay, though down deep in his soul where absolute truth resided, he knew that Eve Stanhope was the only reason he was staying a final night at Stanhope Hall. It was a reason so powerful and compelling, he needed no other.

✒ Higgins's Farm

Two days after the "unfortunate" tragedy that had befallen Burke Stanhope's mulatto woman, Jarmay Higgins sat in his summer house awaiting the arrival of certain key knights, watching his wife arrange a crystal cooler of mint lemonade, finding her distasteful from all angles, from the broad beam of her bent-over posterior to her constant and simpering "happy mood," which enabled her to talk constantly and say nothing.

"Vida Mae, quit fussing," he grumbled, shifting on the uncomfortable wicker furniture and wishing she'd just go and leave him alone—forever.

"I'm trying to make things nice and pleasant for your friends." She smiled and arranged a large tray of sugared walnut cookies, snagging one each time she fussed over it, the tray shrinking while she grew broader.

He watched her with a kind of fascinated revulsion, as one would watch a snake devouring a mouse, easing his feelings of discomfort and guilt with the realization that he had never loved her, never wanted her. Their two daddies had arranged this lifetime of hell for them. Of course in the bargain Jarmay had inherited her daddy's land, and those three thousand acres combined with Daddy Higgins's three thousand acres had made the present Higgins's Farm almost as big as Stanhope Plantation.

"I said quit fussing," Jarmay scolded, shouting it this time.

At the shout she looked over her fleshy shoulder. "You're grouchy, my sweet," she cooed. "Where did my sweet Jarmay go to? Oh, what a lovely man that Jarmay Higgins is, my knight in shining armor, my Romeo, my . . ."

As her singsong voice silenced the nearby bird songs, Jarmay pushed up out of the uncomfortable wicker chair and strode to the door of the summer house, feeling the safest course of action would be to find a vista that did not include her.

Feeling disgust that amounted almost to self-loathing, he stepped out onto the green lawn that swept directly down to the banks of the Mobile River and tried to forget his loveless marriage in pleasant contemplation of his land.

At the edge of his lawn he walked to a small brick path that had been laid by his daddy's slaves and tried to put out of his mind the fat bitch puttering in the summer house, arranging the tea party for the Knights of the White Camellia.

He looked back toward the summer house to see if anyone had

arrived yet. He had said three o'clock, hadn't he? Or was it half past three? It made no difference. They'd be along soon, each bringing a report from his particular field of endeavor. Most important was the report from Stanhope Hall. Had Stanhope taken the warning to heart? In a way Jarmay hoped so. Down deep he didn't care for this sort of violence. Thank God for conscienceless men like Orlando Dow, who could hold the Bible in one hand and drive home a twelve-inch knife blade with the other.

"Jarmay, oh, Jarmay. Carriages are coming."

The shrew voice came from the direction of the summer house; he saw Vida Mae waving a white handkerchief at him. At her side he saw Marshal, a good nigger if there ever was one, a nigger who had known his proper place for thirty-five years and had stayed in it.

"Jarmay! Did you hear? They're coming."

Before his shrill wife could call again, he left the red brick walkway and started off across the lawn, where beyond the wall he could see three carriages just turning in to the rounded driveway, saw Reverend Pounders's silk top hat in the lead carriage. He increased his step, still well behind Marshal, who was moving with remarkable speed in order to be there when the first carriage drew to a halt. Vida Mae moved with less speed, and when he caught up with her, he ordered, "Get into the house. This is a business meeting. No place for a woman."

Then he turned his back on her, though he heard her sniffling and felt gratified by the sound. It had always given him extreme pleasure to make a woman cry.

"Ah, Reverend Pounders," he called out, hand extended. "Good to see you. Please feel welcome. Higgins's Farm is at your disposal."

Wordlessly the cadaverous old man took Jarmay's hand. It was like grasping a cold fish. Behind him now the others were spilling forth from their various carriages: Joel Peterson, his nearest neighbor to the south, a plantation owner who did not stand a chance compared to the gigantic Stanhope Plantation, but a good man nonetheless, a true aristocrat, a loyal Son of the South; following him was Zach Hennessey, president of Mobile Security and Exchange; next came Taylor Quitman; behind Taylor came Dr. Melrose. As these joined the others, Jarmay stood back and opened his arms wide.

"Welcome, gentlemen. We will convene in the summer house, where a light refreshment has been laid for your enjoyment and where our—business concerns can be discussed freely and openly. Please follow me if you will."

He led the way across the lawns toward the summer house, proud that all this was his and these good men were his friends.

"This way, gentlemen. Hurry. There are important matters ahead of us; very important matters. Come, all of you. The South is depending upon us to keep its destiny safe, and we must not fail her."

 *Stanhope Hall*

Sometimes Stephen felt exactly as he'd felt that winter three years ago when he'd been ill and spent seven months in and out of bed. Mostly in. Winter grippe. That was what the London doctor had called it.

Now as he sat perched on the railing in the hot August sun behind the kitchen annex of Stanhope Hall, awaiting Eve for their daily adventure, he felt that same weakness invade his body, though this time it was more pleasurable, as though at the mere thought of her, his bones had grown lazy and forgotten to do their duty. He relaxed on the railing, well aware that his avowed one-night stay had stretched into two and those two into three and three into four and four into five and now was this the sixth or seventh day and did it really matter and did he have a choice? Was he still capable of independent action, or had she worked a spell on him?

He allowed his head to slump forward, his knees to fall apart, and toyed with the cord on his riding jodhpurs. Another ride. Always a ride. She adored her horse Clarissa, and together, every day, they'd met in this spot behind the kitchen annex and walked to the stables together.

Still he must leave here soon, although he had to admit that since that first unhappy day, everyone seemed to have settled down and he seldom saw Mr. Stanhope. According to his aunt Mary, Mr. Stanhope was working on expansion plans for Stanhope Plantation as well as a new series of articles for Richard Gilder's *Century* magazine. In addition, the Tuskegee Institute was in need of funds and Mr. Stanhope was at work on that as well. As all these chores combined, he found it more convenient to take his meals in his study.

There had been a suspect silence from everyone at the table when she had made that announcement, and the silence alone had spoken volumes. But in a way Stephen didn't really object. All meals now were exceedingly pleasant, with David on one side and Christine on the other, an enchanting and incredibly bright little girl, and his aunt Mary presiding at one end and the stern-faced Madame Germaine sitting on her left. Directly across from Stephen, situated where he could feast endlessly on her beauty, sat Eve.

The mere thought caused him to look up in search of her. But he found nothing except the kitchen annex and Katie's backside a distance away as she worked the soil in the herb garden.

Soon. Eve would be here soon and he could wait, though he now wondered how long he should remain at Stanhope Hall. His thoughts of winning over Mr. Stanhope were fast fading. Paradoxically, while he could form no attachment with that distant and troubled man, he felt he was forming attachments that were too strong with almost everyone else in the house. And worse than that, he was beginning to enjoy this way of life. He loved the sun, even loved the extreme heat. He enjoyed the easy camaraderie that passed back and forth among members of the household staff. He'd had many enjoyable and rewarding conversations with his aunt Mary, and he was thoroughly enjoying his friendship with Paris Boley, one of the most remarkable men it had ever been his pleasure to meet. And all these considerations, plus a few more, made even the thought of leaving very painful, though he knew he must.

"There you are."

The soft voice entered his consciousness like a soothing breeze on a hot morning and further postponed the need to think about leaving. He looked up. How was it possible that her beauty seemed to be increasing day by day?

"I'm sorry I'm late." She smiled and walked straight toward him down the gravel path.

"You're not late," he said, leaving his perch on the fence and standing to meet her.

"Mama stopped me," she said, eyes down as she approached. For the first time he noticed a stiff white envelope in her hand. "She gave me this."

"What is it?"

"From Sis Liz. She sent it with one of the girls who look in on her."

"What does it say?"

"She wants to see us."

"Us?"

She nodded with emphasis. "Mama feels it's important. It's the first time she's contacted us since—"

At the end of the fence, she looked back. "I'm afraid we'll have to postpone our ride."

"Shall I go and change?"

"No. It'll be all right." She lifted her head and picked up her full gingham skirts and called back in the spirit of play, "Come on, Stephen, you are about to meet the queen of Alabama."

She led the way across the barnyard and turned right through the broad gates that led to what appeared to be a thick pine woods.

"Is it far?" he called, stepping out in an attempt to catch up.

"It depends upon what you find."

"I don't understand."

"Sometimes there are mushrooms you must stop and pick, other times wild violets, or green pine cones for Christmas wreaths and nuts for September roasting. I don't think I have ever, not once in my life, just walked straight through these woods." She paused. "They found White Doll here."

As she reached this mournful conclusion, Stephen tried to think of something suitable to say and could think of nothing.

The trees were high and thick now, almost obliterating the sun. The underfooting was tricky, with exposed tree roots and dead stumps and slippery pine needles.

"How far did you say?" he asked, amazed at the ease with which she moved through this hazardous terrain.

"Keep your eyes open," she called back, her mood and manner quite cheerful now.

"Eve?"

She stopped and looked back.

"How am I to behave before Sis Liz?"

She laughed. "Be yourself, because she'll know instantly if you're not. I've never seen anyone fool Sis Liz."

Then she was before him, having retraced the half-dozen steps that separated them. Her voice was sweet and close, her face upturned. "She's just a tired old woman," she murmured, "very lonely and very sad. We let her think whatever brings her comfort. And you'll do the same, I'm sure."

She was so near, her manner so loving. He wanted more than anything to touch her face, just to touch that smooth pale cheek, to run his fingers across that small though miraculous slope between her cheek and jawbone, perhaps to dare to graze the corner of her lips, to travel gently on down like a joyous traveler past the angle of her jaw to the slim column of her throat, to where the shoulder angled gracefully out, a miraculous flowing line, so inviting.

And he did so, carefully at first, waiting to judge her reaction, which was minimal except for a faint look of surprise, a slight widening of her eyes.

She returned his gaze with what seemed to be held breath, her throat arching upward as his solitary finger traversed the angle from jaw to neck. Then he noticed her eyes close, mouth fall slightly open, lips parted. For those few brief moments the woods fell away and

Stephen felt as though he were standing on a narrow pinnacle of pure joy, to be touching her in so intimate a manner and not to hear the faintest objection, rather to see a look of sweet pleasure on her face as his finger, joined now by his entire hand, grasped her by the shoulders and exerted a mild pressure and drew her close to him and enclosed her in a light embrace. Now he too shut his eyes, the better to savor the sensation as his left hand, growing incredibly brave, slipped about her waist and flattened itself against the small of her back, thus securing her to him.

For several moments neither spoke. Stephen had the unique feeling that what was happening here he would remember for the rest of his life. At last with great reluctance he ended the embrace in a curious way, with an apology.

"I'm sorry," he murmured, grasping her lightly by the shoulders so that he might see her face and read her expression.

But in truth there was no expression, no indication of whether he'd pleased or displeased her. There was a faint blush of color on her cheeks that he was certain had not been there before. She seemed incapable of looking at him and occupied herself with a quick search around the base of a near tree for something, and still neither spoke, though he suspected that she was as changed as he.

"Here," he heard her exclaim, and he struggled to bring all his emotions under strict control.

"Stephen, here, come and look."

He closed his eyes briefly and then joined her a short distance away and looked down as she pointed out a circle of snow-white mushroom caps encircling a broad-based tree. They were firm, plump, succulent beauties.

She immediately dropped to her knees and, using her skirt as an apron, began to pluck the mushrooms.

He watched her for a few seconds, then kneeled beside her and harvested a few of the mushrooms. He dropped them carefully into her cupped skirts, their hands brushing on two occasions in contact that caused their eyes to meet, then move away in a shared and mysterious knowledge, as though they both were well aware not only of what had transpired, but of what was yet to come.

* * *

Eve wondered . . .

How was it possible that such a simple task of gathering mushrooms, something she'd done thousands of times in her life, should suddenly be transformed into an occasion of pure joy. For that's what she was experiencing now, and she wondered further if she should

have permitted his embrace and knew that she would have been powerless to resist it.

All she knew for certain was that she'd never known such feelings
as were now invading her. As he kneeled beside her over the mushrooms, she found herself focusing on his strong, broad hands, capable
hands, one discolored purple nail as though he'd injured it recently.

"What happened?" she asked, lifting his hand.

He seemed surprised and studied the injured nail for a moment, a
frown on his face, as though trying to remember.

Then he did. "My own clumsiness," he said. "It happened months
ago. Before I left England. A stubborn casement in my father's study.
He wanted it lowered." He grinned. "I lowered it."

"Tell me about your father." She sat back on her heels and knew
they should be hurrying on to Sis Liz's. But just a moment longer in
private. How could it hurt?

The request seemed to catch him off guard. Slowly he dusted his
hands to shake off the dirt of the mushrooms and rested on one knee,
the other raised. "Why my father?"

She met his eyes and the question head on. "Because Mama talks
about everyone else at Eden Castle."

"My father is a difficult man to understand," Stephen began. "I'm
not certain I understand him to this day. I was eight when we went to
live with him at Eden Castle."

"Where did you live before that?"

"With my grandfather. In Dublin. My mother's father."

"Why?"

"My mother had died. And my father didn't want us."

He spoke this so matter-of-factly, as though it were a natural condition of childhood, not to be wanted by one's father. She longed to ask
additional questions but didn't want to appear to pry. He looked
uncomfortable perched on one knee, a smudge near his left temple
where he'd rubbed it and transferred dirt from the mushrooms.

"Wait," she said and reached into her pocket to withdraw a handkerchief. "You have a smudge," she smiled and reached up with the
handkerchief and removed the dirt.

As long as she was there, she allowed the handkerchief to examine
his bruised left eye, the only visible mark remaining from the fight
with her father.

"Speaking of fathers . . ." He smiled and slowly reached up and
captured her hand, handkerchief and all, and removed the handkerchief and pressed her fingers to his lips, never once breaking contact
with her eyes.

And because it seemed the most natural thing in the world to do, she rose on her knees opposite him, only vaguely aware of the spilling mushrooms, and knew what was about to happen moments before it actually happened and felt a surge of excitement that seemed momentarily to rob her of all breath. And when she managed to breathe again, it was just in time, for that most remarkable face was coming closer.

The last short distance was conquered in a mutual effort, her eyes closing at the precise moment she felt his lips meet hers, the sweetest contact, barely touching at first, then the pressure increasing and there was yet another remarkable sensation in this day filled with unprecedented sensations, a taste of sweetness, of caring, of wanting so desperately to please, she him, he her, as though only a miracle of the highest quality would do for both of them, as though as long as it was their turn for this radiant discovery, they both wanted it to be unmatched by any other since the beginning of time.

Still he held her in that slight pressure of a kiss, her first, though she'd dreamed about it many a time, a kiss that now left her head spinning, a roaring in her ears, her knees weak, her heart pounding, a physical disintegration more severe than any she'd ever suffered or enjoyed.

Then like the embrace earlier, it was over long before she was ready for it to be over, her first glimpse of his face one of unbearable beauty, apology mixed with matching enjoyment.

"I'm—sorry if I—"

"No, you didn't—"

"I couldn't—"

"I know."

As their words tumbled out, they kneeled opposite each other and it was as though with this kiss, they both knew that the rules had changed, even the game had changed. All the earlier awkwardness and apprehension that Eve had felt disappeared and was replaced simply with an urgent need to talk about the future, to make certain that this miracle would be given a chance to repeat itself. Fearful that he perhaps did not share her feelings, she sat back on her heels and tried to study his face.

"Stephen, I—"

"Shhh." He smiled and reached out for her again and drew her close, and in that sweet cocoon she knew that he knew what she was feeling, knew that he was sharing it, and that private knowledge brought her incredible happiness.

"I wish we were the only two people in the world," she whispered.

"We are. It's our world now."

"What will we—"

"We'll work something out. I promise. Come," he said at last and stood and offered her his hand. "Sis Liz is waiting."

"She will know."

"Good. Then she'll be the first."

She accepted his assistance and gathered the mushrooms in her skirt and, once up, found his lips waiting for her and wondered how they would be able to conduct themselves without everyone knowing.

"Come on," she whispered and grasped his hand in the manner of someone who never intended to let go and led him at a rapid pace through the pine woods and in a remarkably short time approached the clearing of Fan Cottage and felt a sadness as she recalled the last time she had been there.

"Come on. Sis Liz must be inside. Sometimes she waits for me here, but—"

Before the closed door she came to a halt, and suddenly it occurred to her that she'd never knocked on the door to Fan Cottage in her life. Someone—either White Doll or Sis Liz—had always spotted her coming through the woods and well before she reached this point would have come out, prepared to greet her and make her feel welcome.

Now nothing, not even the customary bird calls that seemed always to surround Fan Cottage. Now there was only silence.

"Do you suppose she's home?"

"She never goes anywhere," Eve said and knocked at the door and at the same time called out, "Sis Liz, we wouldn't have come if you hadn't invited us."

Softly she heard the bolt sliding, heard the pressure of a footstep on the floor beyond, and slowly the door opened and Eve stepped back and joined Stephen where he'd retreated to mid-porch.

Together they eyed the partially open door through which no light came.

"Sis Liz? Is that you?" she called softly.

"Who do you think it is?" came this poor imitation of Sis Liz's once rich and vibrant voice. "I wanted to see you, yes. Those tongueless girls have been killing me by refusing to gossip with me. White Doll used to gossip with me. Now I depend upon you."

By "tongueless girls," Eve assumed she meant Dorie and Katie, both efficient, strong and capable, though not given to idle talk.

"What do you want to gossip about, Sis Liz?"

"Mr. Eden, of course. They've told me a little, about your Papa making a jackass of himself."

Eve smiled and heard a step behind her and saw Stephen silhouetted in the open door. She extended a hand to him. "Come, she's here, not in top form, but—"

He hesitated a moment longer, then stepped all the way in and drew even with Eve where she stood in the fringe of light.

"Sis Liz, may I present Mr. Stephen Eden. He's—"

"I know who he is. Have him come all the way in and stand directly before me."

"I'm fine where I am, thank you, Miss Stanhope."

This voice was not disrespectful, just confident. Eve held her breath to see how it would be received. Sometimes Sis Liz didn't like anyone to be confident except herself.

The two were sizing each other up, the veiled grief-stricken old woman and Stephen, standing just inside the door, neither speaking, though both, Eve was certain, were trying very hard to read the silence.

Finally, "Shut the door," Sis Liz commanded.

Eve protested. "We won't be able to see."

"Nonsense. The best light is the light of darkness."

Stephen obliged, and Eve waited for the shadows to win the day. But they never did. With the absence of the blinding morning sun, there was a pleasant twilight softness where everything was even more visible than under the glare of full light.

"I'm afraid you must forgive us, young man," Sis Liz said now and seemed to sit straighter in the rocker and adjust the black silk veil that obscured her face.

"No need for apologies," Stephen replied. "I'm very sorry for— everything—for your extreme loss, for the senselessness of it. Death is welcome when it is timely; untimely, it is painful to bear and impossible to understand."

There was a pause, though Eve suspected a set of closely listening ears beneath that black veil. "How old are you?" Sis Liz asked, and for the first time Eve saw a blue-veined white hand lift from the arm of the rocker and shift the veil as though it was growing hot and uncomfortable.

"Twenty-two," came the response.

"How is it that you speak with such authority on the subject of death? You're scarcely out of the womb."

"I've always felt an affinity, a kinship."

"With death?"

"Yes. My mother died when I was six. I remember it well."

"Did you love her?"

"My mother? Of course."

"Not everyone loves his mother. I hated mine."

"I'm sorry to hear it."

"Eve, do you hate your mother?"

The unexpected and cruel question caught her off guard. "I adore Mama and you know it."

"Good for you."

There was silence, this one stretching even longer. Twice Stephen turned and looked at Eve as though for guidance.

Then all at once he moved forward until he was standing directly in front of the rocker, forcing the black-veiled head to look up. "We brought you something, Sis Liz," he began, his voice gentle, as though he were caring for a beloved and grieving friend.

"I need nothing."

"Come, Eve. Show her the mushrooms. We picked them ourselves only a short time ago. They are fresh from the ground, and I'm certain still retain their earth taste."

Eve stepped forward and allowed the two dozen or so mushrooms to roll out onto the small table to the right of the rocker. Even in half-light, they glistened like large misshapen pearls.

Slowly Sis Liz reached for one, her gnarled fingers at first having difficulty picking it up, but securing it at last, rubbing it as she transferred it beneath the black veil, the hand reappearing minus mushroom, but a pleasurable sigh suggested that she approved.

"So good."

Stephen nodded. "My father claims he could subsist on nothing else. In certain parts of North Devon, they grow to saucer size."

"Some are deadly."

"Of course. But if you're careful—"

"There's an Irish lilt in your voice."

"After my mother died, I lived with my grandfather in Dublin."

"Why don't you sit down?"

And he did, on the edge of the settee, while Sis Liz angled her rocker about, facing away from Eve now, leaving her feeling the outsider, but not objecting. She found herself a perch on a near footstool and was perfectly content to watch and listen, amazed at this easy and growing rapport between them.

"Now tell me about your plans," Sis Liz asked abruptly.

"My—plans?" Stephen repeated and for the first time he faltered.

"What do you intend to do? What brought you here? Will you be staying? What is your—"

Abruptly Stephen laughed and lifted both hands in a restraining gesture. "Wait, please. One at a time or none at a time preferably. I know someone else who asks questions like that—a volley that leaves one quite defenseless."

To Eve's pleasure, she saw the direction of his gaze shift to her, saw

Sis Liz turn abruptly as though she'd just remembered that Eve was present as well.

"Well for heaven's sake, what are you perched over there for, like some sad Sally-in-the-corner? Come, child, this was all your doing. Sit before me. There comes a time when all age can do is worship at the feet of youth. So much passes me by."

As Eve was settling beside Stephen on the settee, she heard his thoughtful contradiction. "I doubt seriously if much has ever passed you by, Sis Liz," he said.

"You're right, though I am an old maid."

"A deprivation," he said with a smile, "I suspect, that extends only to the absence of a ring on your finger."

Sis Liz's head went rigid beneath the veil. She said nothing. Eve held her breath. No one spoke to Sis Liz like that, except White Doll.

Then she heard a soft and single laugh, like an accidental expulsion of air, followed by another, then yet a third and at last the sound of genuine amusement escaped from beneath the black veil, Sis Liz laughing as Eve had seldom heard her laugh except with White Doll.

"You have picked up more than a lilt from your Irish days, young man," she concluded at the end of the laugh, growing breathless, lifting the hem of the veil and waving it as though in need of air.

"Now I want to take a good look at you," Sis Liz exclaimed and suddenly lifted the black veil and sailed it off her head. "So much for grief," she pronounced almost in anger. "No point to it, no point at all," she said and rose from the rocker and moved toward the shuttered windows. Once there, she threw off the latches until all four shutters had been removed and the small room was flooded with brilliant morning sun.

"There," Sis Liz proclaimed. "That should be enough grieving even to satisfy White Doll. You know we had endless arguments on the propriety of grief. White Doll adored large and noisy and teary funerals. I abhor them. But I played her game for about a week. Thought I was going crazy, all that black and falseness. Now—"

The woman was transformed. This was the old Sis Liz Eve was accustomed to. Stephen was not, and Eve saw him smiling at the old woman, trying to keep up with her in all ways, what she was saying as well as what she was doing. And what she was doing now was fussing with something in the kitchen alcove.

"There!" she pronounced at last, reappearing, bearing a silver tray filled with every kind of delectable sweet imaginable. Eve spotted cinnamon-coated pecans, petit fours, fudge, peanut brittle, dark molasses cookies, spun sugar—a Christmas feast in August that she

placed in front of Stephen on the low ivory table, with a stern order
to "Now eat and let me look at you."

As though her performance was over, she settled back in her
rocker, propped up her elbows and rested her chin on one gnarled
hand. For several moments the spell persisted. Eve, accustomed to
such theatrics, had the advantage and thus was able to focus on poor
Stephen, who, quite obviously, had never met anyone like Sis Liz in
his life.

"Help yourself," Eve whispered. He chose a piece of walnut fudge
and then settled back, chewing contentedly and returning Sis Liz's
merciless gaze.

"I agree with you," he said after swallowing the candy.

Eve saw a perplexed expression on Sis Liz's face.

"Grief," he said simply and selected a second piece of fudge. "We
plan to resist it, criticize those who give in to it, and then ultimately
we succumb to it ourselves. I've never really mourned for my mother.
I look forward to doing so one day."

He chewed contentedly on the second piece of candy. Eve wasn't
certain what he had meant, but it didn't matter. Her attention was
drawn to his lips, enjoying the fudge, the same lips that only recently
had pressed ever so gently against hers.

She felt a pleasant blush that warmed her face. She bowed her
head, afraid that both Stephen and Sis Liz would see her discomfort.

But it was an idle fear as with bowed head, she continued to hear
the two of them speaking together.

"Where did you go after Dublin? I've always admired the Irish.
They are so childlike and apologize to no one."

Stephen laughed and accepted her gift of a sugared pecan. "I agree,
though my grandfather was a warm and generous man."

"Most children are warm and generous."

"He returned us to Eden Castle at my father's request."

"How old were you?"

"I was about eight, my brother Frederick six."

"Why did your father wait so long?"

Stephen shrugged. "He was ill, then he left England for a period of
time."

"He didn't want you?"

Stephen looked up, surprised, though still smiling. "You're absolutely right."

"No, I'm sure I'm wrong. How could anyone not want a child as
beautiful as you surely were."

Eve looked up in this long silence to see them both bestowing on
the other a smile of radiant proportions.

Sis Liz broke the silence by leaning back in the rocker, the picture of contentment. "You know, when one gets to be my age, you become very aware of the quality of one's happiness. Is this an inferior grade? Marred by something beyond one's control? Or is this top notch, perfect in every way?" She shook her head and smiled at a gossamer piece of spun sugar candy.

"White Doll made these only last week. She kept them in an airtight tin and always said they were to be served on special occasions."

A new mood had entered this small salon—not one of mourning, and for that Eve was grateful, but something sad and solemn and very vulnerable. Now she watched along with Stephen as Sis Liz lovingly studied the spun sugar candy.

"Always life has poised me most strangely between extreme happiness and terror." She smiled. "I have never understood the precarious balance or why I am the one selected to endure it."

"Tell me about White Doll," Stephen invited. "Not her death, her life."

Sis Liz seemed surprised by the invitation.

"I'm serious," Stephen insisted. "She seems to have touched everyone I've met at Stanhope Hall. I suspect that you more than anyone knew her to a soul's depth."

Eve sat contentedly to one side of the settee. She knew what was happening even as Sis Liz started to speak, beginning a healing monologue that started with Mammy Fan. And as the tale grew, Eve only half heard the words, concentrating as she was on Stephen, on that remarkable profile, that tenderness of expression, capable of bringing Sis Liz out of herself to the extent that within a short time White Doll had been resurrected, loved, explained, understood and finally put to rest.

Sis Liz's account must have lasted for twenty minutes, her voice alternately strong and aggressive and soft and tender. There was bitterness at the end, though it appeared to be short-lived. Not once, as far as Eve could tell, had Stephen's attention faltered. He had gone with her through a lifetime of devotion, always urging her on without words. When Sis Liz reached the conclusion, the murder itself, she appeared to be drained and sat slowly back in the rocker and said simply, "I wish it had been me. I have nothing left to give this world. I fell out of love with it a long time ago. I try to offend God at least once daily so He will free me in a glorious expulsion."

"Sometimes our offenses are our most treasured contributions to life and the world," Stephen said with a smile.

"What fool told you that?"

"My father."

The announcement seemed to produce a mild repentance. "I can speak only for myself, of course."

"You've just given me a richly detailed account of a lifelong and loving companionship."

Eve saw Sis Liz blink. A shaft of high morning sun cut through the window and highlighted her frail beauty. At first Eve saw suspicion on those lined features. Then slowly it changed to gratitude. Now she stood before Stephen, one trembling hand caressing his hair.

"Most remarkable," was what she said, and Stephen allowed the contact and ultimately stood before her and kissed her hand.

Just when Eve thought that neither of them would ever move or speak again, she heard a rustle and looked up to see Sis Liz moving away from the settee until she was standing at the open front door. "Go on now, both of you, though I'll expect you back this time tomorrow."

When at first neither moved, Sis Liz commanded again, "Go on, I say. Did you hear me? Go and find some dreaming room for yourselves, so that years from now when you're my age and nothing works as it should, and you see all of the strings and none of the magic, you'll have a pristine reservoir of beautiful memories untouched by the passage of time, untouched by cynicism and skepticism, all of which you can take out, gently, one at a time and feed on and derive sustenance from. Then and only then can you remember what the magic was like before the sorrow came."

She turned her back on them and walked out onto the porch as though demonstrating how movement was to be accomplished.

Eve waited for Stephen to make the first move, and he did, reaching out his hand to her, an expression on his face she'd never seen before, but one which she knew she'd never forget, knew further that all she asked of life now was never to be far from that face, that expression of love, that hand that now grasped hers and lifted her up.

Someplace on the front porch, Sis Liz was waiting, and beyond that the world was waiting.

No matter. With every passing moment the gift was confirmed. How effortless and right it seemed, to take the hand of this man when she'd never taken any man's hand before, to stand before him and return his steady gaze, all of it so right, as though each, hidden from view of the other, had been waiting for years—centuries, even—for this moment when they would come together with a simple meaning and understanding that neither would ever be alone again.

"She's a fascinating lady," he whispered.

"I think she's fallen in love with you."

"It's reciprocal."

"Let's walk," Eve proposed.

"Where?"

"Does it matter?"

"No."

They passed Sis Liz without a word, though it was a friendly silence, an understanding silence, with no words necessary. Stephen's hand tightened on hers and she looked around, amazed that the world was no longer a frightening place.

* * *

"Where's Eve?"

As Burke's question flew across the desk with unexpected force, Mary looked up and felt as though she was struggling for balance. She was unaccustomed to being invited into Burke's private sanctum, his study.

When at mid-morning Burke had summoned her, Mary had obeyed immediately, stopping in her rooms to get her leather notebook, confident that the meeting was about the coming weekend, a special weekend for Burke and all at Stanhope Hall, a prestigious gathering including Mr. Booker T. Washington and Mr. Samuel Clemens, the writer from Missouri whom Burke had met a few months ago in New Orleans and who had expressed a strong desire to meet Mr. Washington. She'd come prepared to talk about dinners and menus and sleeping arrangements, and not—

"Mary, did you hear me? Where is Eve?"

There it was again, that same question laced with that new distance, new formality.

"Eve?" Mary repeated foolishly and looked appropriately bewildered. "I'm sure I don't know. I imagine she's in her rooms, or—"

"No, I checked. She's not in her rooms."

"Then perhaps she's out with young Stephen. She's been showing him about."

"Isn't there someone else who could do that?"

"Who?"

At last she saw the assault begin to falter. Now she watched as Burke sat slowly back in his chair and began stacking and restacking the papers before him.

As the high morning sun spilled across the desk, she saw a single ray spotlight his face and thought he looked tired, his face still bearing the scabbed cuts of his foolish bout with Stephen Eden. To the best of Mary's knowledge, the two men had not spoken directly to one another since that morning, even though there had been family dinners with everyone present and accounted for. Yet even then,

Burke had spoken to everyone at table except Stephen Eden, and Stephen had spoken to no one unless spoken to, preferring to spend all his time gazing at Eve, a gaze that Mary found touching and innocent though little more. They both still were children, and she was grateful that Eve had come out of herself to the extent that she could fill his time and show him her most treasured spots at Stanhope Hall.

"I don't like it," she heard Burke pronounce flatly, and she looked up, surprised.

"Don't like what?"

"The two of them, loose like that. Eve has her studies."

"She's keeping up. More than keeping up. Ask Madame Germaine."

"That's your department."

"Then leave it to me and trust me."

He held her gaze, doubt still brewing. Mary tried again to offer reassurance. "Nothing will happen, my dearest, I assure you. Despite your feelings, which usually are quite accurate, but in this case are very wrong, the young man is decent, very personable, very intelligent."

At some point Burke appeared to stop listening. Hurriedly he gathered the numerous drafts of his *Century* articles and appeared to be flipping through them. But despite this performance, Mary knew he was still paying close attention.

"He feels—unwanted here," Mary tried to explain.

"He is unwelcomed."

"Yet he has no place else to go."

"I thought he'd been sent on a mission."

"He has."

"Then let him get on with it."

"We are his kin, blood relations."

"The same blood relations that almost destroyed you."

For several moments she doubted seriously if there was anything she could say that would temper his anger. The truth was the more she was around Stephen Eden, the more she was beginning to learn that this mirror image of John Murrey Eden was quite different from the original; that sincerity issued from his lips, not sarcasm; compassion, not hostility; concern, not conceit; and most important, love, not hate. If only Burke—

"Do you know where your oldest daughter is at this moment?"

She looked up, startled by the persistent question. "Eve is—" She struggled, trying to form an answer. "She—they—I remember—Sis Liz. Yes, we received a note from Sis Liz, requesting to see both of them."

"Why?"

"I have no idea. I was very pleased, though. It's the first time since White Doll that Sis Liz has sent us one of her cards."

"She's obviously feeling better, then?"

"I assume, though the card was a mourning card."

The conversation and the memories that lurked so fresh behind it seemed to plunge Burke into new brooding. Mary knew that no progress had been made in finding the murderers, knew further that none was likely to be made. In a horrible way, what had happened had been overdue. While she was not a true daughter of the South, Mary had been here long enough to discern certain realities, certain codes of behavior. The wise man knew his place and stayed in it. Unfortunately for White Doll, Burke had lacked that dubious wisdom, and lacked it still.

"Mary, are you listening to me?"

She looked up. Had he been speaking?

"I'm sorry. Yes, Eve and Stephen are with Sis Liz. I'm sure of it."

"I was not speaking on that subject."

"I *am* sorry. Then, what?"

"Our company next week."

"Yes, of course." She sat straighter in the chair and tried to shake off this new mood of gloom that Burke had dropped about her shoulders. Suddenly it had occurred to her that Fan Cottage might not be so safe a place after all.

"And here's the guest list. Most of whom you already know. I'll leave seating and menus to you and Mrs. Winegar."

As Burke spoke, Mary scanned the sheet and noticed Taylor Quitman's name. "Will Mrs. Quitman be coming?" she asked, already aware of what the answer would be. Wives never visited Stanhope Hall; something to do with what they perceived her reputation to be. It had bothered her once, though not now.

"No," he said. "No, Mrs. Quitman will not attend."

Mary stared down at the list and felt an ominous burning behind the bridge of her nose. She was so tired of being alone, always alone. Burke's friends, always Burke's friends.

"My darling, I'm sorry—"

The loving voice was Burke's, as were the arms that enclosed her and held her tight, briefly crushing the guest list but not her pain.

She didn't want to cry, though there was much to cry for. But his closeness, coming fast on the heels of his anger, moved her. She closed her eyes inside his arms and gave in to his strength, which seemed never to falter, even under the most difficult circumstances.

"I assure you," he whispered close to her ear, "it's no big loss, the absence of all those feather-headed females, none of whom are worthy to sweep the dust from your path."

"Don't," she whispered and reached up to hush him. She hated to hear that sort of comfort. Quickly she brushed away her tears and allowed one hand to caress his face. She found it after all these years the most moving and remarkable face she'd ever seen and softly proposed, "Come with me. Let's walk to Fan Cottage together and bring the two of them back ourselves."

But she saw the answer in his eyes even before he spoke. "Richard Gilder is coming next weekend. He will expect the entire set of articles to be finished."

She stepped out of his arms. The embrace was over. Unfortunately the hurt was still there.

Burke followed after her for a step. "Are you worried? You said they were to be trusted."

"They are."

"Then—"

His expression of innocence suddenly infuriated her. She couldn't keep up with his mood changes and wasn't certain that she wanted to. "Then I'll go and find them," she announced from the door, a clear tone of martyrdom in her voice, which she loathed.

"Not alone."

"Why not?"

"Do I have to tell you?"

"It's mid-afternoon. Your—friends only operate in predawn darkness."

"They are not my friends."

"You know them."

"Mary, I forbid you."

Halfway through the door, she smiled. At least she had managed to make him angry. And that felt good.

"Mary, wait. I'll get Paris to go with you."

"Surely I don't need his assistance. I'll go myself."

Even as she talked, she was moving steadily down the hall, aware that both their voices were carrying to the adjoining rooms, where servants were already working in preparation for the weekend.

Still she moved toward the far end of the central corridor, half-expecting him to call her back or to send Paris Boley running. But neither happened.

At the end of the gallery she gazed out across the sun-drenched yard, where nothing moved in the heat of the summer day. To the right she saw a small curl of smoke coming from the smokehouse behind the kitchen annex and found it curious. Was Mrs. Winegar already smoking meats in preparation for the weekend? It was far too early. Meats smoked too far in advance retained a strong salty taste.

But it wasn't her concern. Mary glanced down at the guest list Burke had given her. Samuel Clemens, Booker T. Washington, Taylor Quitman, Dr. Melrose—all Burke's friends. No accommodations had been made for Madame Germaine, none even for Mary herself, none for the children.

Suddenly she felt a surge of anger and rebellion. She was nothing more in this house than a servant and a fixture. In a burst of anger she wadded the guest list and hurled it downward and didn't bother to see where it landed, and took the gallery steps running.

She entered the woods and scarcely slowed her pace, unconcerned with all obstacles and all hazards, in need only of freedom and danger.

* * *

Orlando Dow steadied his horse behind the cane brake and kept one squinted eye on the trail of smoke curling lazily upward from Stanhope Hall's kitchen annex. His instructions had been clear. Wait in the cane brake until the smoke ceased, then ride in to the edge of the woods. Someone from the kitchen would deliver a message, which Orlando Dow was to return immediately to Jarmay Higgins's lumberyard in Mobile.

Simple. Orlando relaxed a bit upon his saddle, pleased at the thought of an easy twenty dollars, and a job with so few risks, unlike the one he'd done here several weeks ago.

Orlando kept his eye on the smoke trail and burped pleasurably from his lunch of shrimp and rice. He liked some jobs more than others, but took pride in the fact that nothing was beneath him or above him, not where money was involved. And with these fancy gentlemen who called themselves the Knights of the White Camellia, money was always involved, good gold pieces, all of which Orlando spent on himself, because that's what God had told him to do years ago when he'd first discovered he had a way with words and people. He could get his mouth going fast and recite all the Bible stuff his grandma had beaten into him with a leather strap. But he hadn't been clean then and spruced up, and that's when God came right down to the cot on which he was sleeping out behind his uncle's barn and told him that folks liked their preachers to be clean and well dressed.

Orlando tasted pepper sauce from his burp. *Preacher.* That's the first time he'd ever heard the word, from God himself. God had called Orlando Dow a preacher and that's just exactly what he'd been all his grown-up life—the best preacher in these parts.

Again he glanced toward the smoke trail coming from the kitchen annex. Not clear yet. How much longer? He shifted in the saddle and raised his left leg to brace it against the saddle horn. Listen! Something moving through the woods. A rustling like—

He sat straight and tried to see through the thick mosaic of sun and shadow. Had he misunderstood the signals? Was the messenger to come to him, or was he to watch the smoke for a sign to come forward?

Slowly, all nerves tensed, he eased his legs back down and tightened his grip on the reins. In the event something had gone wrong, it was his desire to make the fastest exit possible.

Now he sat erect and kept his eyes sharply focused on the area of the woods where he thought he'd heard movement. He saw nothing at first, then saw a figure, a woman, quite a figure, for he recognized her instantly, as what red-blooded male in Mobile County would not recognize her, the buxom full-bodied figure of the lady of Stanhope Hall.

Relieved, Orlando Dow allowed himself to relax. She was alone, on foot, and he was well concealed behind the cane brake. He could watch her for as long as she was in his sights, longer if he chose to follow her, but what now struck Orlando Dow was the stupidity of the owner of Stanhope Hall, for allowing his wife to wander unaccompanied through what, even an idiot would assume to be hazardous terrain.

Then all at once she stopped and leaned against a near tree trunk. Orlando, watching closely, was prepared to swear on a stack of Bibles that she was weeping.

Something within him stirred, a curiosity to examine the lady's flesh up close, to see if he could determine the cause of her unhappiness. Perhaps he could even comfort her, and he did have a way with ladies.

He was halfway out of the saddle, having determined that he could best surprise her on foot, when his eye, gazing along the horizon near Stanhope Hall, failed to see the smoke circling upward. The signal: a cessation of smoke.

Damn!

For a moment he balanced precariously on one stirrup, his focus torn between the weeping woman less than fifty feet away and the absence of smoke, which meant that he was to ride in to the rear window of the kitchen annex, where someone would hand him the message.

Suddenly it occurred to him that he could do both, could fetch the message and then return here for a surprise visit with Mrs. Burke

Stanhope. Of course he would conceal his identity. He quickly reached inside his knapsack and found the gray hood that Reverend Pounders and Mr. Higgins had provided them with last week.

With leveled eyes he found her again, collapsed near a tree, head down, clearly distraught. Suddenly he had a hunger for the lady. A little sport certainly would make the long trip out from Mobile more worthwhile.

Then hurry. He swung back into the saddle and carefully led his horse to the left, moving as quietly as possible, not wanting to alert the unhappy lady and warn her in advance. He did not increase his speed until he saw the steep pitched roof of the kitchen annex, the chimney still free of smoke.

Orlando held his position at the edge of the woods and waited, looking in all directions, wanting to see before he was seen. Still he waited. Not a sign of a nigger. No messenger at all with message in hand.

What in the hell?

Annoyed, he steadied his horse and was on the verge of returning to his sport in the woods when suddenly a small window near the north end of the annex was pushed open and the shrew's face appeared, a white kerchief tied about her head.

So she was the one. She gave him a hard look as though trying to identify him, then, as unexpectedly as she had appeared, she disappeared, withdrawing back inside the window and closing it after her.

For several seconds Orlando blinked at the vacuum and rapidly lost all patience. Suddenly he applied his spurs to horseflesh and moved quickly forward until he was even with the small window, which now was closed to him.

He lifted his hand and rapped loudly. "Anybody there?"

He was on the verge of rapping again when suddenly the small window shot open and he found himself staring into the face of the old cook known as Mrs. Winegar.

"I was sent to collect something from you," Orlando said, amazed at how truly ugly the woman was up close.

"I know what you was sent for. Just hold your horses."

"Well, did you signal or not?"

"I did."

"Then where is it?"

"I'm making a copy. Can't give you the original."

With that she disappeared from the window again and left Orlando to look nervously about, cursing the stupidity of women in general and this one in particular. All he needed was to be seen lurking about outside the kitchen annex. Then he'd be no good to any of Jarmay Higgins's friends.

After about ten minutes of waiting he was on the verge of swinging his horse about and returning to the safety of the woods when suddenly the window flew open and there was the bitch again, a large envelope in her hand.

"Here 'tis," she announced. "I think it will interest your gentlemen."

He grabbed it on the first swipe and glared at her. "Thanks for keeping me waiting."

She crossed her fleshy arms on the windowsill. "You'd best take off. And I'd avoid going through the woods, as the mistress just headed that way toward Fan Cottage."

Now it was Orlando's turn to feign surprise. He tucked the envelope inside his coat pocket and swung his horse about and moved at a steady canter toward the edge of the woods. Only once did he look back toward the kitchen annex and when he did the shrew's face was gone, the window closed and bolted.

First work, and now play. Accordingly he patted his inside pocket, where recently he'd stashed the envelope. Then he headed back into the woods, traveling the same path, keeping a sharp eye out on the shadows to the left, hoping that the whore would materialize, weeping against the tree trunk. For as God's man, Orlando Dow would willingly take the place of the tree trunk and that would be true joy, to go where the master of Stanhope Hall had gone, though who would know about it but himself and God, and they could talk and laugh about it later, Orlando and God, for he had never had so good a friend or protector, someone who drank with him and whored with him and laughed with him and provided for him and blessed him with unexpected treasures.

Now where was she?

There she was.

* * *

Mary knew she should not linger in these woods, but for now they seemed a safe haven halfway between the unhappiness she'd left at Stanhope Hall and the unhappiness she'd surely encounter in Fan Cottage. That, combined with the sense of complete disintegration, caused her to lean against a near tree and give in to tears.

Now she sat in a curled position at the trunk of a tree and wept as she had not wept since she was a child. And only when she heard herself in echo, the awful sobbing and sniffling, like an immature schoolgirl, did she withdraw her handkerchief from her sleeve and wipe at her face and thank God there was no one here to see her weakness or to scold her for her self-indulgence.

Listen—

She heard a noise, clear, directly behind her and turned on it. She sharpened her focus on a limited expanse of wood and saw nothing of substance, saw only shadows and ever-changing pools of sunlight. She held still in this awkward twisted position, continuing to look about. Slowly she stood, using the tree for support.

"Who's there?" she called out and was appalled at how weak her voice sounded and backed away from the tree and looked quickly in the general direction of Fan Cottage and wished that she could see it and be within running distance.

But she wasn't, and now she tried to determine whether it might be the wisest course of action to turn about and return to Stanhope Hall.

Then she heard it again, a sound almost brutal in its clarity, the sound of a horse coming from someplace in those deepest shadows to her right. A horse implied a rider and perhaps more than one, for White Doll surely had encountered more than one.

Then she was running, flailing at the low-hanging branches, which seemed suddenly to impede her. Uncertain of her direction, her fears grew, being remorselessly fed by her memories of recent events.

Still she ran, speed increasing, her skirts lifted, fear blinding her, when suddenly, turning her face to the hazards behind, she failed to see the man directly ahead and collided with an unearthly scream which accelerated even more as male arms tightened about her. And over and above the siren of her scream, the last face she saw before she fainted was that of her half-brother John Murrey Eden, a look of concern on his face, and despite her terror, she was pleased to see him though she had no idea how he came to be here, prowling these southern pine woods, so far from England and home.

* * *

"I saw no one in the woods, sir, but then Eve and I were coming from the opposite direction when we encountered Mrs. Stanhope."

"Was she running?" Burke demanded.

"Yes," Stephen said, "She was frightened—"

"That's all."

Burke could scarcely stand to look at the boy, let alone question him. He glanced about at the interior of Fan Cottage and thought it even smaller than he'd remembered it. Of course at this moment it *was* crowded, Sis Liz bending over Mary, who lay on the big four-poster, apparently in a deep faint. Sis Liz was administering a pungent-smelling potion that caused Burke's eyes to burn. He stepped quickly outside onto the porch, where Paris Boley was waiting along with a half-dozen workers who had heard his wife's screams and come running.

Now all Burke was trying to determine was what had happened. What had caused Mary to go pale and lifeless? And had there been a trespasser in these woods? If so, was it a mere transient or someone who wanted to harm his wife, as someone had done harm to White Doll?

He caught Paris's eye and shook his head. The fear was receding, that awful fear that had gripped him when someone—and he literally could not remember who—had come running in to his study and told him that his wife had been hurt and was now at Fan Cottage.

He remembered nothing of his own mad dash to Fan Cottage, remembered little at all except seeing Mary on Sis Liz's bed, Sis Liz bent over her and to one side, Eve looking pale and frightened, and behind her Stephen Eden.

Why was it that disaster always struck when that likeness appeared?

Aware that the question was foolish and unproductive, Burke led Paris back to the door, away from the workers, who had spread out and who now kept a sharp watch on all directions of the woods.

"He says he saw no one," Burke said, keeping his voice down, feeling greater trust in Paris Boley than in anyone present.

"Then he probably didn't," Paris said, "though Billy there said he saw a rider near the kitchen annex about an hour ago."

"Who?"

"He didn't know. Said he had on a fancy vest and coat, said he was a white man."

Burke looked puzzled at this information. A single rider, in a fancy coat? A threat? A happenstance?

The climate of fear was destructive. And Mary *had* been distraught when she'd left Stanhope Hall.

"Is Mrs. Stanhope—"

"Still unconscious," Burke said in answer to Paris's question. He strode back to the edge of the porch and gazed out over the heads of his workers at the benign woods in which now nothing moved.

"Papa?"

The voice was soft and came from behind. He saw Eve, her face mirroring the tension of the day. "Mama's awake now. Sis Liz says you can—"

He didn't wait for her to finish and walked back to the door and was met by two disagreeable barriers, one the obnoxious potion Sis Liz had used to bring Mary around, and the other, Stephen Eden, who stood just inside the door.

"Let me pass," Burke demanded, and even as he approached the bed on which Mary lay, he knew that in his hate for the boy, he was doing greater damage to himself and must soon take steps to curb it before it was too late.

"What is that odor?" he mumbled, and cast a wary eye on the small vial Sis Liz still held in her hand.

"It brought your wife around to consciousness. Try not to send her back again."

"It's all right, Sis Liz."

Mary's intervening voice was weak and drew all attention down to the bed. Burke sat on the bed and clasped her hand, which rested on top of the summer sheet. Her color was not good, and her hair was matted with perspiration about her forehead. But even in distress there was a look of strength about her, as though if everyone would just give her a moment, life would continue. She would see to it.

"My dearest," he whispered. "What happened? Can you tell me?"

She wet her lips as though wanting to speak, though at that moment her eyes grew wide and she looked urgently about. "Eve—Stephen—where—"

"They're here," Burke reassured her.

"Let me see them," she insisted and tried to sit up and failed. Though Burke had no intention of summoning the two, who would only prove a greater distraction, Sis Liz did. When he looked back he saw Eve and the Eden boy standing at the foot of the bed.

Eve, apparently unable to resist the deep love she felt for her mother, came up on the other side and bent down and gracefully kissed Mary's forehead.

"Mama, are you all right? I was so afraid when we found you."

"You found me?"

Eve nodded. "And Stephen. We were coming back from Fan Cottage when we heard your screams."

Burke listened closely, grateful to be hearing at least one account of what had happened.

"Did you see anyone in the woods?" he asked Eve.

The person he wanted least to answer, answered. "No sir," young Eden replied, "though I think I heard a horse."

"You think?" Burke echoed.

"Mrs. Stanhope was crying," the boy added. "It was difficult to hear."

"Then what makes you think you heard a horse?" Burke demanded, still unable to look at the boy.

"Before we heard her screams, I believe I heard the whinny of a horse."

"Papa, I heard it too," Eve said, looking up.

"But you saw no one?"

Eve shook her head and clasped Mary's hand with renewed strength, as though never to let go. "Oh, Mama, I was so scared. All I could think of was—White Doll—"

"All right, enough." This sharp voice of authority came from Sis Liz, who moved into the gathering around the bed, hands waving as though she were scattering chickens. Burke noticed a cool wet cloth in one hand and an attitude of impatience, which suggested she'd heard and seen enough. "Now get out, all of you. Leave Mary here for a while. Feel free to wait outside if you wish. But she must have a few minutes to herself. I'm sure you understand, but even if you don't—"

Burke had heard that tone before, many times since childhood, Sis Liz wielding absolute authority where in truth none existed.

Now he saw Eve vacate her side of the bed and stand back to make room for Sis Liz, who sat close beside Mary and placed the wet cloth on her forehead and gave her a most reassuring smile.

"I'm so sorry," she murmured. "But you see the simple matter is that your misfortune today as opposed to White Doll's good fortune a few days ago is that you have not yet earned your death."

Burke listened, mildly intrigued by what he heard. Apparently everyone else within hearing distance felt the same way, for Eve joined young Eden at the foot of the bed again and both looked down to see Mary paying as close attention as they were.

"Oh yes." Sis Liz nodded. "We earn death, we do, every single one of us. Our concepts are ever so confused, and in a way it is that confusion that keeps us safe. You see, the vast majority of people view life as the prize, when in reality life is the trial and the punishment, death the reward; but you see it must be earned."

Apparently she saw a look of skepticism in Mary's eyes and continued to smooth the cool cloth upon her brow. "Of course you doubt," Sis Liz said with unerring confidence. "We all do from time to time, and with good reason. We cannot know nor can we grasp God's merit plan. Why are two-day-old infants taken, or young soldiers in their prime, or selfless and generous individuals who make of life a rare and rich feast?" She shook her head, and Burke had the feeling she was no longer seeing Mary on the bed.

"God does the judging. It is His system, His understanding. Who would have thought White Doll had earned death before I had? I still can't understand why she was taken in blissful death and I was punished with additional life." She looked puzzled, as though entertaining an old sorrow and an old mystery. "But God decides who gets to go to His kingdom, to His everlasting peace. What a glorious moment death must be—to be aware of so much: past, present and future."

For a moment Burke felt hypnotized by the old raspy voice, though he knew what had happened, that Sis Liz had simply worked out her own form of accepting White Doll's death.

"Ten minutes," he announced from the door, pleased to see that he had broken the spell of his old aunt's madness. "Ten minutes. Then I must take her back to Stanhope Hall. I'm sure she saw no one in the woods, only shadows. It's a climate of fear."

Behind him on the front porch, Burke heard a disturbance of voices, several workers speaking at once.

"The men found fresh hoofprints." It was Paris Boley. "There was a horse, Mr. Stanhope, not ten feet from where they found Mrs. Stanhope."

Quickly Burke moved back out onto the porch and closed the door behind him, not wanting to set off new alarms. At the bottom of the steps he saw two men talking to Paris who had apparently found proof, good men both who'd worked for him for years.

"Are you sure?" he demanded, looking down from the top of the steps.

"No mistake, Mr. Stanhope."

Burke stood at the top of the steps and looked out over the shadowy landscape, tailor-made, or so it seemed now, for villains and villainy.

You have offended the Southern Code.

He heard Taylor Quitman's voice in memory. He would have to take protective measures. He would order his family to stay within the safe perimeter of Stanhope Hall. And beyond that, what could he do but wait and pray that the madness would cease, though in a way he knew better.

"Papa, why are they doing this?" The question came from Eve, who moved close beside him and lightly touched his arm.

"I don't know, my darling," he said and covered her hand with his, newly aware of how precious she was to him, this first, special, beautiful daughter who was living a life of isolation and solitude when she should be at the center of the world, the belle of every ball.

"It sometimes takes a good deal of courage, my dear, to confront madness. There are those occasions when you simply must face it down and make it go away. Do you think we can do that?"

She nodded. "If you can, I can, Papa." She smiled, and in the radiance of that smile Burke suddenly felt strong.

Jarmay Higgins was looking out over his vast lumberyard from his office near the central cutting shed when he saw the scoundrel come through the gate and stand there in his tacky garments as though he belonged.

"Damn!" Hadn't he told the man to come after five o'clock, when all his rich customers had purchased their lumber for the day and gone home to their fine houses? Now what must they think to see someone the caliber of Orlando Dow standing in the center of the Higgins lumberyard as though he had a perfect right to be there?

"Marshal, quick!"

With a snap of his fingers he summoned the muscled black man whose sole function in this world was to do exactly what Jarmay Higgins commanded him to do. "Look! Go get him," Higgins commanded. "Bring him up the back way and into the loft. Stay with him until I arrive."

The black mountain that was his hired man Marshal moved immediately. Jarmay had purchased him years ago, off the block, right before the war, only a lad then, nine or ten, who knew? But even then Marshal the boy had given all the promise of becoming a giant. And that promise had been more than fulfilled. And while the best part about Marshal was his physical prowess, the second-best part about Marshal was, conversely, the microscopic size of his brain. Slack-jawed, dull-eyed, he moved only on command. Now Jarmay watched him go down the narrow winding staircase that led to the ground floor, his arms long and massive at his side, as he headed unerringly toward his target, the grinning jackal of a man named Orlando Dow.

On a curious wave of self-disgust, Jarmay turned back and gazed out over his lumberyard, normally a pleasing sight, with the exception of that one blotch in the fancy coat.

Five—count them, five—wagons were at present being loaded high with fresh-cut Alabama pine.

Jarmay sat back in his chair, remembering with sadness the tensions and conflict that kept his world from being perfect, like those unenlightened few who did not share his love of the Old South, like those who had to be watched constantly lest they make Mobile into a Detroit or, worse, Chicago, or any of those northern hell gates filled with Yankee bastards.

Sobered by his thoughts, he looked back down on his yard in time to see Marshal come alongside Orlando Dow and take his arm and lead him bodily toward the loft staircase and the large room over the cutting shed, a vast cobwebbed place where nothing much was stored now except pieces of old equipment, blades, runners and stacks of warped lumber.

He continued to check the progress of the two men climbing the narrow stairs to the loft door, rickety stairs he'd been meaning to have replaced with some of his own lumber. One day soon he'd do it, as soon as this business was over and Burke Stanhope had been taught a lesson he'd never forget. Then all the Knights of the White Camellia could store their gray hoods and resume their public lives as Sons of the South, though vigilance must always be their watchword, for the true South, the South of the heart and soul, was a delicate blossom whose fragility and uniqueness enraged some and drove them to try to destroy her. And while the Yankee bastards had done physical damage, not one of those dark-blue-uniformed baboons had even come close to harming the soul of the South. That threat, paradoxically, was coming from within, from those most deadly enemies disguised as friends, the scalawags.

So then it was a matter of duty, these unspeakable acts, these unspeakable people. On that positive note, he drew a long breath and adjusted his waistcoat over his paunch and glanced toward the door that would lead him to the staircase, to the loft, to Orlando Dow.

Hopefully the man had something for him, proof that Burke Stanhope was persisting in his treason despite all warnings by the Knights of the White Camellia. Jarmay wouldn't be surprised. It was the mark of arrogance of those such as Burke Stanhope that warnings were seldom effective and never heeded. You had to touch the man himself, for he was incapable of feeling for others. Make the tears spring from a personal agony. Then perhaps with luck . . .

Enough. The white trash Orlando Dow was waiting, though Jarmay vowed not to pay him one penny of the money due him until he'd more than satisfied him that he had earned it. Sometimes preachers were the worst scoundrels of all and had to be watched every minute, lest they use their proclaimed faith as a smoke screen to hide the devil's own doings.

 Stanhope Hall

"Don't go, Stephen, please don't go. You said you'd stay past Friday."

"David's right. I heard you make that promise. I was there," Christine chimed in.

Before these eager and sweet persuaders, Stephen felt helpless and flattered and newly amazed at the unexpected love he'd discovered in this unhappy household.

Now he smiled down on David and Christine, both perched like small birds on the top step of the front gallery, their faces so earnest, so new, reminding him of his nieces and nephews back at Eden Castle, which in turn reminded him of his uncle Richard and the long journey yet ahead of him.

"I can't stay here forever," he said softly, all the while realizing that neither could he leave immediately, and not because of David and Christine's sweet entreaties, but because of their sister, Eve, who had entered his heart on that hot day when he'd first approached Stanhope Hall.

As thoughts of her devastated him anew, he tried to focus on her brother and her sister, seeing in their insistence that he stay awhile longer at Stanhope Hall the same loneliness and isolation he'd first detected in Eve. Apparently no one in the family had contact with the world beyond Stanhope Hall except Burke Stanhope himself. Stephen had been in residence here for over two weeks and no one had come calling; neither had any family members in any combination gone visiting. They never mentioned their isolation, not in so many words, but it was in clear and painful evidence in the upturned faces before him.

In a very few moments, as Stephen knew from the pattern of the last few days, Dorie or Katie or Lucy, one of the young black women who seemed to be in constant movement in and about Stanhope Hall, would come and fetch the children and take them off for their afternoon naps. And if there was a God in heaven, a few minutes after that Eve would appear, having sat at her mother's bedside during her private luncheon to keep her company.

Apparently his aunt Mary had not regained her strength after her ordeal in the woods three days ago, for she had yet to appear at a family meal. Neither had Burke Stanhope put in an appearance. Thus the dining room had been set, meal after meal, for just the four of them: David, Christine, Stephen and generally the grim-faced Madame Germaine.

"Come on, you two. Sandman's awaitin'."

At the sound of the voice, Stephen looked up to see Katie reaching down to both David and Christine, as though she was fully aware that a mere verbal command would be ignored.

"Promise first, Stephen," David demanded in a grown-up tone that sounded eerily like his father. "Promise us that you'll stay at Stanhope Hall past Friday."

Christine added her soft reinforcement. "There are so many trea-sures here at Stanhope Hall, Stephen. We haven't begun to share them all with you."

"Please," David whispered. "We're cousins and we should know each other better before we say good-bye."

It was impossible to resist. "Then I'll stay." Stephen smiled, and saw instant relief accompanied by a wide grin.

"Come on, you two," Katie scolded, "Your mama wants to see you." And with one urgent gesture she indicated there would be no more stalling. Stephen did his part and urged them on, feeling only a little guilty for making a promise that he'd known all along he had no choice but to keep. While the call of duty and responsibility was very strong on one hand, it was as nothing compared to the way in which he fixed his gaze on the doorway through which Katie and the chil-dren had just disappeared, knowing that at any moment *she* would appear, her face reflecting the tone of her meeting with her mother, reflecting as well that deep love she brought to everything and every-one around her.

Thinking about her alone was capable of doing sweet damage, and he stood as though at attention, aware that in a remarkably short time, he'd lost his inner compass, lost his free will, lost his strength of purpose, lost all that was once vital to his life and well-being. For his troubles and sacrifices he had been divinely reimbursed with what surely was heaven's finest gift, Eve's reciprocal love.

Then he heard her—only the slight pressure of a footstep on the lower case of the stairs. In the next second the entire glorious miracle, the most beautiful face and form surely to walk upon this earth, blond hair loosed and flying as she reached for his hand, not taking it —that would have destroyed her spell—but merely touching it, so lightly and whispering, "Come on, let's get out of here, away from this place, just us."

The disjointed invitation told him that something had not gone well during her meeting with her mother. He followed her immedi-ately as she led the way out of the house and cut between the live oaks, heading in an easterly direction, approaching a worn path that Stephen had never seen before. The grasses were higher here. Lead-ing—where?

It didn't matter. A short time later he heard a rush of water and for the first time saw a dark green river up ahead, partially concealed by willows, high banks on the opposite side, with low-hanging Spanish moss trailing gracefully from earthbound trees, like sad women trail-ing their fingers through the swift, clear water.

He had had no notion of a river this size this close. "Eve—"

"Come on." She lifted her cumbersome petticoats even higher and climbed up a steep embankment, the river rushing swift beneath them.

At one point in the climb she stopped and looked around with great stealth and suddenly stepped over the embankment they'd been climbing. For one fearful moment it appeared that she had plunged directly into the river.

"Eve!"

"I'm here, over here, Stephen."

With the next step he saw the natural cave into which she had slipped, saw the short squat tree trunks someone had arranged, and suspected that this was a private place, like his in North Devon, in the old barn halfway between Eden Castle and the cottage of Eden Rising, a geographical accuracy as well as an emotional one.

Once they were safely inside, he sat opposite her on a tree stump and noticed the tension in her face beginning to ease, noticed now other features in the cave itself; a small leather trunk pushed back against the far wall, a weathered and windblown arrangement of dried flowers in an earthenware jar, a book, a fan neatly spread on top of the trunk.

"You've been here before," he observed quietly and noticed that in this shell-like interior, even the roar of the river seemed diminished.

"I've spent a great deal of my life here," she replied. "The best part," she added, and there was that sadness again in her eyes.

"What happened today? With your mother?"

"Mama was not well," Eve said, as though newly saddened by this awareness.

"I'm sorry."

"She's not really ever recovered from her scare in the woods."

"I know. Has the doctor—"

"He's good for nothing," Eve said, looking up for the first time. Her voice drifted along with her gaze, which settled on the cave opening and the river beyond. "Poor Stephen. What a sad tale you will take back to England with you."

"I will take nothing back but the truth."

"That's even sadder."

"How did you ever find this place?"

She smiled. "Easy. Sis Liz says we always find what we need. I found this years ago, right after Christine was born and I heard about death for the first time."

"You came here alone?"

"They were busy with the baby, the whole house in an uproar. Poor Christine. She's been so ill for so long."

"She seems well enough now."

"She adores you. As does David. You're like magic to them, to all of us."

He caught her gaze and held it and marveled at the world for giving absolutely no warning before bestowing these enchanted moments on its poor inhabitants.

"How magic?" he managed.

"You're from the world beyond Stanhope Hall—proof that one does exist, and that with luck we'll all be able to find it one day."

Her mood, her tone of voice, the expression on her face were of such sweet longing. "Has it been so hard for you?" he asked, aching to touch her.

She shook her head. "Not hard in any real sense of the word; not hard like for some. I've never been hungry or cold, never wanted for anything except my own desires. Sis Liz fasts regularly and refuses her shawl regularly and for good measure denies herself at least once a day in order to build her character."

Stephen smiled. "She has a remarkable character as is. I shouldn't think it would need any more building."

"But she didn't come by it easily. She was quite pampered and spoiled as a young girl, like I am. She told me once that she didn't interrupt the vacuum in her head with one hard thought until she was eighteen years old."

Stephen laughed and suspected that Eve was quoting the old woman verbatim. "She's a good woman," he concluded.

"And I adore her. She's made such a difference in my life."

"In what way? Tell me."

At first she seemed taken aback by the question. Slowly she stood and walked to the cave opening, from where she appeared to be gazing out over the river with a new sense of ease and enjoyment in her manner, which pleased Stephen, the tension from Stanhope Hall fading.

"For the same reasons that Christine and David were begging you to stay awhile ago." She looked back. "Oh, I heard." She nodded, hands laced behind her back. "Indeed, the whole house heard."

"I'm sorry for that."

"Oh, no, don't be; even Mama heard it. She asked whose voices were those, and when Katie said David's and Christine's, she said she couldn't remember hearing Christine's voice so strong and clear. That's what Sis Liz did for me. She helped me to recognize my own voice and has assured me that the world one day will find a use for me."

"Have you been isolated here all your life? Was there ever a time when—"

"Oh, no. Isolation doesn't count unless one views one's world as isolated. For a long time I was perfectly content with Stanhope Hall and Papa's visitors and Sis Liz and White Doll and this cave."

Suddenly her voice broke. She appeared to be thinking. "It's only been lately, in the last few years, that I have understood all the restrictions of my life, fully understood this awful isolation."

She moved back to a tree stump and sat, head erect, as though she were in a formal drawing room, her hands folded in her lap.

"Sometimes when I sit here, in this cave, on this spot, I can hear music coming from the Hennessey plantation, or from Mr. Higgins's farm. And sometimes boating parties pass right before me, the most beautiful parties you've ever seen, with ladies in pink gowns and handsome gentlemen in linen jackets, and white satin cloths and bowls of red strawberries and pink carnations, and all the company is laughing and singing, and they never look up and they never see me. Oh, not that I'd want them to. What would they think? Who is that wretched girl living in that cave? But it's a good cave, isn't it? Years ago I brought Sis Liz here and she said it was an enchanted cave."

In that avalanche of words and emotions and sorrows and loneliness, Stephen felt an overpowering compulsion to go to her, to take her in his arms, to hold her until all vestiges of loneliness and sorrow left her.

But of course he didn't. What he did do was walk slowly to a position behind her and in the softest of gestures caress her hair.

"The loss was theirs," he whispered. He ached to touch his lips to such golden silkiness and did. As he bent over, he felt such a longing to keep her safe forever from all future hurts and rebuffs.

"My loss," she contradicted and with one hand reached back and found his and leaned against him, causing a pleasurable weight and pressure that prompted him to close his eyes and look upward toward the damp stones that formed the ceiling of the cave.

"What answer did you give Christine and David?" she asked.

"I told them I'd stay until Friday. It seemed important to them."

"You know why, don't you?"

"A dinner party, David said, of some sort."

"Papa's evening to shine. He arranges similar evenings two, sometimes three times a month, bringing together a distinguished company, generally composed of North and South."

Stephen laughed. "I thought North and South had come together years ago."

"No one's come together at all, under any circumstances, except perhaps at my father's dinner table."

"Who are to be the guests?"

She stood and lightly stretched and walked to the mouth of the cave and peered out over the dark green rushing waters. "Who knows? That's why Mama was so upset. She lost the guest list and menu information Papa had given to her."

"Why doesn't she ask him to make another?"

Eve looked back at his simple suggestion, as though baffled by something. "I don't know. Sometimes I almost think she's afraid of him."

Stephen sat in a straddled position on the stump she'd recently abandoned, content to let her talk about anything, everything. It made no difference to him as long as he could watch her and be with her.

"Of course it's all mixed up now. Everyone's afraid of something, even Sis Liz. Are you ever afraid?"

The question took him off guard. "Of—course," he stammered. "The night before I left on this journey, I went to the old barn . . ."

"Tell me about it, please."

"My old barn is your cave. Do you suppose everyone feels compelled to find a new world for themselves?"

Even as he spoke, she shook her head. "No, only those who find their real world—lacking." She paused. "Could that be everyone?"

He watched her return to the tree stump and sit, a thoughtful look on her face. In an irresistible need, he went to her and drew her toward him, a strong gesture he thought might startle her. But if it did, she gave no indication of it. Rather, he felt her arms move instantly about his neck, and for several long moments they clung to each other.

"My dearest," he whispered. "I cannot leave here without you, you must know that. And I must leave here."

The dilemma, so simply stated, echoed in his ear, without solution until he felt her arms about him ease, felt both her hands forming a soft cup for his face, saw her face emerge with a new and becoming blush.

"Come with me," he proposed.

Certain that he had overstepped his bounds, he watched her face for signs of resistance. Instead she continued to caress his hair, a disconcerting gesture that was wreaking sweet havoc throughout his entire system.

"Sis Liz said you'd ask that," she said, her fingers smoothing back his hair, stopping to caress his ear.

"How did she know?"

"Sis Liz knows everything."

"Will you come with me?"

"How?"

This was not so much a challenge as a need for detail, and though he had not consciously formed a single plan, he was amazed now to find his head filled with the most detailed plans imaginable, as though it had all been worked out in advance in some secret place in his heart.

"We'll go away together," he said simply. "Your father would never approve otherwise."

"When?"

"When he's at his busiest."

"Friday night."

"During the party."

They both stopped speaking at once, a mutual recognition dawning, a new direction underway.

"I love you, Eve," he said in a simple declaration that he had never spoken to a woman before.

"And I love you," she replied.

"Then Friday?" he whispered.

She nodded, and he wished he could move past her beauty and his joy back to the realm of hard thinking and good reasoning. "Where—shall we meet?" he stammered.

"We'll meet at Sis Liz's during the party."

It was a sound idea, a safe place away from the watchful eyes at Stanhope Hall.

"Whom shall we tell?" she asked.

"No one," he said quickly.

"Not even Sis Liz?"

"No one must know."

Slowly she agreed, as though beginning to understand the absolute need to trust no one but themselves.

"Then where will we go?" she whispered. For the first time he saw an expression on her face that suggested she fully understood the magnitude of what they were doing.

"Eve, are you certain?" he asked.

"I've never been more certain," she murmured and kissed him. At the end of the kiss she looked at him. "Do you think I could stay here without you? It was hard enough before. But now every place I went —the dining room, the gallery, the woods, Fan Cottage, everywhere —you would be there, memories of you, echoes of your voice. I'd see your face, wait for your step on the porch—"

He closed his eyes, the better to listen to this sweetest of declarations. He savored it, then persisted with these most important plans, for nothing must go awry, nothing. He couldn't bear it.

"Then listen," he urged and held her at arm's length so their closeness couldn't muddle their minds or dull their brains.

"On Friday evening, after the dinner, when the men go to the library, the ladies the parlor, you pack one small satchel and—"

Abruptly he stopped talking. Already there was a complication. He was going to tell her to go immediately to Sis Liz's and wait for him there. But after the incident the other day, Mary's fright, her certainty that there had been someone in the woods, Stephen now was forced to reconsider his plan.

She waited patiently, as though aware that he'd run head on into a dilemma.

"I want you at Sis Liz's by midnight, but I don't want you in the woods alone," he explained. He looked toward the river, thinking. "Dorie," he said, referring to the young black woman who looked after Eve.

But Eve shook her head vehemently. "A tattletale; she tells Mama everything. Not Dorie."

He looked to her for a suggestion and felt momentarily stunned that they were discussing such a plan, though he knew with absolute conviction that they had no choice. Like her, he could not conceive of life without her.

"Then Katie," he suggested, thinking of Christine's maid, who had seemed almost a child herself and thus inclined to understand their needs.

But again Eve shook her head, only once this time, but enough to convey her doubts about Katie as well. "They are all in cahoots with Mama," she said grimly.

Again there was silence, unbroken except for the rush of the river, which seemed to keep pace with their thoughts.

"Then who?" he demanded. "I don't want you to be in the woods alone."

"There's only one I trust completely," Eve said.

"Who?" he asked hopefully.

"Paris."

Of course. Why hadn't he thought of Paris? He'd liked him from the beginning, though he'd not seen much of him of late. Paris was a perfect choice. But then why the doubt on Eve's face?

"Eve—"

She shook her head. "When we were growing up, Paris was the only one who wouldn't tattle, no matter what."

"Then why are you worried?"

She shrugged. "I think he's changed. Since Papa sent him away to school, he is more Papa's friend than mine." She smiled a sad smile. "You'd think that Papa had enough friends without stealing mine."

For several moments Stephen tried to work his way through the dilemma of whether to trust a man he'd known less than four weeks with his future happiness, his very life.

"Then I'll talk to Paris today," Stephen said.

"Be careful, Stephen. Tell him nothing until you're certain you can trust him."

"I won't. And it's Friday. We'll meet outside Sis Liz's after the dinner party."

She stood up and moved effortlessly into his arms.

"Then what?" she whispered.

"I'll have our horses ready. We'll ride into Mobile," he said. "I know a place where you can stay for the night—"

"Where will you—"

"I'll be close by, I promise. We will leave by train the following morning for New Orleans, where we—will be married."

He spoke the words softly, as though testing them on the air and on her ear.

"Married."

The kiss that followed had little to do with sweetness. Passion, as raw, as insistent as any he'd ever felt, burned through him and caused him to draw her closer than he had any right, a closeness she did not resist but rather seemed to require as much as he, a passion that left them struggling to find new ways around the barriers of garments and distance. And after a few moments, as though by mutual consent, both knowing that they only had to wait a few days and that for now they must be patient, they rested their foreheads against each other, the brief passion having left them mutually breathless, their hands intwined.

"I love you so much," he whispered.

"Friday is so far away," she murmured. "I can't believe you're here. I'm afraid you'll simply disappear like a dream."

"I won't, I swear it."

"And I'll be alone again."

"Never, never."

The conviction in his voice transferred itself effortlessly to his arms. Once again he held her close, as though in an effort to keep her safe from her own fears, her own loneliness.

It occurred to him that they had discussed little beyond New Orleans and marriage. But it didn't matter. After that they would journey together to the west and accomplish Uncle Richard's mission. Then, perhaps, if they so desired, they might travel on to the Pacific Ocean before heading back to England. Such a protracted journey was not scheduled in the original itinerary, but much had changed. He was certain everyone at Eden Point would understand, particularly when he returned with Eve and all could feast on her beauty and sweetness and marvel at the riches that Stephen had discovered in the New World.

But for now he would keep the plans beyond New Orleans to himself and concentrate on their safe exodus from this place, no small feat considering the size and scope of certain obstacles.

"You are certain that your father will be fully distracted on Friday evening?"

"Fully distracted," Eve repeated. "He has been planning this affair for weeks. He admires Mr. Clemens."

"They've never met?" Stephen asked. "Your father and this Mr. Clemens?"

"Only in correspondence. He sent Papa a copy of his new book. Mama's the only one who has read it. She says it's quite good, that underneath Mr. Clemens the writer is a prophet and a reformer as zealous as Papa."

"What's the name of the book?"

"*Huckleberry Finn.* I'm reading it now. Do you know it?"

Stephen shook his head. "Is he quite famous, this Mr. Clemens?"

"I'd never heard of him before he started writing to Papa. He writes under a different name—Mark Twain—and what he really wants apparently more than anything in this world is to meet Mr. Booker T. Washington."

Stephen shifted upon the tree trunk, eager to discuss the specifics of their escape in greater detail and yet interested in the nature of the gathering that was to take place this weekend at Stanhope Hall. Incredibly, for the first time a thought occurred. "They'll come after us," he said, his voice as stark as the thought.

Eve agreed without hesitation. "Of course they will, but they won't know where to find us. And after we're married, I'll send a telegram and tell them of our happiness and not to worry."

She made it sound so simple. And perhaps it could be. Occupied by the festivities, her parents might not even discover Eve's absence until morning. There was a Louisville-and-Nashville train from Mobile to New Orleans. They could be married by noon, the telegram speeding back to Stanhope Hall to arrive before midnight. Only a few hours of anxiety for them, though he regretted even those. But what other way? They would never consent to such a union.

Apparently she caught his mood of concern. She asked again, "What choice do we have? In this both Mama and Papa would block us. They'd send you away and tell me to wait and be patient."

Suddenly she shuddered, as though suffering a fierce chill. "I cannot bear life without you," she whispered.

She lifted her face to him, and to his sorrow he saw tears and understood even more the depth of her isolation.

He kissed her. "Then come Friday," he pledged, "we leave here together."

"Always together."

She walked to the edge of the cave and looked down at the river. "I want to tell someone so desperately." She smiled back at him.

He understood her need but urged her again to wait, then glanced out and down on the river. "Tell the fish," he said and smiled. "They might be interested. I know they would be safe."

She caught his humor and looked intently down at the rushing river. "You, trout, there, have you heard? I am going to marry Mr. Stephen Eden. The next time you see me, if you ever see me again, I will be Mrs. Stephen Eden."

"Is he impressed?" Stephen asked, joining in the fun.

"He seems to be spreading the word." She looked up and moved effortlessly back into his arms. "What, my darling, are we going to do until Friday?"

"I don't understand."

"How do we manage to look normal? I'm absolutely certain that something shows on my face."

He looked closely. Beauty showed, and, she was right, a new radiance.

He shook his head, smiling. "I don't know," he confessed.

"Do we meet?"

"Of course. As we have always met. After lunch."

Again they clung to each other, scarcely breathing, not moving for fear something, anything, would break the trance and the magic, and the mystery would be over, and the world would be plain again. And neither of them could endure that and still survive.

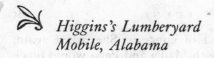

Higgins's Lumberyard
Mobile, Alabama

"Then it's to be the old woman? The mad aunt, the one they call Sis Liz?"

Taylor Quitman looked up at the sound of Orlando Dow's voice, so calmly speaking, and wondered what kind of man was he, and for that matter what kind of men were all of them, huddled up here in Jarmay Higgins's lumberyard loft like night creatures who did not dare expose themselves or their thoughts to the honest light of day.

On the table before them was the crushed "message," spirited out of Stanhope Hall by the traitorous Mrs. Winegar to the villainous Dow, the guest list for the coming weekend, proof that the nigger Washington would once again sit at the Stanhope table.

Finally Jarmay Higgins stirred, a slightly drunken movement, and it occurred to Taylor that most of their late-night meetings were conducted in pleasant states of semi-inebriation, none of them so drunk that they were beyond functioning, the good strong bourbon just rendering their consciences mute, at least until business could be concluded.

"All right, then, it's to be the old woman," Higgins said, slurring his words. "She's lived her life anyway. She's mad as a hatter. And no one will miss her."

"Settled, then."

This strong voice of authority was Reverend Pounders himself, who stood from his perch on a low chair and looked out over the brooding knights.

"It's his own fault," Reverend Pounders went on. "If he had paid heed to us the first time—"

Taylor Quitman spoke up. "I told you, Burke Stanhope will never pay heed. What do you intend to do? Murder his entire family?"

His tone was quiet and ineffective after Reverend Pounders's thundering voice. The slow stares of condemnation came from all quarters. Belatedly Taylor offered an apology. "I'm sorry. Of course we must act again. It would be easier if—"

"It's not easy for any of us," Jarmay Higgins said. "But what are we to do? He's got a nigger running the plantation out there now. You know that for yourself."

Of course Taylor knew it, had known it longer than these men, had been at Stanhope Hall the night Paris Boley had left for Tuskegee, had known then what Burke was educating him for, yet somehow had foolishly hoped it would never come to pass.

"My niggers are talking about it, I can tell you," Jarmay Higgins said. "I heard them the other day. They like the idea of working for one of their own."

"And thus the poison spreads," entoned Reverend Pounders.

"Sorry to have to keep you gentlemen on track, but is it settled then? I must know." It was Orlando Dow, the only one who seemed to be relishing this meeting. "Friday evening, I believe we said. And while you're riding your pretty horses up to the front of Stanhope Hall, I will be paying a visit to the old woman in Fan Cottage. Right? And payment in full is due at dawn the next day, same as always, roadside, like last time, by far the safest. Five hundred dollars this time, gentlemen. Are we agreed?"

He grinned and surveyed the seated men like a grotesque school-master. "Any questions? Any suggestions? Any amendments?"

When no one answered, Orlando Dow moved toward the loft door. "Then if you'll excuse me, gentlemen, my large flock is waiting, the word of God is waiting to be spoken, the collection plate is waiting to be passed."

He started through the door, then stopped abruptly. "Mr. Higgins, could I bother you to call off your watchdog, if you'd be so kind."

Through the shadows Taylor saw Higgins's giant black man named Marshal move from his guardlike position at the door to one side, the passageway down so narrow there still scarcely was room.

It seemed to take the knights several minutes to recover from Orlando Dow and his succinct account of the evening to come.

"Why did you hesitate?"

The first voice to shatter the silence belonged to Joel Peterson, and his question was aimed at Jarmay Higgins, who looked back with a slightly drunken stare.

Joel Peterson repeated himself with elaboration. "Why did you hesitate about the old woman? It seems a logical choice."

"To whom?" Higgins demanded. "Those two females mean noth-ing to Burke Stanhope. You can well see how alarmed he was by the death of the half-breed. He scarcely lost a wink. We're probably doing him a favor, ridding him of that meddlesome old madwoman."

Taylor Quitman felt obliged to speak again, even though he knew in advance he would say the wrong thing. "You're wrong. Burke was very touched by White Doll's death and he will mourn his old aunt as well, I can assure you."

Again he suffered the weight of all eyes, predominant among them Reverend Pounders's. "I'm having trouble understanding you this evening, Taylor," he said with arched formality. "Having trouble understanding your—how shall I put it?—your allegiances, your loy-alties."

Taylor could have predicted that and tried to choose his words carefully. "I have known Burke Stanhope for many years. You see, he believes that his course of action is more right than yours."

"What are you saying?" Reverend Pounders demanded.

"That quite probably you could murder his entire family and he wouldn't change his actions or his words, or his convictions."

This pronouncement seemed to cast the small group into deeper brooding, which was broken by Zach Hennessey's mutter of "I don't believe you."

That rebuttal stirred the others into defiance, and soon they all were on their feet.

"You just wait, Quitman," Jarmay Higgins warned. "He'll take note of us this time, and if not, we'll act again and again until he does."

Taylor shrugged, disliking the division in his own heart, respecting Burke Stanhope, but not his beliefs. "I'll be there Friday, you know that. I've been invited. He will suspect something if I don't attend."

This brought the group to a new silence. Pounders spoke first. "I think you must break with him, totally, as soon as possible."

Higgins objected. "It might be helpful to have someone on the inside, close to him, to help keep us informed."

"Of course. If we can trust him," Reverend Pounders said.

Weary beyond belief of almost everything, Taylor stood, taking several swipes at his coat sleeves in an attempt to rid himself of the clinging sawdust that covered everything. "This place could use a broom," he muttered to no one in particular, though Higgins responded defensively.

"Why? The steam donkeys are going every day and most nights. It is impossible to keep it clean."

Then Taylor turned his attention back to the knights. "Your ability to trust me, Reverend Pounders, is not our greatest problem," he said, heading toward the door. "Our biggest problem," he went on, "is finding the backbone and fortitude to stomach our own actions. Burke Stanhope, in hiring Paris Boley as a general manager, isn't breaking any law."

"The hell he isn't," someone objected.

"Except the Southern Code," Taylor added. "On the other hand, our actions are quite another matter."

"Are you with us or against us, Quitman?" Joel Peterson demanded.

At the door Taylor looked back. "Sit down, Peterson," he commanded gently. "You know I am with you. I wouldn't be here otherwise. I'm saying no more than the rest of you are thinking—that this perhaps had better be the last—of everything—the last ride, the last meeting, the last murder."

He allowed the word to sit on the air and held their respective gazes as though to make certain they fully understood what they had hired Orlando Dow to do.

Then, incapable of staying a moment longer, he pushed open the door and fixed a stern glare on Marshal. Then he brushed past him and made his way down the narrow, sawdust-covered staircase.

God, but he was hot and tired and thirsty. The Blue Hen Tavern wasn't far, was always rowdy and filled with pleasant distraction.

Then that was his destination, though he paused a moment in the cutting shed in fierce though mindless examination of the monstrous silver saw blades.

As he stared at the blades capable of splitting trees in half, he knew he must stay safely within the ranks of the Knights of the White Camellia, for philosophically they were in complete agreement. The only thing that bound him to Burke Stanhope was a shared childhood, now long since forgotten and unimportant.

Abruptly his thoughts came to a halt. Equally abruptly, Taylor Quitman turned and left Jarmay Higgins's cutting shed, moving rapidly out across the darkened lumberyard, heading toward the Blue Hen Tavern, where, hopefully in the chaos of sailors and old soldiers and whores, he might forget the plans that had been formulated for Friday night, forget as well that at the actual moment the brutal crime was being committed, he would be partaking of Burke Stanhope's hospitality, and through it all he would have to play innocent and later outraged.

He shook his head, wondering if such duplicity was possible.

It had to be.

 Stanhope Hall

As Mary arranged a splendid bouquet of dark purple larkspur and yellow daisies in a silver epergne, she was aware of Burke watching her from across the parlor, aware of the look in his eyes and grateful for it.

They had had their reconciliation. She believed him when he told her that of course she and the children were to be included at the dinner in honor of Samuel Clemens, that he could not function without them all at his side.

She'd recovered almost fully from her fright in the woods several days ago and was now hurling herself into preparations for the party tomorrow night, a most important party as far as Burke was concerned and therefore important to her as well. And she was the first to admit that she loved parties, loved giving them, loved preparing this grand old house, airing all the rooms and filling them with huge bouquets of garden-fresh flowers, as she was doing now.

"Does Mr. Clemens have any dietary eccentricities?" she asked, a little startled by how thoroughly her voice had shattered the quiet in the room. Across the parlor she saw the newsprint behind which Burke was sitting. Then slowly it was lowered and she saw his face.

"I don't think so," he said thoughtfully. "I'm sure we will be able to manage."

"Are you looking forward to meeting him?"

"Indeed. As is Mr. Washington."

"Is their cause a mutual one?"

"I believe so. They are approaching it in different ways, but certainly both are reformers of the highest order."

Mary looked down to see an errant larkspur dripping water on the mahogany table. Hurriedly she blotted the moisture with a clean cloth and looked up, ready to converse some more. But the newsprint was back in place, Burke disappeared behind it.

"Where is Eve?"

"I don't know. With Stephen, I imagine. They usually go walking after lunch."

"Where?"

"I don't know. Sometimes to Sis Liz's, sometimes to—"

"How much longer will he be here?" Now the newsprint was lowered, the question blunt.

Hurriedly she gathered the cut stems and stood back to admire her arrangement. "I really can't say, Burke. I have told him he's welcome to stay as long as he wishes."

"I want him gone by the weekend."

Now it was her turn to gape. "You can't mean that. That's tomorrow. He can't—"

"Why can't he?" Suddenly Burke came out from behind the newsprint. "We'll all have multiple responsibilities this weekend, including Eve. She's old enough to work at your side, to help you in all respects. I won't have her shirking her duties."

Gone tomorrow? Surely he wasn't serious. She was on the verge of asking, but she looked across the room to find the newsprint back in place, a convenient fortress behind which he could take refuge after issuing a command.

Without warning, a small revolution caused a sudden heat to sweep across her face. She gathered the last of the stems and left the room and the husband she loved, but could not and would not always obey.

In the shadowed hall she made her way to the parson's bench near the wall and sat, still clutching dead stems and leaves in her hands.

Sit. Just for a moment. There was much to do. Guest rooms to be checked, menus, table service. She wanted it all to be perfect, not only for her guests but for Burke as well.

"Mrs. Stanhope, a word if I may."

She looked up at the voice as though under siege, scolding herself for not being alert to another presence in the corridor. Then she understood. It was Madame Germaine, dressed in black as usual.

"Are you feeling well, Mrs. Stanhope?"

Mary nodded quickly. "You wanted a word, Madame?"

"Several, actually, all concerning Eve and that troublesome young man."

"What have they done now?"

Madame Germaine sniffed, withdrawing a lace handkerchief from her black sleeve and touching it to her nose. "Eve has performed no lessons for well over a week. I make her assignments and she ignores them. The notebooks go unfilled, and the pages unread."

Mary listened quietly, head down, and felt torn. She knew how she should respond as a mother, but she also felt a strong understanding of her beloved truant. Of course the pages were unturned, the notebooks unfilled. A true cause for worry would be if Eve behaved in any other fashion.

"Madame Germaine, you must understand that she is—distracted now."

"My point exactly."

"I promise you it won't go on forever."

"Oh? Is Mr. Eden leaving soon?"

Mary heard a new brightness in the old woman's voice and resented it. "I didn't say that."

"Well, I can assure you that as long as he is here, all three children will accomplish nothing. Even Christine—"

"Perhaps, Madame Germaine, the diversion is good for them. They have no contact with young people, as you know."

"Mr. Eden is considerably older."

"But he is their cousin and is bringing a new dimension, a new perspective to them. I should think that would be educational in its own way."

It was several moments before Madame Germaine could regroup her thoughts. When she spoke, she said simply, "I am at a loss to know my role in all this."

"You are the children's schoolmistress."

"But my pupils are missing."

"Not missing; just temporarily diverted. It doesn't happen often, you must admit. Normally they are apt and diligent students. If they relax for a few days, I'm certain that no permanent—"

She broke off speaking only when she realized that at some point she'd lost Madame Germaine's attention, indeed, had lost Madame Germaine herself, as the old woman seemed fixed on something beyond the door, her face in half-light growing tense.

"There! Look at that!"

With one finger she stabbed toward the doorway and the rectangle of sun beyond.

Mary leaned forward and saw a familiar lavender skirt.

"Mrs. Stanhope, do you see?"

These cold words brought her back in time to see Stephen Eden step up onto the porch alongside Eve. For several moments they appeared merely to be chatting quietly. They were so attractive together, Stephen so tall, one fair, one dark, both—

Mary saw the quick kiss and heard Madame Germaine's shocked gasp simultaneously.

"Did you see?" Madame Germaine gasped again. "Did you see what that young man—"

Torn between Madame Germaine and the lovely tableau on the broad front porch, Mary foundered. Not that she wasn't alarmed by what she had seen. She was, though the kiss was long since over now, the two guilty parties talking low with a prudent two or three feet between them.

"Mrs. Stanhope, you must put a stop to it. Immediately! You must send him away this very day."

This hysterical dictum came from Madame Germaine and bore an uncanny resemblance to the command she'd just heard from Burke.

Send him away. Get rid of him by the weekend.

As the two commands blended, Mary felt a strong impulse to ignore both and started walking down the corridor, keeping her eyes on the beauty beyond the door, the two young people standing on the porch, both revealing such visible and obvious tension. Suddenly Mary knew that there had been other kisses.

She was just this side of the door when apparently they heard her footsteps and looked up, their eyes darting, first at each other and then at her.

"It's just me," Mary said with a smile as she pushed open the screen. She held up crushed leaves and stems she'd been carrying since she'd left the parlor. "Just wanted to get rid of these."

"Mama." Eve smiled.

"Mary." Stephen smiled. Good. They had nothing to fear or hide.

"I was just coming to find you to see if I could help," Eve said.

"The flowers are finished," Mary said, turning back to the porch and brushing her hands together.

"What next?" Eve offered. "Tell me. I want to help. I really do."

"Nothing for a while. Perhaps later you can help with the guest rooms."

"Of course."

Stephen walked beyond Eve and sat on the banister. He seemed desperately eager to convey total relaxation.

It had been Mary's intention to summon Eve to come and help her, but looking at them now, she couldn't separate them.

"A few more minutes, Eve. Then I could use your help in the upstairs guest rooms."

"I'll be along, Mama."

"May I help?" Stephen asked.

Mary laughed. "Men don't attend to guest rooms."

"My father does," Stephen added.

At the door Mary looked back, trying to understand the image of John Murrey Eden folding linens. "I don't believe you." She smiled, trying to make a joke out of her rudeness.

"Oh, but it's true," Stephen protested. "Susan is in the clinic, you see, almost every day from sunup to sundown. My father long ago was put in charge of the cottage on Eden Rising. He does everything a woman does, and Susan claims he does most chores better and with greater efficiency than she."

"The clinic?" Mary questioned, hearing this news for the first time.

"Susan is a nurse. When they first married and came back to Eden, my father helped her convert the main cottage on Eden Rising into a clinic. Then he built another one for them to live in right next to the clinic. Everyone from Mortemouth comes up, and sometimes people come from as far as Exeter. She's really a remarkable woman and a very good nurse."

"I think it would be fun to go back," Eve said softly. "If Mama doesn't want to go, I will."

Mary looked down, trying to tell if Eve was serious. Unable to do so, she pulled open the door. "Well, I can assure you, no one is going anyplace for the time being. We have guests, many of them arriving tomorrow morning, Eve, and I need your help upstairs. So please, as soon as possible—"

And with that she took refuge in the corridor and walked steadily away from the two young people and toward the silhouette of Madame Germaine, who was waiting where Mary had left her near the parson's bench.

"Well?" the old woman demanded in a harsh whisper.

"Well what?"

"Did you speak to them?"

"Of course I spoke to them. You saw me."

"And when will he be leaving? When can this household expect to return to normal?"

"I did not ask Stephen to leave, Madame Germaine, nor do I intend to. He is welcome to stay at Stanhope Hall for as long as he wishes. Is that clear?"

Belatedly she realized she was speaking to Madame Germaine in a tone she'd never used before. It was her intention, by way of apology to Madame Germaine, to summon the truant Eve to come with her immediately, thus dividing the two and leaving Stephen to amuse himself for a few hours.

Resolved, she closed her eyes and walked blind down the corridor and did not open them until she was directly this side of the front door.

"Eve, I want you to come with—"

She stopped speaking only when she opened her eyes and saw the porch empty.

For several moments Mary stood, looking in all directions, thinking to catch a glimpse of them strolling down the avenue of live oaks, in which case it wouldn't be too late to call them back. But the lawn was deserted.

Mary studied the emptiness. Slowly she turned about and saw Madame Germaine still watching her. Not wanting to engage the stern old woman in any form of dialogue, she hurried up the staircase.

Grasping the banister, she sank to a seated position at the top of the stairs, still thinking about that kiss and the radiance she'd seen on her daughter's face. Eve had no experience in matters of the heart, was wholly vulnerable to a young man's charms. And this young man was uniquely charming.

Where had they disappeared to so quickly?

She closed her eyes and tried to relax, the better to rise and face her various duties. It was while her eyes were closed that she heard footsteps below, heavy boots walking along the first floor corridor heading toward the front door.

Carefully she pushed closer to the edge of the staircase and looked down toward the front door. It was Burke in his shirtsleeves, head bent in order to hear the poisoned words that were issuing from the lips of Madame Germaine.

In his hand, Mary observed, was his riding crop. Now and then he bounced it against his leg as Madame Germaine continued to whisper to him. Once it fell silent and he bent low, the better to hear.

Mary knew what was being said and was torn between making her presence known and correcting what surely was an endless stream of lies and distortions, or keeping still, letting Burke digest the lies and act accordingly, as surely he would anyway.

Perhaps it was best that Stephen Eden leave as soon as possible. Hopefully the affection he clearly shared with Eve was new, in its infancy, so to speak, and could be brought to a halt without too much lasting pain or damage to either one of them.

Then she heard Burke's voice, a simple "Thank you, Madame Germaine."

The old woman continued to whisper something else, but obviously he'd heard enough and pushed open the door and left the old woman gaping after him.

Mary stood. The movement caused the old woman to whirl about and look guiltily up. At first she seemed disinclined to speak. Then, "I told him the truth, Mrs. Stanhope, nothing more, nothing less, which is exactly what you should have done."

Mary had no intention of giving the old bitch a response. Besides, she had none to give. Instead she turned about and tried to muster as much dignity and authority as she could, and tried not to think of Burke's destination or what his actions would be. Secretly she prayed that both Stephen and Eve would stay well concealed for the remainder of the afternoon.

* * *

"There he is, over there," Eve observed and pointed toward the large tin shed beneath which Paris Boley sat, dispensing yellow pay envelopes to the field hands. "He looks busy now. You might want to wait."

Her voice dwindled off as the two of them gazed across the hot road made liquid-appearing by August mirages.

"Are you all right?" It was Stephen again, his face nearer and filled with concern.

"Mama worries me."

"Do you think she saw us?"

"Probably. But something else is wrong. I wish that we could—"

"What?"

She looked directly at him, as though to test him. "Tell her?" At the last minute she softened it with a question and waited for his reaction, which was forever in coming and registered more as a look of keen disappointment on his face.

"We could—postpone our departure if you wish," Stephen murmured, coming up close behind her. "But I'm not certain it would be wholly safe to tell your mother."

Pleased by his consideration, Eve took his hand, grateful. "Could we, Stephen? Put it off, just until after this weekend. It's so important to my father, and my mother always wants his salons to be perfection. Particularly this one."

"I understand." He nodded.

"I love you," she whispered.

"And I you."

"Do you still want to speak with Paris?"

"Now more than ever. We will still be needing his services and perhaps now even his advice. New complications—"

She detected a tinge of regret and was sorry she'd caused it. "Just until after this weekend," she promised. "I'll go back to the house now," she said, "and see if I can help Mama."

For a moment Eve regretted the postponement. All the sustenance and nourishment and love she would ever need in her life was readily available there in his eyes. Still how would it hurt, the delay of two or three days, a chance for her to make certain her mother was well and would survive news of the elopement.

Then despite the public place, despite the heat, Eve stepped close to him and stood on tiptoe and was about to deliver a single light kiss when she heard a loud male voice coming from the tin shed, a man shouting something at Paris in anger.

"You're a nigger cheat, that's what you are," the white man shouted as he stood over Paris, a yellow pay envelope clutched in the upraised fist.

When he shouted the accusation a second time, Eve saw Paris bow his head as though weary of the confrontation. She was aware of Stephen starting out around the tree as though prepared to join in the fray if he was needed.

"Stephen, don't," she called out, her voice drowned by the angry man who now had hurled the pay envelope at Paris.

"You're cheatin' us, nigger, you're cheatin' all of us. Don't trust no nigger to give me my pay. Never have. Never will. All of you, check yours," he said to the men behind him. "I'll bet he's done cheated you as well."

As the big man turned to the others, Eve saw Paris slowly rise. "I've not cheated you, Mr. Sizemore. You can check the ledger book for yourself. It's all right here."

But the man whirled about as though the mere sound of Paris's voice had fueled the fire of his anger. "Don't talk back to me, nigger boy. Don't you dare talk back, you hear."

Half-hidden behind the tree, Eve saw a division taking place beneath the tin shed, Negroes drawing together on one side, whites on the other.

She saw Paris turn the big ledger book around as though to allow the man to read something for himself. And that simple gesture seemed to infuriate the man even more, for suddenly he shouted, "I cain't read, nigger. You know I cain't," and he lifted the ledger book and hurled it toward the fields, a gesture of murderous rejection that caused the ledger pages to break open and flutter loose in the hot wind. As Paris was beginning to object to the destruction of the book, the man quickly reached inside the folds of his work shirt and withdrew a knife.

"Stephen, no—"

Her protest came too late, for Stephen, too, had seen the weapon, had obviously seen as well the man's superior size and strength, had seen him lift the knife to Paris Boley.

At the same time the Negroes moved even farther back, a few running out into the fields as though to put as much distance as possible between themselves and the impending violence.

"Mr. Sizemore, please put that away," Paris requested quietly.

"Yes, please," Stephen added, coming up alongside the white man as though merely to relieve him of the knife and that would be the end of that.

But the large man shouted, "Get away, nigger lover," and he held the knife at a more effective angle, this time to include both Stephen and Paris.

Terrified, Eve debated whether to stay and watch or run to the house for help. Stephen and Paris were clearly outnumbered, for their allies, the Negroes, had by now all fled to positions of safety, while the white men held fast and quickly closed ranks behind Mr. Sizemore, a few of them offering to help with their bare fists.

Eve tried to turn about, feeling that some fearful battle was about to take place and once again Stanhope Hall would be plunged into deep and senseless mourning.

In defense against the repetition of such a scenario, she had just started back down the path for help when she saw a cloud of dust on the road, a horse coming fast toward the tin shed. At the same time she saw a blur coming from the shed itself, heard an outcry and looked back to see Mr. Sizemore leap over the table that was Stephen and Paris's solitary defense. As the man lunged forward, knife leading, the others rushed in behind him, obscuring the scene.

At the same time the rider appeared out of the dust cloud, a familiar rider shouting at her to get back and dismounting even while the horse still moved, then running straight into the battle, swinging his riding crop as though it were a machete, boldly pushing aside the brawling men.

"Papa!"

The master of Stanhope Hall had arrived. Relieved, Eve retreated to the tree and clung to it, watching as her father pushed his way forward, his anger seeming to top that of the men.

"Enough!" she heard her father shout as he dragged another brawler from the pile. The table had been pushed to one side during the fight. Eve continued to move toward the shed, keeping a close eye on those near the bottom of the pile.

"Did you hear me?" she heard her father shout as he at last dragged to his feet the red-faced Mr. Sizemore, who shouted in his own defense, "The nigger cheated me."

"Mr. Boley is my general manager. I trust him completely," Burke said, standing before the man and facing down his accusation. "When you accuse him of cheating, you accuse me. Are you prepared to do that? Is that clear?"

Eve couldn't tell if it was clear or not from where she stood in the blazing sun, sweat running down her face, her attention still riveted on the dark interior of the shed where she had yet to catch a glimpse of Stephen. Where was he?

As she heard her father addressing all the workers now, black and white alike, warning them all against a repetition of such a scene, she approached the shed, fear increasing, and at last saw Paris, just struggling to sit upright, his white shirt smeared, an ominous smear of blood on his left shoulder.

Where was he?

The voice screamed inside her head, and at last she was running, throwing caution and prudence to the wind, unconcerned with the near and angry presence of her father, concerned only to learn the whereabouts and condition of Stephen Eden.

She came to a halt, some premonition warning her.

"Stephen—" She whispered his name, and as though in reply, she heard a groan.

She took another step forward, aware of her father approaching rapidly on her right, his voice angry as he commanded her, "Stay where you are."

She obeyed out of habit, though she continued to fix her attention on Paris, who appeared to be struggling up, bringing something with him, his arm placed protectively about familiar shoulders.

"Stephen."

She spoke his name again as he turned toward her on wobbly legs, a bloody cut on his right temple where obviously the table had fallen on him and knocked him senseless.

"Is he seriously injured?" This wintery voice came from her father, who addressed the question to Paris as though the *he* under question was incapable of responding for himself.

"I'm—well, sir," Stephen replied and dabbed at the moist cut.

"May I ask why you felt compelled to come to the counting shed and start trouble?"

Eve gaped at her father's distorted accusation.

Stephen rallied. "I did not come here to start trouble, sir—"

"Then why did you come?"

"I accompanied Eve."

"Why on earth would Eve need an escort to these fields? She's run in them since she was a child."

Stymied, Eve saw Stephen retreat. The truth would never do. "We were simply taking the air, sir," Stephen said at last and did not look up and thus confirmed his own lie.

In the meantime Paris stood steadfastly beside him, a curiously eager look on his face, as though hoping he would be invited to speak.

When her father appeared to turn away in disgust and anger, Paris and Stephen exchanged a glance. Uncertain what to do, Eve ventured forward to her father's side.

"Papa." She spoke his name and saw the fury still in his face as he whirled around on her, riding crop raised, as though he fully intended to strike her.

She heard a man's shout and saw Stephen lunging forward as though to defend her against the raised riding crop—certainly it hadn't been intended for her—and now coming down instead with a stinging snap on Stephen's shoulder, Stephen grimacing as he pushed her to one side, an expression on his face that Eve had never seen before, fury as raw as that on her father's face, the two in senseless confrontation again while Paris and Eve and all the others stood helplessly by, unable to understand this animosity.

"Sir, I beg you. There is no point."

"This is not your household. You have no right to intrude where you are not wanted," Burke said, tracking Stephen as he tried to back away from the range and sting of the riding crop.

"I want you gone," Burke concluded, full voiced and in the event he hadn't been heard, he repeated himself. "I want you gone from here by tomorrow morning. Is that clear? There is no reason for you to remain here any longer."

"Sir, please listen. It was not my intention to intrude. My only desire was to be of assistance to Paris."

The more civil Stephen was, the more outraged her father seemed to become. As he continued to track Stephen around the shed, he was saying the most unjust things.

"If there was trouble here today, I can be certain of one thing: You fanned the flames and you alone."

"Papa, that's not true, not fair."

At the sound of her voice, her father whirled on her. "I told you to go back to the house, didn't I? Didn't I give you that specific command? Or is it possible that under his corrupting influence you no longer find it necessary to obey your parents."

"Papa, please listen—"

"Get out, go on! Now! Did you hear me? I don't want you here." With each utterance he took a step toward her, the riding crop lifted again, while she stumbled back across the road, fear increasing as she realized that she recognized nothing about this man. She felt herself losing balance. Her hands reached out for support and found none and she fell painfully backward, landing flat on her back.

Despite a throbbing in her right wrist, which had taken the brunt of the fall, she scrambled to one side and found assistance waiting.

"Are you all right?"

The voice was familiar and filled with love. She saw Stephen, one arm about her waist, the other assisting her to her feet.

He seemed such a likely comforter, so right, that when the stranger's voice cut down between them, she looked back in new perplexity.

"Papa, don't." She wept and reflexively shielded her eyes as she saw the riding crop in his hand, saw him ready it for a brutal attack this time, Stephen holding his ground, though with head bowed and both arms raised in an attempt to deflect the blows, which continued to rain down upon him.

"Papa, please, don't," Eve cried.

Then she heard a different voice, a usually soft and entreating voice, now raised and forceful. "Burke, stop it. Now!"

Though the riding crop was upraised and ready to come crashing down in mindless repetition, it seemed to hang suspended while he turned to confront the quiet yet forceful voice.

"Mama," Eve said through her tears.

Then Stephen was at her side. She accepted his arms and clung to them and looked closely at his face for telltale signs of the beating and miraculously found none, though his shirtwaist was torn in several places where the riding crop had cut through the fabric and left stripes of red.

She looked toward the shed, where Mary and Paris had led Burke. He was seated, his head down, elbows resting on his knees, breathing heavily, no one speaking, Mary standing protectively over him as though he were the injured party.

Eve waited to see if one or the other of them would come and apologize. The madness had been theirs. She and Stephen had done nothing.

But when after several moments no one seemed inclined to leave the shade of the tin shed, when one of the men brought her father a dipper of cool water from the big barrel, when no one, not even Paris, seemed inclined to come and inquire how Stephen was, Eve felt her estrangement growing. She wiped the residue of tears from her eyes and lifted her now torn and soiled skirts and started running away from this place and from these people.

She knew that Stephen was behind her, and she continued to run until she reached the safety of trees surrounding Stanhope Hall, a cool and secluded place.

She found his arms open and waiting, and she clung to him and tried to apologize, but tears were coming too fast for words. They simply held one another and said nothing for several moments, as though their closeness alone was healing all wounds.

Finally Stephen spoke. "I must leave."

"I know."

"Tomorrow."

"Yes."

She saw the worry in his eyes then. In just the last hour plans had been changed.

"Will you come with me?" he asked.

"Yes," she said, without hesitation.

"Listen to me. Are you certain?"

She smiled at his doubt. "If you left without me, I would die."

"No, you—"

"I mean it, Stephen." She held his hands now, not wanting their pleasant explorations to detract from what she was about to say. "I'm seventeen," she said and held his gaze and saw adoration in it and was grateful for it. "And for sixteen years and eleven months, I have wondered at least once every day what I am here for. What purpose am I supposed to serve? It wasn't precisely unhappiness that I felt, simply a lack of definition."

Still holding his hands and grateful for his attention, she walked with him deeper into the shade trees, feeling stronger and more cer-

tain of her convictions even as she spoke. "Everyone around me
seemed to know exactly who they were and what purpose they were
to serve. Everyone but me."

"Poor Eve."

"Until a few weeks ago when you came walking up between the
live oaks dragging your horse behind you, looking as lost and uncertain as I felt."

He smiled. "I *was* lost and uncertain."

"But you came."

"And the first person I saw was a vision in a white nightshirt staring down at me from the second-floor gallery."

"I wasn't staring."

"You were."

And she was in his arms again, her eyes shut, the better to savor all
the sensations of closeness. "I belong with you," she whispered and
gently touched her tongue to the tip of his ear. "I would go with you
anytime, anyplace, and it is my most earnest prayer to God that we
are never never separated again in this life."

"We won't be separated. I promise."

Once again their lips met with unerring accuracy, and so lost was
she in these new sensations that at first she failed to hear the rustle of
footsteps moving rapidly through the thick brush. Not until she
heard a voice, a quickly apologetic one, did she disengage herself from
Stephen's arms and point to a position behind him, to where a very
embarrassed and weary-looking Paris Boley stood.

"I'm—sorry," the young man stammered and started to back away
from the intimacy on which he had intruded.

"No, wait," Eve protested, remembering that Paris was the one
Stephen wanted to see when this whole nightmare of an afternoon
had started.

"Are you all right?" she inquired softly.

"Your mother wants to see you as soon as possible," he said.

"Where?"

"She took your father back to the house." Abruptly Paris broke off.
He shook his head as though in consummate bewilderment. "I don't
understand. Ordinarily Mr. Stanhope is the model of patience." He
looked straight at Stephen as though the answer to the riddle lay
there. "What happened between you two?"

"Nothing happened between the two of us. I swear it. It was my
father."

"Did your father ever say anything?" Paris asked.

"No. My uncle Richard said something the day I sailed, said that patience might serve me well in America, primarily at Stanhope Hall."

Eve saw him walking a few steps away, his hand touching his bruised right temple. "I'm not certain if all the patience in the world would alter—"

"No," Paris agreed quickly. "He feels badly now, of course. Mrs. Stanhope has helped him to see—"

Again Paris broke off, new puzzlement on his face. "What were you two doing in the fields?" he demanded, as though his mind were recounting the events backward.

"We came to find you," Eve replied.

"Why?"

She looked toward Stephen, feeling he best could answer that. "We're leaving tomorrow. Eve is coming with me. We are to be married in New Orleans."

At first Eve wasn't certain that Paris had heard. His brow furrowed, and he blinked rapidly at Stephen. Slowly he commenced to shake his head. "No, you can't—"

"We are, Paris. We would appreciate your help, but we are leaving here tomorrow night, with or without your help."

Paris turned to Eve as though to appeal to her better judgment. "Your folks, it will kill them."

"No," she said, trying to match Stephen's conviction. "I'd rather have their blessing. But I should think that the events of the last hour would prove to you how futile it would be to wait for such a blessing."

"No," Paris protested again.

Stephen stepped forward. "Your part will be simple, and in a way you will be able to help the others. You alone will know what happened. You can tell all after we are safely on the train out of New Orleans, for we will be married then."

For several long moments Paris did little but stare down at the fallen leaves at his feet. Eve felt certain that they could not count on his help, and in a way she didn't blame him. They were placing him in an awful position, perhaps even jeopardizing his hard-earned post at Stanhope Hall.

Eve felt sympathy for this young man with whom she'd grown up, who was perhaps her best friend. "Paris," she said softly, "remember the time we went in search of the blue trees?"

He did not turn back to her, but she saw him stop, as though he were listening closely to their shared memories.

Now, for Stephen's benefit, she explained. "We must have been five, or was it six, Paris? White Doll had told us that in the farthest corner of Stanhope Plantation, where few people had ever gone before, there were sky-blue trees. They were the exact colors and shadings of a summer dawn, therefore most people missed seeing them. But she said that they were beautiful and powerful, capable of granting wishes if you could only find them and stand directly beneath their blue branches."

She paused, keeping her eyes on Paris's rigid back, confident that he was listening, equally confident that he knew exactly where she was leading with her story.

"Well, Paris and I decided to go look for the blue trees, and we looked and we looked and we looked, and we found ourselves lost and all I could do was bawl, but Paris took me by the hand and said that he would get us back home, that he'd always watch after me and never let me get lost."

Her voice fell as she recreated the scene from the past, the two children, mismatched in all ways, searching for something magic to alter their own realities.

She stepped closer and lightly touched Paris's arm. "If Stephen leaves here without me, Paris, I'll be lost for the rest of my life."

He turned to her, his face in conflict. "Your father will—"

"Be angry, of course. That's why you must help us. He's fond of you, respects you. He'll listen to you."

"Your mother—"

Apparently Paris couldn't even articulate the effect such an action would have on her mother.

But again Eve had a ready answer. "And you can help her as well, by coming straight back to Stanhope Hall and telling them exactly what has transpired, that no one is to worry, and that if we are welcomed, we'll stop by when Stephen finishes his business in the West."

"Where will you go then?"

Stephen came forward. "Back to England for a while, I imagine. But I promise we'll return to America. I feel very much at home here. England, I'm afraid, is dead and over. Here there is life and opportunity and—"

He never completed his thought. He didn't have to. Instead he reached out and drew Eve to him, and Eve saw Paris smile, a faint smile, but better than the doubt she'd seen earlier.

"What do I do?" he asked.

Stephen walked to his side, as though to say that this part of the meeting was his domain. Willingly Eve stepped back, suddenly worn out by the events of the afternoon and the certain knowledge that if they remained here at Stanhope Hall, such scenes would not diminish in frequency or severity but quite possibly could grow worse.

"And immediately following the dinner," she heard Stephen say, "you will excuse yourself along with the ladies."

"Perhaps not," Paris said quietly. "Mr. Washington will be there. In the past, when Mr. Washington is present at table, I've been invited to stay as well."

For a moment Stephen appeared stymied. Paris apparently saw his expression. "I'm sorry. I'll do my best."

Then Eve walked back toward both of them, a simple plan evolving.

"During dinner," she began, "which I suspect you will not attend, Stephen, you will fetch the small gig and our two horses, go to Sis Liz's and wait for me there. After dinner I'll leave with the women and excuse myself on the pretense of going upstairs. Instead I'll slip out through the attic and meet you at Fan Cottage. Paris in the meantime can stay where he belongs and make sure the gentlemen's smoker lasts as long as possible. Then when my absence is discovered, we'll be safe in Mobile, perhaps even on our way to New Orleans, and Paris can explain all, thus putting everyone's mind at ease."

"What about the gig? Where will you leave it?" Paris asked.

"At the boardinghouse," she replied. "The one in Mobile where Stephen stayed before he came here to Stanhope Hall."

Stephen nodded. "Irma Kingsley's. It's down by the waterfront. She's holding my luggage there. She's trustworthy, with a small stable behind her lodging house. I'm sure she'd let me leave the gig there as well as the horses. You could come for them later."

Paris looked from one to the other as though still searching for something to object to.

Stephen said, "I think it's a good idea. Eve is right. You can be of greater help to us here. If you will."

"Of course I will, to the best of my ability. Then I suppose it's settled."

There was something about Paris's abruptness of tone that disturbed Eve. He seemed suddenly distant.

"You'd better get back to the house now," he said to Eve. "I have things to do as well."

And with that he was gone, leaving them both to gape after him, Eve's apprehension clearly mirrored on Stephen's face.

For several moments they said nothing but continued to stare at the place in the trees where Paris had disappeared.

"Can we trust him?" Stephen asked.

"I'm sure we can," Eve said. "He's upset because he is fiercely loyal to my father."

Stephen was standing close behind her, and she leaned backward
into his reliable strength.

"Why is it so difficult?" she whispered and nuzzled the side of his
neck and detected a subtle fragrance she was beginning to recognize
as his.

"It won't be," he whispered by way of response. "Tomorrow evening outside Fan Cottage, you'll be there and I'll be there and we'll
never be separated again. I swear it."

"I still can't believe it," she whispered, "that you're here. What
would have become of me if you hadn't come?"

He kissed her forehead, then the tip of her nose and in the instant
before he found her lips, he whispered, "I would have found you, no
matter what."

Then they kissed and she relaxed into it and responded with a
passion of her own and worried about only one thing now.

How could she possibly survive until tomorrow evening?

* * *

For the first time Mary dared to relax and looked out over her
dining room, filled with glittering guests, all of whom had arrived
promptly at midday in a rush of carriages and introductions: first Mr.
Samuel Clemens, dazzling in his white suit and shock of white hair,
who had said little to her but had bowed in a courtly fashion from the
waist and then allowed Burke to show him up to his rooms, where he
claimed he required only a pot of black coffee and a reasonable quiet
until dinnertime.

Dear Mr. Washington had arrived about an hour later, and he and
Burke had gone directly to the study and passed the afternoon in
quiet seclusion, leaving Mary to welcome Taylor Quitman and attend
to the thousand and one final details regarding dinner. Earlier Dr.
Melrose had sent word that he could not attend, and Burke's editor,
Richard Gilder, had been stalled in New Orleans. So the party,
though small, was still distinguished.

Now, somehow, with the help of God, it had all come together, and
Mary sat back in her chair to relish a quiet moment of achievement.

Mr. Clemens was holding forth as he'd held forth most of the evening, again conspicuous in an immaculate white suit, seeming to
preen himself on his skill in conversational and anecdotal timing.

Seated mid-table, he had effortlessly converted that spot into center
stage and was now thoroughly enjoying Mrs. Winegar's split pea
soup with puff pastry.

Opposite Mr. Clemens, in all ways, was Mr. Booker T. Washington.
From where Mary sat, these two gentlemen resembled the world's

cosmic opposites, Mr. Clemens's pale and fair skin, white suit, white hair, and Mr. Washington's dark skin and black suit, with only a high white brim collar. Thus far the two had exchanged few words other than perfunctory ones. But Mary had sensed in both a great sizing up.

Then there was Burke at the opposite end of the table, looking remarkably intact, considering the spectacle he'd made of himself only yesterday.

Newly moved by her recollection, Mary looked directly at Eve, seated to Burke's right at the far end of the table, the only pocket of taut silence around the table. Everyone else was making that sort of innocuous small talk that aided good digestion and paved the way for more serious discussions later.

Taylor Quitman and Madame Germaine were carrying on a lively conversation about rising prices, while Paris and David were telling Mr. Washington about the size of the trout they were now catching in the upper Mobile River. Even Christine was managing a shy contribution now and then, though occasionally she looked longingly at the empty place next to her, the chair where Stephen Eden customarily sat. Where the young man was, Mary had no idea. She'd not had a chance to speak with him since the unhappy incident yesterday, had not had a chance to speak with anyone except Burke, who, once in the privacy of their bedroom, had responded with customary warmth to her ministrations, had made an apology to her, though she'd told him that there were others more deserving of an apology than herself, to which he'd promised to tender one when time and circumstances permitted.

"More soup, Mr. Clemens?" she asked, seeing the man's spoon at rest for the first time in several minutes.

At first he looked longingly at his empty bowl, still crusty with pastry and cheese. "Ordinarily, Mrs. Stanhope, I'd say yes, but my intuition, always on target in such matters, tells me there are culinary joys and riches undreamed of yet to come, so I will practice at least a degree of prudence and self-control and say no thank you."

"Wise decision, Mr. Clemens." Mr. Washington smiled. "I can personally testify to the bounty of the Stanhope table, and what I lack in words, I allow my girth to speak for itself."

As the two men chatted quietly and easily across the arrangement of larkspur and summer daisies, Mary looked toward the end of the table where Eve sat, head down.

As well as Mary could remember, the girl had said nothing since she'd arrived a few minutes late at table. She looked lovely, wearing the pale blue organdy that Mary had had made by the new French dressmaker in Mobile. She'd done her hair in a french knot, with only small curls left to nestle around her neck, and she wore no jewelry to mar the spotless white field of breasts and shoulders. So striking had been her appearance that everyone at table had grown silent, some, like Mr. Clemens, clearly in appreciation of such youthful beauty, others, like Burke, more condemnatory. But at least he'd been gracious in his introduction of her to Mr. Clemens and had held her chair for her, though immediately thereafter both had fallen ominously silent.

Now the main hum of conversation was taking place between Madame Germaine, who fancied herself to be quite an expert in social affairs, and all other affairs for that matter, and Mr. Clemens, who had settled back in his chair, allowing Katie to remove his soup bowl, thus clearing the way for the next course.

"French cooking is my favorite," Madame Germaine announced now with absolute confidence, as though it had never occurred to her that no one at table was interested in her favorite.

Mary sat back, grateful to the garrulous little Frenchwoman who somehow, despite her arrogant ways, had managed to make a firm place for herself at Stanhope Hall over the years.

"French?" Mr. Clemens replied, with just a hint of archness in his voice. "No, Madame, with your forgiveness, not French, nor English, God forbid, nor German—certainly not German, which, speaking for myself, reminds one of a steady descent into hell, touching bottom in a plate of all grease and soggy starch."

"Oh, sir, what a marvelous description," Madame Germaine gushed, and Mary looked beyond her to see Mrs. Winegar rolling in a cart crowned with a lovely huge prime rib roast, each stave crowned and capped with a curled lace doily and surrounded by steaming vegetables like multicolored jewels.

"But why not French, Mr. Clemens?" she persisted, at her coquettish worst.

"Why not French?" Mr. Clemens echoed patiently, though first he looked about the table as though wondering why someone, anyone, didn't relieve him of this tedious woman. "Boredom, Madame, mainly. Frenchified cooking is the rage now in New York. The chefs should be guillotined on the basis of their coffee alone, which resembles the real thing as hypocrisy resembles holiness."

"Oh, sir, you are a master with words," Madame Germaine flirted. "Didn't I tell you, Eve? Didn't I tell you what an honor it would be to sit at the same table with the genius who created *Huckleberry Finn?*"

Mary watched closely to see if Eve would respond to Madame Germaine's flutterings. If she did, it was not discernible. But she did see a subtle change in Mr. Clemens, whose ego apparently had responded to Madame Germaine, if nothing else.

"You have read it, Madame?" he asked, a look of pleased surprise covering his features.

"Read it! Ah, my yes, haven't we—Eve, and David as well. Haven't we, David?" She didn't wait for a response from either end of the table and rushed on. "From the very time Huck reaches Pap's cabin to his arrival at the Phelps' Plantation, well, it's just the very best American writing I've ever read."

"I agree, Madame Germaine."

Mary looked up at the agreement coming from this surprising quarter. Burke apparently had at last pulled himself out of brooding silence and decided to join his party. "It's fine writing, Mr. Clemens, quite possibly your best."

For a moment Mr. Clemens seemed equally surprised and turned in that direction, holding his neck at a stiff angle as though it were sore. "Praise doubly appreciated," he said with a slight bob of his head. "Your last piece for *The Century* was bold and impressive."

Burke paused before responding, as though having to stop and remember his last piece. "On the generals," he said at last and took the sherry decanter offered by Katie, who looked quite pretty in her dress blacks with a white starched apron.

Astonished, Mary watched Burke closely. She'd never seen him take sherry *with* a meal before.

"It was an interesting job of research as well," he went on, leaning back in his chair, studying the sherry in crystal. "It's remarkable how human virtues and vices are color blind. Neither the blue nor the gray had the market cornered on either."

He sipped again and replaced the glass on the table and appeared to be on the verge of speaking further when, without warning, Mr. Clemens changed both the subject and his choice of a conversational partner.

"Miss Stanhope, speak to me of yourself. How do you survive in this world, in these parts? Do you make music, sing, write verse, dream?"

Suddenly there was no movement at table, everyone gone mute, all now focusing on Eve's slightly bowed blond head.

Speak, Mary prayed silently. *Please keep everything normal appearing. Let Utopia reign at Stanhope Hall.*

"Yes. To all three," came the quiet, low, well-modulated voice, and Mary, pleased that her prayer had been answered, wondered when Eve had developed such a lovely grown-up voice.

"Good for you," Mr. Clemens replied, still focusing on Eve, as though fascinated and pleased by his nearness to such natural beauty. "I assume you will sing for us after dinner while at the same time demonstrating your skill on that Steinway I saw in the parlor?"

At last Eve looked up as though surprised. "I thought you detested parlor music."

This challenge was not impudent, just honest. From where Mary sat, she saw Burke lean forward in his chair as though feeling a need to intercede.

But before he had a chance to say anything, Eve went on. "In *Huckleberry Finn,* while you allow Huck to express innocent appreciation for the music he hears coming from the Grangerfords' backwoods plantation, your own opinion is clearly audible through Huck's, and that opinion is one of caustic sarcasm and condemnation."

Again silence. When and where had the girl learned to speak like that? At what point had the shy child disappeared and this self-possessed young woman taken her place?

Mary motioned quickly for the serving girls to continue filling the platters, for they too had been brought to a halt by this new Eve speaking so confidently and with such authority on the opposite side of the table.

Now Mary focused on Mr. Clemens to see how he was faring. Apparently very well. He grinned broadly, then wiped at his mouth with his napkin, and when he lowered the white linen the grin was gone.

"You *have* read *Huckleberry Finn.*"

"Yes. Several times."

"Then you must read it again, for you missed the point—that it was not the music that I, or rather Huck, was objecting to, but the musical selection."

"*The Battle of Prague.*"

"Do you play it?"

"With a vengeance. But I'd rather sing."

All at once Eve smiled and lightly reached forward and touched Mr. Clemens's hand, quite a coquettish gesture, which seemed to reduce the distinguished gentleman to a schoolboy. "I *shall* sing for you after dinner, that is, if you wish."

Suddenly Mary felt the need to make her presence known. Slyly Eve was taking over, as though she were the mistress of Stanhope Hall.

"What was the musical selection you two were speaking of?" she asked.

"*The Battle of Prague,*" Mr. Clemens replied, scarcely looking at

Mary before turning back to Eve. "Surely the worst musical composition ever composed. Written by one Kotzwara, its sole purpose is to imitate artillery fire, the thunder of hooves and the shrieks of the dying. It is guaranteed to leave scars on the souls of all who hear it."

Eve smiled prettily even as Mr. Clemens worked his way through his long description. When he reached his conclusion, she clapped her hands but once and threw back her head and laughed, as though she knew perfectly well how entrancing a sound her laughter was, how lovely her throat.

"You remember it, Mama. I played it years ago, all the loud chords exploding all over Stanhope Hall. Sir, I'm tempted to go and play it for you this minute," she said at the end of the laugh, "to aid your digestion."

"You move so much as one inch from your pretty perch and I'll ask your father for permission to throttle you, I swear it."

The two were beaming at one another like empty-headed adolescents. Worried by the changes in her daughter, by the rapid transition from a silent Eve to a flirting one, Mary sat straight in her chair, determined to regain control of her dinner party. She must have a serious talk with Eve later, inform her as delicately as possible of all the serious and potentially dangerous consequences of flirting. Men did not always understand, and women always paid.

Now, "Mr. Washington," she announced with a bluntness she did nothing to alter, "I trust your fund-raising journey was a success. At least I certainly hope so."

For a moment it seemed to take everyone at table by surprise, this shift in subject as well as subject matter. Mary held herself in a state of tension, as though she could not possibly commence to eat until she had a response.

Unfortunately Mr. Washington had already approached the prime rib and seemed momentarily loath to leave it. Finally he placed his fork with a morsel of pink meat attached on one side of his platter and smiled patiently. "Fund-raisers are never one hundred percent successful, my dear Mrs. Stanhope. We do the best we can and are grateful to all generous hearts who respond to our needs."

Mary nodded and belatedly realized her ploy had failed, for out of the corner of her eye she saw Mr. Clemens and Eve chatting quietly together, as though now it was time for the party to divide itself into smaller groups. She wished Burke would help, but he seemed strangely subdued this evening, as though fearful of his own propensity to fly into a rage. Fortunately the object of his customary rage was missing from table.

Then when Mary least expected it, she heard Mr. Clemens's voice raised in question to Mr. Washington. "Please, sir, tell me of your Tuskegee. I've heard such grand things about it. A miracle, it's called in some quarters." He wiped his mouth briefly with his napkin and reemerged with a smile. "Less than a miracle in others," he added with just a hint of amused intrigue.

"I can well imagine." Mr. Washington nodded. "Even here in central Alabama, *miracle* is not the word most often applied."

"But what do you care? You have a vision and you are pursuing it. That raises you to the top two percent of the entire human race. I admire it. I stand in awe of it."

As Mr. Clemens's voice filled the quiet dining room, Mary dared to relax and slowly approached the platter of food that Katie had just placed before her.

"So tell me all," Mr. Clemens insisted again, speaking around a mouth full of beef.

Mr. Washington shrugged. "What do you want to know, sir? We started with no enrollment, and for buildings we had the loan of an abandoned church and one tumbled-down outbuilding. Within fifteen years the Tuskegee Institute now has eight hundred students, a staff of fifty-five, property worth two hundred thousand dollars, including a several-hundred-acre farm worked by the students themselves, and one hundred sixty-five graduates already out in this Southern world, spreading what they have learned." He paused and looked with pride at Paris Boley on his right. "This man is a splendid example of why Tuskegee exists."

"And yet it differs from Hampton," Mr. Clemens said, eating steadily as he spoke. "How?"

By contrast, Mr. Washington put down his fork. "Hampton is the Northern white man's creation for uplifting the benighted Negro. Tuskegee is the Negro's own creation, symbolically built brick by brick burned on the place by Negroes, a hand-carved instrument of self-uplift."

At some point Mr. Washington's preaching voice had taken over, a soaring rhythmical voice that could and did effortlessly captivate all. Mary observed that everyone at table was now focused on the distinguished man.

And when no one interrupted with another question, Mr. Washington obligingly went on. "The white man's contribution has only been one of money," he said, speaking directly across the blue larkspur to Mr. Clemens, "and not even all of that. Negroes themselves give generously as much as they can, and as it is with the farm, the brickyard, the sawmill and the print shop, all are extremely profitable."

"But there still are needs for funds?"

Mr. Washington smiled, a rare expression on his long-boned and sober face. "There are always needs for funds, sir, always. The majority of our students can pay nothing, and come to us empty-handed."

"And you take them in?"

"Of course, most of them, if they are capable of striving and succeeding."

"And if they are not?"

"They find their own level, as it is in your world, I'm sure."

The entire focus of the room was now at center table as these two men continued to eat and talk heartily. Beyond the range of conversation, Mary saw Burke watching and listening with a look of amazement. Nothing pleased him more than to provide the setting for such meetings as this. In fact, nothing pleased him more than the rich activity of a good human mind.

"And you believe that can be accomplished by and through education?" Mr. Clemens asked, looking up from his rapidly emptying plate.

"Only through education, sir," Mr. Washington said emphatically.

"And that will solve the problem?"

"Do you know another way?"

"I was just asking." Mr. Clemens smiled and offered a staying hand.

"Tell me if you do," Mr. Washington persisted, revealing his pure zealot colors when it came to the subject of race relations. "The problem can only be solved by the Southern Negro staying in the South, separate but equal, and with God's help and his own intelligence and persistence, demonstrating that he is entitled to full acceptance."

For several moments his preaching voice echoed about the table. Mary sat enthralled along with the rest of them and wished the enemies of such thinking could hear the conviction and resolution in Mr. Washington's voice. It might go a long way toward disarming them, literally and figuratively, for such a voice left no room for debate. The black man and woman and child would not be kept in any kind of slavery, no matter who or what insisted to the contrary.

"It is our opinion, Mr. Clemens," Mr. Washington concluded, "that all Negroes must destroy the stereotype that years of slavery have fixed in the minds of even his friends, and eliminate each of the negative slave characteristics that still cling to him, through no fault of his own, and substitute efficiency for the slipshod work of slavery days, accepted moral standards for the immorality of the slave quarters. So you can see that the Negro needs much more than academic training. It is our hope and dream, indeed, our plan to take young men and women, educate them and send them out as the backbone of a solid and prosperous citizenry."

The silence held for several minutes. Then, without warning, Mr. Clemens made a unique contribution.

"What if you are wrong, sir?" he asked flatly.

Mr. Washington looked up, clearly surprised. "I beg your—"

"What if you are wrong?" Mr. Clemens readily repeated. "And in my opinion you are. Your strategy of patience encourages the permanent legal installation of separatism at every important crossroad of race relations."

Mary saw Burke move up in his chair.

"Separate, but equal," Mr. Clemens went on. "That *is* what you said, isn't it, sir?"

"Yes, but—"

"Do you really think that the Southern mentality is capable of keeping such a bargain, of even admitting its existence? You will get *separate* all right, but I doubt very seriously if you will be able, in good conscience, to apply the word *equal*. Where will your Negro scholar or teacher go to find a post worthy of his training? There is only one choice—to another Negro institution."

Mr. Clemens concluded with a rather sad smile. "The truth is, I'm afraid, that Mr. Washington's self-reliant confidence, assuming proudly that demonstrated worth will eventually get spontaneous recognition, is an unjustified compliment to the human race."

Silence. From all quarters. Mary smoothed her napkin across her lap and found herself in the painful position of agreeing with Mr. Clemens.

But it was not her place to agree or disagree. It was her job to keep the conversation light and relaxed, the dinner party enjoyable.

"You may be right, sir." The quiet agreement was Burke's, who placed his napkin on the table and pushed back in his chair, as though at last he was ready to contribute. "The white community is slow to accept changes here—"

"Everywhere," Mr. Clemens interrupted graciously.

"But particularly here. Still I believe that Mr. Washington's theories are philosophically correct. What comes after them is another matter."

"I agree—"

"Please. Both of you."

It was Mr. Washington, forcefully interrupting both Mr. Clemens and Burke. He appeared to draw a deep breath. Slowly he began to shake his head. "I generally do not allow myself to indulge in Olympian views. There is so much close at hand that needs my attention. What comes in the next century, in the next decade, the next year, even the next month—we will deal with that as it arrives and presents us with its unique problems. For now I must cling to my theory as a drowning man clings to a life raft, and that theory tells me that all Christians must deplore slavery, primarily because it warps the souls of both slaves and masters. That is the foundation for change, on both sides. How we build the edifice of freedom for the black man after that really is unimportant. However, it *must* be built on that foundation and that foundation alone, for all others are bogus and not worthy of our attention or our efforts."

Again in a remarkably short time he had captivated the dining room. Mr. Clemens appeared to be on the verge of response, as did Burke, though both politely deferred and neither spoke and the silence deepened.

Mary prayed quietly that they would leave this vast and unsolved subject alone for now, though she knew very well that it would be pursued later into the night in the smoker, over bottles of Madeira and cigars. Fine. That was the place for it. But not here, not at table.

"My compliments, Mrs. Stanhope," Mr. Clemens said with a smile.

"Thank you," Mary murmured. "I shall convey your compliments to Mrs. Winegar. She has kept all of us well fed and healthy for years."

More silence, punctuated by nothing at all except the occasional clatter of silver on china, and even that was winding down now as, one by one, platters were cleared and the last swallows of wine sipped.

"Mr. Clemens, as you are this country's premier man of letters, answer one question, would you, please?"

Mary blinked toward the charming voice, more grateful than she could ever express. It was Eve again, looking so grown-up, her cheeks flushed.

"Anything, Miss Stanhope." Mr. Clemens smiled graciously and inclined his head. "Anything at all, and if I can't answer honestly, I shall lie with the greatest skill at my command and I pledge to you that you will never know the difference."

"No difference between truth and lies?"

"In most matters, no."

"A questionable morality."

"All morality is questionable. But come, what is this great question? Challenge me. I love a challenge."

Mary watched and listened closely, as did everyone at the table.

"Very well," Eve began and sat up on the edge of her seat and addressed not only Mr. Clemens but the entire table. "If one had to rescue just one book from the flames at the end of the world for eternal preservation, what would you reach in for?"

Mary smiled. The girl would make a brilliant hostess. In point of fact, she was doing a better job now than Mary herself.

"Why?" Mr. Clemens demanded with mock forcefulness. "Is the world on the verge of termination?"

"No, but if it were . . . ."

"One book?"

"Only one."

"Why a book? Why not a painting, a piece of music?"

"Because it's my question and I said a book."

Burke, apparently sensing Mr. Clemens's reluctance to answer and to play the game, tried to intercede. "Eve, perhaps later, after we've all had—"

"No, now, I'll answer now. Thanks anyway for the attempted rescue." Mr. Clemens smiled, waving his hand at Burke in light dismissal.

Now to Eve, he warned, "Of course you know there are several—"

"One."

"Only one?"

She nodded and returned his earnest gaze. Mary found herself along with everyone else waiting with held breath for Mr. Clemens's response.

Finally, "*Huck,*" he said with a sly smile. "I would, out of paternal love and necessity, be forced to rescue my last born. My answer is *Huck Finn.*"

Across the table Madame Germaine applauded daintily. "Bravo, Mr. Clemens. If you hadn't plunged into the fire, I would have."

Mr. Clemens ignored her and turned his attention back to Eve. "Be warned, my dear Miss Stanhope, that it is all soul-butter and hogwash," Mr. Clemens went on, still ignoring the fawning applause coming from across the table. "We authors write books with all our evangelical hearts and souls, hoping to reform, if not remake, the world to one of our own liking. And what happens? No one reads them but pedants and academicians, who take masochistic delight in pawing over them in search of archetypal symbols." He paused for breath, then repeated, "Soul-butter and hogwash. Why do we even bother?"

For several moments Mr. Clemens seemed newly defeated by his own response.

Close by sat Eve, attentive. "Sir, I am neither a pedant nor an academician and I enjoyed Huck and all his adventures and will never forget them, and I haven't the slightest idea what an archetypal symbol is."

Her voice hung like soft music over the table. Mr. Clemens looked sharply at her at first, as though she had attacked him, which, in a way, she had. "A temptress, that's what you are." He smiled softly at last. "All males of the species, beware. Before this young goddess, you are lost and doomed."

"You unjustly accuse me, sir." Eve smiled.

"I do indeed, and I thank you for your kind words, and I breathe a sigh of relief that I am too old to consider you as anything more than a charming table companion."

Eve sat up on the edge of her chair. "Mama, Papa, would you excuse me for a moment?"

Mary looked up in time to see Eve leave her chair. Simultaneously the gentlemen rose, and before Mary could protest, Eve had skirted the far end of the table and disappeared into the parlor.

Mr. Clemens looked concerned. "I—hope I said nothing—"

At that moment Mary heard the soft chords of the old Steinway, coming from the parlor, heard the opening refrain of Stephen Foster's "I Dream of Jeannie," the notes of the pianoforte nothing compared to the voice that followed, Eve's singing voice, growing more spectacular, more pure, almost unbearably lovely by the day.

Across the table she saw Mr. Clemens look in the direction of the parlor and carefully, as though mesmerized, place his napkin on the edge of the table, his entire posture one of intense pleasure as Eve's voice filled the dining room with a heartbreaking memory, somehow conveying the homesickness of a wandering soul for his lover.

At some point Mr. Clemens closed his eyes and lifted his face to the music as though the better to receive it, unencumbered by sight. Mary saw a gratifying smile of pure enjoyment on his face as the song spoke of separation and bitterness and protracted wanderings and unspeakable loneliness, her voice growing richer and purer until the beauty soared as the words approached the end of the song, the pianoforte now falling silent, leaving only Eve's voice to touch the ears and the hearts and the souls of all who listened.

Then it was over.

"Lord," prayed Mr. Clemens and studied the doorway that led to the parlor and continued to look eagerly and hopefully in that direction.

When, after a few minutes, Eve had not reappeared, Mary felt compelled to break the spell. "I'm certain she'll rejoin us shortly, sir."

"You realize, of course, that she is gifted beyond description?" Mr. Clemens said graciously. "The entire world could benefit mightily from hearing a voice of that caliber, if for no other reason than that it confirms the existence of the Divinity. Such a gift as that does not issue from an earthly source."

Mary nodded her gratitude and again looked toward the door and wondered where Eve was and now felt a greater need than ever to rescue the party from the lingering effects of the beautiful song and the perfect voice. "Tell us, sir, if you will, your opinion of our Southern world. You've been investigating us at length, or so we are told. For what purpose, if I may be so bold?"

As Mary endeavored to keep the pulse of the party alive after Eve's mesmerizing song, she felt her attentions torn in two, part of her following Eve's footsteps, which now she heard going down the hall, moving up the stairs, disappearing finally onto the second landing, the other part of her attention on Mr. Clemens's slow and seemingly lifeless response, as though with Eve's departure and following her song, she had taken all the light and life and color of the party with her.

"I am endeavoring to alter my Southern prejudice, Madame," Mr. Clemens began slowly, "commencing with Walter Scott's influence and ending with a redefinition of Southern aristocracy, if you please."

Mary nodded, though in truth she had heard little of what he'd said. Why had Eve excused herself? Why hadn't she returned after her song to enjoy the accolades of the entire table?

Well, no matter. Mary would give her her privacy and perhaps later seek out an explanation of why she left so abruptly after her song.

For now, Mary had her work cut out for her. There was the normal lull that followed a heavy meal, the customary twenty-minute wait before dessert.

Mr. Clemens had apparently sputtered to a halt, and everyone else was busily rearranging their napkins, except for David on her right, who was drawing lines in the white linen cloth with the tip of his fork, and Paris Boley, who had left his chair, whispered something in Burke's ear, waited for Burke's nod and then without a word left the dining room.

Her worry increasing, Mary looked searchingly at Burke for an explanation, for assistance, for anything he was in the mood to give. But apparently he was not in a giving mood, for he reached for the freshly filled decanter of Medeira, filled his glass and offered it to Mr. Clemens.

"Mr. Quitman," Mary began, desperate for someone to take up the conversational pulse which had come to a halt with Eve's exit. "Tell us about Mobile. It's been weeks since I've been to town. Tell us of all the new buildings, the gossip, everything."

She heard in echo the slightly desperate tone in her voice and regretted it, and wondered if perhaps she was not too old for these salons. She used to do them so effortlessly and with a great deal of joy. Now—

"Mobile is—Mobile," Taylor Quitman drawled brilliantly and looked even more uncomfortable than anyone else, if that was possible.

Mr. Clemens stared thoughtfully at the table. Mr. Washington looked straight up at the chandelier. Christine hummed softly on her left, David continued making tracks in the tablecloth with his fork. Madame Germaine smiled inanely at her napkin, and Burke did and said nothing, absolutely nothing.

Where was Eve?

* * *

She suffered only one moment of serious regret, and that was when she passed her mother's rooms. Then the full meaning of this giant step pressed down upon her and she faltered and put down her small satchel and leaned heavily against the door through which she'd passed at least a dozen times every day, every week, every month, every year of her life.

"Mama," she whispered and shivered in the darkened upstairs hall and felt herself to be on the brink of something momentous.

She retrieved her satchel, lightly weighted as Stephen had instructed, with only one change of garments. They could purchase what they needed in New Orleans, symbolic of their new life.

Stephen—

There was a powerful thought, filled with memories, one that quickly erased the doubt and prompted her to pull the dark blue summer cape more firmly about her shoulders and head for the trap door that led up into the attic staircase.

No. Suddenly she changed her mind. No furtive exit for her on this last escape from Stanhope Hall. She could make it easily down the front steps and disappear into the night undetected, she was certain of it.

For now, as best as she could tell, Mrs. Winegar had just rolled in the dessert cart. That should keep them occupied for a while. Then hurry. And she did, lifting the skirts of her dark blue muslin dress, a practical traveling choice, and avoiding the steps that she knew from experience creaked.

In good time she reached the lower hallway and heard the voices from the dinner party increase, everyone apparently talking quite amiably now. She even heard David's piping voice and Mr. Clemens's bold laughter. A nice man, though a troubled one. She liked him and hoped he had enjoyed her song.

Then she took the door running and did not stop until she had reached the beginning of the woods and relative safety. Behind her, a distance away, lamps lit every window of Stanhope Hall. She looked back. How beautiful it was at night! How solid appearing and safe, how fortresslike.

Still the time had come. She felt it in her heart, which now was a curious battlefield of hope and longing, confidence and apprehension. Stanhope Hall was the place of her past, not of her future. That lay somewhere through those inky dark woods, where a man was waiting for her, a glorious man, the most remarkable man she'd ever met or was likely to meet. She took a final look at Stanhope Hall and lifted her valise and ran into the woods.

Surefooted, she made her way effortlessly along the same path she'd run along all her life. How pleased Sis Liz would be, and filled undoubtedly with last-minute advice. Eve would listen politely, as would Stephen. Then they both would kiss her farewell, beg her to try to help the others to understand, and then they'd be off.

Then suddenly she saw it, a faint eye of light, a friendly beacon leading her to her new destiny.

"Stephen—"

She spoke his name aloud and increased her speed and wondered if she had a right to the great happiness that was washing over her, and kept her eye on that beacon of light that surely would lead her to paradise on earth.

* * *

Orlando Dow had been in position about fifty yards from Fan Cottage since dusk. On orders from the Knights of the White Camellia, all he was to do was to set fire to Fan Cottage, and then let nature take its course. If the old madwoman made it to safety, well and good. If not, well and good.

Now Orlando doused the end of the torch in fresh kerosene and looked through the thick foliage of trees toward the front of Fan Cottage. It seemed a tame lesson, compared to the last one. Supporting the torch between his legs, he scanned the front of the cottage and tried to determine where would be the best place to toss it. It all resembled dry kindling; it would blaze well. Then no matter. Light the torch, walk directly up onto the front porch and push open the door and toss it in. With the good southerly breeze of the evening, the flames would spread rapidly, blocking the front door. Addled and frightened, perhaps the old woman would go up in flames along with the cottage.

Orlando Dow felt no remorse, for it was an evil place, this Fan

Cottage was, or so Orlando had been told, the scene of frequent witchcraft, comings and goings of evil spirits and hauntings. It was godless. It deserved to be burned to the ground, and the senseless old woman with it.

On that note of decision he struck a match and held it to the torch and watched the small flame become a large dancing one in a matter of seconds, the night breeze fanning it into a hot glow, which Orlando thrust away from himself lest he get singed by his own handiwork.

He looked back at his horse, secured a distance away, then took a step forward, keeping his eye fixed on the front door.

Listen! Someone's coming—

He lifted his head the better to hear and heard something coming at him from his left, something moving through the dark woods directly toward him. He whirled on the advancing figure and thrust the torch forward, using it like a weapon now.

"Who is it?" he hissed and still could not locate the approaching intruder, blinded as he was by the brilliance of the torchlight. What if Stanhope had set guards in these woods? Why hadn't the knights told him?

Quickly he moved the torch to one side and sent skittering shadows over the tops of trees, highlighting a slim figure, a small satchel clasped in one hand, a surprised look on her pretty face, which turned to fear within the moment.

Orlando Dow blinked, unable to believe his eyes. A gift from God, this heavenly apparition, clearly divine approval that what he was doing was right. It was the eldest Stanhope girl, the pretty one, wandering unescorted, without even the fair warning of a lamplight.

"Whoa there," Orlando Dow called out and stepped forward at the same moment that she stepped backward, clearly sensing her mistake.

"I—thought you were—"

She tried to speak, but fear lodged in her throat and rendered her mute. Dow watched her carefully, sensing that she was ready to bolt.

"Now, who did you think I was?" Orlando smiled, still tracking her, spying by torchlight a short distance behind her a large protruding root which, if he handled her well, would do his dirty work for him. He smiled in an attempt to put her at ease. "You make it a habit, missy, of straying away from the nest so late at night?"

"I thought you were—someone else."

"Who? Now who would you be meeting at this Satan's hour? Bad girl, naughty girl. I wonder if anyone at Stanhope Hall even knows you're here."

With every word he smiled more broadly and continued to track her, seeing precise fear in her eyes now.

"Please," she whispered and shook her pretty head but once. At that precise moment, not looking, she stumbled backward over the protruding root, a terrified outcry leaving her lips as she fell, hands flailing in all directions for support that wasn't there.

Within that same moment Orlando Dow was upon her, the torch abandoned briefly as he followed her down, covering her screaming mouth with one gloved hand, pressing his hand down hard against her face, seeing over his gloved fingers her eyes wide, distended in fear and darting from side to side.

There was a struggle, fearsome for a mere girl, her back arching against him, legs and arms flailing, one knee through the layered petticoats delivering a painful blow to his groin, causing him to wince, then finally losing patience with the impudent bitch and, still holding one gloved hand over her mouth, he lifted his other hand into the air and brought it down in a blow that he delivered to the side of her head and that instantly rendered her unconscious.

He continued to exert pressure even after she had gone limp beneath him. Couldn't be too careful. Women were best known for their treachery, particularly pampered, headstrong women like this one.

At last assured of her unconscious state, Orlando sat back on his heels, still straddling her. *Thank you, God,* he thought humbly. Wasn't God with him at all times? And look at the prize that God had sent Orlando Dow—Burke Stanhope's jewel just wandering these woods as though lost, as though wanting Orlando to find her.

Orlando shook his head. And wouldn't the gentlemen back at Jarmay Higgins's lumberyard be just doubly grateful? Instead of bringing them word of Fan Cottage burning, he could do that plus bring them this rich bonus.

In the flickering light from the fallen torch, he eyed his prize more carefully. At the angle at which she lay, he studied the soft rounded breasts beneath the dark bodice, a full woman's breasts, no girl this. He poked at one with a single finger as though testing a pudding for doneness. Ripe, all right, and Orlando Dow felt appetites stirring. How would it hurt? And who would know?

Then he heard a horse, or horses. Not too far. Coming closer—

His appetites momentarily abandoned, he reached down and effortlessly scooped her up and hoisted her over his shoulders as though she were nothing more than a sack of potatoes. A moment later, still trying to identify the noise and its direction, he retrieved the torch, which still was burning splendidly, and, carrying the girl over one shoulder and the torch in his right hand, he ran toward Fan Cottage and with one mighty effort hurled the torch up onto the porch, saw it strike the front door, saw the fire spread instantly.

Then pleased with his skill in all matters, he tightened his grip on the girl and headed toward the place where he had secured his horse, deposited the girl across the saddle and swung up behind, taking a final glimpse toward Fan Cottage, amazed at the size of the bonfire he'd started.

The entire front porch was now ablaze and burning well, obscuring the door. No one would be passing into and out of that opening for a while.

He stared at the inferno for a moment longer. Then he angled his horse about and plunged his spurs into the animal's flesh. Moving her instantly to top speed, he headed out of the Stanhope woods and toward the road to Mobile, where the Knights of the White Camellia were waiting.

How pleased they would be, those fancy gentlemen, praising Orlando Dow to the heavens for his diligence, his loyalty, his ability to act on his own to the glory and good of the Southern cause.

He tightened his grip on the girl and looked back once to see if he was being followed, though he knew he wasn't for God would not permit it. God Himself had directed this evening, had seen to its success and would not permit anything or anyone to interfere with the execution of His will.

* * *

Despite the fact that Stephen thought he had made flawless plans, he had overlooked one simple fact: that a two-wheeled gig and two horses would not move easily through these dense woods. He had tried three approaches before he could talk Eve's sorrel, Clarissa, and his own borrowed Cicero into proceeding through the darkness, angling them carefully around and through the trees, trying to see all ditches and fallen timber before the horses saw them.

His progress was slow, his nerves taut, and he spent as much time looking backward as ahead, confident that someone had seen him leave the house, had heard him in the barn. The only realization that brought him any comfort was the one that quietly informed him that he had no choice in his actions; neither apparently did Eve. He'd given her ample opportunity to back out, but she was as filled with conviction as he was, that they had no life apart from one another, and therefore had no choice.

"Steady," he whispered to the horses, who were more accustomed to riders than to the harness of a gig. Still he didn't want Burke Stanhope to accuse him of horse thievery along with everything else.

So he'd taken his horse and Eve's and had literally talked the skitterish animals into their bridles and now was trying to talk them through these dark woods, hoping soon to see the lamplight of Fan Cottage.

He looked up in an effort to keep the horses moving forward, and as he did, he saw light in the distance, a mere eye of light at first, torch-sized, no more.

He continued to stare forward, searching again for that single eye of light. Where was it? And who could it be?

"Easy," he muttered to the horses. Then suddenly in the blackness on his left he saw an explosion of fire, no mere torchlight now but a growing, spreading blaze, about fifty yards veering left, toward—

He drew the horses up and heard their whinnying objection. He stood awkwardly in the cramped seat of the gig, keeping his eye on the fire that seemed to be ever growing, coming from—

Dear God.

He retrieved the reins and brought them down across the horses. The gig leapt forward as Stephen struggled for control, all the while watching the blaze increase.

Sis Liz!

Could he get there in time? Was the old woman trapped, or had she escaped to safety? And Eve?

The last question was the most painful. While he was still several yards from the cottage, which was completely engulfed in roaring flames, Stephen abandoned the gig and darted the last distance on foot, his eyes searching the inferno for someone to help, someone to rescue.

He was still about fifty feet away when the heat stopped him and drove him back.

"Sis Liz!" he shouted foolishly, thinking he'd receive an answer.

What to do? The fire must be reported. He couldn't fight it himself. And where was Sis Liz? And where was Eve? And if he returned to Stanhope Hall with news of the fire, they'd never make their escape.

As each unanswered question struck him like a new agony, he closed his eyes against the heat and smoke and knew what he had to do. If Eve had arrived early, she would have gone inside to share her happiness with Sis Liz.

Suddenly he lunged directly at the flames, ripping off his jacket as he ran, futilely beating against the spreading fire, doing nothing to extinguish any single part of it.

"Eve!" He shouted her name over and over again now, hoping if she was within hearing distance, she would answer, but praying that she was still safe at Stanhope Hall, delayed by the society of the evening.

"Please, God," he begged and lifted his arm as a poor shield against the intense heat as the dry old timber exploded in growing flames.

He retreated back to the safety of the gig, where he heard the horses whinnying nervously, their eyes white with fear as they viewed their ancient enemy, fire.

"It's all right," he soothed, rubbing their noses, seeing up close in Cicero's massive white eye an orange-red reflection of the fire itself, as though what the horse feared most originated inside him.

Stephen stood in a state resembling paralysis, not knowing now if this wretched evening would be the beginning of his life or the end of it.

One way to find out. Return to Stanhope Hall, pray to God to find Eve either at table or packing to leave in her rooms. New plans could be made. The same plan executed tomorrow evening. One lost day. No matter. He'd waited all his life to find her. What was one day more?

Soothed by his thoughts, he took a final look at the fire, which showed no signs of diminishing. It could burn for hours. By then he would have the confirmation he needed. As for Sis Liz, may her soul rest in peace, for if she was trapped in Fan Cottage when the blaze started, she would not have had a chance of escaping.

With trembling hands he climbed back up into the gig, secured the reins and felt the horses turn eagerly about.

Strange, but the path behind him now seemed clear and open, as though inviting speed for the return trip to Stanhope Hall.

Eve—where was she?

The question continued to present itself to his mind as though tormenting him for an answer.

Eve. He would find her soon. Of that he was certain. And then his world would be put right again.

 Stanhope Hall

Burke, pleased with the way the evening had gone thus far, had just passed around snifters of French brandy to the gentlemen in the library. Mr. Washington and Mr. Clemens had taken up positions on opposite sides of the room, though that was not unnatural. Burke was certain they would join forces shortly. The sizing up had ended during dinner, and shortly after Eve had sung and departed, the two men had become engaged in a fascinating dialogue concerning the effects of Sir Walter Scott and his works on Southern romanticism. It was the sort of intellectual give-and-take that Burke loved to moderate, prodding when the debate needed a subtle prod, but for the most part staying out of their way and letting two naturally brilliant and original men explore each other's minds.

Eve.

What had come over his foolish daughter? He hadn't the least idea, but he fully intended to explore the subject at length with Mary as soon as this weekend was over.

She had behaved like a common flirt, Eve had. Where on earth had she learned those female wiles? Certainly not from Mary. Mary didn't have a false or coquettish bone in her body. Well, perhaps it was time to ship Eve off to a good Northern finishing school. He knew of several. It would do her a world of good and give them all relief from her growing pains.

Now alone in the library with only the male company, Burke began to relax. Sometimes he had his doubts about women in an intellectual setting. Even Mary had seemed unduly moody tonight, no doubt concerned with Stephen Eden.

Burke turned his back on his company, the better to regain his composure. Anyway they were doing very well without him for the moment. Taylor Quitman had apparently said something to catch Mr. Clemens's attention, and Mr. Washington was doting on Paris Boley, who had just returned from a quick check on the workers' cabins.

"One wonders about the source of such a way of life," Burke heard Mr. Clemens muse now.

From where Burke stood at the fireplace, he saw Taylor Quitman looking about as though in search of a rescue party. Poor Taylor. A fine legal mind, though not much more.

"And what way of life do you have reference to, Mr. Clemens?" Burke asked, smiling at Taylor as he passed, beginning to feel good for the first time in the long evening.

"The Southern way of life, Mr. Stanhope," Mr. Clemens said and sniffed his brandy and touched his tongue to it. "It has proved itself to be so different from the rest of the country, so unlike life in, say, Vermont, or Texas, or California." He shook his head and cradled the snifter closer to his chest. "I can think of only two reasons: parochialism and Sir Walter Scott."

Across the room Mr. Washington laughed. "It is my belief," he began, "that the South is fond of decorating her penitentiary culture with romantic flummery in order to distract herself from the grisly reality of her situation."

"Here, here," Mr. Clemens agreed, and as Burke had privately predicted only a few moments earlier, the two men met mid-library. "I believe it was only a few years ago that I stated that in my opinion Scott had run Southerners mad a couple of generations ago with his grotesque chivalric doings and romantic juvenilities."

"I remember." Mr. Washington nodded. "Still the attitude, the mentality exists, and many of us pay the price for such foolishness."

"I'm sure." Mr. Clemens nodded. "And the only cures are time and progress. Sooner or later all human stupidity is left behind, not necessarily destroyed. Pockets continue to exist, like museum pieces, so we can see what we have left behind in our forward movement and be grateful."

Burke listened to the silence following Mr. Clemens's pronouncement. Taylor Quitman retreated out of the sphere of conversation. He'd been unduly quiet this evening, preoccupied like everyone else. And even Paris Boley, normally talkative, kept his position on the far side of the library as though more than willing to let these two leviathans hold center arena.

But now that they had come together in the middle of the library, they seemed to turn shy, each man refusing to look at the other, as though equally impressed.

Burke watched for a few seconds, debating whether to plunge in and act as catalyst. As he was trying to reach a decision, he heard a disturbance coming from the front of Stanhope Hall, horses driven fast, someone shouting. He listened a moment longer, his attention divided between the curious silence that had invaded his library and the equally curious ruckus being raised near the front gallery.

He exchanged a glance with Paris, who obviously had heard it too. Someone was shouting at the top of his lungs, calling his name now.

"Shall I see, sir?" Paris murmured.

Then Burke heard running outside in the corridor, heard Ben's voice raised in futile protest, then the library door burst open and he saw the young Eden, his face flushed and black-smudged, coatless, disaster written in his eyes.

"Sir, I beg you, come, Fan Cottage is on fire and I can't find Sis Liz or Eve."

"Eve is with her mother."

"Confirm it."

"I beg your pardon?"

"Please, sir, confirm it," Eden begged, appearing almost deranged with his smudged face.

Burke was aware of Paris at his side. "I'll go," the young man offered. As he passed the place where Stephen Eden stood, Burke saw him touch his shoulder as though an alliance existed between these two about which Burke knew nothing.

For some reason the gesture annoyed Burke, as did the entire rude interruption. "If you gentlemen will be so kind as to excuse me," he said to Mr. Clemens and Mr. Washington, who had graciously retreated back to the fireplace. "Taylor, would you look after my guests until I return?"

"But Burke, I—"

"Please, Taylor," Burke insisted, moving toward the door and the place where the Eden bastard still stood. For some reason, each time Burke was forced to lay eyes on him, he took on an even greater resemblance to John Murrey Eden in all respects.

"No, sir, Eve is not with Mrs. Stanhope."

Paris Boley's voice dragged his attention back to the library. As he looked toward the voice, his eyes skimmed Stephen Eden's face. He saw a look of pain, as though he were enduring physical agony.

Then materializing out of the darkened corridor he saw Mary, followed by David and Christine and, bringing up the rear, Madame Germaine.

"Burke, what is it? What—" She stopped short of the library door, apparently catching sight of Stephen Eden and his disreputable appearance. "Stephen, what—"

The young man went instantly to her side in easy familiarity, and again Burke sensed an alliance that infuriated him.

"Fan Cottage is burning," he said, his voice low. "I can't find Sis Liz or Eve."

"Eve?" Mary repeated, the look of bewilderment on her face increasing. "She isn't at Fan Cottage. Why would she be at Fan Cottage? She's been here all evening, with us."

"Where is she now?"

"Probably upstairs in her room."

"Go and see, please, I beg you."

"I don't under—"

"Send someone to check immediately, or, better, let me go."

Burke had heard enough. What right did the bastard have to come running in here, disrupting this most important evening?

"You will not go up those stairs," he pronounced, moving all the way out into the corridor. "You, Madame Germaine, go and find Eve and bring her to us immediately."

With a wave of his hand he set the woman into motion and waited until she had started up the steps before addressing Stephen Eden again.

"Now, concerning the rest of your wild tale—" he began and never finished.

"It is not a tale, sir," Eden shouted. "The cottage is burning, out of control. Please, will you send help?"

Mary moved between them. "Did you see it?" she asked.

"Of course I saw it," Eden replied, the expression of pain on his face increasing.

"And what were you doing in the woods?" Burke demanded, wishing they could move away from the close proximity of the library door, disliking his family problems to be openly displayed in this manner.

For once the young bastard did not have a ready reply. In fact he turned away without answering, thus providing Burke with his first excuse for legitimate anger.

"Answer me," he demanded. "I asked you a question. It was my understanding—indeed, my command—that you were to be gone from here today."

"I was—leaving," the boy murmured.

"Then what were you doing near Fan Cottage?"

"I—had gone to tell Sis Liz good-bye."

"And what is Sis Liz to you?"

"A friend," he replied.

Burke was on the verge of a response when he heard a disturbance coming from the top of the stairs, Madame Germaine hurrying across the landing, a white handkerchief pressed to her lips. "Sir, Madame, we cannot find her. Anyplace," she called down.

Mary turned in a small aimless circle, her voice trailing, "Eve is— someplace. In the house. She would not go wandering off at night, not even to see Sis Liz. She knows better. Doesn't she, Stephen? Doesn't she know it's not safe to go about in the woods after dark? She wouldn't do that, would she?"

Burke watched, puzzled from the door. He understood Mary's line of questioning. What he didn't understand was why she was directing them all to Stephen Eden, and why he had turned his back on her as though refusing to answer.

"Stephen, please give me an answer," Mary persisted.

Finally, without looking at her, he shook his head but once, as though to refute everything she had said. "We were to have met. This evening. At Fan Cottage."

Burke took a step forward. Mary stopped him with a single glance.

"Why, Stephen? Why were you and Eve to meet on this evening at Sis Liz's?"

At last Stephen turned and faced Mary, though it was the face of a man undergoing severe torture. "I love her, and she has led me to believe that she loves me. I asked her to marry me. We were leaving tonight for New Orleans, and she was going to accompany me on my trip west."

Burke heard the words, though his first impulse was to laugh. Eve was yet a child. Marriage? Was the boy as insane as his madman father? Then as all the ramifications and implications pressed down upon him—the secrecy, the deceptions, the long walks, the longer rides, the hours alone—now he knew what had transpired. His beautiful Eve, his sweet, innocent, childlike Eve—

"Damn you," he shouted and started across the corridor, his hands reaching for his target, the young man's throat, no sportsmanlike boxing match this time, now a much simpler goal, to provide death and thus rid him and his family of this nightmare from the past.

With alarming ease and no resistance, he found his mark, the young man glancing toward him with those pain-ridden eyes, then lifting his head as though to accommodate the thrust of Burke's hands. With suspect ease the boy slipped to his knees, offering no resistance as Burke's hand exerted greater strength about his throat, impervious at first to Mary's screams and Madame Germaine's, equally impervious to the sound of more footsteps running, then at last aware of strong arms dislodging him from the completion of this most necessary act.

Despite his fury, he saw Paris Boley on one side and Taylor Quitman on the other and gave in to their respective strengths.

"Have you lost your mind?" Taylor hissed in his ear.

Paris, still holding on to his arm said, "I'll get the field hands to help with the fire."

Reluctantly Burke nodded and watched, breathing heavily from exertion, as Stephen Eden stood on shaky knees, rubbing his throat. "It was not our desire to deceive," he said hoarsely. "You forced us into deception. And if Eve is—"

His voice broke, and without a word he started off down the corridor and out the door and disappeared into the night. A few moments later Burke heard the whinnying of a horse.

"You'd better stay here," Taylor Quitman advised. "I'll go with him, see if there is—"

But Burke had already walked away from the advice and reached the door in time to see Stephen mount his horse. He rode off, abandoning the gig and the other horse, whom Burke now recognized as Eve's sorrel.

She was going to accompany me on my trip west . . .

As the words echoed in his mind, he still couldn't believe them, still couldn't perceive exactly what had happened this evening. Fan Cottage on fire? Why? And where was Sis Liz? And Eve? Surely she would have nothing seriously to do with Stephen Eden.

He heard the others following behind him. Mary was calling to him. Eve's horse was waiting, unattended beside the gig, *his* gig. Was the arrogant bastard going to steal it as well?

"Burke, wait."

But he was not in a waiting mood. The chatter he had heard recently in his library seemed pale and unimportant now. No more talk on what the Southern mind was or was not capable of doing. And perhaps there were greater enemies than the Southern conscience. What about the English one, perverted by generations of inbreeding, sufficient to create a genetic nightmare like Stephen Eden, who in a remarkably short time had disrupted life at Stanhope Hall entirely, had driven a wedge between Burke and his wife, had captivated and poisoned the minds of Burke's younger children, and now had calmly announced that he had every intention of kidnapping his eldest daughter.

This litany of offenses gave him new strength, and using only the loosened bridle from the gig, he mounted Eve's sorrel and turned her about and headed her directly into the dark woods where he saw into the deeper distance, saw a small orange glow that did not belong in quiet woods, and did not even think about what he might do if he found Fan Cottage ablaze and did not find Sis Liz or Eve.

Without warning, grief, premature and painful, joined his fury and he drove the horse deeper into the woods, always keeping his eye on the orange glow that was coming closer.

 Mobile

Jarmay Higgins was cold. Strange. His loft over the cutting shed was hot as Hades during the summer days, but at night it cooled right down as the breeze from the Gulf picked up and blew in through the high, slatted vents.

Then, too, he disliked intensely the way his loft had become central headquarters for the knights, disliked even more how he had become chief-in-charge of all dubious projects, having to wait here alone for scum like Orlando Dow, wait alone for Dow's report, wait alone to pay him off.

Jarmay Higgins peered down into his deserted lumberyard, hoping to catch a glimpse of the scum by moonlight. It seemed time enough. How long did it take a man to ride ten miles out of Mobile, light a torch, toss it at an old slave cabin and ride back?

Abruptly he turned away from gazing down in his empty lumberyard, something bothering him. Why had the knights launched these attacks against two helpless old women? Burke Stanhope would not be touched severely by either death. Better if they had struck Stanhope where it hurt—his immediate family, someone whose absence would cause him continuous and bitter pain.

Pacing now, Jarmay rubbed his arms in an attempt to ward off the cool dampness. He heard a disturbance on the opposite side of the loft coming from the street below. Quickly he moved in that direction, stepping around the stacked piles of old lumber, covered with sawdust.

Looking down, he saw torchlight and revelers, the painted ladies from the traveling theatrical troupe that had been in Mobile and surrounding towns for several weeks. He smiled in reflected pleasure at the white bared shoulders, all the ladies laughing, tippling from dark brown bottles, and in the lead wagon, their head rooster, the cock himself, the man they called Yorrick Harp, once a preacher of the gospel, or so Jarmay had heard, who'd found greater satisfaction and greater profit in owning his all-female touring company.

And they were entertaining. Jarmay had seen their present show several times. They were real charmers, these females, free of inhibitions, dancing, spouting Shakespeare, a few as willing to bare a breast as a smile.

Jarmay rested his arms on the dusty windowsill and watched the midnight spectacle, all cavorting and laughing, a few teasing late-night passersby. He watched until the last bared shoulder had turned the corner and disappeared from sight. Gone. The laughter gone, the color, the joy, the—

"Mr. Higgins."

The voice came from behind and startled him, and he whirled on it, ready to attack. But across the loft, dimly lit by one small kerosene lamp, he saw the disreputable features of Orlando Dow and knew that his messenger had arrived.

"Well?" Jarmay demanded, half in anger that the man had snuck up on him.

"Done." Orlando Dow grinned. "There was quite a bonfire in the woods of Stanhope Hall on this night."

"The old woman?"

"Never saw her. I suspect she's cinder now."

His distance suited Higgins just fine. So the deed was done. Burke Stanhope had just been taught another lesson, though Jarmay Higgins was of the opinion that they were exacting the punishment on the wrong people.

"Wait here," Jarmay Higgins commanded roughly and returned to the old desk on the far side of the loft, where he retrieved a brown envelope thick with bills.

He looked back over his shoulder to see Orlando Dow braced in the doorway, still grinning that insane grin. Did the man have any other expression?

"Is that for me?" he asked.

Jarmay tossed the envelope heavy with bills and saw Dow's good reflexes spring into action and grab the envelope mid-air.

The grin seemed to widen. "Not enough, I fear," the impudent man said. "I found something in the woods tonight I thought might interest you. I brought it along."

Losing patience, Jarmay backed away from the man's babble. "It is enough. Get on with you. It was the bargain."

"Did you hear me speaking to you, Mr. Higgins?" the man scolded. "While I was in the Stanhope woods, I happened to encounter something wandering loose, pretty as a picture, and I said to myself, them gentlemen might want to see this."

Jarmay squinted at the incoherency and tried to play along with the madman. "What was it that you found in the woods?"

"Shall I bring it in for you? It's right outside the door."

As Orlando Dow gestured back toward the open door, Jarmay Higgins peered in that direction as well. Something outside the door?

Orlando Dow placed a finger against his temple, his head cocked to one side, and turned about three times and with a skipping movement disappeared out the door.

All of a sudden Jarmay Higgins's heart accelerated. Something was about to happen, and he wasn't certain if he wanted to be part of it.

He was just starting toward the door with the full intention of closing and locking it when Orlando Dow materialized out of the shadows, leaning heavily to one side, something thrown over his shoulder, something limp like a human form though it was completely encased in a gunnysack.

Jarmay Higgins had no choice but to back away. Orlando Dow moved rapidly through the door and called back orders to Higgins to close and lock it.

"Lock it, I said," the man commanded again, no longer grinning, and proceeded on across the loft, stopping short of the desk by several feet, still grasping his mysterious cargo over his shoulders, his eyes glittering with excitement.

"What is—"

"Bide your time," Dow advised as he kneeled before the desk and eased his cargo off his shoulder and allowed it to fall in a slumped sitting position before the desk on the floor.

As the man fumbled with the cord about the neck, Jarmay circled behind him, trying to catch a glimpse of this unexpected bonus that Orlando Dow had found wandering about the Stanhope woods.

"There," Orlando Dow muttered, an almost reverent tone in his voice, and drew down the burlap casing to reveal—

Jarmay Higgins stared forward. "Christ," he whispered and reflexively crossed himself and saw the soft golden hair first, then the mouth, grotesquely distorted by a cloth pulled into a tight gag, the arched position of her body, her hands tied tightly behind her back, her legs similarly secured with cords about her ankles.

It was her, the Stanhope girl, Eve by name, pride and joy of Burke Stanhope, a natural beauty even now despite the fear in her eyes.

"Where in the hell—" Jarmay hissed and could not finish.

"Just wandering loose, I told you," Orlando said mildly. "She came upon me like she knew me and only backed away at the last, but it was too late then, for old Orlando is a good hunter and knows that sometimes it's what you don't come looking for that you find first."

Jarmay listened, his mind afire with what had just been dumped on the floor of his loft.

Now here was something that would catch Burke Stanhope's attention. Here was a prize capable of bringing him to his knees.

Suddenly the trussed figure stirred. A soft groan escaped from around the gag. She seemed to struggle against her bonds. Orlando Dow drew close as they both focused downward on the girl. Something about her struggle fascinated Jarmay Higgins, and he continued to watch as her head thrashed but once and suddenly her eyes opened.

"Well?" Orlando Dow said a touch of pride in his voice.

"Did anyone see you?" Jarmay demanded, still unable to believe the treasure that had just been brought into his presence.

"An owl maybe," Orlando Dow joked. "I think you will agree, the cost of the evening has just risen."

In all fairness, Jarmay did agree, though he certainly had no authority to act on such a matter. "I'll have to confer with the others," he said brusquely. "In the meantime—"

"In the meantime, the prize comes with me," Orlando said and stooped over the girl, ready to draw the gunnysack back over her head and tie it in place.

"No," Jarmay protested. "Leave her here. I mean, you can't haul her all over town. She's spirited. She'll scream, she'll try to escape, and then where will we be? Leave her here. The loft can be locked securely. I'll call a meeting tomorrow night. I can assure you that you will be adequately paid for these additional services."

He watched Orlando Dow's face, waiting for his decision. The girl had to remain here. She had seen him clearly, could identify him, and once she'd served her purpose of bringing Burke Stanhope to his knees, she would have to be destroyed.

Again he disliked his aloneness in this matter and wanted to summon the other knights for the Stanhope girl to look upon them as well, thus binding them all together in this deed. Jarmay Higgins was smart, too smart to be the scapegoat for anyone.

"Leave her here, Dow," he urged again. "I give you my word, she will be here tomorrow night when you return for double money, and all the knights will be here as well in order to express their gratitude to you for your—creative service."

Apparently the man was willing to listen to reason, for he stood up from bending over her, bringing the gunnysack with him. "Pretty thing, ain't she," he said and grinned. "I was sorely tempted to taste her fruits, but God advised me against it, she being tainted and all, you know."

Jarmay struggled to make the conversational transaction with him. "Tainted, yes," he nodded and for several moments both men continued to stare down on the girl, who now returned their gaze with wide, fear-filled eyes.

"Then I'll leave her with you," Orlando Dow said at last. "She would be a hard piece of baggage to carry through the daytime streets of Mobile."

"Indeed."

"I'll be back tonight."

"Of course."

"And you call the other gentlemen."

"I will indeed."

"Then—"

"Good evening, Mr. Dow."

It was clearly a dismissal, and Jarmay had intended that it sound like one. He did not look up from the girl but charted Orlando Dow's passage across the loft floor. When he reached the door, Jarmay Higgins called out, "Close the door after you."

"I will indeed. We don't want the world looking in on this sight, now do we?"

And with that Jarmay heard a resounding slam and continued to stand still until the footsteps had faded down the loft steps, the whinny of a horse signaling the man's departure.

Then there was only silence and the staring girl, whose frightened eyes seemed to be communicating something else, relief that Orlando Dow was gone and that she had been handed over to Jarmay Higgins.

Relief! The arrogant little bitch. Seed of the arrogant bastard who had systematically thumbed his nose at every sacred Southern tradition. Relief!

Suddenly the sight of her angered him. He wanted to dissuade her in some fashion from her belief that she had greater reason to fear Orlando Dow than to fear him and the other knights. Dow was merely stupid and greedy. He and the other knights were privileged men of conviction who were willing to take great risks for what they believed in.

"Bitch," he whispered and could hardly wait for morning and the chance to spread the word that he had in his possession a grand prize that was sure to capture Burke Stanhope's attention. For now, what to do with her? He couldn't leave her lying about in plain sight, in the event someone wandered up from the cutting shed floor.

He spied under the far eaves an old cutting table with four high standards, one on each corner for directing the course of the wood. It was covered now by a tarpaulin, which in turn was covered with a thick layer of sawdust.

The perfect place of concealment. He could place her on the table, secure her wrists and ankles to the standards, then cover his prize with the old tarpaulin.

He looked back down on her, newly aware of the size and nature of this coup. No mere bonfire, this; no murdered mulatto; no ritualistic march before the historic pillars of Stanhope Hall. With the kidnapping of this girl, they had at last struck a blow at the very heart of Burke Stanhope.

"Oh, my pretty," Jarmay cooed as he bent over, slipped his arms beneath her and effortlessly lifted her. "Don't worry, I'll make you more comfortable," he soothed, enjoying the feel of her young body in his arms, her darting eyes as she tried to see her next destination.

When he reached the cutting table, he placed her on the floor, his eyes lingering on her breasts. Then he threw back the tarpaulin and waved away the clouds of sawdust and lifted her again and placed her at the exact center and released the cords on her ankles and retied them to the two standards at the end of the table. Then he eased her bound hands out from beneath her and secured first one, then the other to the upper standards. The only struggle was when he reached for her right hand, as though she knew all too well that when that one was secured, he would have rendered her helpless.

"No, my pretty, don't worry. Jarmay will look after you." At last the breasts started their delicate movement of breathing again, though now the head thrashed upward as though to see for herself the condition and nature of her new bondage. The same testing went on about her ankles, and apparently having determined for herself that she was pinned and helpless upon this table, Jarmay saw her head roll to one side, saw tears escaping, saw oh, so much as he gazed down on Burke Stanhope's jewel.

In fact, with only very little persuasion he could have watched her for the rest of the night, though such a close and continuous inspection might ultimately prove dangerous, for she was most inviting in her pinned helplessness. No! If Orlando Dow had resisted, then Jarmay Higgins was at least as self-disciplined.

Slowly now he drew the heavy tarpaulin up over her body, pausing before he covered her face. "Get a good night's sleep, my pretty. Busy times ahead."

At last, reluctantly, he covered her face, and tried to anticipate what the reaction of the others would be. He must notify them all come morning, not giving specifics—just tell them it was a matter of vitally important business.

At the door he looked back into the dim recesses of the vast loft, focusing on the old cutting table covered with the tarpaulin and years of sawdust.

She wasn't even struggling. Good. Not aggressive like her father. Undoubtedly she'd already accepted her fate, knew perhaps better than anyone that her days, her hours were numbered; that she would never see hearth or home again.

His thoughts beat upon his conscience like a dirge. Sad, in a way. She was so innocent of the offenses of her father. Yet she was the one who would have to pay the penalty.

Jarmay Higgins shook his head, intrigued by the divergent emotions rushing through him. He glanced a final time toward the table. At last Orlando Dow had earned his pay, though his explanation had certainly been sketchy enough. *Found her?* Made no sense, no sense at all. Orlando Dow said she'd had a satchel with her. Why a satchel?

For a few moments longer Jarmay Higgins tried to deal with the confusion and ultimately dismissed it for the nonsense that it was. "Sleep tight," Jarmay said as he grinned across the shadowy darkness. Then he reached for the single kerosene lamp atop the old desk and left the loft in total darkness, securing both latch and bolt as he went out.

🦋 Fan Cottage

Standing close to Mrs. Stanhope, watching the Negroes beat out the last of the flames of Fan Cottage with gunnysacks wet from the well behind the cottage, Madame Germaine tried to recall the number of times in the last few years she'd secretly vowed to leave Stanhope Hall and this unorthodox family. At least once a year, frequently twice.

Yet here she was, feeling intractable pain on all sides, suffering a degree of pain herself, for hadn't she been there on the occasion of Eve's first step, her first word?

Now gone?

On her left she heard a moan and saw Katie renew her grip on poor Mrs. Stanhope, whose tortured eyes had earlier caught and mirrored the fire. Now, with the flames gone, her eyes resembled two pieces of charred wood. Open wide, they darted as though she expected to see her daughter emerge like a phoenix from the ashes.

"Come, Mrs. Stanhope," Madame Germaine urged. "We can as easily wait back at—"

"No."

The response was firm, though this time Mrs. Stanhope pulled free of Katie's support and stepped closer to Fan Cottage, or what remained of it, which was little: a foundation, covered by a small section of charred roof that had caved in earlier on.

Katie started after her, but Madame Germaine stepped forward with a restraining hand and an unspoken command to let her be. There was a need to know that had to be satisfied. Then and only then could they get her back to the safety of Stanhope Hall.

Stanhope Hall. Dear God, what a muddle was awaiting them there —the distinguished guests abandoned, the servants fled. For everyone had come running to this spot in the woods, such a fearful race, all in their evening finery; even David and Christine, until Madame Germaine had ordered Dorie to take the children back and to stay with them in Mrs. Stanhope's bedchamber until someone came to relieve her.

As for Mr. Washington and Mr. Clemens, they had been left to their own devices, though Madame Germaine had once considered remaining behind to entertain and divert them. But upon hearing the seriousness of the tragedy, she had allowed her emotions to gain the upper hand and had immediately set off through the woods.

Suddenly Madame Germaine looked about, sensing someone missing. Mr. Stanhope. Where was he? He had been here a moment ago, standing over there with Paris Boley, trying to direct the operations, though his own agitation was interfering with his ability to command. Ultimately it had been young Paris who had sent for gunnysacks and ordered them doused in the yard well and commanded two dozen field hands to fight the flames, the entire nightmare taking on an eerie, ghostlike appearance, a macabre dance played out in hysterical shadows.

Now where was Burke Stanhope? Then she saw him wading into the smoke-filled foundation, gunnysack in hand, beating at the remaining pockets of fire as though he meant to do more than merely extinguish them. Not too far away she saw an even more poignant sight: the young Eden, scarcely recognizable as a white man, his clothes blackened, his face blackened, though still he beat on like a madman, whirling on each small explosion of flame, pushing his way through to where larger flames leapt up into the black night. And even after every flame had been extinguished, the young man continued to attack the smoke and the red-glowing embers until everyone, even Mr. Stanhope, stood back and watched him as though at a loss to know how to stop him.

All were silent and staring, except the one who continued to whip the dead ashes, which in turn rose in obscuring clouds about him and added to his grief and discomfort. Over the rhythmic slapping of wet burlap could now be heard a human sound most pitiable, half-animal, half-human, speaking one name over and over in heartbreaking repetition. "Eve—Eve—Eve—"

Madame Germaine closed her eyes and bowed her head. Of course she had suspected for some time that a certain childlike affection had grown up between these two young people. What had so recently disturbed her was the intensity of that affection. All things in moderation, was her motto, even youthful passion. That had been the nature of her objection, and apparently it was well founded. For now, viewing the young Eden, she saw not just a young man, but a young lover if she had ever seen one, one rendered destitute, bereft of reason.

On her right she heard weeping and knew who it was and knew that the tragedy that had occurred here on this fateful night would leave them all forever changed.

Madame lifted her head and looked about in an attempt to determine which pocket of need required her attention first. Surely it was the young man, flailing and sobbing at nonexistent flames in the ruins of Fan Cottage.

But just as she took a step in that direction, she saw movement coming from another quarter, a most unexpected quarter, an ominous quarter.

Burke Stanhope, his eyes leveled, was the one now moving slowly toward the distraught young man. For several steps he dragged the blackened gunnysack behind him. But as he approached the remains of the burned-out cottage, he dropped the gunnysack without looking back and took one step up onto the foundation and then over.

At the same time Madame Germaine saw Mrs. Stanhope look up from her grief and cover her mouth with the soiled handkerchief, as though to stifle any outcry she might feel compelled to utter.

The only one not aware of the silent man approaching him from behind was young Eden himself, who beat at the charred, smoking ruins with renewed fury, the soft repetitive prayer for "Eve—Eve—" quiet now, as though he'd moved into a new phase of sorrow, one that could not be voiced.

To Madame Germaine's left, she saw Paris Boley start forward. Mr. Stanhope made his way through the smoldering rubble, his eyes fixed on young Eden's back, who continued in his macabre ritual, lifting the gunnysack, which seemed to have grown heavier in his fatigue, and bringing it down in a curious slapping motion against the smoking timbers.

Then suddenly young Eden was aware and turned slowly, confronting Burke Stanhope with all the agony a human face could contain and still resemble a human face. For one tense moment the two men confronted each other over a vast distance of hate. And just when Madame Germaine had braced herself for the first blow, she saw instead a most unexpected sight, saw Burke Stanhope offering first one hand and then the other, saying something to the boy as he did so, something so low no one else could hear.

Young Eden dropped his gunnysack and stood unarmed before him, his face filled with grief. Slowly he lifted his head until he was staring straight up at the heavens and issued one animal cry, the force of which caused the hair of Madame Germaine's neck to stand up, a cry that seemed to reverberate through the dark woods, a continuous cry that gradually evolved into one word, one name, one recent inhabitant of his heart who now was gone.

As the cry rose and clung to the night air, Burke Stanhope took the final step across the distance that separated them and drew the young man forward into his arms. Both men turned inward in their grief; no point in further battle, no spirit for conflict, no need to inflict greater pain. For the howl of the young man suggested that at this young age, Fate had dealt him the most severe blow he would ever have to suffer in his life.

As the two men clung to one another, Madame Germaine felt an ominous burning in her eyes. At the same time she saw Mrs. Stanhope turn away, heavily supported by Katie and start back through the woods as though she had seen enough. It was over, the love was over, and now the hate was over as well.

The field hands abandoned their silent staring as well. And throughout all this muted movement, the two men at the center of the ruins did not stir, did not alter their grip on one another in any way. It was difficult to say where the support was coming from, for they seemed mutually dependent, mutually devastated, mutually in need.

At last only four remained—Paris Boley, Madame Germaine, Burke Stanhope and Stephen Eden—and Madame Germaine held her ground until at last Paris was at her side, taking her arm in a gentlemanly fashion, suggesting in a whisper that they return now to Stanhope Hall, for surely Mrs. Stanhope would be in desperate need of someone to help with the guests.

Madame Germaine clung to his arm through the treacheries of the dark woods and looked back only once, to see Burke Stanhope and Stephen Eden no longer embracing but merely standing at the center of the ruins of Fan Cottage, unmoving, not speaking, as though their mutual loss had left their spirits and souls as charred and dried as the ancient timber of Fan Cottage.

 Stanhope Hall

Taylor Quitman had had more than enough. There was just so much duplicity that a man's soul could endure, and he had passed his limit some time ago.

The truth was that the activities of the Knights of the White Camellia had never held great appeal, and now, stuck in the library of Stanhope Hall with these two garrulous and boring men, Taylor listened with relief to the sound of voices outside Stanhope Hall. Someone was returning, hopefully with news, and now he could excuse himself on the grounds of the late hour and rid himself of this place and Burke Stanhope's new grief.

"If you'll excuse me, gentlemen, I hear—"

As Taylor Quitman tried to penetrate the endless pontificating going on in front of the dead fireplace, he paused at the door before opening it, trying for the last time to make sense out of the conversation, each man seemingly trying to outdo the other, one making a statement, the other sniffing, then trying to dispute it.

Intellectuals! Who needed them? This world didn't, certainly not the real world of debts and payments, crime and punishment, of honest labor and earnest causes.

"Gentlemen, I—"

But they were paying no attention to anything but their own voices, raised now, the debate heating over medievalism. Would you believe it?

Having heard enough, Taylor Quitman slipped through the library doors, closed them behind him and hurried down the darkened corridor where old food odors from dinner still lingered.

Now to hear the bad news, look appropriately shocked, then take his leave and beat a hasty retreat back to Mobile.

His thoughts carried him to the front gallery and the late evening softly lit by a full moon. To his left, just emerging from the woods, he saw a sad caravan, the strong acrid smell of smoke accompanying them, a few of the nigger field hands leading, heads bowed, shoulders slumped. Just following them he saw Mary Stanhope, leaning heavily on the nigger woman.

Taylor Quitman played the gentleman and hurried down the steps with the idea of relieving the nigger and escorting Mrs. Stanhope into the safety of Stanhope Hall himself.

"Here, let me," he ordered, and forcibly removed the nigger and took her place at Mrs. Stanhope's side.

"My dear Mary," he whispered and gave her ample support, all the while glancing back to see if he could catch a glimpse of Burke emerging from the shadows.

He couldn't. "Is the fire, I mean, is it out now?"

Mary did not acknowledge his presence in any way, a lapse of good manners peculiar to this lady even under these circumstances. Surely something was amiss, something more than a fire in the old slave cabin and the probable death of the old woman.

"Is she—is Mrs. Stanhope ill?" he asked the nigger.

"Of course she's ill," the woman snapped, anger replacing her tears at the last minute. "She's done lost her baby this night, her Eve."

Stunned, certain that he'd misunderstood the darkie, Taylor looked directly back at the woman. "She's lost—what?" he asked.

"Eve," the Negro snapped. "She was visitin' in Fan Cottage."

Suddenly there was new grief, and the woman bent over and the sounds of weeping seemed to trigger fresh outbursts of grief all around. As Taylor Quitman tried to look in all directions, he felt himself being displaced at Mary Stanhope's side, saw the sobbing nigger take over, her arm thrown across Mary's shoulder, the whole sad procession moving up the stairs, the collapsed Mary Stanhope at center.

Eve? It wasn't possible. Eve had only recently been at table. How could she have left Stanhope Hall so quickly and arrived at Fan Cottage in time for—

Confusion mounting, Taylor Quitman looked about. There! Paris Boley. He could tell all if he wanted to. Sometimes his high-falutin' ways amused the hell out of Taylor Quitman, but for now it was all he had.

"Paris. You, boy," he called out, and waited patiently to be obeyed. When the boy ignored him, Taylor Quitman felt his anger flare. "Boy, did you hear me? I gave you a call."

"I heard," the nigger said. "What is it?"

"Just information, that's all I want," Taylor muttered.

"What?" the nigger demanded, his arrogance seeming to increase.

"The fire—"

"Is out."

"The old woman?"

"Is dead."

"Where's Burke? Mr. Stanhope?"

The nigger bowed his head. "He's still out there. Eve was visiting Fan Cottage. She perished in the fire as well. Now if you'll excuse me—"

The nigger seemed to be crying. For a moment Taylor Quitman couldn't draw sufficient air into his lungs. So it was true. Dead. Burke's baby, dead. Damn Jarmay Higgins and his overzealous bastards.

Did they have any idea what mischief they had caused this evening? Did any of the knights know? If not, then Taylor Quitman would be the first to warn them that there was a good possibility that Burke Stanhope would come roaring up out of this loss like a madman, and if their trail was not well covered, none of them would be safe.

Suddenly, as though newly aware of this urgency, Taylor Quitman started off down the avenue of live oaks as though he intended to run the ten miles back to Mobile. Not until he was almost to the road did he remember his horse, waiting in the stables.

Then he did a quick reversal. The confusion in his head seemed to add to his speed, and as he approached the stables, his ultimate destination was clear.

Jarmay Higgins's lumberyard. He wanted an immediate accounting. Tonight. The plans of the Knights of the White Camellia had tragically misfired.

With the murder of Eve Stanhope they might have witlessly un-
leashed a power upon themselves from which none of them could
ever escape.

* * *

Burke saw the first rosy streaks of dawn on his knees at Mary's
bedside. He'd gone in to comfort her and had found her awake but
unresponsive, simply staring up at the canopy, making no response to
anything he said or did.

He remembered falling to his knees, kissing her hand, so cold, wondering if it was too late to pray.

Now he moved awkwardly, painfully from his position of prayer,
where obviously at some point he had fallen asleep, his head resting
on Mary's hand.

Eve—dead.

He bowed his head into the crumpled bedclothes and tried to find a
safe retreat for his mind so that he could recover at least sufficiently
to go on. But there was no safe retreat. He saw her as an infant—their
first, the most glorious child God had ever created: rosy, golden,
laughing, her dimpled fingers clinging to his one immense one.

He buried his face in the bedclothes and prayed for the courage to
get through one hour of this day. Then at the conclusion of that one
hour he'd pray again for a second hour, and so on for a period of time
that included merely the rest of his life.

He looked up from his prayer beyond Mary's bed and saw the soft
pink of dawn beyond the silk curtains.

"Burke."

The voice startled him. Through blurred eyes he looked toward the
pillow and saw Mary, her hand reaching for his, and he struggled
upward and took her in his arms and they clung together.

At the end of the embrace Burke lowered her gently onto the pillow and studied her drawn white face and thought how ill she looked.

He tried to speak and still found words difficult, for tears were
lurking right behind them.

"I must tell you," Burke said, "Stephen Eden—I brought him back
to Stanhope Hall last night. He was quite—"

Again his voice broke. He stood suddenly from the side of the bed
and walked a few steps toward the window and dawn. "He was out of
his head with grief. I had no idea," he said. "He was so—"

"You—brought him here?" Mary asked.

"Here."

"Thank you," she murmured, and Burke understood the source of
her gratitude and was sorry that his earlier hostility had caused her

pain. He still had many questions he wanted to pose to the Eden lad, but not until they both had recovered.

"Burke, what—"

He looked back at Mary's partial question and knew what she'd wanted to ask and tried to answer.

"I don't know," he said. "The fire was out of control when we got there. Sis Liz generally was careful. I can't believe—"

"It wasn't Sis Liz's fault. I was in Fan Cottage almost every day, winter and summer. Sis Liz was deathly afraid of fire."

"She burned those blasted candles."

"But always took care to make them safe. I swear to you, Burke, it was not Sis Liz's fault."

"Then—"

"It was set—the fire was set."

Suddenly she closed her eyes. Her head pressed back against the pillow.

Helpless, Burke watched her. "Mary, don't," he begged and held her close and watched the sky beyond the window turn increasing shades of rose and pink. A new day, yet Eve was dead.

Dear God, would the pain never end? There was so much to be done—guests to be seen off, investigations to be launched, questions to be asked of everyone.

A set fire?

The question nagged at him. Surely not. One act of violent extremity was enough. The knights were not villains. They were merely misguided Southerners.

"Papa?"

The soft voice startled him, and he looked up from his kneeling position at Mary's bedside. He saw Christine standing in the open door, in a long white nightshirt like a frightened ghost.

Where was Katie? Katie was supposed to be with the children.

"Papa."

"Yes, my dearest," he replied and rose wearily, observing that Mary did not respond at all to Christine's call.

He moved quickly to the door in an attempt to divert Christine before she came all the way in.

"Is Mama—"

"Sleeping, darling. Come, let's—"

"The fire, did Sis Liz die in the fire?"

Burke looked up in one helpless glance toward the top of the door. Two carved dragons looked down on him from wooden korbels.

"Yes," he said, still not able to believe it.

"Where's Eve, Papa? I've looked everyplace for Eve. She's not in her rooms. She's not on the front gallery. Help me find Eve, Papa. I want Eve to stay with me for a while. Please, Papa."

Burke closed his eyes and averted his face as he led Christine blindly down the corridor and thought, now, tell her now, it will not get any easier, tell her now and find David and tell him as well, for they both must know the truth and must learn to deal with it in their own way as soon as possible.

But he couldn't form the words.

No, the message would have to wait, or be delivered by someone else, for he could not reconcile himself to the rest of his life without her smile, her voice, her song, her laugh, her eyes.

"Papa? What is it?"

"Wait in your room, Christine. Please be a good girl."

He abandoned her before the door that led to her bedchamber and fled down the stairs and reached the corridor below and fortunately did not encounter anyone, as though everyone in Stanhope Hall were in hiding against the monstrous grief that had descended upon the house this day. He took the front door running and continued to run, lacking a clear destination, lacking everything except the pain in the center of his heart that would surely, hopefully, kill him. All he wanted now was distance from this house and a safe place to grieve.

He found such a place about halfway down the long avenue of live oaks, at a particularly welcoming tree, whose bark scraped against his face as he pressed against it and whose girth was suitable for clinging to and whose soft moss and promise of shade offered a comfort that allowed him to sit heavily beneath the tree, draw up his knees, cover his face with his hands and weep.

 Mobile

"Higgins? Are you in there?"

Taylor Quitman pounded on the office door of Jarmay Higgins's lumberyard, aware that the noise was attracting attention in the early morning street.

Still he pounded with a frustration made sharper by the fact that late last night, when he'd first ridden in from Stanhope Hall, he had found the gate to the lumberyard locked. So he had been forced to wait until dawn, sleeping on the couch in his law chambers, not sleeping really, seeing in memory that dull orange glow in the night sky of Stanhope Hall and knowing that two had perished.

"Higgins? I know you're in there. Wake up."

Then he felt the heavy oak door give under his repeated poundings, saw a very rumpled and sleepy Jarmay Higgins on the other side.

"There you are," Taylor muttered and tried to push his way into the office. But Jarmay Higgins blocked his passage, his sleepy crocodile eyes opening wide as though at last wakefulness had returned with a vengeance.

"Wait a minute, Quitman," he protested. "You can't—what do you want? Do you know what time it is? Come back after I've had a wash-up and a cup of coffee."

"Something went wrong, Higgins," Taylor Quitman said, keeping his voice low. "Something went very—"

"Something went right, you mean," Jarmay Higgins said and smiled. "Never more right. But I can't talk now, Quitman. Pass the word. We will meet tonight at ten o'clock in the loft, where I will have a grand surprise for all of you."

At that moment a large wagon rattled into the lumberyard. On the high seat sat a most unusual gentleman, a giant of a man, tall, in a long black flowing robe with a mane of steel-gray wavy hair and a full beard. He was maneuvering the horses in an expert manner, with a certain flair. Taylor Quitman stepped away from the door in order to watch, and was aware of Jarmay Higgins standing close beside him, the door no longer a barrier between them as both gaped after the gentleman who resembled an Old Testament prophet. Now he brought the large wagon to a halt directly in front of the office door.

"Good morning to you, man and man," he shouted in a voice that seemed to echo endlessly about the vast lumberyard.

He steadied the horses with that same deep, resonant voice, then smiled down.

"Which one of you gentlemen would be the master of this splendid graveyard for dead trees?"

Jarmay Higgins looked nervously at Taylor Quitman, then shyly raised his right hand, schoolboy fashion. "You are speaking to Jarmay Higgins, owner of Higgins Lumberyard, largest this side of New Orleans."

The man's grin seemed to broaden. He wrapped the reins about the seat handle and brushed a fleck of something from his fine robe. "Then it's you I want a word with, sir," he said and pointed at Jarmay Higgins with a long, impressive finger.

As he spoke, he gestured wildly, and Taylor Quitman sniffed the manner of a theatrical man.

"Catastrophe struck last evening," he said in broad melodramatic tones and bobbed his head toward his large wagon. "Two trunk bottoms fell out entirely, leaving an irreconcilable cavity. And since these two trunks are the nests for spring and summer garlands, we feel we must repair them immediately, lest the shifting seasons be our full responsibility. That, I'm sure you'll agree, is an obligation reserved only for God, or a god, depending upon how you bend your knee in prayer."

Taylor Quitman squinted up at the giant whose features had now been obscured by a blinding ray of rising sun, causing his entire head and shoulders to dissolve into blackened silhouette. He hadn't understood a word the man had said, but nonetheless he was fascinated by the way in which he had said it, and now he felt compelled to listen in the event the man spoke again.

Jarmay Higgins nodded simply. "Trunk bottoms. We can do that, of course, sir, if you'll just—"

"Oh, I knew you could. I just knew you could. Now, a second and more painful question, if you please. This—artistry of yours, how rapidly do you work? Are you a man who must wait on inspiration, or do you see a broken trunk bottom, jot an estimate of length in your brilliant head, calculate the needed timber, summon it forward by your hirelings and fill the hole, presto, done, in miracle time?"

Taylor Quitman glanced at Jarmay Higgins to see how he would respond. When after several moments there was no response, only an expression of bewilderment on Higgins's pudgy face, the giant standing upright in the wagon threw the corner of his cape over his shoulders and with dignity befitting royalty descended from the wagon and appeared on the porch with them, a limited space that had just become more limited, for the man was large in every sense.

"With your kind indulgence and forbearance, sir, allow me to dramatize all particulars of my last question, lest in your mind the fog grow thick and impenetrable and the three of us pass our final days together in these cramped quarters."

Even as he was speaking, he lifted his right arm high into the air, the deep folds of his unique robe forming a kind of batwing. Then he pointed his finger toward the rear of the wagon and gave a resounding snap of his fingers and bellowed, "Come, my fancies." In the next moment the gray canvas flap at the rear of the wagon lifted and Taylor Quitman, watching closely, could not at first believe his eyes, was certain the early morning sun was creating magic where none existed. For what Quitman saw first was a leg, a female leg, a long, lovely, bare female leg, followed by a torso, complete with bared arms and lovely head, a vision, half-clad in the most gossamer of fabrics, transparent to an indecent point, revealing certain features of the female form that in all modesty should never be revealed short of a marital bedroom.

"Come, my fancies, all of you, bring the broken nests, for we needs must have them mended."

The man did not speak so much as he proclaimed, like an actor, a bad actor, who—

But there Taylor Quitman's thoughts were brought to a halt by the appearance of another lovely seminaked female leg. And though he knew he shouldn't be, Taylor couldn't help but be fascinated by the continuing parade of lovely females, four in all, each carrying a heavy trunk between them, one clad in pink, one in lavender, one in blue, one in green, like wisps of the rainbow, all smiling prettily as they placed the two trunks on the steps of the porch, rendering that already limited area totally occluded.

Taylor Quitman felt the railing snug behind his posterior and felt little else as the "fancy" in blue wedged herself tightly against him.

"Show the gentlemen, my pretties, our broken nests," the giant directed, waving his arms high above his head. "Show him the damage so that he may give us estimates on repairs."

From Taylor Quitman's wedged position he couldn't see the damaged trunks, could see little except Jarmay Higgins's flushed face as he, too, apparently tried to digest the near beauty of the four females.

"Birthings have taken place in both nests," the giant went on, in a voice loud enough to carry to the street. "And as you know, birth tends to dampness and dampness tends to rot, and thus is our accounting on your front stoop in this glorious God-given morning. Now what we must know is can you help us, or, more accurately, help our broken trunks. For we must leave this fair city within the span of a cock's crow or else pay the penalty for our freedom. Do you understand? If so, make a sound, any sound."

The four females giggled as though they were well accustomed to the man's gibberish, even understood it, though Taylor Quitman had his doubts. He had his doubts as well that Jarmay Higgins would ever speak again, for the man seemed to have suffered a permanent paralysis of mind and tongue, a state brought on, no doubt, by the lovely buxom beauty in pink who was facing Jarmay Higgins in close quarters.

Well, enough. Taylor Quitman had had more than enough. He knew now who the man was, knew who the harlots were as well, a traveling theatrical troupe owned and managed by one Yorrick Harp, who had arrived in Mobile several weeks ago.

"Higgins!" Taylor Quitman scolded. "Answer the man. Can you mend his trunks?"

Then he heard a sputtering, which he assumed was Jarmay Hig-

gins. "Yes sir, of course, we can mend your nests, or trunks, or whatever—yes, of course, simple, really—"

"When?" The one word question came rapidly from the giant.

"When?" Higgins repeated and briefly disappeared behind a screen
of fancies, who now were trying to angle their way around the
trunks. "By late tonight, no, let's make it first thing in the morning."

"Are you certain? Our zephyr leaves shortly after dawn. We must
be on it, nests and all. Friendly winds aren't sufficient. One must have
reliable wings. By dawn, then?"

"Yes, I'm—"

"Soundly repaired?"

"Of course."

"Strong enough to carry all of Spring?"

"I—of course."

"Do you have any idea how much Spring weighs, my dear sir? But
if you can mend our trunks, then we will be forever in your debt,
won't we, my pretties? Then come, come, we must return to the
others who, lacking our sweet company will mourn themselves into a
stomach ache. What would you say if old Yorrick kept you all amused
with his splendid rendition of Cyrano de Bergerac, followed by Richard the Third. My heart today seems to incline naturally to the de-
formed, the malformed and the uninformed. I hate wholeness, don't
you? Doesn't everyone? Come, come, let's flee this temple of commerce before our souls learn their games."

All the way down the steps, Yorrick Harp "performed," and Taylor Quitman was certain that it was a performance. One by one he
helped the young girls up into the back of the wagon. Taylor observed they wore no shoes. They resembled spirits, something super-
natural, very mythical and incredibly beautiful.

"Stare all you like, gentlemen. God created these beauties for only
one purpose—to please men. Though to look at them now you'd
never believe I rescued them all from nests in falling trees. Discarded
by men, the lot of them. But this very same loving and benevolent
hand reached out and caught them and broke their falls and brushed
them off and reminded them of their purpose while walking this
earth. Now look at them, my jewels. I have many more where these
are stored."

As he spoke, the girls climbed one after another into the back of the
wagon, drawing their gossamer robes about them. Once up, the four
formed a pleasing tableau.

Suddenly the wagon started forward, the giant, Yorrick Harp,
standing upright, driving chariot fashion. "Work your magic, woodsman," he shouted back, "for God has plans for Yorrick Harp. I'll

return at this same hour on the dawn tomorrow to retrieve the trunks, and I and God and all my jewels will be forever in your debt if I find the work complete and whole and expertly done."

Twice he led the horses in a charge around the lumberyard, and Taylor Quitman and Jarmay Higgins gaped without speaking. It wasn't until the wagon had clattered back out onto the street, the beauties gone, that Taylor Quitman could even begin to shake off the mood spun by the outrageous man named Yorrick Harp.

"Do you—know him?" he stammered, aware that Jarmay Higgins had yet to move or speak.

Finally, "No, of course not," the man muttered. "I've seen his show, as who in Mobile has not, with beauties like those there."

As he spoke, he bent over in examination of the damaged trunks.

"If you'll excuse me, Quitman," Higgins muttered now. "Work to do, as you can see. Spread the word, if you will. We'll meet tonight after ten. In the loft. Warn everyone, as always, to take care in arriving."

And so saying, he stepped through his office door and quickly closed it behind him. In the stillness of morning Taylor Quitman heard the latch slide.

Taylor Quitman closed his eyes. Having been up the entire grim night, fatigue was beginning to take a toll. Home then, or, better, to his law office a scant two blocks from here, where a comfortable couch awaited him and, among the dark stacks, an equally comfortable store of good bourbon.

Suddenly Taylor shivered on the steps of Jarmay Higgins's office porch. He looked furtively about, as though Burke Stanhope had already learned his identity.

"Jesus," he whispered and turned up the collar of his rumpled coat and hurried down the steps. Furtively he dashed out into the street, head down, focusing on the safety of his office.

* * *

The manner in which Eve recognized dawn was that the tarpaulin that covered her changed from black to light gray. But that was the only alteration, though she did find that if she turned her head to the left, breathing was easier, the heavy fabric less capable of obscuring her mouth and nose.

Mama.

The thought came unexpectedly and did damage, for in defense against her helplessness, she struggled again, and for her troubles suffered new pain in all parts of her body, her feet and hands alter-

nately burning, then freezing due to lack of circulation, her wrists
and ankles rubbed raw by the thick coarse hemp.

Mama.

The second time the word entered her consciousness, she felt an
unexpected peace and no longer struggled against the ropes, and
closed her eyes.

She thought then how worried her mother would be. And Papa.
Surely Papa had search parties out for her now, or perhaps Mr. Higgins was at this moment riding fast toward Stanhope Hall with the
news that villains had kidnapped her and brought her to the Higgins
Lumberyard and she was waiting there now for their rescue.

The thoughts died for the flawed things that they were. Jarmay
Higgins was the one who had carried her to this table and bound her
to it. And Jarmay Higgins had spoken with her kidnapper in easy
familiar tones; payments had been discussed.

She opened her eyes, having lost the recreated image of her mother's face in new doubt. What did they want with her? And where was
Stephen?

This thought, the face accompanying it, the entire loving recre-
ation, did more damage than anything else, and without warning she
cried out and thrashed helplessly beneath the heavy tarpaulin and for
a moment could not draw breath into her lungs and thought quite
calmly that she very likely would die here.

Again she pulled against the ropes and felt a sharp pain in her
lower stomach, a desperate need to empty her bladder as though at
last the body, recovering from a state of shock, realized there were
certain functions that it had to perform.

The pressure was building, as was the discomfort. Some fastidious
sense of order warned her to keep all under control or else all would
truly be lost.

But it hurt, and ultimately she held still and, lacking a choice, allowed her full bladder to empty in a warm stream of urine that
spread over her backside. She closed her eyes against her own humiliation and hoped that no one would see her until she'd had a chance to
cleanse herself.

As she waited out the spreading wetness, the pain in her stomach
subsided and seemed to take up new residence, in her throat and
head, a searing pain of loss and helplessness.

Would she leave this place alive?

No answer, just silent tears, a sense of mortification, a deeper sense
of terror that the nightmare was not yet over, that the worst was yet
to come.

"Mama, help me," she prayed and tried to think of warm sunny days, the garden ablaze with flowers, and herself and Stephen walking toward the riverbank and their secret cave.

But abruptly she turned her head beneath the tarpaulin. Listen! Was someone coming?

* * *

At first Stephen didn't know where he was. There appeared to be a lace canopy over his head and a flesh-colored oval staring down at him from the foot of the bed. Twice he tried to open his eyes, and both times the heaviness persisted.

Something was trying to warn him against the state of consciousness, something dangerous there, something he could not face. Stay as you are in this safe, quiet, black realm. It's better.

"Stephen, can you hear me?"

He frowned at the persistent voice and wished it would go away. He wasn't ready yet to come back to this world.

Then, without warning, the veil lifted. Fire. There had been a fire. He could smell it in his hair, on his hands, in his garments. In that fire Eve had perished.

His eyes opened, forcing him to confront the knowledge. The safe darkness was over, everything was over, life was over, love was over. Eve was—

He sat up, drawn forward by his thoughts. He swung his legs over the side of the bed.

"Stephen, don't. Stay where you are for a while. You mustn't—"

The voice was near, seated beside him on the bed, a gentle hand on his arm. He looked in that direction and for several seconds worked diligently to bring the face into focus, a kind face that bore a resemblance to the one he'd just lost.

"Please," the voice whispered and he heard tears and knew who was sitting beside him and covered Mary's hand with his own and saw his fingernails still blackened from his vain attempt to fight the flames.

Then her weeping broke into helpless sobs and Stephen took her in his arms and held on tight.

If there had been no elopement plans, Eve would not have been at Fan Cottage last night.

The grief became insupportable and he took the same amount of strength from Mary's arms as he was offering her with his own.

Still, it was his fault. He would have to deal with that, though he hadn't the least notion how to go about it.

Home. Would it help to go home?

The thought held appeal, but the mind broke down while trying to work out specifics. For instance, where was home? Not here. Not England, not Mobile. The last place he had readily identified as home was wherever Eve happened to be.

If that was the case, then home was the burned-down ruin of Fan Cottage.

Now he tightened his grip on Mary's shoulders and held fast against her convulsions of weeping and wished with all his heart that he had perished in the fire with her, for at least that way they would be together.

 Mobile

Twice during this long day Jarmay Higgins had crept away from the demands of his business to check on his treasure. Twice he had climbed the stairs to his loft, his fingers plugging his ears in defense against the shrill whine of the cutting blades below. Twice he had stood in awe at the door and peered into the shadowy recesses toward the old cutting table covered with the tarpaulin, which appeared smooth from this distance, for the Stanhope girl was slim.

Twice as he had thrown back the tarpaulin, his eyes had landed on her full breasts, and twice he had touched them, merely touched, that was all, and had smiled at the pleasure he had derived from that touch and smiled at her terror, muffled completely over the whir of the powerful saws below.

Twice he had studied her in all aspects, still unable to believe who was bound to his old cutting table, and twice he had tried to imagine the chaos and fear of mourning that now was Stanhope Hall. And of course he was curious as to what they were thinking. Did they believe she had perished in the fire? If so, she was his, to do with as he wished. If not, then they could use her as ransom in exchange for banishing the nigger who now served as general manager. But of course the sad truth remained: The girl could identify him now. In a short while Jarmay Higgins intended to make every single Knight of the White Camellia equally visible to her, so that the brunt of whatever the future held would not fall on his head alone.

Now as he climbed the loft steps a third time, he held the lantern high and listened. The saw blades had long ago been silenced, cleaned, and put to bed for the night, the workers all gone home.

Nine-thirty, his pocket watch said. Earlier in the day he'd sent a boy around to Taylor Quitman and all the others, reminding them of the meeting at ten o'clock.

Breathless from his climb, Jarmay withdrew the key from his vest pocket, placed the lantern on the top step and released the padlock he'd put on the loft door this morning for safekeeping. As the heavy lock fell open, he pushed open the door and peered into the dark interior of the loft.

Light. He needed additional light. Quickly he lifted the lantern and carried it to the old desk, and from there he lit the wicks of three other lamps.

Better now. He could see in all directions. The distant cutting table, however, remained obscured in shadow, which suited his purposes until he was ready to display his treasure.

Suddenly he heard the noise of the lower door closing with a bang.

"Higgins, you up there?"

The voice belonged to Taylor Quitman, who led the way for the others, and Jarmay Higgins saw his loft doorway filled with Knights of the White Camellia.

"Gentlemen." He smiled and was just reaching behind for his chair when Taylor Quitman stepped forward and more than filled the silence.

"Are you aware of what happened last night, Higgins? Has your man, Orlando Dow, reported to you as yet?"

His man? Jarmay Higgins looked up. Since when had scum like Orlando Dow been *his* man?

"I know what happened," he said, trying to give the illusion of calm. "As, I dare say, every man here knows what happened."

"Indeed," Taylor Quitman cut in. "And all, to the man, believe you have gone too far this time."

"*I've* gone too far?" Jarmay Higgins repeated, still smiling despite the turmoil building deep inside his gut. "For the life of me, I thought we were acting as a group, all Knights of the White Camellia on behalf—"

He had just begun to enjoy the sound of his own voice when Reverend Pounders interrupted. "We are a group, Higgins. And we are not blaming you, but we do feel that the man Dow went too far. Even in a disciplinary action, a man must be responsible."

"He did what he was told to do, Pounders," Higgins said.

For a moment there was a pause, filled only by uncomfortable shuffling and nervous coughing.

"What we mean to say, Higgins," Zach Hennessey began. "Well, what we want to say is—"

"I know what you want to say," Higgins challenged. "You pay someone to carry out your punishment, but if he does it too well—"

"For God's sake, the girl was killed," Taylor Quitman interrupted, and Jarmay Higgins saw his face torn in grief for his friend Burke Stanhope.

Now, as they muttered among themselves, Jarmay Higgins stole a glance into the far corner of the loft where the girl lay bound and secured. He smiled, enjoying his secret, interested to see how many true colors would be revealed before this night was over.

Joel Peterson now took the floor, his round face flushed with excitement. "You were out there, weren't you, Taylor, at Stanhope Hall when it—"

"I was." Taylor nodded. "And I can tell you, it was dreadful, absolutely dreadful."

Interested in playing with them for a while, Jarmay Higgins issued an irresistible invitation. "Tell us about it, Taylor. Tell us all, if you will."

As the man spun out a lengthy tale of a colorful dining table and distinguished guests, Jarmay wished he would speak louder so that his voice would carry to the set of listening ears beneath the tarpaulin.

"And then what happened, Taylor?" Jarmay Higgins asked, taking only a few steps in that direction, changing the shape of the circle and forcing Taylor Quitman to project his voice toward the old cutting table.

"The boy brought word," he said at last.

"What boy?" Joel Peterson asked.

"The English lad, a relation of some sort to Mary Stanhope."

"He was there?"

Taylor Quitman nodded. "Apparently he happened by shortly thereafter. Everyone left the table and went to the front gallery, from where you could see the glow in the sky over the tops of the trees."

Good, his voice was aimed in the proper direction now; the girl was hearing everything.

"Then what?" Reverend Pounders urged.

Taylor Quitman fell silent, as though not really wanting to go on. "Then nothing," he muttered. "Burke asked me to stay with his guests, which I did, though they did not need or want my company."

Jarmay waited patiently, knowing precisely what would come next.

"Your man went too far this time," Taylor Quitman accused, and the others joined in. Jarmay continued to move slowly but steadily toward the old cutting table, dragging the others behind him.

"I cannot guarantee what Burke will do now," Taylor pronounced, loud enough for all to hear. "He worshipped his daughter, as you all know."

"How is he faring?" someone asked.

Taylor shrugged. "When I left, he hadn't yet returned from the fire. The two of them were still there, that young Englishman and—"

Suddenly there was a moan from the direction of the cutting table. Quitman looked suspiciously about. "What was that? Did you—"

"I heard it."

"Gentlemen, please." Higgins smiled. "I'm afraid it was only my stomach, complaining about my hastily consumed supper, as always."

"Where is your man?" Reverend Pounders demanded angrily. "I thought he was to be here tonight. He is the one who owes us a full accounting."

"He has given one," Jarmay Higgins replied. "Earlier today I paid him the sum due him."

"Then he is not coming?"

"Oh, he may show up, maybe not. The man is his own master. But if he does put in an appearance, it will be because he firmly believes we owe him an additional sum."

For several moments Jarmay Higgins was aware of the men staring at him in the distorting glow of the lamps. Behind him the cutting table was quiet, and thank God for that. He mustn't let her ruin his surprise.

"More money?" Reverend Pounders at last inquired in an arch voice that seemed to represent the tone for all.

"I said so, didn't I?" Higgins nodded.

Self-righteous rage burned across old Pounders's tissue-paper face. "Why should we pay the villain additional sums for disobeying our orders?"

"What *were* your orders, Reverend Pounders?"

"You know very well, Higgins. You were in on the planning."

"Tell me. Anyone of you may speak."

As he threw open the invitation to include the entire membership of the Knights of the White Camellia, he moved stealthily all the way back until he could feel the edge of the cutting table behind the small of his back.

"What is this, Higgins?" Pounders sharply demanded. "Why don't you stay put in one place? Why are you moving about so, playing the fool, and why are you hovering in that dark corner? I say we return to the light and end this discussion and call a halt to all our activities until we can determine Stanhope's reaction to this—new tragedy."

Higgins watched closely, impressed with the man's sincerity. Generally it was not one of Reverend Pounders's most notable characteristics. But now he seemed genuinely upset by the course of events, as did all the others. Just as they were turning to leave, Jarmay Higgins felt certain that the time had come.

"Gentlemen, wait, please, all of you."

He held his position in front of the cutting table. One by one they looked back, and Higgins had a smile for them.

"I must confess I am baffled by your various moods. We have accomplished our goals. We have handed out punishment to the villain who seeks to destroy our Southern fabric—"

"Good God, Higgins," Taylor Quitman exploded. "Haven't you heard anything we have said? Don't you know what has happened? Don't you know the difference between a fire, a simple case of arson, and—"

"Murder. That's what we've done," someone mourned from the back.

"The girl is dead," Quitman went on in a breaking voice. "I was—her godfather. I would never have agreed had I—"

"Then it is the death of the Stanhope girl," Higgins said, "that has affected you and turned you from your purpose?"

"Of course. What else?" Joel Peterson nodded. "I'll never be able to face Burke Stanhope again."

"Yes, you will."

Jarmay Higgins felt his excitement building to almost unbearable proportions.

"I—beg your pardon?" Joel Peterson stammered.

"I said you would be able to face Burke Stanhope again, and the rest of the world as well, and your conscience on top of that."

"You're an insensitive bastard, Higgins," someone called out.

"Am I?" He carried the lantern to the head of the cutting table and was very appreciative of the young Stanhope girl for being so still and not giving his secret away before he was ready.

"Come closer, gentlemen," he invited, waving them forward with the lamp itself, sending skittering shadows throughout the entire loft.

Slowly they came, each wearing a puzzled expression, keeping their eyes fixed on Higgins.

"Come closer, Reverend Pounders," Higgins invited cordially, seeing the man hang back. "You above all must see what I have in store for you. Come, come closer."

He waited patiently until all were arranged more or less to his liking in an uneven circle about the table. "The young Miss Eve Stanhope, eldest daughter of Mr. Burke Stanhope, did *not* perish in the fire at Fan Cottage. Our good and faithful servant Orlando Dow rescued her moments before he threw the torch in. And now, gentlemen, allow me to present—"

With that he placed the lamp on the head of the table, near her face, and slowly drew back the tarpaulin, revealing the girl in full, from her bound wrists to her equally bound ankles, her eyes wide and darting above the distortion of the gag, struggling futilely against her helpless position, then lying still at last, her eyes seeming to meet each face that stared down at her, then moving slowly on to the next, as though recording each set of features.

Jarmay Higgins glanced up from the girl, eager to see the expressions on the faces who looked down on her.

Suddenly, "Dear Jesus," someone whispered. Then, "My God, Higgins, have you lost your—" Then, "I must go. Hurry."

The air was filled with the sound of frantic scrambling, all of the gentlemen moving pell-mell toward the door for a place of safe hiding, for—

"Wait," Higgins tried to call after them. "She is not dead. See for yourselves. Very much alive. Come back, please, and see."

Bewildered, he pointed down at the girl, wondering if they had seen her clearly. But somehow he knew that they had, and knew that she had seen them as well. Only Taylor Quitman remained close beside the table, his face filled with shock and horror and disbelief. Once his hand lifted, as though he wanted to comfort her. Then, without warning, he, too, turned about and ran toward the door.

"Wait, gentlemen!"

This firm command came from Reverend Pounders, who appeared to be regaining his senses. "I'm certain you all know what this means. She has seen us, every one of us."

He looked back toward the table and the girl, who was no longer straining but who now appeared to be listening closely.

"She must be disposed of, Higgins," Reverend Pounders ordered in a voice as cold as death. "And it must be done before dawn. Call your man, Orlando Dow, if you wish, but it must be done or else she will name us all and bring ruination down upon all our families."

The pronouncement hung on the air for several moments, as though waiting for someone to refute or challenge it.

Higgins started around the table. "*You* do it, sir," he challenged. "If you have an appetite for such action. It wasn't my plan."

"What *was* your plan, Higgins?" Pounders shouted back, outraged. "Did you even think once of the consequences?"

"He simply brought her to me, Orlando Dow did. He thought it would please us."

"Please us!" Pounders echoed, his normally sedate voice strained beyond recognition. Now he pushed his way through the men to the door and looked back at Higgins from the cleared path. "Just do as I say, Higgins, as all of us say. Get rid of her, or every man in this room will pay a price beyond your comprehension."

After this tense announcement several of the men joined the reverend at the door. Only Taylor Quitman stood his ground midway across the loft. "Damn you, Higgins." Then he hurried toward the door.

"Do it," Reverend Pounders instructed. "By dawn, or I swear we won't be held accountable for *your* safety."

The threat hung heavy on the air. Jarmay Higgins started to challenge it, but good sense intervened.

By dawn.

Of course Pounders had told him nothing he didn't already know. Still he would have to scout the waterfront haunts for Orlando Dow. And what if he couldn't find him. Why hadn't he returned for his money as he said he would, or had he, too, just realized the consequences?

Jarmay Higgins looked up to see the doorway empty, heard only a last echoing step as the men hurried down the stairs. He looked back at the girl and saw her return his gaze.

"Bitch," he whispered, loathing the sight of her for all the trouble she'd brought into his life.

"Bitch," he said, this time full voiced, and returned to the table and looked down at her close at hand and wondered where that expression of new calm had come from, for surely she'd heard what her fate was to be.

He encircled the table once, still smarting from the recent humiliation at the hands of the others.

"Bitch," he shouted down at her a third time, and felt new fury at that expression of persistent calm, as though from her helpless position she was somehow defying him, proclaiming her own superiority.

Then he felt a hunger growing. Something brutal. It was not surprising. He'd felt it earlier. Now, with the certainty of her fate fixed in his mind, he slowly circled the table, concentrating on those female features that provided him with special excitement—her breasts, the line of her throat, her hips, the inside of her leg, firm to the touch, and she didn't like his touch at all. Look! The calm was gone now from her eyes, replaced by fear.

He stood directly behind her, drawing her hair together in his hand, hearing his breath increase with desire and something more, a need to get even, to cause her the same pain and humiliation that she had caused him.

For several moments he wrapped the long golden hair around and around his hand, pulling it tight against her scalp, feeling her trying to resist the pain.

He was ready now. But he had a job to do first. He must find

Orlando Dow, tell him to come at dawn for what was left of the girl
and do with her whatever he desired, just see to it that she was never
seen alive in these parts again.

The thought caused his excitement to grow. As he looked down at
her, he wondered if she was a virgin, and suspected that she was and
felt his cock grow hard in anticipation of the delights that would
come later.

"My pretty." He smiled and unwound her hair from about his
hand and bent over and placed a kiss on the smelly gag.

As she turned her head away, he smiled and thought how shocked
she would be by things to come if a mere kiss displeased her.

Hurry, find Orlando Dow and come back for a few pleasurable
hours before dawn.

Then all would be well again, the threat of the girl gone, Stanhope
in mourning, lesson delivered, and hopefully heeded.

How topsy-turvey his emotions had been tonight—pleasure, surprise, disappointment, humiliation, desire and now contentment. Everything had worked out, after all.

"I shall return shortly," he whispered and patted her head, and left
the tarpaulin drawn back. No need to hide her now. Everyone had
seen her and, more important, she had seen everyone. If their plans
misfired, they would go down together.

Quickly he stepped through the door, closed it behind him and
tried to imagine her in darkness, what her thoughts were, if she knew
what was yet in store for her.

Interesting questions. Sad to be so young and to die, though what
did it really matter? Nothing in the world ever lived up to one's
expectation of it. So she was better off to be spared the false anticipation and subsequent disappointment.

From this point of view, Jarmay Higgins was doing her a favor. On
that note he stepped out into his lumberyard, took assessment of the
star-filled sky, then started off toward the tent revival grounds on the
outskirts of Mobile, where shortly he would ask Orlando Dow to stop
saving souls long enough to end a life.

Jarmay Higgins would make only one request; that it be as painless
as possible.

🖋 Stanhope Hall

Burke Stanhope watched dawn from the balcony of Eve's bed-chamber, sitting in her favorite rocker, holding her soft white dress-ing gown in his arms, which still bore her unique scent of lavender and rose.

He felt safe here, away from all prying though well-meaning eyes, so he let more tears come. Mary was with Stephen now, though Burke doubted if there was very much anyone could do or say to offer help. The boy had seemed deprived of his senses, still calling Eve's name over and over as though he expected her to rise from the ashes.

Listen! Songs were coming from the cabins, the field hands mourn-ing in their own way, spirituals raised to the dawn, hopefully to a merciful God who might give one and all the courage to meet and shoulder this heaviest of all crosses.

As he thought of her again, he buried his face in her robe and tried not to dwell on his own despicable behavior these last few weeks. For, at bottom, the pain he was suffering most was the pain of complicity. If he had been more tolerant of the Eden boy, if he had been less willful in his own pursuits, if he had been willing to let go of the past as Mary had requested thousands of times, if he had only seen the developing affection between Eve and Stephen Eden, if he had ac-cepted the boy instead of—

"God, help me," he moaned and pressed back against the rocker and looked straight up at the high ceiling and remembered the morn-ing of Eve's birth.

Now he clasped her dressing gown to him in the same manner that, seventeen years ago, he'd clasped the infant, with old Florence scold-ing, "Not so hard, Mr. Stanhope, she's a little lady and needs gentle loving."

Fearful that his own sense of reason was slipping dangerously out of control, he closed his eyes and began to think of cause and blame and responsibility and guilt and all those plain words that somehow softened the sharp edge of grief with distraction if nothing else.

An accident?

It was possible. Sis Liz was old and had persisted with her candle ceremonies, though both Mary and Burke had asked her several times to cease. The old woman had adored candles for their "magic light." All right, then, had it been an errant candle too near a piece of old lace, a willful breeze, the combination capable of producing the in-ferno he'd witnessed last night?

Or was there any reason to suspect outside hands, the damnable knights, who by their own boast had taken credit for White Doll's brutal murder.

No, he couldn't believe the organization would go this far, would be so brazen as to make an attack upon his immediate family. And besides, no one had come forward yet from among those brave cowards who hid beneath gray hoods.

Then accident. It would have to be the cruelest of circumstances, a candle burning too high and no one paying attention.

Now he leaned heavily on the banister and let his head hang down and thought how tired he was. There was no point to any of it, not to life or to death; it was all random, all meaningless.

He closed his eyes, the better to blot out his own bleak thoughts. Eve gone, Eve never to return, a vacuum of such vast proportions. Could he endure it? Did he want to endure it?

 Mobile

Taylor Quitman lost track of how long he had been standing in the shadows across the street from Jarmay Higgins's lumberyard. He'd seen the others quickly depart after having glimpsed the horror of what lay bound to Jarmay Higgins's old cutting table.

Had the man lost his mind?

Then he'd seen the fool himself, Jarmay Higgins, hurrying down the street toward the western edge of town, where the evangelists held their tent meetings, in search of one villain to commit a most heinous crime.

Taylor Quitman leaned back against the rough brick of Penniman's Pharmacy. Even though he felt overcome with horror, there still were strange moments when he was certain he had imagined it or dreamed it, Burke Stanhope's daughter bound and gagged, Eve, the light of Burke Stanhope's life.

Lord, what to do?

He bent low as though in the throes of physical pain, and tried to deal with the truth as he now knew it.

They would kill her. Of that he was certain. On orders from Reverend Pounders himself, and every knight present in the loft had agreed. She had seen too much. She could not be permitted to return to Stanhope Hall and describe at length for her father all of Mobile's leading citizens whom she had seen gathered in Jarmay Higgins's loft.

It had to be. Then why was he standing here, keeping his eyes on that loft, Eve, alone, terrified, and helpless in the dark.

Suddenly Taylor Quitman turned his back on the silent building across the way and pressed his forehead against the rough brick of the pharmacy. If only he had the courage, he would go and rescue her. He could carry her to his office for the remainder of the night, then take her home to safety come dawn.

Wisely the thought stopped. Burke would ask questions. Eve Stanhope would start talking.

No. There was no solution. The girl was doomed, as they all were doomed.

Slowly he waited for the realization to pass, for good sense and better judgment to return. Then he looked over his shoulder at the shadowy facade of Higgins's Lumberyard, his eyes effortlessly finding the loft, though there were no windows to guide his way, merely the gray peeling frame concealing the terrified girl on the old cutting table.

He stared at the building for several minutes, gradually coming to terms with the inevitable. Her fate was sealed. He knew that now. What was more difficult to know and understand was what he should do with his conscience.

*   *   *

Near dawn.

Jarmay Higgins could feel it, the coming of light and, with it, an increase of dread.

Where was the scoundrel Orlando Dow? Jarmay Higgins had searched the outskirts of Mobile, had stuck his head into tent after tent and made inquiry. Time after time he had been told, "Don't know," or "Dow's a hard man to catch," or "May have left town," or "Maybe praying with the ladies up on Larkspur Lane."

Abruptly Jarmay Higgins shook his head as though to cancel the cacophony of voices and turned around on the night street and knew he still had a job that needed doing, and knew deep in his heart that he would not be able to do it.

Then what in the name of God was he to do?

With every step that led back into the city, he pondered his dilemma. He felt used by his fellow knights. Why was this suddenly *his* responsibility? They all were in this together, had been from the beginning.

His lumberyard was ahead by two blocks, a mere two blocks in which to make a momentous decision and then to find the courage to stand by it.

"Damn!"

As anger surfaced, he walked head down and tried to conceive of himself committing the act of murder. How would he do it? In the most recent waterfront murder, the victim's throat had been cut from ear to ear.

No, he couldn't do that. When a person's throat was cut, out of necessity you had to look them in the eye.

Suffocation? There was a thought. Simply hold a pillow over that pretty face until all breath—

No!

Then what? As his dilemma increased, so did his fear, until at last he was running through the darkened streets of Mobile. Long before he was ready for it, he saw his lumberyard, his eyes moving instantly to the loft and his sure and certain knowledge of what lay bound to his cutting table and sure and certain knowledge of what had to be done.

"God," he moaned and stopped on the curb and looked straight up, anger increasing, somehow viewing the whole business as Burke Stanhope's fault, always Burk Stanhope, since he was a child. The Stanhopes had had more land, had made more productive use of it. Burke Stanhope was smarter, more handsome, always more, bigger, better, best; while Jarmay Higgins and his family limped behind, a poor second in everything.

Slowly his anger turned to something else. Then revenge. The sweetest kind. Why not, if he was to get rid of her anyway?

With great deliberation he moved through his gates and carefully locked and secured them. Though dawn was near, there was at least an hour of night left. No early-morning visitors now.

As he stepped quickly across the gravel yard, a strange new thought entered his mind.

What if she had escaped?

As the absurdity grew in his mind, he let himself into his office, dark except for that faint light that always precedes the dawn.

He came to a stop behind his desk and sat slowly, out of breath from his fruitless errand, and looked up at the ceiling.

He rubbed his eyes, which burned from lack of sleep, and made a tent of his hands and rested his forehead and stared down at the scarred desk that had been in his family for over a hundred years, his daddy's desk and *his* daddy's desk, a long line of common woodsmen, who had labored long and mightily for an honest day's wage, and who had never been given anything by anyone for as long as Jarmay Higgins could remember, unlike some he could mention.

Staring down at the desktop, he saw not the scars and scratches of years of boredom, but saw instead Burke Stanhope, riding that white stallion of his, the one he'd owned when he was a boy, riding down Stanhope Lane all the way to the river, riding right past the Higgins farm where Jarmay stood sweating, ax in hand, felling trees by himself, sweat pouring off, suffocating in the heat and the foul odor of his own sweat while Burke Stanhope looked cool and fresh in his white linen riding jacket.

Without warning Higgins's sheltering hands became two fists upon the carved desk. He encouraged such thoughts, for in a peculiar way they made him strong, and he needed strength for what he was about to do.

Slowly he stood and pushed away from the desk and locked his office door. He climbed the loft stairs with deliberation, wondering if she could hear his footsteps, wondering if she knew what was in store for her. Perhaps the shock would kill her. Then good. Job accomplished. He would weight her body and dump it into Mobile Bay at high tide, and within hours she'd be dinner for the sharks.

At the top of the loft stairs he stopped for breath. His hand trembled as he reached toward the lock. Finally the lock gave and he pushed the door open and found himself staring into shadows.

He closed the door behind him and moved to the old desk, where he found a lantern and a box of matches. One strike and he stood in the limited glow of yellow light.

"Eve?"

Then there she was in the glow of the lantern, her eyes catching the limited light as she turned her head at his approach.

He smiled down at her and studied her face, a sweet face, really, beautiful even with the distortion caused by the gag. He would enjoy her lips, he was certain, but if he removed the gag, surely she would cry out.

Then a brilliant idea occurred. Turn on the saws in the cutting room below, the whining, screaming sawblades that were capable of deafening a man if he worked over them too long.

"I'll be right back." He grinned down at her, then ran to the door, half-stumbling down the steps, never breaking speed until he was in the cutting room directly beneath the loft, his hand on the very lever that would activate the shiny blades, which in turn would spew sawdust everywhere and scream like a living, breathing thing in pain.

He pulled down on the lever with both hands and watched with a mixture of awe and admiration as the massive blades whirled into action, the teeth blurring within seconds, until at last they resembled large silver-colored suns spinning out of control, and all the while the scream rose to fever pitch and Jarmay Higgins was forced to cover his ears with both hands.

Then he was running again, back up the stairs, the high-pitched scream seeming to follow him, to increase in volume until at last he was standing over her and couldn't even hear the sound of his own labored breathing.

He noticed that the fear on her face had increased along with the sound of the saw. Now without hesitation he removed the gag, wet from her saliva. As he drew it back, he saw her close her eyes and wet her lips with her tongue and grimace, as though she'd experienced pain in release.

Then there was no further cause for delay. She was here, his prisoner, bound and helpless before him, her screams muffled, night still outside the window, plenty of time for him to enjoy her, to mount her, to at last get even with Burke Stanhope for a lifetime of superiority.

His thoughts helped to increase his appetites. Slowly he leaned over and drew the heavy tarpaulin all the way back. Her lips were moving in some earnest entreaty. Too bad he couldn't hear; besides, he had not come to talk. The first sight of those white breasts as he unbuttoned her bodice caused a pleasurable increase in the pressure in his groin.

As he covered her breasts with his hands, he saw her head thrash, her mouth open in what possibly was a continuous scream, a poor second to the screaming blades coming from beneath in the cutting room.

For several minutes he contented himself with her breasts, examining them at length, rather enjoying the way she tried to shrink from his touch, fascinated by the tears running down her face, her mouth continuously open, either trying to form words or in a scream.

Then all at once he had had enough of her breasts. There were other treasures as yet hidden beneath the dark blue muslin skirt.

"Oh, my pretty." He smiled down at her and saw her terror yet increase. Slowly he stripped off his coat, then his vest, carefully unbuttoned his shirtwaist as the combination of desire and night heat set him to sweating. He loosened the belt on his trousers, then one by one released his buttons for the anticipation of what was about to happen.

He looked down the length of her, then he reached inside his pocket and found his knife, a small sleek penknife, folded in upon itself.

Carefully kneeling between her legs on the table, he unsheathed the blade and commenced to cut the blue muslin dress until it fell away.

He pulled her hips free of white pantaloons and deposited all over the side of the table.

At the same moment that he had rendered her naked, she went strangely silent. In the semidarkness he saw her eyes close, her head arch backward, as though she had at last perceived what was going to happen to her and that further struggle was useless.

He looked the length of her, a young body beautiful beyond description: broad hips; an inverted bowl for a belly, enhanced by the small rise of a dark mound; long, graceful, perfectly shaped legs; that small nipped circle of a waist; the swelling curves of breasts; graceful long white throat—perfection, just perfection. It was now his to do with as he pleased.

In the moment before he lowered himself on top of her, she opened her eyes and met his in a peculiar defiance that seemed to invite him to do his worst. For some reason the expression angered him, reminded him of her father's arrogant superiority. Though once he had thought to be gentle with her, knowing her to be a virgin and not accustomed to the strength of a man, now that one arrogant expression enabled him to thrust into her like an angry bull, disregarding the pain of invasion, disregarding everything except the need to inflict as much discomfort as possible on her, all the while deriving as much pleasure as possible for himself.

* * *

She knew what was going to happen, had known all along that it might come to this and thus was not too surprised, but still hopeful that something would happen to alter destiny.

But when he had momentarily left the loft and turned on the saw blades, her fate had been sealed. She knew then that a decision was confronting her. One, could she survive? And two, did she want to survive?

For most of the long hours bound to the old table, she had little desire to see dawn. Death was ahead of her, she was certain of that. She just hoped it came swiftly.

As he dropped down upon her and she felt a searing pain that radiated deep inside her, she debated the wisdom of surviving only in order to be killed again.

Reflexively she screamed as the pain yet increased, the distortion inside her growing, his teeth chewing on her breasts now, twin pains that seemed to meet inside her head and convince her of the pointlessness and the brutality of this world. That other world of grace and love slipped further away from her until she could say with certainty that it was gone now, as though it had never existed.

Blessedly at some point she lost consciousness for a while, at least that part of her consciousness that recorded sensation. Clearly she hadn't been able to accomplish her death yet, for there still was a weight on top of her, hands moving over her, something moving deep inside her, the man's foul odor suffocating her. But it didn't matter. Death would come. She wouldn't have to wait long. What she had been unable to accomplish on her own, this man could manage for her as soon as he was finished, that is, if he didn't die first, for now she felt his breath hot and labored against the side of her face, felt him give a tremendous shudder, saw a grimace of pain in his eyes and felt him go limp atop her.

Was he dead? She devoutly wished it. But at last the unspeakable weight atop her shifted, pushed up with his hands and looked down on her, grinning, his face red-mottled and sweaty, his eyes watery, a grotesque and evil face that from this moment on would be the centerpiece of her worst nightmares for as long as she lived.

As he crawled off her, she felt him leave something wet and slimy in his trail, like the big garden slugs that crossed the red brick path each morning.

The light of dawn was increasing, and she felt the sharp pain in the pit of her stomach. Her breasts felt raw and bleeding.

Death now? When? And how long would he be content to stand there, staring down at her?

Slowly she closed her eyes, unable to look at him any further. What happened to her now no longer mattered. She was finished. All that remained was the act itself. And that would come soon, would be welcomed, for she wanted nothing more to do with this world. Surely there was a better one somewhere, and all she had to do was leave this one and go in search of that other.

Finish it then, she prayed, and awaited the death blow.

* * *

Jarmay Higgins took all the time he needed to make a full and pleasurable recovery. Never had it been so good, so firm, so resisting. A feast of a female, that's what she was. What a shame to destroy her, thus denying all other males the pleasures he'd recently taken for himself.

But could he now kill her?

No. He couldn't. Then what? She must be gone by dawn or else the Knights of the White Camellia would descend upon him and take their own revenge.

Suddenly he'd had enough of the saws below. The sounds were deafening and beginning to hurt his head. Quickly he drew on his trousers, shirt and vest and hurried down the steps to the cutting room, in desperate need of a period of time for quiet thought and efficient planning.

As he pushed up on the lever and the giant blades whined to silence, he closed his eyes, still savoring the lingering sensations of her body.

The silence deepened as he walked slowly about the cutting room floor. Now what to do? There was so little time. She must be gone by dawn. It was too late to take her down to the bay. Someone would surely see him transporting a body through the streets at dawn. He couldn't leave her here all day, for he was certain a delegation of the knights would pay him a visit at some point during the morning, and if she was still here—

What? What? *What?*

As his dilemma increased, so did the circle of his pacing, a broad range that extended to the loft steps in one direction and the storeroom in the other, where on one of his turns around the cutting room floor he spied two large trunks just inside the storage room door. He passed them twice before he recalled their owner, the bizarre giant who had appeared out of the dawn mist with a wagon full of scantily clad beauties, his jewels, he'd called them, and these two trunks in need of new bottoms.

Distracted, Jarmay Higgins bent low on the third pass to see if his men had done a good job. They had. The smell of virgin pine filled his nostrils as he hoisted the lids and found new gleaming lumber at the bottom, sturdy and solid and well fitted.

He bent over the better to see and knocked once with his fist. Good, strong enough to carry—

He couldn't remember what, and it didn't matter. What did matter was a stray memory that informed him the man had said he would return for his trunk at dawn this morning, something about leaving for New Orleans and points west with his all-female theatrical troupe.

Jarmay raised slowly up. Suddenly his thoughts stopped, intersected by another one, this one powerful beyond Jarmay Higgins's ability to cope with, coming at him with such unexpected force, as though it had been sitting at the bottom of the trunks all this time waiting for him.

He paced once in a limited circle directly around the trunks, never taking his eyes off them, as though the thought was emanating directly from new wood, informing him that there *was* a way out of his present painful dilemma. Still he paced around and around, all the time thinking, *Why not?* How simple. Place the Stanhope girl in one of these trunks and let Yorrick Harp carry her away to the ends of the earth, for all Jarmay Higgins cared. Harp collected females, didn't he, for his troupe of prostitutes? What was she now but a prostitute?

Then it was settled. Yet at the moment of decision, another question presented itself. Should he inform Yorrick Harp of what he was doing or simply deposit her, bound and gagged, in the trunk and allow him to cart her away?

Abruptly the pacing stopped. Had he momentarily lost his mind? Sell her to the man. Surely such a profound judge of female flesh as Yorrick Harp wouldn't have too much trouble seeing the marketability of young Eve Stanhope.

He stood smiling, pleased with himself and his decision. He looked up at the window to see night gone, replaced by the faint gray of dawn.

Hurry then! The man had said he would return at dawn.

Running now, he took the loft stairs two at a time until the need for air caused him to slow his pace, but his mind continued to turn. Of course his story to the knights would be that he had done away with her, that he had weighted her body and, under cover of darkness, taken her to the remote Half-Moon district on the far side of the bay, the side nearest the open sea, and that there he had deposited her and their troubles were over.

Carefully he pushed open the door and didn't bother with the lantern this time. He knew where she was and what he planned to do, and he could do it all in semidarkness.

Accordingly he felt his way across the creaky loft floor, and as he approached the cutting table, he put his hand out and felt warm flesh and decided to place a price tag of five hundred dollars upon her. On the open market anyplace between here and San Francisco, Yorrick Harp could draw at least one hundred dollars per male for the lady's services. And she was young to boot, with many a good year left in her.

No, it was a bargain at five hundred dollars, and it would have to be the sweetest money Jarmay Higgins had ever earned.

Hurry now. Tie the package up and carry her down to the trunk. If she complained, point out the difference between this destiny and the watery grave at the bottom of Mobile Bay.

* * *

About twenty minutes later the job was accomplished. Now where was the bastard? Nervously Jarmay Higgins shifted upon the trunk, deriving enormous pleasure from knowing what cargo the trunk now contained. With the exception of one outcry, the girl had been the model of cooperation, fitting herself neatly into the trunk despite her nakedness.

Listen! In the distance he heard the rattle of a wagon.

As Jarmay Higgins made his way to the door of the cutting room, he knew what he would see even before he saw it. The large wagon moved in a blur past the office door, rattling around in a rough circle, and on the reins was Yorrick Harp, his long gray hair and beard flaring in the wind, his robe a different color this time, bright red, and on the last pass the man waved, a broad gesture over his head.

Now with a loud and melodramatic command of "Animals! Be still!" the wagon rattled to a halt directly in front of where Jarmay Higgins was standing.

It was Yorrick Harp, all right. Red flowers were intwined amidst his long gray locks, and because of the uncertain light of day and Jarmay Higgins's naturally agitated state, he may have been wrong, but he thought he detected lip color and two bright red circles of rouge on Yorrick Harp's face, rendering him more female than male. Atop the red robe was a pendant the like of which Jarmay Higgins had never seen, glittering like the sun itself, diamonds and rubies all inlaid and at least the size of a good orange and resting directly in the center of the man's chest.

"Fair morning to you, woodsman," the giant called out. Wrapping the reins about the wagon stop, he stepped grandly out onto the platform as though he fancied himself royalty.

"Morning," Jarmay Higgins muttered and eyed the back of the wagon and wondered if the old man had brought his pretties this morning.

"Oh, I *am* sorry," Harp proclaimed and moved closer to Jarmay Higgins and reached up to his hair and plucked one of the red blossoms and presented it to Higgins before he even had time to object.

"My jewels had to stay behind this morning. Do you have any idea what is involved in the packing and moving of the cosmos? That's what we must do this grand morning—move the cosmos and have it ready to load aboard the wagons to New Orleans, which is of course why I have come. Not empty-handed, mind you, for I do need assistance when I move the world. So I selected at random these two soldiers from the battlefields of Mobile's streets to give me a hand in retrieving Yorrick Harp's trunks. In exchange for their favors, they have been granted a firsthand look at paradise itself. Come, come, lads. Time is passing, and we must pass with it or be run over by it."

Suddenly he gave a sharp slap of his hand, the sound so echoing and reverberating that Jarmay Higgins jumped as though a pistol had been fired.

At the same time the rear flap of the wagon was lifted and two men slowly emerged, one short, dark, swarthy, carrying a spider monkey on his shoulder, and the other tall, lean, cadaverous-appearing, who landed awkwardly on one leg, which was all he had to land on, the other being missing, though the tattered and patched gray coat told the whole tale, a true Son of the South, defeated every day by new enemies whose names were hunger, shame and pain.

Too bad. Jarmay Higgins had been looking forward to the beauties, none of whom, if memory served him correctly, could hold a candle to the fresh beauty Jarmay Higgins would shortly make available to Yorrick Harp.

"Of course, sir, I remember," he said, and was appalled at how plain and flat his voice sounded after Yorrick Harp's soaring one.

"And I knew you would." Yorrick Harp nodded vigorously and clapped a massive hand on Jarmay Higgins's back and grinned down at him with that dazzling grin and summoned his two soldiers to come closer. "Come, come, one and all. The sun is rising, the drama of the day awaits, and I must have my customary front row seat. Now speak, woodsman. Where are my trunks? Lead the way, I prithee, lead on, Macbeth, before consciousness doth make cowards of us all."

This last was delivered full-bellow to the morning air. The spider monkey hid his face in his owner's jacket. The one-legged soldier hid a smile. And Jarmay Higgins led the way into the cutting room, though he had hoped to do business with Yorrick Harp alone. Considering the nature of what was lying curled in one of the trunks, the fewer witnesses the better.

Still, with no choice but to comply, he pushed open the door and pointed directly into the small storage room off the cutting room and said, "There, sir, good as new, though I have more business to discuss, if I may, in private."

Yorrick Harp started toward the trunks. "What is private, my good man? I'm afraid I don't know that word. We all are playing this game together and we will all go down in defeat together. I know exactly what's in your mind, as you must know exactly what is in mine. The only species entitled to privacy are those with tails and four legs, like my friend there." And he pointed toward the spider monkey, who sat perched on his owner's shoulder.

"They are God's chosen, don't you agree? Look at the intelligence on that face, the sensibility, the wisdom. He has seen it all, knows the answer to the riddle, don't you, my friend?"

Slowly he walked back and lovingly stroked the monkey's head, cupped his hand about it and kissed it with what appeared to be great affection. "Do you know his name, sir?" he asked Jarmay Higgins.

"N-no," Jarmay stammered.

"Abraham Lincoln." Yorrick Harp beamed. "Is it not a rare choice? They called him the ape, you know."

Jarmay Higgins noticed the small dark man smiling, deriving personal satisfaction from the monkey's name as well as from Yorrick Harp's attention.

"Now then, that's enough. Show me my trunks, woodsman, and tell me of your business offer. For within ten minutes I must be gone from your life—but not I hope from your memory, for it is my fondest wish that on the occasion of your death, you will have two last thoughts: the next to the last, of your dear departed mother who, however reluctantly, breathed life into you, and the very last thought will be of old Yorrick Harp and how he appeared before you on this beauteous morning, in sunrise red, with the choicest of blossoms intwined in his locks and a voice capable of earning for him a seat among the gods. Will you do that for me, woodsman, save your last thought on this earth for me? Now, there are my trunks, I'd recognize them anywhere and they look reborn, truly resurrected—"

"Sir!"

Jarmay Higgins felt embarrassed to be shouting in his own cutting shed, but the man was running on and on, all the time drawing nearer to the trunk that contained the Stanhope girl. Higgins felt that some sort of explanation should precede the sight of a naked female body curled in the bottom of the trunk, so he had no choice but to yell. At the same time he lifted his boot and planted it atop the trunk, just as Yorrick Harp bent over to lift it up.

"Sir, I beg you, allow me to—"

"I'll allow you to do anything that pleases you so long as you remove your boot from my trunk."

At that moment Yorrick Harp lifted the trunk lid. The nearest spill of light landed directly on the curved white expanse of a female thigh and buttocks, next on the slim graceful arms bound at the wrists, then on the mussed long golden hair, thrown in disarray over her face and neck.

"What have we here?" Yorrick Harp exclaimed broadly and bent slowly down on his knees and in a hushed tone summoned his "two soldiers" forward in curiosity. The monkey started to chatter, the two men gaped and Jarmay Higgins closed his eyes and thought, *Doomed.*

For several moments there was no sound in the cutting room. Yorrick Harp seemed content to look his fill, and the girl obliged, not moving, unconscious for all Jarmay Higgins knew or cared.

Then questions.

"Dead?" Yorrick Harp asked without looking up.

"No," Jarmay Higgins replied without looking down.

"Used?"

"Yes."

"By whom?"

"Me."

"Local?"

"Yes."

"Name?"

"Eve."

"Is she for me?"

"If you want her. For a price, of course."

All at once Yorrick Harp laughed. He sat back on his heels beside the trunk and threw back his massive head and laughed and laughed and laughed until Jarmay Higgins felt uncomfortable and the other two had withdrawn to safer corners.

"Ah, my dear woodsman, you are not an evil man. Neither are you a good one, and therein lies the grief and tragedy of this world. No, I will not pay you one farthing for this pretty. Nor will I pay you a farthing for trunk repairs now. I will, however, spare your semigood name and reputation by taking this embarrassment off your hands and seeing if you left anything worth salvaging."

He leaned closer over the trunk and smoothed back the long golden hair and spoke so softly that Jarmay Higgins had to listen closely in order to hear.

"My child, can you speak? Do you have the courage to open your eyes and find another world? Come, my beloved. We all are raped at least once on our way to the grave. It comes with a ticket to life. The point is not to care and to rise as soon as possible and walk with dignity no matter what. Do you hear Yorrick Harp talking to you? He speaks the truth."

Jarmay Higgins heard the man speak as though he'd known this piece of used female flesh all his life and was directly responsible for her.

Now he looked up to see Yorrick Harp lifting the girl from her curled position inside the trunk, supporting her, and ordering Jarmay Higgins to cut the ropes that bound her.

"She'll run on you," Jarmay Higgins muttered and withdrew his knife and made two neat slashes about her wrists and ankles and stepped quickly back, fearful that the girl, freed, would turn on him.

For several moments no one spoke. The two "soldiers" drew closer, clearly fascinated. The monkey, Abraham Lincoln, stopped chattering. The only sound in the cutting room was Yorrick Harp's gentle yet persuasive encouragement of "You can stand erect, of course you can. Here. Lean on me, oh, you are so very pretty, beautiful, in fact, and old Yorrick Harp created the word, so I know whereof I speak, and you must believe me, for now your fate has altered, your luck has turned, and in time Yorrick Harp will transform you into a goddess which the entire world will worship. Do you believe me? Can you stand? Of course you can. There!"

With one satisfied sigh Yorrick Harp withdrew his last supporting hand and left the girl standing upright, still in the trunk, though that slight obstruction did not interfere with the stunning whole, the female body in nude and flawless perfection. Jarmay Higgins stared along with everyone else and took secret pride in the fact that he was the only one here who had enjoyed her fully, but he wasn't so stupid as to believe he would be the last.

* * *

Confined in the cramped quarters of the trunk, Eve had found it difficult to breathe, and without sufficient air, she'd given in to an almost pleasurable stupor in which she suffered no pain, no memory, no loss, no fear.

Then someone had thrown open the lid of the trunk. And she'd felt a hand, a massive, warm and very gentle hand, on her thigh and following that had heard the most reassuring voice. Then she'd felt those same hands lifting her up, urging her to stand on her own, though she was certain she would not be capable of such a feat, for her legs felt broken.

Still the voice had insisted with such persuasive gentleness that she could do these things, that she exerted extra effort. Though she'd tried once to cover her nakedness, she couldn't do so and therefore had to assume this was the way they wanted her and it mattered little to her.

Once erect, she found the will and energy to lift her head and stare back at the man with the large gentle hands and compelling voice.

And through eyes swollen from tears, she found herself staring at the most peculiar man she'd ever seen, a giant of a man in flowing red robes with a jewel-encrusted medallion.

Then without warning she felt her knees buckle, and she would have fallen had it not been for the giant, who moved quickly forward and caught her and at the same time drew off the red cape from his shoulders and wrapped it about her, all the time talking. "My beautiful Eve, allow me to introduce myself. I am a simple man named Yorrick Harp, who early on found the world to be an unappetizing place and thus I created my own, the world of Yorrick Harp, owner, manager of the most gifted all-female theatrical troupe in the civilized world. You must come with us and contribute your beauty, for we leave for New Orleans and points west. I promise we will find starlight for you, and you will dazzle the men of the prairies and the ranches and the mountains and the mines. In return, Yorrick Harp's heart will be filled with gratitude and his pockets will be lined with gold."

She heard what he'd said though she understood little, but it was clear that she was being given to this man to cover the tracks of the Knights of the White Camellia. Though she was aware enough to perceive a new set of problems, she was also aware that she would be vigilant in looking for a place and a time to effect an escape.

Thus she nodded obediently to everything the giant said and was grateful for the protection of the red cloak and drew it closer around her. Now she had a glimmer of hope and that was a potent salve. She mustered enough strength to stand alone as the giant summoned forward the two standing in the shadows, a bizarre two, one tall and gaunt and missing a leg, the other short and dark with a monkey perched on his shoulder.

Each man grabbed the end of a trunk and started out through the door. Yorrick Harp called back to Jarmay Higgins. "Lift the other, you scoundrel, and spare my lieutenants. If you're brooding over the lost sale of this invaluable soul, go to the nearest reflecting surface you can find—a still pond, a cup of tea, a cracked mirror—and lean in close and loosen your collar and study the remarkable surface of your neck, unblemished, and remember that if Yorrick had taken it into his mind, he could as easily as not have placed the rope around your neck and stayed to watch you dance on air."

Halfway to the door, while listening closely to everything he said, Eve felt her strength drain from her in a sudden loss of power. Yorrick Harp was there and lifted her effortlessly in his arms.

"In the back," he shouted to the two men loading the trunks aboard the wagon. As he carried her through the door, she saw the most beautiful sight in the world—morning sun, striking every plain surface in the old lumberyard and coating all with rosy orange hues, a dazzling display of color after her long confinement in the dark. Yet with morning light came certain harsh realizations. She had been used, looked upon without garments. What man would want her now?

Stephen—

She must have made a sound, for Yorrick Harp stopped in concern.

"My pretty, what?" he murmured. "You've been through a rough sea, that's right enough. But it's all in how you perceive it. If you perceive it as tragic and irrevocable, then tragic and irrevocable it will be. On the other hand—well, we'll get to the other hand soon enough. For now you must believe me. This was meant to be, and no matter what you did or didn't do, this would have occurred. You would have found me or I would have found you. So instead of being remorseful, realize that fate is working well and destiny is on track. Yorrick Harp is on earth to put things right."

Then he laughed with hearty zeal. "Now, move away, all of you," he commanded the three who continued to stand around as though unable to function without his direction. And as they all did so, he approached the back of the wagon, still supporting Eve in his arms, and bent low through the rear canvas flap and placed her carefully on a straw mat.

As she lay back, she felt new objections coming from her once-cramped body.

"Oh, my poor beauty," he grieved. "I'll drive my horses as carefully as possible," he promised and gave her a final pat on the hand and disappeared immediately. Though she heard voices outside the wagon, she was more fascinated with the interior of the wagon. It was large by any standards, outfitted with hooks attached to a crossbeam overhead. Hanging from these hooks were what appeared to be lifeless dolls of all colors, in all manner of dress, some men, some women and children, the faces most lifelike, some old, some young, their stuffed and lifeless feet swinging grotesquely in the air.

Slowly she drew the red cloak around her. It felt pleasing against her skin, though she knew she dare not lose consciousness completely. It was good to close her eyes, to wiggle her hands and feet, to listen to the men's voices outside the wagon, and at least for the moment enjoy the illusion that she was safe.

* * *

Dawn.

Mary leaned against a white column, aware of her disreputable appearance but for the moment not caring. Earlier in the predawn darkness she'd sent old Ben into Mobile on a fast horse to find Dr. Melrose. It wasn't a question of who needed him. A simpler question would be who was not in need of his medical expertise?

Ben had had plenty of time to come and go by now. Then what was keeping him?

She paced the gallery, her arms crossed against a nonexistent chill, alternately looking down at her skirts, still soiled with the soot and ashes of the fire two days ago, and then looking up toward the road, hoping, praying to see two horsemen returning. Her main concern this morning was for Christine, who had taken a turn for the worse since learning of Eve's death.

Eve's death—

The two words returned in echo to assault her, and in their reverberation, she closed her eyes against the storm of grief that threatened to undo her.

Where was Burke?

She had no idea. They all seemed to be on their own in this tragedy. For the first time since she'd fallen in love with him years ago, she felt so alone now without his support or strength or advice. In this matter he apparently had none to give.

She leaned her forehead against the column in the hope of making her brain stop working. Endless postmortems. They served no purpose.

She heard a footstep behind and looked up and saw Stephen, or at least a facsimile of Stephen. The young man looked ghostlike. He was barefoot, his trousers still bearing the marks of the fire. His once-white shirt looked mottled in the early light of dawn. No coat, no tie, no sign of the young man who'd arrived full of plans for his expedition west.

"Stephen."

She spoke his name, though she wasn't certain that he heard, that he had any awareness that he was not alone.

She started to call again but changed her mind and merely watched him as he stared down the avenue of live oaks as though he were seeing scenes in his imagination that once had existed and now were gone.

"Stephen, come and sit," she invited, still not certain she'd penetrated that vacancy.

"Have they come back?"

His first words were not addressed to her, and she had no idea to whom he was referring. "Who?" she asked.

"The men. Paris took some men back to—" His voice broke. "They were going to search for—"

There was another disruption in thought, and Mary held her position. "I don't understand what you mean, Stephen," she said with all the gentleness she could manage.

She was aware of him standing beside her on the steps, then sitting, each movement as labored as though he were an eighty-year-old man.

At last down, he rested his arms on his knees and folded his hands. "Paris was taking some workers back to Fan Cottage," he said, his voice a monotone, his eyes red-streaked.

She rubbed her aching forehead, wishing that her mind would simply shut down. "Back to Fan Cottage?" she repeated witlessly. "Why?"

"Looking for—"

"What, Stephen?"

"Remains. Skeletal proof—"

Suddenly he stood with such force that she looked up from her own grieving.

"Why?" he demanded of her after he had paced to the end of the gallery and come back again, bringing all his grief with him.

At first she thought she might be able to say something to comfort him. But as he came closer, all she could do was accept with certainty that none of them would ever fully recover from this loss.

With Eve's death, a degree of her love for Burke had died. With Eve's death, old Sis Liz had died. With Eve's death, the once promising and brilliant young nephew standing before her had hopelessly lost his way, and with Eve's death the world at large had lost its savor, its joy, its hope, its meaning.

As soon as one perceives the pointlessness of life, one is ready then to perceive the point of life.

One of Sis Liz's favorite homilies, never fully understood by Mary until this moment.

"Stephen, please," she begged of the young man standing before her as though expecting answers. "I have no answers for you. All I can answer with is my love, my understanding of the pain you are feeling and my pledge to stand with you in any way I can."

He seemed grateful, though he said nothing. He was just turning away when something caught his eye emerging from the woods.

"Paris," he murmured and joined her on the top step and waited for Paris Boley to lead his weary and soot-covered band of workers to a position in front of the steps.

"Nothing," Paris said. "I'm afraid that in our zeal to put out the flames, we apparently destroyed everything, all ashes beaten together. Nothing. We found nothing."

His head was bowed, his hands continuously brushing against each other.

Paris felt responsible, as Mary knew. He had since the Knights of the White Camellia had demanded that Burke dismiss the nigger whom he had hired as general manager of Stanhope Plantations.

Who was right? The question occurred to Mary with all the innocence and substance of a summer breeze.

She looked up to see Paris and Stephen walking slowly away from the gallery, heads down, Stephen's white feet still visible against the dark green lawn.

At that moment she saw horsemen on the road, recognized Ben in the lead and Dr. Melrose trailing behind, balancing his black bag on his saddle.

Come to heal, thank God. Though even as she made a futile attempt to make herself presentable, she knew the doctor had his work cut out for him. She doubted seriously if there was anything in that black bag that was capable of lifting the cloud of death that seemed to have settled permanently over Stanhope Hall.

 Mobile

Eve overheard the man named Yorrick Harp say something to Jarmay Higgins that seemed to silence the awful man.

She heard Yorrick Harp give the other two men a sum of money and thank them for their assistance. Then she heard him bid them all a flowery farewell, and at last she felt the wagon rattle forward, picking up speed as it careened through the early-dawn streets of Mobile.

Then all she heard was the rattle of the large wagon itself and a whistling of wind, as though they had left Mobile for open country.

About twenty minutes later she felt the wagon breaking speed, heard the man yelling at the horses to go easy, felt pressure as they turned sharply to the left, and heard voices then, mostly female, though here and there she heard a male voice rising.

Movement over. She heard the wagon creak as the man jumped down from the high seat, heard women's voices all talking at once, greeting him warmly, and this din was coming closer to the rear of the wagon.

In reaction to what she felt was about to happen, she drew the red cloak more closely about her and was on the verge of pushing up into a seated position when suddenly the female voices outside the wagon fell silent and she heard *his* voice, like a loving father.

"Have I not told you, one and all," he began, "about the mysteries of this world, the riches that go unnoticed or sometimes come when we least expect them, like cosmic gifts to make us forget how truly miserable we are in this realm. Have I told you?"

The sounds of affirmation filled her ears, again female, all clearly adoring of this man who was speaking.

"Well, my pretties," he went on, silencing the very response he had sought to elicit. "This morning, in that predawn darkness when one is tempted to doubt the existence of light altogether, when one wonders why this great ball is spinning out of control across the night sky while we cling to it and suffer and avenge and curse and, worst of all, continue; in that moment of clearest vision, as I drove these noble beasts toward the woodsman's establishment, I thought, Yorrick Harp, why are you doing this, why not simply purchase two brand new trunks from Cabrini's Emporium in New Orleans, latest design for steamship crossing? Why this predawn journey for two trunks that have seen the better part of the civilized world and all the uncivilized world, trunks broken in body and spirit, that perhaps simply want to be tossed on some welcoming refuse heap so that the innate matter contained therein can rot in peace. For in the end, this is all that any of us request of this continuing crucible, the right to rot in peace."

Eve found herself listening to the special music of the man's voice.

"Then, when I least expected it," the man went on, "at the establishment in question, as I was about to conclude my transaction, and in the presence of a noble monkey named Abraham Lincoln, I suddenly understood everything—why I was occupying this space of earth at this time in the history of the world, why I had deposited my trunks with that particular scoundrel of a woodsman. Oh, I'm here to tell you it was a sense of a mystery made clear, and it was glorious."

Suddenly she heard the pressure of a foot on the back of the wagon and saw the canvas flap drawn back, letting in rays of blinding morning sun, from which she tried to protect herself. As soon as her vision cleared, she lowered her hands to behold the strangest sight she had ever seen.

There before her on the greenest of meadows she saw women, countless women, beautiful women, all with painted faces and long hair, a few still brushing their locks as though not quite finished with their morning toilette, a few arranging their garments, though all that could be said of those garments was that they were gossamer in appearance, every color of the rainbow.

Eve blinked, aware that all were staring back at her, yet powerless to alter her focus, for a few were naked from the waist up, parading openly before the men, who were hard at work in the background, loading trunks aboard covered wagons similar to the one in which she was riding.

Still she stared at them and they at her, though some were beginning to smile, one in particular, a tall lovely girl with light red hair and dark violet eyes, and those eyes were now fixed on Eve, though one hand was held behind her back. As she moved toward the wagon, the other women commenced to smile.

"What is your decision, Lily?" Yorrick Harp demanded.

"Of course, she's welcome to stay. In fact, I think we have been waiting for her."

All at once the pretty woman named Lily presented her with a bouquet of wildflowers gathered from the surrounding meadow.

After the presentation of flowers, Yorrick Harp clapped his hands and the chatter fell silent. With all those lovely upturned faces staring at him he asked, full-voiced, "Shall we baptize her then, make her one of us?"

A swelling female chorus of yeses filled her ears. Almost before she knew what was happening, the woman named Lily and a small dark-haired beauty who introduced herself as Violet were beside her.

"Take her to my wagon," Yorrick Harp continued. "Cleanse her and find garments for her and prepare her for baptism. The rest of you, finish your tasks and prepare to leave within the hour. A lonely world is waiting for us beyond that horizon, and we mustn't be late."

"Come, my darling," Lily whispered.

"Where are we?" Eve began and stopped talking only when she realized no one was listening and looked out across the green meadow and saw a dozen men just taking down a huge tent.

Ahead was an immense wagon, with a black canvas covering, with broad gold letters painted on the side that read—

Yorrick Harp's All-Female Traveling Troupe
The Original Adamless Eden

"Here we go," Violet said gently and guided her toward the back of the wagon, where conveniently someone had placed a stepstool, the better to scale the wagon's height.

"Remember, don't be afraid of anything that happens, because you have survived thus far and will survive to grace many another day."

"All you must do—"

"Yes, all you must do is—"

"Is work hard to create a new mind."

"A new mind—"

"That will serve you for what is ahead."

"Do you understand?"

This choral reading sounded continuously in her ears as they assisted her up into the most bizarre chamber she had ever seen, a bed occupying most of the available space, complete with lace and ruffles and dozens of pillows and garlands of false flowers that climbed each poster and joined ranks with the garlands that encircled the canopy overhead.

To one side near the right wall was a large copper pot on a black standard. In this pot she saw live flames licking up, filling the interior of the wagon with a smoky winter smell. A cooking pot?

"Over here, my sweet," Lily invited. Lifting a pitcher of water, she poured it into a china bowl, and into the water she poured a small vial of something, and within seconds the entire chamber smelled of flowers, a too-heavy smell that seemed to produce a curious languor over Eve's mental faculties.

She was aware of the two women guiding her to a small area behind a screen, aware of the red cloak being lifted from her shoulders, of standing naked before them, of sponges being dipped into the fragrant-smelling water, then gently over her body, each woman working gently to remove the bloodstains from her chafed wrists.

A few moments later she felt a towel around her shoulders, felt the same lovely massage extend to a drying motion that seemed to be lulling her into a half-sleep.

"There," Lily whispered and brushed her hair back in long, fluid movements. "How lovely," Lily murmured and asked her if she was ready. Eve didn't understand the question, but it didn't make any difference, for she had understood so little of what had happened.

Then they led her out from behind the screen. With every step she tried to force her eyes open, to force alertness, for she felt that alertness would serve her now. Though both women were still supporting her, she did manage to blink open her eyes and saw Yorrick Harp standing near the open flames of the large copper pot.

He had changed robes. Now he wore white, which floated like a cloud about his mammoth frame, and on his head he wore a tricorn crown of white, the style resembling paintings she had seen of Napoleon, a warrior's tricorn, only this one was satin with white beads and pearls embroidered around its edges. He wore it proudly and looked up as she was led back into the wagon and fixed his hand on that peculiar hat and lifted it and smiled. "A lady to the marrow of her bone. What a distinct pleasure it will be to have you among us."

Then she felt the women guiding her down onto the comfortable bed, arranging her until she was stretched out on its soft surface.

Suddenly something was under her nose that she found unpleasant, a harsh, acrid smell like lye or pure clove.

There was a brief struggle while Violet tried to hold her head. Lily held her hands.

"Don't force her," came the deep voice of Yorrick Harp. "She's made of strong stuff."

In a curious counterpoint Eve heard Lily whisper close to her ear, "Please, one deep breath. It will be for the best."

"Away, I say," bellowed Yorrick Harp. "I believe we're ready now."

At the clap of his hands the wagon flap lifted again and two more women stepped through into the interior. Without hesitation they approached her at the foot of the bed. Each reached out for one foot, and before she knew what had happened, they held her fast. At the same time Violet and Lily lifted her right arm and pinned it to the bed, Lily forcing her hand open, baring her palm.

Eve could not speak, for the languor had deepened, coming from the handkerchief Lily insisted on holding as close to her face as possible.

She tried to lift her head once to see what Yorrick Harp was doing and found only the broad expanse of his back bent over the open flames coming from the copper pot.

Suddenly her thoughts ceased. She looked up to see Yorrick Harp lift something from out of the open flames, a metal rod, quite long, with something glowing red attached to the end, a brand of some sort, spitting heat and red-hot ash as he held it gingerly out in front of him and, smiling, drew near to her and made his way around the women holding her arm, hand open, and she found herself staring up at two small letters, the Y clearly recognizable and co-joined to an H, the entire brand no larger than a peach pit, though it was not the size that promised pain but rather the degree of heat that emanated from it. Now Yorrick Harp was bringing the brand down toward the smooth white tender flesh of her upturned palm.

In anticipation of what was about to happen, she cried out, yet curiously when the red-hot brand seared its way into her skin and she smelled the odor of burning flesh and realized that it was her own, she tried to scream again, but was incapable now of making a sound. She saw Lily and Violet and Yorrick Harp bent over her with concerned and kind smiles on their faces while she struggled to digest the pain.

At some point she saw a convenient and safe blackness heading toward her and she welcomed it, uncertain whether she had risen up to heaven or fallen down to hell, and regretful only that it was so difficult to tell the difference between the two.

* * *

Though he had been drinking all night, Taylor Quitman was far from drunk, which was too bad, for it was a state he fervently desired. He'd stayed in his office and had tried to clear his head of the horrible images that continually presented themselves to his tortured mind; Eve Stanhope stabbed to death, blood running openly from many wounds; Eve Stanhope hanged by the neck from one of the beams in the old loft over the cutting room, Jarmay Higgins on one end of the rope, assisted by the villain named Orlando Dow who had started this whole senseless tragedy.

Angrily Taylor sat up on his mussed couch and eyed the three whiskey bottles at his feet, two empty, one almost empty. And somehow he knew that he would never accomplish complete and numbing inebriation until he made a final trip back to that loft over the cutting room and heard for himself from Jarmay Higgins that the girl was dead.

He moaned, amazed at how his grief was increasing, and hurried down the narrow steps of his office that led to the street.

Dead by dawn and no trace—

It was imperative that he find Higgins and hear from his own lips that the girl was dead. Then it was Taylor Quitman's plan to spend the rest of the day on the waterfront where he felt certain he could achieve a state of complete drunkenness on the home brew notorious to the area.

It was hope that kept a man sober, and as soon as hope was gone, then the will retreated and let nature take over. Unless he missed his guess, he would be senseless, sprawled across some barroom table, by early afternoon.

Two blocks later he paused opposite Jarmay Higgins's lumberyard and studied the gate.

Find out once and for all.

On this note of resolve he started across the street, hurrying through the lumberyard gate and jumping to one side at the last minute as a lumber wagon rumbled through filled with virgin pine.

"Higgins!" he shouted above the rattle of the wagon as he spied at the far end of the lumberyard the one he was looking for.

"Higgins!" Quitman called again. But still there was no response, and tired of being ignored, he ran directly up to where Higgins was checking the inventory on the new lumber and grabbed him by the shoulders and spun him about and demanded, full-voiced, "Where is she? Where is she, Higgins? Tell me or—"

Shifting his ledger book to the opposite hand, Higgins grasped Taylor Quitman by the elbow and walked him over to a patch of purple shade provided by the high facade of the lumberyard.

"She?" Higgins repeated, all innocence. "I don't know what—"

Then Taylor Quitman had had enough of lying and dissembling and didn't give a damn who was listening. He made an attempt to grab Jarmay Higgins by the throat, but the pudgy little man eluded him by jumping to one side and turning the tables on Quitman and pinning him against one of the wooden posts.

"You're drunk," Higgins said contemptuously.

"No."

"Then listen closely," Higgins muttered. "She's dead. Do you hear? That is all you need to know. Dead, Quitman, do you understand? Now if you really want to be of service to the knights, wash yourself up, get some strong coffee and then ride out to Stanhope Hall and help your good friend Burke Stanhope do his mourning. He is no worse off than he was before. What matter to him if he lost the girl in the fire or—"

Higgins broke off. Taylor Quitman tried to still his mind long enough to ask the most painful question of all.

"How, Higgins?" he murmured. "How did you—"

But he couldn't pose the question, for every time he ventured too near to the words, he saw Eve's face before him.

Higgins grinned at his lack of courage. "You don't really want to know, do you, Quitman? All you need to know is that she has gone to a better world, and the Knights of the White Camellia are safe to pursue their common goals for the good and glory of the Confederacy, praise God."

As Higgins waxed eloquent, Taylor moved away.

"Quitman, where are you going? Perhaps you'd better stay for a—"

But there was not a force on earth capable of making Taylor Quitman turn back, certainly not the arrogant voice that was following after him as he stumbled across the lumberyard, trying now to escape the shrill whine of the saw that had started up in the cutting room, and suddenly Quitman knew.

He felt something rise in his throat, though he had eaten nothing, and still the image pursued him, the thick whirling blades cutting into flesh—

With one last surge of discipline he forced his head up and knew where he was going, a place he'd passed countless times near the waterfront, a decrepit rooming house with a small saloon on the street where he could have endless bottles of barrelhouse whiskey, which in turn would produce a drunken stupor, and after that he would kill himself. How? He wasn't certain. Surely he could devise a way. He wasn't a stupid man, just a cowardly one.

There was the place he was looking for, a rundown, paint-peeling harborside establishment with the name of—

Irma Kingsley's Lodging House

Taylor Quitman hurried down the crowded, narrow sidewalk, always keeping his eye on that swinging board sign that promised an end to all human grief and woe.

* * *

Though she had yet to open her eyes, Eve fought her way up from the comforting depths of unconsciousness only to be greeted by a lingering pain on the inside of her right palm and a sense of rattling, bone-jarring movement, the wagon traveling at a high rate of speed over rough road, the thunder of horses' hooves all around her, a curious smell of clove near her face.

She felt cool hands on her forehead and realized that someone was sitting beside her. She opened her eyes and saw the same two, Violet with the short dark curly hair and Lily, tall and fair.

"There, my sweet," Lily murmured and placed something cool on her forehead. At the same time the strong smell of clove came from Violet's side in the form of a small sachet which she held under Eve's nose, and between the cold cloth and the odor of clove, Eve pushed all the way up from the safe depths of unconsciousness and decided that for a while she would have to take her chances in this world.

"Where are—"

"We're on our way to New Orleans," Lily said, her manner direct, as though aware that Eve needed answers now more than anything.

Violet leaned closer. "Are you in any pain? Your hand, I mean. Sometimes it doesn't even phase a girl. Others will be sick for weeks."

"What was—"

Violet removed the spice sachet. "It's the baptism. At least that's what Yorrick calls it. A small monogram of his initials on the inside of your hand. It simply means that you belong to him. Now."

Not likely, Eve thought.

The wagon struck something in the road and both women were hurled to the right, Violet half-flung over Eve while Lily clung to the side of the canvas and looked angrily toward the invisible driver beyond the small opening at the front of the wagon. "Nathan!" she yelled, her pretty face turning suddenly harsh.

"He can't hear you," Violet said, pulling herself off Eve. "We're late, don't you know? Yorrick said we had to make up lost time. The train leaves at six this evening, and we must be on it."

Eve listened as carefully as the rattling wagon would permit. "Train?"

"At New Orleans," Violet said. "Every summer we make this run, because it's important that we get to the higher elevations before

Christmas or we'll either be frozen in or frozen out and neither would please Yorrick, who says the only way to make money is to keep moving toward San Francisco. Have you ever seen San Francisco, Eve? It's so beautiful, isn't it, Lily? So we always leave New Orleans in late August, and generally we reach San Francisco by the turn of the new year. It's a lovely way to pass the months, isn't it, Lily?"

The two women smiled at each other across Eve's confusion. While she sensed loyalty and affection, still she didn't understand why she was here and where they were going.

"Please tell me where you're taking me and what—"

"Well, that's what we've been trying to do," both women said in choral-reading fashion.

Then Lily drew a deep breath and begged Eve to listen carefully. "We are an all-female theatrical troupe—"

"The best in the world, according to Yorrick Harp," Violet interrupted.

"Don't interrupt, Violet," Lily scolded and paused a moment to see if she would be obeyed. And was. "We have an all-female orchestra and we do recitations and excerpts from all the classics, including Shakespeare," she said with pride. "I play Gertrude in *Hamlet*. And my favorite is Viola in *Twelfth Night*. Do you know *Twelfth Night*, Eve?"

Eve was aware of her thoughts moving painfully back toward Stanhope Hall, the wood-paneled library. She even found herself thinking fondly of Madame Germaine.

"We're on tour now," Lily went on. "We will visit mining camps and cattle ranches in the West and we will be welcomed like queens. The men there call us Adamless Eves because no man is permitted onstage with us."

"Is Yorrick going to let you keep your own name?" Violet interrupted.

"I—don't—"

"He should. Don't you think that he should, Lily? Eve. Isn't she the perfect Eve? I don't think we've ever had an Eve before."

"Please, Violet. Let Eve talk. Do you understand now, Eve, where you are? Tonight we will be on the Texas-Pacific train for Dallas, then El Paso, then—"

"I love El Paso," Violet interrupted again. "There is the most marvelous man out there with the most romantic name of Emilio Santa Anna. He is good to us."

"And then Dodge City," Lily went on, giving Violet a withering look. "And then we go up through the mountains, to Leadville. Oh, it's such fun, Eve."

Her voice fell. She leaned close to Eve. "It really isn't so bad," she whispered. "All us girls are good friends and I think we love each other. None of us would have stood a chance if it hadn't been for Yorrick. The world threw us out, and Yorrick Harp picked us up. Discarded, every last one of us, by those we thought loved us. Yorrick is not a cruel father, really, although I know you don't believe me now."

Silence again. Eve struggled to understand all that Lily said.

"Eve, may I ask you a question?"

This came from Lily, whose soft hand was still smoothing Eve's forehead.

"What happened to you? I mean, how did Yorrick Harp come to find you? You're different from the rest of us. We all could see that the first time we saw you."

Eve cleared her throat and wondered how much she should tell them.

"Who is Stephen?" Violet asked.

Eve looked up. "Stephen—"

"You called out his name several times while you were asleep."

Eve bowed her head, unable to go on.

"It helps, Eve, to talk about it," Lily urged gently. "It really does. It helps immensely to remember the love."

"It's like tidying a lovely room," Violet chimed in. "Don't let anything gather dust. Keep it all brushed and polished and aired."

With this quiet urging Eve told all, from Stephen's arrival to their planned elopement, to the stranger she had encountered in the woods, to her kidnapping and imprisonment in Jarmay Higgins's loft over the cutting room, to the—

"Go on," Lily urged, as though she knew Eve had reached the hard part.

And Eve tried, but she could not go on, for she suddenly smelled him again, felt his weight upon her, all the horrible sensations still so alive. Then she was crying, and Lily was holding her and Violet was smoothing back her hair, and both were urging her to cry, for tears were a healing balm.

"Better?" Violet inquired a few moments later. She produced a pink lace handkerchief and handed it to Eve, who still suffered spasms of tears that racked her breathing and left her feeling like a small child.

She took the handkerchief and lay back against the pillows, feeling spent.

"Lily," she whispered. "What happens when we reach New Orleans?"

Lily smiled. "Chaos. That's what happens. We have to pack all these trunks, these musical instruments onto two railroad cars, plus all of us. It takes some doing, I can promise you, but it's great fun watching Yorrick organize something that every year seems to defy organization. Still somehow it always gets done."

She patted Eve's hand. "Get some rest, pretty Eve. I'm so glad Yorrick found you."

What happens in New Orleans?

Pure chaos.

Then a plan began to take shape. Escape. Her last chance. In the chaos of New Orleans. Her father had friends there. She could find shelter and protection, she was certain of it. All she had to do was wait for the proper moment. Then what a simple matter it would be to slip away. She had nothing against Lily and Violet. They had been most kind to her. But she didn't belong with these people, and she certainly didn't belong to Yorrick Harp.

Suddenly a thought stopped her. "Lily," she called out. "I have no clothes."

"Don't worry, dearest. Yorrick provides us with pretty new clothes to wear when we board the train. He says we are walking advertisements for our own theatrical troupe. Ours are there in that trunk. You rest now. I'll get them for you when it's time."

Eve closed her eyes and tried to make her face a blank despite her rising excitement. Then her escape plan would work. It would simply be a matter of choosing the best moment, then slipping away and inquiring of a passerby the way to the Forrest residence or the Fouchons, both men being writers who had visited Stanhope Hall in the recent past, who knew her and who adored her father and who would gladly extend the protection of their homes to her. She was certain of it.

It *would* work. She would make it work. She had to if she ever wanted to see Stephen again or her parents, or David, or dear Christine, and, most important, to tell her father that there were many men in Mobile whom he had sadly misjudged.

Now part of her mind lingered enjoyably on the name Stephen, effortlessly recreating the face and the voice to go with it. Would he still want her? The thought proved too painful to consider.

Though her eyes were closed and she appeared to be asleep, her mind and spirit were soaring with plans for her successful escape and ultimately her sweet homecoming down the long avenue of live oaks, Mama and Papa running to greet her, Christine and David following behind. Paris Boley would be there, and old Florence weeping into her apron, and Sis Liz—

And standing on the uppermost step in his shirtsleeves, his eyes dark with worry, though there would be a smile on his face, would be Stephen. He would fix her with a gaze so filled with love that she would be unable to move until he took her in his arms and held her and vowed to protect her from all future threats and hazards that she might ever encounter in this random world.

 ## Mobile

By noon Taylor Quitman was ensconced at the corner table in Irma Kingsley's saloon, working his way through his second crock of local brew, a barrelhouse whiskey made roughly of black bone meal, gunpowder, creek water and turpentine.

He had kicked off his boots beneath the table and now felt grit from the street through his stockinged feet, still felt everything far too acutely.

He drained the second crock and felt the good numbing in his throat and closed his eyes and wished the sensation would extend to his brain, particularly to the area where memory resided.

He simply hadn't had enough then, that was all. And he had no fear of being recognized, not in this quarter of the city. He was not likely to encounter any colleagues or clients here. The only other "patrons" in this disreputable place were an unappetizing twosome seated at the center table, less than five feet away: a tall gaunt man in the faded gray uniform of the Confederacy, missing his left leg, and his companion, a dark, short, swarthy man, perhaps of Italian blood, who carried a constantly chattering pet monkey on his shoulder. Both men were filthy beyond description, though both appeared to be in high spirits. Apparently there was a celebration of some sort.

The proprietress, Irma Kingsley, a faded blossom if ever Taylor Quitman had seen one, appeared to be bringing out the best for the disreputable two, a bottle of crimson port and two steaming bowls of shrimp chowder and a platter of golden rounds of corn bread.

The odor was appealing and Taylor Quitman was tempted, but food was the last thing he wanted now.

Eve Stanhope dead.

As the refrain filtered through his feverish head like a never-ending funeral dirge, he still couldn't believe it. Briefly he closed his eyes in an attempt to block out the mindless chatter coming from the near table, the men heartily consuming the food as though the last time they'd eaten had been Christmas.

"Let me see the money again," the Kingsley woman demanded, hands on her ample hips, sweat pouring off her face.

The short dark man grinned a sly grin. "Don't you trust us, Irma? We're just your best customers."

"Best, my ass. Biggest free-loaders, you mean; have been for as long as I can remember. Now, let me see your money again. Put it on the table in clear sight and leave it there so when you two get through, I can take my share and have done with you."

For several moments both men continued to eat with crude haste, as though they were fearful that the food and drink would be whisked away before they were finished with it.

When Irma Kingsley demanded again with one shrill wail, "Well?" the one-legged soldier reluctantly put down his spoon and dug into his tattered coat pocket and placed a thick wad of bills on the table. A few moments later the other man followed suit. From where Taylor Quitman sat, the bills looked like singles, though still the thickness of each roll suggested twenty, perhaps thirty dollars apiece—a fortune for the likes of those two.

As the monkey stole a round of corn bread and ate contentedly on his master's shoulder, Irma Kingsley leaned close, clearly impressed, and reached down to touch the money.

Suddenly a dark expression crossed her face. "Not evil money, is it?" she demanded. "Not stolen?"

"No, my dear Mrs. Kingsley," the one-legged soldier said with surprising civility, his voice cultivated. "It's honestly earned and paid to us by a remarkable gentleman in exchange for a job well done."

Irma Kingsley looked skeptical. "Who would hire the likes of you two?"

"Don't know his name," the man with the monkey said. "Didn't ask. Don't care."

"Where did you meet him?"

"Roaming God's green earth, like we always do, lookin' for an honest wage."

"Lookin' for someone to roll, that's what you look for." Irma Kingsley stepped closer to the table, clearly threatening. "Now tell me the truth, one or the both of you—if you expect to finish them bowls of chowder intact."

Impressive bitch. Taylor Quitman was forced to admit that, even though he sided with the two men.

"All right, Irma," the man with the monkey began and shifted the monkey from his shoulder to the table, a gesture that seemed to displease the one-legged soldier, for abruptly he moved his platter to the far end of the table, as though to put as much distance as possible between himself and the monkey.

Taylor Quitman decided to watch the circus for as long as it amused him to do so. Most distracting, the human race, particularly these people who inhabited the nether world.

"—and so this fancy gentleman just comes riding up out of the dawn's darkness and calls out—"

"What were you two doing out so early?" Irma Kingsley demanded.

"Abraham Lincoln had to take a piss," the short man said bluntly. He shoved the food in with one finger, wiped his mouth with the back of his hand and grinned up at the belly laugh coming from Irma Kingsley, and even the reluctant half-smile coming from the wounded veteran.

Taylor Quitman looked out of the window, beginning to grow weary of the threesome and their tasteless humor.

"So, like I was saying, this large wagon stopped and this gentleman said he needed two soldiers of the world, that's the way he put it, two soldiers of the world, for just one hour's labor and he would pay us handsomely if we earned it."

"And what was this important job he wanted you to do?" Irma Kingsley demanded sarcastically.

As they chewed contentedly, the one-legged soldier held up a restraining hand and swallowed and said simply, "Trunks."

"Trunks?" Irma inquired, straddling a near chair with her full skirt in a mannish fashion.

The short dark man nodded. "Trunks." Then he added, "He wanted us to help him pick up some trunks."

"Where?"

"At Jarmay Higgins's Lumberyard."

Taylor Quitman heard the name and looked in that direction as though someone had called out to him.

"And what did old Higgins have to do with all this?" Irma Kingsley asked, leaning her calloused elbows upon the chair.

"He'd put in some new trunk bottoms," the soldier replied.

The other man giggled. "He had put in more than new bottoms. We carried out the trunks, all right, and everything else that was in 'em."

"And what was in them?" Irma demanded.

"A girl," the soldier said. "Or what was left of her."

Taylor Quitman looked up.

Irma Kingsley dragged her chair closer. "Dead?" she whispered.

The soldier shook his head. "No, not dead, though well used. Old Higgins seemed anxious to get her out of his lumberyard, and the man seemed more than willing to take her."

Slowly, like pieces of hurled jigsaw, fragments of the conversation came floating over to Taylor Quitman. He looked over at the three talking quietly together. For some reason their voices had fallen.

"Well, what were we to do?" the one-legged soldier hissed.

"Gentlemen," Taylor Quitman called out and rose on unsteady legs. Grasping the edge of the table, he bore the weight of three surprised and upturned faces. "I couldn't help but overhear," he began. "Whatever your earnings of last night, I'll double them if you'll repeat your tale in full for me."

Belatedly Taylor Quitman regretted his haste. Surely he didn't think for a moment they were speaking of Eve Stanhope. Eve Stanhope was dead. Hadn't Jarmay Higgins told him so? But could Jarmay Higgins be trusted? On any matter?

"Please, gentlemen," he repeated, and managed a step in their direction and was pleased to see that his generous offer had attracted their attention. "What was your fee for the hour's labor?"

"No fee, sir," the short man stammered. "The gentleman gave us twenty dollars to hoist the trunks into his wagon."

"Each?" Taylor Quitman asked, his mind cold sober now.

"No. Together," the soldier said and slowly rose on his one good leg and extended a hand to Taylor Quitman along with a quiet introduction. "My name is Captain William Willing and this is Housy Dunbar and this is Irma Kingsley."

Taylor Quitman nodded to all three. "Then twenty dollars each," he said, "if you will tell me precisely what you did early this morning at Jarmay Higgins's Lumberyard, and what it was that you saw there."

"Are you with the marshal's office?" the man named Housy Dunbar asked suspiciously.

"No."

"Then who?"

"That is not part of the bargain," Taylor Quitman said, a degree of sternness in his voice.

Captain Willing nodded. "Then sit down, sir. It's nothing to us, except your offer which will enable us to pay off this good woman so that we can impose upon her hospitality for another year."

The monkey chattered nervously.

"Shut him up," Captain Willing snapped.

Housy Dunbar hoisted the monkey onto another table, gave him a sizable piece of corn bread, and as the animal ate contentedly, Captain Willing spoke first, his manner direct.

"The man's name was Yorrick Harp. I remember well the name because it suited him—theatrical, broad."

"What happened?" Taylor Quitman asked.

"Well, he told us to climb aboard the wagon and he drove us at a merry speed through the early-morning streets of Mobile and we came to a rattling halt at Higgins's Lumberyard. They seemed to know each other—"

"Who?"

"Higgins and Yorrick Harp," the captain said. "Anyway, he ushered us into a large cutting room."

"Were you alone?"

"Of course. It wasn't quite dawn yet. The workers hadn't arrived."

"Go on."

"Well, in the back room we found the trunks, two of them, quite large. I had a similar one during the war. Lost it someplace . . ."

"The trunks," Quitman prompted, trying to keep the man on track.

"Weren't empty." Housy Dunbar grinned. "Least one wasn't, was it, Captain?"

Captain Willing shook his head. "The two of them, Harp and Higgins, walked away from us, but we could see plainly enough."

"What?" Taylor Quitman asked and felt his heart pounding. "A woman."

"A girl," Housy Dunbar corrected.

"How old?" Quitman asked.

Captain Willing shrugged. "Sixteen, seventeen, hard to tell. She was—"

"Naked." Housy Dunbar grinned. "As the day she was born."

Taylor Quitman closed his eyes for a moment and then opened them. "Was she dead?" he asked bluntly.

"Dead? No," Housy Dunbar said. "Not unless the dead do rise. For that pretty thing stood all the way up with Mr. Harp's help, and it was Harp who gave her his cloak to cover herself and put her in the back of the wagon along with the trunks and took her off Jarmay Higgins's hands, who seemed to want more than anything else in this world to be rid of her."

Taylor Quitman couldn't quite believe what he was hearing. Eve Stanhope not dead? Eve alive, in the company of a man named Yorrick Harp?

A few more questions. To confirm her identity. To be absolutely certain. "What color was her hair, sir?" Taylor Quitman asked of the old officer.

"Fair, sir, golden as the dawn itself."

"Eyes?"

"Didn't see the eyes. She kept them down, like she was ill."

"And was she?"

"I don't know, sir. She looked—abused, sir, if you know what I mean."

Taylor Quitman tried to swallow his outrage.

"Sir, if it'll help," offered Housy Dunbar, "the man, Yorrick Harp, asked her name as he was placing her in the back of the wagon."

Taylor Quitman blinked at the simple statement, as though he knew that in the next few moments he would be tested all over again, for courage, for character.

"And?" he asked, clinging to the edge of the table.

"She told him," Housy Dunbar announced brightly. "Eve, sir. Her name was Eve."

Taylor Quitman closed his eyes and covered his face with his hands. Then not dead. Now what should he do?

"Do we get the double payment, sir?" It was Housy Dunbar, clearly not forgetting the bargain that had started this whole account.

With trembling hands Taylor Quitman reached inside his vest pocket and withdrew his money clip. Without looking, he peeled off two bills and dropped them onto the table.

He heard voices all around, but they seemed to be coming at him from a distance.

"Sir, this is too much—"

One voice drifted after him as he started toward the door, but it wasn't significant enough to turn around and acknowledge.

The true significance was in the fact that he had chosen this pest hole in which to drink himself into oblivion. And the true significance was that Eve Stanhope had survived the night and the brutalities visited on her by Jarmay Higgins, though to what new horrors she had been taken, Taylor Quitman had no idea and didn't even want to guess.

He would not end his life here today for the simple fact that apparently he had a task yet to do, a very important task.

"Sir, are you all right?"

The voice followed him through the smoky room and all the way out into the street, where a hot sun struck him in the face and left him blinded and sobered, head pounding, grateful, yet guilty.

Three words continuously resounded in his ear above the rattling commerce of the street.

She—is—alive.

Now he knew he must find the courage to relay those three words to one man.

 Stanhope Hall

Burke stood over Mary's bed and gazed down at her. He was so worried. She hadn't responded to anything or anyone in two days. Now he reached for her hand.

"Oh, my darling," he mourned and grasped her close and wondered if he had lost three in the fire at Fan Cottage; two to the flames, one later to madness.

But the thought was intolerable. With renewed conviction he lifted her in his arms and walked with her out into the corridor toward the stairs, thinking only if he could get her to the light and sun and air, she would regain her energy and her wits and after a few skipped beats, life for all of them would move on.

Then he heard voices coming from below. He lowered her to her feet, his arms still around her in firm support. "Come on, Mary, someone is here. I want you to come with me."

"Tired—let me—"

"No, you're not tired. Come on. Let's go see together. Lean on me."

She seemed so weak that he was almost tempted to carry her back to her bed chamber. But he saw again that awful vacancy in her eyes and he tightened his grip on her and half-carried, half-supported her down the stairs, listening all the time to the muddle of voices coming from the front gallery. Suddenly he heard the front door slam shut, heard someone shouting his name.

"Hurry," he whispered to Mary, who apparently had heard the shouts as well. "It's Stephen."

They reached the bottom of the staircase together and suffered a near-collision with Stephen Eden, who, after having apparently searched unsuccessfully in every room on the first floor, was just starting up the stairs at breakneck speed, exhibiting more energy, more aggression than Burke had seen since—

"There you are," Stephen gasped. "Please, sir, you must come."

"What is it?"

"A man," Stephen Eden managed, sweat pouring off his forehead.

"What man?"

"A friend, yours. The lawyer. Name of Quitman—"

Taylor Quitman? What was Taylor Quitman doing here? "He says, sir, that Eve is not dead, is alive, and he has proof—"

Burke gaped, incapable for the moment of saying anything. For a brief few seconds he held Stephen Eden fixed in his vision, trying to see through the cruel words. Had the young man lost *his* mind? What would make him indulge in such a poor joke?

Mary—

He glanced behind him to see the same expression on Mary's face: one of disbelief.

"He's outside, sir, please come. *Please.*"

The second plea was accompanied by a firm grasp of his arm as Stephen Eden literally dragged him forward, his words echoing in Burke's head.

Eve is not dead.

Then he saw him through the front door, standing at the bottom of the porch, Taylor Quitman, looking as disheveled as he'd ever seen him, his lathered horse grazing a distance away.

"There he is," Stephen Eden insisted, close at his side. "Get him to tell you what he just told me. Go on."

Slowly Burke started across the gallery, aware of Mary directly behind him on one side, Stephen on the other, doubly aware of Taylor Quitman, who, upon seeing them, appeared to dissolve into new weakness.

"Taylor," Burke demanded. "What is this about Eve?"

Slowly the man looked up. "She is alive, Burke, not dead in the fire. I am prepared to swear to it."

For a moment there was no sound in this world save Mary's outcry and the thunder of Burke's heart beating.

 New Orleans

Eve kept losing track of where she was. When she awakened in mid-afternoon, in New Orleans, she thought she was back in her bed chamber at Stanhope Hall, for she smelled lavender water and assumed that old Florence had filled her pitcher in preparation for her bath after her afternoon nap.

But then the rocking wagon reminded her that she was not at home in Stanhope Hall, that the girl who once had lived there had died and there was a new creature who now inhabited Eve's body.

"Hello there, my pretty."

She turned on her pallet and looked up at the voice and saw the

woman named Lily, whose kind face now stared out of a most fashionable bonnet, the whole vision fashionable—a dark green traveling
gown trimmed in peacock feathers, and a summer parasol clasped in
her hands.

"How beautiful," Eve murmured.

"Nonsense. We all shall pale in comparison to you. Look what Yorrick Harp has found for you to wear."

She stood back to reveal a gown that resembled a summer cloud,
white dotted swiss with the most delicate tint of blue, a low-scooped
neckline and puffed sleeves to match the expanse of the skirt itself—
the most beautiful gown Eve had ever seen. She pulled herself up to a
sitting position.

From behind the screen peered Violet, hairbrush in hand, a corset
tightened about her tiny waist and lavender petticoats billowing in
the narrow dressing area.

"One minute, my sweet, and the tub shall be yours—fresh warm
lavender water. Then Lily and I shall transform you into a vision.
Half an hour until we board the train, and Yorrick wants you looking
your very best."

"Hungry?" Lily inquired and stood directly over her.

Eve shook her head, though in truth she was starved. "Are we in
New Orleans?" she asked.

"We are indeed." Lily smiled and reached into a wicker basket and
handed her a hard roll and a piece of yellow cheese. "Eat, my dearest.
You will need your strength. Though tonight, if Yorrick is true to
form, we will have a banquet on board the train. He says that eating a
good meal on a train as it hurtles through the night is one of life's
greatest pleasures, and we all shall indulge. For now . . . ."

She thrust the roll and cheese toward Eve, and Eve took them and
in private agreed yes, she did need strength, if she was to make an
effective escape in the next few hours.

A few moments later Violet emerged from behind the screen, looking as elegant as Lily in a gown the color of her name, deep rich
lavender with a perky bonnet made of violets that sat well forward on
her forehead, defying gravity. In contrast to these two splendid creatures, Eve felt plain and discarded.

She looked up at the gown hanging on one of the hooks overhead,
the gown designated as hers, and though she found it beautiful, she
might have wished for something more subdued, something that
would enable her to blend in with the crowds at the railway station.

Still all she needed was five minutes to make her way from the
station and seek help from the first constable she met, or else find the
way by herself to the home of her father's friends. Of course word

would be dispatched immediately to Stanhope Hall, and a rescue party would come for her, composed of her father and perhaps even Stephen.

Now in the distance she heard the scream of a steam engine and assumed they were nearing the station.

"Hurry, Eve. We are responsible. Swig down your cider and hop into the tub. We'll be waiting to help."

Quickly Eve swallowed the cider to wash down the cheese and roll and, still carrying the coverlet to hide her nakedness, slipped behind the screen.

"Keep your hand dry," Lily warned. "Burns don't like water. Sponge everything else, and hurry."

She did as she was told and reached for the large sponge and dunked it into the fragrant water and stood on one leg and let the warm pleasing water wash over her.

"What do we do when we reach the station?" she called out, trying to make her voice light and innocent.

"We present ourselves for Yorrick's approval, then we board the train and find our seats. Not to worry; we'll take care of you. Yorrick has given us complete instructions."

Eve moved the sponge back and forth between her breasts. On her left nipple she observed faint purple teeth marks, Jarmay Higgins's panting and sweating atop her—

She ran the sponge around her neck, lifting her long hair. Hurry. Alone, she felt very vulnerable. She needed the safe chatter of Violet and Lily to keep her thoughts from the past.

"Ready," she called out. "I've no towel."

"We have the towels. Come."

At Lily's insistence, Eve moved out from behind the screen and into the soft towels they held extended. She felt them pat her shoulders and back and at the same time drew gently on her shoulders and softly admonished, "Stand straight. It lifts your breasts."

She looked up to see Violet coming at her with a huge pink puff smelling like roses. A few moments later her skin had been smoothed and whitened with the good-smelling talcum, her hair swept up and anchored with a temporary clip.

As the fussing continued, Eve closed her eyes and submitted to everything and took advantage of this interim when nothing was demanded of her to think further about her escape.

"Stand still, Eve. You're wriggling."

The soft reprimand came from Violet, whose eyes caught on Eve's. "You're missing home, aren't you?" Violet said with admirable perception. "You don't have to answer. I know that expression."

Eve was aware of the wagon slowing to a halt. The sudden cessation of noise and movement seemed to jar Violet back to some memory of the past.

"It makes no difference," she said beneath her breath.

"Violet—"

The comforting voice came from Lily, who reached across Eve and found Violet's hand.

"Well, it doesn't make any difference," Violet insisted. "All I want Eve to know is that no matter how much you miss home and family, it will do you no good, because you see, after what's happened to you, your family no longer exists for you. They've no place for you now. You'd only be an embarrassment. So what you must do is stop looking backward."

"Violet, enough, please."

"No, I want her to understand everything now. I want to spare her the days—the months—of agony that I went through thinking they would come for me—*he* would come for me. For they knew where I was, you see. I sent word and I know he received it."

Eve listened to the grim tale and closed her eyes and bowed her head. Not that she hadn't already thought about what Violet had said, but she was certain that Stephen would be different.

"Better?" Lily smiled.

Eve kept silent. She felt Violet behind her, expertly wielding a hairbrush on her tangled hair while outside the wagon the noise seemed to be increasing: shouts, male and female blending; horses whinnying; and the constant chorus of hissing steam engines.

Also from outside the wagon came a voice Eve immediately recognized: Yorrick Harp.

"Did she survive the journey, our rare new blossom?"

"Indeed she did, Yorrick," Lily replied.

"Good. I knew she would. That one has destiny written all over her. Have you seen it yet?"

Lily and Violet exchanged an indulgent smile. "Yes, Yorrick, we've seen it. Destiny written all over her."

"Then prepare her," came the melodramatic command from beyond the wagon. "In half an hour we depart. I shall return to fetch her and escort her personally to her seat on the train. Do you understand?"

"Yes, Yorrick. She will be ready."

As the voices swirled around her, Eve felt her heart sinking. If she was to be held a prisoner here until Yorrick Harp returned for her, then there would be no chance to escape, unless—

"We must hurry," Lily advised. Violet disappeared behind the screen and returned with a chemise and pantaloons and a waist girdle.

"Have you ever worn one of these?" Lily asked, holding up for Eve's inspection the waist girdle.

"No," she replied to Lily and Violet, who instructed her to lift both arms and hold onto the cross bar overhead. This she did, and she felt the corset go around her mid-section, both Lily and Violet moving behind her now, tightening the cross-ties through the hooks and eyes, the corset shutting off her air.

"Enough," she gasped and quickly let go of the cross bar. As her arms dropped, she felt the corset cutting into the lower half of her breasts.

Despite these discomforts she turned slowly to face Violet and Lily and saw a look of wonder on their faces.

"Good Lord," Lily gasped. "Look. I've never seen a waist that tiny in my life. A man's hands could reach—"

"Beautiful," Violet nodded, assessing Eve in the manner of an artist assessing her creation.

"You *can* breathe, can't you?" Lily asked, encircling her, still admiring.

Eve smiled. Breathing was easier now, her body adjusting to the confines of the corset.

As the two women smoothed down the billowing petticoats, Eve watched, fascinated, in the pier glass, studying her face, which in many ways was a stranger's face. It certainly wasn't the little-girl face that had looked back at her from her mirrored dressing table at Stanhope Hall. This woman seemed older, sadder, certainly more frightened.

"Come, we must hurry," Violet urged. "We have her hair to do yet, and her makeup."

Without further delay Eve felt clouds of soft material swirl about her head, felt loving hands guide her through the proper openings until at last she reemerged and watched, fascinated, as Lily and Violet fastened each small button along her wrists. Then both commenced to work on the long row of tiny covered buttons, each button molding the dress to her figure, pulling it snug about her waist.

As the hairbrush scraped against her neck, she looked up to see Violet's expert fingers whisk her long blond hair around and around, a smooth french knot emerging from the blur of fingers and tortoiseshell clips.

Then a leather case appeared in Violet's hand, and Eve was told to close her eyes, to open them, to close her mouth, to lift her chin, to look right, to look left, to moisten her lips, to stand still and not move.

And yet another transformation took place, and Violet emerged from behind the screen with a stylish low-brimmed ivory felt hat with one long graceful white ostrich plume, the most beautiful hat Eve had ever seen. She lowered her head as Violet fixed it in place and anchored it with a hat pin, while at the same time Lily handed her a parasol in matching dotted swiss ruffle, and both Lily and Violet stood back.

"I have never seen anything as beautiful," Violet whispered.

Lily agreed. "Look, please look for yourself."

Eve did, and she was convinced that when she hadn't been looking, the three of them had been joined by a fourth, for she had no idea who that elegant lady was who stared back at her from the glass. She bore a slight resemblance to Mama, but a younger Mama.

"Well?" Violet smiled. "What do you think?"

Eve shook her head. "I don't know who she is."

Lily and Violet laughed. "All this and honesty too. Oh, my dearest Eve, you'll do well. Now who shall go and fetch old Yorrick? I want to see his face."

"I'll go," Lily volunteered and stripped off the large white apron that had protected her own lovely gown.

"I really don't mind going myself," Violet interrupted. "I need to check on my trunks."

Still staring at the woman in the pier glass, Eve detected a longing on both their parts to leave the wagon, however briefly, for whatever purpose.

"Both of you go," she urged. She tried to keep her voice light, tried to convey to both Lily and Violet a sense of ease, of nothing to be concerned about.

"Please," she repeated, stroking the ostrich feather on her bonnet. "I'll be fine. I'd like a few moments alone to study your—artistry, to see how it was done so that I can do it for myself next time."

After several moments Violet and Lily gave in. "Only a minute. We want to be here when Yorrick comes to see you."

Again Eve smiled, hoping to convey that they could trust her completely, all the time trying to still her heart long enough to make immediate plans. Yet what plans could she make? She had no idea where she was. She only knew where she wanted to be. Still she had to try.

"It will be good for her." Lily smiled. "A few moments alone. You see, we are responsible for our own trunks and we both left ours three wagons behind."

"We'll just check." Violet nodded. "And we'll be back in a wink. We promise."

Then the canvas flap was lowered and Eve was alone, her heart pounding. Hurry. Just leave. Now. Calmly, as though she were merely out for a stroll, she lifted the canvas flap, peering out at the wagons, which she observed had been guided onto a grassy island. All around she saw the commerce of New Orleans, saw to the left dozens of men forming a solid line that stretched between the grassy island and the imposing yellow sandstone railway station across the street. These men had formed a human chain designed to transport the trunks and the cased musical instruments, a never-ending supply of bags and baggage, enough to outfit all twenty members of Yorrick Harp's All-Female Theatrical Troupe many times over.

From the wagon she saw children running back and forth among the men working. At the intersection nearest the railway station she saw sandwich vendors and lemonade vendors and flower and fruit vendors. All around on the grassy island she saw the ladies of the troupe, beautifully gowned, their parasols lifted in defense against the hot afternoon sun, a few flirting with the fancy gentlemen who apparently had come to watch the boarding party, others chatting softly in the cool shade of near trees, waiting for the signal to board the train for the trip west.

West. Stephen's destination, and it was to have been hers as well.

For a moment fresh grief threatened to undo her. *Then leave! Now!*

And she did, checking the immediate area for curious eyes. While there was activity all about, no one seemed terribly interested in her. Carefully she made her way down the steps that led to the ground. Once she was down, she opened her parasol and, using it as a shield, glanced about to see if she had attracted any unwanted attention.

Not yet. The movement of the other women was a blessing, for now she was merely one of them, stretching her legs, taking the late-afternoon air before boarding the train.

"Good afternoon to you, miss."

The male voice cut down on her from above and she noticed a man on the high driver's seat, his face obscured by the angle of his brimmed hat.

Quickly she lowered her head and hoisted the parasol higher. "Good afternoon," she called out and decided that he probably was the driver or a stable boy, decided it might be wise not to wait to find out.

Warning herself not to increase her speed, to do nothing to call attention to herself, she walked leisurely across the grassy island toward the curb. There she saw the congestion of foot traffic outside the large doors of the railway station. She thought if she could only make it to that throng of people, it would be a simple matter to move with

them, in what direction it mattered little, only as long as it was in the
opposite direction from Yorrick Harp's wagons.

Now she proceeded on across the cobblestones, daring to think that
she had accomplished it, for she was certain that no one had followed
her. She moved slowly through the throngs of travelers, enduring
nothing more than male eyes that seemed unable to pass her without
a lingering inspection.

But still she kept her eyes down and only looked up to avoid direct
collision. She moved quickly through the crowd, feeling safer with
every step, the shaded portico of the railway station straight ahead
now. Surely on the other side, she'd find a row of carriages for hire.

Then there they were. She lifted her skirts and hurried toward the
carriages and stopped at the first and addressed the driver, a plump
gray-haired man who looked kindly down on her. That look of kindness was almost her undoing.

"Drive away from this place," she murmured, "and I will give you
specific directions later."

Without another word she opened the door and stepped up and
closed it behind her and quickly drew the small black curtain.

With closed eyes and held breath she waited for the cab to start
forward. She thought she heard a voice outside the door but did not
dare look, and she thought she felt the cab give with additional
weight as though the driver had taken on another passenger in his
high seat.

Suddenly she sat up, alert to new dangers. Why the carriage
moving so slowly? Carefully she lifted one corner of the black curtain
and saw the scene outside the window unchanged. All the driver had
done was circle the grassy island where the wagons were being un-
loaded. She could still see the strolling ladies of the troupe, the human
chain passing trunk after trunk into the open bay of a baggage car.

"Driver!"

As she called out, she reached the door handle, ready to make herself plainly understood this time, but the door handle would not give
in any direction.

She heard the carriage come to a halt and listened closely for outside noises and heard nothing but a new silence that caused her flesh
to crawl.

There were threats outside and she wanted no part of them. She
knew that her escape plan had failed, that she was back where she had
started and perhaps worse off than before.

With trembling hands she lifted the window curtain until she saw
the scene complete, a terrifying scene of silently staring faces, all the
ladies of the troupe forming a silent circle around the cab.

Then suddenly the circle moved back and Yorrick Harp appeared, dressed in black. He reached a hand up and opened the cab door and brought his sad face close to hers. "Why were you running away?" he asked.

She tried to draw a breath to calm her fear. "I—want to go home."

"There is no home for you now but here with me."

"No. My mother and my father—"

"You have no mother and father. You are dead to them and they are dead to you."

"Please, let me go—"

Suddenly Yorrick Harp grabbed her by the wrist and led her from the carriage. Though there was traffic moving on the street less than fifty feet away, Eve could not see it, and it certainly could not see her as she was led to a position in the center of the circle, where foolishly she continued to struggle against the viselike grip that Yorrick Harp had on her wrists.

"Those who garbed her come forward," he commanded. "This is all wrong. We must deal with the child first and then later perhaps the woman will blossom."

Eve saw Lily and Violet emerge from the crowd. She tried to make eye contact, but neither woman would look directly at her. Wordlessly they now began to remove the bonnet with the ostrich feather plume, and then the parasol, and Violet moved behind and Eve felt her fingers moving down her back, the billowing dotted swiss falling free from her shoulders until it lay about her feet.

Still the women pressed closer as the corset was loosed and then the chemise rapidly pulled over her head, her hair coming down in the process. Yorrick at last approached with a plain dark blue muslin dress, and while Lily and Violet held her still, he dropped it over her head and shoulders, where it fell shapeless about her.

Eve bowed her head to conceal her tears of mortification. She was aware of Yorrick Harp now forcing her down to her knees, wondering when the humiliation would end.

Out of the corner of her eye she saw Lily and Violet gathering the strewn garments, folding them lovingly as though they were injured children.

Then Eve was aware of new activity in the vicinity of her feet and ankles, felt something hard and cold being fitted around first her left ankle, her right ankle drawn closer and a similar bond attached. Through blurred and terrified eyes she saw leg irons, a heavy chain connecting the two circles of no more than seven inches.

A man Eve had never seen before locked the leg irons into place, and Yorrick Harp ordered, "Rise," and stood back.

Struggling for breath through her grief and embarrassment, Eve felt the cold metal cutting into her ankles.

"Rise!" Yorrick Harp shouted again and again she struggled, fighting against the confinement of the leg irons. Once up, she tried to take a step for balance, but the connecting chain was too short and she tripped and fell to her knees.

She felt movement on either side, felt hands lifting her up, steadying her, a woman's voice, Lily's, urging, "Lean on us. Take small steps. The irons will permit them."

Without looking, she did as she was told and allowed the women to lead her where they wanted in this shuffling hobbled movement, and after a few moments she looked up to find herself standing before Yorrick Harp.

"Look at me, child," his deep voice entreated. And when she didn't, she felt his hand beneath her chin, raising it gently until she found herself staring into his face, his eyes heavy with sorrow, as though he had been struck by a tragedy of unbearable proportions.

"How have I offended you?" he asked quietly. "Except to rescue you from violent death? The man Jarmay Higgins, being both a coward and a villain, sought me out and I gave you back your life. If that is an offense, I'm sorry."

He waited. "Well, never mind, we'll talk later," he said at last, weary, as though he had been made to suffer a great deal.

"You *will* love me before we're finished," he whispered, with remarkable gentleness, "and you will learn to obey me in all matters, I swear it, for I am your loving father now who wants only—"

"You are not my father," she said, keeping her eyes down, uncaring what happened to her. "I don't know you and have no desire to know you, and I swear to God I will never feel anything for you but contempt and loathing."

For several moments the echo of her words seemed to reverberate throughout the circle.

"I am sorry, dearest," Yorrick Harp murmured. "Ladies, escort her onto the train, my private coach, and give her anything she wants, except her freedom. I'll join you later. She'll be difficult, but the best are always difficult."

Then Eve, with the support of Lily and Violet, tried to walk with the leg irons, a harsh confinement that limited her steps to no more than six inches, reducing her gait to a shuffle. She would have fallen countless times had it not been for the support of Lily and Violet, who offered encouragement with each step.

"Take small steps," Lily whispered.

"On your tiptoes, it helps."

Eve continued at her shuffling gait through the gaping crowds. At last she saw the massive train, coach after coach stretching into the distance, the enormous engine up ahead like a black shiny monster emitting steam.

"Up you go," Lily and Violet urged and half-lifted, half-dragged her up onto the platform steps and into the narrow corridor of the coach itself.

As Violet held back the heavy red drapes, Lily escorted Eve into a cozy den of a railway coach with red embossed velvet everywhere—in the window curtains, the draped couch, the red carpet. It was a luxurious nest, quite spacious, considering the limitations of the coach itself.

"Here, sit," Violet instructed. Eve obeyed, eyes down and focused on the despicable leg irons.

Now she was truly lost to all that she had known and loved. She would never escape again, would never even be given a chance to try. All she knew was that she understood nothing, must now hope for nothing, expect nothing, dream of nothing, plan for nothing. She knew with a certainty that caused her shoulders to collapse, along with her spirits, that she would never see her mother again or her father, or her sister or her brother, would never see Stanhope Hall again, would never see her animals again, her household friends, would never see the long avenue of live oaks or the green lawn, never see the ice pond, the lilac hedge, Stephen—

Suddenly, unable to help herself, she bent over and wept into her hands, aware for the first time of the size and scope of her loss—an entire world.

A few minutes later she heard Lily and Violet leave, heard no further movement in the coach, just her heaving sobs, the sense that she was drowning in her own grief, and something else. A presence close by, somewhere—

Slowly she looked up and saw Yorrick Harp seated on the couch opposite her, his huge face a contortion of pain as though he were suffering along with her. In his hand he held a perfect white rose and now extended it to her and waited patiently for her to take it.

"No flower name for you," he said with a smile. "No Lily, no Rose, no Violet. You are and shall forever remain simply Eve."

Eve refused to accept either the flower or his "gift" of the name to her. What gift? She had been born Eve. Of course she would remain Eve.

She moved further into the corner of the couch, and a few moments later she felt the jarring movements of the train, felt the iron wheels shudder and turn, felt the coach itself in creaky movement.

"Now then," Yorrick pronounced, still holding the white rose. "Let me tell you of your future, what is ahead for you and what will be expected of you. Will you listen to me?"

Did she have a choice?

"Our itinerary is Dallas, then El Paso, then Santa Fe, then Dodge City and points west. We will stop in most towns along the way, and we will perform for audiences of varying sizes, under all sorts of conditions, some splendid, some not so splendid. The audiences will be all male, always all male. Our duty is simple, to remind those men of their wives and mothers and daughters and sisters. Occasionally you will be asked to dance with the patrons, nothing more, unless you elect to do so. Is that clear?"

She was only half-listening.

"Have you ever seen San Francisco, Eve, my dearest?"

She did not reply.

"Oh, you will love San Francisco." Yorrick Harp smiled. "Heaven on earth. The most beautiful theaters and the warmest audience you've ever seen. They're waiting for you, Eve."

She looked out the window. The train was picking up speed, the landscape a blur.

"And I do apologize for those," he murmured, pointing down at the leg irons. "I must convince you that you belong to me, and you must understand that, and as soon as you do, life's natural and joyous rhythms will return and we all can get on with the difficult task of trying to figure out a way to survive this bizarre and unpredictable world. Do you understand? Please say that you do."

She glanced at him and assumed he wanted an answer. When she refused to give him one, he reached over and placed the white rose on the seat beside her and patted her lovingly on the shoulder and whispered, "You must learn one very important lesson and learn it quickly, my pretty Eve, and that is simply that I alone am capable of making your life heaven or hell. It's your choice."

As he left the coach, she straightened herself in the seat and tried not to look down at the leg irons or to dwell on the words that he had spoken to her and certainly not to dwell on the pain that had taken permanent root in her heart. For she saw now that she had only two possessions that Yorrick Harp or anyone else, for that matter, could neither touch nor alter. One was her dignity, and the second was her spirit, and those she fully intended to guard with her life, if necessary. For without them, her life was meaningless.

Mary sat to one side of the horsehair sofa in the parlor. She wanted to believe Taylor Quitman's incredible story, and yet she dared not, for it was too absurd, too cruel to be believed. And yet—

"And where did you meet these two, the ones who—"

The faltering voice belonged to Burke, who almost an hour ago had pushed Taylor Quitman down on the velvet ottoman and commanded him to tell his story in complete detail. Throughout the long interrogation the poor man had basically told the same tale over and over again without major variation.

But far and away the most painful face in the room belonged to young Stephen, whose countenance bore a look of confusion at least as great as Mary was suffering. Throughout the entire afternoon the young man had kept well to the far corner of the parlor, listening intently but saying nothing as though he, like everyone else, was struggling with the difficult transition. Eve dead. Eve alive. Kidnapped? Where?

Mary bowed her head, struggling for control, as she had been doing since Taylor Quitman arrived. Now she looked up to hear Taylor say, "It's a boardinghouse near the waterfront, a house belonging to one Irma Kingsley—"

"I know the place," Stephen said, his face alive with hope, at last venturing out of his corner and standing opposite Burke.

Taylor Quitman repeated himself. "As I said, these two were in Irma Kingsley's salon, and I overheard them say they had done a job for a man and had been handsomely paid, by one Yorrick Harp. They had retrieved trunks from Jarmay Higgins's—"

The names all blended in Mary's confused hearing, and try as she could to reconstruct the wild tale, none of it made sense. Eve kidnapped from the woods near Fan Cottage? Eve taken to Jarmay Higgins's Lumberyard in Mobile? Why? Eve held a prisoner under sentence of death? Dear God, why? What crime had her innocent daughter committed to be sentenced to death? And then Eve sold to a man named Yorrick Harp? Who was Yorrick Harp and what right did he have to—

As the puzzling facts swirled through her head, she rubbed her forehead and felt a comforting hand on her shoulder and looked up to see Madame Germaine standing close and sharing her bewilderment.

Burke spoke again, attempting to make sense of it. "Why was she taken to Jarmay Higgins's Lumberyard?" he asked.

Taylor Quitman bowed his head. "He is a Knight of the White Camellia."

Burke nodded with surprising calm. "I recognized his horse that first morning when White Doll—"

As the remembered horror of that tragedy swept over the room, there was a new silence. Mary struggled to keep her mind away from drawing parallels. The men who had murdered White Doll would be capable of anything.

"What I didn't know," Burke went on, his voice level, "was that you too were a member."

"If it helps, I wasn't a very good one. And I knew what Jarmay Higgins was up to, knew that Eve didn't stand a chance. She'd seen us all. She could not be permitted to live."

Stephen stepped forward.

Only at the last minute did Paris Boley succeed in turning him away. Mary saw Paris place a supporting arm about Stephen's shoulder and she sensed a bond of friendship between the two young men and was pleased by it.

Whether anyone else in the room had seen his outrage, Mary couldn't be certain.

"Who intervened?" Burke demanded.

Taylor Quitman shook his head. "I told you—"

"Tell me again."

"No one intervened. When the knights left the loft, Jarmay Higgins had been given clear orders to dispose of her."

Mary bowed her head, unable to conceive of her daughter in such perilous circumstances.

"And you thought he had—disposed of her?" Burke demanded, something cold in his voice, as though at last this round-robin story was beginning to make grim sense.

"I told you, yes," Taylor Quitman repeated.

"Then why did you go back?" Burke demanded.

Taylor Quitman shrugged and moaned. "We've been over this—"

"And we are going over it again."

"Why? You should be in pursuit, before—"

"Because now I don't trust you," Burke said, his voice cold. Everyone looked up, having heard something for the first time that indicated he was beginning to put certain puzzle pieces together, a coherent picture emerging. "Tell me, why did you go back to the lumberyard if you were certain that Higgins had killed her?"

Taylor Quitman shook his head. "Because—I could not bear it."

"Bear what?"

"The thought of—Eve dead."

The two words seemed to hang over the parlor, causing new pain, compounded now by the possibility of hope. Was she still alive? And if so, in what condition?

Then a question occurred to Mary of a very specific nature. "Mr. Quitman," she asked, "did you see her alive?"

The question, though easily understood, seemed to go forever unanswered.

"I—saw her."

"Where was she?"

Mary saw the man look up at Burke, as though pleading to be excused from answering this question.

But Burke gave no quarter, and Mary saw Stephen draw back into the room, Paris behind him, all awaiting Taylor Quitman's reply.

"She was—in the big loft, over the cutting room," he muttered.

"Was she well?" Mary continued. "Was she seated? Was she standing?"

Quitman shook his head, as though unable to accommodate the pain of his reply. "Bound," he said softly. "They had bound her to an old cutting table."

Suddenly Mary covered her ears and wished that she had not asked the question. Kidnappers were not known for their delicacy of treatment. A few moments later she relaxed her hands and heard Burke resume his line of questioning, though from his tone, she knew his suffering had increased.

Finally Taylor Quitman himself seemed to have surpassed the limits of his endurance, and with an anguished curse he suggested, "Why don't you go and see Jarmay Higgins? He is the bastard, he is the one who—"

For several moments the commonsense suggestion went unanswered. Mary's initial reaction was to be cautious where villains disguised as gentlemen are concerned. "No, Burke, please, what if the other knights—"

"They want no part of Higgins, Mary," Taylor Quitman said, leaning forward on the ottoman. "No one planned for this, I can assure you."

"Then how did it happen?" Burke demanded.

"The scoundrel hired by Higgins, one Orlando Dow, went too far, did not understand the basic tactics of the knights."

"Which are?" Burke asked.

Taylor Quitman looked up out of his fatigue and remorse. "I was wrong, Burke, have been from the beginning. I—we didn't like what you were doing—"

"What, in the name of God?"

Taylor glanced nervously toward Paris Boley, in the corner of the parlor, allied with Stephen. "Him," Quitman said under his breath. "General manager in a white man's job."

"Even if that man is qualified?" Burke asked with unexpected gentleness.

For several minutes the two men were locked in each other's gaze. Finally Quitman murmured, "Yesterday I would have said yes."

"Today?"

"No. Not if the results are tragedies of this proportion."

The silence in the room held. Clearly Taylor Quitman had gone through a painful period of growth in the last few days, and as growth of any sort is wont to do, it had left him thoughtful and exhausted.

Now he stood slowly. "I have been wrong. I have contributed to every moment of grief that has descended on Stanhope Hall these last few weeks. And I'm sorry. I think now you must go and see Jarmay Higgins, get him in any way you can to tell you of Eve's fate. And perhaps there is yet time—"

"Yes, please—"

Mary looked up at this urgent plea and saw Stephen halfway to the door, his youthful impatience and his own great need canceling all further discussion.

Then Paris Boley followed, his attitude not unlike Stephen's. "I offer my services as well, Mr. Stanhope. Please allow me to accompany you. Eve is my friend. I am the cause."

Within the moment Paris Boley joined Stephen at the door, apparently ready to go with or without Burke's permission. At last Burke moved forward. "I should be grateful, Quitman," he murmured. "I just wish you had acted sooner." He continued on to the door, to the two young men waiting, stopping where Mary stood. "I must go with them," he whispered and kissed her on the cheek. Up close, she saw the worry and grief and anger in his eyes and realized that he probably was exerting massive self-control. Whether he would ever reinstate Taylor Quitman in his trust, Mary had no idea.

She reached for his hand and detained him a moment longer. "What are you going to do?" she asked and wished that they were alone.

"Talk to Higgins," he shrugged. "See what he tells us."

"What if he tells you nothing?"

"He'll tell us something," Burke said with a smile that belied the ominous tone in his voice.

Suddenly Stephen and Paris pushed open the door. Stephen called back, "We'll get the horses, meet you in front."

The sudden volume and enthusiasm of their voices cut through the lethargy of the parlor and stirred everyone to their feet, and all now were following after Burke.

On the gallery Mary looked out over the lawns, down the avenue of live oaks and thought how often she had seen Eve running pell-mell between those old trees.

Eve—bound to the table—

Behind her was Madame Germaine. "Frankly, I don't believe a word the man said," Madame Germaine whispered. "It's a deception, you know. Don't let them go, Madame, I beg you, don't."

Mary looked up, startled by this suggestion.

"I mean it, Madame. As much as it grieves me to say so, I know our Eve perished in that fire and all this is a subterfuge, a ploy, a tactic to inflict further tragedy upon you and this household."

"No," Mary said and wished the hysterical woman would go away. As she wouldn't, Mary moved to the edge of the gallery, beyond which she saw Burke and Taylor Quitman speaking together while in the distance she heard the horses coming at rapid speed.

Hope. That was what Taylor Quitman had brought to them on this afternoon, hope that Eve was still alive.

A shout went up, and Mary saw all three men riding at top speed down the avenue of live oaks, passing in and out of the shadows until at last they emerged on the sun-drenched road at the bottom of the hill and disappeared into their own dust clouds.

For several moments there was no movement on the gallery. Then at last Taylor Quitman looked back at Mary.

At the same time Mary looked down at him and was puzzled by conflicting feelings. In the past he had simply been Burke's trusted attorney and friend, a frequent guest at Stanhope Hall and always a gentleman of consideration and manners.

"Mary."

She looked at him as he called her name and saw him start toward her and felt no great agitation. Yet he was a member of the Knights of the White Camellia, and as such, he had had an active hand in all the sorrow and persecution that had been visited on Stanhope Hall in the recent past.

"I asked for Burke's forgiveness," Taylor Quitman said.

"Did he give it to you?" Mary asked.

"No."

"I see."

"And you? Do I have your forgiveness?"

"Would it ease the pain that you are suffering?"

"Yes."

"Then you have it. There has been too much pain here. Someone must have a respite." Having spoken, she turned and walked into the cool shade of the front corridor, thinking of Christine and David. She had two other children, and she'd sorely neglected them of late and they must be told the news, that hope once again lived in Stanhope Hall.

* * *

Stephen led the way into the city, Taylor Quitman's words echoing in his head.

Eve not dead, Eve alive—

Faster and faster he rode, though he was unaware of his speed until he looked back to see the other two at least a quarter of a mile behind. Why were they lagging so? They had already wasted enough time in endless talk.

He had been granted a second chance by a most generous Fate, and he had no intention of allowing the trail to grow cold for if indeed Eve *was* alive, then Stephen would give immediate pursuit until he had found her.

The thought pleased him and helped him to race along the dusty road. He looked up a few minutes later and saw the outskirts of Mobile and felt his sense of excitement increase. What if they were to find her this very afternoon, and what if they brought her triumphantly back to Stanhope Hall this very evening! What a celebration there would be!

"Wait!" He heard someone calling to him from behind and looked back to see Burke Stanhope gaining. "Let me take the lead here. I know the way," the man shouted, and Stephen reluctantly agreed and broke speed until Paris and Burke caught up with him.

"Higgins's Lumberyard," Stephen shouted out in the event Mr. Stanhope had forgotten their destination. But then he saw the expression on the man's face, one of cold determination, and belatedly Stephen realized that Mr. Stanhope's loss was as great if not greater than his own.

About ten minutes later Stephen saw him bring his horse to a stop just this side of a busy intersection. Stephen drew up alongside him first, then a few moments later Paris joined them on the other side.

"Over there," Stanhope muttered and reached inside his coat for a handkerchief and wiped his face of dust and sweat and nodded toward a huge lumberyard, the front facade of brown and peeling paint rising at least three stories from street level. In the middle of that field of dry lumber, Stephen saw the words Higgins's Lumberyard.

Still with Stanhope in the lead, the three men guided their horses to the left, toward what appeared to be an office. Without a word Mr. Stanhope indicated they were to follow him to the hitching post, where they dismounted, secured their horses and started toward the office door.

"In here," Stanhope said, keeping his voice low, and drew open the door.

Inside they found nothing except a battered desk covered with invoices and yellow ledger sheets, a smelly dank place that reeked of old urine and tobacco and whiskey. Stephen tried to imagine Eve in such a place and thought how frightened she must have been and felt his anger increase at the empty room, the absence of someone or something to attack.

Then they heard something, worse, smelled something, and looked toward a screened area near the back of the small office.

Someone was back there, quite possibly on the thunder pot from the sounds of escaping gas and the odor itself.

Stanhope led them past the cluttered desk, moving toward the screen until one of their steps struck a weak board and made a noise and a male voice called out from behind the screen, "Who is it? Someone there? Hold your horses and I'll be with you shortly."

"Jarmay Higgins?"

"The same. I said I'll be with you in a moment. Didn't you hear?"

But Mr. Stanhope continued to approach the screen, unmindful now of how many weak boards his boots struck, until at last he stood on the opposite side of the screen and grabbed both ends and lifted it away to reveal a comic sight: Jarmay Higgins, trousers dropped, squatting on a large white porcelain thunder pot, his face red and sweaty with effort and now livid with anger at this rude intrusion.

"What in the—have you lost your—Goddamn it, I said wait. Didn't you bastards hear me?"

Suddenly all the color seemed to drain from his once-crimson face. "Y-you are—"

"Burke Stanhope," came the reply, his voice bearing a remarkable tone of courtesy, which astounded Stephen, for he was fully ready to lift the repulsive little man from his chamber pot and reverse his position, head first.

"Come," Stanhope said, indicating with a gesture that Jarmay Higgins was to rise and follow him. "We need to have an exchange of words," he added. When on the second command the trembling Jarmay Higgins had yet to obey, Stanhope suddenly lunged at him and bodily lifted him to his feet, his flannel drawers falling down around his feet.

Quickly the man tugged them up, covering his private parts, rolls of fat clearly visible beneath the undergarments.

"M-Mr. Stanhope," Higgins stammered, trying to move further back into the corner. "What is it you want?"

"A word, maybe two."

"About what?"

"I was thinking you could tell me that."

"I don't—"

"I have a daughter, sir, Eve by name. I was told she was here."

"Your d-daughter, sir," Higgins repeated. "Not—here, sir, I can assure you. N-Now what would—s-she be doing here?"

Stephen wondered if the stutter was a permanent affliction or merely one of the moment, brought on by fear.

"We were told otherwise, sir," Stanhope went on.

"I—don't know who your—source of information was, sir," Higgins repeated, "but I can assure you he was wrong. I would remember a female as—beautiful as your daughter, and besides, what business would she have at my lumberyard?"

"No business. She was brought here against her wishes."

"Sir, no, you have indeed heard—"

"Do you possess a loft?"

Jarmay Higgins looked taken aback by this change of subject. "A—"

"Loft, sir, a room above the others."

As Stanhope gestured toward the ceiling, Jarmay Higgins looked fearfully up. "No loft, sir. I can assure you—"

"May we see it?"

"What, sir?"

"The loft."

"It's as I said. We possess no—"

Then suddenly there was movement, Stanhope making a direct lunge that drove Jarmay Higgins back, pinning him to the wall of his office, knocking over the screen in the process.

Struggling against the strength of the hands that held him, Higgins gasped, "It's—I'll show you. But you must unhand me first."

Stephen waited along with Paris as Stanhope released Higgins, who scrambled for his trousers where they had fallen to the floor near the chamber pot.

"Leave them," Stanhope ordered.

"But, sir, surely—"

"Where is it, Higgins? Show us now!"

Finally, in an angry gesture, Higgins threw the trousers to the floor. "I'd like to know by what right you barge in here. It is not my obligation to respond to every harebrained charge and rumor that circulates through Mobile."

"Where is the loft?" Stanhope repeated.

Stephen followed the procession out of the office and into a narrow dark corridor, Higgins already out of sight going up the steep steps, Mr. Stanhope ahead. "Do you know a man named Orlando Dow?" he asked, the echo of his voice drifting back down the stairwell.

"Dow?" Higgins mused, no longer stuttering. "No, I think not, unless you mean a customer. And then I couldn't begin to remember all the names of my customers. You realize—"

"No, not a customer," Stanhope replied.

"Still I'm afraid I can't help you."

Stephen went up the stairs after them, stumbling once in the dark, resenting the courtesy in both their voices, as though Stanhope were doing little more than paying a business call.

Then, "What, sir, if I may ask, led you to believe that your daughter was here?" Higgins asked, his voice restored now, not a trace of nerves.

"As I said, I was told so. May we have light?"

"By whom were you told and no, no lantern, not in a lumberyard," Higgins scolded. "Fire is our natural enemy. I'm sure you can understand."

They were at the top of the stairs, in what appeared to be a large and shadowy room, the corners not visible in the present half-light, the only illumination coming from hairline cracks in the high ceiling overhead, which revealed the streaks of late afternoon sun and slivered paths of swirling sawdust particles.

"The loft, sir," Higgins announced, and stood back, apparently resigned to his comic appearance.

Mr. Stanhope looked over the large room. Stephen saw Paris start off on his own in a leisurely inspection tour along the west wall of the loft, his hands behind his back.

"What is the nigger looking for?" Higgins demanded.

"Mr. Boley?" Stanhope inquired.

Higgins continued to glare at Paris, watching every move he made.

"That is Paris Boley," Mr. Stanhope said. "I thought you knew him. Everyone else in the county does. He is the general manager of Stanhope Plantation."

"Well, what's he looking for?" Higgins demanded.

"As I told you," Stanhope said, repeating his words slowly, "we were told—"

"By whom?"

"That my daughter Eve had been brought to this loft against her wishes."

"Absurd, ridiculous," Higgins scoffed. "Sir, I am a law-abiding citizen. You know me. Do you think I would be a party to such skullduggery?"

"Are you a member of the Knights of the White Camellia?" Stanhope's question came rapid-fire and clearly caught Higgins off guard.

"Am—I—?"

"Are you?"

"I don't have to answer that."

"No, but you might want to reconsider."

"Mr. Stanhope."

Paris's voice echoed across the distance of the loft and dragged everyone's attention toward a shadowy corner.

Stephen moved first, hurrying across the old floor, amazed at how loud his boots sounded, as though these ancient dried timbers were ready to collapse at any moment.

He was aware of Mr. Stanhope directly behind him, and behind *him* a sputtering, protesting Jarmay Higgins.

"Sir, I beg you, she is not here, your daughter, nor has she ever been. This is no place for a well-bred young lady, as you can see for yourself. I can assure you, sir, that if your daughter had been brought here, I would have throttled the villain who had touched her and would have immediately seen to her safe return."

Stephen reached the place where Paris stood first. Before him was a high, broad table with a wooden edge running along all four sides, while at each corner he saw four knotted ropes of varying lengths hanging free, as though something or someone had recently been cut loose.

The appearance of the table worked a curious effect on Stephen— the thought, the mere possibility that Eve had been rendered helpless at the hands of such a man. For several moments he stared down at this grim evidence, joined now by Stanhope, who made his way from corner to corner, inspecting the cut rope as though it might reveal a clue to him.

And all the while Higgins talked loudly, sometimes belligerently, always compulsively.

"A cutting table, sir, surely you have seen them before. An old model. We purchased a newer, more standardized model several years ago. Allow me to show you. The blade is fed directly into the precut metal slot, commencing right here," and he pointed to the center of the table, clearly avoiding the grim evidence of the severed ropes.

"What were these for?" Stanhope asked, holding up one of the severed lengths of rope.

"Those?" Higgins parroted. "Why, those were—to steady the lumber as it entered the sawmill. Otherwise slippage, you know, and waste . . ."

For several moments there was no sound in the loft. Stephen felt a strong compulsion to stay close to the table, as though some lingering essence was trying to tell him something. He felt it growing stronger, that specific nightmare sensation that someone had recently been here, someone had recently suffered here, someone had cried out here, prayed here, begged here, all to no avail.

Still the man babbled behind him about cutting lengths and new saws and gave no indication that Stephen was right in his fears. And Mr. Stanhope continued to circle the table, perhaps feeling what Stephen was feeling, but still unable to find anything specific with which to accuse the man.

"Now, if that is all, Mr. Stanhope," Higgins was saying now. "Closing time at a lumberyard is a very busy hour, customers coming for cuts of wood, dropping off orders for tomorrow. If there is anything else, of course, but if not, then I must ask you to leave."

"Mr. Stanhope!"

This strong voice came from Paris, who had at some point moved off into a far corner and was just now emerging, carrying something in his arms—a garment, or so it appeared.

"It belongs to Eve, sir," Paris murmured. "I've seen her wear it before, a dark blue gown, this one, the same, I'd swear to it."

At first Mr. Stanhope seemed loath to touch it and looked at Paris with a glance of anger, as though in a way he resented the discovery.

"Eve's?" he repeated. The name seemed to catch in his throat as at last he touched the dark blue muslin, lifted it, revealing it to be torn, ripped down the center.

Stephen pushed his way around the table and took the gown from Mr. Stanhope. The instant he touched the fabric he knew it was Eve's, though he tried not to dwell on what had happened to her in this place and only gave brief thanks that here at last was proof that she had not perished in the fire at Fan Cottage.

"Higgins!" Stephen shouted, rousing himself from his grief long enough to see the bastard moving rapidly across the loft floor, heading toward the door. "Higgins!" Stephen shouted again, and looked back at Mr. Stanhope to see if he would take the lead. But he saw the man still devastated by the sight of Eve's torn gown and decided that now it was his turn.

"Higgins!" Stephen shouted a third time and started after him and caught up with him as he neared the door and tackled him and felt the flab of the man beneath him like a poorly stuffed feather mattress.

"Wait, I beg you, leave me be!"

As Higgins's indignant protests filled Stephen's ears, he turned the man over and dragged him to his feet and saw the jowly face before him and tried to warn his mind to stay away from the possibility of what this toad of a man had done to Eve. But he could not and he drew back his right fist and let it seek its natural target, a free force of nature that sent Jarmay Higgins reeling backward halfway across the loft floor, collapsing finally on his backside, a fall of such proportions that the floor shook and sawdust clouds exploded in the immediate vicinity.

Just as the man was crawling up in protest of the first assault, Stephen suffered a second image, Eve bound and pleading with this jackal face, and again his fist found its target, the second blow causing Higgins's neck to crack. Again the weight of the man caused a dull thud upon the old boards of the loft floor, and this time as he struggled up Stephen saw the appealing sight of blood, two streams gushing from his nose, the other from the corner of his mouth.

Coming from behind, he heard that voice of caution, not condemning his actions, rather giving him direction.

"Ask him about the dress before you beat him senseless," Stanhope suggested.

"The dress, Higgins?" Stephen demanded, straddling him, pinning him.

"An old one, belonging to my wife." Higgins lied and tried to raise himself and wipe the blood from his nose.

"What is it doing here?" Stephen demanded.

"My wife discarded it, for obvious reasons. I always gather up old garments and bring them here for the purpose of—cleaning saw blades."

"I don't believe you," Stephen challenged.

Higgins continued to wipe at his bleeding face. "I don't give a damn whether—"

Stephen heard Mr. Stanhope behind him. "I know your wife, Higgins, she's quite plump. She could never wear a gown like that."

"Then my daughters, one of my daughters, I don't remember which. I demand that all of you leave these premises immediately, and I might be able to persuade my lawyer not to—"

As he talked compulsively on, Stephen glanced over his shoulder at Mr. Stanhope, who held the gown, sadly fondling the torn lace about the neck. He shook his head, despite the man's incoherent rambling.

"This is Eve's gown," he said with certainty. "I would swear to it. Paris too—"

Slowly Mr. Stanhope moved around Stephen until he was standing directly over Jarmay Higgins.

"My daughter, sir. I demand that you tell me the present whereabouts of my daughter or I will permit this young gentleman to beat you until you are rendered senseless and are unable to speak, at which time we shall wait patiently for you to regain consciousness, whereupon he will start to beat you again. The exercise will bring him incredible pleasure and will bring you incredible pain. And if his arm tires, I shall ask my general manager, Paris Boley, to apply his strong right arm to the task. Is all of this clear?"

Whether it was clear to Higgins or not, Stephen couldn't tell, for he sat up slowly and shook his head, scattering drops of blood over the limited area, and from this bowed position he insisted, "I don't know what you're talking about, Stanhope, and further, I advise—"

Stephen never waited to find out what the man would have advised, for he reached over and effortlessly lifted him to his feet and took aim, this time at his left jaw, and sent his fist flying.

"I'll ask you again, Higgins," Mr. Stanhope said, coming up alongside Stephen.

"I—swear, sir—" Higgins sputtered.

"Don't swear," Stanhope interrupted. "Just tell me, was she here? And if so, where is she now?"

Stephen watched Higgins carefully, trying to read his expression, ready to launch yet another assault.

But after several seconds the man shook his head, his hands covering his battered face, and he started to blubber, a mix of blood and protest, saliva and pleas for mercy, all the time accompanied by a most interesting denial. "I swear I didn't know who she was, I swear, sir. They were the ones who brought her here to my lumberyard, without a yea, nay or thank you, and they said, 'Higgins, do what you must,' and I swear, sir, that was the way it happened."

This disjointed confession left them all gaping at Jarmay Higgins, who now sat childlike on the dusty loft floor in his blood-spattered underdrawers. Strange, it was what they all had wanted, what they had come here seeking, and yet now that they had the certain knowledge that Eve had indeed been held a prisoner here on that cutting table, with those ropes, someone's hands forcibly removing her gown —all this was suddenly a burden that none of them seemed equipped to carry.

Mr. Stanhope moved away first, undoubtedly seeking a moment of privacy before pinning the man down to specifics. At the same time

Stephen looked over his shoulder as though someone had called to him from the cutting table.

"Now, talk!"

This stern command came from Stanhope, who apparently had recovered sufficiently to confront Jarmay Higgins where he sat on the loft floor.

"I'm bleeding," he whimpered.

"Tell me."

"What?"

"Everything. *Now!*"

With fearful upturned eyes Jarmay Higgins started a torturous tale of his own innocence, reluctantly granting permission for the Knights of the White Camellia to use this loft for their secret meetings, and thus it was through this gesture of generosity that he now found himself implicated in the present unpleasantness.

He denied all knowledge of Eve's kidnapping, though he knew about the fire, yes, set by the knights, who had hired one Orlando Dow to do their foul work for them.

"Why?"

This soft question caught Stephen off guard, and he looked up at Mr. Stanhope to see an expression of innocence on his face, as though he sincerely wanted an answer.

"Well, it's him, now ain't it?" Higgins replied, pointing one bloodied finger toward Paris Boley. "Him and all those other niggers you let have the run of Stanhope Hall." Suddenly, as though growing weary of his own explanation, Jarmay Higgins moved straight to the heart of the matter.

"They are niggers, Mr. Stanhope. Can't you see that? Is something wrong with your eyes? And this here is the South, and we have a code here and a certain way of doing things, and you've been trampling on that code for years just like it doesn't exist. And some of us who still love the South and all she stands for can't just stand by and permit that to happen, so we—didn't—"

"The South must change, Higgins," Stanhope said.

"Never," the man replied with jutting jaw and stupid eyes.

"Please," Stephen interrupted, aware of time passing, of Eve alive and missing.

When he received no response from Stanhope, when the look of sadness deepened and when ultimately the man walked into the gathering darkness of the loft, Stephen tried to resume the line of questioning himself.

"Was she alive when you last saw her?" How difficult it was to form the words.

"Yes, alive. Very much alive, though you have only Jarmay Higgins to thank for that."

The man seemed to be gaining in arrogance if not courage. He had managed to stanch the flow of blood coming from his nose and sat with his head upright.

Stephen glanced behind and wished that Mr. Stanhope would rejoin him.

"You see, they had ordered me to kill her, yes they had," Higgins went on. "That was their order and I don't give a damn about them now. They abandoned me, I will abandon them. Each man is on his own and I'll name names if you like, because I don't give a damn anymore."

"Tell us about it. What happened?"

There was a moment's pause. Then, "I gave her away." The man grinned.

"You—what?" This fractured voice was Mr. Stanhope's, who now came up alongside Stephen and gaped down at Higgins.

"I gave her away," the man repeated idiotically. "There was this fancy gentleman who had dropped off some trunks the day before that needed new bottoms. Owned a traveling theatrical troupe. When he came back for his trunks, I told him—everything and he took one look at her and said he wouldn't pay cash for her, but he'd be glad to take her off my hands."

Now it was Stephen's turn to back off, reeling from the horrors that spilled in a continuous stream from Higgins's mouth.

Gave her away. How carelessly he had spoken those words.

It was while he was still walking away, his back turned, that Stephen heard a sudden scuffle, looked back to see Mr. Stanhope dragging the man to his feet, then shoving him up against the wall near the steps, a forceful movement that clearly caught Higgins by surprise and caused his head to collide with the old timber in a resounding blow.

"The man's name, you bastard," Stanhope whispered through clenched teeth.

"Harp," gasped Higgins. "Yorrick Harp."

"The name of the troupe," Stanhope demanded, and when Higgins didn't answer immediately, again Stanhope shoved him backward full force into the wall, cracking the man's skull time and time again.

"Name? I—don't—"

Another shove, another crack, another groan. "An all-female troupe," Higgins gasped. "Lookers, all. Don't know the—name."

"Where were they going? What direction?"

"New Orleans."

Suddenly Higgins seemed to collapse. His head fell forward onto his chest, his legs gave way, and at last Mr. Stanhope released him and stood back as he collapsed in a sprawled heap at his feet.

For several moments there was no sound in the loft save for Mr. Stanhope's labored breathing.

Stephen spoke first, what he considered to be the inevitable. "I'll go after them. They shouldn't be too hard to find."

"They have two full days' travel on you."

"No matter. I will make it up."

"I should come—"

"No, please." Stephen stepped closer. "You return to Stanhope Hall. I swear to you on the love we share for Eve, I will find her and I will return her to you. I swear to God."

Stephen could tell from the look of exhaustion on Mr. Stanhope's face that he didn't quite believe or trust him. Then Stephen heard Paris's voice.

"Mr. Stanhope, please let me go with him. I am the cause. I must—"

"Nonsense."

"It is not nonsense, sir," Stephen interrupted. "I would appreciate his company and his assistance."

Stephen could tell from the indecision washing across Stanhope's face that he was giving the matter serious consideration. He was pleased that Paris had volunteered. The man would be good company and invaluable help.

"You will need—"

"Nothing, sir, except the command to go."

"I'll give you a letter of credit and some cash that should see to your needs."

Stephen nodded. "I have my uncle's letter of credit as well."

"Shouldn't you wait until morning?" Stanhope suggested, not thinking clearly.

"We would lose a night's ride, sir. I'm hoping we can find them still in New Orleans and go no farther."

"And if you don't?"

"Then we will follow their trail until we catch up and find them. I promise you, sir."

Still seeing doubt mixed with grief on Stanhope's face, Stephen walked to his side. "Please, you must believe me. I will do exactly as I say. We will give immediate pursuit. A man who wears robes and who bears the name Yorrick Harp should not be too difficult to find in any community of men. Please believe me, sir, and let us be on our way. Time is our enemy now."

He waited to see what the effect of his words would be on this man with whom he'd been at cross purposes since the day of his arrival at Stanhope Hall.

"You will need fresh horses," Stanhope said at last, and Stephen closed his eyes and breathed a prayer of thanks to whatever gods of reason had intervened.

As he and Paris were heading toward the door, Stanhope stopped them with an additional plea. "Find her. I beg you. Bring her home no matter what. And if you do, I will be forever in your debt."

* * *

There were four important stops during that evening of whirlwind preparation. Burke roused his banker from his evening meal to prepare a letter of unlimited credit and affix the bank seal to it. Then they stopped at the Red Hall Livery and purchased two new horses. And then they stopped at Harmonica's, a well-known emporium that specialized in outfitting parties for the trek west. At last they stopped at Irma Kingsley's, where Housy Dunbar and Captain Willing confirmed Jarmay Higgins's tale of the pretty young girl looking the worse for wear who had been given to Yorrick Harp along with his trunks for use in his all-female theatrical troupe. When the men launched into a description of her physical state, naked, ill appearing, and frightened, Stephen indicated to Paris that he would wait for them outside on the street.

A few moments later they rejoined him at the horses, and he saw the look of despair on Mr. Stanhope's face, clearly matching his own.

"We knew it, of course, didn't we, sir?" he murmured, trying to alter the man's sorrowing eyes. "But she's alive, and that's all that matters. And I swear we will find her and we will return her to you. Do you hear?"

Mr. Stanhope laboriously pulled himself up onto his horse and adjusted the tow line that held the other two horses. "Then God's speed," he said and smiled.

Paris, already in the saddle of the new horse, watched with Stephen until Burke Stanhope disappeared around the corner, heading north out of Mobile. When he didn't speak for several moments, Stephen secured the bundle of garments on the back of his horse and quickly mounted.

"Should we have insisted that he come with us?" he asked Paris, who continued to gaze off into the distance.

Paris shook his head. "If he had wanted to come, he would have, and nothing you could have said or done would have prevented him.

He can't leave Stanhope Hall unprotected now. Besides, he didn't want to come. He's afraid of what we might find."

Stephen listened with rising apprehension. What would they find? Eve alive? Eve dead?

Quickly he shook the thoughts loose and shouted to Paris, "Lead the way—the shortest, quickest way to New Orleans. We'll ride all night."

Paris urged his horse to full speed, and Stephen stayed right behind him and thought curiously of his father, of Eden Castle, of the business he was to have conducted for his uncle Richard.

Everything would have to wait now. Fate had intervened in a way he had never expected.

* * *

Lily Bloom, the abandoned and abused daughter of a Richmond farmer, could not quite make head or tail out of the pretty young girl named Eve Stanhope. As unofficial mother confessor to the Adamless Eden Traveling Troupe of Females, Lily took pride in her ability to draw out the most damaged personalities who found themselves hapless dependents of Yorrick Harp's protection.

But clearly that one slumped in the corner of the coach staring mournfully out the window could present a problem, not only because of her own attitude but because Lily couldn't remember when she had seen Yorrick Harp so excited about a new girl. Obviously he had great hopes for that one, and obviously she didn't give a damn.

"Eve?"

Cautiously Lily approached, aware that there were dozens of tasks waiting for her in the coach behind. The first night out was always hectic, tracing misplaced trunks, so many foolish questions to answer.

But somehow she suspected that her first chore sat slumped right over there, still wearing the drab blue dress, her face bearing the sad imprint of recent tears.

"Eve, my dear," Lily murmured. "This will do you no good, I promise."

Carefully Lily sat beside her and saw her small white hands curled in her lap. It was the sight of those hands trembling that moved Lily.

"Oh my darling," she mourned and reached out for Eve's hands and covered them with her own, and suddenly she heard a sob, repressed, as though someone was struggling with all her might not to cry.

Then the dam broke and Eve sobbed openly and tried to cover her face with her hands, and Lily enclosed her in her arms.

"Is it still the leg irons?" Lily murmured, hoping to quiet the tears at least to the extent that they could talk. "Didn't Violet tell you? We all have worn the leg irons at one time or another. Yorrick must feel that he can trust you." Her voice fell, and she smoothed back Eve's matted hair. "Besides, there are a few girls who actually like the irons, say they would rather have the irons on when we hit a remote mining camp or ranch with nothing between them and those lonely men but—"

She smiled, belatedly realizing that the young girl hadn't the faintest idea what she was talking about and perhaps that was for the best.

Lily continued to cradle the girl, suddenly worried by the sights and sounds yet ahead of her. She looked up toward the narrow door that led out of this coach and into the next one and hoped that the girls were handling themselves well. Most were old-timers, had been on this tour many times. They knew the routine by heart, knew all the stops except the new ones Yorrick scheduled each year, always expanding the length of the tour and his purse along with it.

"Eve, please, don't," Lily urged and withdrew her handkerchief and tried to wipe at the girl's red and swollen eyes.

Suddenly Lily had an idea. "Come, I want you to come with me, now, this minute."

For several minutes Lily struggled against the motion of the rocking train and the all-but-collapsed Eve. Still she managed to make her way to the door and push it open despite the rushing wind, and kept her eyes closed against the hazards of flying cinders and pushed forward, always supporting Eve, who seemed uncaring that they were even moving.

Now Lily guided her through the narrow door and into the next coach and closed the door behind her and heard the din that met them head-on, the entire female company congregated for gossip and rehearsal, while in the background there was the added cacophony of the orchestra, all trying to find a true A, violins crying, flutes screeching, horns burping.

Lily smiled. It was a good sound of energy, and it had been her experience that when the energy was good, the performances were good and the season was good. For this tour Yorrick had selected a different repertoire; all favorites of the men who made up their audiences: *Under the Gas Light, East Lynne*, and excerpts from *Uncle Tom's Cabin*, plus an assortment of readings from *Hamlet, Othello* and *Twelfth Night. Twelfth Night* was Lily's favorite. She played Viola.

"Come on," she urged and looked down at Eve, pleased to see that her hands were no longer covering her face, saw her staring straight ahead toward the noise.

"They're getting ready to rehearse," Lily explained, delighted that her plan had worked, for it seemed as though the movement had distracted her from her deep grief.

Now the girl followed Lily down the narrow corridor toward the chaos of chattering females, a chorus that fell silent the moment they appeared, a transition too dramatic even for Lily, who felt a hot blush on her face as all eyes turned in their direction, all noise sputtered to an awkward halt.

"Well, for heaven's sake, carry on," Lily scolded and placed a protective arm about Eve's shoulders. "I thought Eve might enjoy a rehearsal. You don't mind, do you?"

For a moment Lily wasn't certain if they minded or not. There was sometimes a curious reluctance on the part of the troupe to accept a new member, for whatever reason. If the newcomer was too pretty, there was jealousy; if her voice was too pure, there was jealousy; if her acting ability was superior, there was jealousy.

Finally Lily asked quietly, "Well? Can she watch? Are there any objections?"

After a full minute of silent waiting that seemed more like an hour, Pansy Walker called out from the rear of the coach, "She'd better watch. She'll have to do her part soon enough."

Though it was less than hospitable, the voice did seem to stir the others out of their indecision. Violet emerged from the crowd and urged Eve to take a seat on a near trunk.

"Here, sit," Lily instructed and assisted Eve to the trunk and felt the girl pull against the irons and wondered how long Yorrick would force her to wear them.

"Are you comfortable?" she whispered to Eve, growing even fonder of the girl, as one grows fond of a stray puppy all have abandoned.

Before Eve could answer, Lily heard another voice. "Hungry?"

She looked up to see Pansy offering the girl an apple. Lily smiled her gratitude and looked back to see if Eve would take it, and she did.

Then Pansy drifted back to the rehearsal. One group was getting ready to run the last act of *Uncle Tom's Cabin*, always the most difficult, and always a favorite, while another group was preparing the *Nymphs of the Woods Tableau*. They had many such tableaus in their repertoire. Christian maidens being thrown to the lions, Napoleon at Waterloo, George Washington crossing the Delaware, Betsy Ross sewing the first flag; American history tableaus that always seemed to be great favorites among the men in the West.

"Will you be all right for a while?" Lily whispered and waited for a response and wasn't too surprised when she didn't get one and took a final look at the sad little girl holding the apple in her hand.

"What can she do, Lily? Can she dance?"

Lily looked up, recognizing the voice. It was Marigold, the company's leading actress, leading bitch, flaming red hair, overbearing ways, but she performed everything from Hamlet to Little Eva with flair and vitality.

In answer to her question, Lily smiled. "I don't know. I think it's a bit too soon."

Marigold drew closer. She was dressed in the black flowing robes of Portia and had on far too much eye makeup. "Not too soon. Dallas day after tomorrow. The Palace. She must pull her own weight as we all do. She must do her share."

"No, far too soon," Lily said firmly.

But still Marigold insisted. "Why don't you ask her? Does she have a tongue? Maybe she has hidden talents that no one has ever seen. Or maybe she can do nothing at all and will prove to be dead weight."

"Why don't you just go on back to your rehearsal?" Lily snapped.

"And who are you? Her watchdog?" Marigold snapped back. "I thought Yorrick was her keeper, as he is yours and mine."

Lily bowed her head in an effort to regain self-control. "Marigold," she said, quietly, "please, give her a chance, give her some time, a day, maybe two, then she—"

"I—sing."

This whisper was so low that at first Lily wasn't certain if she had heard it or not. But apparently Marigold had heard, for suddenly she beamed.

"She sings. Did you hear, ladies? A plain brown songbird. Look to your laurels, you singers, and you, too, Tulip, and all of you who fancy the spotlight alone. Here, I present to you—your competition."

With cruel mockery Marigold laughed and stood back and gave a broad theatrical gesture to where Eve sat in less than splendor on top of the trunk, her chained legs clearly visible beneath the plain blue muslin dress, still holding the apple, her head bowed. She looked like anything but competition for anyone.

Still Marigold persisted, with increased cruelty. "Come, sing for us, songbird. Show us what a sparrow sounds like. Show us what you can do. If you do it well, Yorrick may give you the spotlight at the Palace. How would you like that? Have you ever performed in a giant hall filled with thousands of shouting men?"

If Eve was even aware that she was being teased, she gave no indication of it and continued to sit, head bowed.

Again Lily felt the need to intervene, though she wondered if it would do much good, for several other women had now taken up the cry of "Sing for us, yes, do. Show us your style, sing for us, sparrow—"

Against this rising tide all Lily could do was move in closer to where Eve sat and try to deflect some of the jeers and try to formulate a plan for getting the young girl out of here, at least until these bitches came to their senses and recalled their own first days with Yorrick Harp, pain-ridden days without respite, homesick, alone. Why couldn't they remember the simple lesson of life, that what hurts one hurts all?

Yet here they were, almost the entire company pushing closer in cruel curiosity.

It was then that she heard something, a low something, barely audible at first. She looked about, surprised, trying to determine the source, a voice, not singing exactly, low humming really. Was someone in the troupe mocking her further?

Several others heard it as well now, and the jeers fell silent and they looked about, at first one and then the other, as though they, too, were trying to determine the source of the sound. And still it came, so sweet, no words as yet, just a mournful soft melody. And at last and to her great surprise Lily identified the source and could not believe it. It was the girl, Eve, sitting quietly upon the trunk, head still bowed, humming a melody so soft yet so arresting that one by one the taunting voices ceased and all stood still, and almost as though Eve was waiting for their attention, she continued to hum until all were silent around her. Then slowly she lifted her head as though the better to breathe. At last the first words evolved out of the sweet sadness of the song, lyrics telling of a young girl alone, in search of her lover, and with each lyric the voice grew sweeter, stronger, the richest that Lily had ever heard, and still it gained in strength and volume and conviction, the purest of tone, without any sort of musical accompaniment, the crystal-clear words reaching well into the farthest corner of the railway coach.

Not once did she alter her position except for that slight lifting of her head, as though she wanted to make sure all heard her song, the young girl now having discovered her lover dead, holding him in her arms, a red and spreading stain on his shirt.

Then grief in the song, more moving than any Lily had ever heard, the rich voice no longer sweet and soft, but insistent in its variation, in its low, almost guttural tones.

The last few bars spun themselves out with bell-like clarity, tones of such perfection that Lily closed her eyes the better to listen undis-

tracted. Never had she heard a human voice used with greater artistry, greater feeling, greater compassion.

Then it ended on a single note held forever, or so it seemed, and the
last word was one of love, and the note and the tone and the word
seemed to call up all the fragmented pieces of every heart that had
ever been broken and soothed them with the promise of a better day.

For several moments all Lily heard was the rumble of the coach
itself, though even that seemed to have grown quieter during the
splendid song. Now she looked up to see every face in the railway car
transfixed by the beauty of the song, the honesty of the singer, for in
thinking on it, that seemed to be the key—the young girl's honesty.
She had sung simply because it made her feel good to do so.

When the awkward silence threatened to stretch on too long, Lily
looked at the girl to see if she could detect any change in her, to see if
she even knew what she had accomplished, gaining the rapt attention
of twenty women who over the years had hardened themselves to
anything that might even remotely move them.

But as far as Lily could see, the girl had sunk back into herself,
totally unaware of what she had done or of the caliber of gift she
possessed or the spell she had woven on everyone in the coach.

As Lily was looking about, she suddenly caught sight of Yorrick
Harp at the narrow door, his great bushy eyebrows circumflexed
with emotion, as though long after the song had ended, he still was
trying to listen to it in echo.

Then he was moving toward her, walking the length of the coach,
both hands extended, a smile on his face, losing balance once as the
train lurched but righting himself, the women moving back for him,
their attention now torn between Eve and Yorrick as though all knew
that the impending confrontation would be a memorable one.

But if Eve knew he was coming, she gave no indication of it and
continued to sit, looking down, slowly turning the red apple over and
over in her hands.

Lily was tempted to prod her into awareness but changed her
mind. Yorrick was less than ten feet away.

"My dearest child," Yorrick murmured and then he was upon her
and took the apple from her hand and covered her hands with his
own and only then did Eve look up, and seeing who it was, she moved
instantly backward.

But Yorrick made a soothing sound and gently lifted the girl in his
arms, cradling her close. "I shall care for her," he announced to the
coach over the roar of the train. "God has sent us a special gift in this
one, and we shall all take good care of it."

Without a word the women watched as he carried Eve back

through the coach. Lily followed a few steps behind. "Do you need help?"

At the door he stopped. "No; see that they rehearse. My agent tells me we have sold out each performance at the Palace. Expenses are increasing. We must do well on this tour. Do you understand?"

She understood all too well. The economics of a traveling troupe were simple. They lived on revenues from their performances minus a percentage for the theater owners. When the tours did well, they lived well. When they did poorly, they lived less than well.

"Did you hear her song?" Lily whispered, confident that Yorrick had.

He nodded, a residue of rapture on his face as though he were listening to the song in echo. "A gift," he repeated simply, "and I see it all so clearly. No production for this one. Not for her. No makeup, no extravagant gowns, just—Eve, just as I saw her a moment ago. Lord, Lily, what audience could resist?"

Lily smiled. Yorrick had perceived exactly what she had perceived, a new songbird guaranteed to break and capture hearts all the way from Dallas to San Francisco.

"Go along with you, Lily. Take the ladies through the last act of *Cabin*. It was absolutely dreadful the last time I saw it. Go on."

He waved her away, then renewed his grasp on Eve and carried her carefully through the narrow door, heading back toward his private coach.

Lily looked back into the coach filled with strangely subdued women. "Come on, ladies, to work. Yorrick tells me we're sold out for Dallas. You all are professionals in the truest sense of the word. To work!"

With this battle cry she stirred them into action, nursed their bruised egos, salved their wounded pride and set them moving again.

*　*　*

Eve thought, how good it had made her feel to sing, how effortlessly she had transported herself back to Stanhope Hall, to Mama's second-floor bedroom, those endless sessions when Mama had demonstrated how *she* had performed in Sim's Song and Supper Club in London, the cultivated sense of modesty and innocence, stretching the sweet high tones, reaching for the low ones, Mama applauding with such joy when she got it right, patiently telling her to do it again when she didn't, Mama so close, so near—

Then before she had known what was happening, strong arms had lifted her and she had seen Yorrick Harp up close, had smelled him, a peculiar blend of tobacco and spice she was beginning to recognize.

Now she thought back to the extreme pleasure that singing had given her. Who would have thought it? Such a simple act, something she had done all her life with tremendous ease, now capable of transporting her within the instant back to Stanhope Hall, Papa listening in the parlor, and the recent party during which she had sung for Mr. Clemens . . . such a happy time, thinking that in a few hours she would be with Stephen, the two of them racing through the night, soon to be wed, soon—

So many soons and none of them had come true. Abruptly she checked her thoughts, knowing where they would lead her.

Still it was good knowing that if she ever wanted to remember home and what she had lost, all she had to do was sing and everything would come flooding back.

Now she looked about and saw that Yorrick had placed her on his bed in his private coach. And he was there as well, smiling in a near chair.

"Why didn't you tell me you could sing?"

"You never asked," she replied.

Suddenly he threw back his head and laughed heartily for several minutes until he took note of her puzzled expression.

"Is there anything else that you can do that I have forgotten to ask?"

"I can play the pianoforte fairly well. Madame Germaine said I was good enough for the conservatory."

"And who is Madame Germaine?"

"My tutor. And David's, and Christine's."

"And who is David and who is Christine?"

"My brother and sister."

He nodded to everything she said and seemed terribly interested, although she couldn't understand why. Everyone had been telling her to forget the past. Now here he was asking her to remember it.

"Are you aware of the caliber of your voice?" he asked abruptly just when she was getting ready to tell him all about Christine and David.

"Mama said that with practice I could be better than she was."

"Your mother sings?"

"She did once. In London. Before I was born. Before she met Papa."

"And she's the one who taught you?"

"She helped me. Mama told me what to think while I'm singing the words."

"I don't understand."

"Well, for instance, in the song I just sang, when the girl sees her lover killed, Mama said to think of the saddest thing I could remem-

ber, the one sure thing that would cause tears, the one thing that still
hurt."

Eve heard her own words and could not go on. How changed she
was now. When her mother had first told her that, she couldn't think
of a single sad thing. Now all she had to do was close her eyes and her
memory was flooded with grief.

The subject, her tone, the sudden change of mood—something
seemed to work a profound effect on Yorrick Harp. Again he lifted
her in his arms as effortlessly as though she were a feather and carried
her to the cushions beside a cinder-streaked window. She felt comfortable in his arms, no longer terribly afraid, and tried to dismiss all
the images that were causing fresh grief.

"Better?" Yorrick asked. Then, "Look! Food. Are you hungry?"

She *was* hungry. Now she looked up to see a black man in a white
coat standing a distance away. She thought of Paris Boley, though
this man was much older, with white hair.

"Look what has just been served to us," Yorrick Harp urged.

Slowly Eve sat up and saw a cart laden with the most wondrous
foods—a plump golden roast chicken, several rounds of cheese, a platter of biscuits, a tiered arrangement of tea cakes of every flavor imaginable: chocolate, strawberry, lemon. And to one side a large silver
dish filled with dark purple grapes, dew still coating their skins.

"Here," Yorrick urged. "Would you like me to serve you?"

Without waiting for a response he gave a nod to the man behind
the cart and walked with her to a table set up near the opposite
window, covered with a linen cloth, heavy silver and delicate china,
and in the center of the table a vase filled with dark red roses.

"Here we are." Yorrick smiled and held the chair for her.

Then a few moments later he was before her carrying a heaped
platter of food in one hand and a crystal decanter of port wine in the
other.

When at last Yorrick had settled opposite her, she reached for the
golden chicken leg without further delay and closed her eyes at the
first taste of its succulent goodness.

With food and drink she felt her mood lift, her spirits rise, and even
once dared to return the smile that Yorrick Harp was beaming her
way across the table.

Mary had heard Burke's incredible tale of what had transpired in Mobile at least four times. The first time he had delivered it for her ears alone. Then he had told Christine and David. Christine had wept. David had merely stared dry-eyed and had muttered, "I should have gone with Paris and Stephen. After all, I am her brother."

Mary had quickly talked her son out of that foolish notion, and then the two of them, Mary and Burke, had gone to tell the servants and Madame Germaine. Many had shed new tears. All had promised to pray for Eve as well as for the two who had gone off in pursuit of her. All had seemed to listen to the account with a degree of skepticism.

Now Mary sat on the front gallery, her skirts drawn up around her, and she listened as Burke told the tale yet again to a few of his best workers, men who would have to cover for Paris Boley in his absence, hearing slight variations depending upon his audience, emphasizing for these men the details of the fistfight he'd had with Jarmay Higgins, the whole account pushing Mary's incredulity to the brink.

"So I'll be depending heavily on all of you until Paris's return," she heard Burke saying, having at last talked himself out.

One man asked, "And where is it they was heading, Mr. Stanhope?"

"Toward New Orleans."

"Is that where they think Miss Eve had gotten to?"

"Supposedly. She's traveling with a theatrical troupe now, Henry, or so we were told. I'm sorry, I just don't—"

"Well, Miss Eve ought to be at home where she belongs," Henry grumbled, and Mary sensed Burke's frustration, and yet she felt a degree of understanding for everyone who had listened to his tale. In the telling of it he seemed to vacillate between being too vague and too specific. The torn dress; Mary wished she had not heard that. And this alleged theatrical troupe owned by a man with the strange name —what was the connection between them and the fire at Fan Cottage?

"Mama?"

The soft voice came from behind and sounded exactly like Eve. Mary turned about, fully expecting to see a ghost and in fact did see an apparition that resembled a ghost, Christine, who'd suffered perhaps more than any of them since Eve's—

Mary had started to think *death*. "Come," she beckoned to Christine.

Behind Christine she saw an apologetic Katie, Christine's nurse-maid since the day of her birth. "She won't sleep, Mrs. Stanhope. All she says is she has to wait up for Eve to come home. Tell her, ma'am, please tell her that—"

As Katie's voice drifted off into the confusion that seemed to have settled over all of Stanhope Hall, Mary beckoned her youngest daughter to come to her.

As she nestled in Mary's arms, she felt her forehead with her cheek and felt the fever that had been raging for several days. "Why aren't you asleep?" Mary gently scolded.

"Let me stay here with you, Mama. I don't want to be asleep when Eve comes home."

"You must listen," Mary began. "We are not sure—that is, we don't know—what I am trying to say is—"

In her incoherency Mary wasn't quite certain what she was trying to say. In a way she found herself now resenting this "good news" that Burke had brought back from Mobile.

What did it mean? That instead of being dead and at peace, Eve was perhaps alive and suffering even more?

"Mama?"

It was Christine again.

"Mama, please let me stay up until Eve comes home."

"She might not come today," Mary warned gently.

"Papa said—"

"He said only that Paris and Stephen had gone in search of her. That's all. It might take several days. So, you see, you might be wise to go to your room and get a good long nap that will refresh you and make you strong so that when Eve *does* return, you will be ready to greet her."

Christine was listening. "Will you come up and sing a song for me? I miss Eve singing to me. She always sang to me before a nap."

"I'll be up in a few minutes, I promise."

Without a word of protest Christine allowed Katie to carry her back into the cool shade of the house.

Slowly Mary turned around again and saw Burke staring after the workers. It was as though for both of them, the energy of the mind and body was wearing thin.

From where she sat she studied him, this husband of many years, most of them very good, many deliriously happy.

"Christine?"

The question was Burke's, who apparently had seen his frail younger daughter in Mary's arms. She nodded. "She wouldn't stay in bed. She wanted to be awake when Eve—"

She looked out into the green hot distance and rubbed her hands as though she were cold. "I understand—so little," she murmured.

"I know," Burke said with gentle consideration and sat close beside her on the top step and covered her hands with his own.

"I'm afraid that there is nothing we can do now but wait," he murmured. "I take full responsibility," he added. "If only I had accepted the boy instead of—"

Though she agreed with him, she felt that love would be better served if she disagreed. "It wasn't your fault," she said.

He looked slowly around. "Then you understand . . ."

"Of course I do." She smiled and took his arm and drew him closer. "I felt so distant from you of late," she murmured and pressed his arm against her breast and rested her head on his shoulder.

"I have the strongest feeling that Stephen and Paris will find her," he said quietly, "and will return her safely to us."

"Don't," she begged, not wanting to hear more.

Suddenly she shivered.

"Are you cold?" Burke asked, a new tone of concern in his voice.

She shook her head, unable to speak.

"Would you like to go upstairs?" he asked, almost shyly.

"Let's sit here for a while longer. We used to sit like this every evening when we first arrived. Do you remember?"

"Eve took her first steps right there." He smiled and pointed to the grassy knoll just this side of the avenue of live oaks.

"And a good step it was," Mary agreed. "She was graceful even then."

"And so beautiful."

Remembering helped. They sat on the steps in the late afternoon sun and talked of Eve—her first birthday, her first Christmas, her first tooth, her first party dress. And even as they talked, they seemed to resurrect her and that made her seem closer, though Mary knew better and knew further that Eve, at least the one that they had created between them, might very well be dead.

Talked out, Burke at last quietly excused himself and went to the fields. Without Paris, he said, he felt a need to keep closer touch.

Mary watched him until he was out of sight and then bowed her head and said a prayer for all, for Paris and Stephen, for Burke, for Christine and David, for everyone in Stanhope Hall, and most of all for Eve.

Paris was too ashamed to do much talking during the long night of hard riding. With every bone-jarring mile he tried to subdue his excitement over the prospects of this adventure and substitute instead deep concern and fear for Eve Stanhope.

He had grown up with Eve. His childhood was a pleasantly blurred memory of the little blond-haired, blue-eyed girl who was capable of talking him into mischief and somehow capable of talking them both out of trouble as well.

So now the fact that he had been permitted to go on this search with Stephen Eden filled him with a stern sense of duty and responsibility. But also he felt an almost unbearable excitement at this dream come true, a chance, God willing, to see the rest of this land. Once he had thought that he would be doomed forever never to set foot out of Alabama.

Not that he wasn't grateful to Burke Stanhope and Mr. Washington and all the patient teachers at Tuskegee, who had taken on an overcurious little black boy and smoothed the rough edges and taught him how to dress and how to read and how to organize his thoughts and how to be able to articulate them to others.

So while he was grateful for all this, he sometimes felt he'd sold a large portion of his soul into a different kind of bondage and thus would be forced to remain forever in the South.

Now with the outskirts of New Orleans just before them, the smoke from thousands of breakfast fires filling the warm September morning with a blue haze, he was aware of Stephen breaking speed for the first time in several hours. Both of their horses were overheated and lathered; they would either have to rest them here or purchase new ones.

"Straight ahead," Stephen called back to Paris now and led his weary mount head-on into the fringed commerce of busy New Orleans.

Only then did Paris think to call out, "What is your destination, Stephen? We need to—"

"Train station," Stephen called over his shoulder. "Captain Willing said that Yorrick Harp had mentioned catching a train out of New Orleans."

Paris started to suggest that they stop and inquire directly for the quickest route to the train station. But there was nothing about Stephen to indicate he was in the mood to stop for anything. He had set a fast pace, which Paris knew they could not maintain, and now with traffic increasing around them, there was even a good possibility they might become separated in the crush of the crowded city.

As Stephen fought his way through the congestion, Paris did his best to keep him in sight and finally caught up at a crowded intersection.

"I think you're going the wrong way," he said and for the first time in several hours caught a direct glimpse of Stephen's face. Fatigue blended there with grief, though there was the light of new hope, and covering all was a patina of sweat.

"What do you suggest?"

"I don't know. The railway station could be in the opposite direction."

"Where?"

"I said I didn't know. I suggest we make inquiry and at the same time find food and drink. We can't—"

"No, no time."

"We'd better make time or else we will lack the strength to continue."

"Then where?" Stephen demanded.

Paris looked about and saw nothing except small storefronts and a press of black and white faces and an endless stream of wagons all heading into the city loaded with produce.

"Over there," he shouted above the growing din and took the lead for the first time since they'd left Mobile. Up ahead he saw what looked like a tavern sign, and angled his horse through the traffic toward the far side of the road and hoped that Stephen was following.

Together they guided their horses to the hitching post and only belatedly did Paris look up at the black lace ironwork on the balcony above to see a half-dozen white women, scantily clad in chemises and bloomers, leaning over the edge of the balcony.

Quickly he lowered his eyes and kept them fixed on Stephen as he climbed stiffly down from his horse.

"What is this place?" asked Stephen.

Paris shrugged. "It says tavern. I assume we can get food and drink."

"Surely there is a better—"

"Where? Do you want to find it?"

As their tempers briefly flared, Paris backed away from the confrontation. He didn't want to quarrel with anyone about anything. It was just that he was hungry and thirsty and they needed food and a moment's rest before they continued.

Stephen led the way through the tavern doors, and Paris followed. Once inside, he found himself in almost total darkness, though his

vision adjusted rapidly to flickering lamplight spaced at regular inter-
vals and seeming to follow a long, low, tunnellike room.

As they passed through the doors, Paris thought he had heard
voices. Now he heard nothing, but somehow he knew they weren't
alone.

"Anyone here?" he called out, and his voice echoed about the dark,
tunnellike room.

Then Paris knew where they were—in a barrelhouse, an establishment frequented by men whose only intention was to get drunk. He
saw a long row of stacked barrels on one side of the room and a table
filled with pewter mugs on the other. Generally for a nickle, sometimes less, a man was allowed to fill a mug from any of the barrels.

"Come on, Stephen, this isn't what we—"

"Hey, you."

The strong voice seemed to evolve out of the shadows. Paris turned
in all directions. He saw a dozen men in various states of inebriation,
all looking up at the intruders.

"Come on," Stephen murmured, heading back toward the door.

Then, "It's a nigger," was heard by all, and in that instant Paris
realized what he'd done, had grown careless and secure under the
privilege that covered him at Stanhope Hall.

He had only a moment to look back toward the door to see if Stephen had made it to safety, for *his* offense was one of association, and
these illiterate and half-drunken sons of the South would just as soon
attack the companion of a nigger as the nigger himself.

But unfortunately Paris saw that Stephen had not made it to the
door, for at that moment the door leading to the hot street outside
was being blocked by a red-haired giant who was just reaching out for
Stephen, and at the same time Paris felt strong hands seize him from
behind and attempt to twist his arms backward.

"Paris!"

The one sharp yell came from Stephen, who suddenly commenced
to attack the red-haired giant with both fists, a surprise assault that
caught the man off guard, while Paris, feeling he had nothing to lose,
did the same. He jerked forward on the arms that tried to restrain
him and felt their grip break immediately and belatedly realized that
he and Stephen had one advantage—they were not drunk in any degree, which was more than could be said of the men in the barrelhouse.

Then the room exploded into a slow-motion free-for-all, Paris
swinging his fists eagerly with not a great deal of expertise, but fear
supplied him with the will and energy he required. When he had
dispatched one of the rednecks in record time, his enthusiasm grew

along with his confidence and he wheeled on the second, who foolishly had brought his pewter mug to the fray. The dull silver mug
caught what little illumination there was in the room and provided
Paris with the perfect target, and as he swung again the man toppled
backward. The mug of rotgut went sailing through the air and
clanked against the row of barrels, a curious noise that seemed to
sound the alarm, for out of the shadows staggered two more men,
stumbling drunk both of them, but coming fast at him all the same,
one muttering as he drew near, "We got your black tail now, nigger."

Paris, in his enthusiasm to silence the obscene mouth, started
swinging too soon, a premature gesture that, lacking a target, sent
him spinning off balance, and he was stopped by the force of one
well-aimed fist that collided in a blow to the side of his right jaw and
sent him spiraling backward, his head ultimately smashing into one
of the barrels. It was the second blow that rendered him senseless.

He felt the collapse first in his knees, as though someone had removed all the bones and left only the flesh and tissues to support him.
As he fell, he tried to bring Stephen into focus, to see if he was faring
better or worse. Better, he hoped, or else their search for Eve would
be short-lived.

* * *

Stephen flattened three men effortlessly and was ready for the
fourth when suddenly the doors were pushed open and a street constable appeared in his tall blue hat and carrying a billy stick.

For several moments he stood silhouetted against the blazing sun.
As Stephen waited, fists ready for the next assault, the constable took
note of the sprawled bodies and those still standing, and without a
word motioned Stephen to step outside with a wag of his head.

The drunken men all seemed to retreat back to the long row of
barrels. Stephen spied Paris, sprawled near the long table of pewter
mugs. Carefully stepping over the other bodies, Stephen bent down
and with some effort hoisted Paris over his shoulder like a large,
unwieldy sack of potatoes.

As the constable was still holding the door, Stephen walked out
into the light and heat of morning and as gently as possible draped
Paris over his saddle and decided to let him recover at will.

"Friend?" the constable asked with a flat voice that matched his flat
face.

"Yes," Stephen replied.

Slowly the constable shook his head. "Not here. Here you had better make him your manservant. Understand?"

Stephen nodded.

"He waits outside when you eat and drink. Understand?"

Again Stephen nodded.

"Niggers—are—niggers," he concluded stupidly.

The man now stepped back as though he had delivered a hard lesson to a dimwitted child. Stephen watched him walk a few feet away, and then called out, "I beg your pardon, sir. Which way is the railway station?"

The man blinked at him as though the question had offended him. Then in a slow gesture he lifted his hand and pointed with a single finger in a broad westward direction.

Stephen pulled himself up into his saddle, all the time tightening his grip on his reins and those of Paris's horse.

"Easy," Stephen whispered to his horse and urged him forward, leading Paris's horse behind him, aware of the spectacle they must present, though at one point, after receiving several smiles from drivers of passing wagons, a rider drew close and shouted, "Got you one, did you?" Stephen began to realize that this arrangement might be the safest way to travel through the southern part of America, for apparently it was impossible for a white man and a black man to travel any other way.

"You selling him?" a man's voice yelled from a passing wagon.

"No." Stephen smiled and shook his head.

"Is he dead or alive?" came a second male shout.

"Not sure," Stephen replied and tried to urge his horse to greater speed, his feelings of discomfort growing along with his clear perception of this place, these people.

A few minutes later he spied a curved railway track joining the boulevard and running parallel to it.

Then straight ahead he saw a convergence of tracks, and beyond the tracks, about a block ahead, he saw a large yellow limestone turreted building, fronted by a grassy island.

He broke speed. The railway station, obviously. Now what?

Then he heard a slurred inquiry of "Are you all right?" and looked down to see Paris awake, though rubbing his head, trotting alongside him. Apparently he'd slipped free from his horse and had elected to go it on foot for a while.

Quickly Stephen swung down from his horse and led the animals with Paris following behind to the grassy island directly across from the busy railway station.

There were a few people dotted about on the soft grass, obviously travelers waiting for departing trains. In the distance he spied a stream. "Over there," he suggested, thinking the horses could use water as well as grazing grass.

Paris drew even with him and relieved him of one set of reins. "I believe thanks are due for something."

Stephen grinned. "No need. What was that place?"

"A barrelhouse. Cheap rotgut for men who want to get blind drunk."

"Fortunately for us, a few were well on their way."

"Did you—"

"No, I got the luck of the draw. Most fell of their own accord without any help from me."

A few yards later Stephen said, "Here," indicating a partially secluded area. Up ahead a few yards he saw two men lounging near the water, each unrolling small knapsacks, either a late breakfast or an early lunch.

The sight of food caused a turning in his stomach, forcibly reminding him how long it had been since they had eaten or taken liquid. Paris apparently saw the distant picnic as well and volunteered, "Let me go into the station house and—"

Abruptly Stephen shook his head, remembering the cause of their recent unpleasant encounter back at the barrelhouse. "No, you wait here. Watch the horses. I can move more quickly. I'll check on early-morning train schedules while I'm there. It might help if we knew."

Paris agreed, all the time tethering the animals close enough to the stream to drink and to graze.

Stephen started off alone across the grassy island, sidestepping picnickers and small dogs and laughing children. At the edge of the pavement he stopped and saw a long line of cabs waiting for fares arriving, departing. Which way to go? Whom to approach? What questions to ask? And of whom?

 Dallas

Still suffering the humiliation of leg irons, Eve tried to stand after the long confinement of the train journey and immediately felt her knees buckle and sank back into the cushions of Yorrick Harp's private coach. She looked up, aware that Harp was watching her.

"I might do better without these," she said.

"I'm sure you would." He smiled, looking quite grand in a flowing black cape, shiny top hat, black ebony walking stick and blood-crimson cravat. "Still we are our past, and your past unhappily disputes your word. Wait here. I'll call for help."

With that he was gone, leaving her staring out the window at a place called Dallas. She'd never heard of it and had no desire to see it now.

Flat and dusty, the earth seemed to stretch before her in an unbroken line. The landscape for as far as she could see was barren of all that was green and fertile. Dust clouds erupted from behind the hundreds of covered wagons that seemed to press close around the squat railway station. On the boarding platform she saw a sea of men in flat-brimmed hats moving as though they were in a stupor, saw dark-faced Mexican vendors selling something that looked like cornhusks, and she saw a large tent city, row after row of canvas whipping in the strong prairie wind. Directly to the south of the tent city she saw a river, dark brown, with muddy banks. North of the river was what appeared to be the beginnings of a more permanent settlement.

Eve closed her eyes and thought with a longing that was akin to pain of home, of the verdant blue-green Mobile River, of the soft, inviting green lawn that skirted Stanhope Hall on all sides, of the live oaks and their graceful Spanish moss and welcoming shade.

Quickly she opened her eyes to cancel the memory before it did too much damage. Early on in this endless journey she had determined, with Lily's help, that looking back was not the wisest thing to do.

"There you are." She looked up to see Lily smiling down at her, in the company of a woman she'd never seen before, older, with a thick waist and tiny round wire spectacles that sat on the very end of a somewhat bulbous nose. The woman wore a black feather hat with a complete bird perched on her brow, and wore it low over a fringe of tightly curled gray hair.

"This is Mother," Lily said and smiled. "You should have met her before we left New Orleans, but she was very busy."

Eve gaped up at the baffling introduction and the even more baffling woman, who appeared to be equally curious about all aspects of Eve.

"Hello," Eve murmured and tried to read the expression on the woman's face.

"You're too thin," the woman suddenly snapped. "Men like flesh, lots of it. They like to be able to look at it, to touch it, to imagine what it would feel like to lie against it. My first recommendation would be more flesh, lots more flesh."

A strong male voice topped the officious female voice. "Not on your life, Mother!" Yorrick Harp thundered. "We are not aiming for carnal pleasure with this one. Look at her. What does she remind you of?"

Eve pushed back into the cushions, suddenly embarrassed by their close scrutiny, all three of them gazing down at her as though they were selecting a roast from the butcher shop.

"A child," Mother said with a sniff. "She reminds me of a child."

"On the verge of becoming a woman."

"Perhaps, but a thin one."

"A lovely one, every man's dream, the child-bride, the virgin lover, untouched by all hands save God's."

Eve looked down and studied her hands, tightly laced in her lap.

"Look up, my child," Yorrick Harp commanded. "Never be ashamed of anything. Do you understand? You are a rare creation of God's, and therefore among the blessed of the cosmos. You were drawn from a rare design, breathed life into and now here you are, a testament to the genius that is the life force. Nothing—do you understand—nothing must ever cause you to bow your head again."

For several long moments no one spoke, and Eve began to feel a hot blush creep down from her hairline and over her forehead and cheeks.

"There." Yorrick beamed and stood back near the door. "If that isn't the most beautiful sight in God's entire creation, I'm sure I don't know what is. A blushing young virgin on the verge of meeting the world, all new, everything new, untried and untested."

He stared a moment longer. Then, "Well, enough," he announced at last and pushed away from the door and stirred the other two women into action as well.

"Escort our new beauty to the Rail's End. See that she is fed and washed and rested and bring her to the Palace at four o'clock sharp. We will need a short rehearsal before—"

Lily looked up, shocked, "Not tonight, Yorrick. She's not—surely not—"

"Why not?" Yorrick insisted. "I see nothing on her face to suggest a state of unreadiness."

"But the men, the crowds, she's never—"

"Nonsense."

"But she's not ready, Yorrick, please."

"Look at that face. That face was born to a state of readiness and has been waiting for it every day of her life." He whirled about, swirling his satiny black cape behind him. "Besides, she must earn her keep. The free ride of privileged childhood is over. Everyone here puts on the harness sooner or later. And for my pretty, the time has come."

As he exited, Lily called after him. "And what about the irons?"

"They remain. She still has the look of flight in her eyes. We will fix her in a pose before the curtain rises."

"It's unheard of, all of it," the woman named Mother called after Yorrick.

"Then we will be in that most glorious company ever created by the minds of men: the first. Oh Lord, it's grand to be the first at anything. Take care of her, both of you, or it's your hides I'll tan."

All the way down the narrow railway corridor, his voice trailed after him until it disappeared behind the sudden slamming of the door. Then there was only silence except for the muted sounds outside the train window, wagons being loaded with trunks for transport to the Palace, a flat, dusty, barren scene of shouting men and protesting horses and constantly blowing sand.

"Come, child," the woman named Mother commanded, and Eve looked away from the bleak scene to see the woman extending a hand while Lily on the other side did the same.

"Lean on us," Lily advised, "and remember to take very small steps," she repeated, "to avoid tripping yourself."

Once up, Eve did very well, slowly growing accustomed to the irons.

"I think he's out of his mind this time," Lily muttered. "She's not ready. Who knows what she'll do on that stage?"

"Perhaps, though I've never seen him make a wrong decision."

"Men do not come to the Adamless Eden shows to see their sisters or their daughters. They want—"

"I know what they want," Mother interrupted.

"Besides, she is still weak from her ordeal."

"Apparently Yorrick thinks she is ready."

"Well, she isn't. Look at her. She can hardly stand."

Having been talked over and around for long enough, Eve saw the narrow door straight ahead and said in her own defense, "I'd do better without these, as you both know," and indicated the leg irons.

"And you heard what Yorrick said. No one else has the authority to take them off," Mother snapped and at the same time withdrew her support from Eve's right side, momentarily throwing her off balance.

"Mother!" Lily protested, struggling to keep Eve upright.

For several unhappy seconds Eve felt the weight of their eyes, though Lily's were always tempered with kindness.

"Come along then," Mother ordered, and once again Eve felt firm support on either side as they guided her through the narrow door and down the steep steps, where a blast of hot, dusty prairie wind slapped her in the face and caused her eyes to tear.

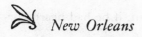 *New Orleans*

"A theatrical troupe," Stephen repeated to a slow-eyed man behind the main ticket counter. "They were to have departed New Orleans sometime yesterday by rail—a large theatrical troupe, primarily women, as I understand it, who . . ."

Stephen ran out of words and allowed his voice to fall as low as his spirits. The old man behind the ticket counter had appeared to grow even more puzzled with each qualifier.

Now he shook his head and scowled beneath his green eyeshades. "I never heard of the likes. Do you want to buy a ticket or not?"

Wearily Stephen shook his head, shifted the package of hard rolls and cheese to the other hand and stared out into the cavernous railway terminal, only partially filled now with travelers. Three trains had departed within the hour.

What now? He had already asked at least a dozen people who should remember such an exotic troupe, yet no one remembered anything. No one even seemed to know what he was talking about.

At the front door he stepped aside to make room for a cabby in a long black coat and flat black hat who was carrying an armload of baggage. As Stephen held the door, the cabby nodded his thanks with a strained expression and muttered, "Don't nobody travel empty-handed anymore?"

Stephen smiled his sympathy and tried to push the doors wider and watched apprehensively as the top part of the precarious pyramid of hat boxes began to shift and topple. Quickly he placed his package of rolls and cheese to one side of the door and stepped forward in time to catch the top boxes until at last the cabby was able to juggle the remaining ones.

"Thanks." The man puffed and struggled to keep the remaining pieces of baggage in balance. "You'd think Harp's girls was still with us."

Stephen waited a moment to see if this new balance would hold better than the first. Apparently it did, for the cabby managed to call back his thanks, to which Stephen nodded and reached down for his package of lunch and pushed open the front doors and stepped out into the rising heat of a noontime sun.

He was halfway across the cobblestone drive, heading toward the grassy island and the cool stream where he had left Paris, when two words registered on his consciousness like thunderbolts.

Harp's girls.

"Wait!" he shouted back toward the terminal doors and broke into a run, instantly reversing his position, not certain if he had heard correctly.

Back inside the terminal he glanced toward the far gate through which he had seen the cabby disappearing. There was no one in sight now. He increased his speed until at last he stood at the high barred gates and looked through to the tracks.

Harp's girls—Harp's girls—

Housy Dunbar and Captain Willing had said the man's name was Yorrick Harp.

Suddenly up ahead he spied the long black coat and flat-topped black hat, standard apparel for cabbies.

"You, sir, please," Stephen shouted and increased his speed through the crowds already gathering for the next train departure.

He was out the door now and onto the hot pavement, which reflected rising heat waves. He tried to shield his eyes with his hands and saw the cabby rapidly crossing the street, heading for his cab.

"Sir, please—" Stephen shouted again, wondering if the cabby had gone conveniently deaf. But at that moment the cabby spotted Stephen and brusquely waved his hand and hurriedly swung up onto the high seat and was in the process of bringing the reins down across the horse's back when, suddenly angry, Stephen made a lunge for the harness, thus prohibiting the cab from moving forward.

"Go on with you. Get away," the cabby snapped. "I'll not pay you a cent. I didn't ask for your help and I ain't gonna pay for it. Now git on with you before I—"

Then Stephen understood. Apparently the cabby thought he was going to ask for a cut of his fare and tip.

"I want nothing except a word with you," Stephen said.

"About what?" the cabby demanded.

"Something you said."

"What?"

"A name. You said something about Harp. You said *Harp's girls.* Do you remember?"

"Sure I do."

"Who is Harp and what did you mean when you said his girls?"

Abruptly the cabby laughed. "Now surely I don't have to tell a young buck like you who Yorrick Harp is?"

Yorrick Harp. That was the name. Stephen reached up and grasped the seat handle as though prepared to pull himself upward. "Tell me who Yorrick Harp is."

"A giant," the cabby said flatly.

"And—" Stephen urged.

"He's a giant of a man lucky enough to own his own harem."

"I don't understand."

"Gals." The cabby grinned. "Plenty of 'em, real beauties, too."

"I'm looking for someone," Stephen confessed at last. "I have reason to believe she is in the company of this—"

"Harp?" the cabby asked, his eyes growing wide with new interest. He patted the seat beside him and obligingly moved over to make room. "Who is it you're missing? Wife? Sister?"

Stephen looked out from the vantage point of the high seat over the grassy island. "A girl," he said.

"Sweetheart." The cabby grinned.

"We were to have been married."

"What happened?" the cabby asked, the light of sympathy on his face.

Stephen counseled himself patience. Time was passing. The sun was climbing. Eve had obviously gone on ahead, somewhere.

"She was—kidnapped."

"And you think she's with old Harp now?" the cabby asked in a gentle voice.

"I don't know. We were told—"

"It makes sense." The cabby nodded. "Of course rumors are always dancing around a man like Yorrick Harp. But I've heard some say that he deals in white slavery."

"Do you know him?"

"Personally? No. He's stuck up, he comes waltzing in here like he owns the place, surrounded by all those gals."

"When did you last see him?"

"Yesterday," the cabby said. "His troupe left here yesterday."

"Headed where?"

The cabby appeared to think a minute, then, "Dallas," he said and sharply nodded his head. "Yeah, Dallas. One of the gals told me Dallas." He shook his head. "We had some excitement here, we did. One of Harp's gals tried to run away. Come to my cab direct, she did."

"What did you do?"

"I took her right back to Harp. He'd have had my hide otherwise."

Stephen listened closely. If Eve was alive, was with the man named Yorrick Harp and on her way to Dallas, then he was wasting valuable time.

"Thanks again," he said and swung down from the high seat, still clutching the brown package that was to have been lunch for Paris and himself.

As Stephen backed away from the cab, he wasn't certain whether to believe anything that the man had told him. A voice of wisdom counseled, believe nothing, believe everything, and waste no more time.

Quickly he made his way through the long line of waiting cabs, running across the grassy island toward the stream in search of Paris. A place called Dallas was their next destination, then. How and when they would arrive, he had no idea. How and when they would catch up with Yorrick Harp, he had no idea. How and when and if ever he would find Eve, only God knew.

* * *

The overpowering smell of manure rose on all sides from the damp straw, but with the first clanging turn of the wheels, Stephen dared to relax.

Across from him on the opposite side of the cattle car he watched Paris hungrily devour the cheese and rolls, the lunch he had purchased hours ago from the vendor in the terminal.

Shortly after the cabby had told him of Yorrick Harp and "his gals," Stephen had learned that there was a late-afternoon Texas-Pacific train heading for Dallas. He had learned further that there were no accommodations for a gentleman wanting to travel with "his nigger," though a sympathetic conductor had pointed out a recently emptied cattle car that was bound for Dallas, empty now and would return filled with Texas beef by the end of the week.

So they had sold their horses for a small profit to a nearby stable master and had just climbed aboard the smelly cattle car when the first shriek of the steam engine was heard, followed immediately by the slow but rhythmic clanging of the huge wheels.

Now as the train increased its speed, Stephen tried to blot out the foul smells around him, convinced that they had made the right decision. Dallas sometime late tomorrow night, and surely that small frontier cow town would not be as skillful at concealing people as was a large cosmopolitan city like New Orleans.

"Sure you don't want any?" Paris offered over the clatter of the wheels and held up a hard roll and a crumbling slab of yellow cheese.

Stephen shook his head. He had been hungry earlier, but the odor plus worry had killed his appetite. There would be stops later, time to jump off and climb back on.

For now, in this first moment of relative relaxation, he found himself hearing the cabby's voice. *"One of Harp's gals tried to run away. Come to my cab, she did."*

Had it been Eve trying to escape?

"Stephen?"

This quiet voice cut into his fear and he saw Paris, who had moved closer on his knees across the rocking cattle car.

"I think we're lucky to have come this far," Paris reassured him. "And all we need, all we'll ever need is the next clue, from someone who has seen them, and sooner or later we will catch up, I swear it. We *will* find Eve, and then—"

Stephen listened, grateful for Paris's conviction. It was the "and then," however, the sudden cessation of Paris's voice that left them gaping at each other, both vibrating with the movement of the train, the great unanswered question mark of the future between them.

 Dallas

Under the constant and watchful gaze of the woman they called Mother, Eve was taken to the Rail's End Hotel in the back of a wagon, through whirlwinds of dust that stung her face and momentarily blinded her to the ugliness of the sprawling settlement. She saw wobbly facades being buffeted by the strong prairie wind, and men riding down the rutted, dusty road, yelling at each other from atop wagons, or stumbling drunk alongside the makeshift board sidewalks. No women, not a woman in view that Eve could see through the grit and dust and perpetually amber-colored sky.

And the odors. Once inside the rough-timbered interior of the Rail's End Hotel, the discomfort of blowing dust was replaced by the discomfort of the most foul odors Eve had ever suffered, a blend of old urine and soiled linen and spoiled food, all mixed together and contained within the closed confines of the hotel whose proprietor had erected a hand-lettered sign directly above the narrow front door warning everyone to Keep this damn door shut or else.

Mother assisted her up a narrow wooden staircase, supporting her when the steep steps proved too much for the leg irons. When they reached the second-floor landing, Eve looked down a dim hallway, the only light filtering in through a tall high window at the end, and from behind each closed door she heard chattering and giggling, sometimes a female voice running the scales, or the discordant sound of an ill-tuned instrument.

Apparently the entire company had arrived ahead of them. Now out of breath, she glanced at the woman named Mother who appeared to be searching each door for a number.

Near the end of the hallway she found it and pushed open the door to reveal a spartan interior: one high window with a drawn yellow shade, two narrow beds, one on either side of the room, each with one blanket and one pillow stacked at the foot, and against the wall was one large chipped pitcher and bowl resting on an upturned wooden crate.

"Dallas," sniffed Mother in clear condemnation. "Come on, let's get ourselves washed up. Now hurry."

Obligingly Eve shuffled through the door, tried for speed and failed and tripped over the leg irons and fell painfully to her knees.

"Small steps," Mother scolded.

"How much longer?" Eve pleaded.

"When Yorrick says so and not before."

Mother went to the bed on the right and commenced removing her hat, still looking about the barren room in a most critical manner. "No water," she complained, tipping the empty pitcher over. "You wait here. I'll fetch some clean towels as well as water."

Without another word she disappeared into the hallway. Before the door closed behind her, Eve heard female voices, excited, greeting the woman named Mother warmly, telling her that they would see her later at the Palace and hurry.

Everyone was leaving. Eve could hear the sharp staccato of their shoes on the wooden staircase, Yorrick Harp's troupe heading for something called the Palace, all leaving her behind, seated on the edge of a bed, staring down at the leg irons.

She bent over and cradled her forehead in her hands, briefly blocking the ugliness from view. Someone would come for her in a few minutes to push her in another direction, to command her to perform in a manner they found pleasing. All she had to do was bide her time and keep strong inside and out and wait for the right opportunity to—

There! Hear it? Footsteps coming. She sat still upon the hard mattress and waited.

More than one coming. Several. Heavy steps like men's boots. And now voices.

"They gotta be up here somewheres. I seen 'em come in."

"You're sure they're on this floor? Maybe—"

"This is the one. Them gals always stay here. I know. Last year I was here when they was."

Somewhere down the long hallway doors were being opened and closed as though someone was looking for something.

She heard a curse then. "Damn, where do you suppose they got to? They jes were here. I saw 'em."

"We'll see 'em tonight."

"I don't want to see 'em at the Palace. I want to see 'em here. What they do here is better than what they do at the Palace. I guarantee it."

Still the voices came closer. Eve looked about for a hiding place. And found none. Even the crawl space beneath the low beds was not sufficient.

Then she saw the door fly open with such force that it banged against the wall and shuddered back and was immediately slammed open again.

She drew herself up, her chained ankles tucked beneath her long blue skirt, and saw three male faces, bearded, their flat-brimmed hats sweat stained, the distinct odor of strong whiskey emanating from their filthy garments. They seemed as surprised to see her as she was to see them.

"Well, lookee here," one said as he grinned down. "See? I told you we'd find 'em."

"She don't look more than a kid," the second one complained, coming all the way into the room and approaching Eve.

"What's your name, honey?" the grinning one asked and bent closer.

She ducked her head to escape his foul odor and saw the third man coming up on the opposite side, a boy really, his face smooth, reminding her of her brother David, older than David but not as old as the two gaping down at her from left and right.

"Seth, you ever seen one of these before?" The one on the right grinned and sat heavily beside her on the bed. His legs spread, revealing worn trousers and manure-caked boots.

"Course I have," the young boy boasted.

"That ain't your ma, you know." The other man laughed. "Ain't your sister either, or your aunts. This one's for fun," he added and leaned against the wall, one boot raised. "Ya ever had that kind of fun before, Seth?"

The boy ducked his head and grew brave. "What's your name?" he asked and she tried to rein in her fear, confident that the woman named Mother would return shortly and clear the room.

"Come on, tell us your name," the older man coaxed. "Ain't gonna hurt none to talk a spell." He stepped away from the wall and moved close enough to lift her hair in his hand, pulling upward with a force that hurt. As she tried to move away, her skirt eased to one side, the leg irons visible for all to see.

"Whoa! What in the—" the older man stammered and joined the others in close examination of her ankles.

"She's gone and made someone mad as hell." The older man grinned, still holding her suspended by the hair.

Slowly one of the men bent over and gave the irons a tug. "Locked," he muttered.

"Well, what did you expect?"

"Who'd you try to run away from, honey?"

Eve looked straight ahead, still held at a rigid angle by the man to her right. She'd never seen this kind of man before, shaggy, more animal-appearing than man, all except the boy, who giggled and watched and said nothing.

But worse than the way they looked was their manner, their attitude, something arrogant and mindless in their faces, as though few forces in this world had ever successfully challenged them.

"So what are we gonna do now?" the older man asked of no one in particular and continued to hold her head rigid. Directly before her stood the boy, a smile on his face as he apparently derived a degree of pleasure by simply looking at her.

"She's a looker," he murmured and lifted one hand to her face, his fingers touching her cheeks, a touch from which she tried to turn away except that the man behind twisted her hair tighter, causing the sensation of sharp needles to cover her scalp, a burning pain that caused her eyes to tear and prompted her to speak on her own behalf.

"Please, let me go," she whispered and tried to reach up toward the hand that held her hair and could not and ultimately had no choice but to sit before them all, the boy's hands now on her throat, his eyes dully glazed, reflecting the pleasure the touch was giving him.

"That's it, Seth, enjoy yourself. I think this little gal is just your speed. Hal and me, we'll watch, give you some hints if we think you need 'em."

Slowly the older man settled back, lifting his boot to the edge of the bed. "My arm's killin me," he grumbled.

"Then let her go," the other man advised. "She ain't going noplace. Someone else has seen to that for us. So just let her go."

Blessedly he did, and Eve felt her head falling forward, her hair cascading around her face. For a moment she was losing balance, in danger of falling over. But the boy reached out and steadied her, his face very close to hers now.

"You okay?" he asked and continued to hold her steady by the shoulders until she sat up and felt the leg irons biting into her flesh.

"Who did that to you?" the boy asked, a new compassion on his young face, where up close she saw the soft fuzz of a beginning beard.

She said nothing, trying to indicate without words that it wasn't important.

"What's your name? Why won't you tell me your name?" the boy asked further, a hurt quality in his face and voice.

"You don't need to know their names, Seth," the older man instructed. "Women like this don't have names, not real ones. They just make 'em up as they go along. She don't have a name. Just call her anything ya like. It don't make no difference."

As the echo of the flat voice reverberated around the ugly room, it seemed to join forces with the awful odors and become a part of it.

"Do you have a name?" the boy asked.

"Eve."

The boy boasted to the older men, "You see, she's got a name and she just give it to me."

The men snickered. "That's likely all she's gonna give you."

"Less you want to give it to her." The older man grinned.

"Bet the kid's never done it like that," he said to the other man.

The boy looked up, interested. "Done what?"

"See, I told you." The older man grinned. "You got no choice, is the way I see it," he added, staring at Eve as though she were an insoluble problem. "You sure as hell ain't gonna get very far up her skirts. So what's your choice?"

Eve listened with closed eyes and felt fear approaching like an old enemy.

She should have been more alert, should have known when she first heard the slamming of doors, the heavy boots.

"Take off her dress," the older man suggested coldly. "Touch her flesh. Then you'll get the feel of what you're gonna do."

At first the boy hesitated, his eyes almost reflecting the fear in hers. But with the constant encouragement of the other two on the bed, the boy moved closer and commenced to unbutton the buttons, which ultimately freed the fabric and made it a simple matter to slide it back off her shoulders, where she felt it fall in a circle around where she sat on the bed.

Suddenly anger joined her fear that again she was placed in a vulnerable and helpless position, and as the boy's hands started down toward her breast, she pushed against him with all her strength and sent him tumbling backward, his head coming into painful contact with the iron frame of the bed on the opposite side, a yelp of pain filling the room, while the other two men laughed heartily and shouted good-natured encouragement at the boy, who only now was stumbling up, rubbing the back of his head, all signs of gentleness and curiosity gone from his face, approaching Eve at a steady pace, calling her, "Bitch" twice, fumbling in his back pocket and ultimately withdrawing a length of cord, no more than two feet, but it was enough, for suddenly he bent over her and in the next instant she felt her hands jerked behind, felt surprising strength in his grip as he held her wrists with one hand and twisted the cord around with the other, pulling the ends tight.

"Go to it, Seth boy." The older man snickered, and as the young boy stood back from his efforts, he never took his eyes off her and those eyes had suddenly gone flat and glazed and lightless, like his two older counterparts'.

Now she saw his hands moving down the buttons of his trousers until at last the pants slipped free of his waist and with a single push cleared his hips and fell to the floor.

"Go, Seth," came a low, guttural mutter from behind.

Eve struggled to escape the approaching nightmare, the boy coming closer, fondling himself now.

She tried to turn away, but from behind she felt a knee in her back, strong hands clasping her head, and still the boy came closer, his hands on her mouth, trying to force it open, the sensation of nausea rising steadily from the pit of her stomach as she felt the boy's hands move into her mouth, one soiled finger parting her teeth.

Beyond the nausea came a sensation of suffocation. They were trying to kill her, for she couldn't breath and he was inside her mouth now, and she was aware of nothing in the room, only the panting terror of her own struggle and the realization that she could not breath.

She closed her eyes, and at the height of her agony she heard a woman's sharp scream.

Her assailants were momentarily deflected by the screams and she saw the boy back away. The woman screamed again and Eve looked up to see Mother, her hands over her mouth, and removed only to release the sirenlike screams that splintered the silence and hopefully raised an alarm.

Then Eve felt a blow to the side of her head. It jarred her teeth and left her mildly stunned, and just as she braced for the second blow, she heard a sharp explosion like gunfire. To her horror the young boy in front of her staggered back, blood spreading on his chest, until he finally fell backward across the opposite bed.

She felt the grip on her hair relax and looked up and saw a man she had never seen before, saw him fill the door frame, a tall, well-built man with graying hair who held a gun in his hand, still smoking from the first shot.

Now with this gun he gestured to the other two men to drag the third one out, and quickly they obeyed. Eve had never seen such quick fear, the bullies going from one extreme to the other.

The woman named Mother was crying openly. The tall man was approaching her now, his face remarkable with its strong jaw, straight nose, and clear, steady, dark eyes that seemed to see directly through her.

With almost graceful deliberation he returned his gun to its holster and bent over and lifted her effortlessly and transported her to the opposite bed, where he rolled her to one side. She felt the cord on her hands giving way before what she assumed was a knife blade. Then a moment later, miracle of miracles, she heard metal on metal and felt a sharp tug as though something more powerful than a knife blade had cut through the leg irons, and blessedly she felt the bondage give way.

She started to speak, felt that thanks were due him. But he lifted one hand and gently smoothed her hair where it had fallen across her face, and his touch was as soft as his eyes. Then slowly he rose from the side of the bed, his tall frame seeming to stretch up to the ceiling.

She watched him go and felt an impulse to call him back as he passed Mother, who stood in the hallway.

If those two exchanged a word, Eve could not hear it. Instead she saw Mother take a respectful step backward, still clutching the towels and now bending over to retrieve something she'd placed on the hall floor.

A pitcher of water, Eve assumed, which she carried in, stopping a moment to peer down the hall after the man.

Once she was inside the room, Mother placed the pitcher in the bowl and, still grasping the towels, looked around at the disarray, the mussed beds, the bloodstain drying on the side of the opposite bed.

"Are you—did they harm you?" she asked. "What did they—"

She cut the question short, apparently aware of what they had attempted to do.

Then, without looking up, Mother made a hushed request. "You will not tell Yorrick, will you?" she asked.

Eve stretched her legs, luxuriating in her new freedom. "Not if you don't want me to," she replied, pleased with the look of appreciation on Mother's face.

"But what about these?" she asked and held up the severed leg irons.

Mother looked newly worried. "I doubt if Yorrick will say anything. He was going to take them off tonight anyway."

"Won't he be angry?" Eve asked.

"No," Mother replied. "I'll tell him who was here, who did it." Now she poured water from the pitcher into the bowl. "Just a touch-up," she said and dipped the corner of a towel in and commenced to massage her brow with it.

Eve lay back on the bed. "Who was the man?"

Mother halted in her scrubbing motions, her eyes over the towel wide and staring. "His name," she said to her reflection in the wavy mirror, "is John Paul Grand."

She smiled at her reflection. "If you were to go to the roof of this hotel," she went on, "and look first north, then south, then east, and then west, everything you would see belongs to the Grand family, one branch of it or the other. Due south of here you will find the beginning of the Grand Ranch. It is rumored that no one has ever ridden all the way to the end of it. John Paul Grand is one of Yorrick Harp's most enthusiastic supporters. Every year he buys out several performances for his men alone."

"What was he doing here?"

"He owns the hotel."

For several minutes the room was silent as Mother proceeded to finish her toilette. "Now, you," Mother ordered brusquely and took her bathwater to the window, lifted the glass, and poured it out onto the street below and refilled the bowl with fresh water. "Hurry. Yorrick wants you there by three o'clock. I'll do your hair while you wash."

All of a sudden the room was filled with activity, Mother pulling her to her feet, Eve testing her new freedom with comic and exaggerated steps, first in one direction and then in the other, even Mother laughing at Eve's pleasure.

"Come, child," she urged. "Off with the old and on with the new," and as she said this, she drew the soiled dress from Eve's shoulders and left Eve marveling again at how rapidly the world could go from ugly to fair, from nightmare to ease.

"Those—men," she began, needing to understand about the hazards of this place.

But Mother dismissed the subject with the simplest of explanations. "Dead. They're dead men. One already is. And John Paul Grand will see to the other two. Before night falls their graves will be dug and filled. There." She smiled, admiring Eve's long golden hair. "How pretty! Your mother must miss doing this for you, poor woman. Hurry now, child; Yorrick is waiting."

To Eve's surprise, she bustled out of the room and returned with a clean dress, plain as the one before, but of a different cut, with a high neck, and endless row of buttons leading to a high white collar and low snug white cuffs.

Once she was buttoned in, Eve glanced in the mirror and saw a plain image looking back at her, her long hair hanging loose and simple about her shoulders, no makeup, no face paint, just a plain face.

"There." Mother smiled. "Come, now, we must hurry." And she

grabbed her hat and was still affixing it as she swept through the door, leaving Eve no choice but to follow, which she did, but first she stole another glimpse in the mirror, seeing not just plain Eve, for there was no longer the look of a child about her. Something had changed, altered, but she couldn't determine what.

"Coming?" This insistent voice was Mother's. Eve took a final look at the image in the mirror, then hurried down the corridor, loving her freedom, thinking about the name John Paul Grand.

At the far end of the hall she saw Mother starting down the narrow steps. To the left she saw a small boy, no more than eight, on his hands and knees with a bucket of water and a scrub brush nearby. The water, she observed as she passed, was red, and the object of his diligent scrubbing was a steady trail of spilled blood.

They are dead men. Their graves are dug.

Quickly she grasped the hand rail, lifted the plain muslin skirt and started down the narrow steps.

* * *

The Dallas Saloon and Opera House was known as the Palace, and was a place of rare luxury for this western outpost. The original Palace had been a canvas tent. But five years ago the city founders, led by John Paul Grand, had transformed the tent into a spacious hall of rough-cut timber. Curtained rooms lined the sides of the proscenium and were available for gentlemen, from which they could watch the entertainment. The rest of the hall was filled with backless benches and could accommodate five hundred eager men. The furniture in the saloon at the rear was of baroque elegance. Fifteen large brass chandeliers imported from Europe hung from the high ceiling. The saloon had enormous mirrors of costly cut glass, the stage was large and accessible and was one of the few opera houses in the West capable of lending itself to a full company finale.

Now it was into this immense and mysterious place that Eve followed after Mother, gaining strength and confidence with every unencumbered step. Pleased to leave the dusty, hot wind of the town behind, she followed Mother through the broad front doors of the Palace and found herself in total darkness. Only after a period of adjustment did she begin to discern wall lamps, faint after the blaze of the afternoon sun.

To one side at the rear of the theater she saw an ornate bar of polished, brass-trimmed mahogany with knee-high cuspidors. There was a man methodically polishing his glassware. He wore a white dress shirt with red satin garters halfway up his sleeves. He was balding, though around the sides of his head were curly red fringes of hair. He possessed an enormous red mustache and a smile to go with it, and he looked up now from his polishing and called out a cheery "Hallo, that you, Mother? You're late. Yorrick has already raised the roof twice."

Eve saw Mother turn on the voice as though under attack. Then all at once the suspicion melted on her face to warm familiarity.

"Amos, good to see you. Where *is* Yorrick?"

As she talked, she made her way to the bar, where the man named Amos turned his back long enough to deposit a polished glass, revealing a brightly flowered backside.

"Harp's in there, putting 'em through their paces." He saw Eve trailing behind. "And who is that?"

Mother glanced over her shoulder. "You know," she whispered to the bartender, who continued to scrutinize Eve from a distance.

"Well, bring her over. Let's take a look."

Mother murmured, "Keep an eye on her, Amos. She has a way of attracting trouble. I'm going in and see if I can read the prevailing mood."

With that she disappeared through heavy red curtains, from behind which Eve heard muted music, a small orchestra of sorts.

For several moments she stood isolated, halfway between the enormous bar and the curtain through which Mother had just disappeared.

"Come closer," the barkeep invited. "Let's have a look. Come on. Can't be shy; not now. Too much has happened."

She started to ask questions, then changed her mind. Just be quiet. And listen. Better to learn.

Finally he smiled and lifted his nose as though sniffing something in the air. "Unless I miss my guess, I smell blue blood. Am I correct? A lady in the bud? You clearly were not born a tart. Old Yorrick's going to have a hard time keeping you from ripening too fast. What's your name? You got a name? I mean a real one, not one Harp has made up for you? Come on, speak up."

"Eve," she said quietly.

A look of incredulity covered the barkeep's ruddy face. "Eve?" he repeated as though on the verge of laughter. "As in Adam and—? Well, I reckon old Harp will let that one stand and leave well enough alone. Eve," he repeated yet a third time. Then, "Come over here, Eve, and set yourself down and tell me about that place—you know what I'm talking about, the Garden of Eden."

"I can't," she said politely. "I'm supposed to go in there," and she pointed toward the red curtains and the theater beyond.

"When Yorrick calls for you and not a moment before," the

barkeep replied sharply. "Come on, there's a seat, and lookee here what I just done."

He pushed forth a high stool from behind the corner of the bar and reached back and withdrew a pitcher of lemonade, pale yellow with ice crystals forming on the side.

It looked delicious and cool. "Would you like a glass?"

"Yes."

"I thought as much," the man said and reached for a glass and filled it.

It was good, cold and tart.

In a remarkably short time she had drained the glass and he had refilled it and had returned to his position behind the bar, leaving her on the high stool opposite him.

"Was it bad?" he asked, methodically polishing his glasses, not looking at her when he asked the question, only looking up when she didn't reply right away.

"What?" she asked, bewildered. "I don't—"

"This afternoon. Those drunken cowhands. What did they—"

"Nothing," she answered quickly, at last understanding and not wanting to talk about it.

"Rumor has it that John Paul Grand has all three of 'em hanging from his big cottonwood out at his ranch. One of them—the kid—was dead to start with, but Grand strung him up all the same. And no one is to go near 'em or cut 'em down till he says so."

Eve looked up, shocked. "Hanged?"

Even as she spoke, the barkeep nodded, at the same time lifting a glass to a near lamp as though to check it for blemishes. "Every last one of 'em," he said. "Three more additions for his collection."

For several moments Eve struggled with this grisly information, uncertain whether to believe that three men had died because of her. "Collection? Of what?" she asked, trying to dispel the image of three men hanging from a cottonwood tree.

The barkeep laughed. "No, Miss Eve. I don't think you are ready for that information yet."

She watched him as he continued to polish his glasses. From behind the heavy red velvet curtains Eve heard nothing now. At some point the musicians had put their instruments away.

"Should I . . ." she asked and indicated with a nod the red velvet curtains.

The barkeep smiled. "I wouldn't if I were you. It's been my experience that Yorrick Harp doesn't ask much of his girls, but he does make a strong request for one thing: obedience. Whatever he tells you to do, do it."

"But the woman named Mother—"

"Is only an extension of Yorrick Harp, as are all his girls, as you will be, given time."

"No," she murmured, disliking the implication.

She held his gaze a moment and was on the verge of saying something else when suddenly the red velvet curtains were pushed open and Yorrick Harp appeared, looking uncharacteristically rumpled and tired. He wore a sweat-stained white shirtwaist, the front of it food-splotched, no coat, and his hair was mussed as though recently he had driven his fingers through it.

The barkeep greeted him cordially. "Good afternoon, sir," he said. "No harm, I assure you. I offered the child a simple lemonade, which I believe she enjoyed."

"Are you all right?" Yorrick asked with great urgency, approaching Eve with his left arm extended, an arm that ultimately settled heavily and yet protectively on Eve's shoulder.

"I'm so sorry for this afternoon," he murmured quietly, walking slowly with her through the red velvet curtains and into the theater itself, immense in Eve's view, row after row of wooden benches on either side of the wide central aisle, which led directly down to the stage house itself.

On the stage, in half-shadow, she saw about a dozen women of the troupe silently gathering musical instruments and pieces of costumes.

As they approached the stage, Eve thought she heard weeping coming from someplace out of sight behind the heavy draped curtains that flanked the stage on both sides.

As they drew nearer, several of the women of the troupe looked up at their approach.

"Hurry!" Yorrick shouted up at the lingering women. "You know what you must do. We will not open tonight unless there is marked and significant improvement by six o'clock. I mean it. I will not take money from my customers under false pretenses. If I don't have a show worthy of their enjoyment and their coin, then I will not open. Mediocrity is unforgivable, morally offensive, and artistically obscene. We have promised them the best, and by God, they shall have it. Go, now, and do precisely as I have told you to do and we will see what resides inside you, what miracles of discipline you can work in less than three hours. Go on with you now, and take that one with you."

He pointed a straight-arrow finger in the direction of the weeping coming from the wings. Again Eve saw all the women look fearfully toward Yorrick Harp. Then slowly, one by one, they left the stage and gathered the one sobbing, the one they called Mother, and they all left together through a side door, disappearing into a blaze of bright afternoon sun.

"Good riddance," Yorrick muttered under his breath, and held his position as though half-expecting someone to come back and make another excuse.

When no one did, he stared down at Eve with an expression she found impossible to read. "Go on up, Eve. We want a special performance, if you will. I have hired a piano man just for you," and he pointed to the right, where she saw a battered upright and a young man at the keyboard in shirtwaist.

"Or would you rather spin the spell on your own as you did for us on the train?"

Confused, Eve didn't know what to say. Perhaps she would prefer to sing alone, for her inner ear always told her when her pitch was off and when it was perfect. Seldom could a musical instrument make the same claim.

So, "Alone," she murmured and hoped she hadn't hurt the piano player's feelings and followed Yorrick up the narrow steps on the left, lifting her skirts, mounting the vast stage house with a sudden and unexpected surge of delight. How many times in her fantasies had she imagined herself in such a setting, when in reality she would open her eyes only to find herself in her own bedchamber or at Fan Cottage or alone on the hot front gallery of Stanhope Hall.

But here she was, at exact center stage, where a single low stool was waiting for her, a soft shaft of light coming from somewhere overhead, brilliant illumination filled with millions of tiny, swirling, colorful dots.

"There," Yorrick said, indicating the low stool. "Sit as you would if you were alone, for the true, the great art of the theater is to behave at all times as though you *were* alone; no posturing, no posing, no falseness, for the discerning patron can see through the pretense. What he has paid his money for is a private, an intimate glimpse of your soul. The good actress makes the patrons think they have seen it. The great ones *allow* them to see it."

Without another word he turned in a broad theatrical circle and started back down the stairs, leaving Eve alone onstage.

Sit as you would if you were alone—

She would never sit facing front. Sideways. That was the most comfortable position for singing.

Singing! A song! Which one? Which one did she feel like singing? Hymns seemed inappropriate, as did the folk songs that her father had enjoyed so much, the songs taught to her by Paris and old Florence, plantation songs mainly.

As she continued to adjust herself to the mood of this vast empty theater, she ran through in her mind possible songs to sing, to no audience, though once as she looked toward the rear of the theater, she saw, silhouetted against the light coming from the saloon, a man, his head and shoulders defined in the contrast of light and darkness. It wasn't Yorrick Harp. Yorrick Harp stood there at the top of the stairs. Then who?

"Are you ready?" Yorrick asked.

"There is someone—"

"It's none of your business. Just sing as God taught you to sing. That's all I ask."

This rebuke, while not angry, was stern, and Eve felt a twinge of resentment at this man who tried to impose his will on hers. She had not been brought up that way. Papa had always shown her respect.

Now she settled on the low stool, eyes down, her head and heart filled with thoughts of her father, of how distraught he must be. And her mother.

She commenced humming, no longer interested in her surroundings or in giving a performance, more for her own comfort and satisfaction, thinking of home, seeing it so clearly.

"The Rose in the Wall." She hadn't sung that in years. It was one of her father's favorites. Now she pretended that she was back in the parlor at Stanhope Hall, Papa in his big chair, his slippered feet propped up on the footstool, Mama sitting behind him with her crocheting and a smile of encouragement while Eve, the child, scarcely eight, lost in her long white nightshirt, her neck curls still damp from where old Florence had given her her nightly bath, smelling sweetly of lilac water, sang "The Rose in the Wall," about an orphan girl who is sent to a cruel home after her parents die and who finds a small garden near the back wall filled with weeds, a patch no one else wants. The young girl plants a rosebush there that grows but never blossoms and everyone laughs at her and makes fun of her. One wet, cold spring the young girl takes ill and dies, and the next day one perfect rose is found blooming in the garden wall, finding light and sustenance despite the cold hard brick.

At some point in the story-song, Eve lost all contact with the reality of this hot, ugly, dusty place called Dallas, forgot even the Palace Theater, forgot everything except the memory of the child with damp neck curls singing for her papa, so pleased when near the end of the song, no matter how many times she sang it for him, she looked up to see his eyes shimmering with tears.

Then the song was over, Eve still seated sideways on the low stool, her hands in her lap, head bowed as the last note drifted up into the dark theater and slipped into silence.

No sound. Either from within or without. She considered looking up to see if she was indeed alone, but something warned her against it, some instinct that suggested the mood should be maintained to the very end to be effective.

At last, from her bowed position, she heard boots devouring the distance between the back and front of the theater as though it was there to be devoured.

Slowly she lifted her head and saw a man, his features not yet clear, a tall man with broad shoulders, a hat clasped in his hands.

Eve held her position and at last recognized the face, the same broad jaw, steel gray hair, stern yet sad eyes she'd first seen back at the hotel, the same man who had rescued her from the drunken men.

"What is your name?" he asked.

"Eve Stanhope," she said and stood up from the low stool.

"Eve Stanhope," he repeated as though testing the name on the air. Then in the most graceful of gestures he bent low, his thick wavy silver hair directly in Eve's line of vision, and lifted her hand and kissed it, a sweetness to his manner that seemed in strange contradiction to his aura of power and authority.

At the end of the kiss he said almost shyly, "I have asked Yorrick Harp for permission to come and fetch you tomorrow at noon. I will show you my ranch and feed you lunch. Do you accept?"

Eve smiled, touched by his shyness. "I'd like that very much."

"I won't tire you, I promise."

"I don't tire easily."

For a moment he looked as though he wanted to say something else, but apparently he changed his mind and took one step back and bowed slightly from the waist, a stiff, small-boy movement, as though a mother at some point in his past life had instructed him in this politeness.

Then he was gone, walking across the stage, the heels of his boots sending back a determined rhythm; a fine figure of a man, Eve thought, watching him go.

Yorrick Harp was at her side, smiling. "Do you have any idea what you have just done?" he asked slyly, with a hint of mischief.

She shook her head.

"Unless I miss my guess, you have just won the heart of the richest man in Texas. Do you know what that means?"

Again Eve shook her head.

Yorrick Harp looked at her as though disbelieving of her response.

Suddenly he threw back his head and laughed, a paroxysm of laughter that left him dabbing at his eyes with a crumpled handkerchief.

"No matter, my pet," he gasped at the end of the laughing fit. "You'll find out soon enough. For now, come. I'll take you back to the hotel. You will perform that song this evening, in this theater, on this stage, and in that precise manner. And it is my conservative estimate that this stage floor will be virtually strewn with men's broken hearts."

He leaned closer to her, smiling, his immense and angular face completely filling her line of vision. The distortion caused her to turn away and start up the long central aisle.

Beyond the double doors was nothing but the same blinding sun and more dust and a greater wind. As she ducked her head against this triple onslaught, Yorrick called out, "Come, child," and extended his hand to assist her upward into a large, elegant carriage.

Inside she found red window shades and black velvet upholstery quilted with tiny pearl buttons. She'd never seen the carriage before. "Yours?" she asked Yorrick Harp as he settled opposite her.

He shook his head. "Mr. Grand's. He's placed it at your disposal. What do you think of that?"

Eve couldn't respond. But she was grateful for all the man's kindnesses and planned to tell him so tomorrow.

As the carriage pulled away from the curb, Yorrick Harp leaned close and placed a finger aside his nose. "Money," he began quite seriously, "is a heavenly tool, my child. You can build with it, but that's all you can do. You must never forget that. Promise old Yorrick you'll never forget that."

Eve was puzzled by the curious remark, not quite certain that she fully understood. Finally she leaned back against the comfortable seat and closed her eyes and without warning felt the most curious sensation, one she had not experienced for so long and never to this degree.

Enjoyment. She was enjoying herself. And was puzzled by it, for she should be frightened.

Shouldn't she?

* * *

Despite the odor of cow manure, the rhythm of the train had eventually lulled Stephen into a deep sleep. Now he heard a silence that awakened him and caused him to sit bolt upright, demanding, "What happened?"

He waited until his heart ceased its runaway beating. Smelly straw stuck to his neck and the back of his head, and he could swear he felt something crawling in his hair.

"Paris," he called out and looked about at the darkness, still trying to understand the lack of movement, the absence of all noise.

"Paris, we've—"

"Stopped. I know," came a sleepy response on his left.

"What—"

"It's all right," Paris reassured him. "Trains do stop, you know. Water, fuel—go back to sleep, it's all right."

Stephen waited out the sleepy advice and continued to peer into the darkness, trying to see something. And he listened closely. There should be engine noises up ahead, sounds, even when taking on water.

Something was wrong. He knew it. But maybe it would be best to find out what and then return with the news.

Carefully he stood on uncertain legs and tried to shake as much of the smelly straw from his clothes as possible. In the knapsack he'd been using as a pillow, he had one change of fresh garments. Though he was tempted to use them now, better judgment intervened. He would need them later when he found Eve.

Found Eve.

Those words echoed through his mind. Back at Stanhope Hall in the first blush of the great news, Stephen had felt so confident that it would be a simple matter to ride forth into this place called America, find her, and bring her back where she belonged.

But America was proving troublesome, baffling in many ways. No matter. For now he must determine why there was this unnatural silence on a train that a few hours earlier had lulled him to sleep with its clangorous noises.

Carefully he moved toward the sliding door, poked his head out and looked in both directions and saw no light of any kind. He heard nothing but crickets and night birds and smelled the damp earth and suspected the worst, that this cattle car had been abandoned on a siding and they were alone, God knew where, while the rest of the train was at this moment speeding toward Dallas.

"Paris!" he shouted full-voiced and at the same time jumped down to earth.

"Paris!" Stephen shouted again, anger rising along with his voice.

"What—"

The sleepy one-word question came from Paris. "What in the—" he muttered and jumped down. "Where are—" he mumbled until the unanswered questions began to annoy Stephen.

"We are on a siding," Stephen explained pointedly. "Where and for how long I have no idea."

"Where's the rest of the train?"

"Gone," Stephen announced.

"Gone—where?"

"How in the hell should I know?" Stephen replied. "And what do you propose we do now?"

"What do *I* propose?" Paris echoed. "Since when is this my responsibility?"

"Well, we can't stay here!"

"Where do you suggest we go?"

They met mid-point beside the abandoned car, their mutual anger and frustration taking a toll. Stephen knew he should back off, knew it wasn't Paris's fault. Still it felt good to shout at someone.

"As I said, we can't stay here. And since this was your idea—"

Paris responded as Stephen hoped he would, with matching anger, both men struggling to maintain their footing on the muddy incline.

"My idea?" Paris thundered and made a fatal mistake, perhaps borne of his own apprehension, of pushing against Stephen. One good push deserved another, and so Stephen delivered one, this one more forceful, shoving against Paris until he fell backward, upended in the mud.

"Damn you," Paris said. On the pretext of examining his garments he lulled Stephen into a false truce, even provoked him to mutter, "I'm sorry," for they *were* friends and were lost in this night together and there was no need to vent their mutual anger and frustration on one another.

He was on the verge of saying all these things when without warning Paris's leisurely examination of his mud-covered garments ceased, and his fist connected in a blow to Stephen's right jaw that up-ended him and sent him tumbling down the muddy embankment, coming to rest in a watery swamp.

Stunned, Stephen massaged the side of his face and at the same time tried to drag himself up out of the water before he slipped too far into it.

Then he heard a mildly apologetic voice coming from the top of the incline. "Stephen?"

Stephen held his position half-in, half-out of the muddy water, not above playing a game of possum when it served his purpose.

"Stephen!" This cry was urgent and accompanied by frantic movement. Ultimately Stephen felt hands beneath his shoulders, lifting him in an attempt to drag him to safety.

Stephen made of himself a dead weight, and whenever he felt tempted to assist with his own rescue, a pounding sensation of his lower right jaw reminded him of the injury done to him.

"Stephen, come on, I'm sorry. I shouldn't—but it isn't my fault and you said it was."

Stephen shook his head, admitting the accusation had been wrong. "Where in the hell are we?" he asked, looking around at a night so dense it refused to reveal anything.

Paris followed his gaze in all directions and returned with a bleak opinion. "Have no idea. I guess we should start walking."

"In which direction?"

"How in the hell should I know?"

"Well, I just asked."

"Then you tell me."

As the two of them scrambled back up the muddy incline, Stephen reached the top first and made his way back to the abandoned railway car and bent low in an attempt to see the tracks close at hand.

Slowly he stood up. "This way," he pronounced and pointed to the track that lay to his left, a short siding that appeared to connect with the main line less than twenty-five yards up ahead.

"Why?" Paris challenged, intolerably stubborn for some reason and growing more so.

"Because."

"Why?"

Stephen hesitated. "It feels right."

"It feels . . ."

Apparently unable to repeat Stephen's foolish claim, Paris made a pronouncement of his own. "The car in which we were riding is facing east. That means it must have been backed onto the siding, which in turn means the rest of the train was heading west."

In the dark Stephen listened closely to this suspect reasoning with as much patience as he could muster. "Look, I'm going this way. Are you coming?" he announced at last, moving toward the door of the railway car and retrieving his knapsack. "Well?" he demanded again.

No answer from the silent, brooding Paris, who stood a distance away.

"I'm leaving, Paris," Stephen called back and picked his way down the center of the railway track, listening for the sound of telltale footsteps, half-afraid he would hear them, half-afraid he wouldn't.

"You're going the wrong way," Paris shouted, his voice growing more distant.

Stephen started to reply but didn't. A few steps later he looked back and saw nothing. Night had devoured Paris and everything else, or else Paris was moving with matching conviction in the opposite direction.

Stephen stared into the night. Gone. Alone. Was this what he wanted? Yes. He took a last look and was tempted to call again. But didn't. He had nothing to say. Undoubtedly Paris would sooner or later find his way back to Stanhope Hall. He could tell the others what had happened, and as soon as Stephen found Eve—

Found Eve.

There they were again, those two words. Would he find her? He must find her for without her he had no life at all.

For over two hours he walked down the darkened railway track, stumbling when he forgot to pick up his mud-encrusted boots. Once or twice he looked back, thinking that perhaps Paris had triumphed over his stubbornness and was following after him.

But each time he stopped, he heard nothing but night sounds and saw nothing but a darkness so dense as to be primeval, a world not only where no light existed but where it seemed no light had as yet been created.

Suddenly he stopped walking and listened. Three more steps and he stopped again, hearing something that sounded like a distant rumble coming toward him, the tracks vibrating. Then he saw a light, a beacon on a locomotive, casting distorted shadows over the night foliage, coming yet closer, a train to be sure, a glorious sound promising light and movement out of this frozen darkness.

The train approached at a slow though noisy speed, the huge wheels setting off sparks in the night as they turned on the iron tracks, coming closer.

Stephen shifted his knapsack from one hand to the other, making ready to leap on the moment an opportunity presented itself.

Then it did, an opened coach similar to the one they had occupied before, a strong smell of manure greeting him even as he ran alongside for a few yards. He tossed his knapsack over the edge and rapidly followed, feeling his legs dragging, pulled along by the power of the train. At last he secured a grip and lifted himself up and lay sprawled facedown in smelly straw, but uncomplaining, relieved only to be aboard the train and back on track.

"Welcome aboard."

The voice came from the shadowy recesses of the car, and Stephen turned to it. "Who's there?" he called out, his pulse accelerating.

"Why don't you come and see?" It was a different voice, this time, clearly more than one.

"Come on, boy, over here, straight where you're headed. Just keep comin'—if you want to stay healthy."

The voices had flat toneless qualities, not precisely Southern. Stephen couldn't place them. But he had no trouble identifying the threat.

All at once he heard scuffling behind him, felt a strong arm about his throat, a knee penetrating his back.

"That's got it," came a voice from the darkness. "Now sit him down there. That's it. Two catches in one night, not bad."

Stephen was aware of the arm around his neck tightening while at the same time he was being forced down into a seated position on the straw opposite someone, for he felt a boot as he went down, and now felt a rope being twisted around his wrists, both arms secured behind him.

"That you, Stephen?"

He looked up into the darkness opposite him, which was beginning to reveal specifics—Paris, bound as he was, arms drawn back. Yet something was different, a sudden sharp glint of light near his throat.

Someone was pressing a knife blade against Paris's throat.

 Dallas

Eve stood in the wings and watched the "Nymphs of the Woodlands" perform their dance, a lovely tableau alternating with vibrant and erotic movements. There were twelve dancers in the number, all clad in gossamer pastels of pinks, lavenders, pale yellows, the gowns fitted below their armpits, leaving bare shoulders, bare arms, and occasionally a bare breast if the dancer became too enthusiastic in her movement.

The audience, a full house, all male, was most appreciative, producing a curious reaction, one minute rapt, held-breath reverence, the next, all five hundred men clapping and whistling and stamping as though heeding a cue of their own.

Eve in her plain dark high-buttoned muslin dress watched, fascinated, as the dancers leapt and pirouetted about the stage, their graceful movements, playing to the background music of Yorrick Harp's all-girl orchestra, a relatively skilled six-piece ensemble.

Eve moved closer, transfixed both by the beauty onstage and the reaction coming from the audience. She began to sense a connection, the girls giving, the men receiving, then both reversing their roles, an excitement that Eve had never witnessed before.

Now she heard a disturbance behind her and looked back to see another group making ready to go onstage. These women were more seriously clad in full Elizabethan costumes. A few of the women were dressed as men, their long hair tucked under velvet caps decorated with colorful pheasant feathers.

She spied Lily in this group. She hadn't seen her since their arrival
in Dallas. For some reason Yorrick Harp had felt compelled to keep
her isolated from the others. She hoped it wasn't a permanent isolation. She loved watching the women of the troupe, studying how
they arranged their hair, the fascinating process of applying face
color, artistically transforming a pretty face into a beautiful one.

These women, or so Eve suspected, were of a slightly higher rank
than the "Nymphs of the Woodland." These women were called actresses, and it was to this group that all the speaking parts were given
in playlets ranging from Shakespeare to the ancient Greeks and all
the stage poetry readings in between. Eve had caught glimpses of
them rehearsing on the train, their voices as beautiful as their bodies
and faces. Everyone appeared to treat them with greater respect.

Onstage the music was racing to a frenzied conclusion. She saw the
nymphs holding out the folds of their long gowns fan-style as they
whirled and dipped, a kaleidoscope of color and movement, building
until at last they whirled one final time and fell onto the stage floor,
motionless, the frantic movement over.

But the stillness did not persist beyond a few seconds, for suddenly
the audience rose like one, shrill whistles punctuating the applause,
some men standing on the long benches, clapping their hands over
their dusty, sweaty, flat-brimmed hats, the collective motion stirring
the lit torches in each wall standard, casting waves of dancing shadows over the men's grinning and appreciative faces.

Eve found herself grinning for no reason other than the sheer exu-
berance and joy and excitement of the moment.

A few yards away stood Yorrick Harp, resplendent in a red satin
suit, satin trousers, long coat with sparkling buttons and a huge red
satin cape with a high stiff collar.

As the nymphs passed him by, he whispered something to each,
sometimes smiling, sometimes frowning, and sometimes his mood of
the moment became the girl's mood. Slowly in this manner they disappeared down narrow steps that led to the dressing rooms.

While the orchestra was still playing an interlude piece, two Shakespearean "men" commenced to carry onstage small set pieces, a large
fake hedge, a stand-up tree, a small round table, two stools, and a
flagon of wine.

The selections tonight were from *Twelfth Night*. Slowly Eve began
to recognize the various characters. Lily was Viola, and there was Sir
Toby Belch and there sweet Olivia and there little Maria, every character pertinent to Shakespeare's great play present and accounted for.

There was a new soberness in the wings, coming from out front as
well as backstage. A select few musicians had launched into a tinkling

Elizabethan selection, a delicacy of sound to set the stage and mood for the scene to follow.

From her vantage point Eve saw the men in the audience settling back reluctantly onto their long benches. She saw a few hurrying down the long central aisle, obviously on their way to the saloon at the rear to ease their thirst and wait out the "serious part" of the evening.

From the front row some of the men called out to the Shakespearean actors, yelling for them to bring back the pretty girls. But from where Eve stood she saw the actors continue to work with dignity, arranging the set pieces to their satisfaction.

As the troupe gathered around Yorrick Harp, there were a few moments of frantic whispering, a few shaking their heads.

But Yorrick Harp stood fast and scolded them in a loud stage whisper. "This is for their souls, whether they like it or not. They cannot live on lust alone. Do you feed a child all of the sweets he demands? These men are our children, our artistic responsibility. We are morally obliged to give them substance. Now, ready yourselves, all of you. Try not to seriously disturb Mr. William Shakespeare asleep in his grave."

Then they were ready, though this was a different mood from the nymphs who had preceded them. As Sir Toby Belch passed before her, Eve saw the woman playing the role cross herself and tug at the painful binding that had rendered her flat-chested. Then all were onstage, and for a few minutes the fascination of a new spectacle attracted the attention of the men, many of whom were drinking steadily as pretty waiter girls passed back and forth down the rows of benches, distributing ales and beers and whole bottles of whiskey for those with the coin to pay.

For several minutes they paid close attention to the world being created onstage. Eve saw the male faces in the front rows, not so much rapt with attention as bewildered by the formal Shakespearean verse.

At some point, in a mass rejection that she could feel, their attention faltered and broke. And though it began slowly, before long they were enjoying their own conversations more than the noble dialogue coming from the stage. At the same time their thirsts seemed to increase and the pretty waiter girls in short white aprons and buttoned-up boots appeared to be running back and forth between the saloon at the back and the thirsty patrons out front.

And still the selections from *Twelfth Night* continued, the actresses looking nervously off to the wings as though in search of Yorrick

Harp, who stood only a few yards from Eve, his arms folded in a defiant gesture upon his chest.

Suddenly someone from the audience yelled an obscenity, a single word. Then there was another, and without warning an overripe tomato landed with a smattering plop right before where Viola stood.

The men cheered, many standing on the benches where, from within the folds of their dusty jackets, more overripe tomatoes and smelly fruits and vegetables were produced and hurled with murderous accuracy at the stage, one head of rotting green lettuce striking Sir Toby Belch directly in the chest.

Eve looked on, horrified, and felt sympathy for the actress, who appeared at first to be merely stunned, staring down at the green slime on her costume. Eve saw her try to wipe it clean, but the residue coated her hands and finally she ran from the stage and was immediately followed by the others. A few were crying, Lily not among them. She stopped before Yorrick Harp and said something sharp to him, then swept past, no longer concerned with her white shirtwaist or pantaloons.

At last the stage was empty except for the set pieces and the messy scatterings of hurled fruit. The men in the audience seemed jubilant.

For several minutes Eve's attention was torn between the chaos taking place in the theater and the matching chaos taking place in the wings, little "Maria" in tears, the other actresses gathered around her in sympathetic support while Yorrick Harp railed first at them, then shook his fist at the raucous men still shouting beyond the stage.

The din was dreadful, the feelings high and rapidly moving out of control. From where she stood Eve saw the women in the orchestra, caught between these two forces, their instruments held suspended in their hands, a few suffering from splatterings caused by the hurled vegetables and fruit.

As the roar increased, Eve began to feel more than apprehension. The men in the audience seemed to be growing angrier, as though not only were they displeased by the Shakespearean performance, their displeasure was increasing because of the empty stage itself. Eve looked back toward Yorrick Harp, who was locked in an angry exchange with the actresses, Lily leading the charge as first she pointed a finger toward the stage and the audience beyond, and then at Yorrick.

Caught between these two forces, Eve pushed deeper into the shadows, wanting only to flee this place of madmen. Was there no law enforcement in this godforsaken place to step in and put the riot down, for that was what it was becoming, men hurling objects across the theater, now at each other, empty bottles, hats, a few trying to scale the partitions that connected with the upper galleries, a churning scene like a volcano on the brink of eruption.

From the increasing sounds coming from the audience, it was only a matter of minutes before the men, most of them drunk now, spotted the small, narrow staircases that led up to the stage. She saw the orchestra nervously gathering their sheet music, the women looking apprehensively up toward the stage as though expecting help to come from that quarter.

But there was no help. Yorrick Harp was still lecturing to his actresses, many of whom, led by Lily, were giving as good as they were getting, an ugly scene in itself, keeping pace with the more raucous one beyond the curtain.

Then enough. Quickly Eve gathered up her skirts, with the thought in mind of easing behind Yorrick Harp and gaining the steps that led to the rear stage door. She could easily make it back to the Rail's End Hotel, go to her room, and there behind the safety of a locked door she planned to wait out this present madness.

A good plan, and she made it past Yorrick Harp and was approaching the top of the steps when she heard his thunderous voice bellow, "You!" an echoing, vibrating solitary word that stopped her in her tracks, and stopped as well all the female squabbling concerning blame and fault and incompetence.

"You, there!" Yorrick Harp repeated and she looked back to see his red-satin-clad arm pointing in her direction and waving for her to come back.

Reluctantly she did.

"Go on out," Yorrick Harp said, a strange fatigue creeping into his voice as though the argument with his actresses had taken a toll.

At first Eve didn't understand and thought he meant for her to leave the theater. He caught up with her, physically turning her about.

"Go out *there!*" he bellowed and pointed toward the stage.

For several painful moments she wanted to believe that she hadn't understood him. But then he put his arm around her and bent close for a ridiculous whisper.

"My pet," he murmured, guiding her steadily toward the curtain beyond which boiled the storm itself, an increasing fury of men's drunken voices. "You go on. Your gentle manner and angel voice will soothe them, I'm confident."

"No, please!" she protested, beginning to understand that he was serious.

"Of course you can. Here, take this stool. It's all you will need. God has generously provided you with everything else."

"No," she begged, confident that she would never survive this ordeal. "I can't. I really can't."

"Go on, now," he urged, shoving a small three-legged stool at her. "Go on, and fulfill your destiny. You will thank me later for providing you with this perfect opportunity. You will be a legend by the end of this tour. Word will spread, I promise, of the child who, armed with her voice alone, quelled a riot in the Palace Theater. Mark my word. It will happen. I have so arranged it. Yorrick Harp has nothing to do with failure and the 'I can'ts' of the world. He will not even move in the same sphere."

He looked back at the sulking actresses. "They have failed, and I move away from them, as does Mr. Shakespeare himself."

He paused as though to allow his words to penetrate. When a new barrage of rotten fruit started to bombard the stage, he renewed his persuasive assault on Eve and pushed her steadily toward the splattered stage, talking continuously about destiny and reputation and Fate and how none of the three could be denied.

"So go on," he urged a final time, paying no attention to the fear on her face, the other actresses drawing near as he pushed her well beyond the safety of the curtains until she was visible to the rioting men, who did not in any way alter their rioting.

"Please," she begged, on the verge of tears, refusing even to turn around and look at the hell's-gate of the audience itself. Something landed perilously close to her feet, a splattering of something. She looked down to see egg yolk smeared across the hem of her plain muslin dress.

"Go on," Yorrick Harp continued to urge. "You must engage their attention. Quickly. Let them see your light. It's more powerful than their angry darkness."

She closed her eyes in terror and turned her back on the men and clutched the stool. "God please help me," she whispered and was amazed at the sincerity she felt in that prayer. With her back still to the audience, she discovered again that delightful magic whereby in thinking of people absent and beloved and of places distant, she somehow was able to transport herself back there and away from this nightmare. And only a few moments later there she was back at Stanhope Hall, with its good smells of citrus and lavender, the heavenly odor of fried chicken and candied sweet potatoes and Mrs. Winegar's buttermilk biscuits, all the odors blending, the entire family half drunk on food and the hot still afternoon where beyond the open windows she heard nothing except the occasional screech of a blue jay and the cicadas objecting to the heat.

"Sing for us, Eve," Papa said with a smile. *"The moment demands it."*

And how happily she obliged. "Yes, Papa," she whispered and took her favorite place in the curve of the pianoforte even though no one was playing it in accompaniment. She smoothed her pale lavender gown and smiled at old Florence, who had suddenly appeared in the door flanked by Dorie and Katie and a scattering of house servants who had been serving dinner, a devoted audience of people who loved her and allowed her to feed on their love daily.

Something was in her hands. She wanted to get rid of it. A stool. Such an ugly one. Where had that come from?

Ready, Papa? What is your choice?

She could have predicted his answer.

"Come Where My Love Lies Dreaming."

Stephen Foster. One of Papa's favorites.

She thought how beautiful her world was, how beautiful this room, these beloved people, that bouquet of pink roses that she and Mama had picked only yesterday morning and that Mama had arranged in the silver vase.

Now she lifted her head and began to sing the Stephen Foster song for Papa alone, unaware of shouting men who seemed to be shouting less, who one by one sat back down as though puzzled, upon their long benches, all beginning to listen closely to the song coming from the stage. A few seconds later entire rows of men slowly reclaimed their seats on the long benches, drinks still in hand, all faces attentive and upturned toward the stage.

The song was going well. Soon Mama would reach inside her sleeve for her lace handkerchief and Papa would cough and turn away so that no one could see him. But most important of all, Eve was deriving enormous pleasure from the sound of her own voice, the ease with which she accommodated Mr. Foster's lovely melody, the music alone carrying the day, effortlessly transporting her from an intolerable and ugly world to one of soft and loving reception, though it too on occasion had seemed like a prison.

Prisons everywhere. Except here. Alone. On a vast stage. Here she was free, at least for the moment.

Perhaps that was all of freedom that anyone was entitled to—a moment, long enough to recognize it, to enjoy it, to revel in it and see clearly what a dangerous and frightening thing it was.

* * *

Lily had never seen anything like it. She stood at Yorrick Harp's right elbow and watched the lovely child make the marauding men her willing prisoners, and she did it all without a weapon, without a prop, without a fake hedge or royal throne or rouged lips, without anything artificial and suspect.

She did it simply by being herself, by standing center stage, that location a wisdom that apparently she was born knowing, for she had moved to it unerringly, not missing exact center by as much as an inch in either direction. And that gentle and brief deliberation had been the first to attract the attention of the five hundred drunken rowdies who earlier had been yelling for the return of the "nekkid wimmen," but who at some point found themselves fatally fascinated by the young girl simply dressed, who stood before them as relaxed, as abandoned as though she were standing in her father's parlor on a pleasant Sunday after dinner.

Listen now! And Lily did and heard the miraculous voice itself, pure, sweet, striking high notes as well as low with liquid ease. From the angle at which Lily stood close to Yorrick Harp, she saw the theater filled with statues, no one moving. Even the pretty waiter girls stood at respectful attention along the far aisle, their trays suspended, mouths open as though they ached to try to duplicate the sweet sounds coming from the stage.

Slowly Lily looked toward Yorrick Harp, knowing she would find an expression as rapt as that of the men in the audience and something else as well, a stubborn pride, as though in the process of singing well, Eve was proving him right.

Song almost over now. Lily heard the refrain cresting toward the climax, the girl still not moving from that magical point at center stage. She looked so small on the massive stage, so alone, and all at once Lily understood at least a portion of the magic she was working on the men. Undoubtedly she reminded them of every innocent and untouchable female they had ever known, mothers, sisters, daughters, all of that innocence and sweetness in one fair-haired young girl.

All around her Lily was aware of the rest of the company gathered silently to watch and listen. Most of the women would be happy for Eve's triumph; a few would be resentful and Lily was sorry about that, for in all ways there was something very special going on onstage.

Song over. One single high note that seemed to stretch directly up to heaven. Eve let it die ever so easily so that one moment you were hearing a musical note and the next, nothing but its echo.

Then silence, as deep and impenetrable as Lily had ever heard. Yorrick Harp stirred, a wide grin splitting his strong, angular features, and Lily saw the expression and knew what it meant, knew that from now on the young girl standing with bowed head before a silent audience of five hundred moved and subdued men could have anything she wanted, for she had indeed proved Yorrick Harp right.

It was Yorrick who broke the spell with slow but steady applause, an echoing sound that seemed to take forever to reach the audience, but when it did, the men caught on quickly enough and within the moment all were on their feet, following Yorrick Harp's lead, a thunderous explosion that seemed to frighten Eve, for she looked up and for just a moment she resembled a frightened animal, a terribly vulnerable look that begged for protection.

And Lily suspected that there were five hundred men ready and eager and willing to apply for the job.

 Somewhere in Arkansas

Bound in seated positions, back to back, thick ropes wrapped about their chests, Stephen and Paris watched for the first streaks of dawn so that they might identify their captors, who, after several hours of torment, had bound them thus, then had taken turns passing around bottles of still whiskey and who at last had fallen into a deep and drunken sleep on the opposite side of the railway car.

"You awake?" Stephen whispered, turning his head as far as the ropes would allow.

"Yes. I'm sorry."

Stephen shook his head and kept a sharp eye on the sleeping men a few feet away. There were four of them. And though the darkness had prevented him from getting a close look, there was enough about them that he did recognize, the talk of good times long gone, the mention of a bank in a place called Texarkana, four heavy canvas bags. Bank robbers, was Stephen's guess, traveling rapidly away from the pursuit of the law.

"Where's Texarkana?" he whispered, watching the darkness beyond the doors which was beginning to show light. With the coming of day, he sensed they should try to make a move.

"Arkansas," Paris replied.

"Where's that?"

"Depends on where we are."

"Where do you think we are?"

"I have no idea, I'm sorry."

Frustration lifted his voice and caused one of the sleeping men to groan and stir. Slowly he sank back into sleep.

"Can you move?" Stephen whispered.

"Only when you do."

"Let's leave here."

"How?"

"By that door. Now."

"Like this?"

"I don't think we stand much of a chance here."

"We'll break our necks in the fall."

"If we stay, they'll cut our throats."

"Do I have anything to say about it?"

"Of course. But I'm leaving."

"It won't—"

"It will. Now on the count of three, slide as far as you can."

Despite Paris's objection, they slid, bound in a seated position, moving through the smelly straw like a single grotesque creature, Stephen always keeping a close eye on the sleeping men.

Poised at the edge of the open door, Stephen looked down at the blur of ground beneath them. Perhaps Paris was right and the fall would kill them.

"Stephen, it won't work."

"It must," Stephen countered with determination. Again he looked back at the four men sleeping, saw a stray arm move lazily up in a drunken yawn. Not much time—

"At the count of three, duck your head, fall sideways and roll. Do you understand?"

He received no verbal confirmation that Paris had understood. No time for asking again. "One—two—three—"

On the third count he followed his own advice, lowered his head well into his chest and rolled off the side of the moving train.

The fall was murderous. At first Stephen thought he'd struck rock, his lungs compressing against his ribs, an awful weight pulling his shoulders back. Following the initial impact, he was aware that they were rolling over and over, a steady descent with the exception that he couldn't breathe. Struggling against this deprivation, he tried to break their fall with his legs and feet, straightening them against any obstacle he could find, and still they tumbled down the grassy slope until he felt the bonds about his chest break loose and he saw Paris roll free, tumbling on down the incline, while he seemed to be losing momentum for some reason and at last came to a halt, lying flat upon his back, though turning quickly over in an attempt to get air circulating through his lungs again.

With a sharp and painful gasp the breath that had been knocked out of him by the fall returned and he gasped once, and then again, a

pleasurable sensation that brought tears to his eyes and a ringing to
his ears.

For several moments he lay flattened upon the ground, waiting for
his restored breath to set everything else to rights. Tentatively he
moved his legs, then both arms, testing the bones, amazed that he had
survived the fall.

Paris.

Quickly he raised up. The loosened ropes fell away from his chest.
He reached down and freed his ankles, then dragged himself forward
on his knees to the bottom of the incline, where Paris lay sprawled.

"Paris!"

Stephen was standing over him and still no response, though he
could see him breathing.

He knelt beside him and gently turned him over and saw his face,
blood streaming from the wound he had received in the barrelhouse
in New Orleans.

"God!" Paris muttered and struggled to an upright position.

"We did it." Stephen smiled, pleased that they were together again
and more or less in one piece.

"They were in the coach when I swung aboard."

"Who were they?"

Paris shrugged. "I didn't ask questions. Bank robbers, would be my
guess. They were coming from Texarkana and going toward Hot
Springs, which means that we're on our way to Hot Springs as well.

"Is that near Dallas?"

Paris looked up. "In the opposite direction."

"The opposite—do you mean we are—"

The incoherency was born of despair. He had understood what
Paris had said, that they were traveling in the wrong direction, were
perhaps miles and days off their course, Eve moving farther away
from him. The thought did damage. He walked a short distance away.

"I am sorry," Paris said.

"It's not your fault," Stephen said, looking down at what appeared
to be a narrow, dusty road a few yards below the tracks. "Where
would you say that road would lead?"

Paris stood beside him, studying the road. "One way to find out.
Come on. We'll have the sun in a few minutes. West. We want to go
west."

Stephen held his ground, pleased by this burst of energy. Paris's
suggestion was a good one. Then he hurried to catch up and reached
the dusty road shortly after Paris. Together they walked, each choosing a rut, each keeping an attentive ear and eye for hazards that might
be lurking in the storm of green on either side.

They walked in silence for over two hours, the rising heat of late summer closing in on them, sweat pouring off their faces and their empty stomachs reminding them again how long it had been since they had eaten.

Abruptly Paris stopped. Stephen, following a few feet behind, almost collided with him. "What?"

Then he saw the dusty road sign almost obscured by the thick green of late summer foliage.

Murfreesboro.

"Do you know where we are?" Stephen asked.

"I know. We had a student from Murfreesboro at Tuskegee. I would say we are about eighty miles from the Texas border."

"Eighty—"

Stephen tried to repeat the words but couldn't. Eighty miles, without a horse, without transportation, countless days lost, Eve steadily moving ahead.

But all was not lost. He still had Burke Stanhope's letter of credit tucked safely inside his shirt, though in their hasty exit from the train they had abandoned the knapsacks.

If only they could make it to this place called Murfreesboro, and if there were horses to buy, he would buy them and purchase a supply of food as well, and with luck they might be back on track.

Stephen scanned the road ahead in search of the beginnings of a settlement, farmhouses, animals, anything that moved and promised a degree of civilization.

But he saw nothing and increased his pace down the road and followed it around the curb and spied just curling over the tops of low-growing trees the smoke of several chimneys, a cluster of low structures, and close by, less than thirty yards away, a strung clothesline from which hung flapping clothes.

"Paris!" he shouted and waved for him to catch up. They stood together, looking out over the small settlement, which seemed to consist of one dusty road, around which was clustered a dozen or so structures, while surrounding these buildings in a wider arc were farms scattered well apart, each textured in various colors of late summer crops.

"Murfreesboro?" Stephen inquired, new hope soothing old despair.

Slowly Paris wiped at the wound on his forehead and did not seem to share Stephen's enthusiasm. "I would think so, yes."

"What's the matter?"

"As I said, we had a student from here at Tuskegee, named Jackson. We all went home for the summer. Jackson did not come back."

He wiped at the persistent stream of blood and sweat that coarsed down the bridge of his nose. "Mr. Washington found out later that Jackson was discovered hanging a few miles from his parents' cabin. His eyes had been gouged out and there was a sign pinned to his body. Niggers don't read books."

Stephen listened and saw old grief and new fear moving across Paris's face. Yet what was their choice? They had to go into the settlement, try to find horses and leave as rapidly as possible.

"Come on," he urged gently and started walking, hoping to dispel the effects of the tragic memory. A few minutes later he was aware of Paris behind him.

Stephen walked in silence, drawing nearer to the clothesline, the first outlying farm straight ahead.

"You wait here," he suggested. "Let me go in alone."

Always keeping a watchful eye on the sagging front door of the dilapidated farmhouse, he moved closer. They needed food and water, to say nothing of two fresh horses and directions back to the Texas border.

He looked over his shoulder to see if Paris was still where he'd left him. He was. Stephen could just see his shoulder beyond a mammoth compost heap, a smelly mountain of rotting vegetables. It was best if Paris stayed out of sight and let Stephen approach the farmhouse alone. The fact of two men of different colors traveling together had caused all their difficulty in the past. Best to allow the farmer to adjust to one color at a time.

He was halfway across the dusty yard and he had yet to see life or movement. Sweat rolled into the corner of his eye, momentarily blinding him. As he rubbed it out, he remembered what Paris had said about the student from Tuskegee who had come home to this place and never returned.

At the bottom of the step he considered calling out, but changed his mind. He stepped up onto the porch and was on the verge of approaching the door when a voice came from inside the darkness of the house.

"Stop where you is or it will be the last step you take on God's earth."

Stephen instantly obeyed and kept his eyes focused on the shadows beyond the door and saw the long barrel of a hunting gun appearing first, leveled and aimed at his face.

Slowly out of the shadows a man appeared, a black man, peering out at him as though Stephen were all of the world's plagues rolled into one.

"What you want?" the man demanded. As he drew nearer to the

door, he steadied the gun and Stephen saw how thin he was. Yet the expression in his eyes was clear enough, hate-filled.

"I said what you want?" the man demanded again and pushed open the door with the barrel of the gun and kept walking until the gun was pressed against the center of Stephen's chest.

"Please," Stephen began, afraid to move.

"Come to rob me, ain't you?" the old man accused, a suggestion of madness joining the hate in his eyes. "Come to take what little I got left. Who done sent you?"

"No one sent—"

"Turn around," came the second command. "Start moving. Back that way toward the woodhouse. Git!"

This last was accompanied by a sharp prod of the gun in Stephen's ribs, and as he turned, he wondered why Paris didn't come forward. Surely he could talk to the old man, make him see that there was nothing to be afraid of.

For a moment he was tempted to call to him, but something changed his mind. There was a demented look about the old man, an unnaturally bright light shining in those dark eyes, as though at some point in the past he had let go of reason and embraced something less demanding.

If this was the case, then Paris was better off where he was. If worse came to worse he could always intervene, though surely the old man did not mean him actual harm.

"Sir, if you would just—"

"I said shut up."

His tone of command left no margin for debate. Stephen looked up to see a crude low structure ahead of him. The woodhouse, he assumed. Surely Paris would emerge at any time and explain to the old black man that he had made a mistake.

But he didn't, and the next thing Stephen was aware of was the gun still prodding him toward the low door, the old man silent except for labored breathing, pushing him into the low, cell-like structure, where a foul smell overpowered him. As he tried to cover his mouth in protection against the poisonous odors, he took a blow to the side of his head, the gun butt probably, not enough to knock him unconscious but enough to send him reeling inside the woodhouse, where he fell facedown in damp freshly turned soil and looked back to see the door swing shut, heard a key turn in the lock, then heard nothing, as though the old man were standing outside, waiting, listening.

Slowly Stephen shook off the blow, rubbed the side of his head and sat up in wobbly fashion and tried to adjust his eyes to the dark interior, where the only source of light came from cracks in the mud-plastered ceiling overhead.

"Damn," Stephen said and rubbed the side of his head and tried to keep his nose covered and wondered what the source was of that poisonous smell, like all the sewers in the world, or, worse, all the graveyards.

Then he saw, though at first he could not believe. Over there, less than five feet from where he was sitting, something not of the damp floor, like a large flesh-colored log, heavily veined, emerged from the dirt floor.

He blinked his eyes, then opened them. Slowly, never taking his eyes off the object, he rose to his knees and crawled forward. And stopped.

It was an arm. A human arm, a white man's arm, which looked as if it had tried to claw its way out of a premature burial, though it was quiet now, frozen in a contortion of struggle and hopelessness.

Quickly Stephen glanced over his shoulder, as though a new threat were coming in through the door. But in truth nothing was coming through the door, and the world outside this nightmare was quiet. Stephen backed away from the horror as far as he could until his back was pressed against the opposite wall, both hands covering his nose in weak protection against the smell of death.

What was he doing wrong? Why were circumstances conspiring against him? No answers. Only the whispers of a morning breeze around the corner of the woodhouse and the buzz of flies in search of carrion that once had been a man.

Paris? Where was he? What was he doing? Why didn't he come to the rescue? Or had the insane old black man already killed him?

 Dallas

Eve stood on the pavement in front of the Rail's End Hotel in the bright morning light and held a handkerchief over her mouth in protection against the constantly blowing dust. Yorrick Harp had produced a different gown for her this morning, pale yellow but as plain as the others, with high neck, buttoned sleeves, with a modest flare.

Now she stood, brushed and dressed on the pavement, not quite certain what was to happen next. Yorrick Harp had told her only that John Paul Grand was to take her to his ranch, a pleasant day's outing, nothing to be afraid of. And of course he would on his word return her to the hotel in time for a nap before her performance this evening.

Yorrick Harp. She knew he was standing a short distance behind her, watching from the cool shade of the hotel porch in a comfortable rocker, his legs spread, his dressing gown open, revealing thin white legs.

She noticed several of the women, also in their dressing gowns, a few drinking demitasses of coffee, all focused on her as she stood alone at the curb.

Across the street she saw a beehive of activity, a new bank being built, one of several, a handsome structure, at least seventy-five men hauling heavy brick blocks.

She drew a deep breath beneath her handkerchief and suffered a momentary displacement, amazed that she, Eve Stanhope, who had never been anyplace except into Mobile on special occasions, was standing here on this dusty street in this place named Dallas. Of course, she wasn't certain, but she doubted seriously if Papa had ever been to Dallas.

She smiled beneath the handkerchief, and thought of the imprisonment that on occasion Stanhope Hall had been, the same rooms day after day, the same people, Madame Germaine, the same instructions, the same faces, the same restrictions, *"Eve, don't go there by yourself." "Eve, mustn't wander too far from safety."*

Well, she had wandered far this time, and safety, as she was beginning to learn, was a privilege of childhood. And with the exception of Yorrick Harp, whom she still did not know well enough to trust or distrust, the last few hours of her life had not been altogether unpleasant.

She had enjoyed her time onstage last night, although she'd been terrified at the beginning. But she'd sung well and she knew it and the men had known it and they had rewarded her by showering her with their hard-earned coin.

Caught up in her recall of last evening's performance, she failed to hear the carriage pull up, a most elegant carriage, drawn by four white horses.

"Miss." The driver smiled and drew open the door and extended his hand in assistance. Once inside, she saw the most luxurious dark blue velvet interior, everything plush and soft. She saw a shadowy figure seated in the far corner, and at first did not recognize him. And then she did.

"Mr. Grand?"

"Miss Stanhope."

Almost shyly he extended his hand to her. Once she was safely within the confines of the carriage, he let her hand go as though to suggest that she could select where she wished to sit.

She sat opposite him, the better to see. Through the small window on her right, she noted the front porch of the Rail's End Hotel. More women had arrived, as though someone had summoned them to see the grand carriage, coming from all quarters, hairbrushes in hand and drying towels. And there was Lily, standing near the steps, smiling at her and waving to her. Then the carriage pulled away from the curb and the hotel was gone from view.

She stared for a moment at the passing scenery outside the window. "Where are the women who live in Dallas?" she asked the silent man opposite her, who had yet to say a word beyond the initial greeting of "Miss Stanhope."

When he did not immediately reply, she saw him staring intently at her, apparently unaware that she'd even asked a question.

"Mr. Grand," she asked, "where are all the women? Do those men out there have wives, families?"

At last he seemed to rouse himself and shook his head and answered with curious formality. "Women do not generally take to the prairies," he said. "A few come, fewer stay."

"Why?"

"Too demanding, too capricious, too selfish, too womanlike. Most females tend to view the prairies as their competition."

She laughed, not certain if he meant it as a joke. "How lonely. For the men, at any rate," she said and tried to imagine Papa and Stanhope Hall without Mama.

"Which is precisely why Yorrick Harp is looked forward to with such great anticipation every year."

"Where are we going?" she asked, enjoying a certain relaxation, as though her instincts had informed her that this man could be trusted.

"For a drive. I hope you don't mind. I'll ask nothing of you except the privilege of enjoying your company, your youth and your beauty while you in turn will be well paid for your time."

"I want no pay."

He smiled. "Your owner does."

"Yorrick Harp?"

He nodded.

"He is not my owner. He thinks he is, but I plan to leave as soon as possible."

"For where?"

"Home, of course."

"Of course."

The quick exchange left her curiously winded. She waited to see if he would say anything else. When he didn't, she looked out the window, amazed that they had left Dallas behind. For now all she saw was prairie, grasses blowing in the wind, a scattering of wildflowers and an endless blue sky.

"It's pretty in its own way," she said. "Quite different from home."

"Where is home?"

"Mobile in Alabama."

"I've been there."

She looked up on a surge of hope. "Do you know my father? Most people do. His name is Burke Stanhope. He's very well known in—"

She stopped speaking only because he was shaking his head even as she spoke. "I think you would like him."

"I'm sure I would."

For several minutes neither spoke. John Paul Grand seemed content to rock with the rhythm of the carriage, all the while never taking his eyes off her, while Eve, less content, stared out the window and thought of home and how worried they must be and thought of Stephen. Did he miss her? If so, why hadn't he come after her?

As her thoughts grew darker, she straightened in her seat and looked across at Mr. Grand, a man about whom she knew nothing.

"And you?" she asked, fascinated by his face, his manner, something about him that reminded her vaguely of her father, an authority, a presence, something intangible that signaled an uncommon man.

"Me?" he asked, as though uncertain what she meant.

"Are you—were you born here?"

He nodded.

"Your parents?"

"Dead. Years ago."

"I'm sorry."

"I'm alone."

She looked out the window at a landscape that still had not changed.

"Is this all your land?" she asked.

"Yes."

"How much?"

"All of it. At least all that we will be traveling over today. You are so very lovely."

This last was said in the same manner as the first, as though it were merely a declaration of fact.

She felt a blush and thought it one of the nicest compliments she'd ever received, so simple and straightforward.

"Thank you," she said and looked up to see him smiling.

"What do you do out here alone?" she asked.

"Cattle," he said. "Hundreds, thousands of them. That's why I'm sometimes in New Orleans and Mobile. We sell Texas beef to Southern markets. It's good beef too. The best."

She had no doubt that it was. "Mrs. Winegar roasts a prime rib almost every Sunday."

"Mrs. Winegar?"

"Our cook."

"If she bought the prime rib in a Mobile butcher shop, there's a very good chance it came from my ranch."

The thought fascinated Eve and she glanced out the window, hoping to catch a glimpse of prime rib on the hoof. "Where are they, the cattle, I don't see—"

"They all are in the southern pastures now," he said, leaning forward. "We rotate them every season from pasture to pasture. It gives the grasslands a chance to replenish themselves."

"Do you have many men working for you?"

"Several hundred."

"Where do they stay?"

"We have accommodations for them."

"Where do you live?"

"You'll soon see."

"Look." She smiled, glancing out the window, at last seeing something different, a patch of dark blue flowers in the prairie grass, growing in abundance, a beautiful natural garden, the first color variation of any significance she'd seen since they had left Dallas.

"Bluebonnets. Would you like to see them up close?"

Before she could answer, he reached across and gave the front window a rap. A moment later she felt the carriage begin to slow until finally they were still. The only movement she felt now was the prairie wind buffeting against the stilled carriage.

A moment later the door opened and she saw the driver standing below the step unit in a stiffened manner as though at military attention. She saw John Paul Grand duck his head and move down the steps and reach back for her, hand extended.

She took it, eager for a chance to stretch her legs, to study the prairie and the blue flowers close at hand. As she reached bottom, a sudden gust of wind lifted Mr. Grand's large white hat and blew it into the air and he didn't seem to notice. It was the little driver who started after it at a comic run.

She laughed as she saw the little man chase the cartwheeling hat and Mr. Grand called after him, "Let it go, Miguel. It isn't important."

But still the driver pursued the hat while Mr. Grand took Eve by the arm and escorted her carefully up a mild incline to a large meadow of blue flowers that were even more beautiful up close.

"Bluebonnets," Mr. Grand announced and bent over and plucked a half-dozen stems, which were indeed adorned with miniature blue bonnets, as deep a blue as in any flower Eve had ever seen.

"Thank you." She smiled and took the small bouquet and waded directly into the center of the flowers and turned in a delighted circle and thought of her mother and her love for flowers.

She looked back at the silent Mr. Grand, who, as always, seemed more than content just to watch her. Then the little driver came running up bearing the very handsome hat, brushing the brim with the side of his arm in an attempt to restore it.

"Keep it," Mr. Grand smiled. "You retrieved it. It's yours."

From where she stood, knee-deep in bluebonnets, Eve saw a look of pleasure cross the little man's face, a dark swarthy face, Mexican, most likely.

Then in a quiet voice Mr. Grand asked him to wait with the carriage, that they would be only a moment.

Still admiring the hat, the driver did as he was told, and Mr. Grand walked to where she was standing in the meadow of bluebonnets. "I wish I were an artist," he said.

"Surely they have been painted before," Eve said, her hand brushing the tops of the flowers.

"I don't mean the flowers," Mr. Grand replied.

She looked up, recognizing another compliment. "Thank you again. My father hired a portrait painter once to paint all our portraits."

"I'm sure they are lovely."

"No, because the poor man never had a chance to paint them. Christine and David came down with measles and I came down with the mumps. It was awful. Papa never tried again."

He seemed to be listening carefully to everything she said and seemed regretful when she stopped speaking.

"You are very kind, Mr. Grand, to invite me on this outing."

"I was afraid you wouldn't want to come; I was afraid you wouldn't accept."

"I was told to accept. But I wanted to anyway."

For a moment her frankness seemed to hang between them and belatedly she regretted blurting the truth. Then he laughed, a nice sound, much better than his brooding silences. He led the way back to the carriage, assisted her up the steps and told the driver who still was busily admiring his new hat, "Let's go home." He climbed into the carriage after her and said not another word for the next half-hour, until, looking out the window, Eve saw a large settlement to the left of the carriage, several immense barns, outbuildings, stables. And on a hill overlooking the settlement, she saw a massive three-story house made of red clay brick, with eight gables painted white running the length of the house, an elaborate gingerbread captain's walk on top of the third story and a broad front porch with intricate capitals decorating the handsome white columns.

Excited, she leaned forward, fascinated by this impressive structure that had arisen like a mirage from the prairie floor.

"Yours?" she asked.

"Home," he said.

Then she saw two horsemen join the carriage outside the window, a clear escort, going with them through the gate over which hung a large wooden sign which said simply Grand Ranch.

Once inside the compound, the driver broke speed, as did the escort horses. At a more leisurely pace, as though someone wanted to give her a chance to see everything, the carriage took the left avenue around the compound, passing several large barns, interspersed with smaller buildings and a large blacksmith shed, two roaring fires visible like jungle eyes in the shadows. All the men looked up as the carriage passed. Most tipped or removed their hats, filling the air with a sense of deference.

As the carriage made its way up the hill, she noticed what appeared to be shops—there a hardware and there a canvas shop and over there a general store, men on the porches, men the customers, men behind the counters, not a woman in sight.

As they approached the crest of the hill, she saw a round-up pen filled with cattle, the pungent smell of branding in the air, at least sixty men working the herd through these pens. Next to the corral she saw a smokehouse, fragrant odors coming from the two brick chimneys on either side.

In no quarter, no matter where she looked, did she see a tree, a shrub, not so much as a bush. The purpose here was pragmatic. Either beauty was a luxury or an impossibility.

The carriage came to a halt. The door opened and there was the driver in his new hat, extending his hand. She crawled down from the carriage and immediately felt the predictable hot wind.

As her hair swirled loose about her, she tried to hold it secure. Mr. Grand was behind her, his hand on her elbow, escorting her across the red brick pavement and toward the high wooden carved front doors, which at that moment swung open to reveal a young man,

Mexican-appearing, in a white coat, his eyes down. On one side of his head, in the vicinity of his ear, he wore a large white bandage.

As he held open the door, he looked up only briefly as Mr. Grand passed through. Eve smiled at him, though she was certain he didn't see, for he closed the door behind them, then disappeared at a fast walk into a hallway near the far end of the foyer.

Eve stared out at the most incredible sight, Mr. Grand's foyer, which was of palatial proportion, a high-ceilinged room with wooden galleries leading around the second and third floors, while at the back of the foyer was a large wooden staircase that led to the second floor. Positioned around the walls of the lower floor were huge mounted antlers. Still there was no color in this huge foyer, only earth tones of brown and beige and bronze, a man's world, where no woman had ever trod, let alone exerted influence.

Mr. Grand seemed more than content to give her all the time she needed in her silent inspection, as though he felt it was important that she see it all at her own rate of speed.

Then, "Come," he said cordially. "You must be weary. This way, please. You can wash; then I have arranged luncheon for us. If that is satisfactory . . ."

Still he seemed so shy, so eager to please her. She allowed him to escort her down the three short steps of the raised foyer, then across the broad-board floor, the heels of her shoes sending back an echoing rhythm as the glassy eyes of dead deer stared down at her.

Just this side of the staircase, he guided her toward a small door, pushed it open for her and promised, "I'll return for you in fifteen minutes, or longer, of course, if you require it."

Inside the door, she turned to confront a small plain room containing one rocker of ancient vintage, one rag rug of faded colors on the floor, a bowl and pitcher of water, no mirror, one towel and one small bar of lye soap. Behind a screen to the left she found a slop jar and a thunder pot. Then when she had despaired of ever seeing color again, she saw on the wash table an interesting and moving apparition: One small pocket of color in a single large sunflower, one blossom only with two leaves in a simple clear glass, standing straight and assertive in all that gray-brown plainness.

She smiled and touched the starched symmetrical petals and wondered who had been sent to fetch that flower and what must he have thought, for clearly it was not a daily errand or even a monthly one. It was simply someone's perception of what a woman would find beautiful. And she did.

True to his promise, in fifteen minutes, just as she was dabbing the towel to her face in an attempt to dry it, feeling refreshed, she heard a knock at the door, smoothed back her hair, took a deep breath and opened the door, expecting to find Mr. Grand, finding instead the white-coated Mexican with the large bandage on the side of his head.

Surprised, she waited for him to speak. But he didn't. Instead he gestured for her to follow him. They had gone a few feet toward the central foyer when suddenly he ran back into the small room and returned with the sunflower in hand and presented it to her as though she had forgotten to take it with her. And all at once she knew precisely who had been sent to fetch the flower.

"Thank you," she said with a smile and wished that he would look at her and not keep his head down, though it occurred to her that his injury, whatever its nature, might be causing him discomfort.

"Your head, how did—"

But he continued to walk, drawing well ahead of her, leading her back across the foyer toward a door on the opposite side. There he pushed open the door for her and she glanced in and saw another immense high-ceilinged room. On the opposite wall was a massive gray stone fireplace, an arrangement of mounted animal horns and, to the left, a large window that afforded a perfect view of the dusty settlement below. Standing in front of the dead fire, she saw John Paul Grand, his hands laced behind his back. He was smiling in pleasure at her, as always.

"Thank you," she murmured to the young Mexican, who closed the door behind her. She held her position, feeling self-conscious. What did he expect of her now?

In her nervousness she glanced to the left and saw two wall displays, collections of something, large black panels arranged on the far wall, each panel containing—from this distance she couldn't see, but obviously Mr. Grand was a collector of something, for something had been mounted with great precision. She was on the verge of asking the nature of his collection when he summoned her to come forward.

"Come, Miss Stanhope. Over here. We have refreshment to revive us from the ride out."

On the table was a pitcher of lemonade, a platter of flat brown cookies and a plate of sandwiches, coarse brown bread filled with some kind of beef. At least it had a brown rim.

"Are you hungry?" he asked.

"Yes," she admitted. "And thirsty."

"Here, drink," he said in a tone of command and pushed the pitcher of lemonade toward her, where apparently she was to serve herself, which she did. "And you?" she asked, indicating his empty glass. "May I pour for you as well?"

He sat opposite her and watched as she poured the lemonade and presented it to him. When after a few seconds he had yet to take it, Eve murmured, "Mr. Grand?" and at last he seemed to jar himself out of his reverie and accept the glass, though not once did he take his eyes off her.

She sipped her lemonade. Quite tart it was, and she recalled the endless tea parties she'd had with Sis Liz and White Doll at Fan Cottage and suddenly she missed them both terribly.

"What's wrong?" he asked, apparently seeing a new expression on her face.

"I was thinking of home."

"This is my home," he said stiffly, his voice filled with boyish pride.

"And most impressive it is."

"I built it myself. My father started it, but later abandoned it. I've done all I can do. I have rooms upstairs that no one ever goes into."

"Why?"

"No need. I've all the room I require here and still sometimes it is not right."

"Not right?" she repeated.

"I miss the open sky, particularly at night," he said, leaning back in his chair. "And the stars. A man really has no need for a roof except as protection against the elements."

She listened closely, eyeing the sandwiches with the thick slabs of meat and wondering if she dare.

"Go ahead. I hope you like them. Sanchez smokes the meat. He has a special formula."

"And who is Sanchez?" she asked, trying to find a small sandwich before she reached forward.

"Cook."

She reached for a sandwich near the edge of the platter and looked for a napkin and there was none, and looked for a small plate and there was none, and brought the sandwich back with her into the chair and held it awkwardly in one hand, the glass of lemonade in the other.

The gesture seemed to please Mr. Grand, and he followed suit and lifted an enormous cut of brown bread and meat from the platter and pulled off a large section with his teeth and chewed contentedly.

She watched him for a moment and knew that ultimately she would have to do the same. "Was that Sanchez?" she asked, referring to the white-coated Mexican with the bandaged head.

He shook his head and continued to chew and finally washed down the mouthful with a long swallow of lemonade. "No, that was Pedro."

"He's injured."

"Yes."

He returned the glass to the table and sat back in his chair and looked at her as though to say, "Your turn."

Up close, the coarse bread smelled of yeast, the beef of blood. She hesitated.

"Go on. The beef is ours. It's very good."

Aware that she could stall no longer, she lifted the sandwich awkwardly with one hand and did as Mr. Grand had done, took a large bite that filled her mouth with the most peculiar-tasting bread. Then she began to taste the meat, chewy and raw, and then something else, something sharp and fiery, the heat increasing as she tried to push it to one side of her mouth with her tongue.

Mr. Grand smiled at her discomfort. "Sanchez's jalapeños," he explained. "They take some getting used to, but they are good for you."

She stared through watery eyes in disbelief at the foolish claim and felt residual heat in all areas of her mouth but was grateful that apparently there was no permanent damage.

"I am sorry," he apologized. "I can't claim to have forgotten how to entertain a lady. I'm afraid I never knew how."

She looked up, interested in this new tone of voice.

"I was born here," he went on, "in the central core of this house. My father came here from Indiana, fleeing the law. He'd taken some money from his bank that didn't belong to him and in an attempt to escape his just punishment, he fled with my mother who was pregnant at that time and brought her here, which the bastard thought was Mexico. Texas had joined the union the year before."

She listened closely, grateful that he was speaking, for it enabled her to keep silent, to refill her glass of lemonade and work at extinguishing the fire still burning in her mouth.

"He pitched a camp on this hill. I was born here. My mother died here. Two weeks after giving birth to me."

His voice had altered, grown softer. "A Mexican woman nursed me and raised me and let me live with her family nearby. Not until I was old enough to be useful did my father come for me, and then it was only to put me to work to earn my keep."

He smiled despite his bleak excursion into his past. "I worked hard for him. Then one day I was forced to kill him."

He allowed the shocking announcement to sit on the air and for several moments made no attempt to soften it or retract it or explain it.

"You had to—" Eve tried to repeat.

"Years ago. He came to visit my Mexican mother. He was drunk. I watched. Sanchez is her natural son and begged him to leave her alone, but he wouldn't, so—".

He looked over his shoulder toward the wall mountings, boasting the collection of some sort. "My mother had been skinning rabbit. The skinning knife was on the table. It was a simple matter."

He looked fatigued by the memory. "So long ago," he muttered. "I miss my mothers, both of them. The dark one and the fair one."

There was such sorrow in his voice, such loneliness. Eve returned the glass to the table and held her position, not certain what she should do.

"Would you . . ." he began hesitantly. She looked up to see a blush on his face. He seemed to lose his nerve and she was grateful for the loss, not wanting even to imagine what it was he was about to ask her to do.

Then, "Would you do a great favor for me?" he asked, looking directly at her.

"If I can," she murmured and saw him leave his chair immediately and go to the large sideboard against the far wall. Once there, he turned his back on her and appeared to be looking for something in the top drawer.

Then she heard him exclaim, "Here it is," and saw him withdraw something, study it with clear affection, then return to his chair, smiling.

"Here," he said as he sat down, his back straight as he extended to her a *hairbrush*.

It was a man's hairbrush, with tortoiseshell backing and soft worn-down bristles, well used by someone.

She stared at it, not certain what he wanted her to do with it.

"I don't—" she began and was not given a chance to finish.

"Brush my hair, please," he asked, his tone plaintive, boylike. "Please, Miss Stanhope, if you will," and he urged the brush toward her. "My mother, my Mexican mother, always cradled me in her arm and brushed my hair when I was frightened. Since then I have always found the movement, the awareness of someone touching my head, my hair, irresistible. But it's been so long. I've tried to imagine the sensations of late, but I can't—"

His voice broke off, though his expression of pleading expectation held steady.

Slowly she nodded her willingness to try and at last took the hairbrush and thought of the Mexican mother soothing the little abandoned boy by cradling him and brushing his hair.

She ran her fingers across the bristles and found them soft as down and took a final look at his face, remarkable in its need, and moved into a position behind his chair and saw him ease carefully back, a new air of tension about him, his hands grasping the arms of the chair as though in full anticipation of the pleasure to come.

Shyly at first, she touched the brush to the back of his head, then touched it again in a gentle sweeping motion about the side of his head. As she applied greater strength, she felt him relaxing even more, all the way back, until his head was pressed lightly against her. She renewed her grasp on the hairbrush and smoothed his hair with one hand and applied the brush with the second stroke, doing it over and over again, establishing a rhythm, a movement from first one side, across the top of his skull and then down the other.

And all the while his pleasure increased as he tilted his head backward. She could see his eyes closed in delight. Still she brushed, down one side, across the top and down the other, and she saw his hands on the arms of the chair become fists, saw his head roll from one side to the other as though to accommodate her strokes.

Suddenly he groaned and bent over, holding his knees, no sound in the room now but muted, heavy breathing.

Eve watched closely as he struggled to recover from his incapacity, rising slowly up. "Miss Stanhope, I'm—"

He had started to say I'm sorry, she was certain, but she shook her head, indicating no apology was necessary. What precisely had happened to him she had no idea.

A few moments later he stood and lifted his face to the ceiling as though in search of additional air, and at last he turned and smiled. "You are so precious to me."

She blushed, finding the sentiment excessive. "We don't know each other."

"I don't think that's always necessary, do you?"

She looked up at him and found his strength appealing, his words romantic, reminding her of Sis Liz's tales of adventure and love.

"Come," he invited, his arm protectively about her. "Let's walk. I'm grateful to you for so many things."

"What?" She smiled. "I've done nothing."

"Nothing?" he echoed. "You have brought beauty and grace to this empty tomb and you have warmed my heart as it has never been warmed before."

They walked to the broad window that looked down the hill to the bustling settlement. "Strange," he mused, "I have everything I want and I have nothing I want."

"Certainly it is within your power to acquire anything you wish."

"You?"

"I don't—"

"Is it within my power to acquire you?"

She started to smile, then realized that he wasn't joking. Uncertain what she should say, she kept silent.

When the silence stretched on too long, she said, "You are a collector," and walked back across the room, heading toward the mounted black panels on the opposite wall.

"What do you collect?" she called back, pleased that she had found a safe and noncommittal subject.

He was following behind her, but had not responded. With each step she looked forward, puzzled that as yet she had not been able to identify the shell-like objects pinned to the display boards, the arrangements symmetrical, row after row across the black panel, all of approximately the same size though some were darker than others, and all resembled—

About ten feet from the black panel, she stopped, having seen. Too clearly. Quickly she covered her mouth with her hand and saw again and still did not believe what she saw.

Ears. The black panel was neatly lined with severed human ears, a few shriveled and discolored with age, others smooth and fresh and pink.

"Necessity, I'm afraid," Mr. Grand announced, and came up alongside her. "It's a very effective method of discipline, far more humane than branding, and I noticed to my deep regret during the meal that you have suffered that pain and humiliation." He indicated her right hand, the small *YH* still pink though no longer painful.

"This way is far better, I assure you."

"Better for who?" she murmured, feeling the room begin to spin in her close proximity to the arranged atrocities.

"I am captain of a very large ship, Eve. Hundreds of thousands of acres, hundreds of thousands of cattle, and I require an army to assist me with my various endeavors. The loyal and obedient worker need have no fear of me. Only the laggard, the disobedient and the runaway."

He stood back and with pride studied the large black panel that contained at least one hundred human ears. He smiled. "It generally makes for a loyal and very dedicated army."

He lifted her hand and kissed her palm and she watched, beyond response. She closed her eyes and tried to still the convulsions in the pit of her stomach, tried also to reconcile her concept of this man who would not harm her with the man who severed ears and then mounted them on a black paneled display board.

"Now, over here," he went on, obviously unaware of her indisposition. "Here we have a sadder story," and he moved back the screen to reveal the second display board.

Still struggling for control, she looked up, braced to find another grizzly display of human ears and saw something different—loose, slightly shriveled and brownish pouches, small, with leather draw-strings, at least as many pouches as ears, all neatly hung from brass nailheads.

"Scrotums," Mr. Grand announced and lifted one from its brass nailhead and handed it to her for her inspection. "Human scrotums. Where the male of the species houses his testicles. Most of the offend-ers were already dead when I relieved them of these. A few true villains were not. They make excellent receptacles for carrying loose change, don't you think?" He reached over to the side of the board and withdrew one. "Here, this is for you. It belonged to the drunken villain who dared to approach you at the Rail's End Hotel."

All the time he spoke, he drew nearer, extending to her a wrinkled brownish pouch. As the human scrotum came yet closer, she tried to move away and saw Mr. Grand before her with his strong handsome face, still speaking madness. "The elasticity of the human scrotum is remarkable. Feel it. Go ahead. Some say it resembles fine leather. Please don't worry. I assure you, every bastard represented on that display board deserved killing several times over. One must maintain order in remote outposts such as the Grand Ranch. There must be a law of sorts, and here it is my law and I am the enforcer. Now come; as I said before, this belongs to you. Here, see how fresh it feels, how elastic. And here are the other two as well if you wish them."

As he reached back and plucked two more from the lower corner of the display board, she shook her head but once, tried to speak and instead of words rising in her throat, she felt the hot burning of the pepper and the beef. She sensed a safe blackness coming at her from all sides and closed her eyes and gave in to oblivion, finding it far safer than this room, this man, this calm voice speaking madness.

 *Murfreesboro*

It was almost dark. Stephen had been held a prisoner since early morning in the foul-smelling woodhouse where near the back wall the remains of a human arm reached upward out of the mud.

Several times he had been tempted to try to break out. It didn't appear that solid a structure, unless of course the insane old black man was waiting outside, gun cocked and aimed at the woodhouse door.

If that was the case, and Stephen suspected that it was, to break out in broad daylight would be foolish. Better to wait for night and the cover of darkness, then take his chances among the shadows of what hopefully would be a moonless night.

So for the last eight hours he had sat in the extreme corner of the woodhouse, his attention divided between the door itself and the inadequate grave, and in this prolonged waiting, his mind had played countless tricks on him. Once he thought he heard Eve outside the door, singing, and that delirium had lasted for several minutes and had almost driven him mad as he talked himself out of the cruel fantasy, then fell into a pit of despair as he realized that instead of being close to him, in reality Eve was slipping further away.

Ultimately reason had intervened and he had regained a degree of control and had passed the swelteringly hot afternoon trying to concentrate on a pleasant memory: the first time he had seen Eve on the gallery, their first kiss in the cave above the Mobile River, their plans to run away, ill-conceived plans, as it turned out.

Now, with dark approaching, Stephen pulled himself up from the damp earth floor. As he stood, stretching the stiffness out of his legs, he heard a footstep. In the distance he thought he heard a neighing sound, no voices, only—

Then suddenly the door was slung open with great violence and only the barrel of the shotgun appeared, followed by the old black man.

Without words the man approached him and prodded at his chest with the barrel of the gun, and with no words spoken, he conveyed that Stephen was to precede him out the door, hands above his head.

Stephen obeyed, ducking his head as he passed through the low woodhouse door and out into the blessed clean air of early evening. Once out, he looked around, struggling for a moment to adjust to light and easy movement. About thirty yards ahead, near the front of the old farmhouse, he saw two horses and a man holding both reins, watching him closely.

Stephen rubbed his eyes and felt the prodding of the gun in his back and continued walking and saw the man coming toward him, recognition dawning with each step.

"Paris?" Stephen called out and in relief saw Paris smile and only then remembered the madman behind him holding the gun. "I was worried about you."

"Worried?" Paris echoed. "No cause for worry, I assure you. Old Man hunted me down early this morning, but he only kills whites, don't you, Man. So he took me to his house and gave me a bath and food, and he said I could have these horses because they're stolen anyway and he gave me a map with a clean route back to the Texas border and he told me further that we could pick up the Texas-Pacific at a place called Sunup, and that beyond Sunup the train didn't stop between the border and Dallas."

Stephen's first reaction was one of pleasure that at last Fate had decided to deal kindly with him, though even as he was enjoying this relief, something kept gnawing at him. It was Paris, his grin, the way he stood on the path, well-fed, cleansed. While he had passed a pleasant afternoon with the mad black man, Stephen had roasted, half dead from poisonous fumes. Paris must have been aware of Stephen's imprisonment, fully aware of every damn thing in this world, yet he had done nothing.

It did not originate with a conscious thought. It was pure reflex, his right hand connecting on the first blow, Paris, surprised, hurtling backward, for the blow had come with accuracy and complete surprise.

Suddenly the old black man rallied, took up a position in front of Stephen as though to prevent a second attack, the barrel of the gun pressed against Stephen's throat, beneath his chin.

"He's not opposed to killing," Paris said, still rubbing his jaw.

"I know," Stephen said. "There's a dead man in the woodhouse."

This seemed to take Paris by surprise.

"Go see for yourself. A white man. Poorly buried."

"Let him go, Man," Paris ordered, and slowly the black man lowered the gun barrel and stepped back.

"Are those horses really for us?" Stephen whispered.

Paris nodded. "I *am* sorry."

Stephen accepted the apology, keeping his voice down. "If you knew I was in the woodhouse, why didn't you—"

"I didn't know," Paris replied. "Not until Man told me you were there."

"Why do you call him Man?"

Paris shrugged. "He says that is his name."

Suddenly the old black man stirred himself out of his lethargy. "What's you two jawing about?"

"Nothing, we—"

"Do you know him?" the black man demanded.

"I do."

"How come you to know a white man?" the black man asked, a hard look of suspicion crossing his face.

Without answering, Paris commenced to walk slowly up the path in the direction of the awaiting horses.

"Wait!" the black man called. "I asked you a question. How come you movin' with a white man?"

Before Paris could reply, Stephen began to perceive a new problem, the suspicion of a black man for a white man, as virulent and suspect as the reverse situation had been in New Orleans.

He caught Paris's eye and read the message. It was time to get the hell out of here. While the black man's attention was focused on Paris, Stephen sidestepped the path and cut slowly up through the thick weeds.

"You ain't answered my question, nigger," the old man said, tracking Paris with the gun as recently he had tracked Stephen.

"I didn't say he was my friend," Paris called out. "I—met him on the rails, that's all."

"Then help me kill him," the black man shouted. "The world's filled with too many white bastards. It's easy to pick 'em off—I blow their guts out and dig a hole out in the woodshed. Help me to kill this one, nigger, you hear me talkin' to you—"

All the time the old man ranted on, both Stephen and Paris were carefully approaching the two horses. Finally, "Let's go!" Paris shouted and knocked the shotgun from the old man's hand, causing it to discharge. He grabbed the reins and swung up into the saddle.

"Keep your head down," Paris shouted and they turned the horses about and headed for the road, hearing the old black man shout curses after them, punctuated by shots that seemed to be peppering the trees around them. And still they rode, heads flattened against the saddles, reins tightly twisted about their hands.

Stephen looked back once and saw the old man still running after them. He clung to the saddle and looked ahead and hoped that at last they were underway in pursuit of their goal.

Eve.

But the thought hurt. Instantly he banished it, and renewed his grip on the reins and urged the horse on to greater speed.

 The Grand Ranch

When Eve regained consciousness she found herself on a stiff horsehair sofa, Mr. Grand bent over her in concern, waving a vial beneath her nose.

She shook her head in an attempt to escape the odor, opened her

eyes and saw Mr. Grand kneeling over her. Standing behind him she
saw the young Mexican with the bandaged head.

I simply cut off their ears. It is more effective than branding—

She tried to turn away from the echo of the voice that reverberated
through her head.

"Brandy," she heard Mr. Grand call out.

"No, please," she protested and struggled to sit up.

"I'm so sorry," Mr. Grand murmured, seated beside her. "Are you
—what can I do—anything?"

She shook her head to all the fragmented offers and waited for the
room to stop spinning. "It's the heat," she murmured.

"Then come, we will find fresh air," Mr. Grand said, and before
Eve knew what had happened, she felt herself lifted in strong arms,
the Mexican boy standing back to make room.

She tried to protest, but protest was useless and she looked ahead to
see the broad veranda coming into view and briefly closed her eyes,
trying to rid her mind of the two collections she had witnessed.

"Here," he soothed and lowered her onto a chaise. She heard a
scrape and saw Mr. Grand dragging a chair close. She drew a deep
breath, beginning to feel restored. "I am fine now," she said.

"You alarmed me," Mr. Grand said.

"I'm sorry."

"I'm afraid Yorrick Harp would never forgive me if I returned you
to him the worse for wear."

The mention of Yorrick Harp cleared her head.

"Are you singing tonight?" Mr. Grand asked.

"I think so."

"Do you enjoy it?"

She looked at him. A peculiar question. She was a virtual prisoner
of Yorrick Harp. Didn't he know that? How was it possible for a
prisoner to enjoy her prison?

Then to her own amazement she heard herself saying, "Yes, I enjoy
singing for the audience. I like the way they listen."

Mr. Grand leaned back in his chair. "I was hoping, and surely it
comes as no surprise, that perhaps you would consider, just consider,
mind you, remaining here with me."

She looked up.

"As my wife, of course," he added, his expression, his manner shy,
as though fearful of her response.

But she was too shocked to give a reply and thus sat silently, not
certain if she heard him correctly.

"Please think on it. You would never want for anything, you know
that, and with you as my wife, I would never want anything. We

could have a good life together at Grand Ranch. Your happiness would be my first obligation, I promise you—no, I swear on it."

His manner had become intense, the way in which he held her hands, his face so close. Then as though unaware that she had not made a response, he assisted her up from the chaise and walked with her back to the steps, where she saw the carriage waiting.

As they stood on the porch, he looked out over his land. "I spoke too soon, didn't I?" he asked. "If I did, forgive me. I don't require your answer now. You will be in Dallas two more nights before Yorrick Harp departs for El Paso."

El Paso! She had not heard of their next destination and wondered briefly what and where El Paso was.

"Before you depart," he went on, "I will come for your answer."

"You don't know me," she said, offering weak protest.

"Not true. I feel as though I have known you always."

"What if I made you unhappy?"

"Then I would learn to love unhappiness."

She looked away, continually embarrassed by his extravagant claims. And it was while she was looking away that he took her arm.

"I do love you, Eve," he whispered. "Please believe that. And if you think someone is coming to fetch you or rescue you, don't," he advised. "For if they were coming they would have been here by now. You are alone, except for Yorrick Harp and his dubious protection."

She started to protest but changed her mind and turned about and faced the carriage. He assisted her up and stayed close while she settled in the carriage seat.

"Thank you," she said.

"Are you sure you are feeling well?"

"Yes."

"Miguel will take good care of you."

"I'm sure."

"I will see you tonight."

"You're coming back into town?"

"To hear you sing, of course."

For a moment their gaze held.

"Until this evening." He smiled and signaled the driver. As the carriage rolled forward, he ran alongside her window. "You forgot this. I want you to have it."

As the carriage accelerated, Eve saw something sail in through the open window and land in her lap.

She looked down and saw the macabre purse for loose change made from a human scrotum.

Quickly she shook it off her skirts and moved to the far side of the carriage. She looked back through the oval window at the rear of the carriage and saw him watching her.

As the carriage rattled beneath the large sign proclaiming the Grand Ranch, she straightened back around in her seat and carefully eyed the grotesque object on the floor, and tried to reconcile the gentle man who had carried her in concern to the front porch, who had seen to her every wish with a man who obviously had committed murder first and then a most hideous form of mutilation.

No matter how hard she tried, she was incapable of solving the problem. It didn't matter. She settled back against the cushions and thought one clear thought, that Mr. Grand was wrong. At least on one score. Someone would come for her, Stephen would come for her. He would find her. She was certain of it.

 The Texas Border

Having ridden all night and all day through a terrain that resembled a tropical jungle, Stephen and Paris found themselves at dawn the following day at a place fittingly called Sunup. It boasted a single-room railway station, a single-room café and a sign that read the last stop in Arkansas for the Texas Pacific Railway.

They had exchanged their horses for fifty dollars and two tickets to Dallas, and now they sat at opposite ends of the station platform waiting bench, having determined during the long hard ride that for the duration of their journey through the South, they would be safer if they claimed not to know each other.

Stephen leaned forward, resting his elbows on his knees. He felt his stomach trying to accommodate the heavy pancakes he had purchased at the café next to the station. The loading platform was empty except for Paris, who appeared to be asleep at the far end of the bench, his head tilted back against the wall, eyes closed.

The train was due "when it got here," according to the man behind the barred window who had cheated them mercilessly in the exchange of their horses.

Now Stephen stood, feeling the need to stretch his legs. Curiously he felt little fatigue, though he knew it would descend soon. When they boarded the train, he would sleep, though past experiences had informed him that things tended to go wrong when one was asleep. In the future it might be prudent if one slept while the other kept watch, like now.

He walked to the edge of the platform and looked down the long empty tracks shining brightly in the early morning sun. No train in sight. He looked in the opposite direction, which hopefully would lead him to Dallas and Eve.

He stood on the edge of the platform, eyes closed, and saw her so clearly, her beauty, her smile, her eyes and hair. They would have been married by now if all had gone according to plan.

Suddenly he felt weak with regret and old grief and felt new urgency as well. Where in the hell was the train? So much lost time. Was Yorrick Harp still in Dallas? And if not, where would he look next, and was Eve still with the troupe? And was she well?

As his thoughts generated new worry, he heard in the distance the first faint sound of a steam engine.

"Paris, wake up," he called over his shoulder, momentarily forgetting that they were not to know each other, at least not until it was safe.

But as he looked back, he saw Paris already awake, stretching the sleep away, the same expression of eager anticipation on his face that Stephen felt.

Then he fixed his eye on the approaching train, the rhythm of the giant wheels clearly audible, the black engine shining in morning light, a miracle that could whisk men in comfort great distances across this vast land.

"Come on," he muttered beneath his breath as he saw the engine breaking speed, the enormous puffs of gray-white smoke filling the sky overhead.

"We're on our way," he heard Paris murmur as he passed behind him, moving on down the platform, not waiting for Stephen's response.

A few moments later the train came to a halt. Six passengers stepped down. Then the porter waved Stephen forward. "All aboard, sir."

Stephen was on the verge of pulling himself into the car when he stopped. "Dallas?" he asked carefully. "This train is going to Dallas. Am I correct?"

The porter nodded, and with relief Stephen swung up into the vestibule and was just turning into the long central aisle when he heard the same porter's voice raised in anger.

"Not you, boy. You drunk? Coloreds sit back there."

Stephen stepped to the vestibule in time to see the porter, himself a "colored," directing Paris toward a coach at the rear of the train. Foolishly Stephen felt an impulse to intervene and would have done so, but he caught Paris's eye warning him against intervention.

Stephen stood in the open door and watched Paris as he moved obediently toward the rear of the train and watched further as the porter shook his head as though with dwindling patience. For one stark moment Stephen was absolutely convinced that he understood literally nothing of the ways of this America.

He leaned out, hoping to see the coach into which Paris had disappeared. But he saw nothing, and no matter. Later he would walk back to make contact. For now all he could do was take his seat and hope that time somehow increased its normal rate of speed, five minutes to each single minute, no, better, an hour per minute so that this railway journey could be accomplished in the blink of an eye and he would look up and find himself in a place called Dallas and would see Eve waiting for him beyond this dusty, soot-streaked window.

The fantasy was pleasing and foolish, and he did nothing to dispel it. As the train rolled noisily forward, he tried to imagine how he would greet her and how she would greet him and knew that their love was of the substance and quality that would permit them to take up precisely where they had left off.

He loved her so and she him and that was all that mattered.

 Stanhope Hall

Burke sat slumped in his big swivel chair and watched as Taylor Quitman drank too much whiskey, bartered too much of his soul and corrupted the chill clean autumn air with too many lies.

Still Burke allowed him to speak on, lacking both the spirit and inclination to interrupt and challenge.

"Dead ends, Burke, one after another. You have no idea."

Oh yes, Burke had an idea, several, as a matter of fact. Of course there would have to be dead ends when each clue led directly to a prominent Mobile citizen, a good, true Son of the South.

"And I have tried, I swear to God, I've tried. You believe me, don't you, Burke? I even hired a man out of New Orleans to assist me. But he's not very effective. People in these parts don't talk easily to strangers, you know that. They just go mute."

Burke watched as Taylor Quitman poured another whiskey and swallowed it in one gulp. His watery eyes met Burke's. The glance held only a moment and was painful. Taylor broke it first by hurrying over to the bench near the door where he had left his satchel.

"Here, do you want to see my notes?" he offered, still breathless from the whiskey. "You will get a better idea of what I have been trying to do."

Burke didn't give a damn about Taylor Quitman's notes. What he had hoped for by now was a strong case with names and faces, a precise charge filed and the slow wheels of justice at least placed in motion. Instead what he had was a drunken attorney who had betrayed him, who didn't dare point a finger of accusation at Mobile's guilty citizens, for the simple reason that he was one of them.

Outside the window, which gave a view of the back garden, he saw a figure in white and for a moment his heart accelerated. It was only Mary, although for one cruel moment, he had thought it was Eve. He had not realized before how similar their walks were.

Burke closed his eyes and found, on the other side of his grief, anger, always anger that his daughter had been taken from him. Was she still alive? And if so, in what state? How frightened she must be, ill, perhaps in desperate need . . .

In a grim counterpoint to these devastating thoughts, he heard Taylor Quitman's voice droning on, speaking lies.

In an attempt to cancel the lies, Burke looked out the window and tried to find Mary again and rest his mind on her lovely countenance, though Mary had perhaps suffered more than any of them during these last difficult weeks. She walked constantly about Stanhope Hall as she was doing now, sometimes engaged in sensible activity, but most of the time just soothing herself with aimless repetition, around and around the upper gallery and then the lower.

And David—Burke couldn't even remember the last time he had seen David, whom he suspected had gone to stay with Cleo and Casey in one of the former slave cabins behind Stanhope Hall.

Burke rubbed his head and made a mental note to check on David. One of his children was lost. That did not mean he was obliged to neglect the other two.

". . . and so, at this point, I must confess, I'm at a loss to know what to do next," Taylor Quitman said and again poured himself a whiskey and drank it.

"Taylor, enough," Burke pronounced, holding both hands up in a staying motion. He stood slowly, feeling one hundred years old, lacking energy, lacking breath. "If you'll excuse me now, I—"

"Burke?"

At the door he looked back. "Yes?"

"I *am* sorry."

"Of course you are."

"Have you heard news from Paris Boley and Stephen Eden? They should have arrived in Dallas by now."

"No. We have heard nothing."

"I'm sorry."

"If you'll excuse me—"

"What should I do?"

"About what?"

"The case, finding the man who—"

Burke turned back from the door. "Try looking in the mirror, Taylor."

"Wait a minute; I resent that. You have no right—"

Suddenly Burke felt a need for fresh air. Quitman could find his own way out. Hurriedly he left the room and made his way onto the back gallery. He looked toward the garden where he'd last seen Mary. Gone now.

He clung to the railing. Somehow he must restore order and purpose to his world. But how? How did one go about substituting hope for hopelessness, faith for cynicism, purpose for dread? At this moment he was prepared to say it couldn't be done. Yet he knew he had to try.

He bowed his head low over the railing and remembered how he used to pray at his mother's knee, simple prayers to make the night end swiftly, the day dawn safely. Well, what harm? Now he leaned heavily upon the railing and tried to remember the religious doggerel of his childhood. At first it came only in fragments.

The blessed Lord Jesus in Bethlehem born, look down from on high and see me to morn, and comfort and hold me in Your blessed care, and ease all my fears and hear all my prayers—

"Mr. Stanhope, Mr. Stanhope."

He looked up at the sound of his name, heard a woman calling to him from the gallery above. It sounded like Florence, crying out over and over, "Mr. Stanhope, please come, please, it's Christine—"

He clung to the railing, weakened by his prayer, and looked up into a September sky promising winter and knew with a certainty that increased his grief and sharpened his fear that no one had heard his prayer, no one was there to hear it, nothing except a blank, unresponding, random cosmos in which a man the size of a speck of dust meant little or nothing.

Eve gone. Now Christine?

 Dallas

On the evening of their last performance in Dallas, Eve sat on one side of the crowded basement dressing room, brushing her hair while all the other women put on lip rouge and cheek color and eyeshadow. She envied them, but again Yorrick Harp had made it clear. No makeup. Not for Eve. The men in the audience preferred her natural.

And she was pleased to admit that clearly they seemed to like something. Last evening she had exhausted the encores that she had worked out with the orchestra and had been forced to sing a final number a cappella, and even then had left the stage under a pleasing barrage of coin and gold nuggets.

In exchange for her success onstage, Yorrick Harp had granted her several favors, such as this small dressing table with the other women and a change of gowns every night—though what she wore could scarcely be called a gown. This new one was lavender gingham with, as always, a high-buttoned collar and long sleeves and a plain skirt that fell straight from her waist without petticoats, without everything.

"Nervous?"

The question came from Lily at the table next to her, who was painting on red bow lips.

Eve watched carefully. She *was* nervous, though it was a good feeling of danger met and conquered. And since she'd been here she had learned a few things about what Yorrick Harp called stage art—how to move about on the stage, how to keep face front, how to hold your head in order to obtain maximum illumination. Still she felt that she performed best when she put everything she had learned out of her head and concentrated on the song, the words and the unique mood they spun. Then she felt that the audience would listen to her forever.

"Are you sure? Your decision, I mean?"

It was Lily again, fully aware, as was everyone in the troupe, that John Paul Grand would be in the audience tonight and at the stage door after the performance awaiting Eve's answer to his offer of marriage.

"You don't have to love a man, you know, to make a good wife," Lily whispered.

Eve started to say something and changed her mind. What was there to say? Sometimes at night just drifting off to sleep, she saw his face in memory, a good face in spite of everything, and heard his voice, a good voice. But then she saw something else in memory, the display boards bearing their grizzly collections, and although Lily and the others had laughed when Eve told them of these atrocities, they had reminded her that he was a very rich man, albeit an eccentric one.

"Hurry, girls, fifteen minutes!"

This cry came from the woman named Mother, who had not come

near Eve since that first disastrous night. Eve had encountered her in
the passageways on several occasions, and she'd merely turned her
face to the wall until Eve had passed.

Now, "You," she called out, pointing directly toward Eve. "Yorrick
Harp demands to see you immediately."

Lily leaned close. "What do you suppose he wants?"

Eve took a final look in the mirror at her plain reflection and stood,
aware of all eyes upon her.

"This way," Mother said, as though Eve didn't know the way up
the stairs.

At the top of the steps she heard the rumble of an audience gathering beyond the stage curtain, louder than usual this evening, or so it
seemed.

She saw the closed door leading to Yorrick Harp's office about ten
feet away and presented herself to the closed door and knocked once
and waited.

Behind, she was aware of Mother lurking about and kept her eyes
straight ahead and heard Yorrick Harp's unmistakably theatrical
"Come!"

Eve drew a deep breath, always a wise first step where Yorrick
Harp was concerned, then pushed open the door and saw him
sprawled on his red velvet lounge.

"Come." He smiled and waved her forward, indicating that she was
to sit beside him on the lounge.

"I have received word from John Paul Grand," he said, leaning
close, his breath smelling faintly of garlic. "He will be here shortly,
and he asked me to bring you here to my office, where he will hold a
personal conference with you."

She listened, head down.

"Are you prepared to meet with him?" Yorrick Harp asked.

"I suppose."

"Do you know what he wants?"

"I think so."

"What?"

She looked up, surprised by his question, beginning to suspect that
Yorrick Harp was the only man in all of Dallas not to know of the
proposal.

"He has asked me to marry him."

This announcement seemed to cast Yorrick Harp into a kind of
paralysis. For several minutes he said nothing, then, "Was he joking?"

"I don't think so."

"And why didn't you give him a ready response?"

"I had none to give him."

"You had—"

As Yorrick Harp's incredulity rose, his voice fell.

Then, "It would be a way out for you," he suggested simply, "but I'm sure you're aware of that. I'm certain that he would marry you first and escort you home second."

Eve looked up, a curious thought troubling her. Did she really want to go back to Stanhope Hall? Apparently everyone there had learned how to get along very well without her. She had been so certain that by now someone would have come for her, one search party or another, her father sparing no expense or manpower in rescue. And Stephen? What of Stephen and their avowed love? But the truth remained. As Mr. Grand had told her, no one had come, no one had even inquired. So either they thought her dead or—

She bowed her head. Somewhere within her there was an instinct toward common sense that told her nothing could be further from the truth, and another instinct toward self-pity that suggested slyly that maybe they *didn't* care. She knew in the past she had been a great cause of worry to both her parents.

"Are you well?" Yorrick prodded. "No cheap emotion please, not as you stand on the threshold of the most important decision of your life. Do you have the faintest idea what it would mean to be Mrs. John Paul Grand? Think, child. You would own a large part of this blasted prairie. You would be mistress literally of all you surveyed. I beg you to think on it very carefully."

His enraptured plea was interrupted by a single short rap on the door. Eve looked up.

"Destiny," Yorrick whispered melodramatically. "Ready?"

She gave no response, for she had none to give. Her spirits had taken a serious tumble a few moments earlier. Now she looked away as she heard Yorrick draw open the door, heard a reverent "Ah, sir," and heard nothing else and at last looked up to see John Paul Grand standing in the doorway.

"I hope I'm not disturbing," he said.

"Not at all," Eve said. "Though I was expecting you after the performance."

"I couldn't wait," he explained. "I've waited too long."

"Indeed you have, sir," agreed Yorrick Harp. "Come, come in. My parlor is yours for as long as you need it. On your feet, girl," he snapped at Eve and for his trouble received a stern pronouncement from Mr. Grand.

"That's enough, Harp. Leave us!" Eve looked up to see Yorrick Harp backing through his own door. Beyond him, she saw small groups of curious women, all venturing as near to the door as they deemed safe.

After his ordered departure and since he had no place else to deposit his embarrassment, Yorrick Harp aimed it at the women. "And just what, pray tell, are you doing? It isn't your cue, is it? No, of course not. Then move back, move back immediately to the waiting area."

Abruptly John Paul Grand slammed the door and shook his head. "I suppose he serves a purpose. He brought me you."

Eve smiled, trying to sort out the rightness of her decision.

"I've missed you so," he said and came directly to where she stood in front of the lounge and took her hands in his and she felt their warmth, their massive size. "You have no idea how I have fought against coming in to see you. But I vowed to wait until this night and it's seldom, if ever, that I don't keep my word to myself."

"My father always said that the bargains one strikes with oneself are the hardest and yet the most important ones to keep."

"Your father was a wise man."

"I miss him."

"I'm sure you do."

The brief conversation died and left an awkward silence. She moved a step away and heard the opening act coming from the stage through the closed door, the wood nymphs charming the hungry men with tantalizing glimpses of bared breasts.

"You're missing the opening," she said.

"I didn't come to see the opening," he replied, his manner changing, more formal, the smile gone, his eyes leveled on her with a disquieting intensity.

"Eve," he began and guided her back toward the lounge. "You must understand, I have never before asked a woman to share my life. I have never truly believed that I needed a woman."

If this was a declaration of love, it was a strange opening, declaring his lack of need for the beloved.

"But now," he went on, and she sensed that a significant qualifier was coming, "the first time I saw you in the hotel, helpless before those bastards who were tormenting you, since that first time when you attracted and held my attention in a way no other woman has ever done, I find that I am at odds with myself."

She listened, head down, beginning to understand how difficult it was for this man to make these declarations.

"Since then," he went on, "I can't sleep, I walk the night away. My house which used to fit me now seems too large, too small, too plain, too fancy. I'm alternately too hot, too cold, too hungry, too filled. I seem to be wholly out of rhythm with my skin and the world."

Abruptly he looked back, his manner plaintive, his voice a whisper. "Will you marry me and set me to rights again? I have no idea what sort of husband I will be. I have never been a husband before. But I can promise you that I will never hurt you, that I will live to protect you and will honor and fulfill every demand you make of me. Do you understand?"

At some point she had become almost mesmerized by his voice. He seemed so in need, and she saw in memory that enormous house sitting atop the hill, looking out over the dusty settlement at its feet, and tried to imagine herself being mistress of such a place.

What happened to the doctor you were in love with, Sis Liz?

Nothing, my child. I learned what it was he loved better than he loved me.

The remembrance of that beloved voice startled her. She hadn't thought of Sis Liz for weeks. How worried she must be.

"Eve? Did you hear me?"

"I heard."

She continued to hear the music coming from the orchestra, saw in memory the nymphs and knew that after the nymphs, there were selections from Shakespeare, and then it was her turn to take the stage and wait for the men to quiet down, that magic feeling when all eyes turned from near conversations, drawn to the stage by her appearance.

Then she had discovered that it was fun to hold them a moment or two longer, hearing their silence increase with anticipation, and she could do all this merely by taking one step toward them, head down.

It *was* fun. Even before she had opened her mouth in song, it was a great deal of fun.

"Eve?"

"I'm sorry."

"You were smiling."

At last she stood, enjoying a lightness of mood that, according to Sis Liz, always signified that a proper decision had been made.

"No, Mr. Grand. I can't accept your offer of marriage."

He looked stunned and disbelieving. "Why?"

She drew near to him, wanting very much to help him to understand. "First and most important, I don't love you."

"That will come."

"No, not for me. I find you interesting and warm and very much in need of a wife, but I am not the one."

"Let me be the judge of that."

"It's my decision."

"I don't believe you know what you are doing."

"Perhaps not. I'm not terribly skilled at taking charge of my own life or actions."

"Then I think you had best reconsider."

Eve shook her head, beginning to dislike his tone, his manner, which had suddenly become hard and arrogant.

"You're incapable. All women are incapable of taking charge of their own lives. They were created to be looked after."

Beyond the closed door she heard the low drone of Shakespeare, heard the pleasing silence coming from the audience, as though the men had at last begun to perceive the difference of these words, if not the importance of them.

She now had only one goal, to bring this matter to a close, to bid Mr. Grand good-bye and move out into the wings so that she could watch the last few lines of *The Merchant of Venice*. Lily's "quality of mercy" speech always gave her goose bumps.

"I am grateful to you, Mr. Grand, for your hospitality, your kindness and most of all for your flattering invitation."

"I did not intend it to be flattering."

"I know, but it was, and I—"

"You must reconsider."

"I can't."

"Yes," he said, insistent, and drew nearer to where she had taken refuge near the door, thinking to open it and in that way end this fruitless encounter. Now as she looked up at him, the anger on his face frightened her. She thought of the mutilated Mexican houseboy and suspected that *he* had seen this same expression on Mr. Grand's face as sentence had been passed.

"Please excuse me," she murmured, no longer wanting to stay in his presence. She was on the verge of reopening the door when suddenly he appeared behind her, one hand forcing the door shut, the other pulling her around and holding her against the closed door.

"I won't be humiliated," he said, his voice so quiet, though there was something different about it.

"It is not my desire to humiliate you," she said and tried to move away from his grasp.

"Everyone will know," he said, both hands on her shoulders pinning her to the closed door.

"I'm sorry for that."

"Everyone," he repeated. "My men will know. They had planned a welcoming party for you."

"I'm sure they will understand," she said and again tried to break free of his grasp and again failed.

For several moments he looked down on her. Then, "Bitch," he muttered, and before she could alter her position or protect herself, he delivered a stinging slap to the side of her face that caused her neck to crack and left a blazing fire on her cheek, her eyes watering.

Just as she was recovering, he slapped her again, harder than the first, causing her to cry out.

She shook her head in order to clear it and tasted blood. Then she heard Yorrick Harp close by on the other side of the door, demanding, "What is taking place in there? I demand to know. I insist upon it."

"Leave us alone," Mr. Grand shouted.

With effort Eve struggled for freedom in the opposite direction, and as she heard him follow after her, she heard the door burst open, heard Yorrick Harp's shocked voice.

"Sir, enough!"

She looked back to see Yorrick Harp filling the doorway, an expression of indignation on his face.

"All right," Yorrick Harp said with dispatch. "I believe the meeting is over."

"She promised me," John Paul Grand claimed and pointed an accusing finger at Eve.

"No, I didn't," she whispered and dabbed at the corner of her mouth.

"Promise or no," Yorrick Harp went on, "you must come with me now. The lady has a performance to give. You may stay and watch if you promise to behave like the gentleman that I know you to be. No more knocking about. My girls must be whole and unblemished. Surely you can understand that."

Eve was aware of Violet assisting her toward the door. She considered staying long enough to thank Yorrick Harp but decided to do so later and was just passing through the door when she heard footsteps behind her and looked back and saw Mr. Grand, his face covered with apology and remorse, the hand that had delivered the blows now outreaching to her.

"Forgive me, please," he said gently. "I had no right. I am sorry."

She started to reply, then changed her mind. Besides, Violet was moving her rapidly out the door and through the crowded backstage area toward the wings that led onstage.

"Are you all right?" Violet whispered.

Eve said that she was and looked out onstage and saw Lily holding forth with the final soliloquy and heard a gratifying burst of applause. The curtain fell and Lily, flushed with success, hurried past.

"They loved it," she said and beamed. "I'm certain they didn't understand a word of it, but they loved it." Suddenly her smile faded and was replaced by concern. "My dear, what happened?" she leaned close in an attempt to get a better look at Eve's face, but then the stage manager shoved her out for a second curtain call and Eve looked over her shoulder and saw Yorrick Harp walking toward the stage door with John Paul Grand.

"What happened?" Lily demanded as she returned, cheeks flushed from her curtain call.

Eve dabbed once more at the corner of her mouth and assured Lily she was fine and looked up and saw the stage had been cleared, the audience silent, waiting.

"It's all yours," Lily whispered. "We'll talk later," and she hugged Eve, and Eve drew a deep breath in an attempt to regain control and was sorry for John Paul Grand and his loneliness, but ahead of her was the empty stage and a waiting audience, the orchestra ready and a song in her head and heart that she knew would please them, and the magical exchange would ease her loneliness, and even though in essence she was a prisoner of this place and these people, something deep within her was being satisfied for the first time in her life. And while she wasn't certain what it was, she intended to explore and develop it fully.

"You're on," the stage manager whispered.

Despite the recent assault by John Paul Grand, she stepped out onstage smiling.

* * *

On the following morning, in a blaze of early autumn sun, Eve stood on the loading platform waiting to board the Texas-Pacific Railway to El Paso. Lily was close beside her. Halfway down the platform she saw most of the women clustered about a young Mexican who was selling something called tamales, a cornmeal concoction filled with meat and wrapped in a corn shuck. They smelled delicious.

All of Dallas or so it seemed had awakened early and had come to the station to bid farewell to the Adamless Eden. A few of the women had found their favorites and were now unabashedly kissing them good-bye, entrancing sights that caused a blush to burn on Eve's face but that she thoroughly enjoyed watching anyway.

"You could be doing that." Lily smiled, apparently observing her line of focus to where three of the girls were delivering warm good-bye kisses to three dusty though appreciative cowhands. "He's here, you know," Lily added, and pointed toward the crowded street beyond the station.

Eve turned quickly in that direction and saw the same enormous carriage that had taken her out to the Grand Ranch, then brought her back. She looked more closely across the distance and saw his face at the window.

"Don't worry," Lily promised. "He won't harm you again, I can assure you."

Though grateful for her assurance, Eve felt no real need of it. Somehow she knew Mr. Grand would not harm her again and perhaps now wanted nothing more than to say good-bye.

"Excuse me," Eve murmured and started across the crowded landing platform.

"No, Eve, wait!" Lily called out, alarmed.

But Eve continued on across the platform, down the steps and approached Mr. Grand's carriage, tentatively at first, and saw his face still in the window watching her.

"Mr. Grand," she said with a smile. "Thank you for coming." She drew near the window. "I was hoping I'd see you again to thank you for—everything, for helping me on my first day in Dallas, for all your kindness and hospitality to me."

She watched his face, still considered it the good face of a remarkable man. He seemed surprised by her appearance, though gradually his features softened into a smile.

"Eve," he whispered, his face bearing the angles of deep remorse.

As he leaned closer to the window, she stood on tiptoe and kissed his cheek and stepped back and saw him touch the place where she had kissed him as though it were a brand, an expression of gratitude in his eyes.

Then she hurried back across the crowded platform, saw Lily waiting for her, a worried look on her face. "What did you do?" she scolded. "You should stay away from him. I would have thought you'd learned your lesson."

"Why? He's lonely, that's all."

She looked back to see Mr. Grand still watching her.

A few minutes later, after all the kisses had been delivered and all the luggage loaded aboard, Yorrick Harp called to the women still eating tamales and signaled them to board the coach that had been reserved for them.

Eve waited, keeping close to Lily. "I wish I could sit with you," she murmured and watched Yorrick Harp sweeping closer, knowing that he would take her with him to his private car where she would pass this tedious journey in isolation except for his endless sermons and homilies.

Their performances here in Dallas had been highly successful, Eve was aware of that. Never had she seen such a beaming, preening Yorrick Harp as the one who approached them now, carrying a silver-headed walking stick and wearing his customary shiny black top hat, which he always wore for traveling.

"And what are you two silly geese waiting for?" he bellowed, seeing Eve and Lily standing alone on the rapidly emptying platform.

"Where shall I sit?" Eve asked, knowing full well what the answer.

"Well, for heaven's sakes, sit where you like!" Yorrick Harp scolded and waved his walking stick at them. "Do you think I have nothing to do but plan seating arrangements for all my girls? Silly Nelly. Go on with you both and sit where you like and do it quickly."

Eve grinned. Lily gave her a quick hug and together they ran toward the narrow steps, Eve scrambling up first, amazed at the sensation of happiness that suddenly swept over her.

As she entered the crowded car, she spied a seat for two on her left and as she made her way to it, several of the women greeted her warmly and she returned their greeting and slid into the seat.

With the first clanking turn of the wheels and the first siren scream of the steam whistle, Eve settled in and leaned back against the seat and loosened her bonnet and thought how at peace she felt, considering.

One day, I promise, you'll find your purpose in life—

Sis Liz. Was this Eve's purpose in life, this crowded railway car on a long journey to a place called El Paso? Perhaps so. Perhaps not. She would have to wait and see.

"Sing for us, Eve," someone called from the rear of the car. "A good luck song for the tour ahead."

As the others took up the request, she handed her bonnet to Lily and turned around and knelt in the seat on her knees, facing her audience, and started to sing, pleased and only mildly puzzled by her curious state of contentment.

 Dallas

"The Palace," Stephen shouted at the first old man he encountered after leaving the train. "Can you tell me where the Palace Theater is?"

"Yes, this is Dallas." The old man scowled up out of his nap, clearly deaf.

Stephen tried again, fully prepared to shake an answer out of him, when Paris came hurrying up from where he'd just departed his coach at the rear of the train.

"Easy," he counseled and turned Stephen away from the old man. "Come on, there are others who are better equipped to answer our questions."

Reluctantly Stephen agreed and advised himself patience. But it was hard to be patient. The railway journey had been endless, this eastern half of Texas a continent wide, or so it seemed. They had had engine trouble about fifty miles back and had lost a half-day, and always he suffered the sense that Eve was moving far ahead of him, would not be in Dallas as he had hoped, the trail grown cold.

Now he followed Paris down the crowded loading platform. All around he saw men in soiled broad-brimmed hats and well-worn boots, faded trousers to match, a town of men, or so it seemed, a town of industry as well, for there was a beginning skyline rising in the east.

At the end of the platform they looked out over a sea of wagons, horses, gigs, the road so crowded that nothing seemed to be moving in either direction. Flanking this road, he saw two narrow crowded board sidewalks, foot traffic flowing every which way, no pattern, a scuffle erupting at the slightest provocation. The "winner" in each case possessed only one clear qualification: physical prowess. And the prize? More elbow room.

Stephen was aware of Paris standing behind him and he was certain he could read his thoughts. That sea of humanity would have to be crossed unless they intended to pass the rest of the day on the high safety of this railway platform.

"Ready?" Stephen called over his shoulder, dreading the plunge into such chaos, unable to bring himself to imagine Eve in such a place as this.

Then coming from behind, he heard Paris's voice, raised, polite and formal. "Sir, I beg your pardon. I'm looking for a place called the Palace Theater. Could you—"

As Stephen turned back, he saw Paris engaged in conversation with a man, dressed as all the others were dressed. There was one point of difference. He was a black man.

In answer to Paris's question the man pointed over Paris's head, due north. "It's that way. Stay on this street. You can't miss it. They don't like us to sit down there. They don't mind if we come in and pay for our whiskey and get out. But you've been warned."

With that the black man strode past and left Paris gaping after him. Stephen rallied first, grateful that the direction had been so simple. "Come on." He motioned to Paris and started down the steps to the

crowded street and pushed his way into the foot traffic and looked
back to see if Paris was following after him. He was, though there
was a look of bewilderment on his face, as though he hoped desperately that sooner or later he would reach a place in this world where
his color did not matter.

About ten minutes later Stephen stopped before the huge towering
frame structure called The Palace.

He stood looking up at the high square roof, clearly the stage house,
and enjoyed a good feeling of certainty, as though he knew that recently Eve had passed through these doors.

Hastily he pushed against the door. And found it locked.

"Damn."

He was on the verge of pounding when from behind he heard a
quiet suggestion. "Try the other one."

He did so immediately and felt this door give and found himself in
a musty interior where at first he saw nothing clearly. Gradually his
eyes adjusted to the semidark and he saw a faint glow coming from
his left, saw a bar with elaborate carved wood panels and red velvet
wall hangings.

Moving carefully forward, he saw beyond red drapes into the saloon itself, saw a barkeep, his head bowed over his work, polishing a
small mountain of glasses.

Paris was directly behind him and whispered a wise suggestion.
"I'll wait here. Go and see what you can find out."

Stephen was grateful for his foresight. No more trouble. That was
his constant and fervent prayer now. Just let him find Eve and take
her away from this place.

"Sir," Stephen began and stepped through the partially drawn curtains and into a ring of lamp light.

The barkeep looked up. "Closed. Your thirst will have to wait.
Come back later and we'll treat you well."

"It's not my thirst that's bothering me, sir. A moment of your time
for a question. That's all I ask."

The barkeep smiled. "A question? Of what nature? I'm not the
smartest man in Dallas."

Stephen eased closer to the bar and looked about at the semidark
interior. Behind him there were small wooden tables and chairs. Most
of the chairs had been up-ended atop the tables, clearly for the purpose of sweeping. Near the back of the saloon, in the farthest corner,
he thought he saw the outline of a man seated, only his head and
shoulders visible.

He was on the verge of taking a closer look when the barkeep pressed him to speak. "Don't have all day, you know. Ask your questions and let me get on with my work."

Stephen took a final look toward the back of the saloon. "Are we alone?" he asked the barkeep.

"We're always alone, from the day of our birth to the day of our death." The barkeep leaned close for a whispered confidence. "He's all right back there. Drowning his sorrows is all, if you know what I mean."

Stephen saw clearly now the outline of a man, solitary, each feature obscured by distance and the slant of the lamplight.

"So, what's your question?"

"A theatrical troupe," he began, "all female, under the management and ownership of a man named Yorrick Harp."

At some point the barkeep started to nod. "What about them?" he asked.

"Are you familiar with them?"

"Of course. Yorrick Harp's ladies have graced that stage in there for years. They've been right here for the past few days."

Stephen closed his eyes, unable to believe his good luck. "One lady in particular, one special lady."

"Name her."

"Eve Stanhope."

The barkeep's face went slack. He gaped at Stephen, then rapidly resumed his polishing. "What about her?" he asked, not looking up.

"Do you know her?"

"There are lots of ladies in the Adamless Eden."

"Do you know the one named Eve?"

For several moments he showed no indication of ever responding again. Then he did. "I know her."

Stephen breathed a quick prayer. It was apparent now that the search was over, all their misfortunes behind them.

"One more question," Stephen asked, hearing a chair scrape behind him but paying no attention to it. "Could you tell me where I could find her? I would be most appreciative."

Something caught the barkeep's eye, just over Stephen's right shoulder. His expression changed from one of cooperation to one of apprehension.

"Mr. Grand," the barkeep sputtered, looking suddenly nervous. "His inquiry was innocent. I didn't—"

As the barkeep's fear increased, Stephen turned to see what was causing it. The man sitting in shadows at the rear of the saloon had now evolved into a whole man, immaculately dressed in a dark suit, expensively tailored, and a white shirtwaist, and the clear unhurried look of authority and self-possession.

As he approached the bar, Stephen extended his hand. "My name is Stephen Eden, sir. I trust I have not disturbed you."

"But you have." The man smiled and in a curious way the smile canceled accusation. Stephen was relieved when he accepted his hand in a firm grasp and moved alongside him at the bar.

The only source of agitation was the barkeep. "I told him nothing, Mr. Grand, I swear it."

The man ignored him and seemed to study Stephen, his smile fading. "My name is John Paul Grand. I own this theater."

Stephen shook his hand, pleased. As owner of the theater, he might be in an even better position to answer Stephen's questions.

"Did you hear my question of this man?" Stephen asked.

"I heard," Mr. Grand said.

"Then perhaps you could answer. I'm looking for a young woman named Eve Stanhope."

"Yes, my fiancée," the man said, and the smile was gone.

Stephen was stunned. "Your—no, perhaps you didn't understand. Miss Eve Stanhope."

"My fiancée," Mr. Grand repeated. "I asked her to become my wife and she said she would. May I ask of your interest in the lady?"

Stephen looked back at the barkeep, who had moved to the far wall and was no longer polishing his glasses. Now his face was a blank as he stared back at Stephen, who was having trouble digesting this latest news.

"Sir, if I may ask again, are you certain we are speaking of the same lady?"

"I'm certain. Now all I must know is your interest in that lady."

"I have no interest if what you say is true."

"Do you doubt my word?"

"No, but there is a way to settle this conflict. Tell me where I can find the lady, and if she tells me of her engagement to you with her own lips, I'll walk away and you will never see me again."

"Her whereabouts are none of your concern," Mr. Grand said, something about his voice and manner growing threatening.

Before such a threat, Stephen had no intention of backing down. He'd come too far to be turned back now by an arrogant son of a—

He stepped forward until he was less than two feet from where Mr. Grand stood. "I will tell you of my interest in Eve Stanhope. Before she was kidnapped and given to Yorrick Harp, she was *my* fiancée, and that is my interest. Do you understand?"

Amazed by his own rapidly surfacing anger, Stephen waited for the announcement to penetrate Mr. Grand's arrogant exterior.

He wasn't certain if it ever did, for the man, with utter aplomb, simply said, "I don't believe you."

"Please tell me where I might find the lady. I'll leave it up to her. But I must see her, not just for my sake but for her family's sake. They are worried to the point of illness about her whereabouts and her safety. One brief conference, sir, is all I require."

But even as he spoke, Stephen saw something unyielding on Mr. Grand's face.

"No, I cannot reveal her whereabouts for her own safety. How do I know you mean her well? Perhaps you are one of her kidnappers."

"No."

"Out of the question."

As his resolution increased, Stephen had heard enough. "Then I will find her without your assistance," he announced. "Surely there is someone in Dallas who knows where the all-female troupe is residing. I shouldn't have to look far."

As he spoke, he started away, still angry that this man had refused him the information he had traveled so far to get.

"Sir, please come back or I'll be forced to shoot."

The voice came from the bar, calm, polite. As Stephen turned, he saw a gun in Mr. Grand's hand. It was a large weapon with an imposing barrel, and it was pointed directly at Stephen.

"Come back, please." Mr. Grand smiled. "I am sorry it came to this, but if indeed you do know the lady in question, then you know her value and how important it is that she have a protector ready to defend her name and honor at all times."

"I meant no harm to either her name or her honor," Stephen said and started slowly back, realizing now his first task was to convince Mr. Grand that there was no need for weapons.

"Sit!" Mr. Grand said, reaching backward with one hand and lifting a chair from atop a table, then placing it in front of the bar.

As Stephen moved toward the chair, Mr. Grand smiled. "I knew you would come after her. Not you specifically, but someone like you. At first she was not willing to give her heart to me, and I suspected there was a tag end of her past somewhere."

Stephen sat in the appointed chair, listening, pleased at how much Mr. Grand was revealing of himself without even knowing it.

She was not willing to give her heart to me.

Now Stephen felt a new surge of concern for Eve. "Mr. Grand, please let us talk. I see no need for—"

He was about to say for the use of weapons when suddenly, coming from behind at lightning-fast speed, he felt a rope draped across his chest, felt it grow taut, felt his arms and hands jerked rigidly behind, felt the rope being looped about his joined wrists, a complete entrapment that had happened in less than a second, or so it seemed. As he looked back, still struggling uselessly, he saw the barkeep, red-faced from exertion, in clear alliance with Mr. Grand, who stood calm and unruffled a distance away.

"You've no right—" Stephen began, still struggling against the ropes.

Mr. Grand appeared to be studying Stephen closely. "You're not American, are you?" he asked, his voice accusing.

"No, I'm not American," Stephen muttered, wondering what in the hell that had to do with anything.

"What then?"

"English."

"Ah, our most ancient enemy. The Red Coats." He smiled at the barkeep. "Amos, do you remember the Red Coats? Do you have a red coat, Mr. Eden? A better question, perhaps, is what business you have in the heart of America, in pursuit of Miss Stanhope. You lied to me, didn't you? You do mean her harm, don't you? *You* are the kidnapper."

"No!" Stephen shouted as the madness continued to spill out. "You're wrong. Her family sent me to find her. All I want—"

"What you want isn't important, never has been, Englishman. This is John Paul Grand's territory. Here all that matters is what *he* wants."

As he spoke, his manner became almost courteous. He circled the chair at a measured pace, fondling something in his hand as he spoke, a blade of some sort, though Stephen couldn't tell for certain.

"And what are you doing in America? Were you invited to come?"

He stood before Stephen as though genuinely interested in the conversation, and Stephen saw clearly the knife, not large, but sharp-edged as a surgeon's scalpel.

"I was sent to America," Stephen began, growing weary of the conversation and apprehensive of the blade.

"By whom?"

"My uncle, Lord Richard Eden of North Devon."

"For what purpose?"

"He made an investment in cattle several years ago."

"Where?"

"Montana."

John Paul Grand laughed. "A foolhardy investment. There are no cattle left in Montana or Wyoming. The blizzards last year killed ninety percent of the herds. The rest have run free. So now you can go home and tell your uncle his investment is lost and that perhaps from now on he should invest in English kippers and leave the New World to those of us who know how to run it."

He laughed again, seeming to enjoy his own humor, and again disappeared behind Stephen's back.

"I do have a favor to ask of you, Mr. Eden, before you depart."

Depart. That was a welcome and encouraging word. "If I can, Mr. Grand."

"Oh, you can," the man smiled. "You have no choice."

"Then what?"

"I would like to have your ear, if I may, your left ear for my collection. I don't have the ear of an Englishman. I assure you I will give it a place of honor and point it out to one and all. I have been told the pain is minimal, and for your trouble I'll provide you with a full bottle of our best brandy." He snapped his finger at the barkeep. "See to it."

At first Stephen was certain he had misunderstood. He thought the man had said he wanted his ear.

"Here it is." Mr. Grand smiled, holding up the bottle of brandy the barkeep had just placed atop the bar. "Would you like some now, to help deaden the pain?"

"Let me go," Stephen said, struggling against the rope. The man was insane. He was convinced of it now, and compounding the fear for his own immediate well-being, he thought of Eve in the company of such a lunatic and began to fear greatly for her.

"You'll take nothing, then?" Mr. Grand asked, returning the brandy to the bar. "I admire your courage. Only a few men have gone through the ordeal sober. And one thing more: I must assure you it will not affect your powers of hearing, so have no fear. And I warn you if you hold still it will go easier for you. Struggle and I have no control over the scalpel. Do you understand?"

The nightmare increased, Stephen aware of his helplessness, doubly aware of the madman circling the chair, scalpel poised, catching the lamplight in bursts of exploding color, coming closer, John Paul Grand bending over, grasping Stephen's head and tilting it to one side.

In a burst of fear Stephen pulled forcibly away. Mr. Grand motioned at the barkeep to come closer. "I may need your help. Would you be so good?"

Stephen glanced at the barkeep and saw a look of reluctance on his face.

"Did you hear me?" Grand called again. "Come, I need you. Or would you rather take his place in this chair?"

Slowly the barkeep laid down his towel and came reluctantly around from behind the bar.

"Hold him secure," Mr. Grand instructed. "I just want the ear, not half of his scalp as well."

From Stephen's contorted position he saw nothing but a distorted corner of the cobwebbed ceiling directly over the bar, heard nothing but the man's voice talking civilly of barbaric matters.

"There will be pain," he warned softly, "and bleeding. You are a normal bleeder, aren't you? Of course you are. And it is not my intention to kill you. You must understand that. You'll be quite alive when I'm finished and as much a man as you ever were before. So enough talk. Are you ready?"

Stephen tried to wrench loose from the barkeep, who was holding his head in an iron grip.

Then the madman was bending over, his left hand clamped rigidly against Stephen's forehead, his right, holding the scalpel, moving closer to his ear. Stephen continued to struggle despite Mr. Grand's whispered warning. "It only makes things more difficult for you." And still the blade came closer until Stephen could feel it pressed against the side of his head. Then the first cut of the blade.

He cried out and heard something, a resounding thud, saw Mr. Grand stand up rigidly, eyes wide, distended in disbelief. Then suddenly he collapsed against Stephen, full weight, and slumped forward half on his knees, half sprawled across Stephen's lap.

As he fell, Stephen looked up and saw Paris, the full bottle of brandy in his hand, where clearly he had used it as a most effective weapon. Paris did not move but eyed the barkeep from a stance of defense, bottle still upraised, ready to use.

"Are you next?" Paris demanded.

Slowly Stephen felt the grip about his head relax, felt the barkeep move away. "No trouble. I promise. Not my idea, his—" Slowly the barkeep came around the chair. "Look," he began by way of apology to Stephen, "he pays my salary, he pays everyone's salary—"

Stephen saw Paris cautiously lowering the bottle. "Are you all right?" he asked of Stephen, and at the same time the barkeep dragged the prostrate figure of John Paul Grand to one side and hurried back and commenced to untie the rope that held Stephen bound to the chair.

"There's not much time," he muttered. "I'm afraid the bottle didn't do permanent damage," he added, glancing down at the unconscious Mr. Grand. "He'll come around shortly, and you two had best be gone."

Stephen looked up at Paris with an expression of gratitude. The barkeep did not have to tell them what they already knew.

"Here," he said and tossed Stephen a towel from atop the bar to stanch the thin stream of blood that was dripping down his ear. "You're luckier than most."

Stephen thanked him, plastered the towel against the slight cut and sidestepped Mr. Grand. "Miss Stanhope—can you tell me where I can find her?"

"Not here."

"Where?"

"Yorrick Harp's troupe left Dallas yesterday morning."

"But he said—"

"He was lying. The lady turned him down flat. And she *is* a lady, with a rare voice. But she's frightened and lost."

Stephen had heard enough. The news both hurt and healed and gave cause for new hope. "Where did they go?" he asked.

"El Paso."

"How?"

"The Texas-Pacific. There's a late-afternoon train. I'd go to the station and stay out of sight if I were you. Every second man you see on the streets of Dallas works for John Paul Grand. Go on, both of you, get out of here and I hope I never see you again."

Stephen wanted to stay longer and hear more of Eve. But he knew they musn't, and he was aware of Paris at his side, literally pushing him toward the red velvet curtains.

"Wait."

At the curtain Paris and Stephen looked back at the barkeep, who stood over John Paul Grand. "You'd better use that bottle on me as well. If I'm on my feet when Grand comes around, he'll suspect. Come on, give me a good one, right here."

But Paris objected to using the bottle again, fearful that he might do too much damage.

"Use what you want," snapped the barkeep. "Only hurry."

As Stephen stood at the curtain, he saw Paris place the bottle of brandy on a near table and assume a foolish-looking pugilistic pose, fists raised in a proper though useless-appearing fashion.

"Will you come on, nigger?" the barkeep shouted, clearly losing patience.

All at once the formal stance was dropped and Stephen saw Paris draw back his fist and deliver a blow of stunning strength and accuracy to the man's jaw. The barkeep collapsed in a heap near Mr. Grand, and Stephen saw Paris rub his hand and reclaim the unopened bottle of brandy. At last he turned to Stephen. "Well, what are you waiting for? You heard the man. Let's get out of here."

As he passed, Stephen had a question. "Where did you learn that fighting stance?"

"At Tuskegee. Everyone said I was pretty good on one condition."

"What's that?"

"That no one was hitting back."

Stephen dabbed a final time at the cut on his ear. Then he tossed the towel aside and took a last look at John Paul Grand, sprawled near the bar.

"Bastard," he muttered.

"Come on," Paris called, holding the door open, letting a square of bright sunlight into the musty-smelling theater.

Stephen moved past him out into the heat of the morning. "I should send a telegram to Stanhope Hall," he said as they made their way back up into the crowded streets of Dallas.

Paris asked quietly, "What will you tell them?"

"The truth—that we missed her here but we are on track again."

They stared at each other, as though both were remembering the hazards behind, anticipating the hazards ahead.

"Let's go," he said. "I'll send the telegram at the station, then we'll find a cool place and share that."

Paris tucked the bottle of brandy inside his jacket. Stephen led the way into the dusty streets, seeing not the crowds or the dust or the hazards beyond, seeing only Eve's face.

 On the Train en Route to El Paso

The train had been rocking steadily along for about two hours, heading southwest from Dallas to El Paso when Pearl, the little blond woman who always played Shakespeare's children, became violently ill and was taken out by two women onto the rear platform for air while the others cleaned up her sickness and tried to keep their own breakfasts intact.

"Should we call Yorrick?" Violet asked of Lily, who was kneeling on her seat looking out over the railway car in clear concern.

"Good heavens, there goes Rose," she gasped, and Eve turned about in time to see Rose make a frantic dash down the aisle, both hands clamped over her mouth. She was joined by Marigold, who, weeping, looked pale, the color of an old sheet. As these two jockeyed for running room, Eve heard a groan directly in front of her and looked back to see Violet sink down in her seat, holding first her head, then her stomach.

Lily turned around in her seat. "Enough," she pronounced and stood and appeared to be surveying the car with an eye of authority. "Listen to me, ladies," she called out, full voice, and was answered by fresh groans, the sound of new vomiting off the rear platform, everyone in the entire railway car or so it seemed falling ill within minutes of one another.

"I'm going to find Yorrick," Lily said to Eve. "Take care of things here as best you can until I come back."

With that she was gone, moving rapidly through the narrow door, leaving Eve with a coach full of sick women who seemed rapidly to be taking turns for the worse.

Slowly she stood, looking in all directions, unable to see how she could be of any help. Then she remembered when Christine had been unable to keep food down, Mama and Florence had made wet compresses for her forehead, sometimes applying them to the back of her neck as well.

Now where to get compresses? Eve looked about, wishing she had a petticoat. And then she thought of someone who did.

"Violet," she called over the seat and saw the pretty dark-haired woman slumped over miserably, a pile of sickness at her feet and more coming.

Hurriedly Eve lifted Violet's feet upward and rested them on the seat and told her to "Lean back, just relax. Take deep breaths."

Weakly Violet obeyed, and as she did so, Eve reached beneath her dress, found the waistband of her full white muslin petticoat and pulled.

"What? Eve, don't—"

"It's for your own good," Eve replied and heard her mother in an echoing memory and tried to recount how many times those words had been spoken to her.

The petticoat freed at last, Eve held it up and decided it would serve perfectly. She glanced back into the coach and tried to make discerning selections based on the color of various complexions. The extreme white and pale green she passed over, but there were several who were healthily rosy, and to those women she called out, "Come, I need your help. Hurry."

To her surprise, they came, although all were older, senior members of Yorrick Harp's Adamless Eden. Still they hurried obediently toward her, stripping off their bonnets and capes as they made their way down the aisle, sidestepping the trails of sickness.

"Anyone squeamish?" Eve asked as they drew near, already busily tearing Violet's petticoat into strips. The woman named Aster who played violin in the orchestra bleakly nodded. "I can't bear the sight of vomit."

"Very well. You go and fetch the large water canister outside the door. It's loosely attached by two clamps. Bring it to us immediately."

Even as the woman moved past, Eve was issuing new commands to the three remaining. "You, finish tearing this into strips of these approximate lengths. When the water arrives, dip them until they are saturated, then bring them back to us. You two, come with me. And bring her."

At the last minute she pointed toward Violet, who lay moaning in the seat behind her. Then she led the way up the narrow aisle, carefully assessing each face as she passed, giving hurried instructions to all. "If you feel ill, move toward the rear platform. Don't wait. Come now. Do you understand?"

Apparently most heard, for a half-dozen fell in behind her as though she were some bizarre pied piper. Eve noticed that the first victims to fall ill were slowly, weakly returning to the coach. They looked pale and wasted.

"Over here," she called to them and found a relatively clean area and began to ease the women down into the seats. At the same time the wet compresses were delivered from the front of the car, the women working with admirable speed, their fancy hairdos quite undone though there was an expression of gratitude on their faces, as though pleased that someone had taken the lead.

"More as soon as possible," Eve requested and continued to ease the ill women down into the seats. "Keep their heads slightly elevated," she called out to her assistants, remembering a dictate from Dr. Melrose regarding Christine. Once the truly ill were settled and relatively calm, Eve gently placed a cool compress on the backs of their necks and another on their feverish foreheads. Her rewards were their pleased groans of "feels good."

The other women quickly learned the mode of treatment, and as soon as a patient staggered back in from the observation platform, one of the makeshift nurses was there to escort them to a seat, whereupon they were given cold compresses and soothing comfort.

In a remarkably short time all were seated in sad rows of limp hairdos and smudged lip rouge, their eyes heavy with the effect of their discomfort. Eve stood back and drew a deep breath, her first in almost an hour. Where was Lily? And where was Yorrick Harp? What she and her limited crew had done was merely a stopgap measure. Some of the women, little Pearl for one, was so sick she could not hold her head up. And there were others who were not faring

well either. Even now she saw one of her "nurses" sink heavily into a
seat, groaning in a way that had nothing to do with fatigue.

As the others moved to attend to her, Eve pushed back her hair and
looked about. They would have to leave this car soon. The heat of the
day was climbing. The stench was rapidly growing intolerable, a new
cause for illness in itself.

She glanced behind her, hoping to see Lily and Yorrick Harp,
someone whose authority at least matched their responsibility.

But the doorway was empty, rattling in rhythm with the train that
was plunging across the southwest prairie, the scene outside the window barren of all life save for an occasional massive herd of cattle and
a few cowhands.

She closed her eyes. To stop the train here in the middle of nowhere would be foolish. Then the nearest town? What was it?

Just then she looked over her shoulder toward the door of the coach
and saw a grim sight coming into view—a very pale and clearly ill
Yorrick Harp, suspended like a grotesque crucifix between Lily's inadequate shoulders on one side and a dapper though determined conductor on the other, both struggling under the weight of the man
himself.

"Put him there," Eve heard the conductor suggest and saw them
lead Yorrick toward one of the front seats opposite where Violet sat
slumped and groaning.

Eve had seen enough, knew they needed help. "Sir," she called to
the conductor who was brushing at his dark blue coat, all the while
eyeing his once handsome railway coach.

"It's terrible," the conductor brooded. "I had no idea it was this
bad."

"The rest of the train?" Eve asked.

"Fine, fine, it's only here."

"A Mexican was selling food on the platform at Dallas," Eve said.

"Tamales," the conductor said with sudden understanding. "It's
happened before. They all should know better."

"We must stop at the next town," Eve said. "They can't—"

"Impossible," the man snapped.

"But we must," she insisted, trying to keep her voice down, not
wanting the others to hear. "They are very ill and need rest and a
special diet."

"And where do you hope to find those things?"

"In the next town."

"Do you know the next town?"

Eve shook her head. Behind she heard fresh moans coming from
Yorrick Harp.

"The next town," the conductor said in a precise voice, "is Abilene. Have you heard of Abilene?"

"Then we'll stop there," Eve said.

But the conductor's manner had changed, his attitude had grown condescending. "I don't think you mean that. My advice is to stay on this train. At least the ladies are safe here. Tomorrow night late, with luck, we will be in El Paso. They have a doctor there—"

"By tomorrow night," Eve said, imitating both his words and tone, "there will be several corpses mixed in with the ladies."

The conductor looked shocked. "Are they that ill?"

"Look for yourself," Eve invited. The man turned slowly about and surveyed the railway car filled with suffering, weeping females. Someone in the back called out in a weak voice, "Help me," and the sad sound seemed to echo pitifully above the rattle of the rails. With each jolt and jar there were fresh moans, fresh weeping, and Eve realized sadly that the ill themselves were proving her point.

"Abilene," she repeated.

"They have no doctor."

"I'm not certain they need a doctor as much as they need rest and quiet and fresh water."

"There is no hotel in Abilene that decent folk would stay in."

"We'll have to manage."

"There are murders every night."

"Who?" she asked, at last shocked.

"Cattlemen who have been on the trail for days. Abilene is the first place for a drink coming up from the Mexican border."

Despite this grim information, she repeated, "As I said, we'll have to manage."

"I have no idea where you will go. The ladies will be fair targets for every drunken cattleman in town."

"We'll do the best we can," she called over her shoulder, feeling that she had talked long enough, confident that she had made the right decision.

But as she approached the seat where Yorrick Harp sat, looking pale and ill, he looked her straight in the eye. "Don't stop," he muttered. "Off schedule now—" Those few words exhausted him and he slumped over, Lily and the others hovering about him in concern, leaving Eve to deal with her confusion.

Don't stop.

They *had* to stop.

There is no doctor in Abilene. The ladies will be fair game for every drunken cattleman—

Eve closed her eyes as though to shut out the echo of the conductor's words. She looked up to see the coach filled with pale, ill women who looked weakly back at her.

Dear God, what to do, she brooded and thought of home, of Christine, how more often than not the mode of treatment for her ills had been merely a cool dark quiet room and fresh water. It was generally a good remedy. And as no one else seemed willing or able to make a suggestion, then they all would have to rely on her judgment.

On that note of conviction she pushed up her sleeves and started down the aisle. Christine. She thought of her sister and missed her with an ache that left her momentarily clinging to the handhold of a near seat.

"Eve, not you—please."

This alarmed voice came from Lily, who hurried toward her.

"No, I'm fine," Eve reassured them all. Then she turned about, thought one last time of Christine, saw her in memory wearing her straw hat with the red plaid bow, the one she had worn the day they had hidden in the lilac bushes and watched Paris and Stephen bathing in the ice pond.

From the back of the coach came a weak cry, "Help me, I can't—"

Quickly Eve put the past behind her and hurried toward the cry of need. Though not the easiest thing to do, it was by far the wisest.

 Dallas

"All aboard!"

From his position of concealment in the baggage car, Stephen thought the words the most beautiful he'd ever heard.

Behind him on the floor Paris lay sprawled in a spread-eagle position. The bottle of brandy and the heat of the day had taken their toll, and while it had not been their intention to remain in the baggage coach, now it occurred to Stephen, why not? If caught, they both had tickets. But this way they could stay together, and in Paris's present condition, Stephen felt certain he required a keeper until he could sleep off the brandy.

Stephen was only mildly tipsy. For one thing, Paris had gotten a head start on the bottle while Stephen had gone to send the telegram to Stanhope Hall.

Then together they'd both taken refuge in the baggage coach, avoiding the stacks of baggage that had been tossed in during the afternoon, staying well out of sight behind each new mountain of crates and boxes. A few moments ago a barred crate containing a goat had been angled into place at the door, then the door had been slammed shut and a moment after that Stephen had heard the all-aboard cry.

Now for the first time since they had arrived in Dallas, he dared to relax and sank pleasurably down, using the baggage as a back rest. His ear throbbed, the thin cut burning with the sweat from his hair. He clamped his hand over it and leaned into the discomfort and found himself eye level with the goat, who stared back with a dispassionate expression, contentedly chewing.

Suddenly weary, Stephen pressed his head back against the baggage. He doubted if either of them had slept four straight hours since they had left Stanhope Hall.

The thought reminded him of the telegram he'd just sent, his indecision in composing the message, the telegraph operator's growing impatience with each correction. Finally what had he said?

From Dallas. Troupe departed. Eve's presence confirmed.
Leaving for El Paso this evening. Hope rising.
                                        Stephen Eden

Hope rising? Would he ever find her? And why hadn't she tried to escape from this theatrical troupe? If she were free enough to sing for everyone, then why wasn't she free enough to run for her life to a position of safety until he could come to her aid?

It was a foolish question, and as though to demonstrate how foolish it was, he was suddenly aware of the goat butting her head against the bars of her cage. And what if freedom were made available to *her?* Of course she'd take it, though soon she would be hunted down and dragged back to her cage, and what would have been accomplished for all her troubles?

Beneath the train's wooden floor he felt the vibration of the heavy wheels picking up speed, an irresistible rhythm that he knew would soon lull him into a sleep as deep as Paris's.

Beside Paris's leg, he saw the empty brandy bottle. Carefully he reached across and retrieved it and stashed it behind a stack of baggage. Best stash Paris in the same fashion. It would not serve if they both fell asleep, only to be discovered by a curious conductor.

Carefully he stood up and grabbed Paris beneath the arms and slowly dragged him into a corner of safe obscurity.

Then he settled down next to him in their private alcove, surrounded on three sides by walls of baggage. Safe now. The train was picking up speed, the rails singing a special song, "Eve, Eve, where is Eve . . ." He closed his eyes against this figment of his imagination, and it was while his eyes were closed that he heard the bolt slide on the baggage coach door, heard voices, male, two, as well as he could determine.

He pressed back against the baggage and thought none too soon had he taken refuge, and with held breath peered out through a nearby narrow slit.

Conductors. Two of them. Both were dragging heavy canvas mail sacks.

"Trouble ahead," one said over the song of the rails.

"That's what I hear. What's up?"

The first conductor dragged the canvas mailbag close to the sliding door. "Pox in Abilene, or so the telegraph man says."

"How bad?"

"Ain't none of it good. But who knows? No doc there. Of course it could be typhoid. All I know is we ain't stopping except long enough to deliver the goat and pick up the mail for El Paso."

The other man lifted his head to the air. "You smell something?"

The first conductor looked puzzled. "Yeah, what is it?"

For several moments both men sniffed and one came perilously close to where Stephen and Paris sat concealed.

"Damn if it don't smell like brandy."

His companion laughed. "You're dreamin', Mitch. Brandy's about as far away as El Paso, late tomorrow. Wishful thinkin'. Come on. We got a full house."

As the two conductors made their way back to the door, Stephen held his position and his breath.

"Sure smells like brandy," the second man said.

"You got one powerful nose, Mitch. Anyone ever tell you that before?"

They left, taking their laughter with them. Stephen held his position, afraid to breathe. Then he did, a long slow relaxing gulp of air. He looked through the slit in the baggage to make sure they were alone.

Sickness in Abilene? Only a brief stop. That was good. Save time. Then on to El Paso.

The thought brought him comfort and heightened his anticipation and allowed him to lay back against the makeshift couch of baggage and take a last look at Paris deep in sleep. Then Stephen closed his eyes and within the instant his dream vision was filled with Eve as he'd last seen her on the evening of their plotted elopement, radiant in white, her hair a halo about her face, whispering close in his ear, "I love you."

Mary stood at the back of the darkened parlor, all drapes drawn, and fixed her eyes on the two tall candelabra, lit and flickering at the head and the foot of the small white coffin, and knew that she still did not comprehend everything that had happened and was grateful for that lack of comprehension.

Surely this wasn't a funeral. Thus far there had been no music, no flowers, no words, no tears, just the darkened parlor and the small white coffin and Burke seated there beside it, in the same bent position in which he'd passed the last twenty-four hours.

To her right she saw Florence. To her left was Madame Germaine, who seemed to be keeping a watchful eye on everyone.

At last it was Madame Germaine who broke the silence. "It's time, Madame. The men have come. Would you give them the word, or shall I?"

Mary gaped at the old tutor as though she were speaking a foreign language. Word? What word?

Apparently her bewilderment was reflected on her face, for she saw Madame Germaine nod at Florence, who stepped out into the corridor and signaled to someone.

At the same time Mary saw Madame Germaine move to Burke's side. She whispered something in his ear and pointed back to where Mary was standing. Slowly Burke turned about and revealed his terrible face to everyone, unshaven, eyes swollen and lost in hollows of sleeplessness.

Now she saw Burke slowly approach the small white coffin, saw him bend over and kiss the coffin. Behind her at the doorway she saw Florence holding David's hand, a frightened David who looked first toward the front of the parlor, then back at Mary.

"Mama."

The voice, usually boisterous and shouting, was shy and apprehensive.

"My darling," Mary soothed and welcomed her son into her arms and clung to him, wishing only that someone would open the drapes. It was so dark in here, the room itself frightening.

For several moments they stood together, both staring at Burke, who continued to hover over the coffin. Then Madame Germaine approached with that expression of indomitability on her face that suggested hard courses of action and straightforward resolve.

"Come, Madame, you must say your good-byes. Not so much for Christine's benefit but for your own. Mr. Stanhope is waiting for

you. The three of you must stand together. It will not go well for any
of you in the future if you don't say your good-byes now."

Christine. She had been so ill.

"Come, David, help your mother. Your father is waiting."

Where was Eve? Eve should be here. Eve adored Christine. Where was Eve?

"Come on, Mama. Papa's waiting."

Mary looked down to see David grasping her hand, trying to lead
her forward. Coming from the opposite direction like a conspiracy,
she saw Burke, his hand extended to her.

"Mary," Burke whispered, and kissed her and led her forward to
that place where she did not want to go. Now in her mind, because it
pleased her mind to think it, she decided that Christine really wasn't
dead. Christine was with Eve; the two of them had gone away together on a journey, as they were always together.

We hid in the lilacs and watched the boys swimming, Christine and me—

*It's true, Mama. Eve let me wear her new straw bonnett with the red
ribbon—*

Before she knew it and long before she was ready for it, Mary
found herself at the coffin's edge, looking down on her youngest
daughter, smiling, as though she were merely taking a nap.

Mary thought the grief would be unbearable, but it wasn't. This
lovely child was her daughter, Christine, and now she was dead and
never again would she suffer from winter's cold, or summer's heat,
never again suffer loneliness, suffer lack of companionship, suffer fear
of darkness, suffer fear of storms, suffer nightmares—

Tell me what happened in 1066, Christine—

So bright, Christine, so pretty, Christine, such a sweet and loving
and giving nature, Christine—

"Good-bye," Mary whispered and lightly touched Christine's forehead, which was cold as marble. She felt a slight pressure against her
skirts and saw David pressing up against her as though competing for
her attention.

"Come." She smiled at David. "Tell Christine good-bye, then we
will leave her with God."

Self-conscious, David stepped forward and mimicked Mary's gesture, touched Christine's forehead, then quickly stepped back.

Burke led her away from the coffin, and all Mary could think of
was how simple, how uncomplicated dying was, everything resolved
within the instant, over and done with, no more struggle, no more
pain, no more fear, just over and done with. How good.

"Are you all right?" Burke inquired.

"I'm fine," she said and found herself wishing that Eve's fate might
be as easily resolved. Not so simple, that tragedy, not so final.

"Come, David," she murmured and pressed her son to her. Outside in the corridor, she heard weeping and knew it was Katie, who'd been Christine's nursemaid since the day of her birth. And there was old Florence who'd served as midwife, Florence who had rocked Christine, soothed her, prepared camphor packs for her every day of her life.

Strange, but as the sounds of weeping increased around her, Mary felt herself growing stronger. It was over for Christine, blessedly over, and for that she was grateful.

"Will you come to the cemetery?" Burke asked.

"Of course. I'll go with her to the end."

As the three of them waited in the corridor for the coffin to be brought past them, Mary walked the short distance to the front door, where a refreshingly cool early autumn breeze was blowing. The summer's heat had at last broken, the summer horrors as well. With Eve's disappearance, the terror caused by the Knights of the White Camellia had come to a halt, as though at last they had committed an atrocity that had shocked even themselves.

"Come, Mary." The voice was Burke's and she turned about to see the small coffin being lovingly carried down the corridor by Ben and Tom and Cleo and Casey, a mixed procession of young and old.

Just as Mary turned about to follow after them, she saw in the distance a horseman at the far end of the live oak avenue, coming at top speed and expertly guiding his mount toward the front gallery of Stanhope Hall.

"Burke!"

The man shouted and Mary recognized Taylor Quitman, though she did not recognize the state of disrepair that attended the man. Taylor used to take pride in his appearance.

"Burke!" Quitman shouted again. Burke glanced through the opened front door, clearly angry. At the same time Taylor Quitman approached the front steps at a run and pushed his way up onto the porch.

As he crossed inside the door, Mary saw him focus on the small white coffin at the end of the corridor. His manner, his urgency instantly faltered.

"Burke, I'm—I have a—I—didn't—"

But coherent words would not come, and Taylor Quitman, once one of the most distinguished-looking men Mary had ever known, made his way in a halting fashion to the nearby staircase and sat heavily on the bottom step. "Christine?" he asked.

Burke looked away.

Abruptly, almost angrily, Taylor Quitman stood. "A telegram. Old man Moseman asked me to bring it out. It's from Dallas."

Mary saw the brown envelope in Taylor's hand. Another death? Word of another coffin to carry out to the cemetery?

Slowly Burke approached the hand that held out the telegram and took it and held it for too long, indicating his fear of what it might contain.

Then as though it were a valuable document, Burke began to move his finger down the envelope flap, causing a clean break.

Mary watched Burke reading the message, his brow knit as though not quite understanding it all.

"Burke."

In response Burke looked at her and Mary thought she saw relief mixed with bewilderment. He lifted the telegram as though he knew all would be interested and read:

> From Dallas. Troupe departed. Eve's presence
> confirmed. Leaving for El Paso this evening. Hope rising.
> Stephen Eden

For several moments after he finished reading, Mary saw him continue to study the message. As for herself, all she'd really heard had been two phrases: *Eve's presence confirmed. Hope rising.*

Suddenly she felt the peculiar sensation of joy coming fast on the heels of sorrow, felt the two powerful emotions blending.

David asked, "Mama, what does it mean? Is it from Stephen?"

She drew him close. "Yes, my dear, the telegram is from Stephen and he says that Eve is alive."

Then Burke was at her side, his arm about her shoulders, and briefly they clung together under the watchful eye of the servants.

A few moments later Burke handed Mary the telegram. She reread it for her own benefit, still putting all her faith in those two phrases: Eve's presence confirmed—hope rising.

Then she folded it and slipped it into the pocket of her dress and felt sorry for Taylor Quitman, who continued to sit on the lower step looking so defeated.

Burke ignored him and led her toward the procession at the end of the corridor and she went with him, thinking this, too, was part of being alive and loving each other and enjoying good fortune and plenty and joy and the richest of blessings, though this was the hardest part. While she was grateful for the news of Eve's survival, a large portion of her heart was being carried away in the small coffin at the head of the procession, her lovely little Christine who had burned

brightly during her few years on earth and who would leave a vacuum that no one could fill.

"Where is El Paso?" she whispered to Burke as they followed after
the coffin out onto the back gallery.

"It's on the western Texas border, close to Mexico," he replied.
"Far away," he added and stepped ahead to be with Christine.

Mary watched him. One dead, one so far away. It was a time for
faith, and she struggled mightily to draw upon hidden resources and
hoped that it would be enough to see her through her grief and the
agony of waiting.

 Abilene, Texas

Still not quite certain why the reins of leadership had been
thrust into her inexperienced hands, Eve stood on the platform between coaches and held on tight against the rocking motion of the
train and watched the flat, dusty place called Abilene come into view.

From this distance it appeared scarcely a block long, with the main
cluster of storefronts lining that one dusty road. There were other
structures scattered about, but now she kept her eye on that one small
settlement, hoping to see something that resembled a hotel, a large
structure that might with luck be able to provide them with rooms,
clean beds and fresh water.

In the railway car behind her she knew the sickness was spreading.
Some of the women had retched themselves empty and yet the spasms
persisted, dry heaves that brought tears to their eyes and left their
foreheads wet with perspiration.

"Do you see anything yet?"

Lily was behind her, having just emerged from the railway coach.
She looked none too good herself, though Eve knew she was tired.
Earlier Eve had conducted a quick questionnaire and had determined
that the six of them who had not eaten any of the Mexican tamales
were the six still on their feet.

"Doesn't look too promising, does it?" Lily muttered, eyeing the
approaching town of Abilene with a skeptical eye.

"Has the troupe ever stopped here before?" Eve asked, on a note of
hope.

"No, Yorrick calls it a barbarous place, says the men there wouldn't
begin to understand our various presentations."

As Lily tried to tuck a stray piece of hair into the french knot at the back of her head, Eve clung to the handrail and let the rush of air flow over her. "Everyone thinks it's the pox, you know that," Lily said.

In answer to Lily's worry, Eve smiled as reassuringly as she could. "We'll find someone to help us, I'm certain. For now, gather all their small baggage and stack it on the observation platform at the rear of the train. Is Yorrick—"

"No better. Worse, in fact. He can scarcely talk, and his fever is so high. Eve, are you sure it isn't the pox?"

"No, of course it isn't the pox. It's bad food, plain and simple."

Lily drew a deep breath. "I'll be in the coach if you need me."

"Keep them inside. I'll try to find out how long we have."

Suddenly the train gave a lurch, its speed broken, the great iron wheels turning more slowly now. The rush of air diminished as well and was replaced by the stench coming from the coach behind. The town of Abilene was growing closer; a dusty, sun-baked settlement, several large herds of cattle now visible, surrounding the town, adding to the stench, a heat-filled pit of dust and foul odors.

Eve closed her eyes and thought briefly of the gardens at Stanhope Hall.

"Miss Stanhope, you must listen."

She saw the conductor hurrying her way, a handkerchief pressed against his nose. "You must get these women off the train as quickly as possible. I have appointed a few men to take care of their baggage. We'll place it all together on the loading platform." He started away, then turned slowly back. "I'm sorry, Miss Stanhope," he said. "I wish I could give you some helpful advice. Abilene is wide open, none of the refinements of Dallas."

She recalled the dusty, crowded streets of Dallas and wondered how she had missed its refinements.

"We'll manage," she said. "And we thank you for all your considerations."

As she moved past him into the railway coach, she was greeted first by a semiconscious Yorrick Harp, who lay stretched out on a cushion for two.

"Is he awake?" she asked Rose, who bent over him, wet compress in hand.

She looked up. "His eyes sometimes open but what he says makes little sense."

He never made a great deal of sense, Eve thought wryly.

"Eve, what's going to happen to us?" Rose asked, looking helpless.

"Nothing is going to happen to us, Rose. We'll be getting off shortly and we'll try to find a quiet place where the ladies can rest and hopefully recover."

"Yorrick has always taken care of us before."

"I know," Eve said, "and he will again. I promise you."

"But none of us know what to do."

On this plaintive tone the train came to a halt and the words carried and the railway coach became silent and Eve looked up to see all looking at her.

She tried to rise to the occasion, and thought of Sis Liz and did a conscious imitation of her queenly stance, her supreme confidence.

It was from this pose that she addressed the coach. "This is Abilene," she said, lifting her voice. "We'll be getting off here. I'll try to find a hotel for us, a place where you can rest and get well. All of you will recover, I promise you that. You must believe that. But you need rest and quiet, and I'll see that you get it."

She bent and looked out the window at the loading platform, saw several groups of people standing about, all male, a few pointing toward the railway coach, others shaking their heads and quickly moving back.

"Those who can walk," she called out, "try to assist those who can't. Your baggage will be seen to, so just move yourselves out as quickly as possible. The air will be good for you, I promise."

As she hurried down the narrow aisle of the train, she glanced to the left where Yorrick Harp lay sprawled. At the moment no one was attending him.

"Mr. Harp," she whispered, kneeling beside him, feeling his brow, which was feverish. "Can you hear me? It's Eve. We're in a place called Abilene—"

Suddenly his eyes opened. They glittered unnaturally with the effects of the high fever. "No," he muttered through parched lips. "Not —here. Don't stop here. Barbarous—"

He made an effort to sit up and failed and fell heavily back against the cushions.

Then she was moving again toward the coach door, already feeling the hot prairie air that seemed to blow perpetually. At the opened door she closed her eyes against the stinging dust and opened them and saw the loading platform emptied now, not a man in sight.

Puzzled, she looked toward the telegraph office, saw the curtains drawn, though she suspected that there were several sets of watching eyes behind the ragged curtains.

Leaning into the wind, she walked up to the door and knocked once and received no answer, and knocked again and called out, "Please, can you hear me? We need your assistance. We need—"

"Go the hell away. We don't want you here. Get back on the train and clear out."

With head bowed she listened to the angry male voice and waited out its tirade. She looked over her shoulder and saw the ladies stumbling off the train, each clinging to the handrail for support.

Behind them, others were coming, the discomfort of illness on their faces heightened by the sudden blasts of hot prairie wind, the odor of cattle dung blending with the heat.

Eve had promised them rest and fresh air. She started to knock again on the telegraph office door, then spied another door on the opposite side of the loading platform. Station Master, the sign said.

She hurried in that direction and found the door closed, but she knocked anyway and called out, "Please, sir. Can you hear me? We are in need of accommodations. Can you—"

"Get away from the door. Get back on the train with all your baggage. We don't want the pox here."

Pox. Of course. They were afraid. "No sir, you're wrong. It's not the pox. I assure you. The ladies ate bad food. That is all."

"Did you hear me? I said get back on the train and take all the whores with you. Don't want you here."

Behind her Eve heard moaning as the women continued to move off the train. As they stumbled out, Eve spied a large tin shed to the right of the loading platform, a place of shade where horses were tethered during the arrival and departure of trains.

"Take them over there," she called to Lily and Rose.

To her left she heard the doors of the baggage car slide open, saw three men push their baggage out onto the loading platform.

"Please be careful," she called out, seeing one of the men lift a violin case clumsily into the air. Either he failed to hear or chose not to, for he dropped it and Eve heard an ominous splintering of wood.

As the confusion increased about her, she looked again toward the telegraph office, then toward the station master's closed door and saw no alteration in either. At last she ran around the station to the front, where she looked the length of the street, a dusty brown deserted place except for horses tied along the side of the road, which suggested their owners were nearby but out of sight.

About halfway down the street she saw a sign that read The Emporium Café. Perhaps they would give her fresh water. As she drew her skirts about her in protection against the wind, she started down the road, looking at the storefronts on either side, a barber shop, the three chairs filled with men, all staring back at her behind the window, a hardware store, another gallery of male faces pressed against the window, a blacksmith shed whose fire was hot though the smithy himself was no place to be seen.

Then there was the Emporium Café, directly to her left, and she climbed the high board sidewalk, keeping her eyes focused on the window behind which she saw no movement.

At the door she knocked and waited and tried to peer in and saw nothing, yet someplace nearby she smelled potatoes and onions frying.

"Is anybody there?" she called out.

She heard movement behind the door, heard a voice, female this time. "What is it you want?"

"Water, please, a full pail if possible."

"None to spare," came the female reply.

"But there is illness."

"We know and we don't want it. Get off my porch and get on back to the train."

Slowly Eve backed away from the café and looked the length of the street and started off in the heat and dust, determined to knock on every door. She knew what had happened. Someone had spread the false rumor of pox and everyone had heard of the deadly scourge, capable of wiping out an entire town with one illness. No wonder they were frightened. She didn't blame them for that. She did blame them for not believing her when she told them it was not the pox, just bad food and not in the least contagious.

She started down the board sidewalk, her own spirits newly defeated by a sly and insidious doubt. It *was* bad food, wasn't it? It wasn't pox, was it? She'd seen food sickness close at hand, in Christine, in David, in Cleo and Casey, the boys particularly, who, according to her father, were billy goats and could eat anything.

But she'd not seen pox, though there had been an outbreak years ago among the workers. She'd not been permitted to leave Stanhope Hall until the illness had been brought under control.

Now what to believe? Time would tell, in a tragic way, of that she was certain. If it was the pox, those who were ill now would within a few days be covered with running sores. Eve remembered an old man, a knife sharpener who, three, four times a year would make his way to the kitchen annex of Stanhope Hall and sharpen every blade on the place in exchange for food and drink. His face was disfigured, and Mama had told her that he had been a victim of the pox, one of the lucky ones who had survived the dread disease, for most did not.

Eve closed her eyes against the remembered disfigurement and thought only of Mama and tried to recall her considerate ways and strength of purpose and tried to duplicate her in all respects as she started toward the next closed door, wondering if there was anyone in all of Abilene who could see their desperate need and come to their aid.

* * *

Stephen tried to keep track of the passing hours by the quality of light that appeared beneath the cracks of the baggage coach door.

During the total absence of light he'd slept, assuming night. Now he began to see gray beneath the crack, sat slowly up from his slumped position next to Paris behind the mountain of baggage and found himself looking straight into the goat cage, the animal staring impassively back.

Paris stirred. "Not the best night's sleep I've ever had."

Stephen saw him staring into space with all the passivity of the goat. Occasionally the train took a sharp jolt and Paris's passivity would fade and he'd grab his head with both hands, and Stephen suspected a hangover.

"Why are we slowing down?" Paris asked.

The train *was* breaking speed. Slowly Stephen stood, using the top of the goat cage for support, and started toward the side door and with effort pushed it open a crack and peered out at a predawn world of empty prairies.

By leaning farther out he saw in the near distance the outline of a country settlement, most of it still cast in night darkness, though here and there a lamp twinkled.

"Come over here," he called to Paris. "The air will be good for you."

"There's plenty of air here," Paris grumbled, and from his slurred speech, Stephen suspected he might be drifting back to sleep. Why not? Let him sleep it off. They were miles from El Paso, of that he was certain. What was the name of the interim town, the one where there was sickness? Abilene, that was it. Then this was Abilene up ahead, where they would make only a brief stop, and then they would be on their way again to El Paso and Eve.

The thought brought him pleasure. What a reunion they would have. How he longed to see her again, to hold her in his arms.

Town ahead.

Quickly he closed the sliding door and returned to his place of concealment next to Paris behind the stacks of baggage. With a sharp jolt the train came to a halt. Silence, strange after so much noise. Stephen peered over the goat cage, heard men approaching the baggage car from the outside.

He heard the sliding door open, heard a man's voice say, "The goat gets off here."

Stephen pushed farther into the corner and watched as the conductors swung up into the baggage car.

"Where in the hell is it?"

"Over there. Hurry up. I ain't lingering here any longer than I have to."

"Did you see them?"

"Yeah. I feel sorry for them, but what are you going to do?"

"Where's the goat going?"

"How in the hell should I know? Read the tag."

"Reverend Justin Kalm. The preacher?"

"Yeah."

Their voices faded as they approached the open door. Stephen heard sounds of effort, heard the goat bleat out disapproval of her rough passage, then heard nothing.

When after about five minutes he still had heard nothing else, curiosity drew him forward, tentatively moving around the baggage toward the open door. Drawing closer to the edge, he saw the two conductors a distance away at the telegraph office, a ledger sheet between them, the telegraph operator signing.

As for the rest of the loading platform, it was empty, no signs of life to the right, no signs of—

Quickly he looked through the early-morning half-light and saw to the right a large tin shed about thirty yards away, and lying beneath the shed was what appeared to be misshapen lumps, perhaps cotton, although at that moment he saw one of the lumps stir, heard a female voice cry out, saw another female near the edge of the shed start toward the distressed cry. As this second figure moved, the tentative half-light caught on her hair, long, fair, like—

"That's done. Thank God. Come on, let's get out of here. You close up and I'll give Henry the signal."

As the two conductors hurried back toward the baggage car, Stephen was torn between trying to determine what was going on beneath the tin shed and his awareness that he must take cover immediately or be found out, a discovery that could undoubtedly mean another delay, time wasted, Eve moving farther ahead of him.

Then he heard the heavy door sliding shut. A few minutes later he heard the steam hissing, trying to build to a head, heard the first grinding of wheels beneath the wooden floor of the baggage coach. Slowly he turned back to his corner and saw Paris still asleep.

Stephen sat slowly beside him and leaned back against the baggage and thought again of that curious company asleep beneath the tin shed, that solitary figure moving through the predawn light.

She occupied his mind for several minutes, and then with resolution he closed his eyes and ordered his mind to shut down as well and concentrated on a state of sleep, of recovery and healing from all past wounds, on the glorious hour, so near, when once again he might look upon Eve Stanhope.

 Abilene

The whistle of the early morning train destroyed the unsatisfying half-sleep in which Eve had passed the frightening night. As the whistle shrieked again, several of the women were disturbed as well. One cried out, and Eve rose slowly and made her way through the sleeping bodies.

Behind her she heard the train come to a halt and considered pleading with the conductors who were dragging open the baggage car door to take pity on them and allow them to board for the trip west to El Paso. Yorrick had been right. It had been a mistake to get off here.

But something intervened, quite possibly exhaustion from having begged half the night, having knocked on every storefront in Abilene, only to be greeted by silence.

Now she tried to soothe the one who had cried out and recognized her as the piano player, Pansy by name. She looked so pale in the predawn darkness, as did all those around her.

It was Eve's assessment that for many, the worst part of the sickness was over. But in order to recuperate they required rest and a light though sustaining diet so that they might regain their strength.

Others she feared were worse off, Yorrick Harp among them. She glanced over to where the man lay at the edge of the tin shed. For the better part of the night he had ranted and screamed under the strain of a high fever, providing all those listening ears in Abilene with proof positive of the pox that was always accompanied by a raging fever.

Now, in a way, his sudden quiet was worse than his rantings. The last time she had checked on him his breathing was scarcely audible.

She heard a sudden scraping and looked toward the train and saw the baggage car door open, saw two conductors leap down, disappear for a moment, then reappear hauling a large cage between them.

She stared at the open door of the train. An easy escape. Two weeks ago she would have taken it in a minute. But not now.

Morning light was rising. All the women were beginning to stir. What would this day bring? They couldn't huddle here forever under this tin shed. What to do?

As the weight of responsibility pressed down upon her, she bowed her head over Pansy's feverish face, exhausted and despairing.

Suddenly she looked up, certain that someone was watching her.

She glanced toward the train, toward the baggage car, and thought she saw a figure standing in the open door of the baggage coach, a tall figure, male, someone who was gazing back at her with matching intensity.

She started to her feet when suddenly he disappeared back into the baggage car. Then she saw the conductors returning.

A few moments later Eve heard the wheels begin to turn and she looked again toward the baggage car just as it rolled beyond her line of vision followed by passenger coaches, the windows empty, all asleep at this early hour.

Then the train was gone, rattling out into the empty prairie, and she continued to kneel at the center of the tin shed, surrounded by ill and sleeping women.

Behind her, near Yorrick Harp, she saw Lily, who had stayed up most of the night and who at last had fallen into a deserving sleep. Lily had complained earlier of not feeling well, and Eve had prayed that it was only fatigue. Now all she knew for certain was that they were stranded and alone in this dusty prairie town, the people of Abilene as hostile as the climate, though she knew they were frightened and for that she could not wholly blame them.

Still one, only one would have to conquer his fear and come to their aid, or else—

She abandoned the thought and focused on the cage resting unattended on the loading platform. Slowly she made her way through the sleeping women, not wanting to disturb them. Once beyond the tin shed she climbed the steps to the loading platform and saw that it was a large female goat with swollen udders. Food—nourishment, for the taking.

She stared down on the animal, who continued to chew contentedly, then looked about at the loading platform as though expecting someone to step forward and claim the animal. But there was no one about.

Then how would it hurt? The poor goat was in sore need of milking, and though she was not an expert, Eve had tagged along often enough into the milking barn as a child, had watched the strong skillful fingers of the milkers, had on occasion tried it herself and been mildly successful.

"I beg your pardon, is that your goat?"

The male voice, so near and sudden, startled her. She rose from her squatting position so rapidly that she lost her balance and sat flat on

the loading platform and found herself looking up at a smiling pleasant male face, a fringe of sandy red hair just visible beneath his flat-
brimmed hat, an ill-fitting black jacket over a faded shirt and well-
worn black trousers.

He offered her his hand and she took it hesitantly and felt callouses.
Once up, she moved quickly back, putting the goat between them.

"No, not—mine," she stammered, "though I was contemplating
milking her."

"Are you hungry?"

"My—friends are." She gestured toward the tin shed and the sleeping women.

The man squinted forward, clearly having trouble seeing the specifics of the tin shed. "What in the—" Slowly he started in that direction, removing his hat, revealing a full head of curly sandy-colored
hair. "What happened?" he demanded, looking back at Eve.

"There was illness on the train, food sickness, nothing more I'm
certain, but I felt they needed rest and water, so I asked the conductor
to stop here, but no one here will help us. They think it's the pox."

As she completed her explanation, the man walked ahead toward
the shed. He placed his hat on the loading platform and jumped
down, stopping at the first woman and bending down as though in
examination.

Eve watched as he made a careful examination of several others.
Then he spied Yorrick Harp at the edge of the shed, with Lily asleep
close beside him. The man seemed to remain bent over those two
longer than the others. Once he looked back at Eve, as though he
wanted to question her. As she started toward him, he met her halfway.

"The man?" he questioned.

"His name is Yorrick Harp. This is his theatrical troupe. We were
on our way to El Paso."

"And you spent the night here, like this?" he questioned, disbelief
giving way to confusion.

"I tried to get help. From everyone. They wouldn't open their
doors."

"There was illness here about six months ago. One family wiped
out except for the husband. It wasn't pox. We don't know what it was.
They're frightened." He retrieved his hat and gave it a slap against
the side of his leg and looked again at the group. "I think you're right.
I think it is bad food, except perhaps for him."

He looked toward Yorrick Harp. Just as Eve was on the verge of
asking further questions, the man introduced himself. "My name is
Pastor Kalm. Justin Kalm. I have a small mission about three miles

out of town. Of course you're welcome to stay there. I'm afraid I only have one wagon so it might take us a while to get the ladies out."

For some reason his kindness weakened her and she fought back tears. She felt herself wavering and in the next minute felt the support of his arms.

"There, are you all right?"

She tried to dismiss the weakness for what it was, hunger and thirst. "I'm grateful."

Up close his shirt felt coarse though freshly laundered, and she was aware of strength in the muscles beneath the shirt, a good figure of a man, capable in all ways.

"Better?" he asked as she felt her strength returning. "You wait here with the others. I'll bring the wagon around to the shed. We'll take the sickest first. Wake the healthy ones so that they can help you."

She started back toward the tin shed when he called after her. "What's your name?"

"Eve Stanhope."

He tipped his hat. "Welcome to Abilene, Eve Stanhope. And don't worry. You'll be all right. I'll take care of you, I promise."

She smiled at him, so grateful, and watched as he lifted the goat, cage and all, effortlessly onto his shoulder and disappeared around the corner of the station. Then she hurried toward Yorrick Harp, who, according to Pastor Kalm, might be suffering from more than food illness.

She bent down and felt his forehead, the fever still raging. Next to him was Lily curled in on herself and sleeping.

"Lily, wake up, we have help. Lily, please, wake."

But as she reached across Yorrick Harp, her hand brushed over Lily's cheek and she felt the same heat she'd felt on Yorrick's forehead.

"Oh, Lily," she mourned and at last saw her eyes open, though unfocused.

"I'm—sorry, Eve," Lily whispered, her voice scarcely audible. "Now who will help you?"

Eve tried to quiet her. "Just rest. We have help. You'll be all right, I promise."

As she stood, she saw a few others beginning to stir, most still too weak to stand, scarcely able to hold up their heads.

A few minutes later she heard the rattle of a wagon and saw Pastor Kalm on a board seat, two horses pulling a sizable flatbed wagon, empty except for the goat.

He brought the wagon to a halt, secured the horses and jumped down. "The sickest first," he called out, moving with speed toward Yorrick Harp and hoisting him up by one shoulder, then half-supporting him toward the waiting wagon.

Eve tried to lift Lily to a seated position and was unable to do so. She saw Laurel, one of her helpers from the train. "Come on, we can lift her together," Eve said and they raised her to an upright position, then to her feet and in similar fashion half-dragged, half-carried her to the wagon, where Pastor Kalm was waiting to lift her over the side and place her next to Yorrick Harp.

"What's your name?" Pastor Kalm asked the woman assisting Eve.

"Laurel," she said.

"All right, Laurel and Eve, select five more of the weakest. Then one of you come out with me, and the other remain here. It may take us a while but we'll get them all out to the mission by noon, I promise."

With dispatch, five of the weakest were chosen and hoisted carefully up onto the wagon alongside Lily and Yorrick Harp.

"Who is coming with me?" Pastor Kalm asked, wiping sweat from his brow with his sleeve.

Eve glanced toward Laurel. She had no preference, and they all had to trust the man.

"You go," Laurel said at last. "I'll stay here. We'll be all right."

Eve looked about. A few of the women were struggling up to sitting positions. She lifted her voice in a brief reassurance to all who could hear. "We will be all right, I promise you. This gentleman is Pastor Kalm. He's taking us to his mission about three miles outside Abilene. Don't move around too much. We'll be back for the rest of you."

She looked out over the pale faces and wide staring eyes. "They're hungry and thirsty," she murmured as she climbed up beside Pastor Kalm atop the high wagon seat.

"We'll remedy both as soon as we get there," he promised and lightly brought the reins down across the horses. As the wagon moved forward, she waved at Laurel. Then Pastor Kalm headed the horses away from town and out across open prairie, where the sun was just rising and painting everything gold and red. Ahead she saw a road that was little more than two wagon tracks, the passage rough, though Pastor Kalm maintained good speed and called out over the rattle, "Hang on. It smooths out up ahead." As Eve looked back to see how the ones in the wagon were faring, she saw Abilene in the distance like a squat cut-out etched against the rising sun.

She tried to relax her grip on the side of the board seat and looked out across the land. No tree was visible, only sagebrush and prairie wheat and here and there the purple trumpet of a persistent prairie thistle. And the wind was still with them, the ever-present wind.

Next to her Pastor Kalm seemed to relax as well, though he maintained a steady pace, heading in an easterly direction.

"Let me apologize for the citizens of Abilene," he began in a quiet voice.

"They are not your responsibility, I hope."

"Oh, occasionally one or two of the men will drift out to the mission. I keep hoping that one day there will be more wives in Abilene. Wives with children will see to it that this road becomes well traveled and smooth as glass. But thus far wives have not fared too well here."

"There are no women in Abilene?" she asked.

"Not many," he said. "The men always come first. Abilene is a new town, a natural intersection of cattle trails and railways. It has a promising destiny. It needs tempering, as do the men who founded her."

"They seemed so frightened," Eve murmured, remembering the closed doors.

"Understandable. As I said, we lost two about six months ago and we thought then it was the pox. Pox comes like prairie fire. There's no defense."

"Then who are your parishioners?" she asked. "If Abilene stays away, who comes?"

"Indians," he said without hesitation. "Kiowas, Comanches, hungry Indians who know that if they listen to me for thirty minutes, they are entitled to a bowl of cornmeal porridge and black bread."

"How do you know if they come for the word of God or for the food?"

"I don't know. But at least for the time they are at my mission they have to put down their weapons and look into a white face and listen to a white man's voice and hopefully find nothing to distrust."

He spoke with such quiet conviction. She noticed his hands holding the reins, calloused working hands that clearly had held a hammer as frequently as they had held a Bible.

"Where are you from?" she asked, hoping that she wasn't prying.

"Canada," he said, "a small town outside Ottawa. I had a comfortable church there, Presbyterian, a comfortable parsonage, a comfortable income, a comfortable bed, a comfortable fireplace, a comfortable table, a comfortable library, comfortable friends."

She smiled at his overuse of the word, his voice gradually converting it into a state to be avoided at all costs.

"Then one day I was studying the small crucifix above the altar,

and do you know that I could not find one angle, one line, one attitude, one essence of comfort in the entire depiction."

He shook his head. "So I gave up comfort and came in search of
need, true need, God-empty need."

"And you found it here?"

"Oh indeed." He laughed and looked at her with the warmest smile
she'd ever seen. "It's such a simple equation really. One wonders and
worries about the denseness of the human race to comprehend it."

"What is that?"

"Comfort and happiness are not synonymous. Oh, we think they
are, but they aren't. The body is truly comfortable only when the
soul is fulfilled, and fulfillment can only be achieved by denial of self,
by giving oneself away to the sorrowing, the ill, the weak and the lost.
And when that happens, there is such a rush of perceptions, everything made simple and clear, and when one least expects it, harmony
is there and joy and unity and beauty and—comfort."

He smiled at the end of his round-robin sermon. Eve watched him
in profile as he stared out across the prairie and she was aware of his
uniqueness, a man at peace with himself.

Suddenly, "There it is," he pointed across the prairie toward a low
clinging structure, scarcely making a difference on the vastness of the
horizon.

She shielded her eyes against the rising sun and saw it clearly, a
plain unpainted board structure boasting a small steeple. Atop the
steeple she saw a wooden cross. Behind the mission, attached like an
afterthought, she saw a second addition, the entire structure resembling the letter L.

"Almost there." He smiled, tightening his grip on the reins. "See, I
told you, about twenty minutes out. Noma will help us. Look, there
she is."

He pointed forward and Eve saw a squat portly figure of a woman
in long skirts, a dark-skinned Indian woman who seemed to sense the
speed of the wagon.

As Pastor Kalm brought the wagon in, Eve saw the woman step
forward, her eyes piercing and dark, though brightening at the sight
of Pastor Kalm.

"Trouble, Noma," he called down as he brought the horses to a
halt. "We'll need blankets and water, and hurry please."

And she did, without hesitation. She simply turned about and hurried as fast as her girth would allow back into the small mission.

"She's Kiowa," Pastor Kalm explained. "She's been with me here
for several years. She never speaks. Her tribe abandoned her."

On this succinct though partial explanation, he hopped down from the seat and moved to the rear of the wagon, hoisted the goat down first, then with care started to ease Yorrick Harp toward the side of the wagon.

Eve stood by, feeling helpless as he struggled with Yorrick, who at that point appeared frighteningly lifeless.

As Pastor Kalm carried him toward the door of the mission, Eve concentrated on Lily, who in all respects seemed as ill as Yorrick Harp.

"Come on," Eve urged, trying as Pastor Kalm had done to angle Lily toward the side of the wagon, then she caught the bulk of her weight as she fell forward. Quickly Eve lowered her to the ground and kneeled beside her. "Oh, Lily, please get well," she whispered, cradling the woman close to her. "I need you. Don't leave me now."

"I'll take her."

Eve saw Pastor Kalm lift Lily into his arms and carry her into the mission.

"Come on in," he called back. "I'll do the transporting. You help Noma in here."

Just as she turned about, she looked out across the prairie and saw a lone horseman in the distance riding toward the mission at good speed. Pastor Kalm saw him as well.

"It's Ramford Towse," he said beneath his breath as though that name alone explained everything.

As the rider drew nearer, Eve squinted into the sun and saw a man with gray hair, stern-faced, thin, guns on both hips.

As he guided his horse in a circle to the front of the mission, he became lost briefly in his own dust cloud. When the dust cleared he appeared to be confronting Pastor Kalm at the back of the wagon.

"Hear you got sickness out here, Pastor?" the man said, his voice accusatory, without inflection.

"Yes, Ram, we do. Some of it could be bad."

"Is it what killed Lucy and Sarah?"

Pastor Kalm bowed his head. "I don't know, Ram. Can't be sure at this point."

For several moments the man looked at the ill in the back of the wagon, looked at Eve on the mission steps, his hand still on his gun.

Finally in a low voice he said, "I've come to help," and in a second he was off his horse, the horse secured, and he was lifting one of the women into his arms and carrying her toward Eve and the mission door.

As he passed without a word into the cool shadows, she saw Pastor Kalm, his head bowed as though offering a brief prayer. Ram Towse. She'd remember the name. At least one in Abilene had come to help.

Still weary, not certain if she'd done the right thing at any point during the last twenty-four hours, Eve followed after Pastor Kalm and Ram Towse into the cool shade of the mission, for the sun had risen and the heat of the day along with it.

Once inside, she smelled a peculiar blend of cabbage cooking and burned-down candles and saw an inviting room, stark in its simplicity, about twelve wooden benches with backs on either side of the central aisle. These benches were now being pressed into service as hospital beds.

At the front of the mission she saw Mr. Towse and Pastor Kalm speaking together. A few minutes later he rejoined her. "I've placed Mr. Harp and the woman close to the front. Ram Towse recommended it. He believes they should be isolated as much as possible. Noma will put the others on the benches near the back."

"Why does he think they should be isolated?"

He did not answer her question, though Eve was certain that he had heard it.

She hurried to the front of the mission, where Yorrick Harp had been placed on one end of the long bench and Lily on the other.

"Miss. I'd stay away." The voice was Ram Towse's. As he turned another of the women over to Noma's care, he hurried down to where she was standing beside Yorrick Harp and Lily.

He took her by the arm and guided her a few feet toward the center aisle. "I'm not certain, far from certain, but their illness is different from the others. My wife and daughter died a few months ago and their only symptoms were a high fever like theirs. The others, as you can see, are slowly recovering. These two are not."

He gestured toward the women at the rear of the mission, who were sitting on the pews, drinking water from a large clay pitcher with Noma's help.

"We'll watch them," Ram Towse offered. "No cause for alarm yet, but until we are certain."

She couldn't argue with his reason. It was just that if something happened to Lily, what would she do? If something happened to Yorrick Harp, what would any of them do?

"I'm on my way back to town," Pastor Kalm called out from the door. "Noma, the goat has arrived. Tend to her. Ram will stay and help, won't you, Ram? Are you all right, Miss Stanhope? Of course you are. I know strength when I see it. Back soon. Take care, all of you."

Then he was gone and Eve heard the wagon rattling about in a sharp turn and she saw only the dust cloud, which soon disappeared, taking the sound of the wagon with it.

She listened to the silence and saw the women stretched out on the rear benches, saw brightly woven Indian blankets beneath their heads. Noma was hovering over the last two, offering them water.

When the last had finished drinking, Noma straightened and looked at Eve. Then slowly the Indian woman bent down to the clay pitcher, refilled the ladle and carried it carefully to where Eve was standing.

The thoughtful gesture moved her, and she took the ladle and drank, slowly at first but the water was so sweet and she was so thirsty that she drained the ladle and wiped the excess from her chin with her hand.

"Thank you," she murmured and looked toward the altar where Ram Towse had placed the two in isolation. Surely they were thirsty as well, and they needed liquid to help break the fever.

"Noma, may I?" and she pointed toward the clay pitcher and ladle.

"No, no water," Ram Towse warned. "Not for a while."

"But their fevers—"

"Will break by themselves or not. There's nothing we can do. Water will not help."

Eve disliked those negative words even under the best of circumstances. *Nothing we can do.* Now she loathed them and started to say as much. Yorrick Harp and Lily were her responsibilities, not this stonefaced old rancher who considered himself a medical authority on all illness. "Mr. Towse, it is my opinion that cool water will help—"

"It will cause them to strangle," he interrupted. "Is that what you want? Now get away unless you want to kill them. I know what I'm talking about. I killed two who were dearer to me than these."

Eve retreated before his anger and his grief. In the manner of an apology, Mr. Towse quietly suggested, "A cool cloth would help. But nothing more."

She bent over and tore a strip from around the hem of her skirt, tilted the clay pitcher until the water had saturated the cloth and placed it lightly on Yorrick Harp's forehead.

The cool sensation seemed to rouse him. He thrashed about on the bench, then opened his eyes and stared straight up at her and caught her wrists and held her. "Don't leave me, Eve, please," he gasped. He started to say more but the words dissipated into a gurgling sound deep in his throat.

"Hush," she whispered, seeing his agitation increase as though frightened by his inability to speak.

As his thrashing continued, she tried to soothe him, was aware of Ram Towse watching, his face etched with concern as though he'd seen this before, knew what it meant.

"Promise me," Yorrick Harp whispered, as though newly exhausted. "Promise you'll stay with me to San Francisco."

"Yes, I'll be with you in San Francisco, I promise."

Instantly he seemed to relax. He turned his face toward the back of the bench. Illness made him seem smaller, no longer capable of blustering at everybody, just frail and human.

She drew a deep breath and was aware of Ram Towse staring at her. She stood with increasing weariness and moved down to where Lily was resting at the opposite end of the bench. Her breathing was even more labored than Yorrick Harp's, fever spots burning on both cheeks.

"Lily, can you hear me?" Eve whispered and sat down beside the bench and tore a compress from her skirt, dipped it into cool water and placed it on Lily's forehead. This same treatment had brought Yorrick Harp to a degree of consciousness. But with Lily, nothing. "Lily, can you hear me? Lily?"

She ceased speaking, realizing she wasn't being heard, and at last she suspected that Ram Towse was right, that this illness had nothing to do with tamales, was something else to be taken far more seriously.

"What is it?" she asked of the man standing near the altar watching her. "What killed your wife and daughter?"

Ram Towse shook his head. "Some say typhoid, others say cholera. Others confessed they didn't know. It just got the two of them. Everyone else in town was all right."

"I'm sorry."

Ram Towse looked out of the window. "It's hard sometimes, living is."

He walked out the back door, taking his grief with him. Eve looked the length of the mission and saw no one. Noma had left, probably to milk the new goat. The women near the back of the mission were resting.

The wagon would return soon with more in need, perhaps more fallen seriously ill. What would she do then? And what would she do if Yorrick Harp died? And Lily?

As the questions warred in her head, she saw, hanging on the altar above the pine pulpit, a crucifix as simple as the rest of the mission, a crudely carved Christ, the knife marks still visible in virgin pine, arms suspended on the cross, feet crossed, face lifted heavenward.

I studied the crucifix and saw no angle of comfort.

She heard Pastor Kalm's voice in memory and for the first time in her life she found herself studying the specifics of this religious symbol, the suffering Christ in the process of dying.

Before now God to her had been little more than a part of Southern civility. One worshipped on Sunday because it was what was done, one said prayers because prayers had been taught and one had to say them, though the words were meaningless, as were the rituals. All of religion, what she had experienced of it at Stanhope Hall, belonged to that category of "proper" behavior that Madame Germaine and Mama were constantly preaching.

She listened to her thoughts, her attention focused on the plain crucifix. She sat slowly on the aisle seat next to Lily. How did one pray when one wanted it to be more than good manners? She felt self-conscious saying words. But in memory she heard a melody, saw White Doll sitting on the porch of Fan Cottage.

"What's that song, White Doll?"

"It's called a hymn. Mammie Fan taught me. God loves music, did you know that, Eve? He will always listen to music from the heart."

Eve heard it, in memory, one of White Doll's hymns,

> Somewhere the sun is shining,
> Somewhere the songbirds dwell,
> Hush, then, thy sad repining,
> God lives and all is well—

To Eve's amazement, she remembered the melody intact along with the words, as though both had been stored in some reservoir of love.

Her voice, low at first, lifted as the words and music returned. As she sang, she felt her heart ease and knew that her song was being heard, knew that there would be strength when she needed it, wisdom when she required it, and direction when she asked for it.

 El Paso

Stephen looked out the train window as the steam engine came to a halt and decided that the farther west they went, the more they left all color behind.

The world he saw through the open doors of the baggage coach was brown, the only variation the shades of brown of the adobe structures that lined the streets and in the dark brown Mexican faces, which seemed to outnumber the whites.

"Come on," he called to Paris, who seemed awake and functioning, having recovered from his hangover, complaining only of hunger, a complaint Stephen shared.

He looked to the right and left of the busy loading platform to see if the conductors were lurking about. Then he jumped down, Paris behind him, and together they blended into the commerce of the platform and headed around the adobe station to the front street, where a large herd of cattle was driving all foot traffic back up onto the board sidewalk.

Fascinated, Stephen and Paris watched as a half-dozen buckaroos skillfully worked the large herd down the center of El Paso, the bleating calves and whining cattle raising their voices in a din of objection, the buckaroos waving their hats at the errant critters, shouting commands in what sounded like an unknown tongue.

For several minutes after the passage of the herd, the street and everyone in it was obscured by a billowing dust cloud. None seemed inconvenienced by it, all willing to wait until the cloud cleared. Then life resumed on the busy street, though it was now mandatory that one took care where one stepped.

Directly across the street from the railway station, Stephen spotted a small clean café directly next door to an immense saloon. "Over there," he said and pointed, his anticipation growing, confident that Eve was here someplace.

The thought caused him to increase his speed and he was halfway across the street when coming from the saloon he heard the sharp report of a gun and looked up toward the swinging doors to see two men supporting a third between them, push open the door and hurl the third man out onto the board sidewalk, where he landed unceremoniously, unmoving.

The commerce of the street seemed scarcely to notice. A few, Stephen observed, looked down at the man, stepped over him as though he were an inconvenient obstacle, then hurried on.

Quickly Stephen and Paris crossed the street. Once on the board sidewalk and closer to the fallen man, they noticed a spreading circle of blood on his back.

"Should we—" Paris began, starting forward in concern.

"No," Stephen said and edged closer to the café, which appeared as neat and clean as everyplace else in the town of El Paso appeared brown and dirty.

Over the door he read a small hand-lettered sign which said Marie's Good Food. Inside, through sparkling clean windows, he saw eight small tables covered with white cloths, though no one was visible through the glass in spite of the fact that he smelled coffee somewhere and bread baking and found both odors irresistible.

"Wait here," he cautioned Paris, who still seemed to be focusing on the body that had just been thrown from the saloon. "And do nothing, do you hear?" Stephen warned beneath his breath. "It is not our war. We didn't start it, we don't even understand it. So wait. I'll try to get us some food."

Paris agreed, though his eyes skimmed over the body that still lay sprawled in front of the saloon.

"Be right back," Stephen promised and pushed open the door of the café and smelled fresh paint somewhere, though the good smell of fresh coffee and fresher bread was winning the day.

For several moments he stood alone at the center of the café. On a high board over the counter he read a hand-lettered menu.

Two Eggs—10 Cents
Beef Steak—15 Cents
Rice and Beans—5 Cents
Pie—5 Cents

He looked behind the counter and called out, "Hello."

His voice echoed and came back to him unanswered. He started to call again when from the recesses of the café he heard a door squeak. A moment after that a young girl, Mexican, very pretty, appeared rubbing her hands on a spotless white apron.

"You want food?" She smiled.

"Please," Stephen replied and glanced out the window to see Paris looking longingly in.

"Are you Marie?" Stephen asked.

"*Sí*, I mean, yes," the girl said. She was young, couldn't have been more than seventeen, Eve's age. "My father say I must speak the English, but sometime I forget."

Stephen nodded, captivated by her coal-black eyes and graceful manner.

"What you want?" she asked and pointed toward the menu on the board. "I fix myself. Special."

"Why special?"

"You my first customer."

Stephen laughed, pleased. "We're honored," he said and looked toward Paris, who continued to stare in as he, too, had caught sight of the pretty girl.

Marie apparently saw the interchange between the two men. She came around from behind the counter. "You know him?" she asked, pointing toward Paris beyond the window.

"He's my friend. We're traveling together."

"Then why he stand out there? Why he not come in?"

Stephen tried to explain. "Some places, he has not been welcome."

"Why not welcome?" Marie demanded, as though offended by someone else's bad manners. "He has very good face."

Stephen saw her walk rapidly to the door, push it open and urge Paris to "Come, I want you inside. Not good to stand on street. No safe."

Stephen saw Paris and Marie exchange a smile and saw him pass before her at the door, apparently captivated by all he saw, for even after they were seated at a table near the counter, Paris never took his eyes off her as she went behind the counter and prepared two heaping platters, both filled with eggs, beefsteak, rice, beans and, to one side, a fresh chocolate pie with a mountainous meringue. A blue-speckled pot of steaming coffee completed the table, which as far as Stephen was concerned was the most beautiful he had ever seen.

"Eat," Marie ordered. And they did, though only now did Stephen notice differences between the two platters; his beefsteak covered one-half of the platter, while Paris's covered the entire platter and hung off the sides. Stephen had two eggs, Paris four, and as they continued to eat, Marie sat down near the counter, her face even prettier when flushed from the heat of her cookstove, and she watched only one, Paris, watched each bite as he lifted it to his mouth, pleased when he showed pleasure, fascinated by him in all respects.

"It's good," Paris declared, looking up with his mouth full and seeing Marie seated a distance behind him. "The best in El Paso, I have no doubt," he added and Stephen saw the girl smile broadly.

"Come, if you're not busy, why don't you sit with us?" Paris invited, and Marie brought her chair up and positioned it next to Paris, the better to watch every move he made.

"Marie, may I ask you a question?" Stephen said, around a mouth full of food.

She looked reluctantly away from Paris.

"Do you know of a theatrical troupe, all women, called the Adamless Eden?"

"A—troupe?" she repeated, puzzled.

Paris joined in. "Ladies who sing and dance for money."

Marie produced a dazzling smile. "Next door. My father will know."

"The saloon?" Paris asked.

"Sí. My father is there. He will know what you ask."

At that moment the front door opened and two men entered, both Mexicans, both well dressed, clearly not buckaroos or trail hands. Marie seated them near the window and served them large mugs of coffee and pieces of chocolate cake. She stayed for several minutes, speaking with them in Spanish, a rapid-fire language that Stephen found fascinating.

Once she laughed, though then she grew quite sober. And a few moments later she came back to their table and sat close to Paris.

"More customers?" Stephen asked. "You're doing well."

"No, no, they are cousins. Don't count. Don't pay."

Stephen was impressed with her business sense and wondered how in this all-male world she had managed to acquire such a potentially prosperous business as this one.

Paris apparently wondered the same thing. "Are you from El Paso, Marie?"

"I was born here. My father from Mexico."

"Are you—married?" Paris asked, at last lowering his fork.

She laughed prettily and shook her head. "No, not married. My father would not allow it. He must choose the man when it's time."

"Seems unfair," Paris commented.

"My father never fair, not always good, but he love me."

She put one-half of the chocolate pie onto a clean platter and invited Paris to try it. "It's my best," she said.

Obligingly Paris took a large bite and allowed the ecstasy on his face to serve as his response.

Marie beamed and drew her chair closer and all the time Stephen noticed the two cousins at the window keeping a close eye on their table.

"You are so beautiful," Marie said now to Paris, with disarming frankness and fixed him with an adoring gaze. "You not from here, not El Paso?"

"No," Paris said. "A long way from here. A place called Alabama."

"Ala—"

"Alabama," Paris repeated, assisting her with the pronunciation, clearly as fascinated by her as she was by him. "In the southern part of the United States."

"You have family? Wife?" Marie asked.

"No, no wife, no family," Paris said and angled his chair to a position the better to look at her.

As the two of them chatted quietly, each growing impervious to everything except the presence of the other, Stephen finished his platter, made an attempt at the chocolate pie, and then, with apology, interrupted.

"Your father, Marie," he said. "Where might I find him? No, Paris, you stay here," he added quickly, seeing Paris start to rise. "It's—safest."

"At the saloon next door," Marie said. "His name is Emilio Santa Anna. Everyone knows him. Just ask for him by name."

Stephen stood. Revived by the good food, doubly revived by the realization that his happiness was perhaps only moments away, he urged Paris to take his time, that he would return as soon as possible, hopefully with Eve herself.

Paris needed little persuasion. He instantly settled back into his chair, legs crossed, his attention focused on Marie, whose eyes were so dark and limitless a man could, if not careful, fall hopelessly into them.

At the door Stephen looked back and saw them in close and laughing conversation. Pleased by the sight, he pushed open the door and out of the corner of his eye saw the two cousins rise.

Were they following him? Surely not. Stephen stepped out onto the crowded sidewalk and noticed the body still there, still sprawled in front of the saloon.

Outside the swinging doors of the saloon, he peered over the top, amazed to find a very luxurious interior, not at all in keeping with the plain adobe exterior. He saw a highly polished hardwood floor and a long, elegant and very crowded mahogany bar. Behind the bar was the standard mirror, though this one sported the enormous figure of a naked reclining woman etched expertly into the glass itself. To the right were a dozen twirling roulette wheels operated by uniformly buxom and decorative women. Behind the mahogany bar he saw three barkeeps in white shirts and black jackets, and to the left of the bar he saw a large dance area and behind that a small raised proscenium, clearly for theatricals.

Encouraged by all that he saw, Stephen stepped through the swinging doors, newly aware that Marie's two cousins were still directly behind him.

Once inside, he glanced to the right and saw a group of men pressed close around a vortex of great strength and greater interest. An animated conversation was going on among all the men, everyone talking at once, though once or twice as if on cue they would fall silent and Stephen heard a deep mediating voice speak only a few words, then the hubbub began again, Mexican voices and American blending.

Now he looked about for someone who might reasonably bear the name of Emilio Santa Anna. One of the barkeeps looked Mexican but he also looked far too young to have a daughter the age of Marie.

Then he spied him. A bent Mexican near the back of the saloon, middle-aged, wielding a broom, his back humped with infirmity, surely old enough to have a daughter like Marie, perhaps too old. Stephen would ask.

He started toward the rear of the saloon, passing close to the busy roulette wheels, which, running together, sounded like a flock of angry birds.

As he approached, the Mexican looked sharply up as though under attack.

"No, please," Stephen soothed. "Are you—Emilio Santa Anna?"

The moment after Stephen had spoken, the roulette wheels went silent.

He was in the process of turning about to see what had caused this sudden silence when suddenly, coming from his left, he caught a blur of movement and felt an arm go around his neck, and felt something cool and very sharp pressed against his throat.

"Hold still," a low male voice advised him from behind, "or your throat will be cut."

A reasonable request, one that Stephen was more than willing to follow. As his captor turned him about, he saw all eyes in the saloon focused on him, a limited focus, for they seemed after a few seconds to lose interest in his predicament. He heard the slow whirl of one roulette wheel, and then another, until at last the din was as thick as before. The only thing changed was the man still holding the knife against his throat.

"Walk straight ahead," the man commanded, and he did because he had no choice. Only now he remembered the dead man on the sidewalk outside and wondered what had been his offense.

"Not so fast," his captor shouted. They were passing the long bar now. All the men drinking looked up with varying expressions on their faces, some merely curious, some smiling as though pleased, others fearful.

At the end of the bar Stephen heard a scuffle outside the swinging doors, heard a familiar voice shout, "Get your hands off—" and looked in that direction and saw Paris similarly restrained, his captor herding him forward, a long blade pressed against his throat as well.

Stephen recognized Paris's assailant as being one of Marie's cousins. Without looking, he knew now who held the knife against his own throat.

"What happened?" Paris whispered.

"What do you think?" Stephen snapped. "Where's Marie? I thought you were—"

"She went out back for a few minutes and this—gentleman insisted that I come with him."

Then the last of the men parted, and Stephen saw the cause of their interest and at first could not be certain what he was seeing.

"Lord," Paris gasped, his vision keeping pace with Stephen's.

At the center of the dance floor, in a seat that more accurately resembled a throne, sat a man, the largest man Stephen had ever seen, five hundred pounds if an ounce, Mexican, his round face blending in an unbroken line of soft flesh with his shoulders, the remainder of his globular form pressing against the ornate arms of the golden chair. His skin was dark, his black hair long, hanging in strands about his broad thick face.

But more bizarre than the man was his apparel. He was dressed in a suit made entirely of an American flag: huge red-and-white-striped trousers, a vest made of a blue field with white stars and a loosely fitting jacket that appeared to be cut from an entire flag.

He was breathing heavily and looking at Paris and Stephen through small dark eyes. His pudgy hands gripped the golden arms of the ornate throne, and Stephen saw a jeweled ring on each finger, diamonds, rubies, emeralds, a glittering array of incredible wealth.

Finally the man spoke, only three words, and at the same time he swatted at a fly with one of his ham-size bejeweled hands and sent rainbows of colors from diamond prisms scattering all over the saloon.

"What you want?" he asked, and Stephen wondered if he should answer.

But when he felt the knife cut sharply into his flesh, he cleared his throat and said as courteously as possible, "We were told we would find a man named Emilio Santa Anna here."

The squinted eyes grew even more narrow. "What you want him for?"

"To ask him questions."

"About what?"

"About a theatrical troupe, about a man named Yorrick Harp."

The words seemed to hang unheeded on the quiet air. Then all at once the flesh of the huge man started to vibrate, only slightly at first, a low guttural laugh that managed to escape through the wheezing, then at last the full-blown and explosive eruption itself, a deep-throated laugh that prompted all those around him to equally maniacal laughter. While Stephen held himself steady against the knife blade, he felt the arm about his chest relax and in the next minute he was freed, the knife gone, Paris freed at the same time, both of them touching their throats now to see if the flesh there was still intact.

After a few minutes the laughter subsided as suddenly as it had started. The large Mexican waved them to come closer. He smiled, revealing a mouth filled with gold teeth.

"I have enemies," he said, winking. "Sometimes they come disguised as innocents." He gestured toward Stephen and Paris as though accurately to describe his enemies. "Once they came dressed as women," he added, the golden smile splitting his dark features. "But I think not you are enemies."

Stephen shook his head in agreement. "I am looking for Emilio Santa Anna."

The man beamed. "I Emilio Santa Anna, bastard son of the bastard general Antonio Lopez de Santa Anna, on whose memory I spit every day."

By way of demonstrating, he threw back his head, cleared his throat and spat a lump of amber spittle onto the wooden floor directly in front of where they were standing.

Stephen stared down at the spittle and felt his stomach turn, his heart still beating too fast.

"And who are you?" Emilio demanded.

Stephen drew a deep breath. "My name is Stephen Eden, and this is—"

"You talk funny."

"I'm—sorry."

"Where you from?"

Stephen glanced back at Paris, wanting assistance. But when none seemed forthcoming, Stephen said, "England."

"I know England." Emilio smiled broadly. "You think I'm stupid bastard like my father."

"No."

"I'm bastard, but not stupid. England red-coat bastards, you try to take this country from us."

"No, I had nothing to do with that."

"Don't say no to Emilio Santa Anna." As the man bellowed at Stephen, every ounce of excess flesh shook.

Stephen debated the wisdom of offering a belated apology for the British Empire over the American Revolution. It seemed far afield from his purpose here.

"Sir," Stephen began. "I just want to—"

"Wait. Hold your tongue," Emilio ordered. "We first must see if you are on the list." With the snap of his finger he summoned an aide, a Mexican of normal size who carried a large green ledger book in his hand.

"Name?" Emilio Santa Anna demanded again.

"Eden, Stephen Eden," Stephen repeated wearily and watched, be-

wildered, as the aide drew the ledger close and studied the entire
page, then firmly shook his head in the negative.

"Too bad," Emilio mourned. "If your name had been on that list, I
would present you here and now with a hundred dollars in gold
pieces."

"I don't understand."

"That list is the name of all the brave Americans who died at the
Alamo, murdered by my bastard father on whose memory I spit every day," and again he cleared his throat and sent a wad flying. "I
personally reward the descendants of each man with one hundred
dollars in gold pieces. There were one hundred and eighty-two. I
have repaid sixty-eight. It is my life's work."

Unable to understand what the man was saying, not certain what
the Alamo was, Stephen was sorry he hadn't qualified for the prize
and now waited patiently while the aide searched the list for Paris
Boley's name.

No, it too was missing. Still the search and brief talk seemed to
have relaxed the crowd. Almost all had returned to their various pursuits, and even Emilio Santa Anna seemed to have relaxed into his
throne, gazing longingly at a platter of roast chickens that had just
been placed on a table to his right by a barkeep.

"I love America." Emilio grinned. "Anyone who speaks against her
in my saloon does not live to speak again."

Now Stephen understood the crime of the dead man outside the
saloon.

"Come closer, Englishman; talk to me. I am Emilio Santa Anna and
I own this saloon and all of El Paso. Tell me of your Roberto Hood.
My dear mother, a saint of a woman, a white woman who was raped
by the bastard general my father, used to send me to sleep with tales
of Roberto Hood, and she told me to be like him, to rob from the rich
and give to the—"

"Father!"

This voice was angry and female and came from the door of the
saloon. Stephen looked up to see Marie, hands on hips, glaring toward
the enormous Emilio, who within the instant seemed to wither.

"Father, how could you?" she scolded. "He do nothing. He with
me. If you hurt him, I never forgive you." As she talked, she moved in
a steady and angry line toward Paris, who obviously had seen her
coming and smiled. As she approached, she took his hand and led him
closer to where Emilio sat, just beginning to attack a roast chicken.
For the first time Stephen saw apprehension on the fleshy face.

"Marie, my daughter," he began and was not given a chance to
finish.

"What did you do to him, Father? Answer me. I step out for one
minute and when I come back, he gone. You not hurt him. He's very
beautiful, don't you think, Father?"

Under this barrage of daughterly fire, Emilio seemed to retreat. "I
do nothing to him, Marie. Look at him. What I do? Your father must
be careful. Have many enemies."

Still clasping Paris's hand, Marie scolded one last time. "*That* is
your only enemy, Papa," she said with emphasis, pointing to the roast
chicken dwarfed by Emilio's enormous hand. Then she led Paris back
through the gaping saloon. Only once did Paris look at Stephen, a
single shrug, as though he were caught in something that was not of
his control. And there was something else in his expression, a look of
rare and extreme pleasure.

"Come, Englishman," Emilio commanded. "Sit, eat with me, drink
with me, and tell me of Roberto Hood and his big friend, what his
name?"

"Little John."

"And there was a woman, what her name?"

"Marion."

"That's it. That's the one. Oh, my mother told it with such beauty,
king wicked like bastard father that I spit on his memory every day."

Again to Stephen's embarrassment an enormous wad of spittle
came flying out between the gold teeth and landed several feet away.

He had no real objection to amusing Emilio with tales of "Roberto
Hood," but first he had a question of his own.

"Sir, please, if you will, tell me where I might find the man named
Yorrick Harp, the owner of the—"

"Girls," Emilio grinned. "Harp's girls. The best. Right?" As he
turned to his aides for agreement, he received it in grinning faces.
"They good," Emilio went on. "Some girls come to Paso and they
nothing but whores. But Harp's girls good singers, good dancers,
good music makers, good girls."

Stephen was relieved to hear it. "Where might I find them, sir? I
would be most appreciative if you—"

Emilio shrugged and licked his fingers and deposited a pile of
chicken bones on the platter, all that was left of the plump chicken.
"How I know?"

"They're here, aren't they? In El Paso?"

Emilio shook his head. "Delayed," he said flatly and reached for the
second chicken.

At first Stephen was certain he had not heard correctly. "What do
you mean?"

"Delayed," the big man repeated. "Eat, you need flesh."

"I don't understand. Delayed for how long?"

"The telegraph man come when—two, three day ago. It say Harp delayed."

Stephen stared down on the man, frustration rising, anger not far behind. "Why?" he demanded, aware that he was attracting attention.

Even Emilio stopped eating and looked up. "Don't know," he repeated with emphasis. "Sickness, I think the telegraph man say."

"Where?"

"I—don't know," Emilio shouted back. "Now speak to me about Roberto Hood while I eat. I like story food. My mother tell story at dinnertime, tell me of my father the bastard general whose memory I spit on every day."

As another wad of spittle sailed out across the floor of the saloon, Stephen turned away and found a near chair and sank heavily into it. For several minutes he sat thus, trying to deal with his despair, combined with new and urgent worry. Sickness? Who? Where? Eve? Pray God not Eve.

With his eyes closed, he smelled something close to his nose and looked up to see one of Emilio's aides holding a glass of amber colored liquid before him. There was a huge foam on the top of the brew that hissed and spewed as though it were alive.

"Drink, my friend," Emilio counseled in a surprisingly soft and gentle voice. "Old Emilio knows sorrow when he sees it. Drink while the head is high. It's our special. We call it pass whiskey. There are secret ingredients I cannot reveal but I can tell you it is a mix of alkali water, alcohol, tobacco juice to give it color and just a dash of strychnine, the last to keep the heart going."

Stephen raised himself slowly and looked into the powerful brew.

"Go on, Englishman. It's guaranteed to end sorrow, dry tears, stop memory and make glad the heart of man."

Such a promise held great appeal. Stephen's disappointment continued to hammer against him in relentless blows. He must find respite.

Finally he took the glass and sniffed at it and touched his tongue to the high foam. Around him had gathered a sizable and grinning audience, though none was grinning quite so wide as Emilio Santa Anna.

"Drink quick," Emilio advised. "Take it all at once. Poison works best when it works fast."

Up close Stephen smelled citrus. In an attempt to escape the despair of this fruitless journey, he tilted the glass and drank through the foam until he had consumed all of it, and his first sensation was that of having swallowed a lighted kerosene lamp. He felt a sudden violent jolt in the pit of his stomach, felt his breath leave his body and his last conscious awareness was one of falling facedown onto the floor, seeing Emilio Santa Anna's spittle rise up to meet him, hearing Emilio Santa Anna's insane laughter still coming at him from the rim of consciousness.

 Abilene

Bent over Yorrick Harp's feverish face, Eve readjusted the wet compress and suddenly thought of Stephen.

Slowly she raised up from the unconscious face before her and tried to deal with the pain of memory. The trouble was she saw his face so clearly, sun-drenched, laughing, saw his hand extended to her, and she closed her eyes against the loss and against the memory as well, for both made her weak and there was no place for weakness in this suffering mission.

"Eve?" The concerned question came from Pastor Kalm. "Are you well?"

She nodded to assuage the fear she saw in his face and saw the same weariness in his eyes that she felt in every bone in her body.

"Come, sit for a moment," he invited. "You are merely human like the rest. You must remember that."

She took his hand and looked back at Yorrick Harp, so ill, and poor Lily, the worst of all.

As she followed after him to the open door, she was torn between the beauty ahead in the pinks and vivid reds of a prairie dusk and the sadness behind, the benches filled with weakened women, though she was pleased to see a few trying to sit up. True, their heads were wobbly, but Noma, the indefatigable Indian woman, moved systematically from one to the other, offering cool water and her own special medicine of arrowroot, honey and alcohol. The Indian medicine was by far the favorite, and those who had consumed a full ladle seemed to be recovering the fastest.

Beyond the open door she drew a breath of evening air and felt a cooling that meant the coming of autumn.

In the distance she saw the man named Ram Towse hanging sheets on a drying line, unaware or uncaring that it was woman's work. "He's been lost since his family died," Pastor Kalm said. "He'll be leaving here soon. He told me he wants to go to the silver mines in Leadville."

Eve listened to his voice, speaking of tragedy and loss and new hope.

"Come, sit down," Pastor Kalm suggested, taking her arm and leading her to the step of the mission porch. "I've watched you work for thirty-six hours straight. You can't go on."

She bowed her head. "I'm not certain what we would have done without you." She recalled how by noon the day before Pastor Kalm had made the last run into Abilene, had returned with the last wagonload of women and word that their baggage was being watched over by the stationmaster, who also had sent the message that Eve had scribbled on a piece of old newsprint informing El Paso that Yorrick Harp's traveling troupe had been delayed because of illness until further notice. She'd signed it Yorrick Harp.

She had done everything she could think of, and yet there still was an overpowering sense of unfinished business.

Slowly she drew her knees up on the top step and looked out over the land. So much land, the horizon unbroken, no variation except in colors of brown. But the sky made up for the lack of earthly color, for there overhead, she had never seen such explosions of pink giving way to lavender, lavender to crimson, crimson to burnt orange.

"It's beautiful," she said.

Pastor Kalm agreed. "Heaven paintings, I call them. I've never seen them anyplace in the world as spectacular as they are here."

"How long have you been out here?" she asked, wanting to know more about him. The recess was good, the air fresh, the sky beautiful. She felt a need to cleanse her mind and heart of the pain of Stephen Eden. Apparently that part of her life was over. Those at home clearly thought her to be dead. Had Stephen returned to England? Quite probably. Then it was over and done with, and all she had to do was figure out a way to live the rest of her life with the loss.

"Please," she went on, "tell me of yourself. From Canada, I believe you said? You fled comfort." She looked up at the dazzlingly beautiful sky. "You may have left comfort behind, but you fled directly into the arms of unbelievable beauty."

He surveyed the heavens with her. "It was a fair exchange. For seven years that has been my roof, though I assure you that in the middle of a winter blizzard it appears slightly less beautiful, less hospitable."

"You came out alone?"

"Not alone," he said. "There are unhappy and lonely people everywhere. I try to offend no man. A rampaging tribe of Kiowas put down their weapons long enough to help me build this mission. They return yearly to see how I am faring."

"They never threaten you?"

"Why should they? I own nothing except the garments on my back,

I have no firearms, no weapons of any kind. All I wanted was a shelter for those who passed this way, including them."

He looked at the simple mission. "Actually I never envisioned anything this grand. But everyone has contributed. The window glass is courtesy of the town of Abilene, the pine timber paid for by a group of men whom I suspect rob banks for a living. I built the benches myself, and I'm now in the process of organizing a school."

"Who will attend your school?"

"Anyone who wants to learn to read, or write, or do numbers, or all three."

He grew sober. "We're so new here, like a newborn infant, all clean slate, and everybody wanting to make a mark upon us. There's room for all, though as always is the case with the human race, we need a tempering now and then, a lesson in how to give instead of take, love instead of hate, create instead of destroy. And no one is exempt from backsliding, for the impulses are universal, positive and negative in each man, and the saint has never lived who has not performed a sinful act, and conversely the sinner has never lived who has not behaved in a saintly manner. So it's all a matter of tempering, of bringing impulses together and making them work in harmony. That is the most blessed state, harmony."

His voice had fallen at some point and she wasn't certain if he was speaking to her or not, but she felt his peace, felt *his* harmony and looked up again at a riotous heaven.

"You make it sound simple," she said. "Life, I mean."

"No, life is never simple," he replied. "The tempering comes in how we approach it, what we do with it, what we do with what it does to us. In you, for example, if I'm not intruding, I sense sorrow, dreadful sorrow."

She looked away, suddenly self-conscious. She was on the verge of answering, in a way wanted to answer when suddenly from the mission door behind them she heard an outcry, looked back to see one of the women, Marigold, standing over Yorrick Harp.

Eve hurried back through the door. "What?"

"He's—dead," Marigold gasped. "Look."

Eve saw his face, a blueish tint, saw his eyes open and fixed and staring.

"Get behind him," she commanded. "Hurry. Move!" she shouted, at last seeing Marigold stumble into action. Then Pastor Kalm was there, looking down puzzled.

"What are you—"

"My sister. I've seen Dr. Melrose do this with my sister. Help her. Get him upright and hold him steady. Hurry."

Together, as the two of them elevated Yorrick Harp to a sitting position, Eve held his face between her hands, felt his skin cold, and watched carefully for the first inhalation of gasped air. It always came with Christine. Dr. Melrose said the upright position caused the fluid in her lungs to shift and drain, thus permitting her to breathe.

"Change places with me," she ordered Marigold. As the woman slid down the bench beside her, Eve gave her further instructions. "Hold his head like this, his chin pointed up."

She waited to see if Marigold had understood. Then she hurried around and sat behind Yorrick Harp, where Pastor Kalm was holding him in an upright position. Exerting all the strength she could muster, she commenced to rub his back in the area of his lungs, stopping to pound with her fists, leaning with all her body strength into the sweat-soaked back.

At some point she was aware of several of the other women gathering behind, watching with frightened eyes as still she massaged and pounded, until at last she heard a sharp gasp of air, heard Marigold shout, "He's—breathing."

A few minutes later, as Pastor Kalm lowered Yorrick Harp back down to the bench, Eve saw his lips no longer as blue, his eyes fluttering open once, then closing again. His breathing was easier.

Of greater concern to Eve was Lily. The woman had shown no signs of reviving. Eve looked mystified up at Pastor Kalm. "What is it?" she whispered.

Pastor Kalm shook his head. "I truly don't know," he confessed. "I've watched both of them and I just don't know. A fever of some sort."

Then Eve remembered a recommendation that Ram Towse had made, that these two be isolated. At the time she had discounted it. "Do you have a room, a place where these two—"

"Back there behind the altar. A small storeroom. I'll move two cots in. There is a large window and good air."

"That will do. I'll stay."

"If it is contagious—" he began.

"Then it is contagious. But I think not."

"You're taking a risk."

"I'd say we have both already taken risks."

Yorrick Harp groaned. She felt his brow still feverish. "Help me move them to the storeroom," she said. "By morning we should know. They fell ill at the same time as the others. There should be improvement by morning. If not—"

With Noma's help they moved Yorrick and Lily into the storeroom at the back of the mission. Quickly Noma departed and returned with a filled pitcher of cool water and several clean cloths.

"Thank you," Eve murmured and placed them on the table. When she looked back, Noma was gone, but Pastor Kalm was still there.

"I'll be outside the door," he said. "One call and I'll come."

"I know. Perhaps by morning—"

"God's will," he said.

"I don't always agree with God's will."

"He doesn't want our agreement. This world is not a partnership."

"What is it?"

"His gift to us, His test of us."

"Sometimes it's difficult to tell the difference."

"That is His intention."

For several seconds he held her in his gaze. "Eve, I shall pray."

"Come morning," she repeated and slowly closed the door on his inner peace and calm acceptance. She looked back at the two on the cots, both so ill. If either died—

Quickly she banished the thought and pushed up her sleeves and hurried toward the pitcher of cool water and placed cold compresses on both their foreheads and bent over Yorrick Harp and saw his breathing improved, and bent over Lily and saw only a pale face, two fever spots on each cheek, heard only labored breathing.

Slowly she sat on the edge of Lily's cot and glanced out the store-room window. The riotous sunset was almost over, the colors fading into night, though at the far rim she detected a band of lavender, the shade of her mother's lilacs in early spring.

Mother. The word worked a peculiar magic in her heart, reuniting her with a place far away, people who once had loved her, a life, an attitude, gone now. Strange, but she'd expected her grief still to be deep. Rather what she felt was a bittersweet longing, a surge of nostalgia, and a renewed awareness that she was desperately needed here.

This was her home now, these people her family. "Come, Lily, try to sit up. You'll feel better for it," and with renewed energy she dragged Lily into a seated position and commenced to massage her back.

It would work. It had to work. She was weary of God's tests and more than ready for just one small gift, that He grant new life to these two who were so ill.

✳ El Paso

Stephen leaned against the cool red tile of Emilio Santa Anna's large adobe house at the edge of El Paso and watched Paris Boley explain in loving and patient fashion the rudiments of elementary bookkeeping.

The audience was large and rapt, made up of Emilio himself opposite the desk where Paris sat and a few of the various "cousins" and "uncles" who seemed to be in constant attendance. And of course Marie was there, her black eyes fastened in unabashed worship of Paris, who seemed more in command, more a voice of authority than Stephen had ever heard.

Whether Emilio had decided that Paris was special because Marie had made that determination, or whether he had discovered for himself that the man was remarkable in all respects, Stephen wasn't certain. All he knew was that a bond of incredible strength was developing between Paris and Marie, and Paris and Emilio, and Paris and the entire Mexican community of El Paso. They came to him with their baffling problems of arithmetic and language and he solved all of them with effective and quiet dignity.

Stephen relaxed anew against the cool tile and decided there were worse places he could wait for Eve. Emilio had assured him that the man Yorrick Harp *would* be along with his girls, that he had been coming this way for years, that the troupe did their show in Emilio's own saloon-theater, and Stephen and Paris were safest waiting right here.

Having no reason to dispute his word, Stephen had agreed. As for Paris, Stephen doubted if he could have torn him away. Listen to him now, sounding like a proper schoolmaster.

"Debit column. Credit column," Paris instructed, holding up a large ledger for Emilio to see. "And over here, profit and overhead. Do you understand?"

Emilio shifted his massive weight in the chair and looked behind at his "cousins" and grinned, as though he'd had something to do with Paris's intelligence. "Smart, this one smart. You listen. You all listen and learn. Not be dumb Mexicans all your life."

As Paris launched into the profit and overhead column, Stephen thought on the subtle changes that had taken place in his friend. Marie was always at his side, his arm about her shoulders, and Emilio had given them his own horse and carriage and Paris was making an inventory of Emilio's endless land holdings, observing in the process a few squatters who were paying no rent, determining that some of his profits from the saloon were walking out the back door in the pockets of his barkeeps, suggesting a system of bookkeeping for the first time so that Emilio could see precisely what he had, which was considerable, and see further that it was being used and developed to the best advantage.

As Paris's voice droned on in an endless recital of figures, Stephen walked barefoot across the cool tile to the open door, which gave a view of El Paso, a brown town, stark behind the white adobe that was everywhere and dazzling bougainvillea in blinding shades of red and purple. The town was growing every day as the Texas-Pacific brought new business, new citizens, new energy and new interests.

"And unless this column and that column match, then it means—"

"Bastards," Emilio grunted, completing Paris's thought for him.

Paris nodded. "Either that or careless inventory."

"Paris take care of Emilio," Emilio smiled. "I appoint you Emilio's pencil. You take ledger books and make marks that make Emilio richer, then Emilio make you rich. Deal?"

Stephen saw Marie move up on Paris's left and reach for his hand, thus wordlessly helping him to frame his response.

"I'll do what I can, Emilio," Paris smiled.

"You do everything. You got good brain."

While Paris and Marie walked arm in arm away from the desk, Stephen watched them, recognizing something between them, the way their hands clasped, the way their bodies leaned together, the way they seemed to move without destination.

"Where's the Englishman?" Emilio bellowed from his throne chair. "Come, Englishman, tell Emilio of Roberto Hood again. The best part when Little Juán falls into water. I be Little Juán. I say his part. Come, come."

Stephen drew a deep breath and decided why not. Telling Emilio the story of Roberto Hood for the thousandth time was better than making himself sick with longing thinking about Eve, watching Paris and Marie, who stood on the porch arm in arm, heads touching.

"There you are." Emilio grinned and waved him forward. "Pass whiskey?" Emilio invited with a mischievous glint in his eye as he shoved a decanter toward Stephen.

Stephen shook his head and leaned back in the chair, wondering if there was any variation of the original fable of Robin Hood he might add to this telling and make it more enjoyable to Emilio, who now sat, eager as a child for the tale to begin.

Just as Stephen was about to commence, he heard a horse in the distance, coming fast, the curious flapping of hooves on hot earth.

"Wait!" Emilio commanded with a stay of his hand.

Stephen looked out at the porch and saw Paris moving toward the rider, who was heading toward the steps, something in his hand. Stephen saw the brown envelope of the telegraph office.

"Message!" the man called out. "For the Englishman."

The rider brought his horse to a stop before the steps. Paris was there to receive the envelope and in turn passed it immediately to Stephen. Their eyes met as they knew the hazards of such a hastily delivered message.

"Shall I?" Paris offered.

Stephen shook his head and was aware of all the "cousins" watching along with Emilio.

Carefully he ran his finger along the envelope and drew out the message.

> From Stanhope Hall—
>
> Continue your search no matter where it takes you or how long. We await your word with newly saddened hearts. Our beloved Christine has died.

There was a date and a signature, Burke Stanhope, though Stephen couldn't see either clearly. All he could see was Christine, bright Christine, telling them about William the Conquerer and the invasion of 1066.

"Stephen?"

He was aware of Paris close beside him. He handed him the message to read for himself. He heard one protest of "No," then saw Paris walk to the edge of the porch, Marie at his side, clearly sensing loss.

Christine dead. The devastation at Stanhope Hall must be complete. Stephen moved out from beneath the shelter of the porch into blazing sun, felt the scorched sand beneath his feet.

"Stephen?"

He saw Paris walking beside him out into the hot desert air. "Is there anything I can do?"

Stephen shook his head. "I wish Eve would come."

"Emilio says they always do."

"But illness. Where and what kind? Is Eve ill?"

His questions drifted unanswered out across the hot air. In the distance he saw dust devils, small swirls of earth lifting into a solitary dance with the wind.

"Come on," Paris urged and took his arm and turned him about where he saw the porch lined with dark waiting faces.

"Bad news?" Emilio called out. "I fix it."

If only you could, Stephen thought, and walked with Paris into the cool shade of the house and took the telegraph from him and put it in his pocket for safekeeping.

He waited wordlessly until everyone had resettled, Emilio directly in front of him, his large face eager with anticipation.

Stephen glanced over his shoulder, expecting to see Paris and Marie, and found them gone. Then he recalled the incredible speed with which lovers could disappear when they were in need of privacy.

"Once upon a time," he began, and Emilio's grin broadened. As Stephen launched forth into the tale of Roberto Hood and his Merry Men, he wished with all his heart that life's stories would end as happily as legend, all sickness healed, all need filled, all dead resurrected, all lost found.

 Abilene

By dawn, God's will had been made clear, and Eve resented it. One was still alive, one dead.

She bent over Lily's body and recalled the woman's kindness to her from the beginning, this small cold hand extended to her in friendship before anyone else had seen fit to do so.

"Oh Lily," she wept, aware of Yorrick Harp, weak, though watching from his cot. She still had no idea of the nature of their illness. It had resembled pneumonia in some ways and in some ways not.

"She was—my best Viola," Yorrick whispered, as yet unable even to raise his head, his long hair and beard damp and straggly from his fever. "She was brilliant."

His voice broke, and Eve saw him turn away weeping, one hand moving slowly up to cover his eyes, as though he didn't want Eve to see his weakness.

She looked back at Lily's face, beautiful still in death, and bent over and kissed her. "Good-bye," she whispered.

"I will say the words over her," Yorrick vowed, wiping at his eyes.

Carefully Eve drew the sheet up over Lily's face and felt newly defeated and bowed her head in an attempt to rest her burning eyes and knew she would have to inform the others but for the moment lacked the courage or the energy to do so.

She suspected that Pastor Kalm was outside the door, where he'd been all during this long night. A single call would bring him running, but not yet.

"Eve."

She saw Yorrick beckoning her to come closer.

"You need to rest," she counseled, sitting on the edge of the cot beside him, arranging the coverlet.

"I must thank you," he murmured, his lips so dry that two cracks caused blood to seep down his chin and into his beard. As she reached for a clean cloth, he caught her hand and held it. "I owe you my life."

She shook her head in an attempt to convey that none of this was necessary. But apparently it was. "I have—no more right to hold you, my dearest. You are free to go where you wish, to do what you wish."

She listened with soft amusement. She'd been "free" for days now, since John Paul Grand had relieved her of the leg irons. She'd been free since the company had fallen ill on the train. At any point she could have turned about and gone in any direction. But she had stayed. She wasn't quite certain why. But she had stayed.

She withdrew her hand from his grasp and again urged him to rest. There was so much she had to do.

"Will you stay?" he begged, growing agitated, as though it were a matter of importance that he learn her plans.

She smoothed back the damp hair that clung to his forehead. "Where would I go?" she asked.

He seemed surprised. "Home, of course."

"Perhaps later."

"I thought there was a young man—"

She looked down, finding the thought, as always, painful. The only good part of the last few days had been the fact that she had been so busy that Stephen had at last been dislodged from her memory.

Now in this new pain of longing she realized his absence from her heart had been only temporary, for suddenly she saw him so clearly, as though he were standing before her, heard his voice in the rising prairie wind.

"I'm sorry," Yorrick murmured. "I didn't mean to cause pain."

She shook her head. "I'll stay with you, Yorrick," she promised, "until it pleases me to leave. But that's always been the case. I thought you knew."

She glanced toward the white sheet. There was a grave to be dug, a sad word to be passed. Lily was beloved by all. The day was marked for grief.

"Eve, one last question before you go."

She waited, amazed at the new courtesy in old Yorrick. Perhaps he'd sweated out his imperiousness in the fever.

"The—tour," Yorrick inquired.

"I sent a telegraph to El Paso saying we were delayed because of illness."

"It was the right thing to do." Yorrick paused. "But not delayed, I'm afraid. Canceled. And so is Santa Fe. We have wasted too much time here. Dodge City will be next. Do you think we can make it?"

"Not right away. You need rest, as do the others."

"Not too long. We must be ahead of the snows of autumn."

He struggled up as though to demonstrate his new energy. "Three days," he muttered, his eyes closing as though the room were spinning about him. "Four at most. And then we'll need wagons, five at least, and a good trail hand. We'll go up the Western Trail. It's a direct route." He looked about with mildly censorious eyes. "Who runs this place?"

Eve smiled. The old Yorrick was returning with each new breath. "A pastor."

"Damn," Yorrick said.

"A good one," Eve added.

"I'll talk to him," Yorrick announced. "Send him to me."

He paused, apparently seeing concern on her face. "My dearest child, this is what I do best, indeed what I was put on earth to do—organize, plan, execute. There are so few of us left, the great entrepreneurs. Don't deny me the privilege of exercising my greatest talent. I arrange the world into pleasing patterns for others to enjoy. And I do it very well, don't I?"

She smiled in agreement. It *was* good to have him back. Unlike Yorrick, she did not like taking the responsibility for other lives, could scarcely manage her own.

"I'll get Pastor Kalm for you," she offered.

"What's his name?" Yorrick asked, a hint of archness in his voice.

"Justin Kalm. From Canada."

Yorrick's eyes slid heavenward. "Is he sincere? I loathe sincere preachers. Well, send him in. I have much for him to do. Three days. Tell the others. And Lily—" His voice fell. "You take charge of them, Eve," he whispered. "Get them on their feet. Keep them nimble. And rehearse them as soon as they are able. Bully them if you must. They respond to bullying."

He raised up, an expression of returning strength on his face. "We're back on track, Eve, thanks to you, and we are more grateful than we can ever say."

Then he lay back down, exhausted. "Lily is dead. My beautiful Viola is dead. Our revels now are ended. We are such stuff as dreams are made on and our little life is rounded with a sleep."

At last the energy, which had been limited at best, was expended.

Sleep then, almost instantaneous, and it was a good sleep, Eve determined, free of fever.

She smoothed his forehead, pleased to find that beneath the thunder of Yorrick Harp lay hidden a good friend, and decent man, though perhaps she'd known this all along.

Eve took a final moment's privacy beside the low window which she'd opened during the night for fresh air. Now it was morning cool and newly perfumed by wildflowers growing close and in profusion. She looked up at the dawn sky to see a new riot of colors that put the colorful dusk to shame. More colors than she had ever seen—soft purples, softer pinks, yellows, ambers, all heralding the light of a new day.

Pastor Kalm was right. The essence was simple. Everyone was given a moment in which to pass a lifetime. Love was the key, both giving and taking. It made no difference.

She heard a knock on the door, heard a familiar voice. "Eve? Are you well?"

It was Pastor Kalm. "I'm fine," she called back softly, and she was.

* * *

Though she was still weakened by her own illness, Violet stood at the edge of the mourners, less than ten of whom were strong enough to walk to the small cemetery behind the mission. Eve was at her side, offering support. Straight ahead was Ram Towse, head bowed. He had been of such help to them all these last few days. And next to him was Pastor Kalm, dignified in his black suit, holding his Bible in his hand, speaking softly to the heavens. "The Lord is my Shepherd, I shall not want . . ."

More tears. Violet was embarrassed to shed so many. But each time she looked at the bound shroud lying beside the gaping grave, she could not bring herself to believe that this was her dearest friend Lily, the same Lily who had helped her through all her nightmares, who had laughed with her, cried with her, comforted her.

"Violet, I'm here," came the voice beside her and she leaned on Eve and marveled at her strength and wished that she could imitate it.

Everyplace that Violet had looked today, it had seemed that Eve was there. With Noma's help, she had sewn the two sheets together to make the shroud. She had helped Noma prepare the noon meal of stew meat and potatoes and had served it herself to the troupe. Midafternoon, Violet had seen her with Ram Towse at the cemetery, both wielding shovels in the hard dried earth, and only a short time ago she had seen her fashioning a crude cross and tethering it with bits of tanned leather that Ram Towse had given her.

"And surely goodness and mercy shall follow me all the days of my life and I shall dwell in the house of the Lord forever. Amen."

As Pastor Kalm's voice came to a halt, the prairie wind took over. Violet clung to Eve's hand and noticed blisters from shoveling the grave.

New grief then, weeping all around, Yorrick Harp watching through the window from his cot in the storeroom. He had not been strong enough to stand.

Then softly, barely disrupting the prairie wind, Violet heard a voice, Eve singing, and the wind fell silent as though to listen.

> "Beautiful Dreamer, Wake unto me
> Star-light and dew-drops are waiting for thee—
> Sounds of the old world burn in the day,
> Love light and moon light have all passed away."

The song helped the grief, the singing more beautiful than any Violet had heard. She looked up to see a new expression on Pastor Kalm's face. Clearly he had never heard Eve sing, and the grief on his face was replaced by a look of wonder.

At some point in the song Eve walked slowly to the head of the grave and sang the last for Lily alone.

> "Beautiful Dreamer, queen of my song,
> Rest while I woo thee with soft melody.
> Gone are the cares of life's busy throng,
> Beautiful Dreamer, awake unto me."

The song was over. Slowly Pastor Kalm and Ram Towse lowered Lily into her grave. Violet wasn't certain if she understood why God needed Lily more than she did. But she would try to accept, try to have faith, as Eve had faith.

Now where was she?

Frantically Violet looked about, having momentarily lost Eve. Then she found her, saw her walking slowly out onto the prairie, apparently unaware of the surrounding emptiness, a small figure in a mussed dress with blowing hair confronting the horizon.

Violet was aware of Pastor Kalm standing close beside her. He too was watching Eve. "I have never heard such a voice," he murmured.

Violet looked out to see Eve walking even farther away. "Should I go to her?"

Pastor Kalm shook his head. "I'll keep my eye on her. You go back into the mission. Help with the others."

Reluctantly Violet obeyed. Her knees felt weak, and she couldn't bare to watch as Ram Towse covered the grave.

At the door of the mission she looked back. Eve was scarcely visible, still walking, head down.

And Pastor Kalm was watching her.

 ## El Paso

"Santa Fe," Emilio repeated and stabbed at the yellowed map with one pudgy finger. "Yorrick Harp always leaves El Paso and heads north to Santa Fe. Miners, trappers, ranchers, priests. Lots of lonely men in Santa Fe."

With dread Paris listened from the far side of the table in Emilio's saloon. He knew that Stephen would not be content to stay here forever, that soon the truth would dawn on him, that something had gone wrong, that Yorrick Harp would not bring his troupe to El Paso this year and he must once again set forth on his search for Eve.

Still Paris dreaded it and for two weeks had postponed reaching any sort of decision of his own. But now his mind was made up and all that remained was to share his decision with Stephen.

"Then that's it," Stephen said, clearly trying to mask the despair in his voice, for Paris knew better than anyone that this had been a bitter disappointment. They both had been so sure that they would find Eve in El Paso. And while Stephen had not found Eve, Paris had found his own heart's counterpart in Marie, in the deepest, most compelling, most accepting eyes Paris had ever seen. At first he had not even taken his own feelings seriously. True, she was thoughtful, sweet and pretty, but what did that mean? The world, even the limited part of it that Paris had seen, was filled with thoughtful, sweet and pretty females. So what was special about Marie?

As though to assist him with his question, Paris glanced sideways to where Marie was seated close beside him, a position she'd occupied almost every minute of every day since he had arrived here. Now she looked up and he saw in her face one single ingredient. Love. For him. She loved him. How uncomplicated. How simple. Paris was loved by Marie. Paris loved Marie.

He reached for her hand and grasped it tightly and understood for the first time since he'd known Stephen precisely how painful this search must be for him.

"Then it's Santa Fe," Stephen repeated, rising from his chair, addressing Paris. "Are you ready to move on?"

Paris started to reply, but Emilio interrupted. "You could wait until next year," he suggested foolishly, an expression of hope on his face. "They come this way every year, Yorrick Harp and his ladies. Something go wrong now. Emilio not know what. But you welcome to stay right here as Emilio's guest until next year."

Stephen shook his head, and Paris saw Emilio's look of disappointment. He liked the Englishman, loved hearing all of the variations on the exploits of Roberto Hood. In the last few days he'd had a monk's robe fashioned for himself after the style of Little Juán and had now replaced his American flag suit with the plain brown muslin of the monastery.

"I can't wait, Emilio," Stephen said. "It's not just our search, you see. Her parents are waiting, worried, as I'm sure you can understand."

"Ah, parent, hard job being parent. Worry all the time, all the time worry, worry."

"Then you understand."

Clearly Emilio did, though there now hovered about the large table a distinct sense of mourning, the imminence of a dreaded separation.

As Emilio talked on about trains and schedules and departures, Paris whispered to Marie, "Come, let's go outside," and she followed after him, both taking the back exit of the saloon, through the kitchen, where more "cousins" were attending large pots of chili, on out into the cool of early evening and a vista that seemed to open onto the entire world.

Paris walked to the edge of the desert and looked out and found the landscape pleasing. The size of the horizon alone would always serve to remind a man of his actual importance in the scheme of things, unlike the South, with its limited vistas and damp heat.

Here the sun was hot and dry and open and honest, and no man, not one since he had been here, had looked at him as anything less than a man. Here he sensed respect, his differences honored, not condemned.

At the edge of the desert he drew Marie close under his arm, and for a moment the two of them gazed out at the vivid setting sun.

"You go?" Marie asked and clung to him.

"Do you want me to?"

"No, oh no, Paris. Please stay. Please."

Her face was so lovely and so near and he kissed her and in her reciprocal affection knew precisely what it was that he had to tell Stephen.

At that moment he heard steps behind coming from the kitchen. "Hurry," Stephen called out. "Emilio said he would give us horses. If we hurry we can catch the train in Seldon. According to Emilio, it goes directly to Albuquerque, then to Santa Fe. It will be cooler riding at night. Easier on the horses. Hurry, Paris."

Paris let him talk his way across the courtyard until he stood directly beside him.

"Marie, please wait for me inside," Paris murmured.

As Marie disappeared back into the kitchen, Stephen apologized. "I'm sorry. I didn't realize you were saying your good-byes."

Paris drew a deep breath. "I wasn't."

"I don't under—"

As their voices canceled each other out, he saw Stephen walk a few steps out into the hot sand. After a moment's pause he looked back. "You're not coming, are you?"

"No."

There was another pause. He saw Stephen shake his head and saw clear disappointment on his face, saw something else—doubt. "Are you certain?" Stephen asked.

Paris replied honestly, "No. I learned a long time ago not to be certain of anything in this hazardous world. You should have learned that lesson by now."

Abruptly Stephen turned away.

Paris hurried to his side. It was not his intention to inflict pain. "You don't need me. You never have."

"Not true."

"Hear me out," Paris requested and prayed that he could be as articulate as possible. "I love Marie and she loves me," he began. "That is the most important factor in my decision."

"You've known her for less than two weeks," Stephen protested.

"How long did it take for you to know that you were in love with Eve?"

Stephen didn't answer.

"And something else," Paris went on. "I'm free here," he said. "I know that sounds simple, but you would have to understand the South. I'm not certain I can explain it, but—"

Stephen waved his hand. "It's not necessary. I was there for a while, remember? I understand."

"I had no future there," Paris went on, wanting desperately to make Stephen understand. "Oh, I was of value to a few, to Mr. Stanhope perhaps, and Mr. Washington, but I always felt as if I was more of an example than a man."

He faltered and wished he had asked Marie to stay with him. Her love gave him strength. "I'm afraid the South was not defeated by the armies of the North but by their own limited visions. Here it is different," he marveled and looked out at the western horizon. "The climate and the space for growth is unhampered by preexisting codes. Here a man—is a man, and is as good as his word and is sought after as his skills merit. So simple."

He paused and found himself listening to his own words and knew that he had said enough to help Stephen to understand.

The silence was long and blending with the silence of the desert.

Finally, "I'll miss you," Stephen said, and Paris looked away and knew that he had two choices: to ignore his emotions or not to ignore them. He chose the latter and felt Stephen's reciprocal embrace and knew somehow that their friendship was not over. They would meet again. The affection was too deep.

At the end of the embrace Paris muttered, "I worry about you. Who is going to keep you out of trouble?"

"I was the one who dragged you clear of catastrophe more than once."

"Will you be all right?" Paris asked, serious again.

"I'll try to manage."

"I know you will find her."

"I have to find her."

"I'll write to Mr. Stanhope and try to explain, and to Mr. Washington as well."

"Just tell them what you have told me."

"There's Emilio," Paris said, pointing toward the mountain in brown monk's robes who filled the kitchen door.

In their final moment of privacy Stephen extended his hand to Paris. "My thanks, my friend."

"Come," Emilio shouted. "Leave while there is still light. It always bring luck."

They walked back to the door. Clearly Marie had already told her father of the good news that Paris was staying, for the man placed his large arm about Paris's shoulder and said, "Good, you good for us. It's good that you stay. I pick you for Marie the first time I saw you."

In less than ten minutes Stephen gathered the few belongings he had collected during his stay at Emilio's. Then he mounted Emilio's fastest horse with provisions strapped to a relief horse behind. It was his plan to ride through the night to Seldon, where with luck he would catch the Atchison-Topeka and Santa Fe for Albuquerque and Santa Fe.

Now he bent over and grasped Paris's hand for the final time.

"When you write to Stanhope Hall, tell them that I have not given up. If Eve is still alive, I will find her."

Paris agreed. "I will. And be careful. Always keep your eyes open."

He started to say more and realized he was just stalling for time, postponing the departure. Finally he let go of Stephen's hand and found Marie's waiting, ready and eager to fill the vacuum.

Then Stephen was gone, riding fast down the dusty main street, heading out toward the narrow trail that cut north across to the New Mexico desert.

"Good luck," Paris whispered and felt Marie's hand tighten. He hoped that he had made the right decision. He felt that he had, for in Marie's grasp and old Emilio's laughing enthusiasm, in the easy acceptance of all the "cousins," he felt something he had never felt in the South. He felt life, the energy, the faith to savor the moment, confident that there would be another, and yet another, a lifetime of such moments, free of threat, a life worth having, accepted, respected, loved.

 Abilene

Eve stood in the shade of the mission porch, gloriously idle for the first time in two weeks, and listened to Yorrick Harp bark orders despite his still weakened condition.

There were five brand new covered wagons in all, four to transport the members of the troupe, the lead wagon to be driven by Ram Towse, who had promised to take them up the Western Trail to Dodge City. There he would leave them and head for Leadville and the silver mines, where three partners were waiting for him, all eager to stake their claim and find their fortunes.

Eve found the scene one of pleasant chaos. She smiled as she watched the various activities, all the women strong again, some growing fat on Noma's good meat and potato stew, all chattering and looking very pretty, the sickness well behind them. Only Yorrick still lacked good color, but even he was improving every day and had claimed at last the time had come to move on.

Near the fifth wagon she saw Pastor Kalm helping Ram Towse load the stores aboard. She focused on Pastor Kalm. They had had long enjoyable walks out into the prairie, and she had learned much from him. She admired his devotion and commitment and more than anything else admired his peace, the deep inner peace that enables one to seek nothing, wish for nothing, miss nothing.

She took another look at the frantic activity going on at the mission and knew she had time to make one last visit to Lily's grave. As she slipped around the side of the mission, she shivered in the cool shadows and looked ahead to the small cemetery, only three crosses, three graves. According to Pastor Kalm, Noma's young son was buried in one grave. He had died shortly after Noma came to the mission.

In the second grave was a man about whom Pastor Kalm knew nothing. He had come walking into the mission out of the prairie two years ago. There was no sign of a wound on him, no visible sign of illness. He was tired and thirsty and hungry, and Pastor Kalm had fed him and cleaned him and put him to bed and had found him dead in his sleep the next morning, no identification.

And the third cross was Lily's.

Eve emerged from the mission shadows into full sun and walked steadily towards Lily's grave, trying to replace the image of Lily dead with the image of Lily alive as she had first stepped forward in Mobile to greet Eve and make her feel welcome with the small bouquet of wildflowers.

Now it was Eve's turn and carefully she picked a half-dozen black-eyed susans bending and dipping in the wind. She placed them on Lily's grave and secured the stems with a handful of sand and slowly stood up.

"Good-bye, Lily," she murmured and stared down at the crude wooden cross she had fashioned. "I'll miss you. I'll never forget you."

She bowed her head and closed her eyes and waited for the grief to pass. A moment later she looked up from the grave, expecting to see the horizon empty, seeing instead less than thirty feet away a group of Indians, about twenty in all, men and women and children, the men astride pitifully thin paint ponies, the women clasping the hands of wide-eyed children with rounded bellies and thin legs.

Their sudden appearance startled her and she backed slowly away from Lily's grave and started to run, then changed her mind. They seemed to be as fascinated by her as she was by them. She remembered, curiously, her brother David warning Stephen to beware of red Indians.

As she turned about, she saw Pastor Kalm standing at the edge of the mission. "Who are they?" she asked.

He met her halfway between the cemetery and the mission. "Comanches. They're hungry. I generally leave food for them beyond the graves."

"Let me help."

"No. They won't come for it while you're here."

"Why?"

"It took me two years to get them as close as the graves. They don't trust us."

Eve looked back out at the group waiting, silently staring. "Are they dangerous?"

Pastor Kalm walked closer, his hands in his pockets. "I suppose they could be. Primarily they're just hungry. Whatever food I leave for them, they take back to the tribe where it is divided among those in greatest need." He looked at her. "Sometimes I wish that the loaves and fishes parable was more than just a story."

She was moved by his concern for these drawn and staring faces. She reached for his hand. "I want to thank you," she began. "Without your help—"

"You would have managed." He smiled.

"No."

"You are strong and very persuasive. You would have convinced someone in Abilene to open their doors to you."

"But you were there."

At some point he grasped her hands and enclosed them between his own, and the focus of the conversation changed from a safe expression of gratitude to something else.

"Eve, could I—I mean, may I speak of something—what I mean is, would you ever consider—staying behind—with me?"

All the time he talked, he was drawing her closer, into an intimacy she welcomed and in a way desired. She enjoyed the strength of his arms, the sensation of being enclosed, and enjoyed his lips, the power of his kiss, lovely sensations all.

At the end of the kiss he seemed content to hold her for several moments, neither speaking, and she felt safe inside his arms, her cheek resting on his shoulder as she continued to feast her eyes on the western prairie and the small band of Comanches.

She blinked her eyes. They were smiling. "Don't look," she whispered, "but I think we are amusing them."

He did look and waved at them, then returned to the matter at hand, a matter apparently close to his heart. "Will you, Eve? Stay with me, as my wife? It's not a bad life, and together we could make it heaven on earth."

She watched him up close. What confused her was not that she was about to say no but how very much she was tempted to say yes.

But she could not and tried to explain. His expression of kindness and understanding suggested that he had known what her answer would be all along.

"I'm grateful to you," she said, "for so much. But there are people I must see before I make a commitment of marriage."

"You're promised to someone?"

"I'm not sure he still wants me. I was thinking primarily of my parents. I must return to them one day."

"I understand," he said, too quickly, indicating that his disappointment was deep.

"Please know that I could be happy here with you."

"Then why?"

She shook her head. "For one thing, I promised Yorrick Harp—"

"Did he do this?" Quickly he turned her hand over and revealed the small brand in the center of her palm. Scarcely noticeable now, she'd never paid any attention to it beyond the healing.

She stared at it as though just seeing it. "How did you know?"

"The others all have similar marks." Suddenly his gentle nature faded. "My God, Eve, they do this to cattle, not human beings."

Slowly she withdrew her hand, not certain that she could explain. "Yorrick has changed," she said simply. "I doubt if he will inflict this," and she held up her hand, "on anyone ever again." She smiled. "Your favorite phrase, I believe, life is a tempering."

Before he could reply she heard a bellowing voice from the front of the mission that put the lie to her last claim concerning Yorrick Harp.

"Eve! Where are you? The early village cock hath thrice done salutation to the morn. Eve? Come, I need you at my side."

Then he appeared like some ravaged Old Testament prophet in flowing gray robes, his long wavy hair whiter, thinner since his illness, though his face broke into a warm smile when he saw her. "There you are. Preacher, hold your ground. I need her light more than you, for my world is darker. Step away. There are savages watching and if you're not careful I will speak their language. Come, Eve, hurry. We have been delayed too long and now we must race with the stars."

Eve smiled. There was this to be said for Yorrick. He never made much sense, but his nonsense always sounded so appealing.

Again she clasped Justin Kalm's hand. "Thank you," she whispered, "for everything," and kissed his cheek, then ran toward Yorrick Harp, who instantly enfolded her in the bat wing of his robe and led her around the side of the mission to where the wagons were waiting.

"He did nothing untoward, I pray?" Yorrick asked as they approached the lead wagon.

"He asked me to marry him."

"What?"

The bellowing explosive word resounded about the prairie.

"I said no," Eve whispered and tugged on his arm in an attempt to calm him.

But for several seconds old Yorrick looked genuinely stunned. "Damn the church," he muttered beneath his breath as Ram Towse took the lead horse. "Damn all men of God. They are farces, you know, all of them, weak sisters who lack the wit to face the real world and so must needs hide behind the spiritual one. Marry you," he repeated contemptuously. "And he would just do it, wouldn't he, and thus deny your gift to the rest of the world."

Despite his fury, he helped Eve up onto the high seat and waved at the wagons behind, filled with the women and their trunks and stores.

As he settled beside Eve, he patted her hand and reached for the reins. "Do you know what Ram Towse has just told me? That we are only about three days behind Iron Adams's fall cattle drive. We'll see their dust cloud about day after tomorrow, and beneath a dazzling night sky ablaze with stars, we will perform for Iron Adams and his men. Oh, Eve, the world is full of such riches, and you haven't begun to taste them. All right, wagons forward."

The last words were a hearty yell, accompanied by a sharp slap of the reins. The wagons moved forward, Ram Towse in the lead, the women with the strongest hands on the reins of the wagons behind, all heading out for the Western Trail that led north to Dodge.

Eve leaned over the side and looked behind to see the other wagons following. As they rounded the corner of the mission, she saw Pastor Kalm standing approximately where she'd left him. She stood up carefully as they passed and lightly threw him a kiss.

When the wagon was even with the three graves, Yorrick stalled to a halt. "Sleep well, my Viola," he whispered, and Eve saw him touch his hand to his forehead.

Then they were moving again, past the waiting Comanches, who appeared to have settled in, as though the antics of the white men were amusing if nothing else.

It was straight ahead then, and Eve settled in the seat next to Yorrick and looked out from horizon point to horizon point and saw nothing to break the solid line, no foliage, no bush, no structure, just limitless space meeting limitless sky and their five small covered wagons were heading directly into the heart of it.

 On the Western Trail

"No more morning coffee," Yorrick Harp bellowed out over the campfire at the end of the third day. A careful check of his map had informed him that they were twenty-five miles short of where they should have been at this time, and he had just informed the women that at last he had discovered the answer to their turtle-slow pace.

Eve wrapped her shawl about her in protection against the prairie chill and was sorry for the ban on coffee, but understood. Nineteen women drinking several pots of Ram Towse's delicious black coffee every morning did not exactly make for breathtaking wagon speed. Every hour during the morning, calls would go up from the wagons behind and the entire wagon train would rattle to a halt and two women would hop daintily down and run a discreet distance out into the prairie and while one held an obscuring blanket, the other would squat. Three or four times an hour, their forward progress would be halted in this manner.

Now amidst groans of protest coming from the women, Eve moved closer to the fire, where Ram Towse was tossing a huge black skillet filled with frying steak and onions. The odor was irresistible.

"You're going to attract every hungry creature within ten miles, Ram," she said.

The man looked up at her. "I hope not. We haven't got enough food to feed that many." He smiled, and she was pleased to see some of his grief tempered by action, a new goal.

"Tell me about Leadville and all that silver," she invited.

He sprinkled a pinch of salt on the cooking meat. "It's there," he said as though she doubted his word. "H. W. Tabor was a clerk in a grocery store who staked his claim, found his vein of silver and now he takes out four million dollars a year."

Eve felt the fire warm on her face, the night chill on her back. "What will you do with the money, Ram?" she asked. "If you find your vein?"

He looked up as though surprised. "You know, I'm not sure. I've been so busy planning to find it, I haven't bothered to think what I would do with it."

He dug the spatula deep into the browning onions. "All I know is that I've been running cattle all my life. I've looked up the rump ends of more beef than I care to count. I thought I had found all the happiness a man's entitled to with Lucy and Sarah. I didn't know God would take them from me and ask me to start all over again."

Eve listened closely. Someone, God perhaps, had asked her to do the same thing.

He reached for his tongs and turned the cooking meat. "I don't know if Mr. Tabor is happy with all his four million a year. What folks say is true, I reckon. Money don't bring happiness. I'm not even counting on it. I'll settle for control. I'm tired of running cattle, tired of chasing around. I just want to sit and have some control."

Eve waited, expecting him to say more. But he said nothing. She rocked gently back and forth, feeling a curious mix of sadness and contentment.

The rest of them were eating now, each plate generously filled by Ram Towse. Even Yorrick had stopped yelling about too much coffee. His appetite had returned threefold after his illness and it was impossible to yell and eat at the same time.

Eve looked about at the tableau and found it unexpectedly beautiful, a small pocket of warmth and fire and human life in this immense night. Death had touched all of them, had brought them together, enriched by the memory of those gone, so grateful for the presence of those remaining. What she felt wasn't exactly acceptance, not yet, just a tempering.

"Sing, Eve. Give us a song."

"Yes, please, Eve."

She looked up and tried to see who had made the request, but she only saw the ladies of the troupe scattered about the campfire, gazing back at her, all relaxed after Ram Towse's delicious meal. Most were already in their blankets, warm and fed and awaiting sleep.

A lullaby, she thought, and recalled the old English lullaby that Mama had sung to Christine. As she started the song, she saw Ram Towse put down his spatula, saw Yorrick draw close on the other side of the fire, saw every face turn toward her as she found the words to the lullaby and added them to the simple childlike melody.

As she sang, she saw Mama in memory, and Christine, saw everyone that she had left behind at Stanhope Hall. Suddenly she was filled with such loneliness that she felt tears behind her eyes and blinked them away, but could not blink away the ache in her heart or the sure and certain knowledge that while she had found love and acceptance here, the largest part of her heart still resided at Stanhope Hall, with her family, with Stephen.

 *Sante Fe*

Half-frozen and almost out of provisions, Stephen had reached Santa Fe on November the seventh. He had missed the train at Seldon, had been told that he would have to wait a week for the return trip and had elected to go the full distance on horseback. He had managed well enough until a thunderstorm in the Sangre de Cristo Mountains. Then his relief horse had bolted and Stephen had been forced to cover the last eighty miles at reduced speed.

On the first night of his arrival, he had been told by the owner of a crumbling mud cantina named La Fonda that yes, the man Yorrick Harp generally brought his beauties here, but no, they had not yet arrived, but would be welcome anytime.

That had been five days ago, and Stephen was beginning to suspect a repetition of his frustration at El Paso. There was this to be said for Santa Fe: It was more diverting than El Paso. From his table at La Fonda near the fountain, he could in the course of the day see the full spectrum of the human circus. Despite its crumbling mud exterior, the cantina was very comfortable inside, cozy even, with surprisingly good food and drink.

As best as Stephen could determine, gambling and liquor and women were the town's three leading commodities. The gambling den in the cantina was always filled, a bizarre mixture of splendor and barbarism, an earthen floor with sparkling chandeliers overhead and cut-glass decanters on the bar.

From where he sat he saw the gaming tables already piled high with gold and silver, Spanish reales, French francs, Mexican pesos and heavy octagonal California gold slugs.

Among the heaviest bettors, he had observed during the last few days, were the Catholic priests from San Miguel Mission, rich Haciendados, American army officers, shaggy-bearded mountain men and cigar-smoking aristocratic señors.

The most popular games were faro, keno and three roulette wheels, and now all the tables were filled, more customers pushing to get in, the din still rising, a sound like hordes of angry insects.

Stephen closed his eyes and warmed his hands over the mug of steaming coffee just poured by one of the pretty waiter girls. No more liquor. He'd taken that vow after the pass whiskey that had almost been his undoing in El Paso.

Also, traveling alone had made him more cautious. He missed Paris, and at times on the endless trail up from El Paso he'd done his share of cursing. But each time he'd taken new stock and realized that he had no hold on any man, and that freedom was a gift a long time coming for Paris.

Still he missed him and would never forget him and hoped that their paths would cross again.

"Hello."

He looked up at the near voice, female, belonging to one of the pretty waiter girls, one he had never seen before, quite plump, her full breasts barely contained by the black dress cut low with a tight white bodice.

In response to the girl smiling down at him, Stephen shook his head politely. "No, thank you, I don't care to dance."

"I didn't ask you to dance," the girl said.

Stephen looked up, surprised. "Then what?"

She glanced over her shoulder as though fearful someone was watching her. Then she moved closer. "I was off last week with a terrible sore throat and I just come on, and the other girls told me you was waiting for someone."

"I am," Stephen admitted, still cautious. Suddenly he heard a shout go up from the roulette wheel in the next room, heard someone level a dangerous accusation, "Crooked game!" As other voices rose in response, Stephen turned back to the plump young girl who was staring down at him with serious eyes.

"Is it—him you're waiting for?" she asked.

His attention divided between the conflict inside the gambling den and the earnest face of the young girl, Stephen floundered.

"Him?" he repeated. "Who do you mean?"

He looked over his shoulder toward the gambling den. Other men were joining the ruckus. A few had guns drawn.

"Yorrick Harp," the young girl said and immediately captured Stephen's attention despite the sudden explosion of a gun, a man's cry, several women screaming, and someone shouting, "Back off, Grasshopper, just put it down."

"Yorrick Harp," Stephen repeated slowly, rising from his chair, thinking news had arrived, this girl had brought him news.

He tried to say more but the shouting increased in the gambling den. More men from the saloon pushed closer to the door, trying to see what was going on. Stephen reached for the girl's arm and looked about for a place where they might speak uninterrupted. He spied a small table at the far end of the bar and steered her toward it.

Just as they reached the table, another shot was fired, more screams, but at the moment his interest was focused on the girl, who no sooner than she was down in the chair jumped up, protesting, "No, I can't sit, not supposed to sit down."

"All right, then tell me. What do you know of Yorrick Harp?"

The sober expression on her face was replaced by a grin. "He's a wonderful man." She smiled. "He come here last year, you know. I sang for him and he told me—"

Impatient, Stephen urged, "Do you have news? Are they—"

"He said I was too young then, but maybe this year I could join his troupe." She clasped her hands together. "I've been practicing all year, I have. That's why my throat was sore. And I was wondering if . . ."

Stephen blinked at her eager face. "But do you have any news?" he asked. "When will they arrive?"

Perplexed, she looked at him. "No, I thought that you—"

Stephen bowed his head to hide his disappointment. False hope. Why was it plaguing him so? The shouts in the gambling den had grown strangely quiet. He looked up to see two men emerge, their faces grim, carrying a large man between them; one had grasped his ankles, another his wrists, leaving a trail of blood on La Fonda's floor as they carried him out the door.

He heard another yell coming from inside the gambling den, saw a grim-faced marshal coming through the front door of the cantina, followed by two men who were clearly his deputies.

"I can sing good now," the girl announced earnestly. "Do you want to hear me? I just know Yorrick Harp will take me this time."

Stephen listened to her enthusiasm and kept one eye on the door of the gambling den. Coming from inside he heard another scramble, heard someone yell, "Goddamn it, Grasshopper, settle down, will you?"

"And his girls are the most beautiful in the whole world," the pretty waiter girl was saying now. "The most beautiful gowns and hats and Yorrick Harp buys them for them and he takes good care of them, least that's what he told me."

"You talked with him?" Stephen asked, thinking this might be a chance to learn something about the man.

"I did," she boasted.

"The girls," Stephen began, "the ones traveling with him? Did you —have you ever spoken with them?"

"I served them regular last year when they'd take their meals in the kitchen."

"Were they—I mean, were any held against their wishes?"

"Against their wishes!" the girl echoed. "Ain't a girl here who wouldn't give a year's wages to travel with Yorrick Harp. He's a magic man, you know. The priests here don't like him, say he's evil, works for Satan. But he ain't evil, he's just—"

Whatever she said was drowned out by new cries, fisticuffs mixed with curses coming from the gambling den.

"So do you know when he'll arrive?" she repeated, leaning close.

Stephen shook his head. "I had hoped you had news. I'm waiting too."

She looked puzzled. "You want to join the troupe? Yorrick Harp don't take men. They call them Adam-less Edens. No men allowed."

"No, I'm waiting for someone who is traveling with Yorrick Harp. At least I hope so."

The girl smiled as though at last she understood. "You're waiting for *her*," she said. "I know all about true love. You can't fool me."

Then she was gone, hurrying back toward the bar where customers were returning after the fight in the gambling den. The noise level in the cantina had increased, as though violence was a natural stimulant.

Two weathered trappers settled in at the brass rail not far from where Stephen sat. As they downed shots of whiskey, Stephen overheard them say, "He ain't never been the same since the blizzard."

"Ruination ruins a man."

"He was passing out gold pieces in this very room not two years ago."

"I remember, had his pockets full of foreigner's money."

"God had His say."

"I reckon."

"Poor Grasshopper. They'll have to find a tall tree in order to hang him."

As Stephen eavesdropped on the two men, he saw a pathetic parade just coming out of the gambling den, an incredibly tall and lean man with the longest legs he'd ever seen, his hands tied rigidly behind his back, a rope about his neck, the marshal on the other end of the rope, leading him through the crowd, the two deputies bringing up the rear.

Grasshopper. He resembled a grasshopper. *Grasshopper—*

Stephen stood up. The name of the cattle agent, the one his uncle has sent him to find.

Grasshopper Teats!

On his feet now, he hurried toward the two trappers at the end of the bar.

"The man's name, please," Stephen asked, pointing toward the procession just leaving the cantina.

The two trappers looked up, their wizened faces bearing the hard proof of many winters, their eyes bloodshot from too much whiskey.

"That there?" one asked pointing toward the door. "His name is Grasshopper."

"Grasshopper what?"

"Teats."

It was the name of the agent his uncle Richard had sent him to find. The second man nodded. "He could have bought and sold this place two years ago. Now . . ."

"What happened?" Stephen asked.

"Foreign money. Syndicate money. Put it in cattle up in Montana and last year the critters froze, every last one of 'em, in the blizzard."

Stephen looked up to see the procession gone. The front door of the cantina closed against the chilly wind.

"You know him?" one of the trappers asked of Stephen.

Stephen shook his head. "Not directly."

"Well, if you got anything to say to him, you'd better say it fast, cause he'll be a dead man by nightfall."

Stephen frowned. "No trial?"

"Why a trial? It's plain hommyside. Killed a man, he did, with about forty people lookin' on. Why a trial?"

"Who did he kill?"

"The fellow on the roulette wheel. It was just a way of Grasshopper getting what he wants."

"What does he want?"

"To die."

"Why?"

"He lost everything. Lost the foreign money, lost his own, lost their trust, lost the cattle, lost his good name, his reputation. When a man loses that, what's the point of going on?"

Slowly Stephen looked away from the two trappers, down the length of the bar lined with excited men, all giving their accounts of the recent killing and all pleased that there would be a public hanging before sundown.

Back at his table, Stephen sat wearily and found his coffee cold, his will newly defeated. No Eve; that trail had grown cold as well.

Ain't a girl here who wouldn't give a year's wages to travel with Yorrick Harp.

Curious, but he had always conceived of Eve as being in desperate need of his rescue. The thought that she might be content was one with which he could not deal.

Now Grasshopper Teats, the man who had first started this odyssey, was destined to die before sundown, thus rendering Stephen's purpose useless. No point in proceeding on to Montana.

He leaned back in his chair and looked straight up at the low mud ceiling. To one side he saw cockroaches burrowing in and out of the hard mud, heard nearby a pretty waiter girl coax a man into a dance and knew that within the hour the man would be relieved of his purse. In the gambling den he heard the wheels spinning again, the games resumed with scarcely a missed beat for a man's death.

Suddenly despair as sharp as any Stephen had ever suffered crushed down on him. What was he doing here? What was the point? Wherever Eve was, she obviously was content.

Then go home, a wise voice counseled inside his head. Go home, deliver the message to Uncle Richard, then try to piece your life

together without Eve, although he knew, as surely as he knew his
name, that if he worked for the rest of his life to obliterate her memory, he could never fully succeed, for she would be with him always,
in quiet moments and in despairing moments, always with him, always inhabiting him, her sweet face, her lovely voice, her kind and
gentle manner.

 On the Western Trail

On the fourth day, exactly as Yorrick had promised, they spied
an enormous dust cloud up ahead that filled the sky.

"Iron Adams and his herd." Yorrick grinned and tightened his grip
on the rein and instructed Ram Towse to move them out at greater
speed despite the small band of Indians that had been tracking them
at a distance for most of the day. According to Ram, speed made
Indians nervous.

Now it was Violet's turn to sit on the high seat of the lead wagon
between Yorrick Harp and Eve. It was the position of honor and all
the women had taken a turn on the long ride.

Violet pressed close to Eve and grasped her hand. "Wait until you
meet Iron. Isn't that right, Yorrick?"

Yorrick smiled, though he offered a caution. "No telling the chem-
istry with originals," he said. He held a tight grip on the reins as Ram
Towse rode ahead on horseback. He shouted back, "Close ranks, stay
together."

The trail was particularly bumpy here, approaching the Texas border, heading into Indian territory. Violet was aware of Eve bouncing
beside her, her sun bonnet hanging loose down her back. "Best put it
on," Violet counseled and lifted the sun bonnet and secured it beneath Eve's chin.

"Look!" Yorrick shouted and pointed ahead to a lone rider who was
approaching them from the north at top speed, circling wide, hat in
hand, waving it at them.

"Iron Adams's rear guard." Yorrick grinned. "Best cover your faces
till we get past the dust."

Violet reached into her pocket for her bandanna and covered her
nose by way of demonstration, then handed one to Eve. She saw Eve
look at it and smile.

Defensively Violet said, "It isn't for looks, it's to help you breathe."

Apologetically Eve tied the bandanna about her face, though Violet
could see amusement in her eyes, an expression that rapidly faded as

the wagon plunged into the thick roiling dust cloud raised by the movement of five thousand head of cattle over summer-parched prairie.

For a few moments Violet could see nothing. She heard Ram Towse shouting for them to break speed and she felt the dust sting her eyes, felt grit between her teeth despite the bandanna.

Then she was aware of Iron Adams's rear guard rider close beside the wagon, his face obscured behind his own bandanna, though his voice was clear as was his enthusiasm as he tried to steady his horse.

"Yorrick Harp, good to see you. This dust will clear shortly. Take the east line above the herd. It's an eastward wind. I'll go tell Iron you're with us."

Yorrick shouted, "We got company," and pointed over his shoulder toward the small band of Indians who reappeared out of the swirling dust.

"Who?" the rider shouted.

"Comanches, I think," Yorrick replied.

"Keep moving ahead at a steady pace. I'll pass the word. We'll make camp over the border. Hope your ladies are rested."

He turned his horse about and lifted his hat and disappeared into the dust cloud.

"Eve, see if the others are behind us," Yorrick shouted. As Eve stood up, Violet extended a supporting hand to hold her steady against the wagon's rocking motion.

"Can't see them," Eve called down. "You'd better slow down, Yorrick."

A few minutes later Ram Towse came riding back, concerned, "What's the problem? You heard Horace. We got to get east of this crap or none of us will be able to breathe. Why'd you slow?"

"Where are the other wagons?" Eve called out.

"Would you ride back, Ram, please," Yorrick asked, "and see if you can catch a glimpse?"

"Where could they be?" Eve worried, still standing up, peering around the side of the wagon.

Violet held her position on the high seat and closed her eyes against the swirling dust. It seemed to be worse now that they had stopped. Ahead she heard the distant sounds of the herd itself, a continuous rumble of moving hooves, the strident calls of one animal to another, a swelling deafening din.

Then all at once Violet felt a slight pressure on her left and saw Eve just jumping down to the ground.

"No, Eve, don't, come back, you—"

But before she could stop her, Eve disappeared around the side of the wagon. "Yorrick, call her back," Violet insisted. "It isn't safe—and you know—"

But Yorrick was already on his feet, his height enabling him to peer directly over the top of the wagon. "Eve, come on back, let Ram—"

From where Violet sat she heard the break in his voice, and knew something had happened that should not have happened, one of those unscheduled turns of fate, the dust cloud, the disappearing wagons behind them and one foolish young woman who did not know that one did not leave the safety of a wagon in the approach to Indian territory.

Now, "Hold your position," Yorrick whispered as Violet stood beside him and saw Eve, bandanna in hand, surrounded by eight Comanches, their ponies forming a tight circle about her, their bows drawn and loaded, arrows aimed directly down at her.

"No," Violet prayed quickly and thought of Yorrick's rifle inside the wagon, but knew by the time he could get it out and load it, Eve could be dead.

"What are we—" Violet whispered.

"Hold still," Yorrick counseled. Now Violet saw Eve turn in a limited circle as though she were trying to speak with them. Violet saw her face lift, saw a smile. Then she came to a halt, as though she knew that nothing she had said or could say would make the slightest difference.

"Yorrick, what are we going to do?"

"Listen!"

At Yorrick's hissed command, Violet heard horses coming at a fast rate of speed, and as she turned, she caught sight of four men riding toward them, while stumbling behind she saw two large white-faced cattle following on a long lead, struggling to keep up with the speed of the horses.

The point rider was a short muscular man, built like a bank vault, his dark eyes and rim of dark hair clearly visible beneath his large Stetson. He rode his horse like he was part of it, and while the riders were still a distance away, Violet saw him point orders to those riding with him, directing one toward the ridge on the left, the other to the right, the third holding the lead of two white-faced cattle.

Relieved, Violet recognized Iron Adams. If there was a solution to be had, he'd find it. It was her conservative estimate that at one time or another every lady in Yorrick Harp's troupe had fallen in love with Iron Adams. He had a gentle way despite his incredible strength. He'd been known to bend a branding iron, then straighten it again, hence his nickname of Iron.

Now as he approached the wagon, Violet saw Yorrick try to wave him back, try to warn him of the potentially dangerous confrontation taking place directly behind the wagon.

But still he came and Violet saw a broad smile on his face as he approached, clearly unaware of anything amiss.

"Mr. Harp," he called out with unfailing politeness. "I had heard you were ill and the troupe had turned back."

"Not ill, recovered, thanks," Yorrick stammered. "We have—trouble."

He pointed behind the wagon and ceased talking. Violet saw Iron Adams come to a halt about twenty feet in front of the wagon, saw him motion for the rider holding the cattle to halt as well.

From where Violet stood, she could see him trying to peer around the wagon. A few moments later he edged close enough to the wagon to speak. "Who is the idiot?" he demanded angrily. "One of your ladies, I imagine. Doesn't she know never to leave the—"

"New, I'm afraid," Yorrick Harp apologized.

"Dead, I'm afraid," Iron Adams countered.

"Please, we must do something," Violet begged. "She just didn't know."

Again she saw Iron Adams peer around the wagon. "How many are there?" he asked.

Yorrick answered. "Eight on their ponies."

"That means there are eighty someplace close by."

Violet looked back over her shoulder. The grim tableau had not altered, Eve held a prisoner at the center of the Indians, their ponies pressing closer in, forcing her to stand still, the bows still drawn, arrows poised.

Slowly Iron Adams reached into his holster and withdrew his gun and held it out of sight near his saddle horn. He motioned to the man behind to come closer. Violet heard him give orders to ride back to the herd and bring help.

But as the man was handing over the lead to the cattle, a new sound cut through the whistling prairie wind, faint at first, then growing clearer, a woman's voice, singing her heart out in a familiar tune of "Jenny Crack Corn."

Violet looked at Yorrick who in turn looked at Iron Adams who in turn looked at his man holding the cattle who in turn looked back at Violet who peered over the top of the wagon and saw Eve, seated flat on the ground now, still imprisoned by the eight Indian ponies, her head lifted up, singing full voiced, "Jenny Crack Corn and I don't care," a smile on her face, her head keeping time with the music, not a sign of fear visible in any aspect of her posture.

Iron Adams ventured closer. "Is she drunk?" he asked Yorrick Harp.

Yorrick smiled weakly and shook his head, "That's Eve, just Eve."

Violet then noticed the Indians holding the poised bows look at each other, then look down at the woman seated flat on the ground singing, and in the process the bows dropped lower, the arrows no longer poised and aimed.

And still the song floated out over the prairie, gathering in strength and enthusiasm as a good polka should, and Violet saw Eve's feet moving in time to the music, saw her relaxed and leaning back, her face lifted, eyes closed, fairly well belting out: "The fox in the chicken house and I don't care—"

Verse after verse, each crazier than the one before. "Fleas in the flour and I don't care." Violet giggled. "Where did she learn those?"

Yorrick shrugged. Iron Adams stared in disbelief as the voice grew yet louder, more abrasive. Then he gave Yorrick Harp muttered instructions. "I'm going in. They may be only hungry. That's why I brought these," and he motioned toward the cattle. "I'll try to lure them out of the circle, and if I can I'll pick up the woman and I won't stop until we're back in camp. Whatever happens, you go ahead as soon as I've got the woman."

Violet interrupted. "The other wagons—that's why she went back."

"They're already heading into camp," Iron Adams snapped. "Ram Towse led them in. You got separated in the dust. It's our party now."

He gave his man additional instructions, which Violet couldn't hear. All the time Eve's voice rose even louder, each refrain of "The master's gone away," topping those before it.

At last all was ready, Yorrick on the reins, Violet still peering around the side of the wagon.

Iron Adams muttered, "The crazy bitch," and started his horse forward at a slow pace, leading the two cattle behind until at last he'd cleared the wagon and was wholly exposed to the Indians.

Violet could tell that Eve had seen him as well, though the song never faltered. "Bats in the belfry and I don't care—" the song going faster, picking up new momentum, new excitement as now she sang, "Skunk in the buttermilk and I don't care—"

With held breath Violet peered around one side of the wagon, Yorrick around the other and saw the Comanches focused on Iron Adams, who held his position for a moment, giving them all the time they needed to see the fat well-fed cattle. And still Eve's singing increased, a more discordant screech Violet had never heard, amazed that such awful sounds could come from the same voice that had in the past moved entire audiences of men.

Now Violet saw Iron Adams moving slowly up an incline to the left, taking the cattle with him. Once up, he dropped the lead and allowed the cattle to graze free. At first the Indians didn't move. Then she saw one start slowly toward the cattle, then another, and yet a third, all bows lowered, Eve and her song abandoned for two fat cattle that could feed a starving tribe for several days.

Afraid to breathe, Violet saw Iron Adams watch the Indians until they had scaled the incline, all clustered around the cattle, none of them paying the slightest attention to the screeching female seated cross-legged on the prairie floor.

A moment later Iron Adams rode close. "If you shut up singing, I'll try to save your life," he shouted. The song ceased and quickly she grabbed his arm and he scooped her up onto the saddle behind him. As he accelerated to top speed, he passed the wagon and motioned for them to follow and the last thing Violet saw was Eve, her arms about Iron Adams's waist, clinging for dear life, her face pressed against his broad back.

* * *

Eve clung to the thick-waisted little man who had lifted her effortlessly from the prairie floor and felt the strength in his muscles as he urged his horse to top speed, his head bent into the wind.

Behind she heard Yorrick Harp's wagon rattling across the bumpy terrain and tried to calm herself from her recent fear. The Indians had appeared so quickly out of the dust, had surrounded her before she knew what had happened. At first she had planned not to be afraid. After all, she had confronted Indians before at Pastor Kalm's mission outside Abilene. There they had appeared merely shy and hungry.

But these had been different, fierce, angry appearing, encircling and imprisoning her within the moment. The song had been merely a measure of self-defense, to keep her spirits up.

Now she looked behind to see the Indians riding off in the opposite direction, taking the cattle with them. About fifteen minutes later she looked ahead and saw the herd all grazing placidly, and there, farther to the right, she saw the other wagons joined with three others in a circle, saw a large group of buckaroos freely mingling with the women, saw all look up at their approach.

The man brought his horse to a halt directly in front of a large campfire, from which delicious odors were filling the early dusk sky.

She saw beef roasting on a spit, saw two immense kettles bubbling and smelled coffee.

"Give me your hand," the man commanded, and she saw an expression on his features not unlike that of her Indian captors, fierce, angry.

"I can do it," she claimed and hopped down to the ground and was aware of the others running toward her, of Yorrick just guiding his wagon into place behind her. She heard Violet cry, "Are you all right, Eve?" She heard all these things but something in the man's face held her attention, a fury that she knew would not be abated until he spoke to her.

"Do you have any idea how damn near you came to being a squaw woman?"

Eve bowed her head, aware of all the other voices falling silent as though the better to hear her scolding. "What's a squaw woman?" she asked.

He stood his ground directly in front of her. "A squaw woman," he said, his voice echoing loud and clear about the quiet prairie, "is a white woman who is captured by Indians, who is systematically raped by every Indian male in the vicinity who has the appetite for such sport, and who is then left for anyone who wants her on a permanent basis and if no one claims her she is left for the vultures."

Eve tried to swallow and couldn't, tried to look up and meet his anger and couldn't.

He stepped closer and in one angry gesture scooped the hat from his head, revealing thick black wavy hair. "Yorrick says you're a greenhorn, so on the basis of your inborn stupidity, I'll let it go. But I'm warning you"—and he stepped closer and wagged a finger directly in front of her face—"if you even think of jeopardizing these good people with such a harebrained action again, you'll answer to me. Is that clear? Is it?"

Eve drew a deep breath in an effort to swallow everything, the man's arrogance, as well as the close attention of the others. "Sir, could you tell me—"

But his anger had reached the point that he could no longer speak. He turned his back on her and walked away and left her gaping after him.

Only Violet stayed at her side. "Don't worry," she whispered. "He'll come around."

"Who cares?" Eve murmured and retreated to Yorrick's wagon and blessedly heard the others start to chat among themselves. As she reached the wagon, she looked back and saw the man on the far side of the clearing, in close conference with his friends, and once she saw him shake his head, as though still unable to digest her foolish action.

"Who is he?" she asked.

"Iron Adams," Violet replied. "He's generally courteous to a fault. I've never seen him so—"

She didn't stay for Violet to finish but crawled up into the back of the wagon, where her comfortable pallet was waiting. There she stretched out and closed her eyes and continued to see the Indian faces in memory and knew that everything the man had said was true, knew that she had been wrong and foolish and knew that she would have to find a way later to apologize to all.

For now she was tired and wanted to sleep and hoped that her dream images of Stephen would be strong enough to blot out Iron Adams's angry face.

* * *

When she awakened it was night outside the wagon, and she heard Marigold's voice in the near distance reciting Desdemona's lines from *Othello*, heard Yorrick Harp's rich mellow voice reciting Othello's. She sat up, lost for a moment, and rubbed the sleep from her eyes and ventured to the end of the wagon and peered out at a most unusual sight.

The night sky was clear and filled with a million stars. In the clearing, around a roaring campfire, sat a large company composed of at least fifty buckaroos, the ladies of the troupe scattered comfortably among them, while on the other side of the fire Yorrick and Marigold played the death scene from *Othello*, played it beautifully according to the enraptured faces of this mixed audience, their rapt expressions highlighted by flickering firelight.

Eve watched, moved by the unique beauty of the scene, by the vastness of the night sky, the crystal-clear, slightly cold air, the horses grazing beyond the wagons, and beyond them five thousand head of cattle, though even they too had fallen politely silent as though in appreciation of Shakespeare.

The scene was over then, the applause warm and sincere, and Marigold and Yorrick took countless bows. As he was turning about after the fourth bow, Yorrick apparently saw Eve seated on the rear of the wagon, for in the next moment she heard him call to her and wave her forward to the area designated as the stage. Though she tried to protest, she found it useless as several of the women looked up as well.

Reluctantly she approached, smoothing her dress wrinkled from her nap, and pushed back her hair. As she took her place near the fire, she saw Yorrick smile, felt a warm clasp of his hand, and both gave her strength and confidence.

"Sing for them," he whispered. "They are lonely men."

She saw a man with an accordion close to the fire, saw another with a harmonica and started to give them the key for a Stephen Foster melody but at the last minute she changed her mind, remembering one of the hymns that White Doll had taught her.

Not certain if the musicians would be familiar with it or not, she started it alone, her voice low on the opening lines, hearing the hymn's harmony inside her head, closing her eyes as the words returned after all those years:

> "I never will forget the day,
> I heard my mother gently say,
> You're leaving now my tender care,
> Remember, child, your mother's prayer—"

Her voice felt well suited to the cool quiet night air. The words were ready for her when she needed them, and at some point the harmonica joined in, doing the harmony for her, a skillful musician.

It was not her intention to sing all four verses, but she did simply because it pleased her to do so and clearly it pleased the men. On the last stanza, when she sang softly of a mother's death and of years gone by, she saw a few of the men look down in close study of the earth, and she brought the hymn to a close on the promise that there was another home they would one day share.

She looked out over the company and heard no sound, as though unwittingly she'd hypnotized them.

Then there was movement coming from the back of the crowd, the man himself, short, broad, the firelight catching on his dark features and thick curly hair.

"Miss Stanhope,"

"Mr. Adams," she countered.

"I—we—"

"I'm sorry for my thoughtlessness this afternoon."

"No, I'm sorry for—"

The crowd was moving closer, as though fascinated by this splintered dialogue.

"The song was—" Again Iron Adams broke off, apparently unable to finish.

She smiled. "Did you prefer it to the one I was singing this afternoon?"

Iron Adams grinned.

"Do you polka, Mr. Adams? Come."

So pleased was she that he was no longer angry with her, she nodded to the accordion and harmonica player to join her and she broke into a spirited rendition of "Jenny Crack Corn" and was pleased to hear a fiddle now coming from somewhere pick up the melody, adding volume, and at the same time she saw Iron Adams smile and open his arms to her and they commenced their polka around the campfire, in a limited circle at first. But as the music accelerated, they threw away their caution and picked up their speed and she felt his arms tighten about her in a grip worthy of his name and she clung to him, laughing, and heard laughter all around, saw everyone in a blur on their feet, hands clapping as their mad polka continued, the circle growing wider, the movement broader until the velocity at which they were dancing forced her head back and she found herself staring straight up at the star-filled night sky whirling about overhead while the thunderous applause of the company filled her ears and her heart.

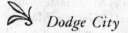 *Dodge City*

On the morning of the tenth day, in a driving rainstorm, having left Iron Adams and his cattle four days behind in a place called Oklahoma Territory, Eve sat in the back of the lead wagon opposite Violet and stared out at the river of mud that served as Dodge City's main street and through which Yorrick Harp and Ram Towse were trying to guide the wagons.

Overhead, stretched across the street, flapping in the rain, she read a banner that said,

Welcome to Dodge—The Beautiful Bibulous Babylon of the Plains

Violet saw the sign and made a sound of mild contempt. "Used to be," she said over the rattle of the wagon. "Used to be my favorite, Dodge, but no more."

Eve drew the shawl about her head in weak protection against the chill damp wind. She leaned out at the risk of getting soaked and looked up and down the main street on the high board sidewalks and saw no sign of life.

"Where is everyone?" she shouted over a clap of thunder and drew her head back into the wagon and waved at Henry, one of Iron's men who was driving the wagon behind. Iron Adams had loaned Yorrick four men to drive the wagons, as the women were beginning to complain of callouses on their hands from holding the reins. The men were to wait at Dodge until Iron brought the herd through.

Now in answer to her question, Violet shook her head. "Inside most likely, but even on a sunny day Dodge isn't what it used to be, not after the Murphy Movement."

"What's the Murphy Movement?" Eve asked and felt the wagon tilt dangerously to the right in a sinkhole of mud.

"Prohibition," Violet called back. "But it doesn't mean much here. Mr. Masterson just pays the bootlegger and calls his bar a drugstore."

Suddenly the wagon tilted even farther and Eve felt herself sliding across into Violet's lap. In the wagon behind she saw Henry's look of alarm, saw him stand up in the seat and wave frantically at them.

"Yorrick," Eve called through the front of the wagon. "I think we're stuck."

"Damnit, I know it," Yorrick yelled back and tried once more to urge the horses forward.

As the wagon rocked back and forth, going nowhere, Eve settled beside Violet for warmth and information. "Who is Mr. Masterson?"

Violet looked at her with eyes wide in disbelief. "George Masterson owns the Varieties Opera House and Saloon. It's where we will perform. Surely you've heard of his brother."

Again Eve shook her head, feeling cold and uninformed.

"Bat Masterson," Violet announced.

"Who is he?"

"Bat?" A look of incredulity covered Violet's face. "A gunfighter. Yorrick told us once that according to rumor, Bat Masterson had killed thirty-eight men, not counting attacking Indians."

Eve scowled at the endorsement and thought it a ludicrous one at best. "Come on, let's see if we can help."

But just as she started to her feet, a very wet and muddy and weary-looking Yorrick Harp stuck his head through the back flap.

"We are immovable," he announced sadly. "The wet earth has captured us and here we sit."

Violet peered out the flap at the other wagons. "All of us?"

Yorrick nodded. "I'm afraid so. When we stopped, we sank. There is a lesson there, I'm sure, and as soon as I am dry and warm, I'll pursue it. For now we must walk, not far, to the Varieties and perhaps someone will spy us sinking into the mud of Babylon and come to our aid."

"Walk?" Violet exclaimed and peered out at the storm, which seemed to be increasing. The storefronts across the way were totally obscured by a solid sheet of rain, the mire of the road under the wagons beginning to resemble a broad red lake.

Then Eve had an idea. They had stopped the night before last for wagon repairs at a place called Cottonwood. She and the other women of the troupe had wanted a bath, had been in desperate need of one. But the proprietor of the small hotel had informed them water was limited and they were not dirty enough.

Now in the event the same rule applied here in Dodge, Eve smiled, pushed off her shawl, moved to the rear of the wagon and took one giant leap out into the mud and the rain, landing in muck up to her knees, the deluge instantly soaking her to the skin.

She wiped the rain from her face and found herself staring at several unbelieving faces, Violet among them.

"You wanted a bath?" Eve called out over the pounding rain. "This walk will assure us of one. I'll see to it. Come on."

After several hesitant moments Violet dropped down next with a massive splatter, then the six women in Henry's wagon followed suit, and slowly Eve worked her way down all five wagons until the muddy street was filled with giggling women, a few trying futilely to keep the mud damage to a minimum and finally surrendering to it completely as though they were children.

"Which way?" Eve shouted to Violet as they came to an intersection.

Without speaking, Violet pointed straight ahead to a large box of a building, the word *Varieties* painted on the side.

"I assume they know we're coming," she called to Violet, who walked next to her.

Apparently beyond speech, Violet wiped continuously at her face, trying to clear the mud and rain.

Then straight ahead Eve saw the doors of the Varieties Opera House and Saloon open, saw a group of men, perhaps a dozen in all, led by a man in a dark blue suit, a glass in his hand, emerge. They came out as far as the overhang would permit without getting wet.

"Hello," she called up. "We're with Yorrick Harp. Our wagons are stuck. We had to walk."

She thought she'd made perfect sense, therefore couldn't understand the blank, down-staring faces of the gentlemen, all of whom shifted their drinks to the opposite hand and continued to stare down and say nothing.

At last the gentleman in charge seemed to stir himself out of his hypnotic state. "No, I'm afraid it won't be possible," he said with curt politeness. "Yorrick Harp is late. By two weeks. The Opera House is now—otherwise engaged."

Eve blinked up at the man and shivered and tried to explain.

"There was illness, the entire company outside Abilene. It caused the delay."

"I'm sorry," the man repeated with stubborn civility. "It's as I said, we are now otherwise engaged and—"

Suddenly Eve had had enough of the polite though overbearing gentleman. She was freezing, and up and down the steps behind her she heard teeth chattering. It was her intention to move straight through those handsome wood-carved doors of the Varieties Opera House and Saloon, taking the ladies with her and into the warmth of the huge fire, which she could see from her present vantage point and which smelled so inviting.

Now she strode to the doors, pushed them open and motioned the women to go inside, and they did, despite the man's glaring look of anger.

"Miss, you can't do that."

"I'm afraid we have to do it, sir. The ladies are—damp."

"That is not my concern."

"It should be when we all have traveled a great distance to fill your hall."

"That is not the point," he protested, his distress increasing as the women continued to file in. Eve followed at the end, eager to see the famous Varieties of Dodge City. Even Iron Adams's men had described it as "gleaming," "swell," "palatial" and "luxurious," with clean, sparkling glasses and gold spittoons.

Now as she stepped inside the doors she saw a large, unadorned, stark room with rough uncovered tables, mismatched chairs, a splintering floor, a few unshaven men with their hats on seated at the tables, two dogs asleep in front of the bar, which did not in any way resemble a bar and was topped by a hand-painted sign that read Drugstore.

She took in the drab scene and decided that Iron Adams's men had been on the trail too long. To the left she saw a large graystone fireplace, the source of the delightful smells and inviting warmth. At one side of the fireplace she saw a middle-aged man seated, a dapper gray bowler hat perched at a backward angle on his head. Opposite him at the fireplace, his legs spread akimbo, she saw a second gentleman, taller, older, a flat-brimmed hat atop his head, his face practically obscured by a large handlebar mustache. In his lap she saw what appeared to be a cat, yellow, curled comfortably into a ball before the warmth of the fire. Both gentlemen looked tired and old, gray showing in their hair.

"Miss, I must ask you—"

It was the blue suit again, looking none too pleased.

"And I must ask you," she cut in. Then she remembered her manners. "My name is Eve Stanhope. And yours?"

Clearly her courtesy had caught the gentlemen off guard. She remembered Sis Liz telling her that courtesy always caught a rascal off guard. Still he replied, "My name is Masterson. George Masterson."

"Are you the proprietor of this place?"

"I am."

"Then could you please direct us to the baths? Are they straight on back, through the kitchen?" As though answering her own question, she started off across the floor.

Mr. Masterson made an attempt to block her. "Is your hearing impaired?" he demanded, his manner arch, his voice sarcastic.

All right, she'd tried to be polite. Now it was time for another approach. "No sir," she said, summoning as much dignity as her soaking wet and mud-covered garments would allow. "My hearing is perfect. Unhappily none of what you said matters very much, for we are in desperate need. Now if you will go deep inside yourself, pushing aside your pomposity and your arrogance, I'm sure you will find a stray instinct toward humanity. Only a wisp will do, and we'd be most appreciative. Then within the hour I'm certain that Yorrick Harp will walk through those doors. If you wish, you can tell him about the hall being emptied or closed or otherwise engaged. I really don't care. Our needs now are obvious and simple. Will you point the way to the baths, or shall I go and find them for myself?"

Her angry voice reverberated in echo throughout the saloon. Then she heard solitary applause coming from the gentleman in the gray bowler hat beside the fire. Without looking around, he suggested in a kind deep voice, "You never did know when you were bested, George. Believe me, the young lady will have her hot bath with or without your direction."

The man in the dark blue suit glanced toward the two sitting at the fireplace. "I was thinking of you, Bat. You said you wanted privacy."

The other gentleman spoke up, the one stroking the cat. "Give them what they want, George. I for one would like to see what's beneath all that mud."

Grateful, Eve looked in their direction and started toward them with the idea of delivering her thanks in person when suddenly she felt a firm grip on her arm and saw Violet at her side, a pinched expression on her face.

She was about to pull away when she heard George Masterson give a resounding clap of his hand, and a moment later she saw the kitchen door open and a plump Chinaman peer through the door.

"Ling-Three, fill the baths," Mr. Masterson ordered, "and send someone out to clean up this mess."

As he stared down at the muddy floor, Eve followed his focus and apologized, though the floor probably could have used a scrubbing before they arrived.

"Thank you," she said with renewed politeness and pointed the women toward the kitchen door and the man named Ling-Three.

Eve held her position until all the women had disappeared into the kitchen, then she glanced toward the two men at the fireplace. "Thank you," she called out and wanted to say more but Violet was there at her elbow, tugging at her in a most annoying fashion.

Reluctantly Eve followed after her through the door into what appeared to be a large and dingy kitchen. To the right, standing over a black cookstove, she saw another Chinaman, who looked up as she entered.

She saw the women disappearing through a door on the left and would have followed after them had it not been for Violet, who was still clinging to her elbow as though for dear life.

"What's the matter?" Eve demanded.

"Do you know who they were?" Violet gasped and pointed back toward the main saloon.

"The man said his name was George Masterson."

"Not—him. His brother, the other one," Violet stammered. She turned away in clear worry. "We shouldn't have come. I knew we shouldn't have come. Santa Fe would have been safer. Someone should warn Yorrick."

"Warn him of what?" Eve demanded.

"Those men, Bat Masterson, Wyatt Earp."

"They looked harmless to me."

"They are—dangerous," Violet whispered.

Eve listened, ready to offer additional comfort, but suddenly she heard a scuffle coming from the saloon, men shouting, one man in particular, whose voice she recognized as Yorrick Harp's.

"Oh my God," Violet gasped and backed up against the near wall.

Eve moved quickly back to the door and pushed it open a crack and saw Yorrick, mud-covered, surrounded by the men whom Eve had noticed earlier slouched about the tables of the saloon. She'd assumed then they were trailhands or drovers, but now the manner in which they surrounded Yorrick and Ram Towse and the four other drivers led Eve to believe otherwise. There were at least two dozen of them. Their guns were drawn and they surrounded Yorrick and the others and held them at gunpoint just inside the door of the saloon.

Eve watched through the crack of the door, amazed at how quiet

Yorrick appeared. No Shakespearean quotations now, no bombast or theatricality. He looked merely cold and wet and defeated as he lifted his hands high into the air.

"Masterson?" he called out in a subdued voice.

Eve looked at Violet. "Weren't we scheduled at all for this place?"

Violet held her position against the kitchen wall. "We're late, remember?" she reminded Eve, "and in the past we always have come by rail. Men have never traveled with us before. It's the strange men that are making them nervous."

At that moment another voice coming from the saloon caught Eve's attention. She looked back to see George Masterson approaching, after having been in conference with the two men at the fireplace.

"The women can stay overnight, Harp. You and the other men will have to find other lodgings."

"I won't leave my girls alone."

"You don't have much choice." Masterson looked toward the fireplace and the two seated, one stroking the cat. "My—guests must be cautious. As I said, the ladies can stay overnight, then you all must leave. I'm sorry. Be on time next year."

With that he walked back toward the fireplace and left Yorrick standing inside the door with the others, all still surrounded by the gunmen, who had not moved except to raise their guns to a more fatal angle.

For a moment Yorrick seemed incapable of speech or movement. For ever so long he stood looking from one to the other, occasionally lifting his arm to shake loose some of the wet, clinging mud. Then at last, "Masterson, I must talk to my girls."

"Not necessary."

With that Eve had had enough of the bullying, assertive Masterson and pushed open the door with a suddenness that caused three of the gunmen to whirl on her.

"Don't!" Yorrick shouted and the sudden cry seemed to stir everyone in the saloon into nervous movement.

Eve stared at the gunmen, then saw George Masterson hurrying toward her, his face livid. "You could have been killed!" he shouted.

"I want to speak with Yorrick," she said, meeting his anger.

Finally George Masterson lifted his hands in a despairing gesture and motioned for Yorrick to come closer. "Hurry and then leave and take those men with you and get out of here."

As Yorrick drew near, he grabbed Eve by the elbow and propelled her a few feet away from where George Masterson stood, arms crossed.

"What is going on here?" Eve demanded, keeping her voice down.

"Bad timing." Yorrick sighed and looked heavenward. "How was I to know?"

"What?"

"That those two would be meeting here."

"Why are they afraid of us?" she whispered back, looking beyond Yorrick's shoulder.

"It's not you or the girls. It's Iron Adams's men, any man. Too many try to start fights with them, draw guns on them. Some have no reason, some have good reason."

As Yorrick stopped whispering, Eve saw the two men at the fireplace exchange a few words, saw a smile on the face of the one with the mustache, and then they both settled back into a relaxed silence.

"They don't look very fierce," Eve whispered.

Suddenly George Masterson issued a stern command. "Say your say, Harp, and get those men out of here. You've never traveled with men before. Why now?"

Yorrick smiled broadly, though nervously. "As I said, Fate had a surprise for us in Abilene in the form of illness. Instead of going on to El Paso, we took the Western Trail by wagon train. You don't expect my ladies to handle reins, do you?"

"All I expect your ladies to do is get out of here first thing in the morning, and you can leave now and take the men with you."

As Masterson pointed toward Ram Towse and the four drivers, Yorrick whispered to Eve, "Now don't worry, it's the unexpected that frequently provides the greatest bonus, though I must confess at the moment it eludes me."

"Where will you—"

"Down the street, a third-rate fleabag called the Hudson. I'm counting on you to look after the ladies, and I'll check with the Denver and Rio Grand to see if I can't get us out of here by tomorrow at the latest."

"Railway?" she asked hopefully.

He nodded. "To Denver, then on to the Tabor Grand at Leadville and we're back on track."

"Finished, Harp?" Masterson demanded.

"We are." Yorrick smiled pleasantly. "Now look to my girls," he advised Eve, "and look to yourself as well." He seemed to see her clearly for the first time. "You need—cleaning," he said with a wave of his hand. Then abruptly he turned about and waved a cheery greeting to the two men at the fireplace. "My thanks to you, gentlemen, for your understanding. Sorry we can't perform for you. The loss is most assuredly yours."

Eve smiled. The old actor was back, despite the change of plans and muddy garments. Now she heard him scatter the gunmen as though they were fat geese.

"Shoo, shoo, all of you, put those barbaric things away. Anything capable of snuffing out life should be classified an illegal obscenity and banned from the planet, and I don't just mean firearms. A harsh word, a falsehood, a cold welcome—all are capable of snuffing out life."

As he babbled on in loving and familiar fashion, the gunmen moved back as though Yorrick's words were weapons against which there was no defense.

Eve stayed long enough to watch the grand exit, and it *was* grand, a bit of Shakespeare, a line from Rostand, words beautifully and non-sensically arranged that somehow got them all out of the door and back into the rainstorm, which showed no signs of ceasing.

For several moments a stunned silence seemed to hang over the saloon, punctuated at the end by a woman's sharp scream. Eve ran back into the kitchen, through the side door and into the baths to see the women, most in states of undress, three already in the large copper tubs with Ling-Three pouring water.

"What's the matter?" Eve demanded.

"It's c-cold water," Rose shivered.

Eve drew a deep breath, rolled up her sleeves, took the large kettle from Ling-Three and patiently explained, "Hot water, Ling-Three. We must put the kettles on the stove and bring the water to a boil. It must be hot."

Clearly the little round-faced Chinaman had not understood a word she'd said.

"Come, ladies," she called. "We must do our own work. Marigold, bring that kettle, and Violet, find some more wood for the stove. Hurry, before we all catch our death of cold."

* * *

It was eight o'clock that night before all the women had had a hot tub and put on warm garments, which Ram Towse had left in a trunk outside the door of the Varieties Saloon. Now all were tucked in for the night in the large dormitory above the kitchen, enjoying bowls of Ling-Three's hot chicken stew. Violet and Eve were alone in the baths, Violet just finishing, Eve slumped on a near bench, too tired to move.

"Come on, Eve, you're next," Violet urged. "I'll fill the tub for you myself."

"No need," Eve murmured, eyes closed. "I'll just sleep here."

"No, you can't. I'll be back in a minute with the water. Get those things off."

Slowly she stood and knocked enough mud loose to find the buttons on her skirt. She stepped out of the garment and shivered and sat back down on the wooden bench.

"Here we are," Violet announced cheerily, looking very rosy and scrubbed after her own bath. "In you go," she ordered, and Eve obeyed.

As she crawled over the high rim of the tub and sank down into the warm water, she closed her eyes against the pleasurable sensation.

"Scrub while the water is hot," Violet advised. "Do you want me to?"

"No, you go on upstairs, see that everyone is settled. I'll be along in a minute."

Violet gave her a warm smile and bent over and kissed her on the cheek. "Hurry," she called back and disappeared up the narrow steps that led to the sleeping rooms overhead.

Alone, Eve slipped down into the copper tub and looked up at the old wooden-beam ceiling overhead and heard the rain still coming down and heard the kitchen quiet. Ling-Three had gone to bed. She heard the dormitory overhead quiet as well, the women exhausted after their hectic arrival.

Eve reached for the sponge and filled it with warm soapy water and squeezed it playfully over her stomach and breasts and in the quiet of the bath she sensed memories waiting for her, Stephen the most difficult of all.

In the darkness behind her closed eyes, she saw his face in perfect detail, his eyes, the strong line of his nose, his mouth—

The memory hurt too much and softly she began to hum, always a good remedy to any pain, a mindless melody at first, then, as always happened, the song filled her attention and demanded all of her concentration. She found words to go with the melody, an old favorite, a camp song she enjoyed singing very slowly and very softly, not at all in its usual lilting rhythm:

> "Oh, my darling,
> Oh, my darling,
> Oh, my darling Clementine—"

As Eve recalled the words, the melody grew stronger, and even as she sang, she was transported back to Fan Cottage, to White Doll and Sis Liz sitting opposite her at the tea table, both of them smiling at the little girl named Eve who sang her heart out in the old camp favorite:

"You are lost and gone forever,
dreadful sorry, Clementine—"

Lost and gone forever? Was she?

As she sang, she heard a single step outside the bath door, looked in that direction without losing the words or the melody and saw someone push open the door, only a crack, and she saw silhouetted against the kitchen wall the clear outline of a dapper bowler hat.

Still she sang. She didn't care if he listened. That's what songs were for.

 Santa Fe

Plump Sarah proved a blessing, for once she got over her disappointment at not being able to join Yorrick Harp's traveling Adamless Eden, she served Stephen morning, afternoon and evening with devotion, and she was good company.

Stephen was grateful, particularly on the afternoon she introduced him to a man named Cody Tanner, the barkeep at La Fonda, a man who seemed to know a great deal about Yorrick Harp and his "traveling gals."

"We missed 'em this year," Cody said, smiling at Stephen from behind the bar. "They're always good for business, those gals are. Sarah here was going with them this year."

Stephen listened sympathetically and stepped closer to the bar. Only yesterday he had been on the verge of sending Burke Stanhope a telegram, telling him that Eve's trail was lost and cold. Then he was going to retrace his route on the Atchison, Topeka and Santa Fe back to El Paso, say a final good-bye to Paris and Marie, and then return to Mobile and ultimately to England.

But all that was before Sarah had calmly mentioned that Cody Tanner knew Yorrick Harp's entire schedule, knew precisely where he'd be and when he'd be there.

At first Stephen had doubted the claim. It was obvious that something had gone wrong with that schedule. The troupe was supposed to be in El Paso. They weren't there. They were supposed to be in Santa Fe. They weren't here.

Cody Tanner disappeared behind the bar, was gone for a few minutes, then reappeared and handed Stephen an advertisement.

Yorrick Harp's All Female
Adamless Eden Traveling
Theatrical Troupe

It read across the top in bold print. Then it listed the female names who were members of the troupe, then there was a line that read simply:

Girls—Girls—Girls—Girls—Girls

And beneath that, it stated:

Grand Tour from Mobile to San Francisco
with performances in
Dallas, El Paso, Santa Fe, Dodge City, Denver, Leadville,
Cheyenne, Granger, Promontory Point and San Francisco

Stephen read it twice, aware of Sarah and Cody Tanner watching.

"You know someone traveling with Harp?" Cody Tanner asked.

Sarah volunteered the information. "It's his sweetheart." She smiled sadly. "They was to have been married."

Stephen could tell by the look of curiosity on Cody Tanner's face that he was dying to hear all. But he lacked the energy for retelling the tale that still haunted him every night.

Sarah murmured, "Can you help him, Cody? He has no one."

Stephen started to protest his helplessness, but Cody interrupted. "Let's go to the telegraph office," he said briskly. "Let's talk to Virgil. It seems to me it would be a simple matter to contact Dodge, and I think Elmer's still on the key up there. All we have to do is find out if he has seen Harp and take it from there."

Stephen looked up with renewed hope. "Is that possible?"

"Sure it is." Cody Tanner grinned. "Come on. Sarah, you watch things here for me. I'll go with him. I need to stretch my legs before the night crowd."

In the next moment Stephen found himself in the company of Cody Tanner, making his way across the square in the chill dusk of autumn toward the telegraph office just beyond the Palace of Governors. There were only a few people on the sidewalk.

"Early winter," Cody Tanner commented, sniffing at the night air. "You can feel it."

In all honesty Stephen was feeling little except the tension of fresh hope. If they could contact Dodge City and *if* they could learn of Yorrick Harp's precise schedule, then it would be a simple matter to select a location and wait for them, for Eve.

"I take it you been a lookin' for a long time," Cody Tanner said sympathetically.

"Since late summer. She was only a day ahead of us at one point."

"What happened?"

"Everything that could possibly happen."

Cody seemed to understand. "Come on, in here," he directed and pointed to a dimly lit office connected to the railway station, adobe exterior, mussed and worn interior with a large railway map of the United States on one wall and a telegraph map on the other.

Behind the cluttered desk sat a thin, graying man who looked suspiciously up over his specs as they came in.

"Don't worry, Virge, it's just me, Cody."

Virge put down his pen where he'd been working on account books. "Who cut you loose from behind your bar?"

"A fella has to stretch his legs sometime."

"You bring me a free sample?"

"Didn't know you wanted one."

"Cody, you bastard, you know better than that. Can you feel the nip in the air?"

"Sure can. Early winter. Didn't I say so?" he said to Stephen. "Early winter."

Throughout this maddening exchange Stephen with great effort bided his time and moved close to the telegraph machine, eyeing it hopefully, aware that in a short time that small key would either send his spirits soaring or plunge them to new depths.

"Who's he?" he heard Virge inquire.

"He's searching for Yorrick Harp and his troupe of girls. You remember Harp?"

Virge grinned. "I remember his gals better."

"Well, what we want you to do, Virge, is to get on that key to Dodge and see if he's in those parts and if so what is his new schedule? This gentleman feels an urgent need to catch up with them at some point."

"Why?"

"I told you, Virge," Cody scolded. "He's got a lady friend traveling with them."

"Well, she won't be no account to him if she's been traveling with—"

"Just get behind the key, Virge," Cody interrupted.

Half-afraid he would lose control during this pointless banter, Stephen took refuge at the window and looked out at twilight, the sky a dark blue with fiery streaks of bright orange and red and no wind blowing. Just cold and still, a winter sky.

A few moments later he heard the sharp staccato music of the telegraph key, heard Cody ask quietly, "Elmer still up that way?"

"Is if something ain't got him."

For several minutes the only sound in the room was the unique music of the telegraph key, a series of uneven dots and dashes, a mystery to all save the initiated who worked the telegraph offices.

Curious, Stephen turned away from his vigil on the cold empty road outside the window and watched the concentration on Virgil's face; his upper teeth pulled on his lower lip as he relayed the message.

"When will—"

"Shhhh," Cody interrupted, a finger to his lips, and again there was silence except for the irregular counterpoint of the telegraph key.

Then Virgil was finished. He pushed back his green eyeshade and lifted his arms into the air in a stretching movement and at the end of a yawn said, "Course the office may be empty now. Suppertime, you know."

"I thought the machines had to be manned at all times," Stephen said, worry rising.

"Oh, they do. But we're talking about Dodge. They do things their own way up there."

"How long a wait?"

"If someone's at home, we should know in a few minutes; if not—"

Stephen turned away without giving Virge a chance to voice the alternative. He moved back to the chilly window and heard the two behind him in easy conversation.

Then a few minutes later, "Listen!"

Stephen heard it first, the telegraph key moving of its own volition, tapping out a message.

"Hurry," Stephen begged and saw Virge at last slip into his chair, pencil in hand, listening carefully to the metallic click, scribbling as fast as the key moved while he and Cody stared down over the top of the counter, intrigued and slightly intimidated by the miraculous advances of modern science.

After several minutes the telegraph key went silent, though Virge continued to write. At last he tore off a piece of yellow paper and sailed it toward the counter.

"Don't know if that helps you or not, but there 'tis—"

Quickly Stephen grabbed for it and read:

> Harp in Dodge. Booked on Kansas-Pacific for
> Denver this P.M. Closed shop here.

Stephen read the short message again, not immediately able to determine if there was cause for hope or not.

"Closed shop here," he read. "What does that mean?"

"Probably it means the club is gathering," Cody explained.

"What club?"

"Earp, Masterson, God knows who else. Those fellas get nervous when there are too many guns in town. Dodge is their home. The town usually obliges them."

Stephen listened carefully, not understanding a great deal of what was being said. He trusted Cody Tanner and now extended the cryptic message for him to read.

After a few minutes of silent reading, Cody Tanner looked up, a smile on his face. "Do you want me to tell you what I'd do if I was in a life-and-death pursuit of a lady traveling with Yorrick Harp?"

Stephen waited. He didn't have to follow the advice, but he was curious to hear it, for at this point the message made little sense to him.

"All right," Cody began. "As I read it, this means that Harp is off schedule. For whatever reason he got to Dodge late and the town was closed. Now if I was a young buck in heat, I'd hop on the Atchison, Topeka and Santa Fe tomorrow morning and take me a ride straight up to Denver. But I wouldn't hang around in Denver because I know for a fact that Harp plays several theaters there. The Criterion, the Orpheum, the Brown Palace, and with the run of luck you've been havin' if I sent ya to the Orpheum, old Harp would show up at the Brown Palace so—"

Cody drew a deep breath and walked to the large railway map pinned on the far wall. He reached up and pointed to a dot of a town just below Denver and west of it.

"Leadville," he announced. "The Tabor Grand at Leadville, the fanciest opera house, according to Harp's girls, between Dallas and San Francisco. They wouldn't miss it for the world. If your gal is traveling with Yorrick Harp, she'll show up at the Tabor Grand within the week. I'd bet my life on it."

"What's in this place called Leadville that warrants an opera house?" Stephen asked.

Cody smiled. "Silver. Tons of it. But that doesn't concern you. That's where I'd go if I wanted to meet up with Yorrick Harp. Would you agree, Virge?"

Stephen looked back in time to see Virge nod broadly. "Leadville," he repeated. "A sight to see in itself. The Atchison, Topeka and Santa Fe will take you right into Denver, two days, three if you hit snow. Leadville's just a holler away once you get there. Lots of stages coming and going."

"What's the name of the opera house," Stephen asked.

"The Tabor Grand," Cody replied.

"More than one in Leadville?"

Cody Tanner grinned. "Just the one, and once you've seen it I think you'll agree that one is all they need."

Then his decision was made. Stephen walked to the window and looked out at the cool clear crisp Santa Fe evening and dared to think that perhaps his long search was coming to an end. One more train ride, one more town, one more theater and perhaps he'd find her.

He rested his forehead against the cold window glass and closed his eyes and prayed that it would be so.

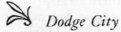 *Dodge City*

In a state of apprehension, Violet waited behind the kitchen door and peered out at the two men at the fireplace who had just come down for breakfast. She glanced toward the front door, praying that Yorrick Harp would come at any moment with news of their scheduled departure from this awful place.

Violet eased closer and sipped at the mug of steaming coffee that Ling-Three had just handed her. Eve was supposed to have been standing here waiting for Yorrick's word, but Violet had tried to awaken her twice in the second floor dormitory and twice had been unable to arouse her from what apparently was a deep sleep. Let her rest; that had been Violet's decision.

As for the other women of the troupe, they were packing, preparing to leave, disappointed that the two men downstairs had ruined their engagement here. Still all were eager to move on to Denver and Leadville and were now waiting for Yorrick, who had gone to the railway station to purchase their tickets to Denver.

Behind her in the kitchen she saw Ling-Three hurrying to put the finishing touches to two heaped breakfast platters. Violet held the door for him as he staggered forward under the weight of an incredible amount of food: eggs, sausage, bacon, corn rolls—

As she was surveying the bounteous platters, she heard the front door open and saw Yorrick Harp, his billowing black cape swirling in with the cold wind.

Halfway across the large saloon she saw Yorrick glance toward the fireplace as though someone had called to him. Puzzled, she leaned farther out from the kitchen and saw the man in the gray bowler hat motion for him to come close.

Yorrick declined with a polite smile and indicated he had more pressing duties, whereupon one of the men on the opposite side of the saloon came up behind Yorrick and forcibly assisted him toward the two men at the fireplace.

Violet held her breath, wishing that Eve were here. Eve always seemed to know what to do. Now Violet saw the two at the fireplace placidly eating breakfast as they spoke, the one in the gray bowler smiling, which Violet took as a good sign until she heard Yorrick's protest, "No, impossible, absolutely impossible, out of the question. We were told that the Varieties Saloon was otherwise engaged, and now we have made new plans."

The louder Yorrick's voice rose, the softer the man in the gray bowler seemed to speak. At the same time three more gunmen from the opposite side of the saloon joined their colleagues, until at last Yorrick Harp was again surrounded by drawn guns.

Violet saw Yorrick's head bow, saw him reluctantly hand over to the man in the bowler what appeared to be railway tickets.

Everyone was smiling now, even Yorrick, though his was a smile without warmth, and as he at last turned away from the confrontation, Violet thought she had never seen him look so defeated. As he started toward her, he turned down the high collar of his cape and steered her steadily into the kitchen and closed the door.

"Are you all right?" she whispered. "When do we leave?"

"Where's Eve?"

"Sleeping."

"Awaken her."

"Why? She—"

"I said awaken her. Now!"

As he delivered this last word in his best bellowing command, Violet retreated as far as the steps. "I'm sure she's awake now. I'll get her."

"I'm sorry for shouting," Yorrick apologized and sat heavily on the edge of a near table. "They—demand now that we stay. They want a performance this evening. They want Eve to sing."

Violet frowned at the bizarre request. "How did they—"

"Masterson heard her singing last night, in her bath, apparently. He wants to hear more."

Violet listened closely. "Don't worry, Yorrick. Eve will sing for them, and then tomorrow at the latest we will be on our way to Denver. It's only a slight delay. I'll go and fetch her."

But as she started up the steps, she heard a commotion coming from the dormitory, saw several ladies running toward her, all talking at once, all very agitated. When they saw her, Mother called out, "Violet, come quick. Something awful. It's Eve."

Violet had just started up the steps when suddenly Yorrick pushed past her. She reached the top of the stairs behind him and saw a most fearful sight, Eve in her white nightshirt, sprawled facedown on the floor not three steps from her cot.

As Yorrick scooped her up in his arms, Violet listened to a splintered account from the ladies.

"She awakened—"

"—and asked why it was so hot."

"I went to get her some water, but when I got back—"

"She tried to get out of bed—"

"She just fell. We tried to—"

"It's all right," Violet soothed, trying to still her own pounding heart. She saw Yorrick carry Eve back to the low cot and place her gently down. "She's on fire," he murmured, covering her forehead with his massive hand. "Listen."

At his command, the dormitory room fell silent and all heard the labored breathing, the telltale wheezing. Violet was the only witness to the look of despair on Yorrick's face as he bent over Eve. Then suddenly he was on his feet shouting orders, "Cold cloths, all over her body, keep her cool. I'll be back in a minute."

As he ran toward the top of the steps, the women scattered. At the landing he called back, "Violet, don't leave her. Do you hear me? Do not leave her."

Violet was amazed that he would even feel the need to issue such an order. Of course she had no intention of leaving her. "Come, ladies, to work. Fetch a pitcher of water, Rose. The rest of you, give her air, stand back."

After having mobilized the entire room, Violet felt herself strangely without a task. She sat on the edge of the cot and looked at Eve and found the sight distressing.

"Oh my dearest," Violet grieved and touched Eve's hands and felt them as hot as though she'd touched a live ember. The rain yesterday, the wet clothes, the fatigue had all conspired against her.

Then Violet saw Rose just climbing the stairs, a filled pitcher of water in her hand.

"Will she—I mean is she—"

"Of course she will," Violet snapped in an attempt to discourage the bleak incoherence. "Come on now, you heard what Yorrick said. Let's keep her cool."

As Rose and Marigold drew down Eve's nightshirt, Violet dipped a clean cloth into cool water and placed it on her forehead.

The sudden change in temperature elicited no response. The only change that Violet could discern was that Eve's breathing now could scarcely be heard at all.

* * *

Dr. Timothy Costley, Dodge's leading physician—Dodge's only physician—looked down at the young girl and thought what waste for such beauty to die so young. And she *was* dead, he was certain of that, or would be soon despite the affection he felt coming from her friends, particularly from the weird geezer in the black cape who stood at the foot of her bed, his head uplifted, lips moving as though in continuous prayer.

"Double pneumonia, I fear," Dr. Costley announced and knew he had to say little more.

Behind him he was aware of weeping and wished he could say something to ease their tears. He looked over his shoulder and saw the man named Ram Towse, the one who had come to fetch him. He stood at the top of the steps, weeping openly. Obviously the young girl had been beloved by all. Too bad. Wasn't it always so? The good go first; the selfish and self-centered always seem to find the key to survival.

Dr. Costley tried to monitor his thoughts as he fished through his black bag in search of a placebo, something to make the witnesses feel better, something to make *him* feel better, something that would have absolutely no effect on the inevitable end result of this ravaging illness.

Near the bottom of his bag he found a small vial of camphor. The odor was strong, medicinal, though impotent when pitted against the poisonous fluids filling both her lungs and slowly suffocating her.

"Here." He smiled and offered the vial to a small dark-haired woman who was kneeling on the opposite side of the cot, her eyes filled with tears.

As she took the vial, he tried to respond to her bewildered expression. "Let her breathe it. Sometimes it helps."

He shrugged and knew that everyone knew the truth, that she would not survive through the night, that come morning there would be a brief funeral, a fresh grave in Boot Hill and life would go on.

Though he was in his mid-forties, having practiced here for fifteen years, one simple fact never ceased to amaze Dr. Costley: that no matter what, no matter how harsh the injury, how brutal the slash, how deep the bullet wound, how repulsive the atrocity, how premature the birth, how deep the grief, how senseless the persistence, life and the living *did* go on. He had come to view it as a kind of irrational solution to an irrational problem.

Behind him he heard a familiar step, heard the women move back and looked over his shoulder to see Bat Masterson drawing near, his gray bowler in his hand.

"Will she survive?" Masterson asked, looking down at the young girl.

Dr. Costley shook his head. "No, I'm afraid not, sir."

"Too bad. She sang like an angel. See her to the end, Costley. You'll be paid, as I'm sure you know."

Then Masterson disappeared back down the steps, and Dr. Costley drew a chair close and settled in, waiting for the end.

It wouldn't be long. He was certain of that. Her lips were already beginning to turn blue.

The weeping had started again. The women huddled together in their grief. The giant was at prayer. Mumbo-jumbo, in Dr. Costley's opinion. But if it helped, let them have it.

Costley was a man of science and knew better, knew that poisonous fluids filling both lungs meant death, and that was that and there was nothing that anyone on earth could do to alter it.

* * *

For three days and three nights Violet did not leave Eve's bedside. Others came and went—Dr. Costley, Yorrick Harp, even Mr. Masterson. But Violet remained steady at her side, though she dozed occasionally on the pallet she'd made on the floor.

Why life was persisting was beyond Dr. Costley. He said he'd never seen anything like it, a fever raging this long, fluid building, not getting worse, not getting better.

Yorrick Harp stood at the foot of the bed, his face lined with new worry. Now he looked at the doctor as though there was something he wasn't telling them. "Doctor, this is clearly a battlefield, isn't it?"

Dr. Costley looked up. "I—don't understand."

"I know you don't, and I just this minute realized your stupidity could cost us more than we are willing to pay."

"Sir, I beg your—"

"There are conflicting forces at war over the possession of that girl's soul. Is that correct?"

Violet looked up, amazed at what he was saying.

"Answer me, physician," Yorrick commanded. "This is a battle," and he pointed down at Eve, who appeared dead, her face chalk-white, her hair plastered in sweat against her forehead, no movement except for the scarcely discernible rise and fall of her breathing.

Suddenly, "Come," Yorrick ordered and strode past Dr. Costley to Eve's side, bent over and lifted her, sheet and all, ignoring the protestations of Dr. Costley.

"No, Mr. Harp, I won't permit it, I can't permit it. Mr. Masterson said I was responsible—"

"You!" Yorrick bellowed. "Who are you to be responsible for her? You are nothing to her, she is nothing to you. There must be affection and love with responsibility. Otherwise it becomes that most deadly of human motivations—duty."

He shuddered visibly and turned his back on Dr. Costley and addressed the women. "Come, we must hide her from those forces who seek to take her from us." He started toward the door. At the top of the steps, he turned back to Dr. Costley.

"Physician!" he shouted. "Is there a church in this hell hole?"

"No, I'm afraid not."

"I thought as much. No matter. Come, ladies, one god will serve as well as another."

Still grasping the lifeless Eve close to him, he led the way down the narrow steps, Violet directly behind him, through the baths and into Ling-Three's kitchen.

"Ling-Three?" Yorrick called out, moving directly to where the Chinaman stood, peeling potatoes.

"Would you be so good as to loan us your god for a brief period of time? There are forces in pursuit of this one, and we must get her into close proximity with a god, with any god. I've always admired yours. May we borrow him for a short while?"

A broad smile broke through Ling-Three's solemn moon face, and immediately he motioned for Yorrick to follow and led them through the kitchen and down a dark narrow corridor.

"Too many," he called back to the women, and Yorrick agreed.

"Wait here," he commanded, though to Violet he invited, "Come with us."

And she did, following them into a small room, stopping just inside the door, startled by what she saw.

There were Chinese red candles burning everywhere, hundreds of candles all leading stairstep fashion to a small altar, above which hung the portrait of a stern-faced oriental.

"Lao-tse." Yorrick smiled with warm familiarity and approached the altar with respect.

"Here," Ling-Three offered, pointing to a small couch. "Put lady here."

As he pushed the couch to a position before the altar, Yorrick carefully lowered Eve, covered her with the sheet and stood back.

"Taoism." He beamed.

Violet was aware of Ling-Three hurrying about into darkened corners of his temple room, doing something, she couldn't see what. Within a few minutes she began to smell something pungent and suspected incense, several sticks burning all at once, filling the small temple with the strong scent.

"Watch her," Yorrick commanded of Violet. "Stay close while I pay my respects."

As she took up a position directly beside the couch, she saw Yorrick in flickering candlelight approach the shrine, his head erect, his bearing straight.

He spoke directly to the portrait, while to one side Ling-Three grinned, pleased.

"The perfect man employs his mind as a mirror. It grasps nothing, it refuses nothing. It receives, but it does not keep."

Ling-Three's smile broadened. Yorrick spoke on. "What is light without dark, pain without pleasure, hunger without satiation." Then suddenly he lifted his arms to the shrine.

"No more words, Lao-tse. Give us the art and healing of silence. Win back this child of light for the benefit of a dark world. Remind us that those who know do not speak, and those who speak do not know."

Then he fell silent. He drew up a stool and sat slowly, and Ling-Three joined him on his right, both men facing the shrine, faces upturned, the incense growing thick and pungent about the room.

Self-consciously Violet looked toward the closed doors and wished briefly that she'd been left on the outside. But she hadn't. Yorrick had asked her to "attend Eve," and that she would do. She wasn't quite certain what had been accomplished by bringing her down to this small and private shrine.

One god will do as well as another—

She hoped so and settled on the floor beside the couch and took a close look at Eve's lifeless face. In an attempt to distract herself from her own grief, she concentrated on the flame of a single red candle, studied the way it dipped and danced under the whimsy of every passing breeze.

* * *

She must have fallen asleep, for the next thing she heard was a voice so soft, so near and weak.

"Violet . . ."

She pushed slowly up from the floor and looked about, trying to determine who had called to her. "Violet, where are you?"

She looked down at the couch. And saw Eve. Her eyes were open.

"Eve," she whispered, unable to believe what she was seeing, the girl pale but awake, her breathing easier.

"Eve," Violet said. Then, "Yorrick," she called out and saw him still seated before the shrine, in the same position, Ling-Three beside him.

He turned at her call, smiling as he saw Eve awake. "Our silence worked, my friend," he said to Ling-Three.

The three of them stared down at Eve, who returned their gazes with a puzzled expression. "Where am I?" she asked and held her hand up to Yorrick, who took it and kissed it and sat on the side of the couch.

"In a safe place, my pet. You've been on a long and difficult journey, but you're back now. When you're feeling stronger, you must tell us about it. News of the other world always makes for fascinating listening, don't you agree, Violet?"

For a moment Violet was incapable of agreeing to anything. She couldn't stop the tears of gratitude, yet she knew she must tell the others.

She kissed Eve's forehead and felt it blessedly cool. She looked up at Yorrick, still puzzled, "What—how did—"

But Yorrick smiled and dismissed her questions. "We did nothing. Opposites are always the essential elements of any game. The dark side of life has its integral part. The cards must be shuffled, thrown into chaos in order that there may be a significant development of the play. Now go and tell the others that Eve has returned."

* * *

Eve had no idea where she'd been and at first had no idea where she was, waking up in Ling-Three's shrine filled with red candles and the smell of incense.

But after four days of drinking Ling-Three's Chinese mystery tea, of enjoyable chats with Ling-Three, so named because once there had been a Ling-One and then a Ling-Two before him, after four days of trying a few steps across the room, she was beginning to feel stronger in every sense of the word, and bored.

At last on a bright cold Sunday morning, Yorrick Harp appeared in the doorway with a broad smile on his face, wearing his traveling cape and tall silk hat and holding something behind his back.

"We're free to go, according to Mr. Masterson, who is so very grateful for your recovery that he has sent Dr. Costley back to Chicago and has promised to allow Ling-Three to do more than feed his belly, and that, my pet, is what we might be tempted to call real progress."

Eve sat up on the side of the couch, trying to see what Yorrick was concealing from her. Then he held up a lovely autumn-colored wool traveling suit with buttoned jacket and warm fur collar.

"Put it on," he said. "We're leaving within the hour. Denver in two

days. No performances for you, however, until we reach Leadville, a
week from this evening. Then if you're feeling—"

"I feel fine."

"Then you'll sing in the Tabor Grand, the most elegant opera
house in all the west, the same stage on which Oscar Wilde has performed and Sarah Bernhardt and Lola Montez, and now—you."

She sat up, cross-legged, in the center of the mussed couch, tired of
inactivity, longing for the feel of a stage again, the lovely feeling of a
responding audience.

"Will you be ready, my pet, for the Tabor Grand?" Yorrick asked.

"I'm ready now," she said and left the couch on still wobbly legs
and approached old Yorrick without a hint of shyness and hugged
him about his great massive neck, exactly the way she used to hug her
father, and felt Yorrick hold still for her affection, then turn away and
gruffly order her to dress, though he sounded strange, sniffling as
though he had just caught cold.

 Leadville

Stephen had stopped in Denver only long enough to purchase
new clothes, a pair of boots and a heavy fleece-lined mackinaw in
protection against the biting wind he'd felt all the way up on the
train from Santa Fe.

He had considered sending a telegram to Burke and Mary Stanhope concerning his great luck, his change of fortune, telling them
that his search was almost over, success at hand.

But he'd changed his mind. Wait until Leadville, then send the
happiest telegram of all:

> Found Eve. She is well and with me. Home soon.
> Love, Stephen Eden

Now in an attempt to escape the spitting snow that had been falling all day in Leadville, Stephen sat in Phil Golding's saloon beneath
the Tabor Grand Opera House and looked out over the colorful
sights made more appealing by his own buoyant frame of mind.

Cody Tanner had been right. He'd never seen anything quite so
elegant in all of America as Leadville's Tabor Grand Opera House.
One of the pretty waiter girls had given him a complete tour earlier
in the day, had shown him the four-story building, plain red brick on
the outside but on the inside boasting the most modern of everything.

Seating eight hundred easily, the Tabor Grand was furnished with flowered carpets and patent opera house chairs upholstered in wine red plush. The ceilings were adorned with frescoed allegorical paintings, and the curtain alone cost one thousand dollars.

After a complete tour the pretty waiter girl had brought Stephen here to Phil Golding's saloon, "the neatest in Leadville," where tall-hatted theatergoers and opera fans could down a jolt or two of red-eye and play a hand of stud poker during the long intermissions.

Now at ten o'clock at night Stephen sat almost alone in the elegant saloon. The theater crowds had gone back up to see the last acts of *As You Like It*, starring Helena Modjeska. Stephen had considered joining them but had changed his mind. He wanted no man's thoughts, not even Shakespeare's, to interfere with his own on this evening.

When he'd first arrived from Denver by stage earlier in the day, he had established everything he wanted to know from the ticket seller behind the gilt booth inside the Tabor Grand Opera House. Yes, Yorrick Harp and his all-female troupe were scheduled to arrive day after tomorrow. They were to play five performances in Leadville. Yes, there were tickets available for all five performances.

Stephen closed his eyes and downed a shot of whiskey and smiled, recalling his joy at that moment, defeat transformed into victory. Eve soon.

"Refill?" the man behind the bar inquired, smiling.

Stephen hesitated. Why not? He had until day after tomorrow, a mere two days, though they loomed before him as endless as two centuries.

"Please," he agreed.

"You're new here," the barkeep commented, refilling Stephen's glass.

Stephen said he was.

"Where from?" the barkeep asked. "Don't mean to pry none," he added.

"No, it's all right," Stephen said. "Are you Phil Golding?"

The man shook his head. "Naw, Golding owns the place. I work for him. My name's Dick Crawford. This is my domain," and he gestured to the elegant, well-stocked bar.

"Not a bad domain," Stephen commented and sipped at his refill and found it several cuts above the usual red-eye he'd found in other bars.

"Nothing but the best for Tabor Grand customers," Dick Crawford said. "On clear orders from Mr. Tabor himself. You here to mine?"

"No. My name is Stephen Eden. I'm from North Devon in England and I'm waiting for someone."

Apparently it took Dick Crawford a time to digest all this information. He repeated the one point that seemed to interest him the most. "England?" The light of recognition dawned on his face. "There was a man, an Englishman, here not too far back, named Wilde, Oscar Wilde. You know him? Fancied himself a poet, though a bit foppish, he was. He could drink though."

Stephen had heard the name, little else. "No, I'm sorry."

"Claims he was a genius. But you couldn't tell it by the poetry he gave us."

"What did he give you?"

"A pain in the ass and a lecture on the practical 'Application of the Aesthetic Theory to Exterior and Interior House Decoration.'"

Stephen laughed and downed his drink and decided it was better talking than brooding. Time seemed to pass faster.

"Another?" Dick Crawford urged and held the bottle up, waiting for Stephen's signal. He gave it.

"And who is it you're waiting for?" He stopped pouring and looked apologetic. "I'm sorry if I ask too many questions."

But Stephen reassured him it was all right, all the while debating how much to tell him, how much to keep to himself.

After three more drinks he ended up telling Dick Crawford everything, an earnest and lengthy tale that apparently held him spellbound from start to finish.

"Well, I'll be damned," Crawford muttered when Stephen reached the end of the story. "And you think she's traveling with Yorrick Harp?"

"We were told so, yes, by people who had seen her."

"Back in Mobile?"

"Yes, back in Mobile."

"That's a long way away. A lot could have happened."

"She's with them, I know."

"And you left your friend in El Paso?"

"Yes."

"I've been there. It's a hell hole. Give me the mountains any day."

For several minutes Dick Crawford was silent, clearly trying to digest all aspects of his tale.

"I know Yorrick Harp," he said at last.

"Tell me about him."

Crawford shrugged. "What's to tell? He herds those girls of his all over the country and keeps them on a short leash and tells 'em where to sit and where to stand and they seem to love him for it."

"Is he—I mean, does he—"

Dick Crawford looked up at his incoherency and slowly understood. "No, no, I don't think so. He treats 'em good, real good. He just never lets 'em forget who's in charge. And they're talented, his girls are. Always a favorite here. Our miners appreciate a pretty face more than they appreciate fancy words and poetry." He looked up at the ceiling, where in the theater above Shakespeare was going on.

"No, they'll all come down out of the hills for Harp's gals, mark my word. This saloon will be packed."

Stephen studied his empty glass and considered having another and changed his mind. His head was beginning to feel heavy. A brisk walk through the high cold mountain air back to his boardinghouse would put him to rights, and then he would pass the night beneath the feather comforter dreaming of Eve.

"Calling it a night?" Crawford called out from the end of the bar where he'd gone to wait on two men who'd just come in.

Stephen waved. "See you tomorrow," he called back and pointed toward the coins he'd left on the bar.

As he passed the men at the bar, he overheard one say, "Bad storm coming . . ."

"Good night," Dick Crawford called out.

Stephen drew on his heavy mackinaw and turned the collar up and pushed open the doors of the saloon and stepped out into a field of swirling white, the snow yet increasing, obliterating everything across the street. He bowed his head and kept close to the side of the building and in this manner felt his way back to his boardinghouse a block away, grateful for only one thing, that the storm had come now, in plenty of time to blow itself out so that the day after tomorrow would dawn clear. For he intended to be at the stagecoach terminal two blocks away early that morning, to check thoroughly on every stage from Denver until at last he found the one he was looking for, found Eve and took her in his arms and held her close with no plans of letting her go again in his lifetime.

 Denver

Eve had never seen anything so beautiful in her life. From the window of her room on the second floor of the Brown Palace Hotel, she stared down at a dazzling winter scene, one she'd never seen before, of snow and ice sparkling, coating everything in a brilliant high noon December sun.

Still weakened by her recent illness and forbidden by Yorrick to step so much as a foot out of the hotel, she was forced to watch the other women romping and throwing snowballs in the park across the busy street that fronted the Brown Palace. From time to time one would look up and wave at her, and she would wave longingly back.

"I don't see how it would hurt," she complained to Violet, who had kindly agreed to sit with her.

Patient as always, Violet looked up from her knitting. "Not hurt? And you not a week from getting up out of a death bed?"

"I wasn't dying."

"You certainly had us impressed."

Annoyed but unable to argue with Violet's love, Eve turned back to the window. It wasn't just the miraculous snow that had attracted her attention. She wanted to see all of Denver, the most beautiful city she'd ever seen, this hotel the most luxurious.

"Violet," Eve called softly back to the woman knitting peacefully before the small fire. "If I dress warmly, put on everything I have, please let me go down for ten minutes—only ten."

In answer to her heartfelt plea, Violet laughed, though it was a sweet sound of sympathy. "I can't, and you know that." She came up alongside Eve where she stood at the window, the light of a plan dawning on her face. "I'll tell you what. I'll get dressed and go down and bring up some snow for you. I can't believe you've never seen it."

"I haven't, I swear it," Eve confessed. "And will you? I'd be so grateful."

With a look of indulgence Violet placed her knitting on a table and started the endless task of dressing for the weather.

"I'll walk down to the front door with you," Eve volunteered and reached for her shawl and looked back to see the put-out expression on Violet's face.

"Well, what harm?" Eve protested. "I didn't say I was going outside, just to the lobby. I was there this morning for breakfast in the dining room, remember? Yorrick said nothing about staying in this room, just the hotel."

"You're supposed to rest this afternoon."

"I'll go to bed early tonight."

Even as Eve spoke, she knew Violet would give in. And she did with a resigned shake of her head.

"Come on, then, and tomorrow I'm going to ask Yorrick to let someone else watch you. You're impossible, worse than a child."

Delighted, Eve ran out into the broad handsome corridor and looked both ways, hoping to see someone. Anyone. She was hungry for chatter and people and movement.

"Come on, Violet, hurry, please. Don't lag."

As Eve lead the way down the corridor, she stared fascinated at the closed doors, one after another, all in a row, and wondered what was going on behind each door.

"Pull up your shawl around your throat," Violet scolded. "Yorrick wants you well for Leadville, and if you're not, it will be my neck."

At the top of the broad marble staircase that led down to the luxurious lobby, Eve stopped, fascinated by the sight of handsome men in tall hats and elegant women with bustles and fur capes. Everyone looked so confident.

"You wait here," Violet ordered. "I'll bring you back a snowball."

Eve agreed obediently and watched as Violet moved down the stairs and through the crowds onto the lower floor, heading toward the glass doors at the front of the hotel. She waited until Violet had slipped past the doorman and disappeared into the snowy street beyond. Then quickly she drew the shawl up about her head and ran down the steps and turned to the left, where earlier she'd spied a small side door. She just wanted to stand in the snow for a few moments, to touch it, to feel it on her face. How many times she'd read "The Snow Princess" to Christine, both of them trying hard to imagine what snow felt like.

As she spied the side door, she started toward it in eager anticipation when she saw a large carriage outside, saw a man pull open the carriage door. Though well bundled against the blowing snow, he was covered with ice. Eve saw him reach back and assist a woman. Wrapped in a beautiful long white ermine cape, she appeared frozen, snow caught in her hair, while behind her struggled a second woman, this one dressed in black, wearing a black cape, and she too assisted the man with the woman in white fur, the three of them struggling toward the side door of the Brown Palace.

"See to the horses," the man shouted back at the carriage as he pushed open the door. A strong gust of wind cut into the warmth of the hotel. Eve drew back for protection into a small alcove, and to her surprise saw the snow-covered threesome following after her, the two still assisting the woman, who looked ill and faint.

"Let her rest for a minute," the woman in black requested. "She must catch her breath."

Eve drew back as far as she could in an attempt to stay out of the way. But all at once the gentleman glanced directly at her.

"You! Are you a maid? Of course you are. Would you do me a favor? Go and fetch Mr. Merchant at the front desk. Tell him that Mr. and Mrs. Tabor have returned and must speak with him immediately."

Eve saw the poor woman looking quite ill and frozen and started off immediately across the crowded lobby toward the desk.

She located Mr. Merchant on the first request and got his attention when she told him that Mr. and Mrs. Tabor had returned and must see him immediately. A stricken look crossed his haughty face, and with one pointed finger he commanded Eve to lead him to them immediately.

She led the way back across the lobby, enjoying immensely her role as messenger in this drama, feeling once again to be in the flow of life and mystery. Finally she brought him to the small alcove where the lady apparently had partially revived, though her lips were still blue from cold and her hands were trembling.

"Mr. Tabor," Mr. Merchant gushed. "What happened?"

"Blizzard," the man said wearily.

"How far did you get?"

"Damn near to Leadville. The road bed was giving way on the last mile. An avalanche. Too risky. No one's going to be going in or out for a while. Ah, my dear," he said at last, looking toward Eve. "Here, for your trouble," and before she could protest, he reached into his coat pocket and handed her a large shiny silver dollar. He turned about immediately and commanded the woman in black, "Help me with her." Then to the woman he urged, "Come along, Baby Doe."

Together the three of them, including Mr. Merchant, assisted the woman in white ermine and gave her escort all the way up the broad staircase.

Eve followed after, wanting only to return the silver dollar to the gentleman. She'd not run the errand for money.

But at the top of the staircase she saw Violet cradling something in her shawl, saw her back out of the way as the woman in ermine and her attentive entourage passed by.

As Eve caught up, Violet whispered, "Do you know who that was?"

Eve shook her head and stared fascinated into the shawl filled with white fluffy snow.

"Mr. and Mrs. Tabor," Violet went on, her voice a reverential whisper. "He owns the opera house in Leadville where we'll be tomorrow."

Slowly Eve placed her tongue on the snow and shook her head. "No, I think not."

"What do you mean?"

"They couldn't get through—something about an avalanche. Oh, Violet, the snow is beautiful. Thank you. Here!" She grinned and handed Violet the silver dollar and imitated Mr. Tabor. "For your troubles."

She took the shawl filled with rapidly melting snow and started down the corridor toward her room. "Where's Yorrick?" she called back to Violet. "Perhaps you'd better tell him about the road and the blizzard. According to Mr. Tabor, no one is going in or coming out for several days."

Violet hurried down the steps as Eve gathered the shawl filled with snow and ran back to her room and placed the shawl on the table and discovered only cold water, the snow melted.

No matter. She went to the window, expecting to see the women still in the park below making snowmen and hurling snowballs. But she saw nothing except swirling whiteness, the storm obliterating everything, a curious sensation as though she were standing alone on an isolated pinnacle of warmth and dryness.

Apparently they wouldn't be going to Leadville. Apparently they wouldn't be going anyplace for a while. Suddenly tired, she drew a chair close to the window and stared out at the swirling wind-driven white world.

So far from home. She wrapped her hands, still cold from the snow, in a dry shawl and thought of summer's warmth, the ice pond on a hot afternoon, the long second-floor gallery of Stanhope Hall where she used to press her cheeks against the cool varnished wood, Sis Liz's mint lemonade, Mama's lavender water . . .

Did that place really exist or was it merely a figment of her imagination?

There was one other persistent fragment from the past. Stephen.

 *Leadville*

For six days the blizzard raged, the worst in over fifty years according to old-timers who could remember such things.

For six days Stephen stared despairingly out at the white world and knew what it meant, knew that he had lost track of her again. On the seventh day, when the storm still showed no signs of blowing itself out, he seriously doubted the wisdom of further pursuit.

A regular resident now of Phil Golding's saloon, Stephen had not tried to make it back to his lodgings since the third night, when two other men had left the saloon and never been seen or heard from again.

"Someone will find their bones come early spring, I'm afraid, halfway down the mountain," Dick Crawford had said and he urged Stephen to remain in the saloon, as a dozen other men were doing. More had come in last night, and Dick Crawford had managed to find warm blankets for them. There always seemed to be endless pots of hot coffee and good venison stew coming from the kitchen.

Stephen looked up from his corner near the back of the saloon and saw the poker game in progress again, four weathered miners who paid no attention to the storm and looked up from the cards only long enough to drink and eat.

On the far side of the saloon he saw the new arrivals from last night, a group of three who had stumbled in half-frozen and spent the better part of the early morning in hot baths.

And Dick Crawford was on duty as always, trying to keep the massive fire fed and everyone's spirits high.

"You, Eden, come on, breakfast," he shouted. Stephen waved back to let him know he had heard even if he didn't move right away. He sat up from his pallet and looked out the two broad windows flanking the door and saw the same unchanged white world, blowing snow, the street in front of the Tabor Grand one massive snowdrift, the mountain road down to Denver all but obliterated by avalanche, the telegraph lines down, no way in, no way out, no word in, no word out, nothing.

His bleak thoughts had the effect of literally beating him down. He stretched out on his pallet and looked up at the ceiling and tried to deal with his flagging spirits and tried to reach a decision on what he should do next. How long he would be trapped here he had no idea, and what would Yorrick Harp do after the blizzard ended? Would he wait for the road to be cleared and come on into Leadville? Or would he leave Denver immediately and make his way to San Francisco and the Gold Coast? The man was unpredictable. Stephen had learned nothing the last few months if not that.

"Drink this, and then I want you to come and meet one of the men who arrived last night."

He looked up at the voice, saw Dick Crawford, his normally pleasant face strangely sobered. In one hand he held a shot of whiskey and in the other a mug of coffee.

Stephen sat up and took the coffee and shook his head to the whiskey, puzzled by Dick's sober attitude. He looked toward the bar and saw a middle-aged man, gaunt, tired-appearing, undoubtedly one of the miners who had stumbled in last night, looking the worse for wear. Now Stephen was bewildered as to why Dick Crawford wanted him to meet the man and said as much.

"Who is it I'm meeting and why am I meeting him?"

Dick Crawford looked briefly up at the ceiling. "His name is Towse. Ram Towse. He saw your Eve in Dodge City only a few weeks ago." He bowed his head. "I'm sorry, Stephen, she's dead."

The last word seemed to hang forever on the still air. Stephen tried to repeat it and couldn't and had to settle for, "Dodge? Who is—what did you say his—"

"Come on," Crawford insisted. "He's willing to talk, and I think you must hear what he has to say."

Slowly Stephen looked toward the man at the bar, who returned his gaze with a sympathetic expression.

Then Stephen led the way across the saloon, Crawford directly behind him, ready with introductions. "Mr. Towse, this is Stephen Eden. Please tell him what you've told me."

They shook hands. Stephen peered closely at the man. Rough-cut, obviously he'd spent most of his life out of doors.

"You a friend of Miss Stanhope's?" Mr. Towse asked almost shyly, one hand brushing his still snow dampened flat-brimmed hat.

"I am," Stephen said, fighting off some inclination to despair. It could be a false rumor, the wrong person. "You saw her?"

"Oh, indeed, I did see the lady. I gave the gals escort all the way up from Abilene. Miss Stanhope rode in Mr. Harp's wagon. We had good talks together, she and me. Prettiest of 'em all, she was, with a voice like God's own angel—"

"Up from Abilene?" Stephen repeated, drawing closer, aware of Dick Crawford behind the bar, pouring another shot of whiskey.

"They were all sick, you see," Ram Towse went on, "and Miss Stanhope nursed them. And she sailed through that sickness just fine. And then Iron Adams let four of his men go 'cause old Harp needed trail hands, cause the ladies weren't very good at it and it was when we got to Dodge that Miss Stanhope took sick and Earp and Masterson was there and didn't like four strange guns in town and ordered us out. But she died that night, and I didn't want to stay around after that anyway. So I left to meet my partners here in Leadville, and we'd just started mining when the blizzard hit."

Stephen listened, frowning at the entire explanation. He glanced at Dick Crawford, whose expression was one of concerned sympathy.

"I'm sorry, Stephen," he muttered.

But Stephen wasn't certain what he'd heard, and what he understood had to be rapidly denied.

"The lady, Miss Stanhope, you say? What was her given name?"

"Eve."

"What did she look—"

"Long gold hair, the longest I've ever seen."

"She was ill?"

"Terrible."

"What?"

"I heard the doc tell Mr. Harp pneumonia, heard him say she was dead."

"Come on, Stephen, drink this," Crawford urged and shoved the double shot toward him.

But Stephen didn't want whiskey. He wanted to find something in the man's story to refute, some small detail previously overlooked that would signify to all that it was false identification.

"What was the name of the manager?" he challenged.

"Yorrick Harp. Weird duck."

"Where did the troupe originate?"

"How in the hell should I know? I joined them out of Abilene."

"Eve Stanhope?"

"The same."

Stephen tried to think of another safe question that would produce an answer that would bring him comfort. But he couldn't.

"Look, I'm sorry to be the bearer of bad news, I am. I was fond of her myself. She was a pleasure to watch, like God had sent us down this pretty gift to help us get through life."

Stephen walked slowly to the windows, past the poker game and the others huddled about the fire. He heard Dick Crawford call after him once, then heard only the crackle of the fire, the persistent whine of the blizzard beyond the window, an occasional slap of the cards and the laborious beating of his own heart as he struggled to digest the man's news, not certain whether to believe it, unable to find one good reason not to.

Several times during this long and frustrating journey he'd frequently worried that she might be dead. But he'd never played host to the thought for long. Now to hear it from someone else—

He leaned against the cold window and watched the chaos of tumbling, blowing, swirling snow and found the disruption of orderly nature a perfect reflection of his own thoughts.

Eve was dead.

He closed his eyes and pressed harder against the frozen glass. No matter which avenue of hope or despair he explored in any direction, he found that he could not move, could not plan a course of action.

It was as though at last exhaustion and grief had produced a paralysis and he was helpless in the throes of it.

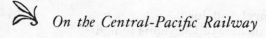

"Keep well under your lap robes, ladies," Yorrick Harp shouted out over the rattle of the railway coach. "With God's help, San Francisco in a week. But first a few one-nighters here on the Northern Route."

Violet, seated with Eve in the rear of the coach, tucked the heavy woolen lap robe about them both and looked out at the white landscape. The train was pulling a steep grade made doubly treacherous by the high snowdrifts on either side of the track. The storm was over here, though it had still been raging when they left Denver.

"You all right?" Violet whispered to Eve, who sat in the window seat staring out at the snow, still fascinated by it. From time to time Violet noticed a residual weakness in Eve, a tendency to do just as she was doing now, sit with her hands in her lap and stare into the distance as though she were seeing something that no one else could see.

Violet heard Rose ask Yorrick, "What stops are we making, Yorrick? And for how long?"

From the front of the coach Yorrick raised up. "Three in all," he said. "Cheyenne tonight, Granger the day after, and Promontory Point the day after that. I have sent advance word via telegraph. They are looking forward to welcoming us, and the audiences should be good."

Violet recognized all three stops. Though they were good-size settlements, the theaters were crude and cold, the audiences farmers mostly. Still at the end was the crown jewel, San Francisco.

"So you might break into your groups," she heard Yorrick advise, "and run a rehearsal. We owe them our best, as always, and I shall see that they get it."

Violet saw him turn to leave, then abruptly he stopped. He looked back over his shoulder toward the rear of the coach where they were sitting. Slowly, using the hand straps overhead for balance against the rocking train, he made his way down the aisle, his eye on Eve.

As he approached, he looked questioningly at Violet, who in turn shrugged. If he wanted information he would have to ask Eve.

He slipped into the empty seat in front of them and looked closely at her. "Are you still angry with me?" he asked gently and at last summoned Eve back from whatever horizon she'd been visiting.

"No."

"It was for your own good. You were very ill, whether you believe it or not. This is not suitable weather for someone recovering from pneumonia. How *do* you feel?" he asked.

"Fine," she replied, strangely subdued.

"Up to singing for the ranchers of Cheyenne tonight?"

"If you want me to."

Yorrick smiled. "Then rest," he advised and stood up and took a closer look at Eve, as though he saw a subtle change in her but was unable to identify it. "Watch after her, Violet," he said, a tone of love in his voice. To Eve he said, "You know where my coach is if you need to—"

He never finished, apparently saw no need to speak for she'd gone off again, gazing out the window, her face a calm mask, the only expression a slight sad smile.

Violet watched Yorrick as he made his way back down the railway car, stopping to chat along the way. She settled as comfortably as possible into the cushions in a sideways position, the better to keep her eye on Eve.

"Eve, what is it?" she murmured and reached across for her hand.

Startled, Eve looked at her. "I'm sorry. What did you say?"

"I asked if there was anything wrong. You looked so—"

Eve glanced out across the endless fields of snow. "I was thinking of Stephen."

"The one you were going to marry?"

"Yes. Sometimes I can go for hours without thinking of him. Then the memory of him comes back and he's so real—" She broke off and looked quite undone. "Oh, Violet, how long does it last? The hurt?"

Violet started to suggest that Eve should have been over it by now. But she didn't. Clearly this had been no ordinary attachment. "Tell me all about him," she suggested. "Tell me everything from the first time you saw him until the last. Please. I'd love to hear."

At first Eve looked at her with a disbelieving expression. Then it was clear that the invitation held great appeal for her as well.

She turned toward Violet, at last ignoring the snow outside the window. The two of them cuddled beneath the warm lap robe, and Eve began. "He came riding up our avenue of live oaks on a borrowed horse named Cicero, and he was the most beautiful man I have ever seen."

Violet listened with rapt attention for over two hours while Eve spilled her heart out in loving detail until Violet felt she knew this man named Stephen Eden, and more important, she had a new understanding of what Eve had lost, a deprivation of the heart from which she might never fully recover.

Several hours later Yorrick returned to give them instructions for getting off the train at Cheyenne. "And when you get to the hotel, rest. Performance at eight-thirty."

Violet saw him look again toward the rear of the coach and apparently was pleased by the sight of Eve in motion, reaching up for her hat box, safely emerged from her bleak mood. Violet waved at him and smiled in an attempt to signify that all was well, at least for the time being.

Of one thing Violet was certain. The bond of love that had existed between Eve and the gentleman named Stephen Eden was no ordinary bond, was made of richer stuff, not easily ignored and probably never forgotten, all of which meant simply that Eve Stanhope would suffer the pain of his loss all her life, in retrospective moments like train rides and just before she stepped onstage.

Violet looked up, suffering the weight of a new perception. Perhaps it was Eve's lost heart that helped to provide her audience with such pleasure.

* * *

Thomas Horan, editor and owner of the Cheyenne *Independent Daily*, wrote the following:

> Let us describe the central jewel in Yorrick Harp's crown of jewels known as the Adamless Eden Troupe.
>
> There she stands at center stage. She is of middle height, of slim form though rounded where Venus was rounded. Her complexion is as pure as marble, a pair of dangerously pretty blue eyes, a slightly Roman nose, a prettily formed mouth. Her long silken hair is brushed meticulously down her back and over her shoulders and resembles cascading gold.
>
> How sedate she looks as she stands there, head bowed, the stage barren of all decoration, all pretense stripped bare.
>
> Then she shows her little white hands by lifting one to the collar of her dress. See how simply her dress falls, simple blue, simple cut, simple elegance with its pinched waist to set off her flawless form. No wonder that a weary rancher would willingly pay—not one dollar, but all that he has in his purse for a glimpse of such female perfection. And all this before she opens her mouth in song. And then we know we will not have to wait until we cross the heavenly threshold to hear the sounds the angels make, for Grace and the kindness of God has sent one to stand among us and fill our ears and minds and hearts with the most beautiful sounds this side of heaven. . . .

Mr. Lewis Richardson, owner and editor of the Granger *Telegraph*, wrote the following:

> Eureka! We all exclaimed a day or two ago when we received word that Mr. Yorrick Harp was returning with his splendid Adamless Eden—All Female Theatrical Touring Troupe. The ladies are truly a favorite of this region and the day or two warning gave us all the priceless gift of anticipation. But, good Lord! And I must confess my pen is still shaking even as I write this sentence, none of us were fully prepared for the splendid addition to the troupe of a songbird who answers to the name of Miss Eve Stanhope.
>
> Centered on the bill, following the Nymphs of the Woodlands and Excerpts from Shakespeare, she takes the stage simply adorned, beautiful and graceful. The effect is unequaled. Some indulging god must put on a pleasing aspect to enable her to conquer the formidable enemy of three hundred strangers so advantageously.
>
> But conquer she does as surely as Napoleon conquered, gathering up our weary and distracted hearts in the palm of her pretty white hand and singing to us as our mothers once sang, our wives, and sisters, the epitomy of female grace and loveliness and purity.
>
> On dark nights, on distant ranges, many a rancher huddled cold about a campfire will close his eyes in search of something warm and pleasing and will find—her in their dreams. . . .

Mr. Wayne Mathison, reporter for the Promontory Point *Leader*, wrote the following:

> It was an auspicious evening in more ways than one, the opening of Brockwood's new theater saloon and the emergence of a stunning new star in Mr. Yorrick Harp's Adamless Eden.
>
> The auditorium departs from the conventional horseshoe pattern and is shaped rather like a funnel. It is so narrow that we, leaning out of one box, could almost shake hands with our opposite neighbors. The tableaus in which the ladies posed were wonderful, with a good addition being the Statue of Liberty, newly erected in New York Harbor and a gift to America from the citizens of France. Vive la France.
>
> Then suddenly the stage below went empty. The stage lamps flickered in the absence of movement.

Then quite unexpectedly a single young woman took the stage and in her stunning simplicity put to shame all of the barbaric red and yellow splashes of paint and bizarre Venuses and Psyches posing on the walls. The songbird called the Lark by some is wonderfully well ordered and marvelously beautiful, surpassing even the legendary Lily Langtry, whom this reporter has had the privilege of seeing on two different occasions.

This Lark is different. She sings without artifice, as though singing was her natural God-given state. The audience, wholly masculine, was captivated and refused to let her leave the stage until after two A.M., when Mr. Harp himself took the floor and placed a protective arm about the young lady's shoulders and led her from the stamping, applauding audience.

Even then it was after three A.M. before they could convince the audience that she would not be back and reluctantly they filed out into the early dawn cold and took up a steady vigil outside the Gaslight Hotel where she had gone to pass what was left of the night.

The following morning there were two hundred men at the railway station waiting to see her off with the rest of the troupe. Their next stop, San Francisco, and what a magnificent encounter that should be, the gifted Lark and the rich Gold Coast. . . .

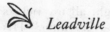 *Leadville*

It was three days after the blizzard ended before the mountain road leading into Denver was cleared sufficiently for a stage to pass over it.

Now as Ram Towse lined up to buy one of the first tickets, he had mixed and urgent motivation for doing so. Supplies, for one. Leadville had been stripped clean of everything while it was isolated from the rest of the world by the blizzard. His partners had gone back up to the mine, and Ram Towse had volunteered to go into Denver for supplies. He would return on the stage the following morning.

His second motivation for getting out of Leadville had been even more urgent. He felt a strong need to escape the constant questions of Stephen Eden, who had driven him to distraction during the blizzard. Isolated as they had been in the Tabor Grand Saloon, it had taken

Eden a full day to recover from the blow of Ram Towse's bad news, that Eve Stanhope had died in Dodge of pneumonia.

But then, in trying to deal with his grief, he had followed Ram Towse everywhere, begging for stories, for accounts, anything, no matter how small or insignificant, that he could recall regarding Eve Stanhope.

Ram Towse had damn near talked his lungs out. Of course he felt sorry for the lad, but now he had nothing more to say.

As he bought his stage ticket to Denver, he looked forward to a quiet morning's ride down the mountain, all thoughts of blizzards and lost time and Eve Stanhope and grief behind him.

He breathed a sigh of relief as he swung up into the coach and saw one seat left at the window, though his relief was short-lived as he heard a familiar voice call his name. "Mr. Towse, good to see you. I wanted to say good-bye. I had no idea you were leaving Leadville this morning."

He looked up to see Stephen Eden in the far corner, now standing, asking the man next to him if he would be so good as to change places, which the gentleman did, and before Ram Towse knew it, he was seated next to Stephen Eden as he'd been next to him for the last several days, facing another barrage of questions, all concerning Eve Stanhope.

Ram Towse tried to be courteous in spite of everything. "I didn't know you were leaving Leadville either."

Eden straightened himself in the seat. "Nothing to stay for," he said, and again Ram Towse heard the loss in his voice and regretted it.

"Going home?" Ram Towse asked.

"Back to Mobile for now, via Kansas City. Bought all my tickets from the station agent. I must tell her parents—everything." His voice fell, as though he were aware of how difficult that task would be, and again Ram Towse ached for him, but there wasn't a damn thing he could do about any of it.

"I'm glad for this opportunity to thank you," Stephen Eden said and extended his hand. "It will mean a great deal to her parents to have the information of an eyewitness. I had hoped—"

Then the stagecoach started forward with a lurch, and Ram Towse never heard precisely what it was that Eden hoped for. But he vowed to be patient with the lad during this trip, to repeat all he knew about the last days and hours of Eve Stanhope even though it pained him to do so. It was the least he could do for a young lad so far from home who had lost his love.

* * *

As the stage terminal and the Denver Railway Terminal were one and the same building, they disembarked from the coach together. Again Ram Towse felt talked out. But when a bitter cold wind cut into his face, when he was aware of his feet like blocks of ice from the long trip down the mountain, and when Stephen Eden pointed to a saloon that glowed a warm orange from a roaring fire just inside the terminal door and suggested a parting drink, his way of saying thank you, Ram Towse was hard put to find a reason to say no.

A few minutes later they both were settled before the fire, boots raised to the warmth, drinking good house whiskey. Now apparently it was Stephen Eden's turn to talk, telling Ram Towse the whole sad story from the moment of his departure in Southhampton, England, to his less than cordial reception at Stanhope Hall in Alabama, an endless narrative during which time the single drink of whiskey gave way to full bottles, all supplied by an obliging pretty waiter girl.

And Ram Towse listened intently to the compelling tale, the intimate detail of their first kiss, their plotted elopement, and he found himself enjoying the warmth of the saloon, the good whiskey and the earnest young face opposite him speaking of love.

Three hours later, talked out and quite drunk, Stephen slurred something about being tired and put his head down on the table and appeared to be fast asleep.

Ram Towse, faring better only because he could hold his whiskey, tried three times to rouse him. And couldn't. He looked about for assistance and saw only the crowded saloon, travelers arriving and departing, no one caring about a heartbroken young Englishman.

What to do? Ram Towse stared down at Stephen and again tried to rouse him with a good hard shake of his shoulder and couldn't, and considered just leaving him, and couldn't quite bring himself to do that either. At last he stood up and reached down for Stephen and dragged him to his feet and draped his arm about his shoulder and urged, "Come on, lad. I'll put you on your train for home. After that you're on your own."

Once on his feet, Stephen seemed partially to revive, enough to where he could walk with support from Ram Towse. As Towse paid the barkeep on his way out, he asked, "Trains for Kansas City?"

"Straight ahead. Can't miss. I was afraid your friend was having too much."

Ram Towse shifted Stephen's weight and left the saloon and looked straight ahead through a maze of railway tracks, trains going every which way, the loading platform crowded, the early evening wind cold and growing colder.

"Come on, lad," Ram Towse urged. "Not far now. Then you can

sleep it off in comfort until you hit Kansas City. My advice would be for you to return to your England and forget the pretty lass, though I won't be so foolish as to say you'll ever find another like her."

Ram Towse knew the boy wasn't listening, was beyond hearing, but it helped to talk as he lugged him toward the train. A few minutes later, out of breath, he came to a stop before the passenger coach.

Ram Towse renewed his grip on Stephen and looked down the platform and didn't see a conductor in sight. Well, nothing to do but get him safely on board and settled in a seat. Then, his duty dispatched, Ram Towse could see to his own business of provisions and return in the morning to the Leadville mine, where surely his fortune was awaiting him.

With considerable effort he maneuvered Stephen up the narrow stairs and into the railway coach, empty except for an old woman who appeared to be snoozing at the far end. As for proper seating, Stephen could sort that out with the conductor when they got underway.

Carefully Towse lowered the lad into a seat, lifted his feet until he was curled quite peaceful appearing in a deep sleep aided by an ocean of good whiskey.

"Good luck to you, lad," Ram Towse murmured and took a final look. Then with increased step he left the railway car and hurried back across the rapidly filling loading platform, heading toward the heart of Denver, where he'd purchase their needed supplies, and find a warm lodging house for the evening, find a full bottle and do as the lad had done, drink himself to sleep in defense against the misery of this world which never seemed to abate, but only got worse.

 Stanhope Hall

It was the letter from Paris, though Burke couldn't argue with the young man's apparent happiness, and it was his continuing worry over Eve, no word from Stephen, that now prompted him to take refuge from his silent house in the deeper silence of his study and write a letter to a friend in Washington, a powerful friend who would respond to the charges he would level in his letter by immediately dispatching a federal investigator to Mobile.

Charges! Burke stared down on his desk. What a strong word for such a weak action. But what else could he do? Could he point a finger at the guilty parties and charge them with murder, with kidnapping, with arson?

Of course not. He lacked evidence, he lacked clues, lacked—everything. So all he could do was inform his highly placed friend that the clandestine organization known as the Knights of the White Camellia, barred along with the Ku Klux Klan after the civil conflict from ever regrouping and taking action again, had indeed regrouped and were now taking heinous action.

Charge! Was that a charge? It sounded more like ladies' gossip in an afternoon salon. Still it was all Burke could do that even faintly resembled action, and in this agonizing waiting of almost four months for his life and his heart to mend, for his family to recover from the tragedies of August, he needed to take action, even if it was a weak and elusive one.

Letter written, he quickly reread it, signed it, addressed it and decided to take it in to Mobile himself. Perhaps it was futile, but at least he was moving, doing something.

As he stood up from his desk, he heard a footstep outside his study door, saw Mary passing in a hurry. A thought then occurred. Invite her to go with him into Mobile. The outing might do her good. "Mary?"

He waited, expecting to see her come back to the door. When she didn't, he called again and came around from behind his desk. "Mary, a word, please, if I may."

From the door he saw her continue on down the corridor as though she hadn't heard his call. At last she turned back, though the expression on her face alarmed him. She seemed distracted to the point of illness. "I can't find David," she said, hysteria rising. "I've looked everywhere. Oh, Burke, what if—I can't—"

Instantly he caught up with her and tried to draw her into his arms, all the while offering reassurance. "He's on the back gallery," he said calmly.

"No, I looked—oh, dear God, Burke."

Hurriedly he took her by the arm and led her, despite her protestations, back down the corridor to the rear gallery, where, pointing to the left, he saw David and Madame Germaine, both bent over a book, Madame Germaine reading, David looking bored as always.

At the sight of her son, Mary closed her eyes in relief and hurried down the gallery, scolding both Madame Germaine and David. "Why are you out here? It isn't safe. Madame, you know it isn't safe. How many times have I told you. Come, David, we'll continue your lessons in my rooms. There no one will see us or bother us or hurt us. Come, my dearest, you frightened me to death. If I lose you . . ."

Her voice trailed off, apparently unable to articulate such a nightmare. As the two hurried back past Burke, he saw the expression on

David's face, part plea for help, part helplessness against his own mother, for of late Mary had refused to let the boy out of her sight. For the last few weeks she'd even taken to sleeping on a small cot in David's bedchamber.

After Mary and David had passed him without a word, Burke looked back to see the stern countenance of Madame Germaine staring at him from the end of the gallery.

He started to speak to her, but what was there to say? She didn't need an explanation. She understood what was going on. Everyone understood. It was just that everybody lacked a solution.

Then go and post the letter to Washington. Set something in motion even though it was a weak something. And while he was in town he could check with the telegraph office, see if Stephen had sent word of his whereabouts.

In deepening anger and frustration at his own state of helplessness in the face of his changed family, he abruptly turned his back on Madame Germaine's relentless stare and started off at a fast pace toward the stables. He hoped that Cotton Man was up to a good hard ride, for Burke ached for the feeling of speed and movement, a sense of control over his own destiny.

It had been months since he'd known such feelings, and it was not good for a man to be without them for long.

 Aboard the Kansas-Pacific Railway

A lost number of hours later, Stephen heard a voice, insistent and loud directly above him, felt a hand on his shoulder, shaking him. "Come along, sir. I need your ticket. We're almost there. You've slept the whole trip, night and day. I've worked around you the best I could. But now—"

Stephen tried to elevate himself to a sitting position, tried to identify the voice speaking to him and saw through unfocused eyes the dark blue coat and hat of a train conductor. Where was he? The last conscious remembrance he had, he was sitting in a saloon in Denver with Ram Towse. How he got from there to a moving train, he had no idea, but—

"Ticket, sir, I need your ticket. Can you hear me?"

At last he found it and presented it to the conductor and allowed his throbbing head to rest against the cushions and closed his burning eyes.

"Wait a minute, something's wrong here," he heard the conductor say and found himself in total agreement. Something was wrong here and in the rest of the world. Eve was dead and Stephen could do nothing to deny or refute it. All he could do was try to accept it.

"Your ticket," the conductor went on.

"What about it?"

"It's wrong."

"What do you mean, wrong?"

"It's for Kansas City."

"Yes, that's right."

The conductor looked about as though for help, then said, "You're on your way to San Francisco."

"I—what? I don't—"

"You must have gotten on the wrong train."

Stephen looked out the window and saw verdant green farms. What had happened to the Rocky Mountains and snow? He had no idea.

"I'm—sorry," he said to the conductor and tried to say more. But the words wouldn't come and the throbbing in his head was increasing and all the people staring from the rest of the coach seemed to be burning holes in him and finally he bent over and covered his face with his hands and felt completely lost, going in the wrong direction, adding days of misery to this journey, postponing the dreaded announcement he must make at Stanhope Hall.

"You got yourself into quite a pickle, didn't you?" the conductor scolded. "Nothing to do but to ride on to San Francisco, then reticket back to Kansas City. You'd better pay more attention to your business from now on. You hear? This country isn't for going to sleep in."

Stephen listened, his hands still covering his face, knowing he should say something, apologize, but he felt bereft of words, of thought, of hope.

At some point the angry conductor stood up. "Devil rum. If you've sold your soul to it at this early age, then you're truly a lost man. And a dead one as well, you hear what I'm saying to you?"

The conductor made his way down the narrow aisle, though on two occasions he stopped and chatted with a passenger, then all looked back at Stephen with stares of condemnation.

He endured it. What choice did he have? He'd worked out in his own mind what had happened. He and Ram Towse had stopped in the saloon in Denver. He remembered that much, but he remembered nothing beyond. Obviously Ram Towse, thinking to be of service, had put him on the train, not knowing it was the wrong one.

No matter. He felt defeated by Fate and destiny. Hope had died with Eve. Now every moment was an endurance test, something to get through in order to make it to the next one, and then the next, a lifetime of such labor, and it mattered little where he passed this life sentence—here on this train, in England, anyplace, noplace—

"Here, young man, you must read this and heed its message."

He looked up at the sound of a hard female voice and saw a middle-aged woman, quite thin, with a sharp nose, staring down at him with joyless eyes. She was thrusting a pamphlet at him, and he took it and took as well her lecture and condemnation.

"What a sight you are," she murmured. "One that would break any mother's heart, your clothes smelling of brew. The devil's got a hold of you and you must shake him loose."

Then she was gone, taking her knife-sharp features with her, leaving him holding the small pamphlet.

He looked down and read—

> I stand for Prohibition
> The utter demolition
> Of all this curse and misery and woe;
> Complete extermination, entire annihilation,
> the saloon must go!

He read it twice, then placed it in the seat beside him. Despite the nature of the message, he found the words suitable to his mood. Annihilation, extermination, misery and woe.

Suddenly his grief vaulted and he leaned forward again in his seat and covered his face with his hands.

 San Francisco

Five hours later he found himself on the streets of San Francisco, lost as always. He'd reticketed back to Kansas City on the Central Pacific, but the train was not scheduled to leave for eight hours. He had left the railway station, hoping to find the ocean, a secluded beach, blue water, forceful waves. His head was still heavy and throbbing from the drink and his despair.

He'd thought he smelled saltwater and had followed his senses for several blocks, then had lost both the odor and his way in the crush of San Francisco traffic, the streets crowded with elegant carriages, all filled with laughing ladies and well-dressed gentlemen. There were shouts everywhere; vendors, cabbies, a sidewalk monkey that reminded him of Housy Dunbar and Mobile, which in turn reminded him of Stanhope Hall and Burke and Mary Stanhope, which in turn reminded him of Eve and suddenly he broke into a run as though to outrace his memory and collided awkwardly with a long line of people who shouted at him for his clumsiness and told him he must take his place at the rear of the line and to make certain that he did as he had been told, two large gentlemen gave him escort. As soon as they had resumed their places, he looked up and determined it was a theater, with a brightly lit marquee that read Alhambra Theater, San Francisco's Finest.

Just coming into sight on his left was a large theater poster. Curious as to the attraction that would draw such a large and prosperous-looking crowd, Stephen stepped out of the line and moved to a position directly in front of the poster and saw two words plainly printed that had been on his lips since he'd left Mobile:

Yorrick Harp

He stepped closer, stunned, the irony of the moment all but crushing him. At last he'd found them, Yorrick Harp's famous Adamless Eden All-Female theatrical troupe. And Eve was dead.

"Are you in line or not?" an impatient male voice called out.

"N-no," Stephen stammered. "I'm not in line." He moved nearer to the poster and read a list of female names, then in bolder print, he read, "The Lark," whatever that was.

He bowed his head before the poster and wondered if any purpose would be served by going around to the stage door, seeking an audience with some of the women, perhaps with Yorrick Harp himself. Could they tell him anything that he didn't already know? Could they tell him anything that would ease his grief, help him understand why Eve had been taken from him?

"Flowers, sir, for your lady?"

He looked away from the theater poster to see a bent, gray-haired old flower vendor. Her chin was covered with warts and whiskers and her lips were blue from the chill night air.

He found coins in his pocket and purchased a small bouquet of pink roses and hoped it meant a cup of hot tea for her later that night. He held the roses in his hand, feeling foolish, when suddenly a large wagon rattled up to the curb and he saw three flower merchants transporting enormous bouquets of flowers down a narrow side alley that led to the stage door.

He was curious, and with nothing better to do, he followed after the parade of elegant flowers. How would it hurt to look backstage? If he saw a friendly face, he'd make inquiry of the girl named Eve Stanhope. If he didn't, he'd leave immediately and go in search of the ocean. It mattered little to him one way or the other.

All he knew for certain was that he could not survive another account of her death.

 ## The Alhambra Theater

And still the flowers came, all for Eve. Violet had never seen so many flowers. Eve's opening last evening had been spectacular, a sold-out and most appreciative house, standing room only, all of San Francisco giving their hearts to the Lark, who in turn had sung hers out for them.

Now as Violet looked about at the crowded backstage area, a mere half-hour before curtain time, she saw Mother directing more flower deliveries toward the back wall.

"Over there, and be careful," she heard Mother scold, enjoying her close proximity to a celebrity the magnitude of Eve Stanhope.

Violet held her position a distance away. She longed to suggest that politeness cost nothing and served both the giver and the receiver.

"Watch out!" Mother bossed, "and as soon as you put them down, leave immediately. Do you hear me? No free show here for anyone."

Violet looked heavenward and was about to return to Eve's dressing room when she heard Mother's voice take a particularly cruel turn.

"Wait a minute! You! Just where do you think you're going dressed like that! This is a theater, not a saloon. Now get out before I call a policeman and he'll put you where you belong."

Violet looked back across the crowded stage area and saw a young man, quite disreputable-looking, in need of a shave though he carried a small bouquet of pink roses at an awkward angle and seemed shy and ill and so lost.

Before Mother's barrage of insults he retreated immediately. Violet felt sorry for him, some poor lost soul who had been transported by Eve's voice. She started off in the opposite direction toward the dressing rooms when suddenly she stopped, some vague and instinctive element of recognition dawning.

Someone very recently had described that young man's face to her in great and explicit detail. She looked quickly back and saw him disappearing through the stage door. She noticed that Mother had relieved him of the pink roses. Where had she heard of that face?

Without knowing why, she was running after him. She hurried

past the flower merchants, past the surprised look on Mother's face, until at last she stood on the darkened stoop of the stage door and saw him walking in a shuffling motion about thirty feet ahead, going into the night and the crowded street beyond.

Should she call? "You!"

She waited with held breath as he walked a few feet on and then at last turned, his face even more recognizable despite its present ruination. She *did* recognize him. She was certain of it. Someone had told her of this face, those eyes, that mouth—

As he walked slowly back, she felt suddenly self-conscious. As he stopped less than five feet in front of her, she knew she owed him an explanation. "I'm sorry. I—thought I recognized you."

"I've never seen you."

"What's your name?"

"Eden. Stephen Eden."

Violet gasped. Of course. *Of course.* Then she remembered. Eve. The long and painful description on the train from Denver, Eve speaking endlessly, lovingly of this countenance, this man, this love.

"Oh, Mr. Eden, I can't—I can't believe it. You must come. Please."

"Did you know Eve?"

"Did I—know her? I know her still. Come, she must see you, she must—"

"But she's dead."

"Dead? No, come, please," and at that she reached out and grabbed his hand and dragged him back into the stage door, despite Mother's protests, despite everything. Midway across the backstage area she stopped, unable to propel him farther.

The other women apparently caught her sense of excitement and gathered close while she at last abandoned his hand, though gave him clear orders to "Wait! Wait right there. Don't move, promise me you will not move."

He looked so confused, so lost, but there was no time to explain, for now she ran as fast as she could toward the dressing room down the corridor, flung open the door and saw Eve seated at the dressing table, brushing her hair, saw her surprised reflection in the glass.

"What is it, Violet? Is something—"

But Violet smiled, scarcely able to contain the happiness she felt. "Come, quick, Eve. Hurry, I beg you to—"

"I'm not finished here."

"Yes, you are. Now *come, please!*"

At last, despite the bewildered expression on Eve's face, Violet saw her rise, saw her start toward the door, Violet in the lead, grabbing Eve's hand now as earlier she had grabbed Stephen's.

She led her to the end of the corridor, to the beginning of the backstage area, and then she knew her direction was no longer needed for she felt Eve pull away, saw her stop, stare intently across the crowded area which had miraculously cleared, no obstacle at all between herself and the stunned young man who now in turn caught sight of her and on whose face broke the light of a thousand suns, all grief lifting, replaced by disbelief at first, then briefly doubt, then confirmation as Eve took the first step, weeping openly, speaking his name, at first a whisper, then a call, then a cry that seemed to motivate both of them until at last they were moving toward each other, arms open and coming together in an embrace so close, so moving that Violet felt her own eyes fill with tears and let them brim over as the two of them were doing, Stephen's hand cupped about Eve's head, holding her close, his face a contortion of joy and weeping as he spoke her name over and over and over again.

For several long minutes nothing stirred in the backstage area. Even the stagehands watched, as though they sensed something special taking place.

At some point Violet was aware of Yorrick Harp at her elbow. "And who is that?" he whispered, nodding toward the two who continued to hold each other.

Violet smiled with pride. "That's her young man. Stephen Eden."

Yorrick seemed surprised. "So he caught up with her at last."

Violet looked up at him. "You knew he was following us?"

"No, I just knew he would be a fool not to." He looked amused for a moment. "I wonder what took him so long."

Then Yorrick Harp watched in silence along with Violet and all the others as at last the embrace altered, at least to the extent that now they appeared to be studying each other, Eve gently tracing her finger down the side of his jaw until he captured the exploring hand and kissed it and again enclosed her in an embrace of such strength and duration as to suggest to all those watching eyes that he intended never to let her go.

* * *

Eve, in a state of shock, clung to him, though now and then she felt compelled to see his face, to make certain that this was not a dream. For she had dreamed of him so often, only to awaken to an empty room.

Then she heard Yorrick Harp, saying, "Come, both of you," and felt his arm around them, leading them into her dressing room.

"You need privacy," he said from the door. "I'll move the Lark to the end of the bill. It will give you time to recover, will heighten the audience's anticipation."

Then he was gone, closing the door behind him. Eve looked up again into the face she'd carried with her in memory every day since she'd left Stanhope Hall.

"I can't—believe it," she whispered, still in his arms, content to stay there.

"Nor I. I was told you were dead."

"By whom?" she asked, shocked.

"A man I met in Leadville named Ram Towse."

"You were in Leadville? When?"

"A week ago. I can't remember—"

"Oh, my darling—"

Again he enclosed her in his arms and found her lips. Their kiss, the first real one, stirred sensations deep within her and she clung to him for breath and balance and gave thanks for his safe arrival, though he looked so tired.

At the end of the kiss she led him to the couch and sat with him and knew they each had endless tales to tell and that they might as well make a start, but the comfort of the couch was so appealing and how effortlessly she found her way into his arms again, found his lips, and decided words could wait, forever if need be.

Stephen was with her, they were together, and that was all that mattered, all that had ever mattered.

*   *   *

In her arms he lost track of time, his mind still trying to sort out the confusion of Eve dead, Eve not dead, Eve gloriously alive and responding to him as she had never responded before.

He knew they must talk soon, so much to ask, so much to tell, but for now all he wanted was to hold her close, to kiss her over and over again, to feel her close to him, a true resurrection that had left his heart soaring, his head spinning.

He heard a soft knock at the door and a woman's voice. "Eve, fifteen minutes. Will you be ready?"

She looked up at him, a radiant smile on her face, then answered the voice on the other side of the door. "Yes, Violet."

"Where are you going?" he asked, alarmed, and renewed his grip on her hands.

"Come on, I want you in the wings. Will you come?"

Of course he would, and he watched from the couch as she drew the hairbrush through her long hair and watched her adjust the collar of her gown and thought, she'd changed in certain ways, seemed older, more confident, and if it was possible, more beautiful. He'd never seen such beauty as that which caught his eye in the reflection of the oval mirror.

He stood up then and moved toward her, unable to permit the smallest distance to come between them. It could happen so fast, separation.

From outside the door came a male voice, slightly melodramatic. "Come, Eve, dearest. All of San Francisco is waiting, as I promised it would be. Bring your young Romeo with you. Perhaps he will inspire you to even greater heights, though I doubt if that is possible. Even if you sang with greater perfection, this world still would only be able to listen with imperfect ears. So bring him anyway, if for no other reason than to still the hearts of the rest of the ladies who are fluttering about like wounded butterflies, their hearts aflame with speculation."

At the end of this theatrical monologue and in answer to Stephen's bewildered expression, Eve laughed. "It's Yorrick. He's harmless. Come along. I will sing only for you this evening."

Stephen followed her out into the crowded wings, where he saw the women in their various garb from Shakespearean pantaloons to pastel gossamer gowns, all very pretty, all gaping at him.

Then before them was a giant of a man in a red satin cape and wavy gray beard and thick shock of white hair and somehow even before introductions, Stephen knew that he had at last found Yorrick Harp.

"Mr. Stephen Eden," the man said in a splendidly mellifluous voice that seemed to echo endlessly about the backstage area. "You must be warned. Eve's heart is no longer exclusively her own. Everyone standing about you enjoys a small portion of it, and that great mass of ladies and gentlemen beyond the curtain are waiting for what is left. I hope you were brought up in a loving and giving atmosphere, for I'm afraid you must share, and sharing comes easier to those who have been instructed in the art at an early age."

At first Stephen had no idea how to reply to this bombastic man who, while he appeared to be good-natured, also appeared to be quite serious.

Then he felt Eve close beside him. "I've kept a secret from you, Yorrick," she said with a smile. "I have two hearts, one of which has been exclusively reserved for Stephen Eden all my life."

She spoke these words for Stephen alone, and he derived strength from the sentiment and joy from the lips that had spoken it and rapture from the deep blue eyes gazing up at him.

Yorrick smiled. "For you, Eve, anything is possible. Now get on out there. Don't keep them waiting a moment longer. It is too cruel."

Stephen saw him gesture toward the immense stage, empty now save for one small stool. From beyond the closed curtains he heard the din of the very large audience, the crowds, the traffic jams in front of the Alhambra Theater, and realized they all were coming here.

"Come as close to the curtain's edge as you can," Eve whispered, taking his arm and leading him forward. Behind, he was aware of the rest of the women following after, was aware of Yorrick Harp taking up a position directly beside the burly curtain puller.

"Don't make a move, my good man, until I give you the word. We're dealing in magic from now on."

"Stay close," Eve whispered and reached up and kissed him. "Oh, Stephen, I was so afraid I had lost you."

He wanted to reply, but then she was gone, walking directly out onto the vast and empty stage, head down. He saw Yorrick Harp motioning for him to come close. As Stephen drew near, Yorrick murmured, "I envy you. If she has indeed given you her heart, you are without question the richest man on earth."

"I was afraid I wouldn't find her."

"I always knew you would."

Stephen was surprised by the man's confidence and started to ask how he was so certain, but then Yorrick Harp placed a finger to his lips. "She's ready." Stephen looked out to see Eve seated on the low stool, head bowed, saw Yorrick give the signal to the curtain puller, then saw the huge stage flooded with light as the curtain lifted, heard the audience, once restless, grow quiet.

Then he heard the first delicate tones of a violin, the melody, Stephen Foster, and within the moment other stringed instruments had joined in. Once through the central melody, the musical instruments receded into the background and Eve looked up.

With the first few bars Stephen closed his eyes and felt the wonder of the audience, of the ladies closing in around him. Her voice had changed as she had, deeper, fuller, richer, moving effortlessly from love ballads to camp songs to folksongs, the transitions impossible to determine, a seamless artistry, until at one point he forgot he was watching Eve and succumbed to the spell of the woman onstage and allowed her to take complete control of his mind and emotions, leading him effortlessly through the sorrows of a young lover, the grief of a widow, the wonder of a child, the joy of a mother, the repentance of a sinner, the rapture of a saint, song after song, story after story, world after world all presented by a voice that seemed capable of creating anything until at last she stopped, stepped back from her low stool, bowed her head and walked slowly off the stage.

It was the thunderous applause that shattered his mood; that, and

Eve's presence before him, her cheeks flushed, tiny jewels of perspiration on her forehead, her face uplifted and eager as a child for praise. "Did you like it? Stephen?"

Beyond words, aware of everyone watching him, well aware of his own incapacity to speak, all he could do was draw her close into his arms and hope that he could manage a degree of control.

But Yorrick Harp saved the day by reminding Eve that the applause was showing no signs of ceasing and that her presence was required onstage.

"I'll be back," she whispered, her eyes dancing. Stephen watched her walk onto the empty stage with such poise, such simple beauty, heard the audience on their feet now, saw the front of the stage lined with elaborate baskets of roses and orchids, the ushers having trouble keeping everyone in their seats.

But once she was center stage, Stephen saw her calm the audience by merely standing before them, head bowed. Then she waited patiently for everyone to return to their seats, and when that remarkable silence once again filled the theater, she lifted her head, no musical accompaniment this time, and though her voice was scarcely audible, he heard the haunting opening tones of the old English folk ballad "Greensleeves," and she was looking directly at him now, her voice, each tone crystal clear, the words so simple, the expression of love profoundly moving.

He heard sniffling behind him, saw Yorrick Harp withdraw a handkerchief. "She's never sung that before. That one is for you." Now he saw the same indisposition sweeping the audience, all held enthralled by the slim girl with long blond hair whom first he'd seen peering down at him in her summer chemise from the second-floor gallery of Stanhope Hall.

When the explosion of applause shook the theater again, a terrible thought occurred to Stephen. Why on earth, given her clear gifts, her growing reputation, her dazzling future, would Eve Stanhope ever want or consent to be his wife?

The thought hurt. The doubt almost destroyed him. He couldn't live without her, yet what right had he to deny her this rich future?

Behind him over the thunderous applause, he heard a woman's voice. "My name is Violet. I believe you brought these for Eve."

He turned to see the little dark-haired woman who had first dragged him back into the theater from the stage alley. In her hand she was carrying the small nosegay of pink roses he'd purchased from the old flower vendor outside the theater. Compared to the massive bouquets of flowers on stage, they looked so plain.

"Go on," Violet said. "Give them to her."

Stephen took the roses and thanked her and looked back out on-stage and watched Eve in her triumph and feared again that the moment he had found her, he might have lost her and this time for good.

*   *   *

Certain that everyone would understand, Eve, still stunned by the miracle that had occurred this evening, begged off going to the after-theater party at Bella Union and summoned her carriage. Still holding Stephen's hand and his bouquet of roses, she led him back down the alley, past waiting crowds of admirers and well-wishers and into the privacy of her carriage.

"We'll go back to my rooms at the hotel," she said.

"You could have gone to the party."

"No, I didn't want to go. Did you?"

"No, no, of course not."

She settled close beside him and wondered where the stiffness had come from, this new formality. Twice she started to speak and changed her mind. Perhaps he was only tired.

They drove in silence to the Crescent Hotel and went up to her rooms on the second floor, a comfortable suite that afforded a lovely view of San Francisco Bay.

"Are you hungry?" she asked as she closed the door. "They have a very good chef here."

She watched him go to the window, saw him shake his head to the offer of food, then saw him survey the furnishings of the large sitting room.

"Very pleasant," he said from the window.

She laughed and dropped her cloak on a chair, still worried about this peculiar change in him. "We've not always been so comfortable."

"Nor have I."

She looked up. "Stephen, what is it?"

"You sang beautifully."

"Thank you."

"The audience was most appreciative."

"They were kind."

"Are your receptions always this—warm?"

She moved carefully forward, not wanting to say the wrong thing, saddened that she had to be aware of saying the right and wrong thing.

"Sometimes less. It depends."

"On what?"

"Where we are playing."

"I don't understand."

She sat on the settee and leaned back, thinking that if she appeared at ease, he might relax as well.

"Sometimes we play in remote rural areas," she explained. "The ranchers, while appreciative, sit rather like small boys in Sunday school."

"Everyone can't be a sophisticate."

"I didn't say they could."

He turned his back on her and appeared to survey the night scene of San Francisco. The silence went on too long. For several minutes she was quite content just to study him, to match the reality of the man with the memory that had fed and sustained her for so long. The match was perfect, the reality even richer except for this new and awkward tension between them.

"Stephen, I—"

"Everyone was so worried—"

They both spoke at once, each canceling the other out.

Eve apologized. "I'm sorry. Stephen, come and sit down. Let's talk. You first. I want to hear everything. I think I need to hear everything. Then I'll talk and you can listen. Please, come and sit beside me."

She watched his face, disheartened by the hesitancy she saw there. She drew a deep breath and reached out for his hand and saw him sit a distance apart, stiffly, his hands on his knees in a strangely formal pose.

"It was terrible," he said by way of a beginning. "We all thought you had died in the fire."

And thereupon he commenced his tale, an account that lasted over an hour, during which time Eve never stirred, never altered her position except to weep softly when he told her of the death of Sis Liz, an incredible tale, Paris accompanying him, always a step behind Yorrick Harp, sometimes moving ahead, a few names that she instantly recognized, John Paul Grand, Ram Towse, others she'd never heard of before. About an hour and a half later he fell silent, then said, "I have tragic news. Your father sent word to us in El Paso of Christine's death."

Eve stared at him for a moment, her mind still reeling from all she had heard. Now Christine—dead. No.

Slowly she turned away and hid her face in the arm of the settee and wept openly and was only vaguely aware of his hands on her shoulders, turning her about to the comfort and shelter of his arms. She clung to him, still weeping, and tried to resurrect Christine's face in her memory.

Some time later, wept out, she rested her head on his shoulder and thought of Stanhope Hall. "Mama?" she inquired.

"Is well as far as I know. I haven't been in contact since El Paso."

"Where you left Paris?"

"Yes."

"Was he going to marry the girl named Marie?"

"I'm sure. By now he probably owns half of El Paso."

"Good for Paris."

"Are you better?" he asked, leaning close, some of the awkward tension gone along with the tears and the telling of his story.

She touched his face. "Thank you for coming for me. Some of the ladies tried to tell me that it would be for the best if I forgot you."

"And did you?"

"Never," she said with conviction.

"Now tell me what happened. Everything."

And she did, hesitating only briefly when she reached the nightmare of Jarmay Higgins's rape. For a moment she saw him look at her with an expression of acute pain, and again he reached for her and drew her close.

A few minutes later she went on and left nothing out, described John Paul Grand and his ranch and his grizzly collection, described the terrible illness of the ladies in Abilene, the wagon train to Dodge, her own illness there, Ram Towse's understandable confusion concerning her death, for Yorrick Harp had told him that the doctor had pronounced her dead, told Stephen every incident, every episode recounted in full until at last, exhausted, she looked beyond his shoulder and saw the first rosy streaks of dawn.

For several moments they sat, mutually exhausted, side by side. "What are you—"

"When will you—"

Again as they verbally collided, Stephen rose and went to the window. She watched him, tried to read his mood. He seemed to be growing more distant, and that frightened her.

"Stephen, what—"

"Do you enjoy being with Yorrick Harp's troupe?" he asked bluntly.

"Yes, I enjoy it very much."

"You are magnificent onstage."

"I sing for myself. Sometimes for Papa and Mama, sometimes for Sis Liz, always for you."

He looked at her, then again turned his back on her. For several moments Eve held her position by the settee. Perhaps he had come all this way only to find something he didn't like. Perhaps the women had been right. A raped woman was an undesirable one. Perhaps along the way, like Paris, he'd found someone else. Against the onslaught of these grim thoughts, and because she had to know, she said quietly, "Stephen, I love you. I have never ceased to love you. And if you still want me, I—"

Slowly he turned back to her. The sun, rising rapidly, obliterated his features. She moved around the couch in an effort to see him more clearly.

"I—you—shouldn't leave the troupe," he said haltingly. "I would have no right to ask you—"

Then at last she understood and went to him and took his hands, so relieved. "I wouldn't leave the troupe," she reassured him. "Not for a while. But I don't want to do this forever. Surely you know that. I want our home one day, our children, our life. I'm certain the time will come when I will be perfectly content to sing only lullabys."

She saw the relief and joy on his face and found her way back into his arms and clung to him and nestled deeper into that magic hollow between his jawline and his shoulder, and knew that there might be more auspicious moments in her life but never a happier one.

At that moment she heard a soft knock at the door, heard Yorrick Harp's generally booming voice strangely subdued though as melodramatic as ever. "Romeo and Juliet, your friar is here, bearing a large bottle of champagne and a larger weight of curiosity. May I enter?"

Eve looked up at Stephen with an expression of weary though loving indulgence. "I suspected he'd be around. Shall I let him in?"

"You'd better or he'll awaken the entire hotel."

She opened the door to find Yorrick leaning against the frame in a rakish pose. His black shiny top hat tilted down low over his forehead, his black cloak flung back, revealing a mussed shirtwaist that spoke of a long and rowdy party.

"My dearest Juliet," he said sadly. "Your admirers at the Bella Union were bereft by your absence. They sent this along with a loving warning, that if you are not present at their festivities on Christmas Eve, they will form a pact and commit mass suicide and the weight of all their souls will be on your conscience."

"Come on in, Yorrick," Eve invited wearily, knowing he would anyway.

She put the champagne on a near table and went immediately to Stephen, where she found his arm opened to her and she slipped beneath it effortlessly. Their alliance seemed to plunge Yorrick into deeper gloom. "I came by—what I mean to say is—I've made accommodations for you, Mr. Eden, in this hotel. Can't have you staying here. My girls have pristine reputations. They are my responsibility."

Amused, Eve listened and kept silent, rather enjoying seeing old Yorrick flustered and out of sorts.

"Did you get all your talking over with?" he asked, pacing nervously about the sitting room. "I can't imagine what more there would be to say. You talked the night away, and I trust it wasn't a waste of night."

"It wasn't, Yorrick," Eve reassured him. "Anything else?"

"Yes, of course. I—what I mean is—well, I was wondering—"

Suddenly even he became annoyed by his stammering. "Damn it, what I must know is, have I lost the rarest songbird I've ever had, or have I gained a young assistant?"

Eve glanced up at Stephen and decided to let him answer.

A moment later, "The latter," Stephen said, "though we are going to be married."

Eve closed her eyes in silent joy and heard Yorrick's cry of delight. "Married! How marvelous! We'll plan it all, the most magical of all human rituals. When? How soon?"

"Eve?"

She looked up to see Stephen waiting, apparently willing to let her make this decision. Quickly she thought. *December twenty-first, Christmas next week. Then New Year's. Not New Year's Eve, not the end of something. Then New Year's Day.* "We'll be married on New Year's morning, on the stage of the Alhambra Theater with all the ladies as my attendants."

Yorrick Harp looked heavenward with an expression of pure rapture on his face. "Perfect, perfect, it's perfect, isn't it, Mr. Eden? It will be a ceremony to remember, I can promise you that. Oh, my darlings." And suddenly he was upon them, enclosing them in his cape, an embrace of massive though sincere proportion.

He stayed a moment longer and focused all his attention on Eve. "I have no words to express my happiness for you, for both of you. I can only thank you, my dearest Eve, for the immense joy you have given to me, to all of us. And if this young man can give to you even a fraction of the joy you have given to others, then he is welcome among us, is blessed among us, and is from now on a member of our rare and unique family."

Clearly it was a blessing, and Eve was grateful and saw the two of them shaking hands.

"Now, I do hate to spoil things," Yorrick said abruptly, "but there is a performance tomorrow and the New Year is ten days away and I must, for all our sakes, insist upon decorum and propriety, without which we slip effortlessly back into the jungle, all progress lost. Come, lad, I have comfortable rooms for you, and in addition I have a matter of great urgency I would like to discuss with only you. Kiss your bride-to-be and no need to wish her happy dreams. Look at her face."

Then he was gone and Eve saw Stephen approach her slowly. "Are you certain?" he whispered as he embraced her.

She put her arms around him to complete the closeness and found his ear for a whispered message. "I know nothing else for certain except I must be with you until the day of my death."

She was ready for his kiss, more than ready with matching passion and felt his tongue warm inside her mouth and wondered why she had set so far a date. Ten days. A lifetime.

"Come, children, enough. Passion grows by being tempered. Denial makes the blood run hotter. Come."

Stephen started toward the door, then turned back. "I should send a telegraph to Stanhope Hall."

"Let me. Just a minute." Eve hurried to the desk and penned a short message and handed the notepaper to Stephen.

He read it and smiled. "I'll send it first thing tomorrow."

"Come, come," Yorrick Harp urged. "To bed, my pet. The magic you spin requires incredible energy. You may not know it, but I do. To bed, to sleep, perchance to dream, as I'm sure you will. Lovely dreams all too soon come true—"

Then they were gone, the door closed.

The first of January 1890. Ten days away. Could she wait? Slowly she stretched out on the settee and looked up at the high ornate ceiling and thought *Mrs. Stephen Eden*, thought the words over and over again, fell asleep thinking them.

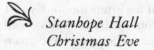 *Stanhope Hall*
Christmas Eve

Burke was aware of the incredible effort on the part of everyone to make this first painful holiday as normal as possible for David's sake, for everyone's sake.

Now he watched as old Ben fed another massive log into the fireplace in an attempt to dissipate the chill rainy dark December day. Behind Burke, working silently, were Mary and David, draping strings of popcorn and cranberries on the small fir that only that morning he and David had felled at the edge of Stanhope Woods. In the past the decorating of the tree had been a noisy laughing time, Eve curling strings of berries about her neck, Christine wrapped in warm blankets on the sofa before the fire, calling out directions to everyone in her sweet voice.

Without warning Burke felt a pain of loss that could not be endured and bent low over his glass of port, his eyes closed, and waited until the pain eased.

Behind, he heard Mary instructing David to keep the strings away from the candles. Her voice was low, almost a whisper, with none of its usual vibrancy and color. If David even gave a response, Burke did not hear it.

To one side on the big round table, he saw a lavish display of Christmas treats, the handiwork of the new cook. Taylor Quitman had told him of Mrs. Winegar's involvement with the Knights of the White Camellia, and Burke had dismissed her immediately and hired in her place a little Frenchwoman named Estelle, a long-time friend of Madame Germaine's. She had proved herself to be an artist in the kitchen, and now the Christmas Eve table was a picture of yule cakes and candies, fruit meats, spiced nuts and a steaming wassail bowl with sprigs of holly tucked about the silver footing.

There was only one problem. No one had gone near the table. David had invited Cleo and Casey to come, but as yet they had not appeared. Madame Germaine was always present at the Christmas Eve party, but now she was nowhere to be found. It was as though all knew that sadness and loss would be present in the Stanhope parlor this year, and no one wanted any part of it.

Burke drew a deep breath and drained his glass of port and hoped it would fortify him against the chill outside as well as the one inside. "It's perfect," he said, turning to face the two decorating the tree. "Quite the finest I've ever seen."

Mary looked at him as though doubtful.

David disagreed. "The tree last year, the one Eve found growing behind Fan Cottage, was much better, taller, fuller, everything. This one is too small."

Burke struggled against a new wave of despair that threatened to engulf him. "What do you think, Mary? You're our true expert."

She shook her head. "No, Christine always had the knack for judging trees. Remember she and Eve found the one last year together. Eve told me that Christine had guided her directly to the tree, said she'd dreamed about the location and there it was."

Mary's face lit up as she relived the memory of her two daughters, one lost, one dead, though for all Burke knew they both were dead by now.

Discouraged by the realization that the past was all that could bring a light to Mary's face, Burke retreated back to his chair before the fire, poured another glass of port and leaned back into the cushions. It didn't matter how hard they tried; the present was intolerable, the past unbearable, and as for the future, it was nonexistent.

The last word he'd had from Stephen Eden had been weeks ago. Burke could only assume that tragedy had struck again, knew the accounts that settlers brought back with them of the West, of marauding Indians, strange illnesses, drought, storms, a hard land, a harder life. How foolish Burke had been to send two boys, unarmed, both sheltered all their lives. How foolish.

Again he drained the port and refilled his glass and thought he heard the sound of a horse over the steady rain, listened closely and heard nothing but the silence of the room and of his heart.

"Burke, come," Mary called. "We need your height for the star. Will you help?"

He had just started out of his chair when he heard a knock at the door, saw old Ben leaning around the corner. "Mr. Quitman, it is. He says it's urgent." So Burke *had* heard a horse. Quitman? What did the man want now? Burke had not seen him for weeks, wanted nothing more to do with him.

But as he saw Mary and David hurry toward the door, Burke followed after and felt the damp chill coming from the corridor and saw its source, the open front door beyond which he saw the gray cold wet December day.

"For God's sakes, close the door, Quitman," he shouted and approached the man, then stopped abruptly, appalled by what he saw.

Taylor Quitman looked half-dead, looked thin, unshaven, his clothes unspeakably dirty, eyes bloodshot. Now Burke saw him reach inside his pocket with a hand that trembled and withdraw a slightly damp brown envelope.

"A telegram," he said and smiled weakly. "I go by Moseman's office every day, sometimes twice a day to see if there are messages. Today there was this one."

He thrust the envelope toward Burke, who held his position, aware of the corridor filling with people, all those absent from the Christmas Eve festivities suddenly appearing for the bad news. And for some reason he knew it was bad news and looked helplessly back at Mary, who stood clinging to David, her arms wrapped tightly about him as though the power of the message might be capable of taking him from her.

Briefly Burke closed his eyes, but not to pray. He'd long since abandoned that futile ritual. There was no one in heaven interested in his loss or his grief, so why mouth empty words?

Without further hesitation he opened the envelope and read the message. Only three words long. He read it twice, then a third time and could not read it the fourth for the tears in his eyes.

"Burke, what is it?"

He was aware of Mary at his side and handed her the simple message, which said:

Coming home—
Eve

He heard Mary's cry of joy and reached for her and drew her close as the message moved down the corridor, passing from hand to hand, every reaction the same, first tears, then laughter, then more tears until at last the corridor was filled with life and movement and warmth and hope.

"When?" Mary asked, breaking free of his arms long enough to wipe at her eyes. "When? She doesn't say when she's coming?"

Burke grinned. "We'll wait for her. At least we know she's alive."

At that moment Cleo and Casey ran down the corridor toward David, who in turn shared the good news and excitedly invited them to "Come on into the parlor. You must see the Yule table, come."

And Madame Germaine was there, hugging Mary, and Mary returned the affection. "Tell Estelle the food looks so pretty. Have you seen it? Come, the fire is warm. You, too, Florence, wassail is waiting."

As the women retreated back down the corridor, Burke started to follow after them. He stopped and looked toward Taylor Quitman, who pushed open the front door as though he knew he wasn't wanted here.

"Taylor."

Burke stopped him just this side of the door. He approached slowly, trying to fight through the warring emotions of his heart. Finally he smiled and placed a forgiving arm around Quitman's wet and bowed shoulders. "Unless you have other plans, why don't you spend Christmas with us? Come to the parlor. We've wassail and good food. You're welcome to stay."

To his amazement, Taylor Quitman turned away and hid his face and wept like a child.

"Come, Taylor," Burke urged gently. "Eve's coming home. You brought us the message and I'm grateful. Come, it's Christmas and we all could do with a bit of warming."

At last, wiping at his eyes, Taylor rejoined him. Burke glanced the length of the corridor, saw Mary coming toward them, smiling. She took Taylor by the arm, and together the three of them walked into the warmth and gaiety and laughter of the parlor.

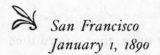 *San Francisco*
January 1, 1890

At 7:30 on the morning of January 1, 1890, after a sold-out performance the night before, Violet, her head covered by a shawl, slipped into the first balcony of the empty Alhambra Theater, her sense of anticipation almost unbearable, her happiness even greater.

What a beautiful and memorable day this was going to be, and she didn't want to miss a moment of it. She had promised Eve that she would meet her in the dressing rooms later and help her dress. The ceremony was scheduled for one o'clock in the afternoon.

But for now Violet wanted to see Yorrick work his special magic on that immense empty stage house, for he had promised Eve and Stephen that he would transform it into paradise.

Now Violet settled comfortably in one of the plush front row balcony seats and stared out and down over the semidark cavernous theater. Inside her pocket she reached for a hard roll she'd taken along with an apple as she passed the breakfast table in the Crescent Dining Room. She planned to be here in hiding all morning and to miss nothing, for Yorrick had kept his design secret for the last ten days, though he'd been in endless conferences with San Francisco's leading set designers and flower merchants.

Comfortably Violet settled back and munched her roll and thought about the remarkable Stephen Eden, how to the best of her knowledge the entire troupe of ladies had fallen in love with him.

A bit lovesick herself, Violet drew a pleasurable sigh and thought of the number of hours that Stephen Eden and Yorrick Harp had spent sequestered in Harp's office. "A surprise for the entire troupe, following the wedding," Yorrick Harp had announced with customary theatricality.

Suddenly on the stage below she saw the carbon arc lights come on, then saw a large shaft of sunlight flooding the stage. She looked up toward the top of the stage house, a sky light, she'd never noticed before.

A few moments later she saw an army of workmen pour onto the stage. At the rear of the stage house, she saw men attaching a cyclorama to a large rod that followed the curve of the stage house. A short time later the rod was hoisted high into the air and a lovely pale blue silk cyclorama filled the back of the stage. Here and there she noticed white puffy clouds that had been handpainted by a consummate artist.

Then she saw Yorrick just emerging from the orchestra pit, a black coat thrown dramatically over his shoulders, a large notebook opened in his hand as he shouted orders toward the men and gestured broadly toward stage left. At that moment an immense flat wagon painted to resemble white marble was dragged onstage. Next Violet saw columns, huge, Greek, again painted to resemble white marble, carried in and placed upright in fitted holes that had been cut into the wagon.

Next she saw a domed top with elaborately carved border frieze lowered carefully onto the column. The center of the dome had been removed, thus permitting the natural shaft of light from the skylight to spill directly down onto the marble floor.

After three hours of labor the workmen stood back, all peering nervously toward Yorrick Harp, who stood downstage, carefully studying his design.

"Gentlemen, behold the Temple of Aphrodite," he proclaimed, arms spread wide. "Goddess of love and beauty. It is perfection."

And it was. Violet had never seen anything so beautiful, the blue sky, the pristine white Greek temple, the dazzling shaft of brilliant sun spilling onto the temple floor, clearly the spot where the bride and groom would stand.

And while she had not yet looked her fill at the temple, flower merchants arrived, dozens of them, carrying in topiary trees of pink and white roses, a veritable forest of roses, the taller ones placed in a border against the blue sky, the shorter ones lining the white satin path that had just been unfurled and that led from the steps of the Greek temple to stage left, where Eve would make her entrance.

Violet closed her eyes to rest them from the excess of beauty and smelled the perfume of roses already wafting up to the balcony. Onstage the scent would be intoxicating.

Through it all Yorrick watched and corrected and grew angry and placid and instructive and pleased. At last he stood on the edge of the stage and looked out over his handiwork and quickly shook hands with the two men nearest him and bowed formally to the workmen as they, too, took a final exhausted look, for it was nearing twelve noon and they had been working since eight o'clock.

Then, alone, Violet saw Yorrick walk slowly across the stage, checking, adjusting the cyclorama, testing the steps leading up to the Greek temple, standing for a moment in the shaft of noon sun.

It was magnificent. Violet had never seen such a transformation. In no aspect did the stage resemble a stage. It was a page from a beautifully detailed Greek history book, the white marble temple gleaming like a jewel against the blue sky, the soft pink and white of roses lending color and scent.

Violet saw Yorrick turn full front, facing the theater. She ducked lower, not wanting to be discovered. From this crouched position she saw him descend the steps down to the orchestra pit, reemerge in the center aisle and walk slowly back until he stood directly beneath where she crouched in the first row of the balcony.

"Do you approve, Violet?" he asked very softly.

Startled, Violet made a face and wondered how he knew she was there, but then Yorrick knew everything. "Yes, it's beautiful, Yorrick," she said.

"My design, you know, every last bit of it."

"I know."

"Well, what are we standing about for? In less than an hour the miracle and mystery will commence, two trying against all odds to become one. I'll tend to the groom, you the bride. Hurry now. The sun will fall on the Temple of Aphrodite at just the proper angle at one o'clock sharp. Let's see if for once in the history of this world, man and nature can work in perfect accord."

"Yes, Yorrick."

As he disappeared under the balcony beneath her, she took a final look down on the dazzling stage and saw the pool of sunlight in the temple spreading. Yorrick was right. At one o'clock it would completely fill the temple, and Stephen and Eve would recite their vows bathed in sunlight.

* * *

Madame Simone of Paris and San Francisco had made Eve's wedding gown, and Violet, along with the other ladies of the troupe, stood by and watched, less than ten minutes before the ceremony started, as Madame did the final fluffing and straightening.

Made of ivory taffeta, the gown was cut straight in front, with alternating tiers of lace and satin insets, all drawn back into a five-tiered bustle, again of lace and satin inset, each bustle caught up with handmade white satin roses, a cascading effect culminating in a glorious train of alternating layers of white lace and white satin. The bodice was fitted, cut low to reveal her beautiful back and shoulders, the sleeves softly draped and caught up with white satin roses on each shoulder.

Rose had put Eve's hair up in a stylish chignon, with loose curls framing her face, real white roses caught beneath the curls. She would carry a single long-stemmed white rose.

It was a gown and a vision fit for the Temple of Aphrodite. Through all the primping and fluffing and straightening and adjusting, Eve stood, head bowed.

The other women looked lovely in their pale pink gowns and bouquets of roses. Beyond the stage, Violet heard the ladies in the orchestra warming up.

Then Yorrick Harp, looking quite distinguished in his good dress blacks, his shoes polished like mirrors, a single white rosebud in his lapel, appeared before them. He came directly to where Eve stood. Madame Simone saw him coming and moved back, as did all the women, sensing the privacy of this moment.

Yorrick circled Eve once, his face filled with a glowing look of love. He stopped directly in front of her and gazed down into her face for ever so long. Violet thought he would never speak.

Then he did. "I was traveling once in India years ago, and I was told there was a magic man in the neighborhood who could tell me my past as well as my future. I was young then and not wise and sought the man out. He told me my pride was my curse, had always been, that in the year eight hundred B.C. the gods had taken my beloved daughter away from me because I had challenged the heavens. He told me I would never be reunited with her until I repented."

He lightly touched Eve's face. "I don't remember having repented, but I think I'm reunited with her."

Eve looked up at him, and there was a special exchange between the two. As she leaned forward to kiss him, the women in the orchestra commenced the wedding march and the ceremony was underway.

* * *

Father Lourence Johnson of St. James Episcopal Church, resplendent in his gold and white brocade robes, performed the service and smiled with curious approval on the Temple of Aphrodite and took his place in the sunlight. Violet heard the wedding march commence and stood on the first step of the temple and saw Eve and Stephen step out onto the white satin carpet and knew if she lived to be one hundred, she'd never again witness such beauty.

Stephen was handsome in formal blacks, Eve on his arm, his hand covering hers, an expression in their eyes as they looked at one another that suggested they were totally unaware that a party of almost seventy-five friends was looking on. Yorrick led them to the temple steps. Eve kissed him again, then walked with Stephen into the pool of cascading sunlight where Father Lourence was waiting.

The ceremony was short, less than twenty-five minutes, the vows read, promises and simple gold bands exchanged. Then the wedding kiss, a clear-eyed expression in both their faces as they studied one another, then a slow coming together of these two who had waited so long, through such a cruel separation and arduous search.

Still the kiss persisted, Eve and Stephen framed between Greek columns, sun spilling over them, the scent of roses permeating every corner of the theater.

And still the kiss persisted, Father Lourence smiling, then ducking his head to hide his smile, a few of the women giggling until at last Yorrick motioned for the orchestra to commence playing the spirited wedding recessional, and only then did they part and even then reluctantly. As they stepped out of the Greek temple, the women hurried forward to offer them love and congratulations, and during this interim of hugs and kisses, Violet saw Yorrick guiding the caterers in, pointing out where the wedding cake was to go, a stunning confection, an exact replica of the Temple of Aphrodite, and next to the wedding cake pink champagne and next to the champagne a buffet that extended the width of the stage and was laden with every foodstuff imaginable, every delicacy from caviar to shrimp to lobster to oysters, roast turkeys and hams, a feast befitting the occasion.

* * *

Whereas before the ceremony Eve had appeared pensive and withdrawn, Violet observed her now, a whirl of light and color and laughter, her hand always clasped in Stephen's, the two of them greeting everyone, thanking them for their part on this special day, their private inspection tour of the transformed stage and finally back to Yorrick Harp, who was just lifting his glass in toast.

"Friends all, as many arrows loosed several ways come to one mark; as many ways meet in one town; as many streams meet in one salt sea; so may a thousand actions, once afoot, end in one purpose and be all well borne, without defeat."

"To Mr. and Mrs. Stephen Eden, whose love will enrich the world, our blessings for years to come." He lifted his glass and waited until the others had done the same.

Then he went on. "Before Mr. and Mrs. Eden leave our company for their private honeymoon destination, I would like to make an announcement that concerns us all." He turned back and drew Stephen and Eve close. "With the help of this remarkable young man, I am pleased to announce that at dusk on February sixteenth, Yorrick Harp's Adamless Eden will sail from New York Harbor on the Cunarder *Etruria*, and on April sixth we will open to a London audience at the Haymarket Theater."

A sudden rush of excitement swept through the women. Violet couldn't believe her ears. For years Yorrick had been promising them a European tour. They'd largely discounted it as so much idle talk.

"Wait!" he commanded, his hand upraised. "After London we will cross the channel to Paris, Venice, Florence, Rome—"

As he called off most of the major capitals of Europe, the ladies hugged and kissed each other and pressed closer to Yorrick for details.

"But first," he shouted above their excitement, "we must complete our West Coast tour. Two weeks at most. Then we will leave for New York."

As the excitement rose again, Stephen this time lifted a staying hand, the other as always holding Eve close. "Before London you will need a rehearsal hall. I offer you on behalf of my father and my uncle the Great Hall of Eden Castle. You are warmly invited."

At last the women could be contained no longer. As a deafening squeal filled the air, Violet saw Stephen and Eve run offstage, the ladies in pursuit, and out the stage door where an elegant carriage with a driver and two footmen were waiting.

The last Violet saw of Eve was her lovely face in the window, flushed with happiness as she waved good-bye.

 Bridal Suite—Cliff House
San Francisco Coast

To be touched in love, to share one's body in love, to see joy, delight, pleasure on the face of the beloved, these were the miracles that enchanted Eve for the next two days.

She loved to watch him. He was like an unexplored and exotic country and she the intrepid explorer. She was fascinated by the way the sun filtered through his hair in patterns on his cheek, the way his dressing gown hung on his shoulders, the soft canal at the nape of his neck, the small scar on his left temple, the result of a childhood dispute with his brother, Frederic, the tiny black mole to the right of his navel, the soft white skin of his buttocks, the tightly coiled hair of his inner thighs, his feet, the most beautiful feet she'd ever seen.

Now at last he stirred in his sleep in the big four-poster and looked drowsily up. "Good morning," he said with a smile.

She bent over from where she sat cross-legged in bed next to him and kissed him and lingered long enough to smell his hair. She loved the smell of his hair.

On one side of the grand bed lay their wedding finery in a discarded heap where the night before they'd slipped it off in order to serve the passion that had been building for a lifetime. Thus far they had not seen fit to dress beyond their robes. Food had been delivered earlier that morning and sat untouched on a table outside the door.

"What are you doing?" He smiled up at her following the kiss.

"Memorizing you."

"I already know you by heart."

Then she found that she was incapable of staying out of his arms and lay down beside him and studied the lace canopy overhead and thought that from now on she would secretly associate white lace with sexual passion, for every time she had received him, she had looked up at that same lace through eyes blurred from her own pleasure.

She felt him nuzzle her ear. "Should we do something foolish like get dressed today? We have to go back tonight, you know."

"No," she said firmly in a negative response to everything. "Why couldn't Yorrick have given us a week?" she protested.

"He wants to finish this tour and get back to New York."

"Did you really help him with the European tour?"

"He had letters of invitation from several European theaters. I only gave him my advice on the ones I felt he should accept."

"London first?"

"Then Paris."

She turned on her stomach and found a small scar beneath his chin which she'd never seen before. "Are we really going to Eden Castle?"

"Of course we are."

"Do they know?"

"I've written. We finish this tour on the twentieth of January. We sail from New York February sixteenth."

Quickly she calculated the time. "Three weeks. We will go home."

"Home," he repeated.

Suddenly she felt a splintering of emotion, longing to see her home but fearful of her father's reception of Stephen.

Apparently he read her thoughts, saw the doubt on her face. "You must see them before we leave for Europe."

"What if they won't accept you?"

"I could wait in Mobile."

"No," she said with conviction. "No," she repeated. "You'll be with me. We'll go home together or not at all."

Home. For her Stanhope Hall. For him Eden Castle. What their reception in either place would be she couldn't imagine. For all their sakes she prayed it would be gracious and accepting. If not, they would make their own world, for with Stephen, as she had known since the first time she saw him, all things were possible.

Los Angeles

After a triumphant West Coast tour in which Eve and the ladies had played to standing room only every night, it was decided that Yorrick would take the ladies of the troupe directly back to New York on the Union-Pacific Railway. There were new costumes to be fitted for the European tour, new numbers to rehearse, new set pieces to be built, dozens of chores before they sailed for England on February sixteenth.

Stephen and Eve were to leave on the Southern-Pacific Railway for Mobile and Stanhope Hall, and after a short visit, would rejoin the troupe in New York in time for the sailing.

Now on the crowded platform of the Los Angeles railway terminal, Eve tried to kiss all the women good-bye. The Southern-Pacific train was leaving first, in only a matter of minutes. She had a special hug for dear Violet, whom she promised faithfully, "I'll be there in New York, Violet, don't worry."

At the door of the train she saw Stephen and Yorrick in last-minute conversation, steam hissing all about them. At last the all aboard was called and Stephen hurried over to where she stood, surrounded by the women of the troupe.

"Take care, all of you," Eve said as she waved.

As she stepped up into the train, she saw Yorrick lift his face for a kiss and she delivered it with a smile.

To Stephen he said sternly, "Be at the Cunarder dock on February sixteenth. The *Etruria* sails at dusk."

"We'll be there. I swear it."

"And take care of her. She is now your sole responsibility."

"I'm aware of that," Stephen replied, "and more grateful for it than you can imagine."

They hurried to their compartment and opened the shade and saw the women and Yorrick still on the platform, waving.

Eve settled into the seat and caught Violet's eye beyond the window and threw her a special kiss and was amazed at how much she already missed these remarkable women who had become like sisters to her.

As Stephen settled beside her, she enfolded his hands in her own and leaned back against the cushions, exhausted from the excitement of departure.

"Home," he whispered close to her ear, their foreheads touching.

She studied his face, so close, and marveled at its special beauty and recalled her father's irrational and violent hostility toward Stephen, recalled other nightmares as well, White Doll murdered, Sis Liz murdered, Christine dead, Jarmay Higgins, the loft, the pressure and smell of the man, endless pain and terror.

She shuddered and closed her eyes and saw in memory the Knights of the White Camellia staring down at her and wondered how long she would have to live with the pain of those memories.

"Are you all right?" Stephen murmured.

"I was thinking of home." She sighed, suffering a mix of dread and excitement.

Mobile
January 27, 1890

In the last light of day Jarmay Higgins saw the man enter his lumberyard, his Yankee clothes, if nothing else, giving him away. A federal investigator if Jarmay had ever seen one.

Behind Jarmay in his office he heard the nigger, Marshal, sweeping, indolent lazy movements typical of the breed. Jarmay had been on his way home after a hard day, had been looking forward to the peace of Higgins's Farms. But instead here he was watching the stranger, who in truth was no stranger at all. Jarmay Higgins had heard rumors of his arrival in Mobile over a week ago and knew that this was the Yankee investigator folks had been talking about, the same who had been poking his long Yankee nose into everyone's business.

"Leave off with the floor," he muttered over his shoulder to Marshal. "Get me a lantern—hurry."

After issuing the command, Jarmay moved back to the window, keeping well out of sight, watching the Yankee bastard peer into first one bin, then another. He was smoking a pipe, Jarmay Higgins just noticed it, saw the wreaths of smoke curl lazily up into the chill winter air.

Damn! "Marshal!" In growing anger he looked over his shoulder to see the stupid black giant still lazily sweeping the floor, Higgins's earlier command had gone completely unheeded.

"A lantern. Now! You dumb black bastard."

At the last minute it occurred to him to lower his voice. He didn't want to attract attention prematurely. He knew it was only a matter of time before the Yankee discovered his office on the far side of the lumberyard and came calling. God alone knew what the others had told him.

Now Jarmay Higgins peered out the window, watching every

move the Yankee bastard made. Jarmay knew the questions he'd been asking, about the Knights of the White Camellia and the missing Stanhope girl. Well, let him come. Jarmay didn't have a thing to hide that he hadn't already hidden, except one, and he was going now to check on that.

"Marshal, damn you. You gone deaf?" In his fury at the sight of the nigger still sweeping the floor, Jarmay effortlessly grabbed the long broom handle from the slow-eyed man and gave him a sound crack on the head.

As Marshal buckled to his knees, Jarmay hissed, "Now do as I say. Do you hear, you black baboon. I need a lantern. Go and fetch one from the cutting room and bring it up to the loft. And hurry."

Jarmay watched as the nigger continued to rub his head. He saw a small stream of blood glistening on the black forehead. What the hell. A beating now and then was good for niggers, reminded them who they were.

But when after several seconds Marshal still had not moved, Jarmay lifted the broom handle and struck him again and yet a third time. "What's gotten into you, nigger?" he demanded.

At last, holding his head, Marshal staggered up, though for good measure Jarmay gave him a sound whack directly across his shoulders and smiled as Marshal cried out.

See? They didn't understand much but they understood pain.

Now he hurried back to the window to see the Yankee investigator standing at the center of the lumberyard, looking about as though trying to decide which way to go next.

Quietly Jarmay slid the bolt on the door. Oh, he'd let him in soon enough, but not until he was ready. Then Jarmay started up the loft stairs and pushed open the loft door and peered into the shadowy room and wished that Marshal would hurry with the lantern.

Jarmay Higgins was looking for one specific item that had caused him trouble in the past and that now could perhaps put a rope around his neck if he didn't find it first. The dress, the Stanhope girl's dress. Stanhope's nigger had found it and that one discovery had caused Jarmay Higgins to endure a beating he would not soon forget or forgive.

Now he couldn't remember whether he'd come back and gathered up the torn dress and destroyed it, or was it still up here, waiting to get him into more trouble. For Higgins was certain the federal investigator was here at the request of Burke Stanhope and was further certain that Stanhope had told him precisely what to look for and where to look.

All right then, find it, destroy it. He was certain it was still here, for he had not come up to this loft since his unfortunate encounter with the English boy who had damned near torn up his face with his fists.

Still smarting from that humiliation, Jarmay started across the creaky loft floor, trying to peer ahead into the darkness. The light of late afternoon was fading fast.

"Marshal, up here," he called back through the gathering shadows, in desperate need of a lantern.

Quickly he circled the cutting table, scuffling his boots as he went, hoping to find the small pile of heaped material. Had Stanhope taken the dress with him? No, he didn't think so. Jarmay could still recall the expression on Burke Stanhope's face as the nigger had brought it to him.

Suddenly he felt the old floor beneath him give in a mighty crack like echoing thunder. He froze as though standing isolated on an island, and with the most tentative step, he felt his foot plunge directly through the rotted timber, felt himself falling, grabbing frantically out at the cutting table, hanging on, though his right foot and leg were dangling free beneath the floor, the rest of his body twisted at a distorted angle as he clung to the edge of the table and tried to see the extent of his predicament.

"Damn," he gasped. "Marshal!" he shouted and saw clearly what had happened, his foot and leg had fallen through a rotten timber.

"Marshal, where in the hell are you?" He tried to lift himself from this imprisoning position, but every time he pulled himself up by the table, the other timbers seemed to shift and crack and he imagined with horror the entire ancient floor giving away and sending him plummeting to the shed below.

"Jesus," he murmured and felt shooting pains in his trapped leg and tried again to alter his position so that the jagged pieces of wood wouldn't cut into the flesh of his leg, and as he twisted against his imprisonment, he felt behind for something to grab hold of and felt a soft mound of fabric—the gown, cut and torn, belonging to Eve Stanhope.

"Good." He smiled despite his predicament. Then, "Marshal," he shouted and at last saw a dull orange glow moving at a snail's pace up the loft staircase, heard at the same time the rhythmic thud of Marshal's boots and at last saw the man filling the doorway, holding the lantern out in front of him.

"Over here, you idiot," Jarmay called.

At last he saw Marshal turn slowly toward the cutting table, saw his face in the dull glow coming from the lantern, his eyes heavily hooded, resembling a crocodile, his mouth perpetually open.

"Over here, can't you see?" Jarmay Higgins shouted and at last he saw Marshal start slowly across the floor, his brow furrowed, as though he couldn't quite understand why his master was sprawled one-legged upon the floor.

But with every step the large man took, Jarmay felt the floor shudder and vibrate, the old timbers objecting to Marhsal's massive weight, and yet all the time he came closer.

"Wait!" Higgins cried. "Wait right there," he commanded a second time, and at last saw Marshal come to a halt, the lantern flickering and casting distorted shadows over the high ceiling.

"What are you staring at, you ape?" Higgins cried out. "Go downstairs and find a rope. Put the lantern down and back away slowly and go back down to the cutting room."

But even as he spoke Marshal came closer, the old wood floor groaning continuously under his massive weight.

"Stop!" Jarmay Higgins shouted, trying desperately to scramble free of his imprisonment. "In the name of God, stop, you fool!"

At last Marshal did, though he was so close now, less than ten feet, the floor giving visibly beneath his weight. Jarmay tried to calm his shattered nerves and speak slowly so that the dim-wit could understand precisely what he wanted him to do.

"Listen to me, Marshal," he began, puzzled by a strange new expression on Marshal's face.

"Marshal, back away, slowly," Higgins commanded. "Go back down to the cutting room and bring a long, sturdy rope. Are you understanding me?"

Jarmay Higgins looked closely over the flickering lantern light, not certain if Marshal understood or not. There still was something moving on his face, something Higgins had never seen before, an expression that curiously resembled a smile.

"Damn you, Marshal, move!" Higgins ordered and saw the black man take one step back, then lift the lantern high, spreading the light as though he wanted Jarmay to see his face.

And Jarmay saw it clearly, and saw that it *was* a smile, a wide jack-o-lantern smile, revealing missing teeth.

"M-Marshal, do as I say. I need your—"

But all at once the black man lifted his head, cleared his throat in a rough, raw, guttural sound and sent a large slimy wad of mucus sailing directly toward Jarmay, where it landed on his left cheek and slid down into the corner of his mouth before he could wipe it away.

Spitting, coughing, struggling to wipe his face clean, Jarmay jerked about in a spasm of revulsion and anger, flailing out and reaching for the dress and using it as a cloth and smelling the girl's old urine as he did so and feeling a sickness rise up in his throat.

"Damn," he gasped. "Damn your black hide, you son of a bitch." In his anger he continued to wipe at his face and only at the last minute did he look up to see a fearful sight, Marshal slowly, deliberately tilting the lantern, pouring a trail of kerosene along the old timbers, backing his way to the loft door.

"No," Jarmay pleaded. "No, Marshal, what in the—"

Pinned and helpless, Jarmay watched Marshal stand erect then, taking the lantern with him, the smile on his face growing wider until at last he broke into a laugh, a deep-throated sound that Jarmay had never heard before. Even before he bent over for the final time, Jarmay knew precisely what the black man was going to do, knew as well that such small annoyances as federal investigators and torn blue gowns and kidnapped girls and Southern Codes no longer mattered. Nothing mattered except Marshal's boot pressed against the lantern, which now sat on the floor precisely at the end of the kerosene trail.

"Marshal!"

Higgins had time for one last terrified scream. Then the boot pushed the lantern over and the small flame jumped forward as though eager to become a larger one and raced along the kerosene trail, coming closer, the flames spreading out, hungrily devouring the ancient wood floor while Jarmay Higgins, pinned and trapped near the cutting table, had no choice but to watch oblivion come.

"God help," he screamed as the flames, ever growing, leapt forward onto his jacket and his last thoughts were of his mother, that hard-driving shrew who had beaten strength into him.

"Mother," he cried out and felt the heat sear his face and felt the old floor, aflame around him, crackle and give way. In his fiery descent, his last breath was spent in cursing the nigger Marshal who had repaid Jarmay Higgins's kindness with treachery.

* * *

Burke Stanhope rode in with David the following morning and watched along with most of Mobile as the fire brigade put water on the stubborn embers of the now charred ruins that once had been Jarmay Higgins's lumberyard.

David, close beside him on his own mount, appeared fascinated by the amount of destruction.

Burke closed his eyes against the smells, the lingering heat, the scent of smoke and ash, so reminiscent of that other fire, the one at Fan Cottage, that nightmare that still plagued him in his sleep every night.

"How many dead?" he heard a voice call out from the opposite curb.

"Everyone as far as we can tell. Mr. Higgins himself, God rest his soul."

"What started it?"

"Some saw a big nigger run out of his office just before the flames broke. They're lookin' for his man, Marshal."

"Awful."

Burke opened his eyes. He'd seen and heard enough and remembered the night that he and Stephen Eden and Paris Boley had paid a visit to Jarmay Higgins in his loft, remembered the smells, the cutting table with severed ropes still attached, and then the worst sight of all, Eve's gown, torn, abused, filthy.

"Come on," he muttered to David. "Let's go home. Work to do. I want you to look at the ledger books with me."

David started to protest but apparently changed his mind. "Coming, Papa," he said and took a last look at the smoldering ruins that had once been Jarmay Higgins's lumberyard.

"Is that the place, Papa," David asked, "where they took Eve?"

Burke nodded. Apparently the boy had overheard everything several months ago.

"Then good riddance," David muttered. "And we might want to keep our eyes open for any man wanting a place to work, you know, a place to hide or rest."

Burke smiled, pleased with the bright young face before him. "We will indeed. Come on, your mother's waiting dinner. This afternoon we'll go over the ledger books."

David angled his horse about and guided him carefully through the crowds still gathering to watch the fire.

When they reached the flat expanse of road that led north out of Mobile toward Stanhope Hall, David called back, "Race you—"

Belatedly Burke accepted the challenge and saw his son spring forward, already an expert horseman, a nourishing sight to see such youth racing into the future.

As Burke prepared his own horse for speed, he thought again of the fire, thought of Jarmay Higgins dead. It was an empty victory, an unsatisfying retribution. Even in his worst fury and deepest grief, Burke had never wanted anyone dead. All he'd ever wanted, all he wanted now was to have Eve back.

Then he urged his horse forward and saw David a distance ahead and knew he'd never overtake him and perhaps that was as it should be.

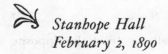 *Stanhope Hall*
February 2, 1890

Mary had the habit of doing her needlework in Eve's room.
The light was good, the memories rich, the gallery nearby where the
two of them had enjoyed endless chats on every subject imaginable.

Now for the first time this winter she threw open the gallery doors
and smelled early spring, a lovely scent of damp earth and growing
things, a beginning warmth in the air to dissipate the chill of winter.

She placed her basket of needlework beside the old rocker and
stood at the gallery railing and peered out and saw the lawn just
beginning to turn green in spots, saw the azalea hedges showing pink
and white buds, the long avenue of live oaks as solid as ever with
trailing, graceful Spanish moss that lifted in the slight breeze.

She saw a carriage then, quite large and elegant, on the road below.
It appeared to slow down as it approached the avenue of live oaks,
and then it stopped directly at the bottom of the hill.

Mary stood for a moment, her eye on the driver in the high seat,
who seemed to be taking his instructions from someone inside the
carriage. Still she waited, watching the carriage door for a sign of life.

Then she understood. Probably a land speculator looking for the
Higgins farm. Since Jarmay Higgins's death, Mrs. Higgins had been
trying to sell part of the property. Mary had seen several large carriages rumble past on their way to inspect the Higgins land. Undoubtedly this one was lost and in need of direction.

As she turned away, she saw the carriage door open, saw a hand
reach out for the door handle, then she saw a woman alight. She
appeared to stand beside the carriage door and peer up toward Stanhope Hall.

Lost. The woman was clearly lost. With a sigh Mary thought that
she'd go tell old Ben to walk down and direct the carriage a few miles
down the road to the Higgins farm.

But as Mary turned back for a final look, she saw the woman take
one step forward, saw even from this distance her lovely gown and
perched hat and dainty parasol, saw her take another step, then another, and Mary held her position at the railing, her heart beating too
fast, some element of recognition dawning.

Eve?

For a moment she was torn between holding her position at the
railing and running down to the porch below. She had to be certain.
It would be too cruel if—

The woman spied her and Mary saw her lift a gloved hand and
wave, saw the perched bonnet fall off, saw a lovely long cascade of

golden hair and the recognition was sealed, for Mary had brushed and combed that hair from the moment of her birth. Then she heard a distant cry of "Mama!"

And Mary was running back through the upper corridors of Stanhope Hall, down the stairs, crying out with each step, "Burke, come, oh come!" until she was on the porch and down the steps and looked up to see Eve running toward her, skirts lifted, and at last they came together in a loving embrace of need and joy and relief, each clinging to the other, Mary weeping openly and doing nothing to hide it as she clasped her daughter to her.

"Oh, Mama," Eve said as she wept, faring none too well herself. At last Mary released her to the extent that she could see her face clearly and saw a beautiful face, the same Eve, though older, the eyes wiser.

"Oh, my dearest," Mary said again. "I can't believe it's you."

"I missed you, Mama, so much."

"And I you. We were afraid—"

"I know. So was I. I'm home now."

"Yes."

Then suddenly she felt tension in Eve's body and looked back over her shoulder and saw Burke on the porch, David at his side, saw a press of servants including Madame Germaine, as apparently Mary's cries had raised the entire household.

Mary stepped back. It was Burke's turn, and as he started slowly, disbelieving, down the steps, she saw breaking pain on his face, saw Eve start toward him with a simple whisper. "Papa, I'm here." While he was still a distance from her, he opened his arms, tears streaming. "My Eve," he murmured and enclosed her in his embrace and buried his face in her hair, though Mary knew he was weeping.

She gave them several minutes alone, then motioned for David to join them. She saw Eve wipe uselessly at her tears and kiss David, who merely blushed and stepped back. And then the three of them were in each other's arms, a quiet healing communion with no words spoken except the language of the heart, which seemed content for now to hold, to touch, to gaze.

"I—can't believe it," Mary said at last. "You're so beautiful."

"And you as well."

"Come inside," Burke invited, still holding Eve's hand.

"Papa?"

"Yes?"

"I'm not traveling alone."

The announcement caught all by surprise. Eve looked back down the row of live oaks to where the carriage was waiting on the road. She walked a few steps away and with a wave of her hand summoned the carriage forward. As the driver pulled near the front porch, Mary tried to see in the rear windows, but they were heavily curtained.

Eve said, "My husband is with me," and she stepped up to the carriage door and as it opened Mary gaped forward and saw—

"Stephen!" With a cry of joy she embraced him, thought he looked older, perhaps thinner, but like Eve, he was handsomely dressed, his smile as warm as ever.

"Mary," he said. "It's good to see you."

"You're married, you say?" she smiled, secretly pleased and not terribly surprised.

Eve reached eagerly for his hand, "In San Francisco, Mama, the most beautiful wedding. There were newspaper reporters there. I will read to you the accounts—"

Abruptly she broke off and Mary looked up to see the cause of this new tension and saw Burke standing a distance away, his eyes locked on Stephen Eden, who apparently had just felt the weight of his focus and who now turned to confront it.

Eve went to Burke's side and took his hand. "Papa, Stephen is my husband now. All I ask is that you receive him with courtesy for all our sakes."

For several moments Mary could not interpret the expression on Burke's face. Still suffering shock from Eve's arrival, he looked at Stephen, then started slowly toward him and at last extended his hand in the warmest of greetings. "Welcome home, Stephen," he said, "and thank you for bringing Eve back."

In a surge of joy Eve and Mary embraced again, then Madame Germaine came joyfully forward, followed by old Florence and Ben and Katie and Dorie, a laughing, talking, pocket of life and thanksgiving played against a backdrop of a pale green lawn and budding azaleas and lined sentinels of impassive live oaks that had watched over the comings and goings, the sorrows and joys of Stanhopes for two centuries.

*　*　*

For almost two weeks Stanhope Hall hummed with the sound of voices. Endless talking, endless sharing, endless tears and laughter and anger and pride and suspense as the odyssey was told and retold by Stephen and Eve.

Eve loved hearing Stephen's account, particularly his tale of Paris and dark-eyed Marie. They were married now, for Burke had received a lengthy letter.

And Eve loved to sit and hold Mama's hand and tell her of the performances, the audiences, read the accounts of critics to her and watch the light of pride in her eyes, and she enjoyed watching Stephen and Papa share cigars and brandy after dinner, the entire party moving nonstop from the dining room to the library, where there was always another tale to be told, another sorrow shared, another triumph relived.

One morning, midpoint of the visit, Eve drew on a light shawl in protection against a gentle spring rain. With Stephen and Mary and Burke in attendance, she made her way to the family cemetery and knelt at Christine's grave and tried to tell her good-bye, but she could find no words to ease the grief in her heart and she wept unashamedly and at last turned to Stephen for the support of his arms and the healing power of his love.

On the following day, in bright sunlight, she and Stephen visited the charred ruins of what once had been the most magical place in Eve's world: Fan Cottage. To her pleasure she saw a small wild azalea bush with white buds growing at the exact center of the destruction, and she thought of Sis Liz and knew what a large portion of the magical old woman lived in her heart, was with her every moment of every day and perhaps was never more with her than when she took the stage before a large audience.

Long before they were ready for it, the calendar informed them it was time to leave.

On a crisp bright February tenth the carriage was brought around front, with David on the high seat next to the driver.

Stephen and Eve came out onto the porch with Burke and Mary, and good-byes were started, first the servants and Madame Germaine. Then the four of them walked down to where the carriage was waiting.

"And how long will the tour last?" Mary asked.

Eve shook her head and saw the sorrow on her mother's face and tried to alleviate it. "Only through the summer, I think."

"Then you're coming home?"

Eve looked to Stephen to reply. "Hard to say now, but don't worry, Mary. We'll be back before you know it. I promise you."

Then Eve saw Stephen approach her father, hand extended. "Thank you, sir, for your faith in me."

"My apologies—"

"Are not necessary."

Eve saw her father renew his grasp on Stephen's hand as though reluctant to let him go. "Tell your father, tell John Murrey Eden that Mary and I would be honored to receive him at Stanhope Hall. Tell him that for me—please."

Eve saw the two men exchange a glance, and then they embraced warmly and with clear affection. She saw her mother smiling and went to her and kissed her.

"I love you, Mama. I can't begin to tell you how many times in the past all that kept me strong and on track were thoughts of you."

They embraced a final time and Eve clung to Mary and kissed her, then kissed her father and at last took Stephen's hand and followed him to the carriage.

She saw nothing clearly, saw everything clearly. Though her eyes were blurred with tears, she knew that her mind and heart and soul had been formed in this place by those two people, and whatever triumphs she might enjoy in this world, they would always deserve the true thanks and her deepest gratitude.

"Are you well?" Stephen murmured and put his arm around her and drew her close.

"I'm well," she replied and knew she probably wouldn't make a truer claim in her life.

New York Harbor
Aboard the Etruria
February 16, 1890

After a warm and loving reunion with Yorrick Harp and the women of the troupe, resplendent in their new feathers and fineries, the handsome Cunarder the *Etruria* set sail for Southampton, England, at twilight.

It was a glorious winter sunset. Eve watched as Stephen and Yorrick talked excitedly of the tour to come. She sensed a bond of affection developing between the two men, Yorrick, who had passed a lifetime with women, blossoming and relaxing under the tempering influence of good male companionship.

Eve sat with them in the salon for the first few minutes of the departure. Then as she saw the New York skyline slide past beyond the large window, she excused herself, wrapped her cloak more closely about her against the chill ocean breeze and hurried through the crowds up to the top deck.

A sizable gathering had already formed at railside to see the new phenomenon in New York Harbor, the Lady of Liberty, given to the citizens of America by the citizens of France only a few years before.

The sunset was vivid. Eve had not seen sky colors so dazzling since Abilene, at Pastor Kalm's mission. She looked up now to see bands of fiery red and orange intersected with winter gray, the lady's massive torch of liberty illuminating the darkest part of the sky.

Eve found a spot next to the railing, and looked up at the statue breathtakingly beautiful, immense, her torch extended heavenward, her eyes clear and leveled, the folds of her robe falling gracefully down to her sturdy base.

"Liberty enlightening the world," a gentleman instructed a child nearby.

Enlightening the world. A tall order.

"Look! New Americans!" another voice shouted and pointed toward a large ship just entering the harbor, the decks filled with bearded men holding fast to the hands of solemn women and wide-eyed children.

Eve leaned against the railing and watched as the ship passed before them and thought of her own recent journey across America, thought with fondness of Justin Kalm, remembered his peace, his words.

"We're so new here, a clean slate, and everybody wanting to make a mark upon us. There's room for all, though as is always the case with the human race, we need a tempering now and then, a reminder of how to give instead of take, love instead of hate, create instead of destroy—"

Eve shivered in the cool ocean breeze. Perhaps a difficult lesson for a rich, ambitious and energetic land.

She felt arms about her waist, heard a beloved voice close to her ear. "I wondered where you were," Stephen whispered. "I missed you."

Eve took a final and hopeful look at the Lady of Liberty and the ship filled with new Americans.

"I'm here," she said and turned to kiss him.